The Natives of Sarawak and British North Borneo

Vol. II

outlook

Henry Ling Roth

The Natives of Sarawak and British North Borneo
Vol. II

Reprint of the original, first published in 1896.

1st Edition 2022 | ISBN: 978-3-36827-512-9

Verlag (Publisher): Outlook Verlag GmbH, Zeilweg 44, 60439 Frankfurt, Deutschland
Vertretungsberechtigt (Authorized to represent): E. Roepke, Zeilweg 44, 60439 Frankfurt, Deutschland
Druck (Print): Books on Demand GmbH, In de Tarpen 42, 22848 Norderstedt, Deutschland

THE

NATIVES OF SARAWAK

AND

BRITISH NORTH BORNEO

Based chiefly on the MSS. of the late Hugh Brooke Low
Sarawak Government Service

BY

HENRY LING ROTH

AUTHOR OF

"The Aborigines of Tasmania," "The Peasantry of Eastern Russia," &c.

WITH A PREFACE BY

ANDREW LANG

OVER 880 ILLUSTRATIONS

IN TWO VOLUMES—VOL. II

LONDON
TRUSLOVE & HANSON
143 OXFORD STREET & 6 SLOANE STREET
1896

PRINTED BY
TRUSLOVE AND BRAY
WEST NORWOOD S E

CONTENTS.

VOL. II.

	PAGE
CONTENTS OF VOL. II. ...	iii.

CHAPTER XVI.
HABITATIONS ... 1

CHAPTER XVII.
WEAVING, DYEING, AND DRESSMAKING, TRIBAL DRESSES, DRESS IN DETAIL ... 29

CHAPTER XVIII.
FASHIONABLE DEFORMITIES ... 77

CHAPTER XIX.
PAINTING AND TATUING ... 83

CHAPTER XX.
WAR AND WEAPONS ... 96

CHAPTER XXI.
HEAD-HUNTING ... 140

CHAPTER XXII.
THE SUMPITAN AND OTHER POISONS ... 184

CHAPTER XXIII.
PEACE, SLAVES AND CAPTIVES, HUMAN SACRIFICES, CANNIBALISM ... 202

CHAPTER XXIV.
GOVERNMENT, TRADE, MINING, MENSURATION, NATURAL PRODUCTIONS ... 224

CHAPTER XXV.
BOATING, SWIMMING, RIDING ... 246

CHAPTER XXVI.
MUSIC ... 257

CHAPTER XXVII.
LANGUAGE, NAMES, COLOURS ... 267

CHAPTER XXVIII.
ARCHÆOLOGY, JARS, ALLEGED NATIVE WRITING, NEGRITOES ... 279

APPENDICES.

I.

VOCABULARIES.

Sea Dyak, Malay, by H. Brooke Low	i.
Rejang River Dialect, by H. Brooke Low	xlv.
Malay, Kanowit, Kyan, Bintulu, Punan, Matu, by H. Brooke Low	xlvii.
Malay, Brunei, Bisaya, Murut Padass, Murut Trusan, Dali Dusum, Malanau, by C. de Crespigny	xciv.
A Collection of 43 words in 24 different Districts, by Rev. C. Hupé	xcix.
Collection of nine words in eight dialects, by Ch. Hose	ciii.
Kayan, by R. Burns	civ.
Sadong, Lara, Sibuyau, by Sir Sp. St. John	cix.
Sabayau, Lara, Salakau, and Lundu, by Rev. W. Gomez	cxiv.
Sea Dyak (and Bugau), Malau, by Mr. Brereton	cxvi.
Milanau, Kayan, Pakatan, by Sir Sp. St. John	cxix.
Ida'an, Bisaya, Adang (Murut), by Sir Sp. St. John	cxxiv.
Lanun, by Sir Sp. St. John	cxxx.
Sarawak Dyak, by Rev. W. Chalmers	cxxxii.
Iranun, Dusun, Bulud Opie, Sulus, Kians, Punans, Melano, Bukutan, Land Dyaks, Balaus	clvii.

II.

ETHNOGRAPHICAL NOTES TRANSLATED FROM DR. SCHWANER'S "BORNEO:"

I. The Barito River Basin	clxi.
II. The Kahaijan River Basin	cxcix.
NOTES FROM MRS. PRYER'S "A DECADE IN BORNEO"	ccviii.
,, ,, PROF. KÜKENTHAL'S "FORSCHUNGSREISE"	ccix.
NOTE ON BURIALS	ccxi.

III.

NOTE ON SKULL MEASUREMENTS	ccxi.

IV.

BIBLIOGRAPHY	ccxii.
INDEX	ccxviii.
LIST OF SUBSCRIBERS	ccxxxviii.

CHAPTER XVI.

HABITATIONS.

LAND DYAK houses—Twelve in a row—Separate houses—Description of parts—A house at Stang—Dimensions—Description—Detached houses—Single blocks—Lower verandahs—Poor buildings—Dirt—Position of the Stang house—House *antus*—*Langs*—Middens—Tributes—Cradles—*Tabu*—Jungle treasure houses—Rotan and gomuti palm fibre—Smoked roofs—Pillows—Flooring—Absence of streets - SEA DYAK houses—Long houses—General description—*Bilieh* or private apartment—Life in – Utensils—Fire-places—*Tempuan* or general thoroughfare—Women work here—*Ruai* or verandah—Open on all sides—Fire-places—Stores and treasures—Heads and charms, &c.—*Tanju* or open-air platform—For paddy drying—*Sadau* or loft—Shifting quarters—Searching new grounds—Marking-out—Omens—Collective labour—The exodus—The *rusilan*—A large Sibuyau house—Stockades—The longest Sea Dyak house on record—Plainness—Cleanliness—Smells—Incised doors—Slab bark walls—Roofs—MALANAU houses—Lofty buildings—KAYAN houses—Chiefs' slab seats—Reason for high posts—Low rooms—Large houses on Baram river—Good workmanship—Omens—Co-operation—Quick erection—Little furniture—Raised seats—Kenniah close packing—DUSUN houses—Vermin—Second story—A neat clean house—Bambu roofs—Whole houses of bambu—Kiau houses—Vermin—New houses—Omens—MURUT houses—Poor specimens—Low roofs—Origin of barrack houses—Not conducive to progress—PATHS—Curious means of communication—Near houses—Over hills—BRIDGES—Elegant constructions—Tree trunks.

THE late Mr. Noel Denison has given us many accounts of houses built by the Land Dyaks. "The houses of the Singhi Dyaks are constructed in blocks of perhaps twelve in one row, the platform in front being common to all, the verandah which is closed in front is supported on straight posts, the wall behind and before being upright." (Denison, ch. ii. p. 19.)

At Tringus: "The houses are all separate, but run so close together that they touch; the connection from the platform in front of the houses, which are all distinct, is by means of bamboo *batangs* or bridges, though the platforms often approach one another so closely that no bridges are required (*ibid*, ch. iv. 39) . . . . the names of the various parts of a Dyak house vary a little with the various tribes. The platform in front of a house is called the *tanju*; the verandah *awach*; the sloping roof, which can be raised or lowered from the end of the house roof, or is perhaps a continuation of it, is the *kumban* (window). On entering a house, the door *tiban* of which is generally made of bilian or some other hard wood, we come across a passage between the fire places called the *ladang*, while the fire place itself is called *apuk*. There are often two fire places right and left. The shelves above, used for storing household goods, wood, etc., are called *piyu* or *pyu*; the room itself is the *arun*; the raised seat at the end of the room, used as a sitting divan and sleeping place for strangers, is the *jangan* at Tringus, and *bakowse* at Gumbang. I have written that there are sometimes two fire-places; it happened to be so

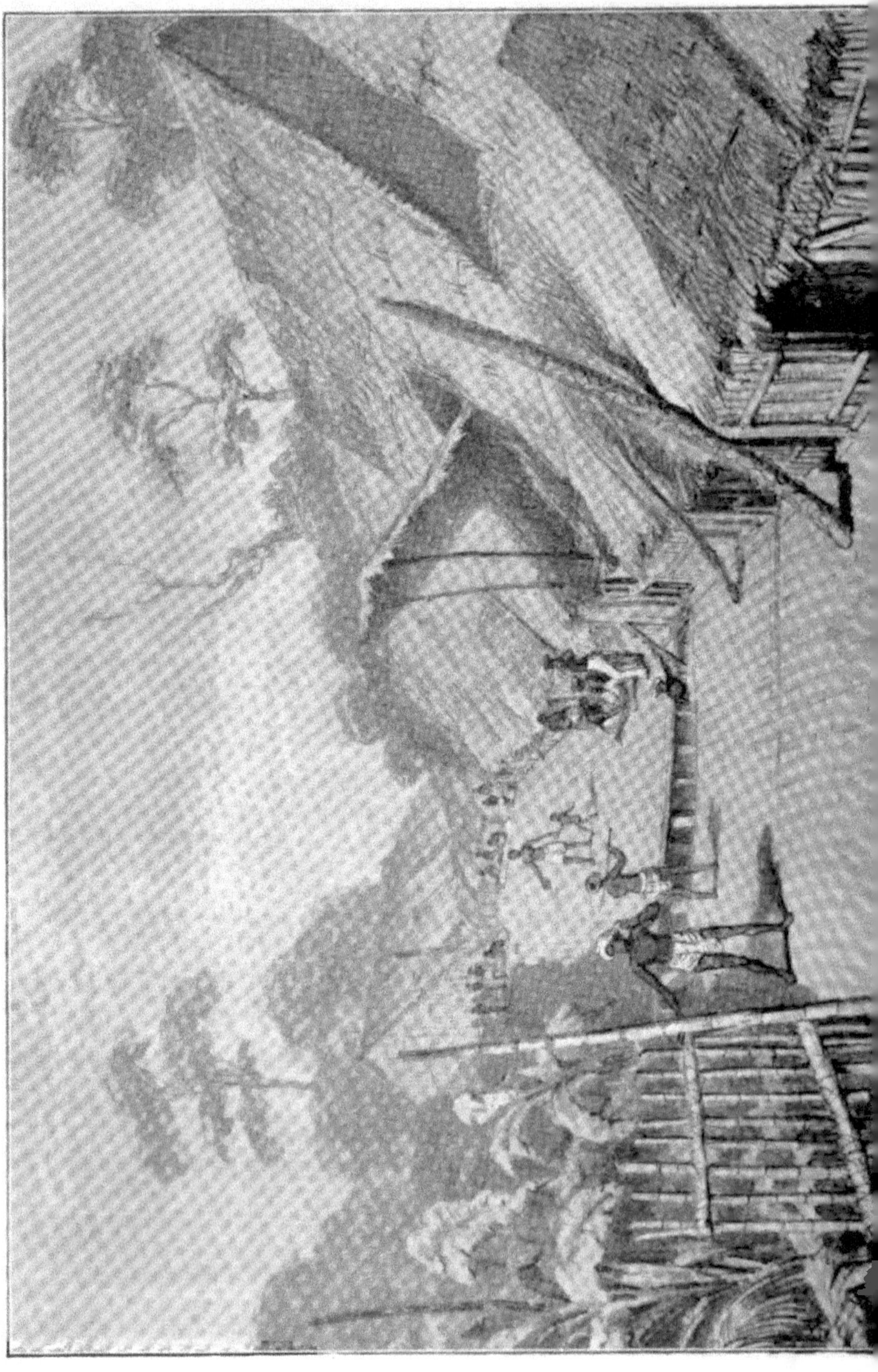

in the house I was describing; in other houses I found only one fire-place to the left of the door, the *piyu* being on the right." (*ibid*, ch. iii. p. 39.)

"At Stang there was a house like that of the Sibuyaus. The house is some 90 feet in length with 8 doors, and stands about 4 feet from the ground. There is a verandah in front 24 feet broad running the whole length of the building and behind this is another verandah 15 feet in breadth. This latter is covered by the roof which slopes down to within 3 or 4 feet of the tanju, and is supported by a split bamboo wall. Behind the outer verandah is a passage 1½ feet in breadth, running parallel the whole way with the verandah, terminating at each end in a wooden door, and into this passage the 8 doors of the house all open. Between this passage (which is the thoroughfare through the house) and the inner verandah, firewood, etc., is stored, and light is admitted by the roof being made to rise and fall in the usual Land Dyak manner. The roof slopes down at the rear of the building as low as it does in front, while the side walls constructed of attaps come down as low as 4 feet from the ground. The rooms are small and there is a door of communication between each of these, so that there is no difficulty in passing from one room to another. The whole of the front verandah is surrounded by a split bamboo fence 5 feet high, erected to keep out fowls and protect the children from falling over. This (and one a little smaller at Sigu) is the best Land Dyak house I have seen and it should be taken as a pattern by all our Land Dyak tribes." (*ibid*, ch. vii. 74.) "While on the subject of the village I may here mention that some of the Simpoke houses are constructed differently from those of the Stangs, etc., many of the houses are detached, and have no front verandahs, and are built higher from the ground." (*ibid*, ch. vii. 76.) "The houses of the Lanchang Dyaks and in fact of the whole Bukar tribe stand in blocks some 160 feet in length, raised about four feet from the ground. The roof slopes down at the back of the house till it reaches and rests on a boarded wall three feet high, the roof opening over every room forms the windows, admitting light and air in the Land Dyak fashion. In front, the roof is the same, and rests on a boarded wall or partition which encloses the inner verandah twelve feet broad, and outside of this there is another verandah or platform, ten feet broad, generally a foot or two lower down. The bamboos of which these are constructed are most slovenly and loosely placed and the whole building has in fact a most forlorn and wretched appearance. In some of the rows or blocks, in front of every door a portion of the roof is continued over the outer verandah to form a small fowl-house or coop, but this is not universal. The Bukars are the only Dyaks I have met who feed their pigs in the verandahs; this is done in the lower verandah. The interior of a house is divided into three compartments fifteen feet in breadth. The first compartment entered from the door has a fire-place on each side with a passage between into the next compartment, which may be said to be in the same room, there being nothing to mark the separation but a thick bamboo joist in the floor. This second compartment, which is used as the sleeping or lounging place, is about twelve feet in length. In the third compartment, also twelve feet long, are stored the household goods—jars, guns, swords, charms, gongs, baskets, cloths, etc., etc., and here under the raised roof a portion of the floor is railed off for storing bottles, jars of arrack, oil, etc., etc. The sides of the houses are all of planking and the floors of *lantis*. The above account of a Bukar Dyak house describes the habitation of Pengara Guddus." (*ibid*, ch. viii. p. 83.)

"The effluvium arising from the accumulation of dirt and refuse in this village was really fearful. The houses being built on the level ground, there is no natural drainage, and the Dyaks have made none for themselves." (*ibid*, ch. viii. p. 84.) "Around the houses the filth, offal, refuse and mud create such a stench that it is at times unendurable." (*ibid*, ch. viii. p. 85.)

"In one thing the Grungo excel every other tribe of Dayaks I have ever seen, and that is in dirt; their houses were dirty, their mats were dirty, and their little children could only be described as positively filthy." (St. John i. 147.)

The Rev. Mr. Chalmers thus describes the Land Dyak village of Staang near the left branch of the Sarawak river. "It is built on a high, steep hill, and the houses are reached by a rugged path, which consists of steps cut into the face of the hill, strengthened by pieces of

NIBONG PALM. *Oncosperma filamentosa*.
(Blume's Rumph. 96 t. 82-103; Mart. Nat. Hist. Palm iii. 312 t. 150-153.)

THE NIPA PALM. *Nipa fruticans*.
(Martin's Nat. His. Palm iii. 305 t. 108.)

bamboo. Here and there huge masses of limestone rock tower above the surface; but in general the hill is covered with a dense undergrowth of ferns and shrubs, and above these rise jungle and fruit trees in abundance; the latter consisting of plantains, durians, and many kinds of palm, as cocoanut, sago, nibong, näuh, pinang, etc. As one ascends, there is heard the unceasing dash and ripple of streams innumerable over their rocky descents, and every now and then one comes upon a bamboo seat and *panchur*. As the village is neared, a cluster of fine yellow bamboo (*bŭlu gading*) comes in view, and close by this is a small but tolerably lofty bamboo stage, on which are placed *Antu* offerings, to which a ladder is sometimes attached to help the *Antus* in their ascent to get their dinners. They pay no worship to the bamboos, but the *place* is sacred, and here they generally await the bird omens before setting out on their journeys. The houses are few or numerous according to the population, and each house contains from three to four *langs* or family apartments. They are built on posts from four to twenty feet from the ground, and are entered by means of ladders (notched trunks of trees) or by an inclined plane of bamboo. At Tabiah there is one ascent of this latter kind at least 200 feet in length. . . Among the posts below the houses, the dogs, pigs, and fowls quarrel and flourish, the ground there is little else than an immense midden : it receives all the dirt of the house, and this is rendered still more unsavoury by that of the pigs, etc., so that the thick *Rottan* mats which are laid over the floors of *lantei* are quite necessary to keep down the stench.

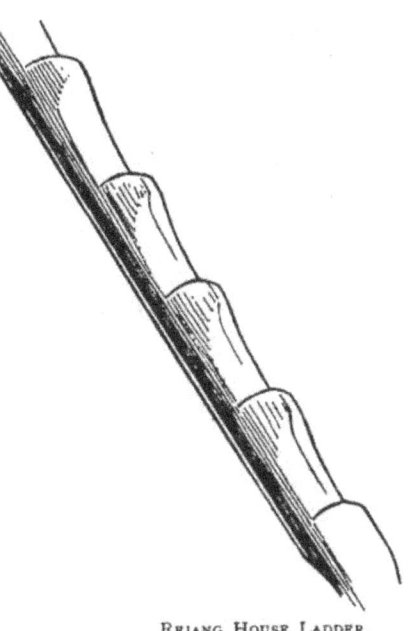

REJANG HOUSE LADDER.
(Brooke Low.)

"Each family or *lang* pays a tribute of two *passus* of rice or three rupees in money to the Government. A *lang* consists of a married couple and their family; the Orang Kaya, widowers, widows, bachelors, and unmarried women pay nothing. Each *lang* has a separate *ramin* or apartment in one of the long houses, and the children and unmarried girls of the family sleep in this room (which is sometimes pretty large) with the heads of the family; the lads of the village as soon as they are old enough to work on the farms, have to take up their quarters at night in the *panggah* or head house." (Occas. Papers.) "One or more cradles, formed of the hollow stem of the sago-palm, or a block of wood, in which a cavity has been made, slung from the beams of the house by ropes attached to both ends of it, adorn the room." (Low, p. 280.) "When a new *bŭtang*, or row of houses, is built, those who live therein may not eat some kinds of jungle vegetables, or fish with *tuba*, or seek rattans in the woods, till the house has been doctored, a pig killed, and a feast held." (Chalmers in Grant's Tour.)

"The Lanchangs had just repaired and in many instances entirely rebuilt their houses, they had consequently put them under pamali for four days, two of which had already expired." (Denison, ch. viii. p. 84.)

"A man being told to make a regular flight of steps to his house instead of the old notched ladder replied, 'No, that would be *pamali*.'" (Chambers, Miss. Field, 1867, p. 69.)

"The Sikongs and neighbouring tribes and besides them the Gumbangs construct small houses in the jungle, in which they keep their most cherished valuables. This is done as a precaution against fire, and I noticed that these houses were only fastened by a rough wooden bolt." (Denison, ch. v. p. 52.) "The Goons and Tabiahs have also this custom." (*ibid*, ch. vi. 62.)

"For binding the timbers of a house together rotan is largely used." (Crossland.) "The gomuti palm is likewise much in request for the same purpose. The cordage it produces from the hairy-like filaments, which are interwoven round the stem and about the axils of the leaves, is of excellent quality, and of great service, on account of its durability." (Low, p. 40.)

DESIGN BURNT ON A ROTAN MAT (*tckar rotan*). Muruts of Upper Labut River in North Borneo. Total length of mat, 8ft. 10in.; width, 3ft. 2½in.; length of decorated portion, 2ft. 5in. (Edinboro' Mus.)

In the Upper Sarawak Dyak houses "the whole room looks black from smoke, which has no other escape than the door and one large window. This latter is merely a large hole left in the roof, and in rain must be shut with a shutter made of palm-leaves. The room is lighted by the fire from the hearth, and by a little torch made from the gum of a tree put into bamboos, and used as oil. The sleeping-place is before the fire, on mats spread out at night; pillows stuffed with grass, etc., are made use of, and coverings made of the rinds of certain trees." (Houghton, M.A.S. iii. 199.)

"The floor is always formed of strips split from large bamboos, so that each may be nearly flat and about three inches wide, and these are firmly tied down with rattan to the joists beneath. . . . they form with a mat over them an excellent bed. . . . When, however, a flat, close floor is required, excellent boards are made by splitting open large bamboos on one side only, and flattening them out so as to form slabs eighteen inches wide and six feet long, with which some Dyaks floor their houses. These with constant rubbing of the feet and the smoke of years become dark and polished, like walnut or old oak, so that their real material can hardly be recognised." (Wallace i. 121.)

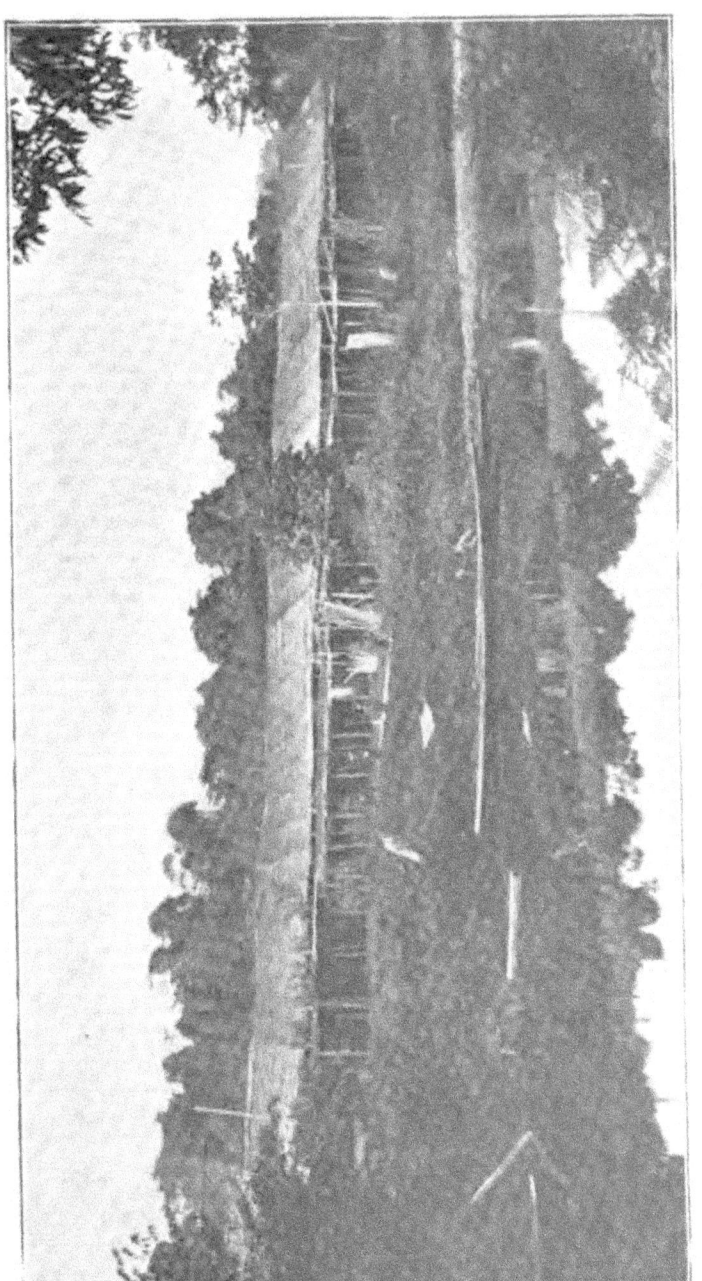

A Rejang River Sea Dyak Village House.
(From a photograph by Mr. Lambert, of Singapore.)

"In describing Peninjau Mr. Hornaday remarks: "The houses stand just wherever they can find standing-room, with no order or regularity

EXTERIOR OF SEA DYAK LONG HOUSE.
(By Mr. W. T. Hornaday. "Two Years in the Jungle.")

whatever, not a sign of anything like a street nor even a good path anywhere. They were of course built along the side of the mountain, usually with the open side uphill, and all were elevated on posts which were from six to eight feet high on the upper side, where they were the shortest." (p. 485.)

The following description of a Sea Dyak village house is by Mr. Brooke Low, and is based on earlier accounts of the houses of the Undups by the Rev. W. Crossland :—

" A Sea Dyak Village is a terrace upon posts varying in length according to the number of houses of which it is composed, and as the various houses are built according to a single scale and measurement and by a combination of labour, they rarely fail to present a uniform and regular appearance.

" There is always a ladder at either end of the terrace by which to ascend, and sometimes one or more towards the centre of the *tanju* or open-air platform. The roof is thatched throughout with the same material—shingles or palm leaves—if the latter, the *nipa (duan apong)* leaves are used where procurable, and where not the *pandanus (duanbira)*. The flooring in some villages is made of palm trees split into laths (*nibong* = wild varieties of *areca*?); in other cases of cane, or bamboo, or even twigs. The laths of split bamboo allow a delicious current of air to permeate the apartment. The outer walls are of plank, the inner of bark. No nails are used, the beams or rafters are lashed together with rattans or secured by wooden pegs. The posts are innumerable and of hard wood. The village is surrounded at its base by a wooden palisade which is itself protected by *chevaux de frise* of pointed bamboo. The village is divided by a plank walling into two main portions, the front and the rear. The former partakes of the nature of a very wide verandah, and is open throughout its entire length. The latter occupies the rear of the entire building and is sub-divided into apartments, one for each family. Between the plank wall and the edge of the *ruai* is the *tempuan* or footway, a narrow passage running through the centre, so that a person may walk from one end of the village to the other without encountering any obstacles.

" Every family thus possesses a compact little residence to themselves, comprising a *bilieh* or room where they can enjoy privacy when they like, a *tempuan* or thoroughfare where they pound their rice and pile up their firewood, a *ruai* or verandah where they receive visitors, a *tanju* or open-air platform where they air their things and lounge in the cool of the evening, and a *sadau* or loft where they keep their tools and store their paddy.

" The *bilieh* or private apartment is furnished with a swinging door which opens outwards, and is closed by means of a heavy weight suspended to a thong to the inside. The door can be secured when required by means of a bar. If the room be unusually large, it may have two doors for the sake of convenience. Figures are sometimes carved or painted on the door—saurians among others, grotesque images of supernatural beings, and indecent caricatures of the human person.[1] There is no window such as we understand, but

---

[1] "The inner walls of the houses of the Benoas were ornamented outside with grotesque figures—some representing the inevitable crocodile, in various positions; another, a man being swallowed by a crocodile." (Bock, p. 137.) " Another of the carvings represented a Dyak riding on an animal meant for a boar; while on a third wall was depicted a Dyak returning from a head-hunting tour, with a head in his left hand. Further down the room was hanging suspended against the wall a small model of a house, somewhat resembling a Noah's ark, from the door of which protruded a carved serpent, which was represented to me as being a valuable medicine for the stomach." (*ibid*, p. 138.)

a portion of the roof is so constructed that it can be raised a foot or two by means of a stick to let out the smoke or to admit the fresh air. If the neighbours are near relations or intimate friends, as is often the case, a hole is cut in the wall which separates the room to avoid the necessity of a roundabout way into one anothers' apartments, and some villages are so arranged that one can traverse the entire length of the rear section of the building, by means of these apertures, without appearing on the verandah at all. There is no furniture in the room—none, in fact, being required. The floor is the occupiers' table, and they squat to their meals. But there are plenty of mats to sit upon, and baskets to pack their clothes in. Their cups and plates are hung in rows upon the walls as much for ornament as for use. Their valuables, such as old jars, gongs, etc., are ranged on three sides so as to present the most imposing appearance of wealth. But the room is stuffy and untidy, and no wonder, seeing that there is but one for each family, and this one is used as a kitchen as well as a mess room, as a nursery as well as a bed chamber. There can be no absolute privacy unless the door is barred to exclude the neighbours. Boys and girls keep running in and out, and the dogs are always on the watch in the *tempuan* to spring in whenever the door swings open. The floor is swept after a fashion, but the room is never deserted, and the roof is simply black with soot. The refuse is thrown into the piggery and poultry yard, which occupies the area or waste space under the house. Very little stench, if any, reaches the apartment from the ground, as the floor is raised too high above it to be affected by it. The *dapur* or fire-place is the only real piece of furniture in the room. It is built either to the right or to the left of the door set up against the wall of the *tempuan* and resembles an open cupboard, the lowest shelf resting upon the floor, and the upper shelves being of lattice-work instead of plank. The former is boarded all round and filled with clay. This is the fire-place, and it is furnished with a few stones between which the pots are set.[1] The shelf immediately above the fire is set apart for smoking fish and meat, etc. The shelves above this again are filled with firewood, which, being thoroughly dried, is ready for use. The women, who do all the cooking, have also to keep these shelves supplied from the pile in the *tempuan*. As the smoke from the wood fire is not conducted to the roof by means of a chimney, it spreads itself throughout the loft and blackens the beams and rafters until it finds its way out by the open window.

SLAB DOOR OF UNDUP HOUSE.
The upper pivot is fastened by rotan to the post B, but the lower pivot drops into a socket let into A. The door is held closed from the inside by a bar of wood which is dropped into catches pegged to the posts.
(From a sketch by Mr. Crossland.)

[1] Elsewhere Mr. Brooke Low in his notes says: "They make a *palan*, or raised platform, and under it light a fire and heap it with dry twigs, and fill the platform with split wood for drying as *bekal* (fire-wood). From the fire they take brands for other fires."

"The *tempuan* or general thoroughfare is between the *bilieh* and the *ruai*. It is three feet in width and is paved with wood. It is furnished with a ladder or notched stick by which to reach the loft, a family mortar where the women pound their paddy with wooden pestles to free it from the husk, and a pile

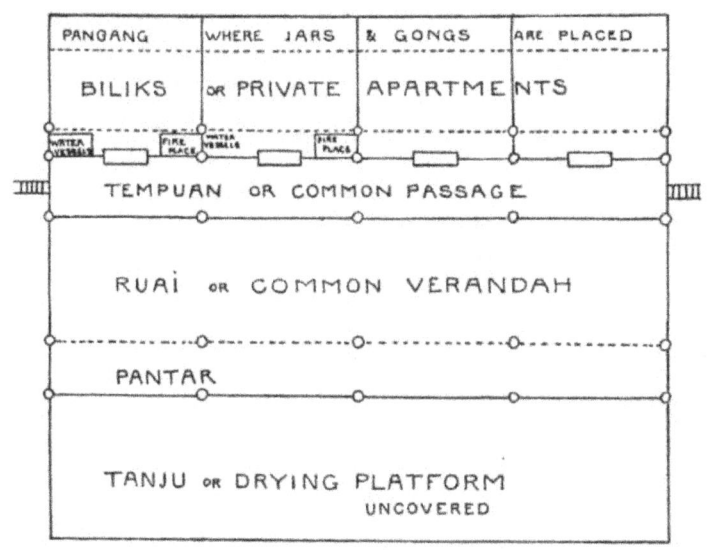

```
| PANGANG   | WHERE JARS   | & GONGS       | ARE PLACED |
| BILIKS    | OR PRIVATE   | APARTMENTS    |            |

        TEMPUAN   OR   COMMON   PASSAGE

        RUAI   OR   COMMON   VERANDAH

        PANTAR

        TANJU   OR   DRYING   PLATFORM
                      UNCOVERED
```

DIAGRAMATIC PLAN OF SEA DYAK HOUSE.
(F. W. Leggatt.)

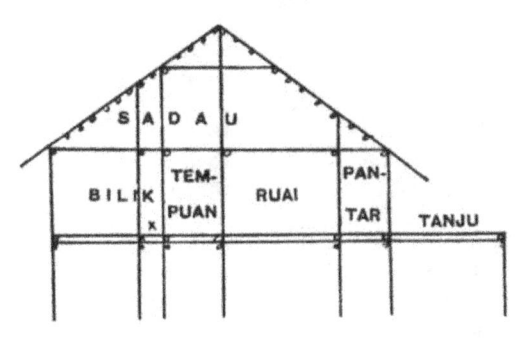

```
        S | A | D | A | U
BILIK | TEM- | RUAI | PAN- |
    x | PUAN |      | TAR  | TANJU
```

X Fire Place

DIAGRAM OF SECTION OF SEA DYAK HOUSE.
(From a sketch by Mr. Crossland.)

or two of firewood reared by the men for use inside. This passage is also used by the women to winnow their rice in, feed their dogs, and attend to their chickens, and by the men to wash the dirt off their feet when they come home from their work. The wall of the *tempuan* is sometimes elaborately painted in various patterns, and the spears of the family are thrust into the skirting board so as to be handy.

"The *ruai* or verandah is in front of the *tempuan* and is as nearly as possible the same size as the *bilieh*, from which it differs principally in being open on all sides and without any partition. It is therefore a cooler and more agreeable place and as such is frequented by both sexes for the purposes of conversation, discussion, and indoor pursuits. Female visitors are usually received in the *bilieh*, but male visitors are invariably received in the *ruai* and only enter the *bilieh* when invited to do so to be introduced to the women and to share the meals. They sleep in the *ruai* along with the boys and bachelors, and sit there all day when they have nothing better to do, conversing with the head of the family and chewing betel. The floor is carpeted with thick and heavy mats of cane interlaced with narrow strips of beaten bark.

INSIDE VIEW OF UNDUP SHINGLE ROOF.
Shingles about 30in. long and 4in. to 14in. wide, according to splitting power. They are tied on with rotan through a single hole only.
(From a sketch by Mr. Crossland.)

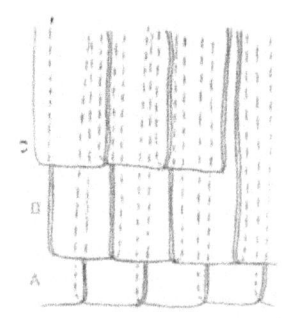

DIAGRAM to show method of laying on an Undup Shingle Roof. The lowest row A overlaps from left to right; B overlaps from right to left; C overlaps same as A.
(From a sketch by Mr. Cross and.)

Over these are spread other mats of thinner and finer texture. There is a small fireplace between this and the next *ruai* for the men to warm themselves at when they get up, as they usually do, in the chill of the morning, before the sun has risen above the trees; the fire is allowed to go out in the middle of the day, but is revived towards the evening when it is getting dark, but still too early to light the torches.[3]

[3] "As a rule the houses are provided with a couple of sliding doors, and they seldom have more than two openings which serve as windows, whatever the number of occupants. Three or four families, or more, reside together in the same habitation. Internally, the house is divided longitudinally by a bamboo partition. One of the long compartments so formed serves as a sleeping place for the unmarried youths and men, and as a general living-room for all the occupants; while the other compartment is sub-divided into a series of smaller rooms for the married members of the family and the women. In front of the door of the long room, adjoining the ladder, is often an open platform or balcony of bamboo or wood, which is used for various domestic purposes—drying rice, or laying 'the clothes to dry.'" (Bock, p. 197.)

"Some *ruais* are provided with a *panggan* or bedstead with plank sides in one corner of the room for the men to sleep in, but this is not always the case. If the head of the family has made it for his own use and if he be a chief or rich man he will fix his gongs of various kinds around it for the sake of show; his weapons will be within reach and his war dress will hang from the roof where it can be seen to the best advantage—a skull cap of wicker work with its nodding plumes, and a skin jacket decorated with the tail feathers of the war bird of the tribe. But the most valuable ornament in the *ruai* by far is of course the bunch of human heads which hangs over the fireplace like a bunch of fruit; these are the heads obtained on various warpaths by various members of the family, dead and living, and are handed down from father to son as the most precious heir-looms, more precious even than the ancient jars which they prize so highly. The next ornament of paramount importance is the bag of charms which is fastened to the centrepost and which is in like manner handed down from generation to generation, and about which there is a great to do if any of the charms are lost or stolen. Other posts are often adorned with trophies of the chase, horns and such like of deer and wild cattle, and the heads of animals such as bears, monkeys, and crocodiles killed by the young boys. The empty sheaths of the swords and knives of the family are suspended on wooden hooks, while the naked blades are placed in racks above their heads.

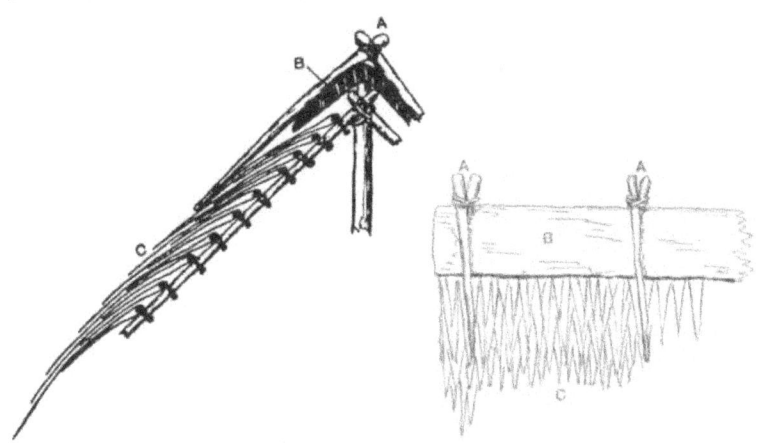

DIAGRAMS to show method of Undup *nipa* palm thatching. A stakes to hold on ridge capping; B ridge capping a piece of wood; C *nipa* thatch.
(From sketches by Mr. Crossland.)

"The *tanju* or open-air platform is in front of the *ruai* and is railed at the edge, but the rail is often so slight that it is unsafe to lean against it. The flooring is usually of ironwood the better to stand exposure to the weather. It is used as a lounge in the evening, the view from it being extensive and the breeze refreshing. While the sun is shining the paddy is put out to dry as are the clothes and a variety of other things. The family whetstone and dye vat are kept here under the eaves of the roof.

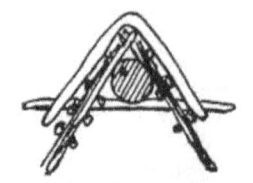

"When the roof is completed the ridge is closed by bending over it sheets of bark, which are kept down by long horizontal pegs driven through the bark beneath the ridge. At intervals also logs of wood tied at top are placed astride the ridge to keep the bark in its position."
(From a sketch by F. W. Leggatt.)

"The *sadau* or loft is used to stow away the baskets and agricultural instruments during the season they are not in use. The paddy is stowed away here in tubs of bark and also the seed for next year's farm. Young women often sleep here and so do the young men and boys who are unprovided with curtains when the mosquitoes and sandflies are troublesome down below. They burn a fragrant bark to keep off the mosquitoes.

"Whenever it is deemed expedient by the Sea Dyaks to shift from one locality to another, or to abandon an old habitation in favour of a new one, a general meeting is convened to consider the proposition and the desirability of the measure is fully discussed. If a move be decided upon a few experienced men are deputed to select a site and to report on its adaptability.[4] If there be no reason to be dissatisfied with the choice, others are sent to hear whether the birds they venerate are for it or against it. Three days in succession they visit the spot and if the bird omens be favourable they proceed to work at once, and on the following morning the men turn out in a body with axes and choppers to hew down the jungle which is then left to dry. Another general meeting is thereupon convened to determine the question of the *tuan* or chieftainship, the measurement of the timbers, and the sequence of the rooms. It is customary to place the richest people in the centre of the village that they may exercise hospitality to all comers, and the boldest at either extremity so that they may defend the approaches if called upon to do so. The next move is to appoint an evening for the people to meet at the site of the new village. The ground is then cleared and measured out and pegs are put in where the posts are to stand. A piece of bamboo is then stuck in the ground, filled with water and the aperture covered with leaves, a spear and a shield are placed beside it, and the whole is surrounded by a rail. The rail is to protect the bamboo from being upset by wild animals and the weapons are to warn strangers not to touch it. If there is much evaporation by the morning the place is considered hot and unhealthy and is abandoned. Half-a-dozen people or so remain to keep watch and beat their tomtoms all night to frighten away evil spirits. Their friends return early in the morning and if all is well they set to and dig the holes, commencing with the chief's quarters and working simultaneously to

DIAGRAM to show how the sticks of *nipa* thatch are tied on to the roof.
(Sketch by Mr. Crossland.)

NIPA LEAF
Folded over stick. 30 to 35 are strung on a stick with rotan, care being taken that they overlap.

[4] Suitability consists in rising ground, nearness to a good supply of water and of firewood. (Crossland, Miss. Life, 1887, p. 162.)

left and right of him. Every family must kill a fowl or a pig before the holes can be dug, and the blood must be smeared on the feet and sprinkled on the

INTERIOR OF A SEA DYAK LONG HOUSE
(From a sketch by Mr. H. H. Everett, in Mr. Hornaday's "Two Years in the Jungle.")
(NOTE.—It is not usual to husk the padi on the ruai but on the tempuan, which is narrower, and therefore vibrates less.)

posts to pacify *Pulang Gana*, the tutelary deity of the earth. The posts must be planted firmly, for if one were to give way subsequently it would be regarded as a disastrous event and the house would be abandoned. All combine to labour collectively until the skeleton of the village is complete, and then every family turns its attention to its own apartments. When the building is sufficiently advanced to receive them they pack up their valuables and convey them by water if practicable, halting on the way until they obtain a favourable omen, when they proceed rejoicing.[5] Their valuables and cotton stuffs may not be moved into the house before themselves, they must be taken with them; this is required by custom. Before the village can be occupied a pig must be killed and its entrails examined and if the reading be unsatisfactory it is abandoned. After everything is settled a cup of *tuak* (toddy) is passed round.

"When a family proposes to leave the village and remove elsewhere it must give an *ensilan* (propitiatory gift?) or be responsible for the consequences if a death ensue; a fowl, or a bit of iron, or a pig if the village be a large one is usually given."

The large Sibuyau habitation in Lundu has been thus described by Sir Jas. Brooke: "The common habitation, as rude as it is enormous, measures 594 feet in length, and the front room, or *street*, is the entire length of the building, and 21 feet broad. The back part is divided by mat partitions into the private apartments of the various families, and of these there are forty-five separate doors leading from the public apartment. The widowers and young unmarried men occupy the public room, as only those with wives are entitled to the advantage of separate rooms. This edifice is raised twelve feet from the ground, and the means of ascent is by the trunk of a tree with notches cut in it—a most difficult, steep, and awkward ladder. In front is a terrace fifty feet broad, running partially along the front of the building, formed, like the floors, of split bamboo. This platform, as well as the front room, besides the regular inhabitants, is the resort of pigs, dogs, birds, monkeys, and fowls, and presents a glorious scene of confusion and bustle. Here the ordinary occupations of domestic labour are carried on—padi ground, mats made, &c., &c. There were 200 men, women, and children counted in the room and in front whilst we were there, in the middle of the day; and, allowing for those abroad and those in their own rooms, the whole community cannot be reckoned at less than 400 souls. Overhead, about seven feet high, is a second crazy storey, on which is stowed their stores of food and their implements of labour and of war. Along the

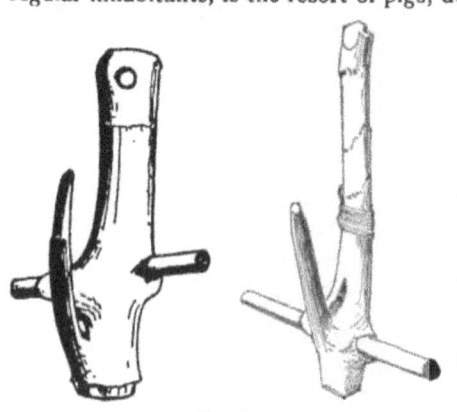

Hooks.
Made out of natural forms with gutta.
(Hose Coll.)

[5] The old women carry the fire, the young ones rice boiled in bamboo. The old men carry their precious jars, the wives the clothes and mosquito curtains, the smaller fry whatever they can. (Crossland, *ibid.*)

large room are hung many cots, four feet long, formed of the hollow trunk of trees cut in half, which answer the purposes of seats by day and beds by night." (Keppel i. 51.)

Sir Spencer St. John measured a Sibuyau house on the Lundu as 534 feet long containing 500 people. (i. 7.) It is of either of these two houses that I think Mr. Marryat writes "the town was surrounded by a strong stockade[6] made of the trunks of the kneebone [*nibong*] palm, a wood superior in durability to any known. This stockade had but one opening of any dimensions." (p. 73.) Another house also of the Sibuyaus on the Senange branch of the Simunjan river "is partially fortified with logs of trees," and is 257 yards = 771 feet long. (Mundy i. 232.) This house is the longest Sea Dyak house on record. "Most of the Sibuyau village-houses are raised about eight feet above the ground; but some are twelve, and others again only four or five. Externally, they are all weather-beaten, gray, and wholly unpicturesque-looking structures, but sometimes are very prettily surrounded by banana and cocoanut trees. Within, they are clean enough, because all the dirt and litter falls of itself through the slatted floor; but the ground underneath is usually covered with litter, perpetually wet and mouldy from the water thrown down through the floor above, and, being the favourite resort of the pigs of the village, often smells horribly. Sometimes the pigs are kept in a sty underneath the long-house. As a matter of course, the old villages are the most foul smelling." (Hornaday, 467.) Elsewhere the same traveller records on the Simunjan (p. 356): "Each door was one wide board with a projecting point at the bottom for it to turn upon in lieu of a hinge. On one of the doors nearest us I noticed a figure of a crocodile rudely carved in low relief. The outline was very good, but no time had been spent in working out the details. The side of the house, which was enclosed, and also the ends, were made up of wide slabs of bark lashed to the framework. The roof was of *attap* or large square sections of palm-leaves sewn together and lashed to the rafters in courses, like shingles."

The Rev. Mr. Horsburgh, who lived among the Balaus, thus describes the roof material: "The roof and partitions are composed of *attaps*, a kind of thatch. . . . It is made of the leaves of the Nipa, a palm which grows in the mud on the banks of the rivers, and differs from most other palms in having no trunk, being merely a collection of fronds proceeding from one root. Each frond consists of a stem or midrib about twenty or thirty feet in length, on each side of which grow a series of leaves, two or three feet long, and two

---

[6] "Some villages are intrenched and provided with a strong palisade formed of the trunks of nibong palms, which shelters them from any sudden attack in case of unexpected hostilities." . . . On the upper Doeson the palisades consist of ironwood. "There also the habitations of the Dyaks are raised much higher above the ground, that is, on posts twelve to fifteen feet high, and they are moreover of very considerable dimensions, as 140 feet long and more; the walls and the roof consisting merely of tree-bark Such a large habitation will contain twelve or fifteen families, so that occasionally they shelter forty or fifty individuals. The Pari, or Parei Dyaks, celebrated for the bold incursions they make on their neighbours as well as the savageness of their customs, and who live inland toward the Koti river, have, it seems, houses which are several hundred feet long and which shelter 400 or 500 individuals. It thus comes about that their villages consist of only one or two sheds of equally colossal dimensions." (S. Müller ii. 359.)

or three inches broad. To form attaps, the Dyaks cut off these leaves, and double them over a stick a yard long, making them overlap each other, so as to be impervious to rain. They then sew or interlace them all firmly with split rattans; thus forming a sort of leaf-tile, at once strong and light, and well adapted for excluding both sun and rain." (p. 16.)

"The natives of Sarawak depend a great deal on the various barks of those trees from which it can be stripped in quantities without splitting. They house their paddy in the bark of the *Impenit* tree, and one good coil or strip can easily hold a ton of paddy; again, they greatly depend on the *Ramin* tree for covering the tops of the roofs of their houses, as it is perfectly waterproof and very durable; the bark of the *Baru* tree is strong and handy for fastening things together and lasts for several months, thereby dispensing with the use of rattan, which naturally every year grows scarcer in the country, and therefore more expensive." (S.G. 1894, p. 121.)

"The (Milanows) houses were formerly built on posts of hard wood, raised about 40 feet from the ground, for protection against their enemies. Several of these houses still stand, but they are never replaced or rebuilt now, as, under Sarawak rule, peace and order have been restored." (Crocker, Proc. R. Geogr. S., 1881, p. 199.) But in Sir Sp. St. John's time the houses were still "built on lofty posts, or rather whole trunks of trees, as a defence against the Seribas." (St. John i. 35.)

"On the way up to Mukah I stopped at Lelac, where are the remains of a long Milanow house. The iron wood posts are still standing, although great forest trees have grown about and among them. Menjanei, one of my Milanow chiefs, who was with me, said that his great grandfather, named Bugad, was the chief of Lelac, and in consequence of the inconstancy of his wife, he called in the aid of the Kyans and destroyed the place, and all his own people who happened to be at home. The ruins are 96 fathoms (672ft.) in length." (Hose, Proc. R. Geogr. Soc., xvii., 1873, p. 133.)

Capt. Mundy incidentally refers to the Milanow village of Palo, then recently destroyed by the Kanowits, which, "like Rejang, is, or rather was, a collection of houses built on the summit of immense piles, forty feet from the ground." (ii. 124.)

On the Limbang river, Sir Sp. St. John finds "the old posts of the houses are removed; being of iron wood they will last for a century. In fact, in many of the villages they have them, descended, it is said, from a long line of ancestors, and these they remove with them wherever they may establish themselves. Time and wear have reduced many of them to less than five inches in diameter, the very heart of the tree, now black with age and exposure." (ii. 32.)

As to the Kayan houses on the Baram river, he says: "Siñgauding's house was of a similar construction to those of the Sea Dyaks, . . . with small doors about two feet above the floor, leading into the inner rooms." (*ibid*, i. 101.)

"Every Kayan chief of consideration possesses a kind of seat in a huge slab cut out of the buttresses of the tapang tree; and this seat descends from father to son, till it is polished and black with age. Siñgauding gave me one,

Town of Kenowit, Rejang River.
(Drawn by Mr. B. Urban Vigors. *Illus. Lond. News*, Nov. 10, 1849.)

measuring ten feet six inches by six feet six inches." (*ibid*, i. 102.) "I looked about the house to-day, and though it is boarded all through, and, therefore, more substantial than those of the Sea Dayaks, yet it did not appear so bright and cheerful as the light yellow matted walls of the latter. I never saw so much firewood collected together as in these houses: on a fine framework, spreading partly over the verandah and partly over their rooms, many months' supplies are piled even to the roof." (*ibid*, i. 109.)

The Kenowit village, where afterwards a fort was built, and where Messrs. Steele and Fox were murdered, is thus described by Sir Sp. St. John: "The village consisted of two long houses, one measuring 200 feet, the other 475. They were built on posts about forty feet in height and some eighteen inches in diameter. The reason they give for making their posts so thick is this: that when the Kayans attack a village they drag one of their long *tamuis* or war boats ashore, and, turning it over, use it as a monstrous shield. About fifty bear it on their heads till they arrive at the ill-made palisades that surround the hamlets, which they have little difficulty in demolishing; they then get under the house, and endeavour to cut away the posts, being well protected from the villagers above by their extemporized shield. If the posts are thin the assailants quickly gain the victory; if very thick, it gives the garrison time to defeat them by allowing heavy beams and stones to fall upon the boat, and even to bring their little brass war pieces to bear upon it; the Kayans will fly if they suffer a slight loss." (*ibid*, i. 38.)

This building would appear to be the same as that mentioned by Sir H. Keppell (Meander i. 177.) and by Captain Mundy, who says: "I could just stand upright in the room, and looking down at the scene below might have fancied myself on the top-mast cross-trees." (ii. 125.)

On the Baram river the "houses usually stand about 20 feet above the ground, on huge posts made of *billian* and other hard woods, and sometimes are 400 *yards* [sic] in length, and often hold over a hundred families; a shingle roofed verandah runs along the front of the house for its entire length, and from this there is a door leading to each room in the house, the said rooms each measuring some 7 yards in length by 3 in breadth, and containing five people on an average. Excellent workmanship is displayed in the construction of these houses, which are very massive throughout, the floors (to mention one item) being usually of planks about 30 feet long and 4 feet wide, with a thickness of 2 inches. All the parts of the house are made ready for putting together, and then on a given day, when the omens have been consulted, every man, woman, and child lends a hand, each contributing in one fashion or another a measure of assistance towards the labour of erecting the structure, and while this is proceeding a few small boys are told off to beat gongs and make a noise in order that bad omens may not be heard after a good augury has been obtained.

"These long houses are sometimes erected in two or three days, all labouring to the greatest extent of their capacity, while the chief keeps order and gives directions, and the amount of work which is crowded into so short a space of time is wonderful to contemplate. The furniture of these dwellings consists of a fire-place, a few rude stools, and chairs carved out of one solid block of wood, are sometimes to be seen; huge slabs of wood, measuring 8 feet by 7 feet, are used for seats, and a description of shelves are sometimes put up in order to provide beds for the young unmarried men; mats, very neatly made of rattans, serve as sleeping mats, and to cover the floor; and the firewood is all stacked ready for use in the empty space above the room." (Hose, xxiii. J. A. I. 161.)

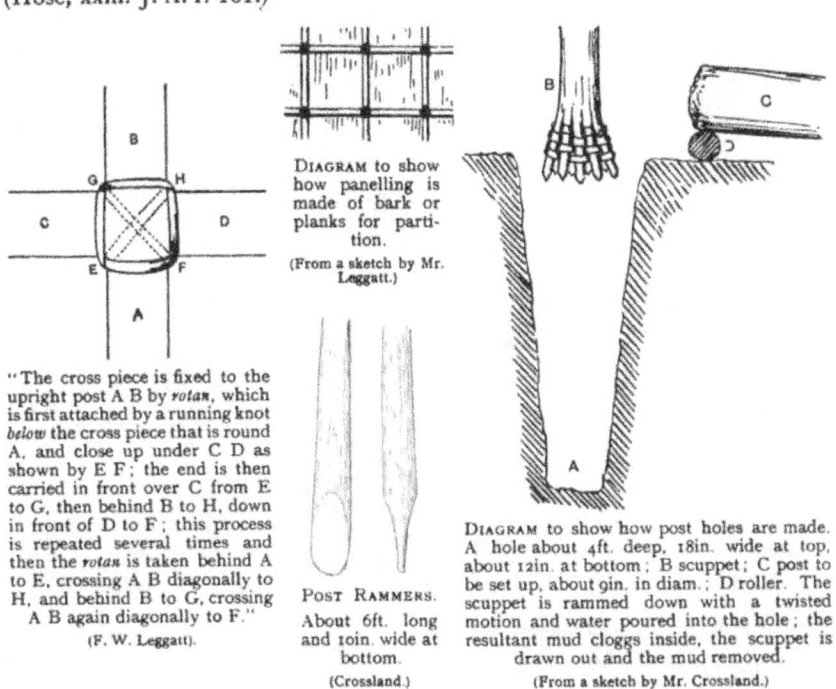

DIAGRAM to show how panelling is made of bark or planks for partition.
(From a sketch by Mr. Leggatt.)

"The cross piece is fixed to the upright post A B by *rotan*, which is first attached by a running knot *below* the cross piece that is round A, and close up under C D as shown by E F; the end is then carried in front over C from E to G, then behind B to H, down in front of D to F; this process is repeated several times and then the *rotan* is taken behind A to E, crossing A B diagonally to H, and behind B to G, crossing A B again diagonally to F."
(F. W. Leggatt.)

POST RAMMERS.
About 6ft. long and 10in. wide at bottom.
(Crossland.)

DIAGRAM to show how post holes are made. A hole about 4ft. deep, 18in. wide at top, about 12in. at bottom; B scuppet; C post to be set up, about 9in. in diam.; D roller. The scuppet is rammed down with a twisted motion and water poured into the hole; the resultant mud cloggs inside, the scuppet is drawn out and the mud removed.
(From a sketch by Mr. Crossland.)

Bishop McDougall mentions the raised seats of polished wood, round the Kyan rooms (Mrs. McDougall, p. 158): "Kiñah houses are packed close together, and there are originally three in a row, without any intermediate space. The floor is only four feet from the ground, and anyone can jump in." (Brooke Low.)

"The houses [at Tambunan] are roofed with bamboo, and frequently the roof is horizontal, making these dwellings look like cages. . . . The people are sadly infested with lice." (Witti Diary, 29 Nov.) Mr. Hatton complains he "had to bend almost double to walk about in a Dusun's house. The roof was covered with the smoke and dust, and there being no chimneys to conduct away the smoke from the cooking-fires, it curls up and hangs about the house, and finds its way out through holes in the roof." (Hatton, p. 165.) "The Danas people have a kind of second story to their houses to which they climb in the wet season, when all the lower part is under water. They told me that in the wet season the whole of the plain was a sheet of water for more than a month." (Hatton Diary, 11th April.) "The

Bungal Ida'an (Dusun) house in which we lodged was the best I have ever seen among the aborigines: it was boarded with finely-worked planks; the doors were strong and excellently made, with a small opening for the dogs to go in and out; everything looked clean—quite an unusual peculiarity. The flooring of beaten-out bamboos was very neat, and free from all dirt, which I have never before noticed in a Dayak house, where the dogs generally render everything filthy. As this was the cleanest, so I think my friend the Bisayan chief's house on the Limbang was the dirtiest —to describe its abominations would turn the reader's stomach." (St. John i. 248.) " The dwellings which, near the coast, are generally of *atap* or thatch made from the leaves of the *nipa* palm, are here (among the Dusuns) nearly entirely of bamboo, the roof being thatched with *atap* of cocoanut or the sago palm." (Burbidge, p. 255.)

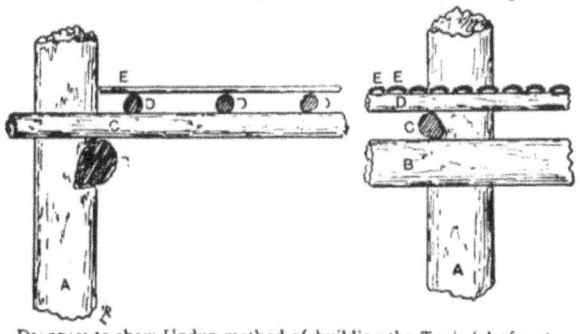

DIAGRAM to show Undup method of building the *Tanju* (platform). A main post; B beam; C cross piece; D joists; E lanties of *nibong* palm (if rich), of bambu (if poor).
(From sketch by Mr. Crossland.)

"The Dusun long house is built like those of the Muruts and Bissayas on the Limbang with the single exception that the floor is not so high above the ground and that the front is open or nearly open while the front of the Murut houses

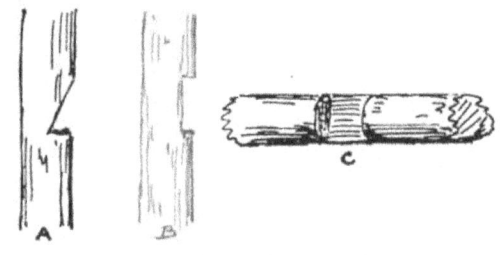

CUTS IN POSTS
For supporting beams, cross pieces, &c. Cut as A when the cross piece is left in the round and as B when the cross piece is cut similarly to C.
(From a sketch by Mr. F. W. Leggatt.)

is closed, and besides the doorway there is a narrow opening along the whole length of the building which serves as a window and can be used as a loophole against the enemy when attacked. Nor did I see any stockaded Dusun house in North Borneo. The house is completely built out of neat bambu, the main entrance is at the end of the house. On the left is a verandah roofed over against sun and storm; on the right are the long rows of chambers for women and married people; the unmarried have no chambers. Above the property of the inhabitants is stored. . . . At the end of the house is a raised platform for visitors. (De Crespigny Berl. Zeit. N. F., v. 335.) Elsewhere the same traveller says everything is kept as clean as a new pin." (Proc. Roy. Geogr. Soc. ii., 1858, 344.)

Among the Kiaus Sir Sp. St. John discovered a "house better arranged than the ordinary Sea Dyak ones. Instead of having the whole floor on a level with the door, they had a passage leading through the house: on one side the private apartments; on the other, a raised platform on which the lads and unmarried men slept. We found this very comfortable as the dogs were not permitted to wander over it." (i. 312.) "Some of the tribes in the Tawaran have followed the Malay fashion of living in small houses suitable for a single family." (*ibid*, i. 374.)

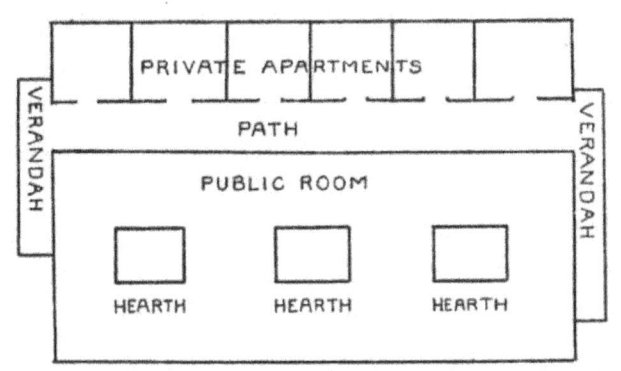

```
┌─┬──┬──┬─PRIVATE APARTMENTS─┬──┬─┐
│V│  │  │  │  │  │  │  │V│
│E│  └──┴──┴──┘  └──┴──┘  │E│
│R│         PATH             │R│
│A├──────────────────────────┤A│
│N│                          │N│
│D│      PUBLIC ROOM         │D│
│A│  ┌────┐  ┌────┐  ┌────┐  │A│
│H│  │    │  │    │  │    │  │H│
│ │  └────┘  └────┘  └────┘  │ │
│ │  HEARTH  HEARTH  HEARTH  │ │
└─┴──────────────────────────┴─┘
```

PLAN OF LARGE DUSUN HOUSE AT KIAU. N.W. Borneo.
(After Burbidge, p. 96.)

"Dusuns are decidedly of a social turn of mind, assembling in small working-parties, after the day's toil is done, at each other's houses. Light is

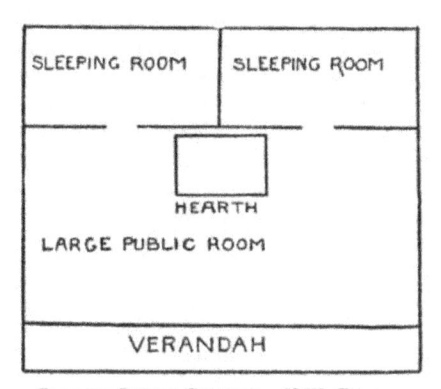

```
┌──────────────┬──────────────┐
│ SLEEPING ROOM│ SLEEPING ROOM│
│              │              │
├──────────────┴──────────────┤
│                             │
│         ┌────────┐          │
│         │        │          │
│         └────────┘          │
│           HEARTH            │
│   LARGE PUBLIC ROOM         │
├─────────────────────────────┤
│         VERANDAH            │
└─────────────────────────────┘
```

PLAN OF DUSUN COTTAGE. N.W. Borneo.
(After Burbidge, p. 85.)

admitted by windows and small doorways in the plank sides; the shutters have rattan hinges. In some houses the whole of one side of the public apartment is open. As there is no special outlet for the smoke, the roof and nearly everything inside is black and dirty. A house lasts from five to seven years when it falls or is pulled down, the plank sides being used again for the new one. Some of these planks are of great age, and it is wonderful how smooth they are considering the tools at their command. The floors are made of bamboo; the bamboo is split from end to end when green, then each joint is cut through in many places; after this operation the bamboo is forced open and laid flat on the ground, heavy stones being placed on it to keep it so until dry, when it remains perfectly flat and soon becomes beautifully polished, but, I am sorry to say, affords a splendid covert between the tiny cracks for numerous specimens of most disgusting insects. The bugs which infest these floors, at times become sufficiently troublesome for the Dusuns even to take an interest in their ever-increasing numbers. It is no uncommon sight to see a Dusun who is patiently working at a rope or fishing-net, suddenly jump up and commence scratching himself; then he walks to the fireplace, on which he proceeds to boil some water in his small earthenware cooking-pot; this, when ready, he pours over these bug-infested planks, and once more proceeds with his occupation. As most Dusuns at home wear the chawat, their interest in these pests may be well understood. . . . The fire is made on a mud hearth, and has a light bamboo framework built over it, for drying rice and placing a few earthen cooking-pots." (Whitehead, p. 105.)

"Among the Dusuns, on building a new house, to insure the inmates from devils and bad luck, a long ceremony is held over a pig. This animal is tied down and a nice tray is placed over it to keep off the sun; the priestesses and the female occupants of the new house stand in front of the pig with the household bunches of charms, and coco-nut-shells filled with water, with which the pig is sprinkled; after nearly an hour's incantation, accompanied by the klicking of small flat pieces of metal held by the women in their hands, the pig is taken by the men into the new house and there killed, and afterwards forms part of the evening's feast." (*ibid*, p. 110.)

As we have seen above, Mr. De Crespigny has referred to the Murut houses; in the same paper he also refers to stockaded Murut houses (p. 328) but he describes none. For the only account of a Murut house we must tender our thanks to Mr. O. F. Ricketts: "Murut houses are of the most temporary description; in the case of the interior tribes it is owing to the fact that they shift their locality about every year in order to take up fresh land for their paddy; but in the case of those in the lower river it would appear to be to save trouble as the land they cultivate is always close to them, being planted in alternate years. A house that is 250 to 300 feet long containing about 30 doors is the largest built and is the exception, generally being half that size ; the plan is much the same as those of other tribes, one half length ways being divided into rooms for the families, the other half forming a verandah but closed in, a space being left all along the wall about a foot wide for lights; this can be closed by a plank which slides over the aperture. The roof is generally too low for a European to walk under upright and the floor requires treading with caution, though the Muruts themselves stump over it as if it was solid brick." (S. G., No. 347, p. 214.)

It will have been observed that by far the larger portion of the natives live in long houses where by means of their large numbers the people are better placed for withstanding attacks. As Sir Sp. St. John remarks of Pangalan Tarap, that much harassed village : " The detached house system, so progressive with security, does not answer in a country exposed to periodical incursions." (ii. 29.) It seems, however, to have been the opinion once that the life in these long houses was better than that in detached ones. Thus Bishop Chambers wrote in 1859: "I am persuaded that this social and communal life has had a great influence in preserving the people from barbarism ; and that the consequent shame of doing anything condemned by their code of morality exercises a very powerful influence in preserving them from acts of fraud, baseness and cruelty." (Miss. Field, 1859, p. 58.)

But a more intimate knowledge of this life in the long houses has not confirmed the Bishop's opinion. As a Batang Lupar correspondent of the " Sarawak Gazette " put it as recently as 1894 (p. 67) : " The practice of herding together in long houses prevents mental and moral improvement and hinders advance in gardening and planting and agricultural development generally."

" The Land Dyaks carry their paths straight over the mountains, irrespective of height or difficulty of ascent, the idea of making a détour round the base never seems to have struck them." (Chalmers O.P., p. 5.) " The object of the paths, until recently, has seldom been to connect the villages, and render communication between them easy, but this has generally been fortuitously brought about by the paths leading to the farms of the neighbouring tribes meeting each other."

"All the paths of the Land Dyaks are formed of the stems of trees, raised two feet above the ground, on supports placed under them. Sometimes larger trees are employed, but the usual size is about three inches in diameter ; the bark from the upper surface, as they lie in their horizontal position, together with a portion of the wood, is cut off, so as to leave a flat rough surface for the foot of the wayfarer ; in good roads, and where bamboos are abundant, these canes are employed, two large ones laid parallel with each other, forming the breadth of the path; but as bamboos more readily decay than the wood of which the more common path is made, these, though much preferable when new, and in dry weather, are more troublesome when old and decaying, or from the slippery surface of the bamboo on rainy days." (Low, p. 285, &c.)

These bambu paths are called *batangs*, and most writers have given accounts of the awkwardness they experience in walking along the top of them. Sir Charles Brooke describes these paths as "an introduction to a new style of walking, resembling tight-rope manœuvring more than any other. Some of these trees were six or eight feet above the ground." (i. 18.)

"In some of the Land Dyak villages the custom prevails of carrying the *batangs* and bamboos which constitute the road immediately under the houses and verandahs, thus laying the unwary traveller open to receiving slops and refuse on his head through the *lantis* above, besides keeping the path always dirty." (Denison, ch. viii., p. 87.)

"It is no easy matter to move about at any time in a Land Dyak village, where the paths are but batangs, and where filth, offal, and dirt surround you on every side; in the dark it was simply out of the question" (*ibid*, ch. iii., p. 30.); but Mr. Grant mentions once (p. 7), that "cocoa-nut leaves were laid down where the path was dirty, and over these we passed till we arrived at the Orang Kaya's house."

Miss Coomes tells us that once at Lundu: "Mr. Gomez proposed a walk round the village, there being what he called a *good* road. In front of the Dyak houses there is indeed a very good path, being in some parts three feet wide, beneath a grove of palm-trees; but, beyond that, it puzzled me sadly to find any path at all. Mr. Gomez led the way; and, although a tall stout man, he was often hidden by the long grass. I had to fight my way through the bushes, and returned, after an hour's ramble, wet to the waist."

DYAKS USING AXE-ADZE.
(From a sketch by Mr. H. H. Everett, in Mr. Hornaday's "Two Years in the Jungle.")

(Gosp. Miss., 1858, p. 119.) Mr. Burbidge speaks of "a rather rough walk through long grass, in which ugly concealed logs were plentiful." (p. 60.) "In carrying a path along the face of a precipice, trees and roots are made use of for suspension; struts arise from suitable notches or crevices in the rocks, and if these are not sufficient, immense bamboos, fifty or sixty feet long, are fixed on the banks or on the branch of a tree below. . . . When a path goes over very steep ground, and becomes slippery in very wet or very dry weather, the bamboo is used in another way. Pieces are cut about a yard long, and opposite notches being made at each end, holes are formed through which pegs are driven, and firm and convenient steps are thus formed with the greatest ease and celerity. It is true that much of this will decay in one or two seasons, but it can be so quickly replaced as to make it more economical than using a harder and more durable wood." (Wallace i. 122, 124.) Mr. Grant (p. 49) likewise refers to pegs being driven into the mountain paths. On the Jagui mountain, Mr. Denison says: "The climbing was of the steepest description, being simply a series of steps or pieces of wood placed zig-zag along the sides of the hill, like ladders, and occasionally perpendicularly. We counted no less than 2,476 of these steps, some of which were the roots of trees, and I may describe my progress as an eternal getting upstairs." (ch. iii., p. 31.)

There are many bridges, and they "are generally very picturesque. They are made where the river is narrow, and where two trees, one on each side, overhang the stream. Amid the branches of one is placed a long thick bamboo, which reaches to the branches of the tree on the other side; but if it prove too short, two bamboos are lashed together with rattans and creepers. This is the footway. Next, long thin bamboos are suspended from the upper branches of the trees, the lower ends being tied to the footway before made, and fixed crosswise below it. Rattans and creepers are also brought into requisition, to strengthen and steady the bridge; these are the suspenders. Another bamboo is tied along the suspending bamboos, on each side the footway, to serve for railings. The general appearance of this primitive bridge, with a rapid stream running under it, is very pretty, especially as the banks of the rivers are in general beautifully lined with trees and masses of rock. By a sloping ladder of the usual description, the bridge is connected with the banks on each side of the stream, but the whole thing is more picturesque to the eye than safe for the person of the novice in jungle travelling." (Grant, p. 33.)

Mr. Denison speaks of a bridge amongst the Grogo Dyaks "which was constructed of jungle wood and bamboo and was 138 feet in length and most skilfully put together." (ch. iii. p. 28.) Mr. Wallace says "some of these bridges were several hundred feet long and fifty or sixty high. . . . . The bridge is partly suspended and partly supported by diagonal struts from the banks, so as to avoid placing posts in the stream itself, which would be liable to be carried away by floods." (i. 114 and 122.) Sir Hugh Low describes the bridges (p. 286) and Sir Sp. St. John remarks on their lightness and elegance and also on their apparent flimsiness (i. 139). Mr. Burbidge complains that "the only bridges across the streams were formed of a single tree-trunk, often a very slender one not perfectly straight, so that when a particular part of it was reached in one's journey across, it had a treacherous knack of turning round and landing one in muddy water up to the neck. The natives are used to

SEA DYAK ABODE AND BRIDGE.
(Sir Chas. Brooke's "Ten Years," i. 220.)

such slender makeshifts for bridges, and, being barefoot, are as sure-footed as goats." (p. 60.)

UNDUP BAMBU DESIGN.
(Crossland Coll.)

DESIGN ON BAMBU BOX.
This design is made the reverse way to those below; the black portions still represent the natural outer skin of the bambu.
(Amsterdam Mus.)

LEAF
wrapped round dragons' blood. ¼ real size. S.E Borneo.
(Leiden Mus.)

DESIGNS ON BAMBU BOXES. ½ real size.
(Crossland Coll.)
For method of engraving, see p. 241.

CHAPTER XVII.

WEAVING, DYEING, AND DRESSMAKING. TRIBAL DRESSES. DRESS IN DETAIL.

WEAVING, DYEING, AND DRESSMAKING.—Weaving—Dyeing—Weaving—Eye for colour—Native cloth — Cotton — Jacket making—Petticoat making—Lanun cloth—*Chawats*—The *Artocarpus*—The *Kulit tekalong*—*Antiaris toxicaria* - Bark cloths—*Artocarpus elastica*—*Lamba* fibre (*Curculigo latifolia*)—A jacket made of a towel—Great variety in dress.
TRIBAL DRESSES.—LAND DYAKS: Sauhs, Serambo, and Singe general dress—The *Rambi*—Method of fastening petticoat—Tringus dress—Curious head dress—the *Seladan*. SEA DYAKS: Love of finery – Ornaments— Batang Lupars — Drowning through weight of ornaments. MALANAUS: General dress. DUSUNS: General dress—Breast cloth. MURUTS: General dress.
DRESS IN DETAIL. — Corsets—*Rambi (rawai)* — *Tinchien* — *Tina-lumiet* — Land and Sea Dyak corsets—JACKETS: Varieties of. PETTICOATS: Ornaments to—Expensiveness—Shortness of—CHAWATS: Description—Tribal disposal of—Variations of—Trousers coming in. HIP LACE: Description—Value of. MAT SEATS. RAIN MATS. HEAD DRESSES: Great varieties of—Beads—*Labongs*—*Selapoks*—Bark fillets—Hair dressing—*Balong*—Heads having—Hair cut to look fierce—Flowing hair—Grotesque caps—*à la Chinoise*—Flowers— Children's head shaving—Hairpins—Coloured beads—Cloths—Sou'westers—Monkey skins. EAR ORNAMENTS: *Grunyong*- Ear lobe extensions— Ugliness of — *Langgu*—*Tinggu* — Animals' teeth — Heavy brass earrings — *Tusok pendieng*—Buttons—Discs or ear plugs—Verdigris. NECKLETS, ARMLETS, LEGLETS: Porcelain—Shell—Tapang wood—Animal teeth necklaces—Charms—*Simpai lengan*—*Rangki*—*Tumpa*—*Kongkong rekong*—*Tinchien*—*Tunjok*—*Nghrimoks*—*Selong*—*Lukut sekala*—Spiral collars.

WEAVING, DYEING, AND DRESSMAKING.

"THE cloth which the Balaus weave is of two kinds, striped and figured, the former for their jackets, and the latter for their *bidangs* or petticoats. The former is made by employing successively threads of different colours in stretching the web; the latter is produced by a more difficult and elaborate process. After the web has been stretched (for which, in this case, undyed thread is employed) the work-woman sketches on the extended threads the pattern which she purposes shall appear on the cloth, and carefully notes the intended colours of the various scrolls. Supposing she intends the pattern to be of three colours, blue, red, and yellow, she proceeds as follows:—She takes up a dozen or a score of the threads of the web (according as the exigencies of the pattern will permit her) and wraps a quantity of vegetable fibre tightly round those parts of them which are intended to be red and yellow, leaving exposed those portions which are intended to be blue. After she has in this manner gone over the whole web, she immerses it in a blue dye, which, while it takes hold of the exposed portions of the threads, is prevented by the vegetable fibre from colouring those portions which are intended to be red and yellow. After it has been dried the vegetable fibre is cut off; and when the web is now stretched out the blue portion of the pattern is seen depicted. In a similar manner the red and yellow colours are applied, and thus the whole web is dyed of the required pattern. The weft is of one uniform colour, generally brown." (Horsburgh, p. 43.)

Dusun Loom.
(Brit. Mus.)

Of the Sea Dyaks Mr. Thos. S. Chapman writes: "At present there are only two kinds of looms, the *tumpoh*, at which the weaver sits on the floor and uses the hands only; and the *tenjak*, at which the weaver sits on a bench, and uses hands and feet, the latter working treadles. The cloths are much better and closer woven in the *tumpoh* looms. Both looms are picturesquely clumsy, and the work slow. . . . The natives here do certainly seem to me to blend their most brilliant dyes by instinct. I once watched a woman arrange the coloured threads for a tartan, and she evidently worked neither by rule nor pattern, indeed, she consulted me now and then, but I evading to give any advice, she finished her design and the tartan eventually turned out charming, to my great admiration. Then there is no lack of industry among our native women weavers (for women only, as a rule, weave out here) and no lack of energy in learning the craft, which is tedious enough even when learnt: but their love for their old fashions and customs stands much in the way of improvement." (S.G., 109.)

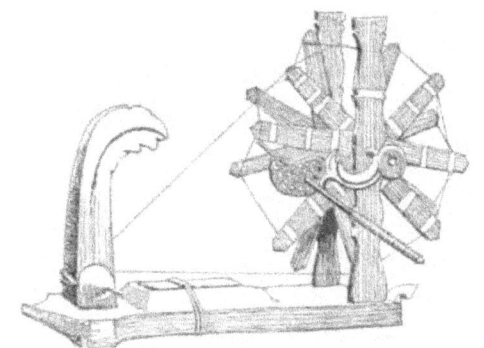

Gasieng inggar, DYAK NOISY SPINNING WHEEL.
(Brooke Low Coll.)

MODEL OF COTTON GIN.
S.E. BORNEO.
(Leiden Mus.)

Speaking of the Sea Dyaks generally Sir Spencer St. John says: "All their clothes are made from native cloth of native yarn, spun from cotton grown in the country." (i. 29.) "The women manufacture a coarse cloth; making and dyeing their own yarn, beating out the cotton with small sticks, and, by means of a spinning-wheel, running it off very quickly. The yarn is not so fine as what they can buy of English manufacture, but it is stronger, and keeps its colour remarkably well; and no cloth wears better than Dayak cloth." (*ibid*, i. 74.)

"They grow their own cotton and weave it, but they never manufacture enough in the piece for a garment. The fabric is however particularly strong and serviceable, especially in the dense woods and tangles. . . . I have often worn them myself, and found these cotton stuffs of the greatest service as a protection from thorns." (Bishop McDougall, T.E.S. ii. 28.)

Referring more particularly to cloth-making among the Skarans, Mr. Leggatt has communicated the following to me: "The method of making a jacket is about as follows, and refers to a little girl's jacket (aet 7), but as the female jackets are all made on the same principle, this one will serve as a very good example. The strip of cloth is about 56 inches long, and about 11½ inches wide at one end, and 10¾ inches at the other (it is characteristic of these cloths that they are all slightly narrower at one end than at the other). Two pieces of about 10 inches deep each are first cut off to make the sleeves, which come to about five inches wide each at the shoulder end, while at the wrist end, in order to make them narrow, a triangular piece (*a*) is cut off one side only, so that when sewn together the seam does not run straight. The piece of cloth, now about 36 inches long, is folded over in half (*b c*) and a hole (*d*) cut out for the neck, and from this hole the front part is cut straight down to *e*, forming the opening of the jacket. The cut edges are hemmed much the same as European hemming. The sides are then sewn together by cross stitches, in much the same way as we lace up boots with a single lace. Under the armpits, both in the sleeve and the jacket, a ventilation hole is made by simply leaving the parts unsewn. In order to fasten the jacket in front, a thorn, or wood, or bone pin is skewered through the cloth on one side, and some thread let into the edging of the other side is slightly twisted round the peg much as a halyard is made fast. Now buttons are frequently used, but they do not make button-holes, nor loops, but twist the thread round the button, holding the thread, when doing so, very like a sempstress when she is sewing on a button."

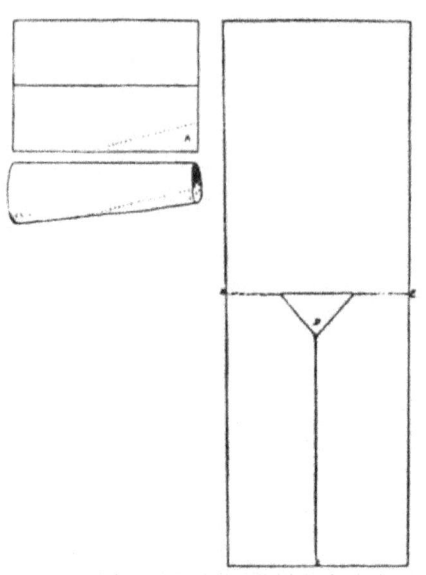

DIAGRAM to show how a jacket is made from a piece of cloth (see text).

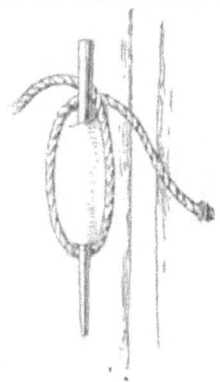

SKEWER acting as button. Sakaran Dyaks.

The dyeing by the Skarans is similar to that described by Mr. Horsburgh. "It takes several months to dye and weave a piece about 45 inches in circumference. These petticoats are woven in circular pieces, same as our pillow cases are manufactured; they are then cut into two, so that two petticoats are made out of the one original piece. The ends are properly sewn together, in the European style, and not sewn together in the same way as the sleeves are attached to the jacket body. The backs of the jackets appear to bear a sort of tribal badge in the pattern, and, in the case of the Sekrang and Saribas, this pattern is worked into the cloth while it is being woven, the thread of the pattern being put through at the same time as the warp. In the case of the Balaus, the pattern is made on another piece of cloth, and a piece of the back of the jacket cut out and the badge piece fitted into its place. The dye on the back of the jackets is made very faint, or that part of the jacket is left undyed, in order to leave a light background for the dark badge." (*ibid.*)

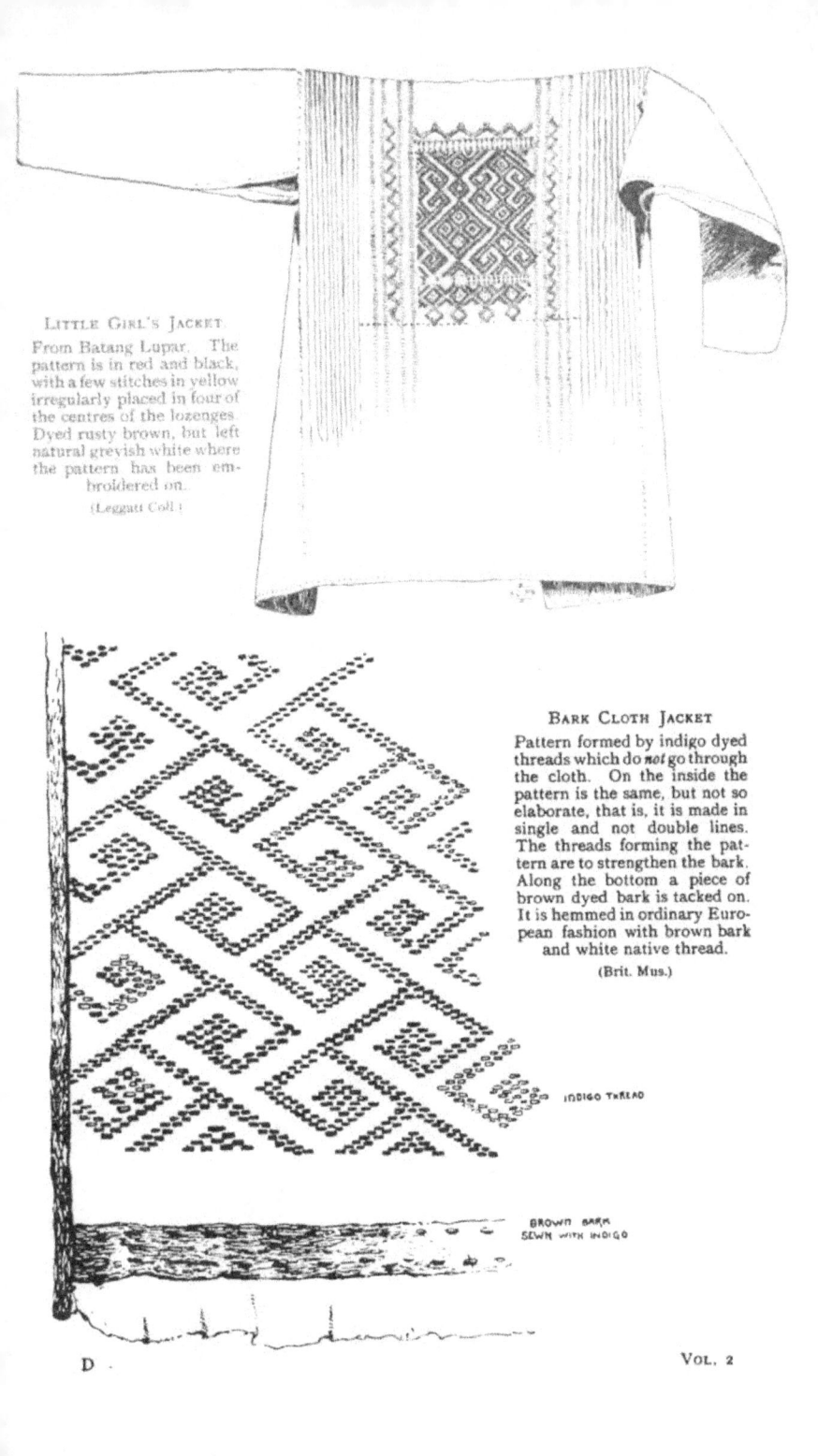

LITTLE GIRL'S JACKET.
From Batang Lupar. The pattern is in red and black, with a few stitches in yellow irregularly placed in four of the centres of the lozenges. Dyed rusty brown, but left natural greyish white where the pattern has been embroidered on.
(Leggatt Coll.)

BARK CLOTH JACKET
Pattern formed by indigo dyed threads which do *not* go through the cloth. On the inside the pattern is the same, but not so elaborate, that is, it is made in single and not double lines. The threads forming the pattern are to strengthen the bark. Along the bottom a piece of brown dyed bark is tacked on. It is hemmed in ordinary European fashion with brown bark and white native thread.
(Brit. Mus.)

INDIGO THREAD

BROWN BARK
SEWN WITH INDIGO

INSIDE OF SAME BADGE to indicate how the pattern is worked on.

HAND WOVEN BADGE.

Forming the back of jacket worn by Banting women. The cloth of this pattern is black, the pattern red and white. The jacket from which it was taken was a sort of (? European) red twill. Width at top, 14½in.; width at bottom, 18½in.; length, 18in.

(Leggatt Coll.)

"Spinning and weaving is practised but little by the Kayans, but almost all the other races in Borneo manufacture some kind of cloth. The patterns of these cloths are very artistic, the dye used being made from the fruit of the rattan, the juices of various roots, and the sap of some trees. The yellow dye used by the Dyaks is known as *Intamu* and the red as *Jeranang.*" (Hose, J. A. I. xxiii. 165.)

"The Lanuns also furnish a cloth which is highly prized among every class of inhabitants in Borneo; it is a sort of checked black cloth, with narrow lines of white running through it, and glazed on one side. This was formerly made entirely of native yarn. It is also worthy of notice that this cloth is dyed from indigo grown on the spot." (St. John i. 259.)

Of the Hill Dyaks, Sir Hugh Low writes: "Their dress, when they have property sufficient to obtain one, is the long cloth, or *chawat*,[1] the manufacture of the Sakarran Dyaks; but poverty more frequently compels them to supply its place with a rough substance made of the bark of several trees, particularly that of the genus *Artocarpus*, which produces the bread-fruit." (p. 240.)

"There is the tree *Kulit Tekálong*, which the Dyaks pound until it becomes soft in texture and then manufacture into the *bajus* (jackets) and *chawats* (so familiar to those who have lived in Dyak districts), and very pleasing to the eye too are these garments, in hue reminding one of the colour of a new saddle, whilst in length of time they wear quite as well if not better than a garment of 'bazaar cloth.'" (S.G. 1894, p. 121.) Evidently this note has brought the following from a correspondent on the Batang Lupar: "*Tekalong* bark in former days, when cloth was not to be had, was always used by Dyaks for their *chawat* (waist-cloths); it is even now used by Dyaks in the *ulu*, or heads of the rivers, where cloth is expensive and by persons who cannot afford to buy cloth. Dyak *puah* (blanket, or night covering) is still much in use, but the old *kibong* (mosquito curtains) composed, as the *puah*, of the *Tekalong* bark have been given up. A *Tekalong* tree has somewhat the appearance of the *Padalai* fruit tree. When the tree is large, long strips of bark, let us say up to ten feet, can be obtained; but when the tree is small and like *babas* growth of course only small strips can be got. When small the tree is called *Temeran.*" (S.G. 1894, p. 146.)

"The bark the Sea Dyaks employ for caulking is very tough, and, beaten out, serves to make useful and comfortable coverlets, as well as waist-cloths and head-dresses." (St. John i. 70.)

"The inner bark of a tree called *ipoh* by the Dyaks and *tajam* by the Kayans, and which appears to be identical with the Upas tree of Java *(Antiaris toxicaria)*, is used for clothing, and the young tree is grown for this purpose in Dyak gardens; the bark is not pulled off until a year after the tree has been felled." (Brooke Low.)

"The Kayans use the bark of a tree to make coats and waist-cloths, and I have even seen a mosquito curtain formed of this material." (Hose, J.A.I. xxiii. 165.)

[1] The two *chawats* in the Leggatt collection are 66 inches long, width at front end 12 inches and at back end 10¾ inches; length of fringe 10 inches. There is much European material in these two specimens.

"Among the Muruts the bark is peeled off a tree in broad strips and is very united and flexible; it is then hammered all over with a heavy wooden instrument, which has a flat surface on one side cut in deep cross lines like a file; this breaks up the harder tissues of the bark and reduces it to a very pliant, though by no means united, texture. The bark being full of rents and

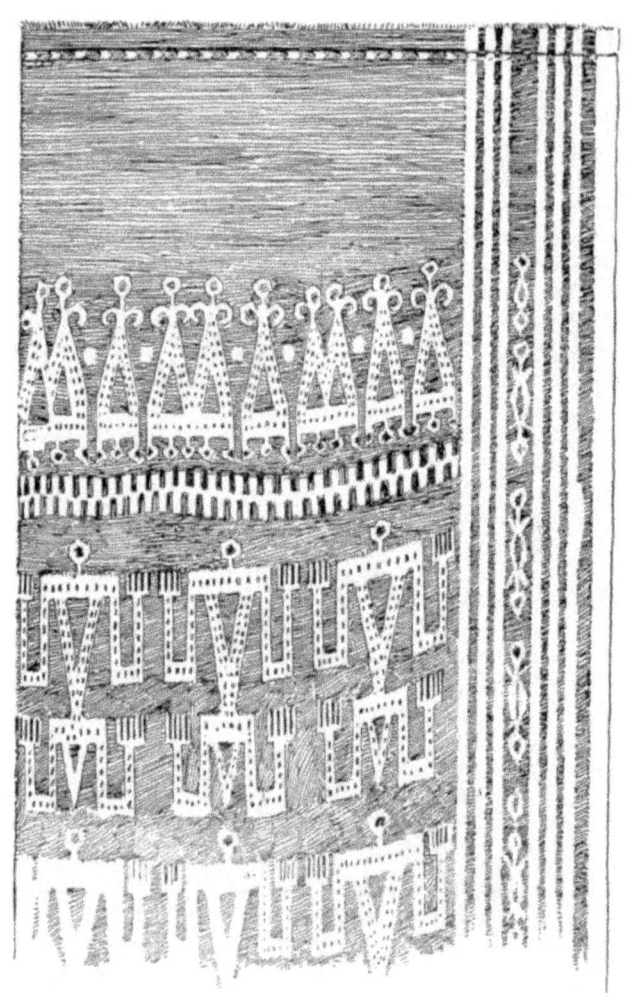

DYAK WOVEN BLANKET.
The warp threads on the right dyed light green and red before putting on the loom. The cloth itself is dyed a dark brick red. To prevent the edges fraying a double chain stitch in alternate green and white thread is run along the bottom. The whole blanket is made by sewing on to it a similar piece of cloth with same pattern, but left handed, giving a total width of about 35in.; length, 6ft. 6in.
(Leggatt Coll.)

holes, this difficulty is overcome by transverse darning: one of these coats[2] now before me has no fewer than 270 transverse strings on the back alone, each thread penetrating the outer surface only, and assists to work out a cross pattern for ornamentation. The size of a strip of bark for a *baju* is about five feet by eighteen inches. This after being prepared is folded in half: the half for the front of the jacket is divided right down the centre; the sides are stitched up, leaving holes for the arms; from the back of the neck hang narrow strips of bark or long streamers of coloured wool. The bark is mostly reddish brown; but the best kind is white, the texture being more united and requiring little or no transverse stitching, but is occasionally ornamented with coloured patterns in wool. The sewing-thread is made from pine-apple leaves, which plant was growing in a semi-wild state on some hills near, the fruit being apparently valueless to the Muruts." (Whitehead, p. 75.)

Mr. Burbidge says of the bark cloth[3] *chawats* of the Muruts that it "is the produce of *Artocarpus elastica*. The inner bark is stripped off and soaked in water, being afterwards beaten to render it soft and pliable. Of this, *chawats* or loin-cloths and jackets are commonly made by the Muruts on the Lawas and the Limbang rivers, and it is also still used by the Dusun villagers on the Tampassuk, notwithstanding their skill in preparing, weaving, and dyeing the *Lamba* fibre." (Burbidge, p. 155.)

Mr. Burbidge speaks of Dusun. ". . . netting needles of wood, similar in principle to our own, and of weaving instruments, by means of which a strong and durable cloth is made from the macerated fibre of a species of *curculigo* called *lamba* by the natives.[4] This is afterwards dyed with native grown indigo. . . . I noticed a small basket of true cotton of excellent staple, but it is not much used, *lamba* fibre being obtainable in any quantity from the jungle without any trouble, and its fibre is more readily worked with the help of rude implements. For sewing thread we found our hostess using the fibre of pine-apple leaves (*Ananassa sativa*), which serves the purpose well." (p. 252.)

Of this *lamba* amongst the Dusuns, Mr. Whitehead says: "The lengths of fibre which run in parallel lines along the underside of the leaf are separated and tied together. . . . The fibre is wound round a stick, and when sufficient has been obtained is woven into a hard cloth on the small Dusun looms." (p. 180.) "He gave an old woman a towel which she folded in half, sewed up the sides, leaving holes for her arms, cutting a slit in the middle for her head, and in a few minutes was wearing this novel garment." (p. 189.)

Mr. Witti noticed among the Dusun that "the homespun of these people is not uniform bluish gray but striped with black." (Diary, Nov. 20th.)

[2] Mr. Von Donop notes the bark coats on the Papar Mountain; he says they won't stand washing. (Diary, 24 May.) At Pomatum "I was shewn a small shrub called *Home*, the leaves of which closely resemble that of a young *cinchona succirubra* in appearance. It is used as a dye in the place of indigo. The leaves are boiled and the thread or cloth is immersed in the liquor. The plant, they told me, was ready for plucking three months after planting." (*ibid*, Diary, March 4th.)

[3] Sir Sp. St. John remarks that the men had broad belts of bark worn over the *chawat* like the Sagais of the eastern coast. (ii. 129.)

[4] Elsewhere (p. 155) he calls it "*Curculigo latifolia*, a yellow flowered broad leaved weed, often seen in great abundance on old cultivated plots near the houses."

HEM (FRONT)

HEM (BACK)

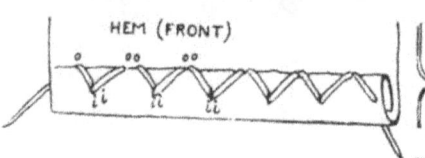

SEAM OF A DUSUN COAT.
Made with native thread. The coat is of coarse palm leaf (?) fibre, the sleeves of European (?) woven cotton. It is hemmed with European tape in ordinary European style.

DUSUN SHORT COAT HEM.
Beginning at the left the thread in the hem at the bottom comes out in front at *o*, goes in at *ii*, out at *oo*, then back in again at the first *ii*, out at the second *oo*, and in at the second *ii*, and so on.

SEAM on a very rude thick bark jacket from Kina Balu.

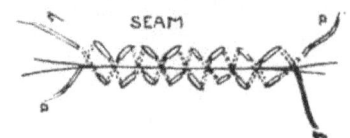

SEAM

SEAM on the side of the same coat, sewn with two threads.

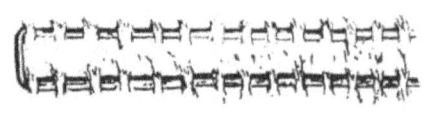

INDIGO THREAD run through a Dusun bark coat to strengthen it.

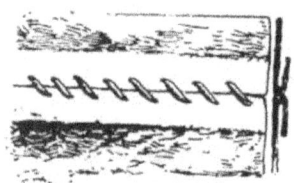

SEAM on a Rejang River Dyak coat.

SEAM of a bark jacket in which the back is made in two pieces. From Long Bléh.

JOINING of a piece of loin cloth of the Rejang River Dyaks. From the top downwards on the surface the thread comes out at *o* and goes in at *i*, then out at *oo* and in at second *i*, out again at same *oo* and in at *ii*, out at *o* and in at *ii* again, and so on.

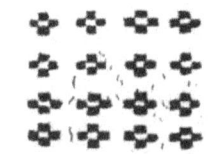

STRENGTHENING THREADS of a bark coat made into a pattern of little crosses.

DOUBLE THREAD SEAM on a bark cloth; also ornamental double thread running through without seam. From Long Bléh.

SEAM on a Rejang River Dyak coat.

SEAM of a Dusun shroud. The ends of the cloth are overlaid and first one end *a* sewn and then the other end *b* by separate native thread.

SEAM on a Dyak cloth coat.

NOTE.—All the above examples I have taken from articles in the British Museum. Mr. Crossland informs me the Undups make a true needle out of thin brass wire.

Lieut. De Crespigny found the Muruts with "good cotton out of which they made coarse cloth." (Berl. Zeit. N.F. v. 325.) While of this people Mr. O. F. Ricketts writes: "Weaving is very little done and only by the people of the far interior." (S. G., No. 347, p. 214.)

The dress of the peoples varies in every detail throughout the country. It will therefore be the better way to take first general descriptions of the dresses of the various tribes and to supplement these with details of the special articles of clothing and ornament.

TRIBAL DRESS.

LAND DYAKS.

"The men of the Sauh tribe as well as those of Serambo and Singhi generally wear a dark blue or black head-cloth, and sometimes also a cloth of Malay pattern, a necklace of two or three strings of beads, the only colours used being red, white, black, and yellow. On great occasions brass wire rings are worn half way up the arm to the elbow, and above this armlets of the *rotan ijuk* which are replaced by silver armlets among the upper classes when in full dress. Round the waist is worn a cloth called the *chawat* by the Malays, and the *taup* by the Land Dyaks; this is a long cloth twisted round the waist the ends being allowed to hang down before and behind. The *chawat* or *taup* is generally of black or dark blue cloth, and sometimes of scarlet colour, but, in jungle wear and among the poorer Dyaks, this is often changed for the inside of the bark of the *Artocarpus*. Among the Dyaks this tree is known as the *bayu*, among the Malays the *temarang*. (Denison, ch. iii. p. 25.)

"On the right side the Land Dyak suspends a small basket, often very prettily plaited, to which is attached a knife in a bamboo sheath, the latter sometimes tastefully carved and colored. The basket, knife, and fittings are called the *tunkin*, the basket itself is the *tambuk* and holds the siri leaf and is made to contain two round little cases for lime and tobacco called *dekan*, and a piece of the inner bark of the *bayu* tree, while the knife in its sheath hanging on the outside of the *tunkin* is called the *sinda*. A sword or *parang* is worn on the left side, the one in general use is that called *buco* by the Dyaks and *tunduk* by the Malays, another *parang* used is the *bye* of the Dyaks and *kamping* of the Malays. Ear-rings consisting of a single ring of broad flattened wire or else pieces of thin round bamboo $\frac{1}{4}$ of an inch in diameter, and some two inches long, ornamented with the black thread-like bands of the lemmun creeper, are worn through the lobes of the ear. A jacket of some coarse cloth often of Sea Dyak manufacture completes the costume, which may in fact apply to all Land Dyak tribes visited by me, though I may add that on festive occasions, the head-men sometimes wear a necklet or *bobut* of wire, on which are strung opaque beads of a dark green and blue colour, with which are mixed kejang, deer and bear's teeth. The armlets or *mannu* are made of brass wire and rotan twisted together, and very neat they are. Ear-rings, *shibu*, are worn of wire twisted round in a coil and hanging from the ear by single bend of the same.

"The women of the above mentioned tribes wear a necklace of two or more strings round the neck, red, yellow, and black coloured beads being used. On festive occasions this becomes a heavy mass of bead-work, as it is worn in many coils. Round the arms, between the shoulders and elbow, armlets are worn, made of the red wood of the heart of the tapang tree, which becomes hard on exposure to the atmosphere. Brass rings cover the lower portion of the arm from the wrist to the elbow, but never above it. The dress is a *sarong* or waist-cloth called the *jammu* made of coarse cloth generally of Sea Dyak manufacture, and brass rings are worn on the legs below the knees. Round the waist hanging loose over the loins partially covering the *jammu*, are coils of split rotan fastened together by small brass rings; these coils of rotan are called *rambi* (*uberi* by the Sennah Dyaks) and are made of the rotan *padina* stained black, which colour is the only one in use amongst these tribes. Bands of small fine brass chains some three inches in breadth (*sabit*) are worn round the loins mixed with the *rambi*, and at feasts silver coins are worn on the edge of the *jammu*, and as a kind of belt round the loins. I must not forget to mention that the *jammu* is fastened round the waist by a string of rotan, or twisted lengths of the *ijuk* fibre from the *No* palm or other substance. This string is worn loosely next to the skin, round the waist, the *jammu* is drawn round to the hip and then folded back across the body, the string is then pulled over it and this keeps the cloth in its proper place and position round the waist. (*ibid*, ch. iii. p. 26.)

"I now come to describe the dress of the women of the Tringus tribe, and in describing them I include also the Gumbang women and those of the other tribes I am about to visit, who all wear nearly the same attire. The body is naked to the waist; below this is worn a short *jammu* or waistcloth, generally of a dark dirty-blue colour, with frequently a red border or edging. On great occasions, and even in general wear, silver coins are often fixed to the end of the edging. The *rambi* of thin narrow split bamboo is worn in four or five coils round the waist, and is stained red and not black as with other tribes. This is allowed to hang loosely over the loins, and mixed with it are very fine brass chains called *sabit*, which are worn in coils to a thickness of three or four inches. The ankles are ornamented with brass rings, which are also worn above the knee, between the wrist and elbow, and above the latter nearly to the armpit. Bracelets of the kima shell, which when long worn resemble ivory without its yellow tinge, are in constant use; sometimes as many as four of these bracelets (besides the brass ones), are worn on each arm, say two below and two above the elbow. The neck is graced with thick coils of red or black beads. Unlike the other Dyak tribes I had visited, the women of which went bare-headed, these Dyaks and the Gumbangs wore a peculiar and fantastic head covering made of beads, strung perpendicularly on a circular wire frame, about eight inches high, made to fit the head at its base, but tapering upwards to the top (which is open) to about one half the circumference of its base. When worn by the priestesses, or *bilian* as they are called, these head-dresses are closed at the top, when they are often surmounted with a tuft of feathers or hair. The beads are always of the same colour, viz.: red, yellow, black, and white. These curious head coverings are called *burang* by the Gumbang and Tringus tribes, though, I believe, they are also known as *segubak* and *sipia* by other Dyaks; they are worn by the women of every tribe from Gumbang to the Sadong, the Land Dyaks of which district also make use of them. The Singhis, Serambos, and Sauhs are the only tribes without the *burang*, and these are again the only tribes who wear the *seladan*. Among the Dyaks I am now about to visit, a cloth skull cap, fitting close to the head, made of blue cloth, with a little red trimming, is much affected by the women." (*ibid*, ch. iv. p. 40.)

"The chawat is generally of blue cotton, ending in three broad bands of red, blue, and white. Those who can afford it wear a handkerchief on the head, which is either red with a narrow border of gold lace, or of three colours like the chawat. The large flat moon-shaped brass earrings, the heavy necklace of white or black beads, rows of brass rings on the arms and legs, and armlets of white shell all serve to relieve and set off the pure reddish brown skin and jet black hair." (Wallace i. p. 104.)

Sir Hugh Low speaks of the young men covering "the upper portion of the arms with rings of the black *iju*, or horsehair-like substance, plaited very neatly. This, to the eye of an European, is the most becoming of all their adornments, the dark black of the material contrasting agreeably, but not too decidedly, with the brown colour of their skins. . . . Amongst the tribes on the western branch of the Sarawak river, the dress of the women is increased by the addition of an article called by them *Saladan*. It is made of a bamboo, split, flattened, pared thin, and dyed black: being thus prepared, it is fitted to the body, and secured in its form and position by brass wires passing across its breadth, which also serve for the purposes of ornament; they are placed at the distance of about one inch apart from each other. Girls begin to wear it at the age of five or six years, and as it is made on the body it is only removed by destroying it when a larger one is needed.[5] This curious article of dress is confined to the tribes of Sarawak called Singhie, Sow, Serambo, Bombuck, and Peninjow, who in their dress also differ from the other tribes of the Hills in this, that their women wear no beads for ornament, and the men only those of two colours—black and white. Transparent beads are not esteemed by any of the tribes I have visited; small and opaque ones alone being valued by them. The colours most in demand are the two above mentioned; but yellow and red are also much sought after. The girls of the tribes on the western branch of the Sarawak river never wear the brass wire above the elbow-joint of the arm, nor have I seen them use the white bracelets so common in the others of the southern river, the use of which amongst these tribes is apparently confined to the men." (Low, p. 240.)

Sea Dyaks.

"Love of finery is inherent in the young of both sexes; the elderly are less fond of it, and often dress very shabbily and save up their good clothes for their offspring. The ordinary male attire consists of a *sirat* or waist-cloth,

---

[5] See *infra* for difference between the Land and Sea Dyak corsets.

a *labong* or head-dress, and a *takai buriet*, or seat mat; the full dress consists of the above with the addition of a *klambi* or jacket, and a *dangdong* or shawl. The ornaments are *grunjong, langgu, tinggu, kongkong, rekong, simpai, tumpa, tinchien, ngkrimok* or *unus*. The female attire is very simple, consisting of a *bidang* or short petticoat when at home, and a *klambi* or jacket when out of doors. By way of ornament the women wear in addition to the finger rings, necklaces, and bracelets which are described later on, other ornaments peculiar to their sex, styled *balong, tusok penchieng, tina, ranghi, lumiet* or *tinchien, selong* and *gelang ghirieng*, all of which are described in due order." (Brooke Low.)

Top view.

View from below.

Side view.

MALANAU GOLD BUTTONS.
Worn along the sleeves of women's jackets. Weight, ⅜oz.
(In the possession of Mrs. F. R. O. Maxwell.)

Tanjong takup, or SHELL VINE LEAF.
Worn by little girls.
(Brooke Low Coll.)

LITTLE GIRL'S GIRDLE AND SHELL.
W. Borneo.
(Leiden Mus.)

The dress of the Batang Lupar people is thus described by the Rajah as being very "plain, and their costume is far from graceful. Boots of brass wire are attached to their legs from ankle to knee, a scant cloth around the middle, and strings of brass rings, beads, and wires encumber their bodies all the way up to their breasts; bead bracelets are around the neck, and armlets of brass encircle the wrists, to correspond with the leggings. This is full dress; but when in mourning, they cast off these ornaments and use stained rattans around the waist instead, to be replaced by the finery when a head is brought into the country, for gaieties prevail on such occasions. How they can clamber hills and mountains, and work at farming, with such a weight attached to their bodies, is a marvel. Several have been drowned in consequence of these weights, when their small boats have swamped. They also sleep in this gaudy paraphernalia, and one has some cause to pity the bed-fellows of these brazen images." (ii. 168.) Mr. D. S. Bailey writes from Simanggang thus: "A girl from Rantau Panjai, in the *ulu*, was being conveyed to her wedding feast, when the boat upset, and, as is usual in such cases up river, the enormous weight of her brass ornaments carried her to the bottom immediately." (S.G., 1895, p. 14.)

SKARAN GIRLS.
The one on the left has a *chimpoke* (sacred flower) in her hair.
(Crossland Coll.)

MALANAU.

His Highness has given the following description of the dress of one of this tribe: "His skull-cap of many hues had long feathers standing upright from it; a maias (orang utan) skin jacket hung over his shoulders. He was further adorned with feathers both before and behind, and sundry strings of beads hung dangling about. A breast-plate of tin, with the edges slightly carved and perforated with holes, was attached to the jacket; his under-garment consisted of a red cloth, and his legs were free of any incumbrances. The ends of the red cloth were long, and prettily embroidered with beads; the short sword of his country, with the convex and concave blade, hung at his waist, and human hair, stained various colours, fastened to the hilt, the belt being composed of beads." (i. 302.)

THE DUSUNS.

" The Dusun women have perhaps one of the most picturesque dresses of all the Bornean tribes; they wear a fairly long petticoat of home-made cloth, dyed indigo blue ; above this skirt and over it for a few inches are coils of black and red rattan ; below these hang rows of red beads, closely threaded to a depth of six inches or so ; sometimes numerous brass chains hang above the beads. The bright metal cylinders worn by the Patatan women were seldom worn by the Dusuns round Kina Balu. Until they are mothers, a strip of blue trade-cloth is worn over the breasts, which is kept in its place by numerous coils[6] of red rattan ; these coils, like those round the waist, are tied together in quantities of six or eight. The women file their teeth like the men ; their eyebrows are shaved into narrow arched lines ; as a rule, the right ear only is pierced. Their coiffure is simple, the hair being tied in a knot on the top of the head, through which a bone hair-pin, attached to a string of beads, is stuck, the beads being wound round the base of the knob. Some of the women wear coils of thick brass wire round their wrists and ankles, one old dame having a pair of solid brass anklets, several pounds in weight, which she always wore. A cowl is worn during field work, as a protection from the sun. Children run naked until about four years of age." (Whitehead, p. 106.)

THE MURUTS.

"Their usual dress consists of the 'chawat,' though some of the more civilized wear jackets and head-cloths in addition, and some even trousers. The hair is worn long, parted in the middle, and then tied in a knot at the back of the head with a pig's tusk, sometimes ornamented with a tuft of hair or a tassel at the largest end, passed through the knot as a hairpin; often a piece of bone (see p. 59) somewhat arrow-shaped and slightly carved is used for the same purpose. They wear no brass earrings as many other tribes do; the usual thing is a piece of bamboo, or rather a section, about a quarter-of-an-inch deep, and in circumference rather smaller than a cent piece, into which a piece of mirror is fixed; this forms the earring, which is inserted into the

---

[6] This strip is mentioned by Sir Sp. St. John (i. 248, 306), Mr. Von Donop (Diary, 22nd May), and Mr. Burbidge (p. 156).

lobes of the ears. Some of the interior tribes wear a large round earring either of bone or ivory with a knob of agate in the centre, about three-quarters-of-an-inch long. These have rather a curious appearance and in circumference are about the size of a half-crown. Bead necklaces are much worn by the men, some of them being of considerable value, consisting of large agates; few wear bracelets or amulets, and these are generally of inferior quality. The women are short and dumpy, and one who is good-looking is very much the exception; they wear the short petticoat, reaching from the waist to the knees; in the lower river most of them wear jackets, in the interior nothing else. They have the same necklaces and earrings as the men, and, in addition, bracelets of beads and strings of beads on the head to as many as six rows; these fit the contour of the head, and if continued to the top of the head would form a cap: the hair is smoothed down and the end is brought up and passed through inside the strings of beads, forming a long loop a little to one side of the head. Brass rings round the waist, so common amongst the Dyaks, are unknown; the only ornament is a belt of several strings of small beads worn just over the petticoat." (O. F. Ricketts, S.G. No. 347, p. 214.)

"The native women inland wear short *sarongs* of *Lamba* cloth, reaching from the waist nearly to their knees, and a profusion of stained rattan coils, brass wire, coloured beads, and other trinkets around their waists, and heavy rings of brass on their legs, or coils of brass wire on their plump and dusky arms. The younger ones wear a strip of dark cloth across the breast. . . . The hair is often gracefully wreathed up with a string of red or amber coloured beads, sometimes with a strip of the pale yellow nipa leaf, in its young state, and the contrast is very effective." (Burbidge, p. 156.)

DRESS IN DETAIL.
CORSETS.

Regarding the curious corset referred to in the above descriptions, there are several varieties among the various tribes. At Si Panjang (Land Dyaks) the women "wore brass wire over and mixed with their rotan *rambis*." (Denison, ch. v. 56.) The Serins (Land Dyaks) wear the *rambi* of black and red rotan mixed." (*ibid*, ch. vii. 78.) Madame Pfeiffer describes the Land Dyak corset, called *raway* or *sabit*, " as 7 to 9 inches long, and covered with innumerable brass or lead rings and weighing 15 to 20 lbs." (i. 79, 88.) The Rev. W. Chalmers says: " The stays are made of the bark of some tree, ornamented with brass wire," and that " it does not improve their looks, however much it may add to their comfort, as it gives the body somewhat of a barrel-ly appearance." (Miss. Field, 1859, p. 148.) Mr. Hornaday thus describes this garment: " The *tinchien* is the body ornament of the Ulu Ai and Ngkari women. It is composed of some eight or ten parallel rows of large brass rings long enough to encircle the waist. They are strung on rattans and connected with one another by a network of cane inside. The ends of the band are furnished with a pair of vertical plates of the same metal, the outer edges of which are curled, the one inwardly, and the other outwardly, so as to catch one another, and effectively lock in the body. The rings (with the exception of every alternate one, which is an ordinary finger-ring), are long and broad, and rudely engraved a variety of patterns. These rings cost eight shillings a string, and a complete set of ten would cost five pounds.

RING of a *rawai* made of rotan with fine brass wound round.
(Canterbury Mus.)

CHAIN BAND, *tali mulong*. Of antique pattern; worn over the *rawai*.
(Brooke Low Coll.)

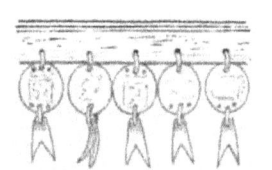

Senawir. BRASS HOOP AND SILVER COINS.
Worn on top of the *rawai*.
(Brooke Low Coll.)

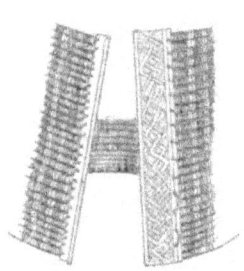

FRONT OF WOMAN'S GIRDLE.
With brass clasp, and made of brass rings strung on rotan. W. Borneo.
(Leiden Mus.)

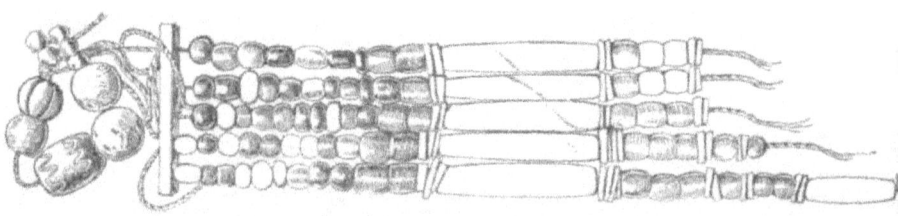

GIRDLE of glass and shell beads, called *entelo*. Worn hanging on to the end of the *rawai*.
(See pp. 51, 55.)
(Brooke Low Coll.)

"The *tina* are slender hoops of crimsoned cane, worn round the waist, and look like whalebone when coloured black, as they invariably are in mourning costume.

"The *lumiet* is the *rawai* of the Malohs (Malaus) and is a much esteemed body ornament of the Sakarangs. It is composed of a series of cane hoops covered with an infinity of diminutive brass links. A few of the hoops are made larger than the rest so as to hang loose on the hips. The series that encase the waist and the stomach fit close and are pinned together with brass wire; they sometimes are worn up to the nipples, but not every woman can afford to be at such great expense." (Brooke Low.)

"The Dusuns, a tribe of Dyaks on the north coast, wear immense rings of solid tin or copper round their hips and shoulders." (Marryat, p. 79.)

"These curious corsets were models of rigidity and closeness of fit, and being brightly polished, gave the young ladies quite a substantial air." (Hornaday, p. 485.)

A writer in the Field, Dec. 6, 1884, says: "I had the opportunity of examining carefully a Sea Dyak brass corset, which differs from the Land Dyak one, in so far that the brass wire is wound horizontally round the waist, and therefore moulds itself to the shape and movements of the body in a more pleasing manner than the Land Dyak corset, in which the wire is placed perpendicularly, and always remains stiff and rigid. The latter must be for the wearers uncomfortable to a degree, as they can hardly bend the body at all, while the former is not such an impediment to motion, and rather enhances the gracefulness of an elegant figure. Those brass corsets are rarely taken off, and when they are the operation of doing so is somewhat ludicrous for lookers on, but not so by any means for the unfortunate wearer, as I once had the occasion of judging. The girl I saw had to hang by her hands to a bar of wood, whilst a friend slipped her brass cuirass inch by inch upwards and over

"Narrow Garment to fall fore and aft of the body. Hole in middle to pass the head through. The under part is bark cloth, the upper, of a woven fibre cloth, is covered with six rows of discs from 4 to 1in. diameter, made of shell and sewn on, bordered with small rubbed down shells (*terria*). The edges are bound with red cloth and the ends fringed with black human hair." Double length, not including fringe, 4ft. 5in.

(Brit. Mus.)

her head." They will not part with these corsets. Mr. Hornaday gives a similar account of the method of taking them off. (p. 450.)

JACKETS.

"Land Dyak jackets, or *bajus*, whether the fighting padded ones, or the ordinary ones, are without sleeves, the shoulder, however, being so cut that it sticks out like the scales of an epaulette." (Grant, p. 17.)

Among the Sea Dyaks, "the *klambi*, or jacket, is manufactured from yarn spun from their own cotton. There are several kinds of these, but the one known as the *klambi burong* is considered the best. In all of them the sleeves are open in the armpit, and the pieces sewn together with twine. The edges

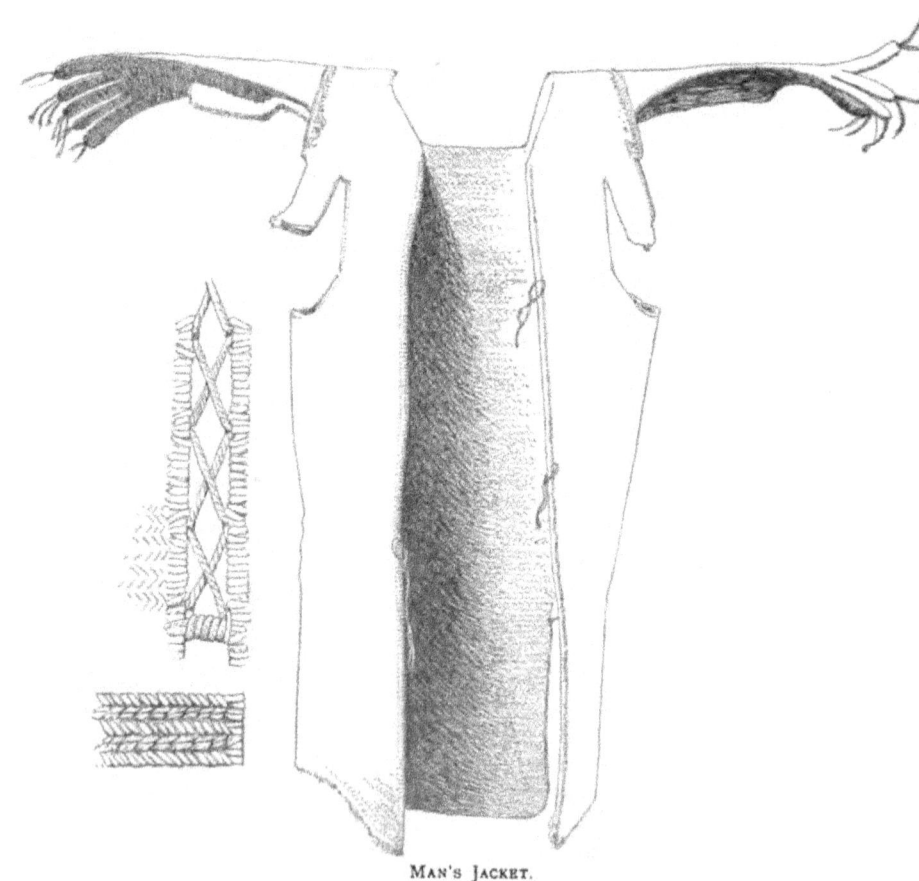

MAN'S JACKET.
Open in front. Made of three pieces of peculiarly-woven (?) cloth of brown cord, laced together at the edges. Lappets to fall like epaulets over the shoulders, their lower ends slashed, and beneath them are smaller lappets of cotton originally red and blue. Length, 4ft. 1in.
(Brit. Mus.)

are bordered with scarlet cloth. There is another kind much worn by the Sakarans, which resembles a waistcoat more than a jacket, being without sleeves. The Ulu Ais manufacture a coarse white jacket striped with blue.

DYAK MAN'S JACKET.
Of woven light brown fibre with pattern painted or printed on, joined in front and at sides, leaving neck and arm holes.
(Brit. Mus.)

The *klambi subang* manufactured by the Sarebas is of finer and closer texture than any other, and is in consequence far more expensive. The thread of which it is wrought is procured from the Malays, and is of a red colour. The lower portion of the back is embroidered with gold and silver thread, with a fringe of silk depending from it.

"The *klambi*, or jacket, worn by the women, is, if anything, larger than that worn by the men. The patterns are precisely the same, but the texture is finer. The Sarebas women wear another jacket dyed a ruddy brown with mangrove bark, with a square embroidery on the back, and a fringe of hawks' bells." (Brooke Low.)

"The jackets are ornamented with fringe." (St. John i. 29.) "The women's jackets among the Sakaran reach nearly to the knees, and are brown in colour; among the Balaus they are bright red, and reach to hips only; and among the Sarebas they are nut-brown, and reach to knees. The dresses of the Sarebas are the best embroidered, as they are cleverest in all needlework." (Leggatt.) "The *dandong*, or shawl, is worn slung over the shoulder." (Brooke Low.)

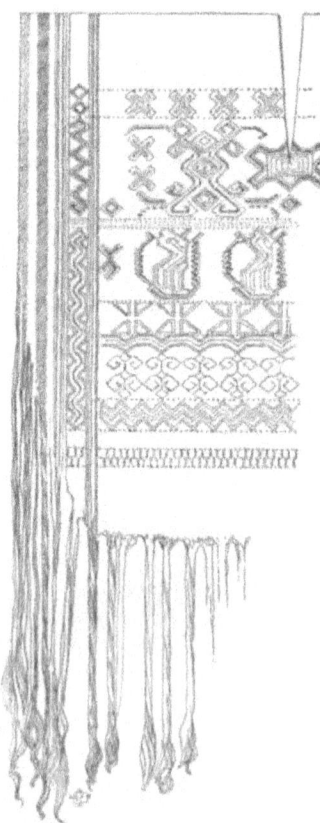

UNDUP GIRL'S SLEEVELESS JACKET
of unusual shape.
(Crossland Coll.)

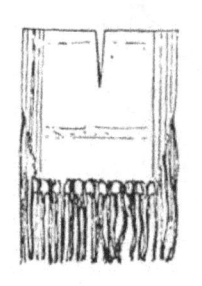

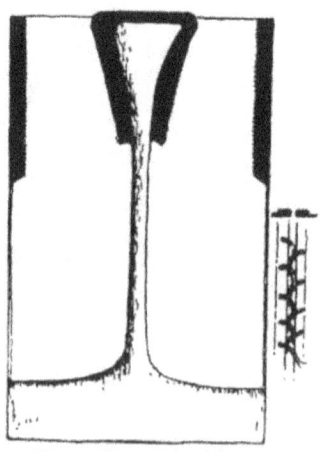

WHITE BARK BALAU JACKET
Made for Land Dyaks. Neck and arm holes bound with black cotton.
(Canterbury Mus.)

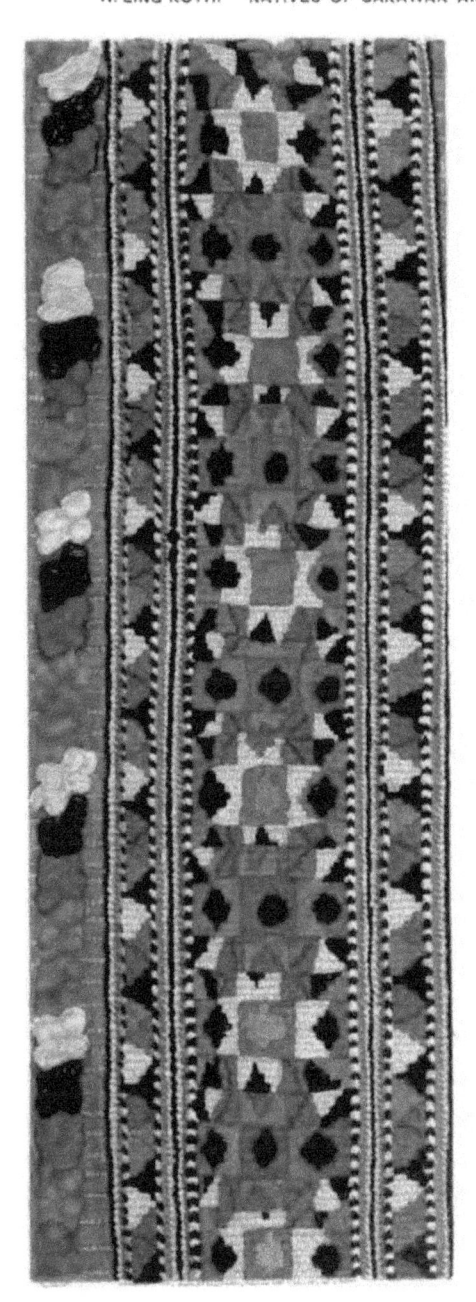

H. LING ROTH.   NATIVES OF SARAWAK AND BRIT. NORTH BORNEO.

PATTERN ALONG BACK RIM OF SEA-DYAK WOMAN'S
JACKET; WORKED ON ENGLISH RED CLOTH.
(LEGGATT COLL.).

BORDER DOWN
FRONT OF THE
SAME JACKET.

Dress in Detail.

PETTICOATS.

The Land Dyaks woman's petticoat or "*bidang* is of the size and shape of a kilt. A belt holds it round the waist, and it descends to the knee." (Grant, p. 17.) "Silver coins are freely worn round the edges of the *jammu* (petticoat) of the Sering and Simpoke women." (Denison, ch. vi. p. 76.)

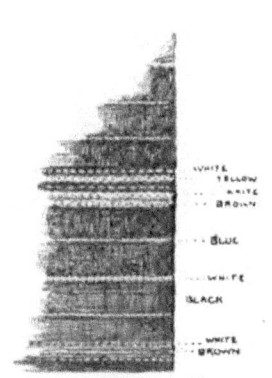

END OF A PIECE OF CLOTH
to show how they arrange their colours.
(Brit. Mus.)

PATTERN ON UNDUP WOMAN'S PETTICOAT.
(Crossland Coll.)

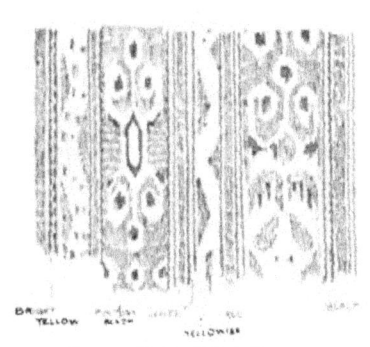

REJANG RIVER DYAK CLOTH.
(Brit. Mus.)

The Rev. Mr. Horsburgh relates: "On one occasion I saw the daughters of several Sakarran chiefs clothed in loose dresses composed of shells, beads, and polished stones, arranged with great care and considerable taste. The dress, which was very becoming, hung as low as the knee, and as the young ladies walked along, the stones of which it was composed rung upon each other like the chime of distant bells. These dresses are very expensive, costing some seventy or eighty reals a-piece (about £12), and are therefore not common." (p. 11.) "In the wealthier Undup tribes the women wear round their petticoats strings of silver coin, the united value of which, in many cases, will amount to above £10. . . . . To an European fresh arrived the dress looks scanty; but, when he lives amongst them and has seen their walks and their work, he cannot but admit that it is admirably adapted to their condition." (Crossland, Miss. Life 1865, p. 655.)

"The Sea Dyak *bidang* is a short petticoat reaching from the waist to the knee, and is kept in its place by being folded over in front and tucked in on one

SAREBAS WOMAN'S PETTICOAT.

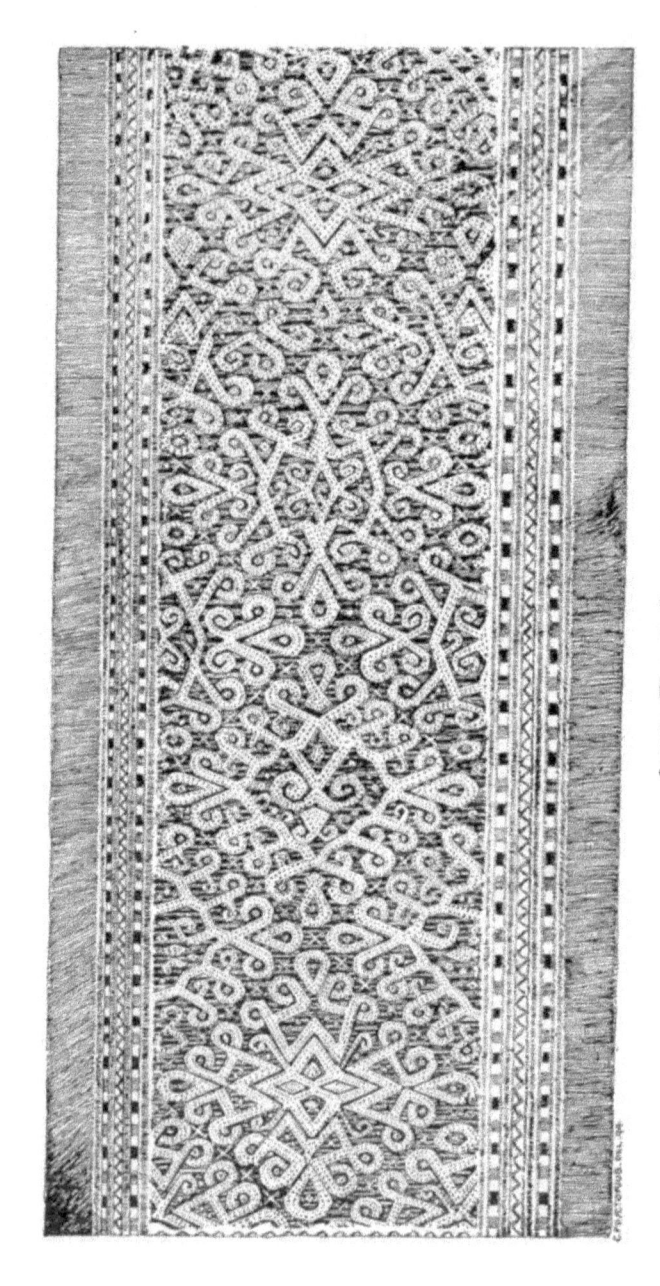

Width, 17in.; length of piece drawn, 36in.; the circumference of the petticoat formed by sewing the two ends of half a piece of cloth together is 46in.; the whole piece of cloth from the loom being about 92 or 93in.

(Leggatt Coll.)

side. It is manufactured from their own cotton fabric, which is first partially dyed and then worked into a variety of patterns to which the most fanciful names are given. The *bidang* worn in mourning is stained a deep indigo blue, and is called *kain baloi*. A lighter shade is worn out of mourning, especially by the Ulu Ais, and is often adorned by them with small cowries or pearl buttons, and fringed with *grunongs* or little tinkling bells." (Brooke Low.)

"The Kayan women's frock covering is more capacious in drapery than those used by the Dyaks." (Brooke ii. 225.)

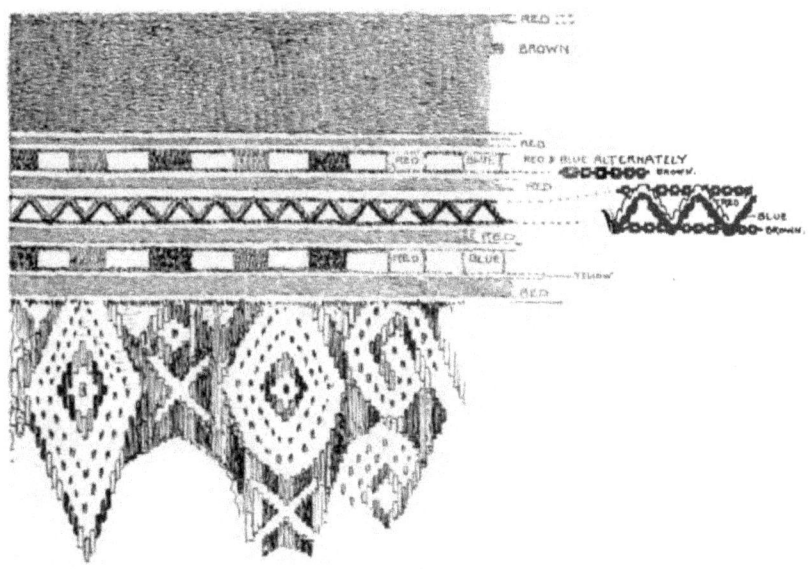

BORDER OF THE SAREBAS WOMAN'S PETTICOAT.
Illustrated on opposite page.

"The dress of the Kayan women is a cloth reaching from the hips to the ankles, tied at the hips, but open all down one side, leaving room for them to walk easily. They wear a string of beads round the waist." (Hose, J.A.I. xxiii. 167.)

Of the Ida'an young women's petticoats Sir Sp. St. John says: "They were larger than usual, a practice that might have been followed with advantage by their elders." (i. 248.)

Mr. Witti remarks on the scantiness of the petticoats of some Mount Dulit Dusuns—"regular female kilts, which do not incommode them in climbing steep hill-sides or ascending a ladder." (Diary, 16 Mar.)

Among the Adang Muruts the "petticoats are of the shortest, sometimes not eight inches broad, and are scarcely decent." (St. John ii. 115.) "A few of the young girls have petticoats composed entirely of beads on a groundwork of cloth or perhaps bark." (*ibid*, ii. 129.)

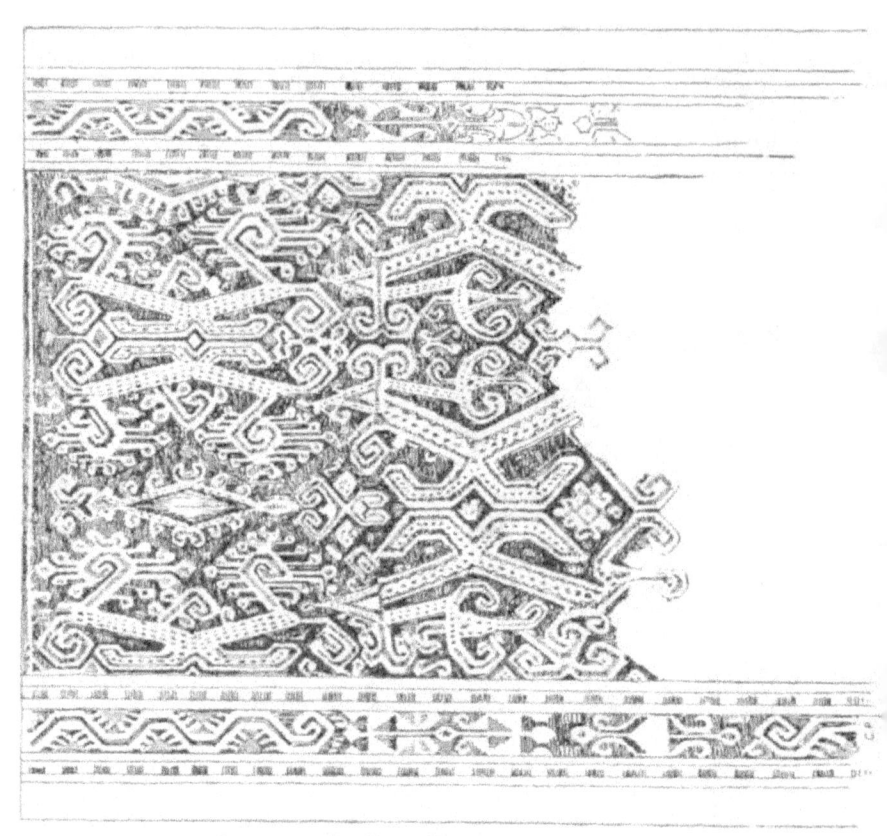

PATTERN OF SEA DYAK WOMAN'S PETTICOAT.
Dyed in shades of brown varying in intensity, with a few more reddish lines running through. Method of dyeing same as that described on p. 29. Width (top to bottom), 18½in.; circumference, 46in.
(Leggatt Coll.)

CHAWATS.

"The *sirat*, called *chawat* by the Malays, is a strip of cloth a yard wide, worn round the loins and in between the thighs so as to cover the front and back only; it is generally six yards or so in length, but the younger men of the present generation use as much as twelve or fourteen yards (sometimes even more), which they twist and coil with great precision round and round their body until the waist and stomach are fully enveloped in its folds. It requires considerable practice to enable one to dispose of so much cloth gracefully about the person, but more time is spent by these young dandies of the forest than one would imagine, in order that they may appear to the best advantage; and the Ulu Ais seem to excel all other tribes in the skill and taste which they display in the disposal of this personal attire. One end is so arranged as to fall over the coils in front and dangle between the legs; the other is hitched up behind so as to hang at the back like a long tail, or is looped up at the hip to droop on the right thigh. The former plan is adopted when no *takai buriet* (seat mat) is worn, so as to cover the hindquarters as much as possible. A practised eye can tell in a moment to what tribe or section of a tribe an individual belongs, not merely by the length of his waist-cloth and the way in which it is wound on, but also by its colour and the fashion in which it is decorated at its extremities. White, as being the plainest and most unpretending, is worn in mourning and during outdoor labour; it is cheap and will wash. Dark blue, however, is the commonest throughout the country when out of mourning; it wears better, shows the dirt less, and is singularly becoming. Both kinds are sometimes bordered at the edges with scarlet flannel. Prints and shawl patterns are affected by the young men of the Ulu Ai and Ngkari tribe; crimson, and saffron, and orange by the young of the Lamanaks and Sakarang tribes. A *klapong sirat*, or tail flap, is often worn by the elder men of the latter tribes; it is of a dull white colour with a fringe to it, being made of home-grown cotton; it is prettily and fancifully embroidered with coloured thread and is sewn on to either end of the *sirat* to hang before and behind. The younger men and boys prefer the fringes, *kabu sirat*, manufactured by the Malays, or ornamental borders of coloured flannel." (Brooke Low.)

Among the Kiaus Sir Sp. St. John found "chawats were decreasing, and trousers coming in." (i. 320.) Among the Main Muruts the chawats "are often absurdly small, not even answering the purpose for which they are intended." (ii. 129.)

HIP LACE.

A garment perhaps mentioned by Mr. Horsburgh (*supra* p. 51) is described by Sir Sp. St. John as worn by Si Obong, the wife of Tamawan, a Kyan chief: "The most curious part of her costume is what I must call a hip-lace of beads, consisting of three strings, one of yellow beads; the next of varied colours, more valuable; and the third of several hundred of those much-prized ones by the Kayan ladies. It is difficult to describe a bead so as to show its peculiarities. At my request, she took off her hip-lace and handed it to me; the best appeared like a body of black stone, with four other variegated ones let in around. It was only in appearance that they were let in; the colours of these four marks were a mixture of green, yellow, blue, and gray.

"Were I to endeavour to estimate the price in produce she and her parents had paid for this hip-lace, the amount would appear fabulous. She showed me one for which they had given eleven pounds' weight of the finest birds' nests, or, at the Singapore market price, thirty-five pounds sterling. She had many of a value nearly equal, and she wore none that had not cost her nine shillings."[7] (i. 119.) See illustration, p. 46.

[7] Round the waist the women wear four or five coils of large stone beads—red, blue, and yellow—which form a support to the sarong, or petticoat. Curiously enough, while various miraculous and valuable qualities are attributed to most of their personal ornaments, these waist-bands seem to be the only articles valued as heirlooms. The women attach great value to these rows of beads, especially if they are not new; and when I wanted to buy a set, the answer was that it had been in the family so long, and dated back to so remote a date (*tempo doelo*), that they could not part with it. Sometimes they tried to recount the pedigree of the article, but could never get further back than their great-grandmother. (Bock, p. 188.)

MAT SEATS.

"The *takai buriet*, already referred to, is a small mat which is tied round the waist with strings so as to cover the hindquarters and furnish the wearer with a clean portable seat at all times, and at all seasons. The mat is of split cane and woven into an endless variety of patterns and decorated in a variety of ways, use being made of coloured flannel, nassar shells, and European pearl buttons for this purpose. Sometimes a bear's skin or a panther's skin is cut to the required size and worn in lieu of a cane one, and when this is set off with the requisite beadwork of the country it forms a most handsome ornament to the person." (Brooke Low.) Mr. Hornaday (p. 392) says the "mats are shield-shaped of many colours, and one was ornamented by a border of cowries sewn on close together all the way round." The Rajah also mentions them. (i. 302.)

"The Dyaks [? Dusuns] here all eat monkeys and preserve the skins, which they fasten round their waists, letting the tails hang down behind, so that in the distance they look like men with tails." (Hatton, Diary, 18 Mar.)

SEAT MAT OF SARIBAS DYAKS.
Worn to prevent owner sitting upon damp places, thorns, &c. ornamented with black, yellow, and white woollen cloths or flannel and European porcelain buttons. Length, 23in.; width, 14in.
(Edinboro' Mus.)

Dress in Detail. 57

Rain Mats.

"On their backs the (Balow) men and women carry a neat mat basket suspended round the forehead, and when it rains a mat covers the head and the basket, and throws off the rain from their persons." (Sir Jas. Brooke, Mundy i. 237.)

Head Dresses.

The Tringus head-dress has already been described. Among the Si Panjangs "the *bilian* or female doctors or prophetesses wear a strange cover to the *burang*, or bead head covering. It is of wood, circular, made to fit the top of the burang, and prettily ornamented (inlaid) with tin. A short stick covered with the feathers of the *enchalang* or horn-bill is stuck in the centre and gives the whole a very curious effect. I have seen this covering to the head-piece in no other tribe." (Denison, ch. v. p. 56.) The Serin Dyaks also wear the conical head-dress of the Tringus. (*ibid*, ch. xiii. p. 78.) Mr. Wallace notes the conical hat. (i. p. 107.) "The Lanchang men and women wear a large round hat (see p. 63), fitting tight round the head by a band on which is raised the flat cover about two feet and more in diameter." (Denison, ch. viii. p. 84.) "Some wore a small cap of red cloth, ornamented with pearls, shells, and brass leaflets and with a long feather of the beautiful argus bird. Others had a piece of bast tied round their heads like a bandage, the ends of which were frayed out and looked like cocked-up feathers. A man so got up looked very funny: above—all decoration, below—nakedness!" (Pfeiffer, p. 88.) Sir Hugh Low (pp. 179, 240) and Mr. Grant (p. 17) also refer to the bark head-dress dyed yellow.[8] "Some of the Ballau young men wear head-dresses composed of the hair of their enemies, dyed red." (Horsburgh, p. 11.)

"The Semproh, Sebongoh, and other tribes on the southern branch of the Sarawak river, are fond of ornaments of opaque and very small beads which are worked into very

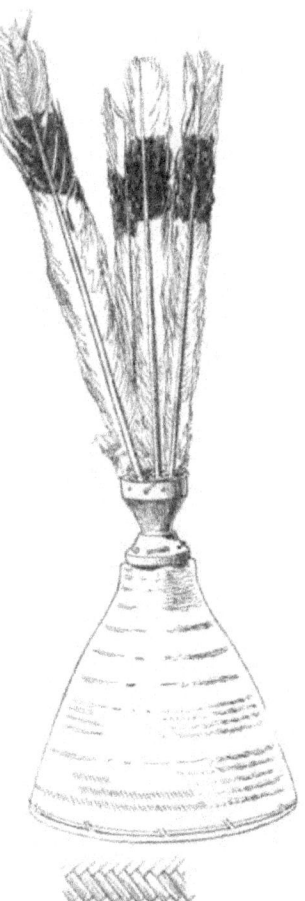

Dyak Conical Cap.
Made of closely-interwoven crimson-dyed palm leaf. Wooden plug at the apex *(a)* into which is fixed a tuft of long white feathers with black stripe. Diam., 7in.: height, 21in.
(Brit. Mus.)

[8] Mr. Bock noticed it among the Tanjoeng (p. 131) dyed red, blue, or yellow.

pretty head-dresses. This ornament is made of the strung beads of various colours, disposed in broad transverse bands: they are about four or five inches in breadth, and open at the top, so that they resemble a broad fillet." [9] (Low, p. 241.)

"The *labong*, or head-dress, is a piece of cloth a yard or two in length and wound round the head in the style of a turban, but so disposed that one end stands up straight from the forehead. But there are various ways of wearing, binding, coiling, &c., whereby one tribe may be distinguished from another. A white *labong* is frequently the sign of mourning. Saffron and orange are favourite colours among the Lamanaks and Ngkaris; black prevails among the Sarebas settled in Kajulan. The Ulu Ais affect shawl patterns and *buntas*, and the Sakarans of Gutabai use Javanese handkerchiefs edged with scarlet and yellow. By others, young as well as old, a kind of cap called *selapok* is much worn. It is made of plaited rush or cane, sometimes coloured and sometimes plain, as well as coarse or fine; and is shaped either to fit closely to the skull or to resemble an ordinary square cap. (See p. 60.) Fillets or head-bands of the same material and variable quality are also worn with an open crown and bordered with scarlet cloth. The Kiñahs wear bark cloth round their caps (as we wear crape round our hats) to show they are in mourning." (Brooke Low.)

It is I think of the Sarawak Dyaks that Mr. Marryat writes: "Their hair fell down their backs, and nearly reached their middle: it was prevented from falling over the face by a fillet of grass, which was ornamented with mountain flowers." (p. 11.)

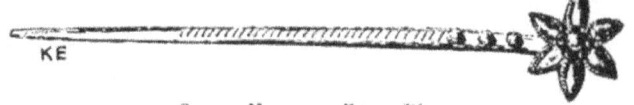

SILVER HAIRPIN. Baram River.
(Peek Coll.)

"The Sea Dyak women make no attempt to part their hair but push it over the forehead and gather it into a knot at the back of the head—a plain or fancy one as the occasion may warrant. They use no oil of their own manufacture, but all who are able to afford the luxury may obtain it from the Malays. The hair is not so long as it might be, and is frequently cut short during dangerous illness. The circumstances of their lives are not favourable to a luxuriant growth. They have in common with the men their full share of exposure to all weathers, together with hard work out of doors as well as in doors. Flowers are worn in the hair as ornaments—red and green being the favourite colours. The *balong* is a chaplet of odoriferous berries worn by marriageable girls.

[9] The hair is straight and black and is kept cut rather short by both sexes, but if permitted would grow to a great length. . . . "The chiefs adorn their heads with the feathers of large birds, which are stuck erect in a bandage encircling the head, in a manner precisely similar to that adopted by the aboriginal natives of South America. The chiefs of a friendly tribe, which visited Sambas in 1833, were all thus decorated." (Earl, pp. 258, 262.)

"The men dress their hair in a variety of ways. The genuine Ulu Ai fashion is to let the back hair grow long and flowing, and to keep the front either shaved or close cropped. The Ngkasi style is to shave in front and to keep the back hair close cropped, to shave again across the back of the head but to leave two parallel rows of hair and a tiny lock beneath them in the centre. The Kayan method of dressing the hair is, however, fast becoming the fashion among the dandies of all the tribes, *e.g.*, to permit the back hair to flow to its full length over the shoulders and to grow the front hair over the forehead long enough to form a Grecian fringe. When it is inconvenient to have the back hair streaming over the shoulders, they twist it and tuck it carefully into the turban." (Brooke Low.)

The Sarebas Dyaks' hair "is cut in such a manner as to give to their features the most savage-looking appearance, being shaved from that part of the head near the temples in an arched form, so that the ends of the two arches meet in the middle of the forehead in a fine point: the hair is cut short in front, but left long and flowing behind."[10] (Low, p. 179.)

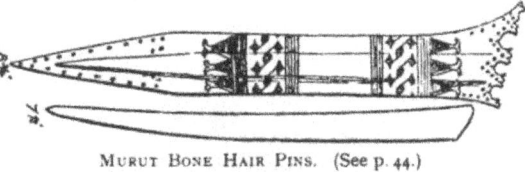

MURUT BONE HAIR PINS. (See p. 44.)
(Hose Coll.)

WOMEN'S WOODEN COMB. Kina Bulu. (See p. 63.)
(Brit. Mus.)

"The head-dress was a clean turban of bright scarlet cloth, neatly wound around the head, with a loose end falling over the left ear. The crown of the head was wholly uncovered, and a profusion of jet black locks fell over the top of the turban." (Brooke.)

PALM-LEAF KAYAN CAP.
(Brooke Low Coll.)

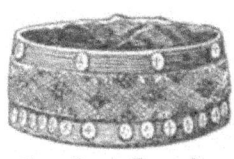

UKIT GIRL'S BEAD CAP.
(Brooke Low Coll.)

WICKER-WORK FOUNDATION OF A KANOWIT FUR CAP.
(Hose Coll.)

"The Sarebas are rather fond of ornament, and wear grotesque caps of various coloured cloths (particularly red), some of them square, others peaked, and others like a cocked hat worn athwartships, and terminating in sharp

---

[10] "The hair is cut short below the occiput, while on the crown it is allowed to grow to a great length, sometimes reaching to the knees. This long hair is rolled up in chignon fashion." (Bock. p. 131.)

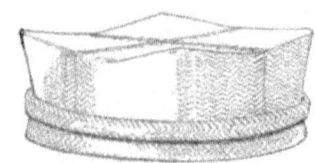

PLAITED HAT. (See p. 58.)
(Canterbury Mus.)

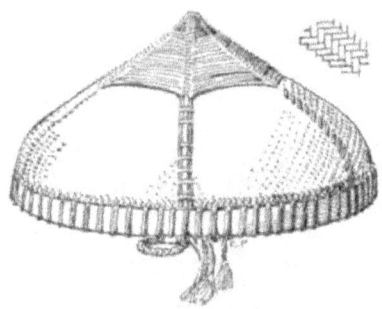

CAGAYAN SULU PLAITED ROTAN HAT.
Partly stained with native dyes. The centre-line as shown is stained red; with dark brown strips on both sides. The edging along the bottom is a lighter brown. No lining.
Diam., 14⅔in.
(Edinboro Mus.)

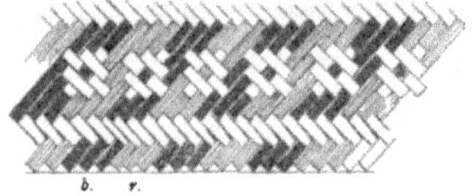

SAKARAN MEN'S MAT CAP.
b., black plaits; *r.*, red plaits. Diam. of brim, 6¼in.; diam. of hole on top, 3½in.
(Leggatt Coll.)

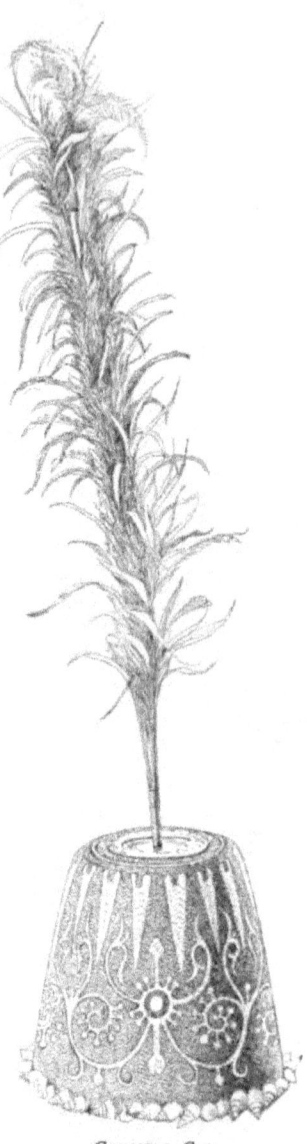

CONOIDAL CAP
of plaited narrow strips of pale (buff) reed, painted with scroll and vandyked patterns in dark crimson. A row of small pinkish white shells round lower edge. In centre of crown is stuck a tall plume (height, 21in.) of small downy white feathers attached to slips of bambu. Height of hat, 5¼in.; diam., 6in.
(Brit. Mus.)

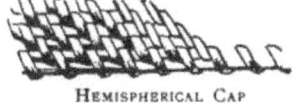

PALM-LEAF HAT.
(Leiden Mus.)

HEMISPHERICAL CAP
of plaited rattan, with star-shaped
covering of coloured glass beads,
and plume of black and white
feathers on top.   Diam., 7in.
From Dutch Borneo.
(Brit. Mus.)

FINISHED HAT.
Sambas (Dutch Borneo.)
(Leiden Mus.)

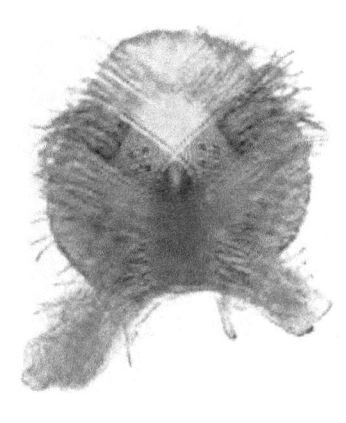

HATS in process of manufacture.   From Sebelau, Sambas (Dutch Borneo).
eiden Mus.)

points on the top of the head. These head-dresses are ornamented with tufts of red hair or black human hair, shreds of cloth, and sometimes feathers; but what renders them laughable to look at is that the hair is cut close to match the shape of the cap; so when a man displaces them, you find him

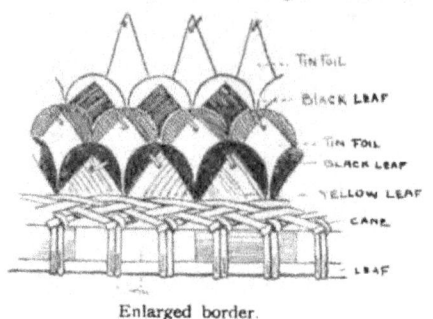

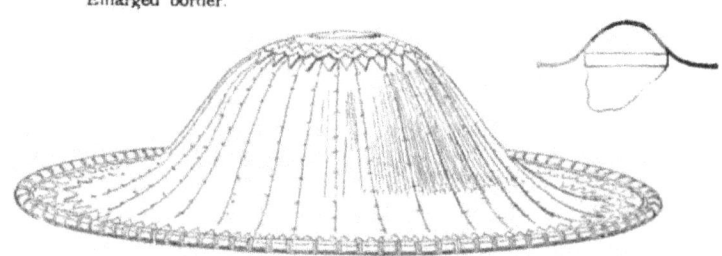

Enlarged border.

SADONG DYAK MAN'S HAT.
With domed top made of radiating crimson-coloured strips of leaf. Diam., 15in.
(Brit. Mus.)

bare of hair about the forehead and posterior part of the skull, cut into points over the ears, and the rest of the skull shewing a good crop of black bristles." (Keppel i. 224.)

The hair of the Sibuyau, long and dark, "was twisted up at the back of the head, the frontal arrangement being something between a braid and the costume à la Chinoise." (Mundy ii. 115.) "A fillet of plaited cane is worn round the head, into which the long hair may be tucked up if it should at any time incommode him. It is considered a shame to a woman to have her head shaven or her hair cut short. A woman generally wears her hair tucked up at the back in a loop resembling a single bow." (F. W. Leggatt.)

"Both sexes of the Balaus are fond of adorning their hair or head-dresses with flowers, generally large bright red and yellow blossoms, which become their dark complexions exceedingly well." (Horsburgh, p. 11.)

"The Kayan and Kenniah men wear on the top of the head only a cap or large tuft of long hair which hangs down the back, all the rest of the scalp being shaven. This way of wearing the hair is, I consider, the last remnant of the Chinese pigtail, and I firmly believe that the Kayans, Kenniahs, and Punans are all descended from a Chinese stock." (Hose, J.A.I. xxiii. 167.) Among the Kyan women a "small ribbon of beads attached to some cloth is often worn on the head to confine the hair so that it shall fall evenly over the shoulders." *(ibid.)* The Kyan women "wear head-dresses in many instances, generally red turbans . . . allowing their hair to fall loosely down their backs, or else they wind it round the head-gear when it encumbers their movements." (Brooke ii. 224, 302.) Sir Sp. St. John (i. 103) says their hair is bound with white fillets.

"Among the Dusuns the heads of the children are shaved for the first few years, after which the hair is allowed to grow. The young men do not shave their heads or cut their hair until they become fathers; consequently many youths have fine heads of long black locks, which they generally tie up beneath their head-cloths *(cigare)*." (Whitehead, p. 105.) "The women use bamboo or wooden hair-combs made by their lovers or husbands, and this is their only toilet article." *(ibid*, p. 109.) See p. 59.

CONICAL HAT.

Formed of four pieces of leaf overlapping, painted in red and black, with a band of scroll pattern and dentated borders. Dutch Borneo. (See p. 57.)

(Brit. Mus.)

Among the Tinagas Dusuns (Mamaguns) Mr. Witti noticed "the splendid heads of hair among the *male* population. Their hair is mostly three feet long and is worn tied up in a knot behind when at work or on the tramp, but when at ease it is loosened. It is a curious sight to see a number of men combing each other's hair and forming a chain in doing so. But their hair is by no means so thick as to support the theory of an improvement of the Dusun race by a mixture of Chinese blood." (Diary, 24 May.) Speaking of the same people, he says: "No vanity whatever about the girls; they are smutty-faced and toozle-headed. We yesterday passed a number of rustic damsels whose hair was quite carroty from neglect." (Diary, 29 Nov.)

Sir Sp. St. John mentions that among some Ida'an he met with "the young girls had the front of the head shaved, after the manner of the Chinese." (i. 249.) At Niasame, writing likewise of the Dusuns, Mr. Hatton says: "They

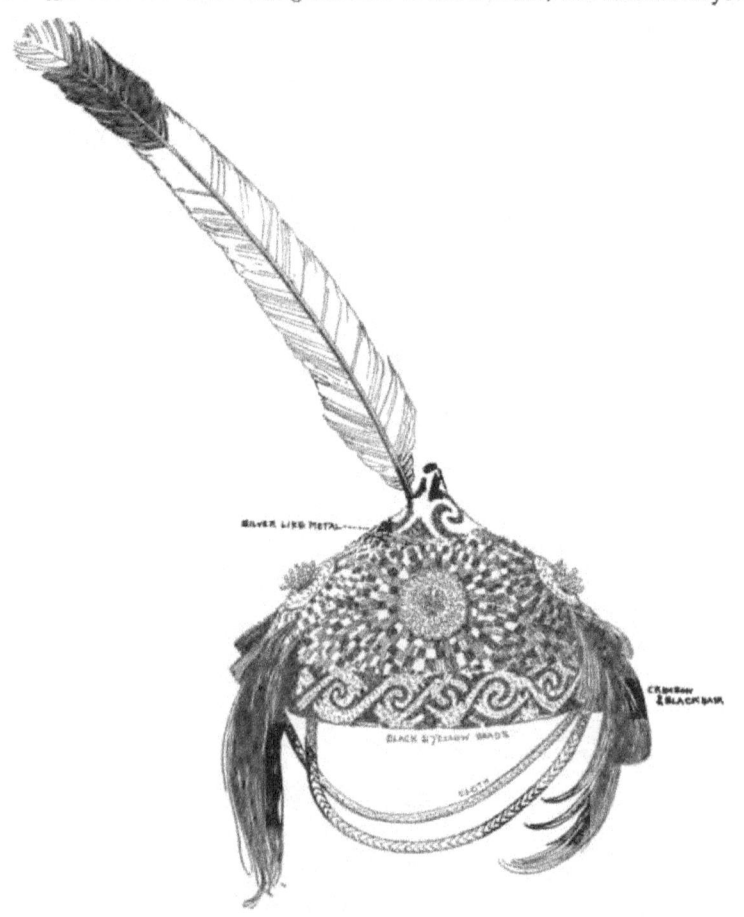

KAYAN HEAD-DRESS. Baram River.
(Hose Coll.)

shave their heads like the Chinese, leaving a patch at the back and two small tufts at the ears." (Diary, 8 April.)

"The Muruts on the Limbang river, like those seen near the coast, often wear their hair tied in a knot behind, and keep it in its place by a great pin, fashioned something like a spear-head both in size as well as in appearance, which is made, according to the means of the wearer, either of brass or of bamboo." (St. John ii. 90.)

Their hair "is often very gracefully wreathed up with a string of red or amber-coloured beads, sometimes with a strip of the pale yellow nipa leaf in its young state, and the colour contrast is then very effective." (Burbidge, p. 156.)

The Sin Dyaks wore "a head-cloth of common blue calico, fastened on by a plaited rattan, which was passed over the top of the head-cloth and under the chin." (Hatton, Diary, 18 Mar.) And the Dusuns of Toadilah wear "a black piece of cloth round the head, kept on by a band of red rattans." (*ibid*, 31 Mar.)

Mr. Witti met some Dusuns who had "sou'-wester" hats "consisting of deer or bear skin, the hair outside." (Diary, 16 Mar.)

Describing the Saghai Dyaks on the S. E. coast of Borneo, Mr. Marryat (p. 79) says they "are dressed in tigers' skins and rich cloth, with splendid head-dresses made out of monkeys' skins and the feathers of the Argus pheasant."

EARRINGS.

"The heavy metal earrings are, I believe, made in moulds, and many are beaten out with hammers: each tribe of the many scores in Sarawak wear different earrings. . . . What few metals the Dyaks possess of gold are bought from Malays and Chinese." (F. R. O. Maxwell.)

"The *grunjong* of the Sea Dyaks is worn in the rim of the ear, which is pierced along its entire length to receive the numerous rings of which it is composed, and it looks uncommonly pretty on the person; but when it is discontinued for a time, as it often is, from choice or by necessity, as in mourning for instance, and the holes are plugged

SEA DYAK PAIR OF EARRINGS (back and front). Composed of penannular brass wires graduated in size and fastened to plaited cords, with loose brass pendants attached at intervals in front.
(Edinboro' Mus.)

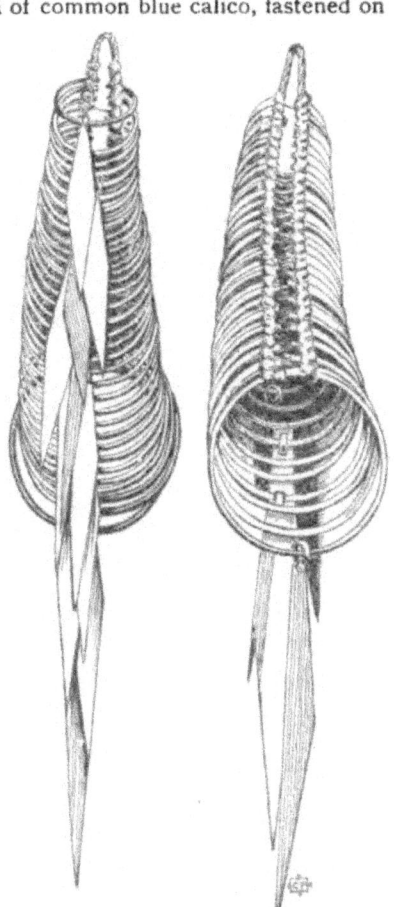

with wooden pegs[11] to keep them open, the cartilage looks hideously ugly and disfigured by slits and sores. The rings are of brass, and smallest at the top, gradually increasing in size until they reach the bottom. A very great many are worn in each ear by the young and vain—as many as twenty holes by the

DYAK BRASS EARRING.
Furnished with aiglettes. Real size. Weight, 1½oz.
(Leggatt Coll.)

young men—while elderly men are content with fewer. The variety worn by the Ulu Ai and Ngkari are strung with white cowries, which are kept in

[11] S. Müller met with plugs 2-3in. in diameter; the women do not wear them quite so large, but embellish them with thin plates of gold in front. (ii. 352.) The Punans asked Mr. Bock for his empty cartridge cases to put through their ears. (p. 74.)

Dress in Detail.

their place by a ruby bead at either end of the line, and are heavier by far than the plain brass *grunjongs* used by the Sakarans." (Brooke Low.) His Highness also refers to the ugliness of the ears when the rings are taken out, and to their jagged, broken appearance, and the ulcerated sores and discoloured places to be then seen. A lady newly out from England thought they looked as though they had been gnawed by rats. (i. 108; ii. 210.) Madame Pfeiffer counted fifteen rings in one ear, the largest ring hung as low down as the shoulder, and was certainly three inches in diameter. Attached to the latter were a leaf, a flower, a small brass chain, and some other article. (p. 87.) The Land Dyaks told Sir James Brooke (Mundy i. 63): "When you meet a Dyak with many rings in his ears, trust him not, for he is a bad man." They were referring to the Sarebas and Sakarans.

The *langgu* of the Ulu Ai is borrowed from the Punan, and consists of a small but heavy coil of brass or copper. The Lamanaks wear larger but lighter ones of lead. Boys sometimes wear a narrow strip of scarlet as a pendant to the ear, or a wing of the golden green *Chrysochroa (? Buprestis)* beetle.

The *tinggu* is a pendant worn at each ear to droop on to the shoulder, and is only worn by over-dressed

YOUNGEST DAUGHTER OF THE CHIEF OF KANOWIT.
(By Mr. B. U. Vigors, *Illus. Lond. News*, 10 Nov., 1849.)

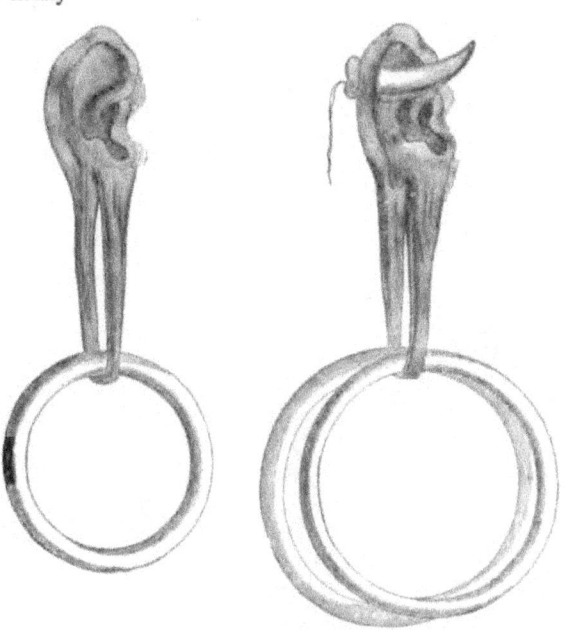

EARS OF NATIVES [? Dusuns].
At Gunong Tabor on Panti River (E. Borneo).
(After Mr. F. S. Marryat.)

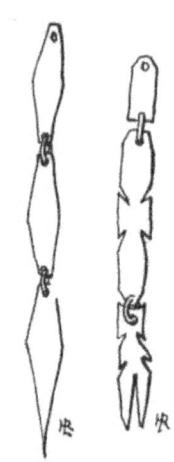

Ulu Ayer and Sarebas Brass Earring Pendants.
(Crossland Coll.)

Gutta Ear Plugs.
Worn in the lobe. ½ real size. From Long Wai.
(Brit. Mus.)

Udang, Kyan Ear Ornaments
(of canines), with gutta knobs.
(Hose Coll.)

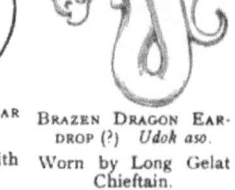

Brazen Dragon Ear-drop (?) *Udok aso.*
Worn by Long Gelat Chieftain.
(Brooke Low Coll.)

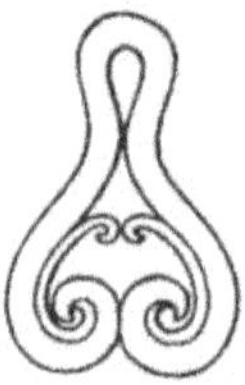

Sea Dyak Ear Ornament (?)
(Brooke Low Coll.)

Udang beto.
(hornbill imitation.) Worn in ear by Kayan chief.
(Brooke Low Coll.)

Ear Ornament (?)
(Brooke Low Coll.)

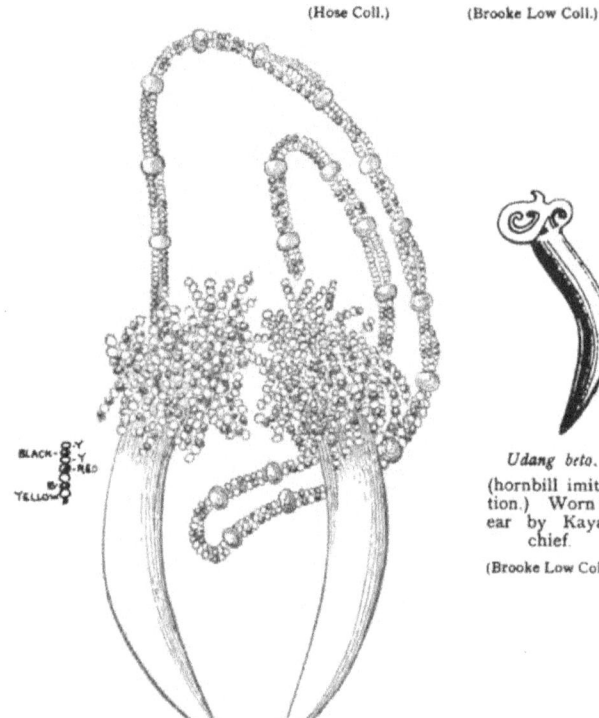

Kayan Ear Rim Pegs (Teeth).
From Fort Kapit, Rejang River.
(Brit. Mus.)

Ear Ornament.
(Brooke Low Coll.)

Ear Pendant.
(Brooke Low Coll.)

Ear-lobe Plug.
3¼in. diam.
Bejaju, S.E. Borneo.
(Leiden Mus.)

Ear Peg (?)
(Brooke Low Coll.)

dandies. It is decidedly ornamental, being made of thin crescent-shaped plates of brass stamped and fringed with metal. (See p. 66.) These ear-rings, especially the heavy shell ones, oblige a man to lie flat on his back when he is going to sleep, it being painful to rest on the sides of the face.

The Sibuyaus wear " ear-rings apparently of a kind of mixed metal, and of very large size; but by no means a becoming ornament, being so disproportionate to their small and symmetrical figures." (Mundy ii. 115.)

Mr. De Windt speaks of a Kanowit (?), who, in addition to a dozen small rings in the lobe of the ear, had a pair of wild boar's tusks thrust through point outwards. (p. 69.) Sir Sp. St. John (i. 100) says: "They are tiger-cat's teeth, stuck through like a pair of turn-down horns." He also says the Kanowits "draw down the lobes of their ears to their shoulders by means of heavy lead ear-rings." (i. 39.) "The Kayans' ears are similarly pierced and an animal's tooth pushed through." (Brooke ii. 224.) "Kayans and others wear tiger-cat teeth in the tips of their ears. The points of Dians (a native of the Rejang river) I observed turned upwards, which is not usual, and he said it was an old custom revived by a chief named Hang. The Uma Lesongs wear two such teeth in each ear, the upper one pointing upwards, the lower one downwards; those who are unable to procure the genuine article wear imitation ones carved out of horn or bone." (Brooke Low.)

" In the ears of the Kayan women there are heavy brass or leaden ornaments attached, and the aperture occasioned by these weights is often large enough for a man's hand to be passed through. . . . . Those who marry Malays cut their ears off short and join the ends, and after a time very little mark is observed. . . . . They have rings of ivory and beaded rings in their ears, and a tiger's tooth through each lobe. Hung to the women's ears are ponderous bits of lead or brass." (Brooke ii. 224, 225, 302.)

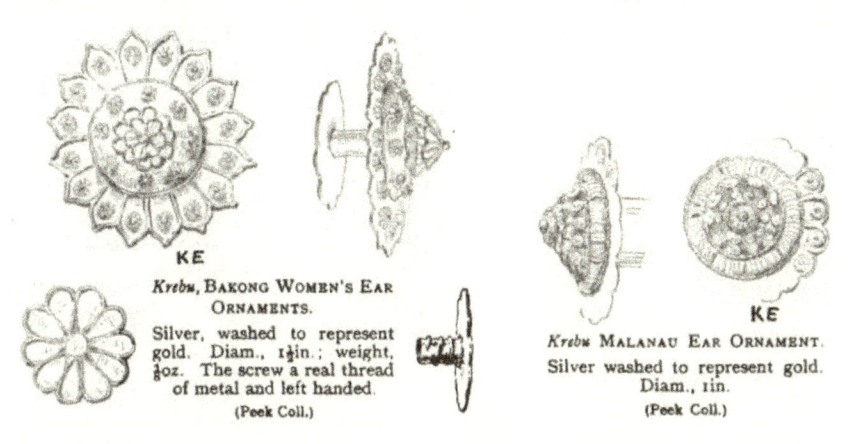

KE

Krebu, BAKONG WOMEN'S EAR ORNAMENTS.
Silver, washed to represent gold. Diam., 1½in.; weight, ½oz. The screw a real thread of metal and left handed.
(Peek Coll.)

KE

Krebu MALANAU EAR ORNAMENT.
Silver washed to represent gold. Diam., 1in.
(Peek Coll.)

" None of the Kayans or Kenniah races wear nose or lip ornaments. They pierce holes in the ears of their children when the latter are from two to three years of age. From these holes—in the case of a girl—they hang heavy weights, adding to them yearly, till the opening in the elongated ear-lobe is sufficiently large to allow of the girl inserting through it her own head; in the case of some women I have seen as much as two pounds weight depending from the lobe of each ear. The men wear light ear-rings, and the lobes of their ears usually hang down about 2 inches."[13] (Hose, J. A. I. xxiii. 167.)

"The women of this and other tribes wear in their ears ornaments of gold or silver, which are of such an extent of surface as entirely to conceal that organ : like the bracelets, the pattern is stamped upon them from the back, and the thin plate is soldered to a small tube which passes through the hole pierced in the ear, and is fastened by a nut in the manner of the more elegant ear-ornaments of the Malayan women." (Low, p. 181.) "Among the Rejang Dyaks this article is called *tusok pendieng*." (Brooke Low.)

"The poor little infants' faces are horribly distorted by the discomfort and weight of these masses of metal, which they are obliged to wear at the earliest age." (Mrs. McDougall, p. 155.) Mr. Crossland once gave some buttons to some Undup girls : "The buttons excited universal admiration, and were eagerly sought for as earrings. I tell you I can put my little finger into the hole without giving pain. The way they do it is : first they make a small hole, which they gradually enlarge by plugs of wood increased in size—the buttons they fasten by putting a piece of wood into the shank. The small buttons really look pretty, the contrast being good—the raven-black hair, copper-coloured skin, the rich gold of the button. The gold earrings of the country are of filagree work, the gold being tinged a dull red, which would lead those who did not know to suppose they were not really gold. I have a ring of pure gold from the upper country, which makes my English gold look like silver." (Miss. Life, 1864, p. 651.)

"Many of the Adang Murut men and women wear round flat pieces of metal or of wood in the holes of their ears instead of earrings, while others have heavy pieces of lead, dragging the ear down to the shoulder, like the Kanowit tribe, I suppose to enlarge the holes to the proper proportions." (St. John ii. 115.)

"The Muruts also wear many rings of lead up the rim of the ear." (*ibid*, i. 29, ii. 124.)

---

[13] "A child's ears are perforated when it is only six months old, and from that day the hole is forcibly increased in size, till the lobe of the ear forms a loop from one to four inches or more long. At first wooden pegs are placed in the hole, these are afterwards replaced by a couple of tin or brass rings." Those who are poor use a rolled up leaf instead. "Gradually the weight is increased by the addition of other larger rings, till the lobe of the ear often gives way under the strain and splits. I have counted as many as sixteen rings in a single ear, each of them the size of a dollar. The rings are generally made of tin," they can be removed and replaced at leisure ; the slit of the ring is made to hang lowermost. "Among the Tring and Long Wai Dyaks, they average 3oz., 330 grains troy. Sometimes discs of wood, often coloured or otherwise ornamented, and varying from one to one and a half inches in diameter, are inserted into the openings." The helix of the ear is also pierced or slit in several places, and pieces of red or blue ribbon or cord are tied, or buttons, pieces of wood, and feathers inserted. The elongation of the lobe of the ear attains its greatest development among the Tring Dyaks. A Tring woman, from accurate measurements taken by me, had a total length of ear, 7·1 inches ; with length of the gash in the lobe, 4·75 inches ; and with the distance between the level of the chin and the bottom of the ear, 2·85 inches." The men do not carry the fashion to such extremes as do the women. Besides this central slit in the lobe of the ear, the Tring women pierce one, two, or three additional holes in the loop of flesh on either side. (Bock, p 186.)

"Among the Niasame Dusuns earrings are not at all popular." (Hatton's Diary, 18 April.)

"The Mount Dulit Dusuns have earrings which dangle one below another, all three of brass wire coiled into a spiral. The lowermost is fixed into the ear lobe, and is 2½ inches in diameter; the two smaller ones are fixed into the margin of the ear. . . . A profusion of brass wire attached to the ear shell we found customary with the Dyak tribes on the left side of the Pagalan River. There it seems to be an ornament proper, and not a piece of armour as I understand it. At Salimbitan elderly females wear enormous earrings of brass, which purposely they never polish, the verdigris being considered to add to the ornament, at the same time they carry little children about who play with these poison coated trinkets. . . . The women on the Upper Kimanis wear a plug stuck through the ear lobe coloured red, black, and yellow, and which has the shape of an acorn." (Witti's Diary, 16 March.)[13]

NECKLETS, ARMLETS, AND LEGLETS.

In the early portion of this chapter in the full descriptions of the dresses of the natives frequent reference was made to their necklaces, armlets, &c., and to the varieties of beads which found favour in the different districts.

"The Sikong women seem to prefer wearing more white beads mixed with black in their necklaces, Tringus showing a strong partiality for red and black." (Denison, ch. v. p. 52.) "The Si Panjangs wear chains of black and red beads (I saw a few of blue[14] colour) round the neck like the Gunibang and Tringus women, differing herein from the Sikongs and Si Baddats who affect black and white beads." (*ibid*, ch. v. 56.) "Among the Simpoke and Serin women silver chains round the neck were far from uncommon, these latter being also affected by the men." (*ibid*, ch. vii. 76.) "The Serin women also wear broad shell armlets." (*ibid*, ch. vii. p. 78.) "The Upper Sarawak women wear a white porcelain ring as an ornament on the upper part of the arm." (Houghton, M.A.S. iii. 198.) "For ornaments, they wear bracelets of the red wood of the heart of the Tapang tree, which, after exposure to the air, becomes black as ebony, and being without its brittle qualities, is more durable; and broad armlets, which are made of the shell *(Kima)* from the coast of Celebes, and which, when polished by length of use among the

---

[13] Mr. Bock thus describes the method followed by a native in making tin earrings: Taking a long, straight piece of bamboo, the hollow of which was the same diameter as it was intended that the earrings should be, he fixed on the top of it the half of a cocoa-nut shell, with a hole bored through, in which the upper end of the cane was inserted, the whole forming a tube, with a cup at the top. Wrapping the tube in a cloth, he melted the tin in a small ladle, and poured it into the cocoa-nut cup, till the tube was filled. When the tin was cool, he opened the bamboo tube, and took out a long, straight, round rod of tin; which he then bent round a thick, but smooth, piece of wood, forming a ring, with the ends not quite meeting. (Bock, p. 67.)

[14] "The women adorn their heads and necks with little blue and white beads, the manufacture of Great Britain and China, which are eagerly sought after for the purpose." (Earl, p. 262.) Both sexes appear to place high value on their necklaces, which generally consist of cornelians 2 and 3 inches long, mixed with small balls of gold hollowed out like our bells. The greater part of these cornelians found among the Dyaks would probably have been brought to them in bygone times by Arab merchants who then carried on trade with Borneo. (S. Müller ii. p. 354.) See illustration on p. 72.

Dyaks, resembles ivory, but never acquires its yellow tinge, always remaining of the purest white colour."[16] (Low, p. 240.)

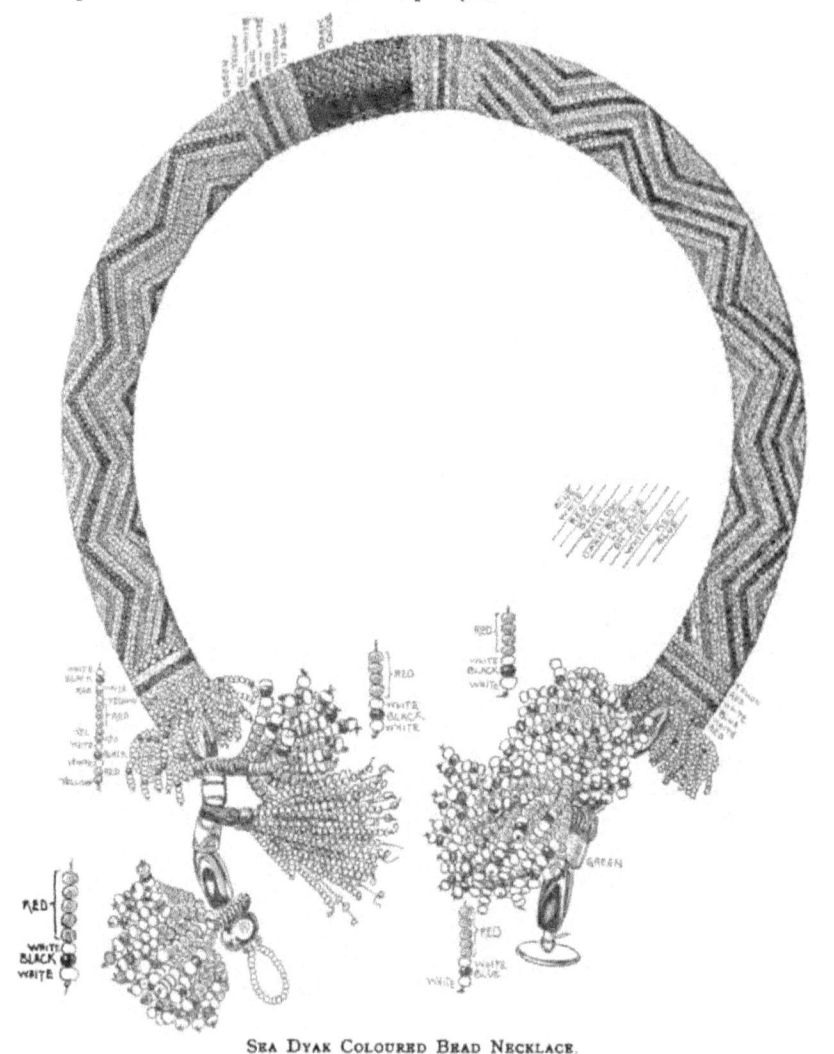

SEA DYAK COLOURED BEAD NECKLACE.
Worn by men and women. The beadwork covers a piece of wrapped rope about ⅜in. in diam.
(Leggatt Coll.)

[16] The Bukkit men, as well as women, wore round the arms and neck strings of a kind of bead made of a small marine shell (sp. of *Nassa*), from which they cut the whorl away, leaving only the part round the mouth; the columellar lip is much expanded in these shells. The traders from Passir and Tanah Boemboe get these shells from the coast, and exchange them for gold dust and wax. Nowhere else in Borneo have I noticed these *Nassa* ornaments, though occasionally in other parts I have seen a *Helix Brookei* worn as an ornament, or to form the tops or lids of the arrow cases. (Bock, p. 244.)

Dress in Detail. 73

At Sambun village the Rev. Mr. Chalmers "noticed some *teeth* necklaces. They consist of two or three rows of beads, next a row of small shells, and then a row of pigs' or bears' tusks fixed in a circular frame. Bears' tusks are valued here at at least two rupees per tusk, so that when there are from thirty to forty in one necklace, they form a rather expensive ornament."[10] (Miss. Field, 1859, p. 134.) Sir H. Keppel met a Singie who " was ornamented with a necklace of bears' teeth; and several had such a profusion of small white beads about their necks as to resemble the voluminous folds of the old-fashioned cravat." (i. 147.)

Mr. Grant speaks of a similar "necklace, to which is attributed a charm; it is composed of bears' tusks and teeth, the

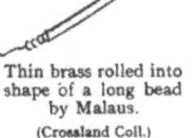

Thin brass rolled into shape of a long bead by Malaus.
(Crossland Coll.)

points stuck outwards, and the intervals between their roots filled up with large blue beads of unknown origin and manu-

Undup Bead Necklace Tassel Ends.
Made of bits of red and yellow European cloths.
(Crossland Coll.)

facture; the circle to which these are attached is of rattan, covered with red cloth. . . . These necklaces give a wild and imposing appearance to the wearer, but poor men do not often boast the possession of them. Bears are not very numerous, and each tooth costs somewhere about 1s. 6d. to 2s. sterling, or its equivalent in rice or paddy." (p. 43.)

Reed Necklace.
On European thread; the ends joined by piece of lead wire.
(Leggatt Coll.)

L 9 3/4

[16] " At Sabutut several of the men wore a necklace of tigers' teeth, fastened by their roots to a brass wire, in such a manner that the sharp points stand outward, and present a formidable defence for the breast. Beads and cowrie shells are inlaid among the teeth in a neat manner." (Doty, p. 298.)

ARMLETS.
(Brooke Low Coll.)

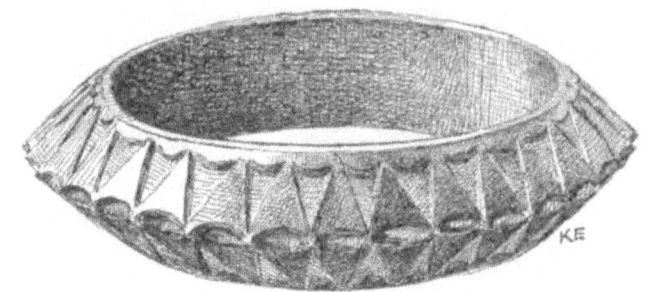

Simpai DYAK MAN'S BRACELET.
Of hard black wood. Inside diam., 3½in. ; weight, 6½oz.
(Peek Coll.)

KADAYAN BRACELET.
2⅜in. diam. ; weight, 1⅜oz. Copper, with three silver wires running round. (Joint shown in illustration). Baram River.
(Peek Coll.)

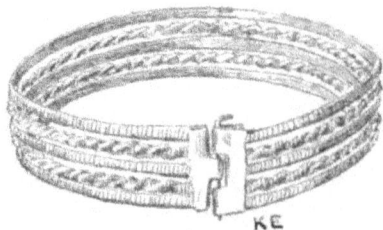

Gelang.
(The second and fourth ring *appear* to be made of European prepared metal). Baram River.
(Peek Coll.)

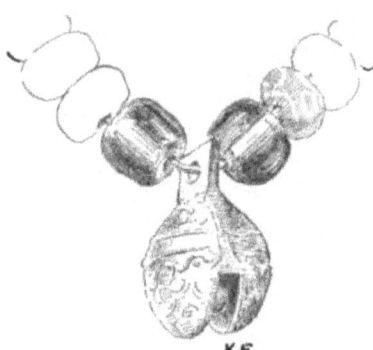

HAWK'S BELL ON KAYAN NECKLACE.
(Peek Coll.)

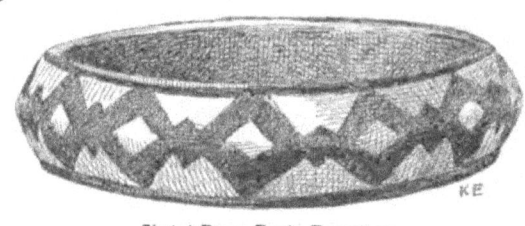

Simpai DYAK BOY'S BRACELET.
Tinfoil inlaid, dark wood (like that of a palm). Internal diam., 2½in. ; weight, 1½oz.
(Peek Coll.)

SHELL ARMLET.
Dammar seam, inlaid with cowries.
(Brooke Low Coll.)

PORCELAIN ARMLET.
(Canterbury Mus.)

KNEE RING.
(Brooke Low Coll.)

The following is a list of Sea Dyak ornaments for neck, arm, and leg wear drawn up by Mr. Brooke Low:

"A *simpai lengan* is an armlet, or as it is literally translated, a loop for the arm. It is worn above the elbow-joint and is often of dark wood or carved ivory, but the kind most generally in use is formed from the base of the cone of the *Kima* shell *(Conus Guratensis)*, and is grooved on its upper surface. The cavity is filled up with resinous substance, and studded with the scarlet seed of the *Michelia* or with a few Nassar shells. It is a most becoming ornament, but extremely expensive—a pair of the largest and best costing £6. Occasionally two are worn on each arm, but this is considered bad taste and is discouraged.

"*Rangki* are the same as shell armlets already described under the name of *simpai lengan*, and are worn by the women. They are only worn upon especial occasions, and form part of the full dress of a woman of fashion. As they are far smaller in size, and not so well finished, they are less costly than those worn by the men. Some eight or nine, however, are worn upon each arm, the more the better in their opinion.

"The *tumpa* or bracelets worn alike by men and women are of three descriptions, and are called *tumpa gelang*, *tumpa bala*, and *tumpa unus* respectively. The first are of brass, the second of ivory, and the last of plaited fibre. The two first consist of some sixty close-fitting rings commencing at the wrist and reaching half way up the arm; a few in the former are made to hang loose on the back of the hand and being engraved are styled *tengkelai*.

"The *tumpa bala*, or *tumpa godieng* as they are also called, have been adopted by the Sea Dyaks within the last few years from the Tetaks and Segaus; they are now made in china and gold in Bornean bazaars.

[The Sarebas and Sakaran women have their arms "adorned with bracelets of silver very neatly made, being formed of thin plates of a broad and convex shape, so that they stand out from the arm; they have the patterns stamped upon them from the inside, and wear them from the wrist up to the elbow, eight or nine in number; they do not, like the women of some other tribes, wear brass wire above the elbow-joint." (Low, p. 181.) The Undups have silver "bracelets, reaching from the wrist to the elbow, nine in number, cost about eight dollars, nearly two pounds. I weighed a set the other day, and found there was three-and-a-half dollars' worth of silver. Those who cannot afford to buy silver, buy brass rings, fifty in number, for each arm, and some sixty; these cost nearly six dollars." (Crossland, Miss. Life, 1865, p. 655.)]

"The *tumpa unus* are only worn by young people too poor to afford any other kind; they are merely rings of plaited gomuti palm fibre worn in heavy masses on the wrist.

[Sir Hugh Low considered the arm, leg, and necklets, made of the gomuti palm fibre with its deep black and neat appearance, more pleasing to the European eye than the brass or bead articles. (p. 41.)]

"*Kongkong rekong* signifies 'collar for the throat.' Necklaces of European beads are worn by the young of both sexes; the ends are furnished with tassels of minute beads or bats' fangs. They are worn loose round the throat, and button in front, the tassels resting on the chest. Lamanak lads are fond of a large gold button as well as the tassel, but this is not universal even among their own tribe. Frequently several necklaces are worn, especially by the women. These necklaces of beads seem to have superseded the more savage necklaces of human teeth, etc., which were the fashion a generation ago, and is one proof of the civilising influence of the European government.

[Madame Pfeiffer (p. 87), Lieut. Marryat (p. 15), and Sir H. Keppel (i. 147) mention necklaces of human teeth.]

"The *tinchian tunjok* are the rings worn on the fingers by both sexes. They are commonly made of brass, variously but rudely engraved and are not soldered at the ends; other metals also are used but less frequently, such as copper, lead, tin. Gold and silver rings are procured from the Malays and used only by the tribes living in close proximity to them. Shell rings are less uncommon.

"The *ngkrimoks* are hoops of cane worn immediately below the knee-joint, and covered with an infinity of diminutive brass rings. The hoops, some eight or ten in number, are strung together with coloured rattan, to preserve a compact and regular appearance. The *ngkrimoks* are worn almost exclusively by tribes of Sakarang and Lamanak origin; the Ulu Ais and Ngkaris use the *unus* instead, and this consists of innumerable rings of plaited fibre, worn in heavy masses, as many as 300 at a time upon each leg. The palm from which the fibre leg rings are made, is called *apieng* by the Dyaks and *limak* by the Kyans.

"The *selong* are dense coils of thick brass wire, many fathoms in length, and of enormous weight, worn on the leg from the ankle joint to the thigh; they are not worn every day, as may readily be conceived.

"Bunches of sweet smelling leaves are often stuck in the armlets." (Brooke Low.)

"The Kyans have no knowledge of the manufacture of glass or beads—a description of ornament of which both the Kayan men and women are very fond; some of the beads in their possession are very old and greatly prized by the owners, being valued by them from 60 to 100 dols., and the most valuable of which are known as *Lukut Sekala*. Their armlets are usually of ivory, bought from the Chinese and other traders, and the women may sometimes be seen with as many as thirty bangles of ivory rings on each forearm." (Hose, J.A.I. xxiii. 166.)

Sir Sp. St. John, when among the Muruts, writes: "The girls twist about a couple of fathoms of brass wire in circles round their neck, rising from the shoulders to the chin, forming what appears a stiff collar with a very broad base; it is, however, no doubt more pliant than it appears. . . . Heavy necklaces of beads are worn by the men as well as by the women." (ii. 119, 129.)

"The Dusuns at Toadilah all wear brass collars, bracelets, and anklets" (Hatton Diary, 31 Mar.); and Mr. Witti describes some other Dusuns (?) of whom "the men wear on a rattan string round their neck a short knife, the handle of which is invariably a boar's tusk. It looks quite a pretty addition to their scanty wearing apparel." (Diary, Nov. 22.) "The Tinagas Dusun men and women alike wear the neck spiral, and the former also a closely fitting spiral around the biceps." (*ibid*, Diary, 24 May.)

CHAPTER XVIII.
FASHIONABLE DEFORMITIES.

TEETH: Filing to point—Concave filing—Flatten horizontally—Black stain—Not the effect of betel—Dogs and Europeans have white teeth—Toothache—Filed down short—Black resinous juice—Protection to teeth—Brass studs—Incisors removed for *sumpit*—Filed to point—Brass wire—Stained black—Ground down—Caries—Brass plates hooked on—Brass plates rivetted on.

HEADS: The Milanau head flattening—Sign of beauty—Description of instrument—Tender solicitude of mothers—Twelve months' cure—Instrument used during sleep—Three months' cure—Female children only—Result on skull—Occasional deaths—Child lies on its back—Size and weight of instrument—Chinese coin—A Vrolik Museum skull.

CIRCUMCISION. KAYAN MUTILATION. CICATRICES. EAR LOBES. DEPILATION.

TEETH.

"The invariable Lundu custom of filing the teeth sharp, combined with the use of the betel-nut turning them quite black, gives the profile of the Lundu a very strange appearance. Sometimes they render their teeth concave by filing." (Marryat, p. 79.)

"Most of the people coloured their teeth black by means of the juice from a climbing plant. The Balaus and Undups occasionally file their teeth horizontally, while the Balaus, Undups, and Skarangs file them to points. Until files were introduced the filing was done with a stone, or with wood, water, and sand. The Undups, Skarangs, and Saribus drilled holes in their teeth by means of a piece of steel rubbed between the hands." (Crossland.)

Speaking of the betel chewing, Mr. Treacher says:—"It tinges the saliva and the lips bright red, but, contrary to a very commonly received opinion, has no effect of making the teeth black. This blackening of the teeth is produced by rubbing in burnt cocoanut shell, pounded up with oil, the dental enamel being sometimes first filed off. Toothache and decayed teeth are almost unknown amongst the natives, but whether this is in some measure due to the chewing of the areca-nut I am unable to say." (Jour. Straits Asiatic Soc., No. 20, p. 58.)

"Like many other races, the Land Dyaks file their teeth into points, and flatten them horizontally by the same means, and they also stain them black, for 'dogs have white teeth,' they say." (Grant, p. 97.)

A writer in the S. G., No. 102, says, white teeth are unpopular with them owing to dogs and other animals possessing that colour of teeth.

"So among the Dusun the teeth are filed down short and blackened; this does much, in a European's idea, to spoil the good looks of these people, but they equally object to the long white teeth of Europeans." (Whitehead, p. 106.)

The Rev. F. W. Leggatt informs me "the teeth are often blackened for prevention of decay; or for beauty. The blackening is done by taking a piece of old cocoanut shell or certain woods, which are held over a hot fire until a black resinous juice exudes. This is collected, and while still warm the teeth are coated with it. In the case of decayed teeth this resin dries as a coat of enamel or varnish, covering the nerve and thus protecting it. Teeth are also frequently filed like the teeth of a saw, and blackened, after which brass wire is cut into short lengths and driven in as studs into holes previously drilled in the teeth. Or the stud ornament may be adopted without filing the teeth. Another mode of treating the teeth of the upper gum is to file them off almost level with the gum. It is very rare to see a Dyak with a good set of teeth." Mr. de Windt (p. 86) and Mr. Hose (J. A. I. xxiii. 167) give similar reports.

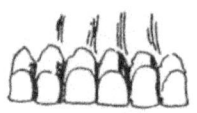

TEETH IN A BORNEO SKULL.
(Mus. Roy. College of Surgeons, obtained from the Anthropological Institute.)

Of the Dulit Dusuns, Mr. Witti writes (Diary, 16th March): "They do not file their teeth, but break the upper incisors to gain a stronger blast at the sumpitan, or blow-pipe."[1]

Among the Rejang Dyaks: "The upper incisors of both sexes are often filed into a single sharp point; a hole is bored through the centre of each and filled with brass. The enamel is scraped off with a rough stone, and the teeth are rubbed with leaves which stain them black. The lower incisors are ground down to half their natural size and blackened in the same fashion, but are neither pointed nor studded with metal. Caries is rare, and the natives seldom suffer from tooth-ache. The teeth are naturally beautifully white and regular, but it is the fashion to disfigure them in this manner as they approach the ages of puberty—boys do it when they begin to care to please the women. They dislike white teeth and consider them hideous. I once saw a Sakarang wearing over his natural teeth a thin brass plate (*lios*) cut to resemble a row of pointed teeth; this was worn over the upper incisors and hooked into the molars. I believe the boy picked up the notion from the Mentuaris or Malohs (Malaus), but I do not imagine it is common with his tribe, as I never saw another with it either before or after." (Brooke Low.)

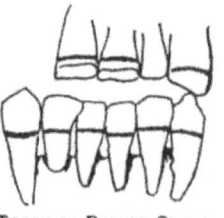

TEETH IN BORNEO SKULL.
"A fine groove has been carved in the enamel, across the front of each tooth. This notch is seen filled with betel on all incisors and the lower canines."
(No. 283, Barnard Davis Coll. Mus. Roy. College of Surgeons.)

TEETH IN A SKULL FROM BANJERMASSING, showing small brass pegs with rounded heads let into the two outer ones; the centre tooth shows hole only drilled to the pulp cavity. (No. 279, B. Davis Coll. Mus. Roy. College of Surgeons).

At Lake Padang Mr. Hornaday "took advantage of their good humour to ask them about the little metallic

---

[1] "This singular practice we have since met with among all tribes along the shores of the Pagalan, excepting the Dyaks of Dalit proper. It reminds me of the frontal fitting of the teeth in use among the Malayans around our coasts, and also among the Dusuns who chew beetle and sireh. In each case the peculiarity applies to both sexes. With Dusuns it is a bad joke to ask a 'fading' woman how often she has had her teeth filed, the operation being performed about once every ten years." (Witi *ibid*.)

plates on some of their front teeth, which looked like gold. I found that each upper incisor and canine tooth was capped by a smooth plate of copper, held in place by a pin driven into a hole in the tooth. The Dyaks showed me how the hole is drilled (with a bow), and one imitated the agony they endure during the operation. He was a good actor, and his facial and bodily contortions and writhings excited roars of laughter."

From the Baram river Mr. C. Hose writes: "The teeth are filed by nearly all the races of Borneo at any age, and in many cases drilled with holes in which brass wire is inserted." (J. A. I. xxiii. 167.)

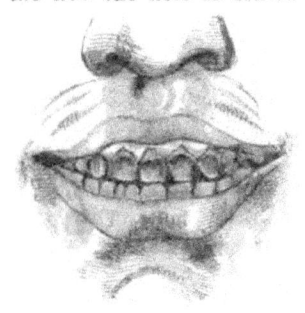

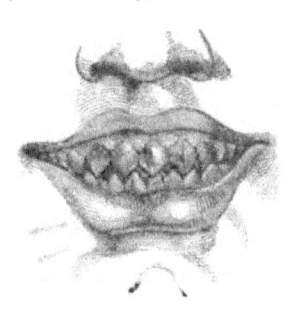

DYAK TEETH FILED CONCAVELY.
(After Lieut. F. S. Marryat.)

DYAK TEETH FILED TO A POINT.
(After Lieut. F. S. Marryat.)

The Rev. W. Crossland informs me "that some of the Undups obtained a piece of brass plate, which they filed out to look like teeth, inserting it over their teeth in order to look fierce, but the custom is not by any means universal."

HEAD FLATTENING.

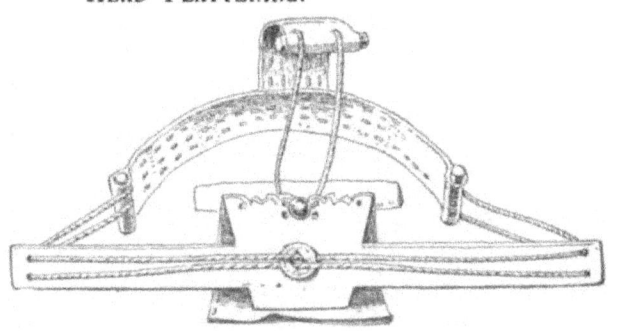

Mr. Crocker found in one tribe only that the parents flattened the heads of their children, and he believes this practice is confined entirely to the Milanaus. He says: "It is considered a sign of beauty to have a flat forehead, and although chiefly practised on female children, boys are occasionally treated in the same manner.

MILANAU FEMALE INFANT HEAD DEFORMER; the horizontal piece in the centre is the pad which presses on the child's head.
(Brooke Low Coll.)

When a child is a few days old, an instrument is applied to the forehead, a small cushion being placed underneath, and under that again some green banana leaves. By an ingenious arrangement of strings equal pressure is brought to bear on the forehead, and the final tightening is done in front by a contrivance which has the same effect as a torniquet. I have often watched the tender solicitude of the mother who has eased and tightened the instrument twenty times in an hour, as the child showed signs of suffering. The chief object is to get the child to sleep with the proper amount of pressure on the instrument. Before the child is twelve months old the desired effect is generally produced, and is not altogether displeasing, as it is not done to the extent of disfigurement, which I believe to be the case amongst some of the American Indians." (J. A. I. xv. 425.)

In forwarding me a specimen of a head flattening instrument, Mr. Chas. Hose writes: "The *Tadal*, as it is called by the Bintulu Malanaus, is only placed on the child's head during the time that it is asleep—the moment the child wakes it is taken off. Its use is first commenced when the infant is fifteen days old, and is continued until the third or fourth month. In the early stages only very slight pressure is applied, but gradually it becomes more and more severe. Only female children have their heads flattened in this way. If too much pressure is used in consequence of the frontal and occipital bones being approximated the parietals are prevented from joining, and the soft hole-like depression with which every child is born remains in the adult. If the child is not well looked after the board often injures the nose, and occasionally deaths are caused by the use of these *Tadals*, but not often. The cushion is placed on the child's forehead, and the bands being placed over the top and round the back of the head, the strings which hold the bands in position can thus be adjusted without disturbing the child lying on its back." The instrument Mr. Hose has forwarded is 12in. long and weighs 9½ ozs., a weight of itself sufficient to cause compression on the soft bones of a child. "The Malanaus consider flat faces more beautiful than others." It is curious that in the instrument sent me by Mr. Hose, as well as in the one in the Brooke Low Coll. and in the Dresden Museum, a Chinese coin should be used as a torniquet.

Dr. A. B. Meyer suggests that a very symmetrical skull in the Vrolik Museum, Amsterdam, from Banjer, may be artificially deformed.

CIRCUMCISION.

Circumcision is practised, but it is not universal or obligatory. (Brooke Low.)

KAYAN MUTILATION.

Particulars of the Kayan sexual mutilations have been deposited in the British Museum.

CICATRICES.

The Sea Dyaks do not make any use of raised cicatrices to ornament the body, but they are proud of scars nevertheless, and especially if they are regular and symmetrical. They are particularly proud of their vaccination marks if they show out well,

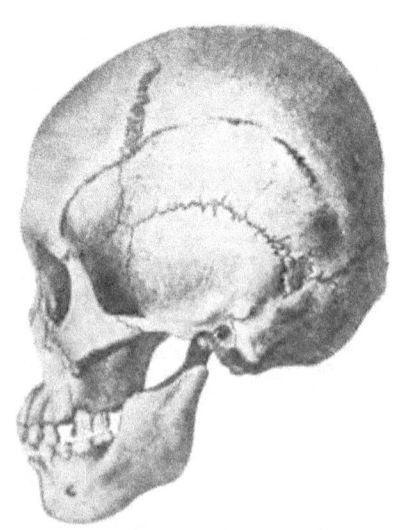

ARTIFICIALLY-DEFORMED SKULL OF MALANAU.
(Dresden Museum).

and are equidistant apart. The women often prove the courage and endurance of the youngsters by placing a lighted ball of tinder on the arm, and letting it burn into the skin. The marks thus produced run along the forearm from the waist in a straight line, and are much valued by the young men as so many proofs of their power of endurance. (Brooke Low.)

EAR LOBE EXTENSION.

The extension of the ear lobes is treated of in the chapter relating to dress in the part devoted to earrings.

DEPILATION.

" The prejudice in favour of a smooth face is so strong that in the whole course of my experience I have never met with a single bearded or moustached Sea-Dyak, although it cannot but be manifest to a close observer that were they only so disposed they could produce a thicker crop than the Malay. This is evident especially in the case of old men and chronic invalids who by reason of age or infirmity have ceased to care much about their personal appearance and whose chins are rough in consequence with a bristly growth. The universal absence of hair upon the face, on the chest, and under the armpits would lead the superficial observer to infer that this is owing entirely to a natural deficiency, whereas it is due in great measure to systematic depilation. *Chunam*, or quick lime, is frequently rubbed into the skin so as to destroy the vitality of the follicles. The looking glass and tweezers are never out of the hands of the natives, and they devote every spare moment to the conscientious plucking out of stray hairs. It is likewise the fashion for both sexes to shave the eyebrows and pluck out the eyelashes. The growth upon the pubes in both sexes is often copious enough—some few Loweas object to even this, and either crop it close or remove it altogether.

SILVER NIPPERS.
For depilation. Length, 2⅝in. Baram River.
(Pook Coll.)

Female Sea Dyaks eradicate the hair off the pubes. I know a Malali at Kanowit who is bearded from ear to ear, and when he shaves which is every now and then, his chin and cheeks are quite blue; he was a Mentuari of unmixed blood." (Brooke Low.)

Mr. Leggatt tells me some old Sea Dyak men shave their heads. He knows "one Dyak who wears a remarkably thick beard. But the hair of his head is also peculiar, being in thick wavy ringlets. I have never met with a native with woolly hair or anything resembling negro hair." Sir Chas. Brooke speaks of the "abominable practice of plucking or shaving eyelashes which often brings ophthalmia and weakness of eyes" (ii. 171); and of the Kayans he says: "their eyebrows are shaved with the lash plucked out which gives them a staring look devoid of expression." (ii. 224.) "Both men and women of the Kayan and Kenniah races at the age of fifteen pluck out their eyebrows and eyelashes." (Hose, J.A.I. xxiii. 167.) "Among the Dusuns hair is seldom allowed to grow on the face, most men being provided with a small pair of tweezers, with which they jerk out all stray specimens, the importation of small looking-glasses by ourselves giving a fresh impetus to these hair-jerkers. One old man here had a long grey beard and was the only bearded Dusun I ever saw." (Whitehead, p. 105.) Mr. Von. Donop writes: "I notice the Dusun men very seldom have any hair on their face. Mr. Witti tells me they are very proud of it if they have any."[1] (Diary, 28 May.)

[1] "I never saw a nearer approach to a beard among the men than a few scattered hairs over the chin and upper lip." (Earl, p. 258.)

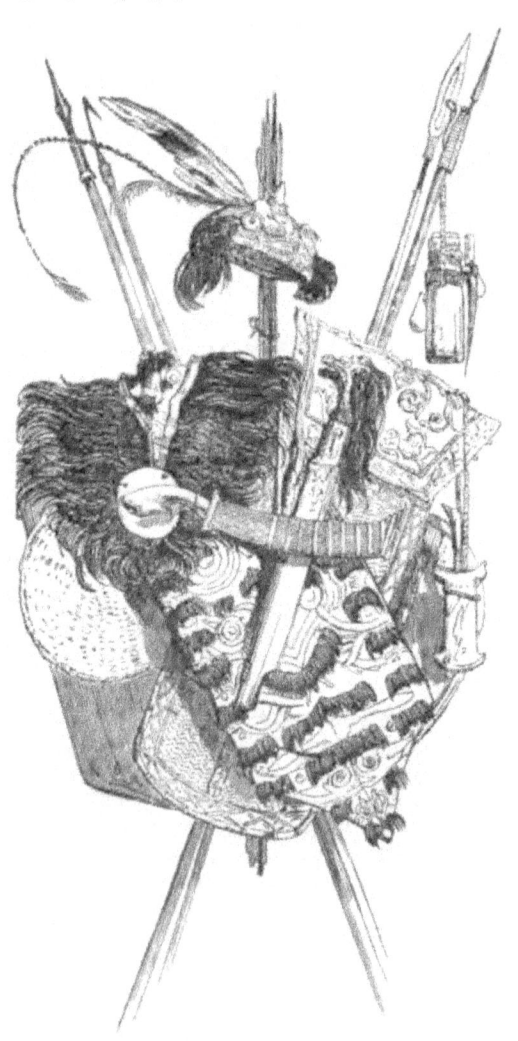

TROPHY. DYAK AND KAYAN WEAPONS.
(By Mr. B. N. Vigors, *Illus. Lond. News*, 10 Nov., 1849.)

CHAPTER XIX.

PAINTING AND TATUING.

PAINTING: Feet and fingers—Women. TATUING: Undups' needles and method—A new fashion with Sea-Dyaks—Poor art—Blocks—Needles—Inflammation—Payment—Beautiful work—Elaborateness—Kayan patterns—Great variety—Method of tatu-ing—Chief—Women's thighs—Arms—Kayan fondness of tatu-ing—A sign of valour—Kenniah women—Curious Kanowit marks—Intricate patterns—Kalabits—Bakatans—Imitation beards—Malanaus—Punans—Their method—Dusun patterns—Sign of prowess—Sign of murder—Muruts—Sign of bravery—Sign of cowardice—Strange objection to copying—Mittens—Dutch Borneo patterns.

MADAME PFEIFFER says the Dyaks "do not tatu, but occasionally colour the feet, nails and finger-tips a red brown." (p. 79.)

Among the Sea Dyaks "the men never paint their bodies, but the women after bathing often colour themselves from the waist upwards with turmeric to render themselves yellow and attractive. The result is far from agreeable to the eye of an European, but for this they care little so long as their efforts to please are appreciated by the men of their own race, which appears to be the case." (Brooke Low.) "The Undups, who are only slightly, if at all tatued, use three needles stuck in a piece of soft wood, the needles being bound round together with fine cotton at a fixed distance from the points so as to prevent them striking too deep. A small native hammer is used to strike the wood with. The outline of the pattern is marked out with clay and gunpowder is used to make the design permanent." (Crossland.)

"*Tatuing* prevails to a small extent among the Sea-Dyaks, but it is by no means universal among them. It is besides a custom of very recent introduction but is steadily gaining ground, though as yet it is confined to the male sex. I have seen a few women with small patterns on their breasts, but they were exceptions to the rule and were not regarded with favour. The marks or patterns are found more commonly on the arms, shoulders, and thighs; occasionally also on the forehead, throat-apple, chest, and ulna. The patterns are small, of a bright blue tint, and supposed to improve the appearance of the men. They have no other use or signification whatever, being neither distinctive of race, family, rank, nor of individual. The pigment employed is a solution of soot (dammar-soot), which is rubbed into the skin after it has been punctured. Tatuing has not yet acquired the dignity of a profession. Few Dyaks are really able to puncture with skill, although many of them can trace designs; but as their own designs are poor imperfect imitations of the Kayans, they disfigure the skin rather than adorn it. They say they are able to eradicate the pattern by puncturing it over again with the acrid sap of a forest tree. The designs employed are not numerous, although four are in common use. The practice is simple, but requires practice like most things. The design is first carved on wood in

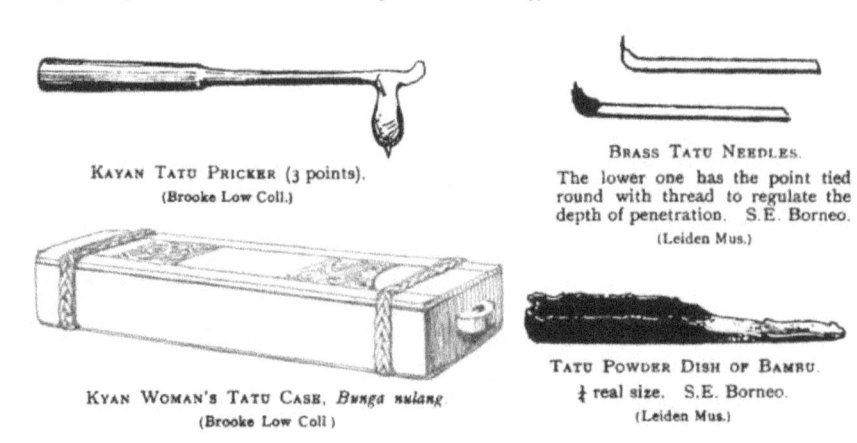

KAYAN TATU PRICKER (3 points).
(Brooke Low Coll.)

BRASS TATU NEEDLES.
The lower one has the point tied round with thread to regulate the depth of penetration. S.E. Borneo.
(Leiden Mus.)

KYAN WOMAN'S TATU CASE, *Bunga nulang*
(Brooke Low Coll)

TATU POWDER DISH OF BAMBU.
¼ real size. S.E. Borneo.
(Leiden Mus.)

TATU MALLET, S.E. Borneo.
(Leiden Mus.)

TATU SOOT HOLDER. S.E. Borneo.
(Leiden Mus.)

relievo; it is then smeared with the sooty preparation and printed on the skin. The figure is then punctured in outline with a set of needles dipped in the ink (for such it is), and afterwards filled up in detail. More ink is poured on to the skin and allowed to dry into it. Rice is smeared over the inflamed surface to keep it cool; if this is not done, it is apt to gather and fester. The limb operated upon must be kept free from wet, and must not be scratched however much it may itch. The operator of course requires to be remunerated, but as he is not a professional he is satisfied with a moderate guerdon. Among the Lugats there was a certain Aman Jerin who was partially but beautifully tatooed in patterns of a bright blue tint." (Brooke Low.)

"The Kanowit, Bakatan, Lugat, Tanyong, Tatau, Balinian are all more or less tatooed, both male and female. . . . The Bakatan and Lugat are most elaborately tatooed from head to foot." (Burns, Jour. Ind. Arch. iii. p. 141.)

"The Kyan men and some of the women," according to Bishop McDougall, "are tattooed in the most complicated and grotesque patterns.

TATU BLOCK.
Used by Kenniah men. ½ real size.
(Hose Coll.)

TATU BLOCK.
Used by Berawan men. ½ real size.
(Hose Coll.)

TATU BLOCK.
Used by Kenniah men. ½ real size.
(Hose Coll.)

TATU BLOCK.
Upper Kapuas R. ¼ real size.
(Prof. Molengraaff Coll., Leiden Mus.)

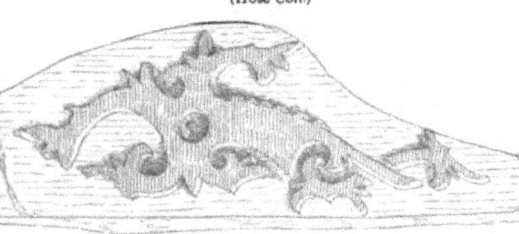

TATU BLOCK.
Used by Lelak men. ½ real size.
(Hose Coll.)

THREE TATU BLOCKS.
For Kayan women's thighs.
(Brooke Low Coll.)

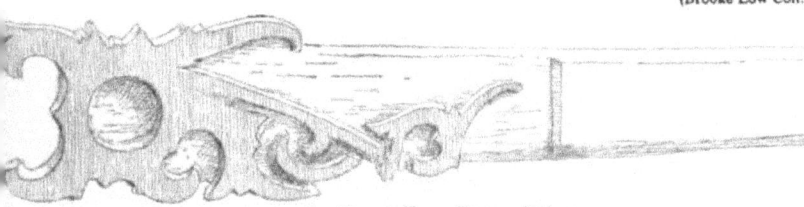

KAYAN TATU BLOCK, *Kalong*.
Very light white wood; length of imprint, 6in. Baram River.
(Peek Coll.)

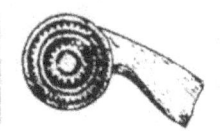

FIVE TATU BLOCKS. Upper Kapuas R. ¼ real size.
(Prof. Molengraaff Coll., Leiden Mus.)

When you look at them closely, the invention displayed in them is truly remarkable; but at a distance, they give a dusky, dingy appearance to the men, as if they were daubed with an inky sponge. Nature having denied them beards, they try to make up for the deficiency by the quaintest serpentine curly locks tattooed along their faces, and always bordered by a vandyke fringe, which must task their utmost ingenuity." (Mrs. McDougall, p. 154.)

Mr. Burns says : " The Kayan men do not tatoo, but many of the higher classes have small figures of stars, beasts, or birds on various parts of their body, chiefly the arms, distinctive of rank. The highest mark is that of having the back of the hands coloured or tatooed, which is only conferred on the brave in battle. With the women, the arms, from the elbows to the points of the fingers, are beautifully tatooed, as are also the legs from the thighs to a little below the knees, and likewise the upper parts of the feet; and those of very high rank have in addition one or more small spots on the breasts. In tatooing the performer pricks the design or pattern with three

Tatu Blocks.
Used by Berawan men. ½ real size.
(Hose Coll.)

needles, and afterwards smokes it with a dammon torch, by which process a beautiful dark blue is produced ; frequently inflammation of a serious nature follows. The operation of tatooing begins when girls are about four or five years of age, at first the hands and feet, and afterwards, previous to arriving at the age of puberty, the other parts are finished." (Jour. Ind. Arch. iii. 145.)

Of a Kayan chief Sir Sp. St. John wrote : " He is but slightly tatooed, having a couple of angles on his breast, a few stars on his arms, his hands as far as the joints of his fingers, and a few fanciful touches about his elbows "; and of the Kayan women : " As yet, I have seen but the few women who bathe opposite to the ship. They are generally tatooed from the knee to the waist, and wear but a cloth like a handkerchief hung round the body, and tucked in at one side above the hip, leaving a portion of the thigh visible. When bathing, their tatooing makes them look as if they were all wearing black breeches." (i. 99, 102.)

"Si Obong, the Kyan chief's daughter, had her arms much tatooed and she was also ornamented in that manner from just under the hip joint to three inches below the knee." (*ibid*, i. 121.)

Painting and Tatuing. 87

The men were "slightly tatooed with a few stars and other marks." (*ibid*, i. 98.)

"The Kayans are particularly fond of tattooing; the women more so than the men. A Kayan woman is tattooed on the upper part of the hands and over the whole of each forearm; on both thighs to below the knees, and on the upper part of the feet and toes. The pattern is so close that at a slight distance the tattooing appears simply as a mass of dark blue, and the designs—some of which are very pretty—usually consist of a multiplicity of rings and circles. A man is supposed to tattoo one finger only, if he has been present when an enemy has been killed, but tattoos hands and fingers if he has taken an enemy's head. The chiefs, however, often break through this rule, and have the whole of their hands tattooed if they have been on a

TATU MARKS
on arm of Kapuas Kayan captive woman. ½ real size.
(Copied from life by the Rev. W. Crossland).

TATU MARKS
on arm of Kapuas Kayan captive woman. ½ real size.
(Copied from life by the Rev. W. Crossland).

TATU MARK
on Kayan captive woman's elbow. ½ real size.
Copied from life by the Rev. W. Crossland).

TATU MARK on Punan shoulder.
(After Bock.)
This pattern very common among the Undups.
(Crossland).

single war expedition. The Kenniah women do not tattoo their thighs and legs as much as the Kayans, but they usually have their feet and hands and forearms thus ornamented. The men have designs on the underside of the forearm and sometimes on the thigh, and different races are characterised by different designs."[1] (Hose, J.A.I. 166.)

"Some of the Kanowit men are curiously tatooed; a kind of pattern covers their breast and shoulders, and sometimes extends to their knees, having much the appearance of scale-armour. Others have their chins ornamented to resemble beards, an appendage denied them by nature." (St. John i. 39.)

Mr. De Windt describes some Kanowits as being all tatued "from head to foot with most intricate patterns, and others representing birds, beasts, fishes, etc.: while round the face and throat the marks were made in imitation of a beard, an ornament which none of the tribes yet met with in Borneo possess. . . . Jok was tattooed from head to foot so thickly as to cause his body to look at a distance of a light blue colour, but a very small portion of his face around the nose and eyes, being left *au naturel.*" (p. 68.)

Sir James Brooke speaks of a Kanowit chief "profusely tatooed all over the body." (Mundy ii. 123.) (See *supra* illustration of tatued Kanowit chief, p. 29, vol. I.) "The Kalabits have long lines right down the arm from the biceps to the hand." (Hose, J.A.I. xxiii. 169.) "The Bakatans tattoo their faces and chests to such an extent that only a small portion of the skin of those parts is free from it." *(ibid,* p. 167.)

TATU MARKS sent me by the Rev. F. W. Leggatt. 1 and 2, *Trong*, ornament on breast; 3. *Trong*, on arm or breast; 4, ornament on throat; 5, *Trong*, on breast or arm; 6, no information given; 7, *Entadu*, on breast; 8, *Kala*, scorpion on arm or breast.

(Nos. 2, 3, 4, 5 and 6 were copied from life by Mr. Leggatt himself on the Sakaran river; Nos. 1, 7, 8 were drawn for him.)

Lieut. De Crespigny also says: "They tattoo themselves from head to foot in the most beautiful manner." (Proc. Roy. Geogr. Soc., 1873, p. 133.) Of these same people Sir Charles Brooke says the lower parts of cheeks "instead of being clothed with whiskers were tattooed; this ornament passed round the chin." (ii. 302.) Mr. W. M. Crocker likewise says: "The Bakatans are

---

[1] The Hon. Capt. Keppel describes a native from the Koti River (Dutch Borneo) a Kayan prisoner, as follows: "The lines, correctly and even elegantly laid in, of a blue colour, extended from the throat to his feet." (i. 87.)

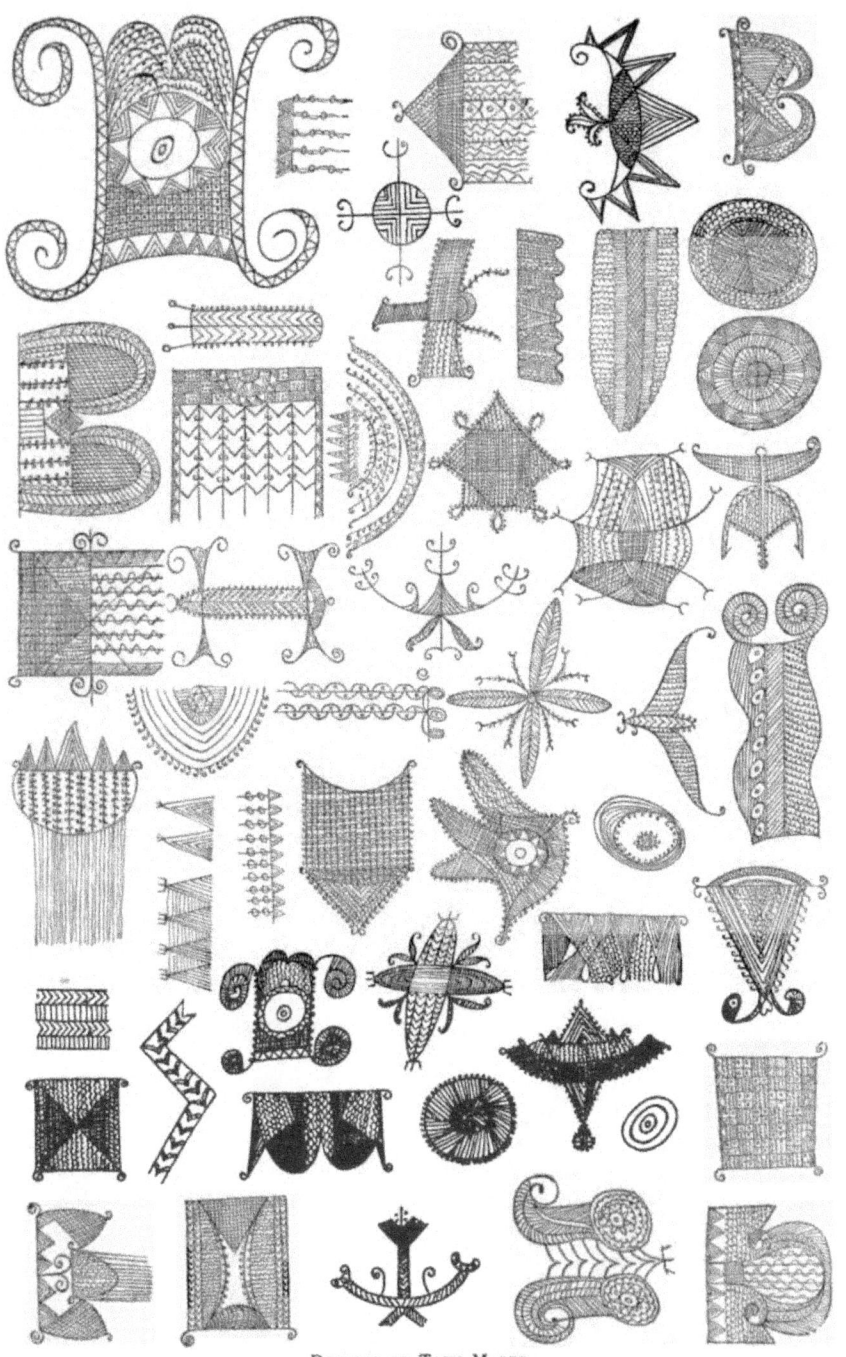

DESIGNS OF TATU MARKS.
Collected by Dr. Wienecke (Military Surgeon) in Borneo.
(Leiden Mus.)

profusely tattooed even to the hands and face, the latter probably intended to resemble a beard." (S.G., No. 123, p. 5.)

"The more primitive branches of the Malanaus practise tattooing, variously arranged in their different countries: some are nearly covered, others merely have anklets, bracelets, or necklaces, with a star or two on their breasts. The further removed they are from civilisation, the more thickly are they generally found to be tattooed." (Brooke i. 73.)

After Mr. Hose's very distinct statement, "the Punans do not tatoo" (J.A.I. xxiii. 167.), it seems strange to hear Mr. De Windt's account of tatued Punans: "Mrs. Lat and her two fair daughters. We found these (unlike the Kayans) tattooed over the face as well as body, and each wore the short skirt of the Kanowit. . . . On re-seating ourselves in the *ruai*, L. happened to notice the intricate and really beautiful tattooing on the body of one of the younger men. The latter, seeing this, asked us through our interpreter if we should care to be operated upon in a similar manner, this being considered a great honour to a guest; and no sooner had we accepted the offer than an old woman made her appearance armed with the necessary implements, and with the aid of a pair of very blunt needles, and a peculiar species of dye obtained from a tree, succeeded, after a good hour's work, in embellishing us,—L. with a ring on each shoulder (the sign manual of the tribe), and myself with a bird, whose genus it would puzzle most naturalists to determine, but which was popularly supposed among the Poonans to represent a hornbill, on the arm. Strange to say, neither L.'s punctures nor mine showed the slightest signs of inflammation afterwards, and the figures are far more distinct than they would be had Indian ink or gunpowder been used." (p. 86.)

Among the Ida'an Sir Sp. St. John saw men with "a tattooed band, two inches broad, stretched in an arc from each shoulder, meeting on their stomachs, then turning off to their hips; and some of them had a tattooed band extending from the shoulder to the hand." (i. 249, 374.)

Lieut. De Crespigny says: "The only parties among them who tattoo are those who have killed an enemy. The tattoo is invariably a broad band from the navel up to each shoulder, where it ends abruptly. A smaller band is carried down each arm, and a stripe drawn transversely across it for each enemy slain. I am happy to say I saw but few men tattooed, but one young fellow had no less than 37 stripes across his arms. Upon my enquiring where he had been so fortunate, he pointed towards the river Labuk." (Proc. R. Geogr. Soc. ii., p. 348.)

According to Mr. Whitehead (p. 106): "Some of the men are slightly tattooed with a few parallel short lines on the forearm."

Writing of these people Mr. Witti says: "There is nothing new about the Tolungun men, except that they tatoo themselves. The effect produced is quite the same as frequently seen on a stripped 'Jack.' I told our self-pricked friends here that white men do the same thing, for this and that reason— though I am not aware really of any reason at all; however, I thus learnt that tatooing here distinguishes the men who have slain a foe in an inter-tribal war. There are five such warriors in the three houses of Bundo. The ornament begins below the stomach and rises to the shoulders, like the skirt of a coat,

LONGWAI WOMAN'S TATUED HAND.
(After Bock.)

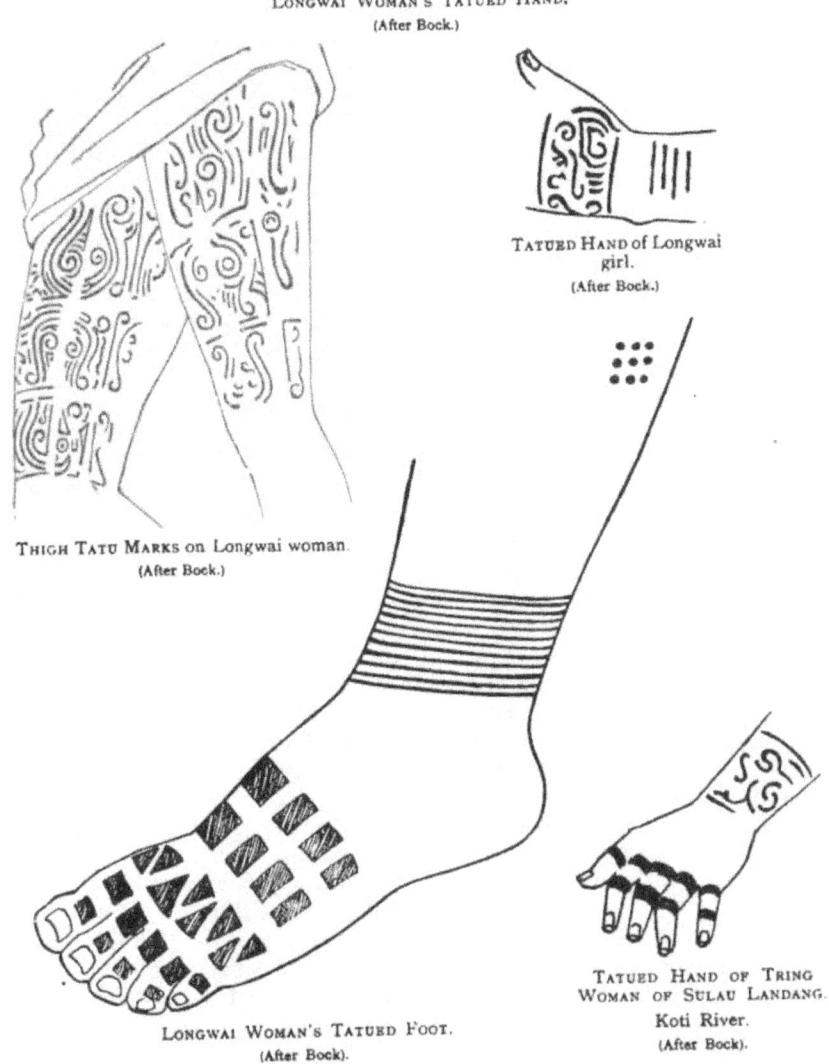

TATUED HAND of Longwai girl.
(After Bock.)

THIGH TATU MARKS on Longwai woman.
(After Bock.)

LONGWAI WOMAN'S TATUED FOOT.
(After Bock).

TATUED HAND OF TRING WOMAN OF SULAU LANDANG.
Koti River.
(After Bock).

then down the upper arms; here the two parallel broad stripes end, and the fore-end, on its inner side, shows a number of narrow stripes. These latter are more numerous if the man-slayer be at the same time well-to-do." (Diary, Nov. 19th.) And again: " It struck me that nearly all the men of Tamalan are tatooed, even mere lads. They are marked on breast, shoulders, and arms, the same as our friends of Upper Sugut. But, while with those tatooing distinguishes the hero of an inter-tribal war, here at Tamalan it signifies something very different. When remarking about these signs of prowess, they at once said their custom was different from the people of Bundo, Kagasingan, Lansat, Morali, &c.; and then we heard a tale which betrays a horrible side of the Dusun character, although they spoke with glee, like little children talking about their sport, and they laughed good-humouredly to our cross-questions about slowly extracting blood from their victims, or preserving their heads, &c. This *costumbre del paes* consists in the following:—When they had been damaged in their plantations and other property by the Sulus, they kill every Suluman they can get hold of. The Mahomedan chiefs, in order to keep the river open, then used to reconcile them by giving the aggrieved community some slave to dispose of; this is done by tying the slave up and spearing him through the thorax, which accomplished, the men in the village each take a cut at the quivering body. Whoever does this has a right to tattoo himself. They afterwards bury the dead, without retaining the skull, for the Sulu chiefs do not wish them to do that! They assure us they are not the same tribe who are reported as catching the blood of such victims in small bamboos, on purpose to sprinkle it over their fields; but they are certainly the same people of which the Danoa men, pointing to E.S.E., said, ' Don't go there! they are bad.'" (Diary, 30 May.) Mr. Hatton remarks of some Sin Dyaks (? Dusuns): " They are painted and tattooed in a peculiar way" (Diary, 18 Mar.), and he adds they are "tatooed with blue all down the arms, breasts, and legs." *(ibid.)*

The Muruts appear all to tatu. The Adang Murut women, met by Sir Sp. St. John, were tatued about the arms and legs. (ii. 115.) "The Muruts here are much tatooed. Those men who have fought, or have gone on bold or risky expeditions, are tattooed from the shoulders to the pit of the stomach, and all down the arms—three parallel stripes to the wrists. A headman, or rather a sometime headman of Senendan, had two square tatoo marks on his back. This was because he ran away in a fight, and showed his back to the enemy. Another and braver chief was elected in his place." (Hatton, 6th April.) . . . Of the Ghanaghana men "scarcely a man of them was untatooed." (*ibid*, 10th April.)

Describing the Murut women, Mr. Whitehead remarks: " Several Muruts were tattooed on their chests or thighs. Whilst busy drawing a peculiar tattoo, the Murut caught my eye and immediately covered the mark over. The tattoo was a peculiar one, resembling a three-legged dog with a crocodile's head, one leg being turned over the back as if the animal was going to scratch its ear. The reason the Murut gave for not allowing me to sketch this mark was that his wife was expecting a child, and he was afraid of my eye affecting her." (pp. 70, 73.)

At the present time Mr. O. F. Ricketts writes from the Trusun about the Muruts: " Tattooing is only carried out to a very small extent, many do not tattoo at all, the men have some simple design just above the knee-cap, or

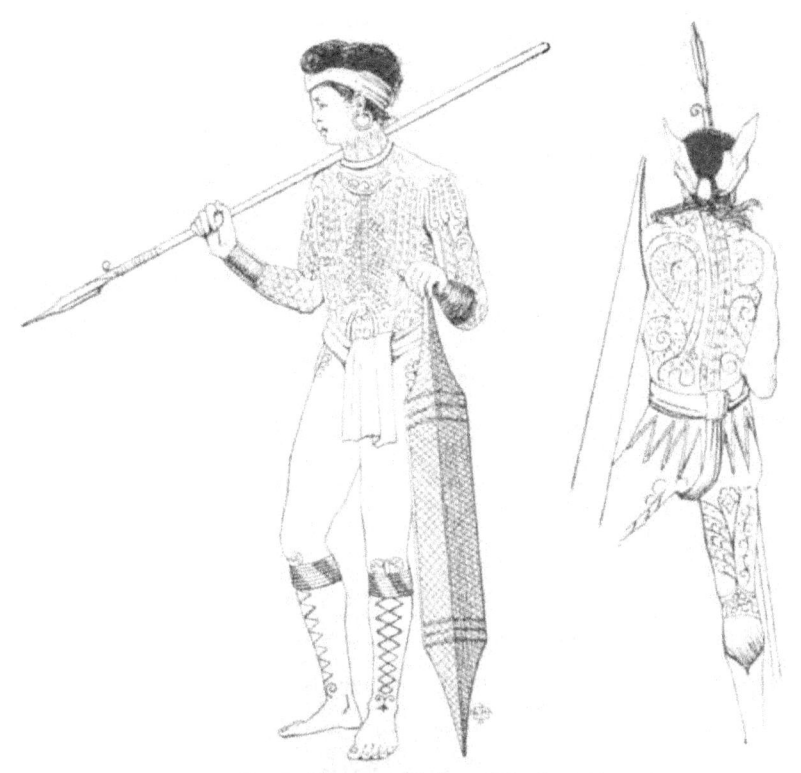

TATUED NGADJOES (Natives of Southern Borneo).
(After Dr. Schwaner).

plain circles on the chest; the women have fine lines tattooed from the knuckles to the elbow, which gives them the appearance a little distance off of wearing black mittens." (S.S. 347, p. 214.)

The following is condensed from Mr. C. Van Den Hamer's account of Biadju tatuing. The different patterns are practically only more or less elaboration of the same designs. Some have only a pattern (*boenter*) on the calf, others the pattern (*manoek*) on the arm, and so on, without intending to have more done. The coast people have mostly given up tatuing, but the Oet Danoems, of the Uplands, still practice it. The boys are tatued as soon as they begin to wear the chawat There appear to be no ceremonies or fastings in connection with it. The operator has a small brass style with bent point, and a small hammer of light wood. The pattern is drawn on with dammar soot and gold dust. The boy lies groaning on the ground. Owing to the inflammation only a little can be done at a time. The style is continually dipped in soot and water, and the blood wiped away with a bunch of bast. The inflammation is allayed by salt, the sores turn to a whitish colour, like *korap*, and then to a leady blue, and are indelible. The first pattern (*boenter*) is put on the calf, and consists of a circle of 5 cm. radius, with check pattern inside. It looks like a piece of plaster. Then the arms are done with five patterns (*manoek*), two inside and three outside—a spiral with a few curved lines; from the commencement of the spiral rays stream out with flourishes. The general form of the *manoek* is that of a wing. The smallest pattern is on the back of the wrist. To save pain they are put on on alternate sides. From the wrist to half up the upper arm, 2 parallel lines are drawn, with lozenge designs in between with a dot in the centre. It looks like a row of buttons. There are also designs (*sala pimping*, *sala* = between) between the *manoeks*. On the wrist is the design *matan poenai doehin bambang* ⌐⌐⌐ which is also met with on the throat. The *toeres oesoek* (lines of the chest) flows in three parallel lines from the navel up to the pit of the neck. On either side of these lines are about 29 rays (*rioeng*), on the outside of which are two lines, *toeroes taehaloeh* (head) *naga*, flowing from the navel to the breast nipples. On each breast (?) are the *naga* and dragon's head, with open jaws, teeth, and tongue distinctly drawn, eye less so, facing each other. These have the usual surrounding flourishes supposed to resemble the *palas*, a native shrub. The *manoek oesoek* is put on the muscles of the neck; it looks like the *samban*, a well-known breast ornament, which the inland youth wear on a cord round the neck. The nipples have circles, *tamboeling tosoe* (nipple), tatued round them. The *batang rawang* are lines which run from the chawat, parallel with the *toeroes tahaloek naga*, to the shoulder joint, where they join the leaf or wing pattern, *dawen baha* (shoulder). This latter pattern fills up the upper part of the arm. There were here nine rays and twenty-two flourishes. The *boewoeh sapoei* is a sort of collar pattern—it has two adjuncts, the *matan poenai* and *doehin bambang*. Two lines, *rampai baha*, run from the nape of the neck into the hair. It is said, with some up-country people these lines recurve behind the ears, flow over the temples, and end in a curl on the cheek. Down the spine there are five parallel lines, *batang garing* (ivory), like the *toeroes oesoek*. Over the whole surface of the trapezius muscle, rays, crosslines, and flourishes are drawn, which hang down from the collar like fringe. There are six *manoek* on the upper part of the back. An old man from the Manoehing river, uplands, had on his hips a zig-zag pattern called *penjang* (charms). On the back of the hands there are various forms, such as a crossed S with four dashes at the intersection, a swallow, cross, &c. Some have nothing on their hands. The Oet Danoem women have two parallel lines, with cross-lines, from the knee to the tarsus; on the thigh they have a pattern like the *sambas*; from the *boenter*, on the calves, to the heel there is a barbed line called *ihoeh* (*ekor* = rank) *bajan* – on the right leg it is called *bararek*, and on the left leg, *dandoe tjajah*. Brave warriors have such a *dandoe tjajah* on the elbow-joint, with a cross, called *sara pang matan andau*.

"According to the belief of the Biadjus tatuing takes the place of clothing, and turns to gold in heaven. The following account gives an idea of the cost:—the *boenter* costs 25 cts.; the *toekang langit*, on the hand, 10 cts.; the *toeroes oesoek* 1 fl.; the two dragons 2 fl.; the *manoek oesoek* 2 fl.; the *dawen baha*, on the left and as well as on the right arm, 4 fl.; the neck 1 fl. I do not know the cost of the other patterns.

"It is generally mentioned in the Sangiang saga that *Tèmpoen Tèloen*, in long past times, journeyed through many tracts of the earth, and let himself be tatued in certain localities according to the customs of the country, and in this manner introduced it into these parts. *Tèmpoe* is lord and *Tèloen* the name of his slave mistress; thus *Tèmpoe'n* or *ain Tèloen* means, master of *Tèloen*."

"Tatuing operations commence at an early age, and the first designs are generally traced on the calves, arms, and chest. As the individual increases in age, the operations are continued, and are extended to all the other parts of the body, so that there are some men who are completely covered from chin to foot with lines and drawings, representing flowers arranged in festoons." (S. Müller, ii. 352.) "Women are not tatued." (*ibid*, p. 353.)

According to Mr. Bock, among the Modangs the decoration is one of the privileges of matrimony, and is not permitted to unmarried girls. (p. 67). . . . "The Tandjoengs do not tattoo as a rule. I only found one with a + on his arm. (p. 130). . . . At Benoa the men were all tattooed with a small mark ⌒·⌒ either on the forehead, the arm, or the leg. (p. 139) . . . Tatooing is followed by all the tribes of Kotei, with the exception of those in the Long Blèh district; and some of the designs have very great artistic merit. The marks are either on the arms, hands, feet, thighs, chest, or temple. The women are more elaborately "got up" than the men, and seemed proud of displaying their skin-deep beauty. The more intricate patterns are executed by professionals, who first cut out the outlines in wood, and then trace the design on the part of the body to be decorated, filling it in with a sharp-pointed piece of bamboo, or a needle dipped into a pigment prepared for the purpose from vegetable dyes. The operation is very painful, and often takes a long time to execute, and the marks are absolutely indelible. The tattooing takes place, in the case of men, when they attain to manhood; and, in the case of women, when they are about to be married. There is an old woman of sixty, the marks on whose thighs were as distinct and bright as when they were first executed, perhaps forty or forty-five years previously. Different tribes, and different individuals of the same tribe, have different methods of tattooing. In some it is the forehead or chest; in others, the hands or feet; in others, the thighs that are tattooed. The greatest slaves to this fashion are perhaps the damsels of the Long Wai and Tring tribes, who unite in themselves the fashions of nearly all the other tribes. Whereas the others are content with ornamenting only one part of the body at a time, a Long Wai or Tring lady must be tattooed in various parts of the body." (pp. 189, 190.)

NOTE.—The statement in Jour. Anthrop. Inst. xvii. 322 and copied by Prof. Hain (p. 147) that the British Museum possess a portrait of a Tring priestess tatued should read that a plate taken from Mr. Bock's book has been hung up for public inspection.

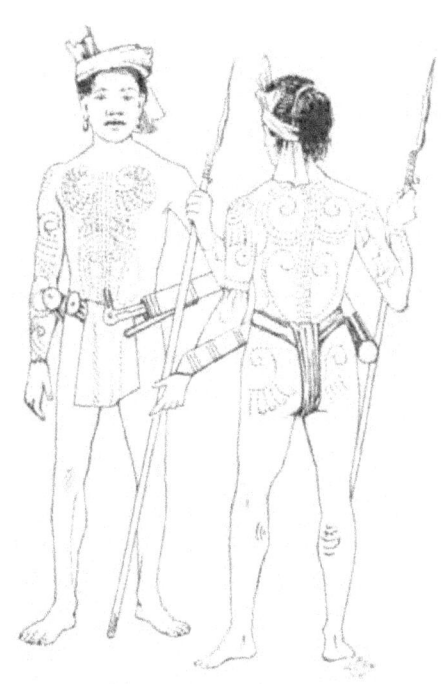

TATUED DYAKS (? Kayans).
(After Prof. Veth)

CHAPTER XX.

WAR AND WEAPONS.

WAR: CAUSES OF WAR—General causes—Feuds—Old quarrels—Tribute—Reprisals—Nabai's feud—Helens—Women an incentive—Love of robbery under arms—'To ease a sore heart'—Debts—Chivalry—WAR EXPEDITIONS—Formidable character—Announcing an expedition—The spear token—Preparations—Women's precautions while men away—The start—No hurry—Result of delay—Time no value—A grand sight—Camping places—Precautions—Explorations—War council—Traders decoyed—Retaliation—Crossing war paths—WAR ALARMS—DEFENCES—*Pagars*—Tactics of the invaded—Hiding treasures—Fires—Steep hills—*Chevaux de frise*—AMBUSHES—Luring on the enemy—Ambuscades—Dressing up as friends—Flank movements—*Ranjaus*—Stray invaders—SURPRISES—The Sauhs' annihilation—Prowling attacks—Dusuns *versus* Lanuns—Attacks at dawn—Kanowits' methods—Burnt chillies—Fight with Steele and Fox's murderers—Attacks in absence of men—Breach of hospitality—Allies killed *faute de mieux*—HOMERIC COMBATS—Fights for the slain—Saving heads—Guarding relations—Desperate hand-to-hand encounters—Chivalry—EXCITEMENT OF WARFARE—Mad with excitement—Quarrels amongst parties to an expedition—No mutilations—All is spoil in warfare—ORIGINAL DREAD OF FIREARMS—Mr. Dalton's notes on war.

WEAPONS: GENERAL WAR COSTUME—Sea Dyaks—Helmets—Jackets—Thighs unprotected—Kayans—Accoutrements—SPEARS—Lances—Wood javelins—SWORDS—Hill Dyaks—Sea Dyaks—*Parang pedang*—*Parang nabur*—*Parang ilang*—Good steel—Good smiths—SHIELDS—Method of using—BOWS AND ARROWS—Mr. Skertchly's remark—Undup children—Mr. Earl's statement—Testimony of an old Dutch soldier—Dr. Lewin's authority.

WAR.

THE CAUSES OF WAR.

"It may be observed that their causes for war, as well as its progress and termination, are exactly the same as those of other people. They dispute about the limits of their respective lands; about theft committed by one tribe upon another; about occasional murders; the crossing each other on the war-path; and about a thousand other subjects. . . . In short, there is nothing new in their feelings, or in their mode of shewing them; no trait remarkable for cruelty; no head-hunting for the sake of head-hunting. They act precisely on the same impulses as other wild men: war arises from passion or interest; peace from defeat or fear. As friends, they are faithful, just, and honest; as enemies, blood-thirsty and cunning, patient on the war-path, and enduring fatigue, hunger, and want of sleep, with cheerfulness and resolution." (Keppel i. 301, 304.) According to Mr. Dalton (p. 9): "The Daya are, generally speaking, peaceable; the petty feuds among themselves may be traced to the horrid custom of ornamenting their houses with human skulls, procured by way-laying individuals of a different tribe, and to decorating their children with the teeth; or to disputes about particular tracts of forests." Old feuds are a fruitful source of the wars and quarrels of the present day. "The

Sow and other Dyak tribes once made an incursion into the Puttong country and killed eighteen persons. This was simply the continuation of an old feud." (Keppel Meander ii. 17.)

" Many of the feuds in which the Dyaks of Sarebas and Sakarran are now engaged, are quarrels which arose in the times of their ancestors[1]; and the ostensible object in carrying on of which now is, that their balance of heads may be settled; for these people keep a regular account of the numbers slain on each side on every occasion: these memorandums have now, perhaps, become confused amongst the sea tribes, but amongst those of the hills, where fewer people are killed, and fighting is less frequent, the number to which each tribe is indebted to the other is regularly preserved. A hill chief once told me that he durst not travel into another country, which he wished to visit, as their people were the enemies of his tribe; when I asked him in surprise, having supposed that he was at peace with everyone except the people of Sakarran, he told me that in the time of his grandfather, the people of the other tribe had killed four of his, and that in retaliation his tribe had killed three of the other, so that there was a balance of one in his favour, which had never been settled, nor had any hostilities been carried on for many years, yet all intercourse between the tribes had ceased, and they could only meet in a hostile character." (Low, p. 212.) Mr. Grant reports much difficulty in settling feuds: " At night we had a good deal of *Bechara*, in reference principally to the demands made upon one tribe by another, for certain fines or debts, in acknowledgment of supposed victories gained in the olden time. It appears that formerly, when a party of any tribe took some heads from another, not content with that, they must needs demand certain gongs and jars from them, in acknowledgment of their having been defeated. This was, I suppose, looked upon in the light of a tribute. . . . At any rate, one tribe making such a demand upon another, causes the latter, in order to get the wherewithal to pay, to remember some old feud and successful onslaught on a third tribe, and so the wheel is set in motion, after having been at a stand-still for years. I have put a timely stop to all this." (Grant, p. 61.) The Muruts also have their feuds. They "are not by any means a warlike race, for, taking them altogether, they are great cowards; they do not organize large expeditions to go on the war-path, . . . though on one occasion they combined to resist the attack of a party of Kayans, when they killed some sixty of them. The worst feature in their lives are the inter-tribal feuds above mentioned, which have been carried on amongst them from time immemorial, and which they are totally unable to settle themselves. Indiscriminate head-hunting, simply for the sake of obtaining heads, is the exception rather than the rule, but when making reprisals against another tribe, they will try and get one if possible with the least danger to themselves, and the head, instead of being hung up in a head-house, as is the custom of the Land Dyaks, after having been feasted over, is put away with the rest in a basket in some corner of the house. Each house has its own feuds, and carries them on irrespective of the

---

[1] Mr. Hupé refers to hostilities which broke out on account of some losses which one party had incurred 15 years previously when 300 people were killed (p. 314).

others; the usual way being for a small party to go and fire into an enemy's house, trusting to chance that they may kill some one, and then they return home more or less satisfied; they sometimes lie in wait in jungle to make their attack on an enemy if their omens are good, and on these occasions they sometimes get a head, though more often from some woman or child who happens to be working in a paddy field. They are not particular as to whether they kill the individual who made the last attack on them, anyone in the same house, or living on the same stream, will equally satisfy them, thus complicating the cases." (Ricketts, S.G. No. 347, p. 213.)

Of a Dusun feud, Mr. Witti writes: "Nabai has a feud with Peluan, the adjacent district south-west, and that is what makes Jeludin [the Nabai chief] so miserable. Thus I learnt the account there is running between Nabai and Peluan. Killed by Nabai, 16 people, of which 6 men, 3 women, 2 children; Nabai paid blood-money for five people and a half, Peluan for two. Peluan, therefore, appears debited with eight dead and a half. The chronological mark here is worthily selected, it is formed by the smallpox epidemic. To himself, I explained he could no longer receive from Peluan a slave for the purpose of sacrificing it in amends for the murder of Ah Hok, a Chinaman, who last year went trading in Peluan, after having lived a while in Jeludin's house. Jeludin was in that matter offered a slave-woman, a short time ago, but he sent her back on the ground that she was not young enough. What business has this Jeludin to try and get his blood-thirstiness quenched on account of an outsider who went to Peluan, as the man went up the Kimanis entirely at his own risk? And then, Ah Hok's death was brought about in retaliation for a Peluan mother and two children, who were murdered by Jeludin, with his own hands, in his own village." (Diary, 19th Mar.) Of this same feud he writes two days later: "Having to act as intermediary in bloody feuds like these would be repulsive if it were not for the sake of an experiment. I do not pretend to say for the sake of peace, for these tribes have so few mutual interests, that peace between them will ultimately have to be the object of rigorous measures on the part of the Government. But it will be a source of some interest if we succeed in accomplishing our round from one tribe to the other, each of which threatens to blowpipe, shoot, and behead anybody who may come from the opposite camp. To-day, the Dyak Ankaroi complained that two years ago Jeludin and party carried off his wife and two little children (girls) whilst he (Ankaroi) was absent from home. At Petikang, Jeludin put all three to death in that cruel manner called *ambirus* (making a spirit). Ankaroi and his friends offered Jeludin all they had to ransom those captives, but in vain. On that Ankaroi took an oath not to touch any woman until he shall have killed Jeludin. I now quite understand why my *ex-officio* friend is in such an awful funk, notwithstanding the long odds on the side of Nabai. But how can I decently ask the bereaved party how much he would take in cloth, brass, salt, jars, and cattle to make it up? I had much sooner express my sympathy with Ankaroi by giving him a Henry-Winchester, latest model. As it is, the Peluan people understood me so far correctly, that they asked me to bring about a meeting with Jeludin, for the purpose of estimating the amount of blood-money, should Jeludin wish to pay up. They make it a condition that I myself shall be present to keep the other party from treachery. I agreed to let Langadoi, the elder of Peluan, know after my return to Nabai. Ankaroi alone asks such heavy damages that I have but little hope. What I wonder at is which of the two parties has misrepresented the facts of the case most ?" (*ibid*, 25th March.)

They have their Helens too. Thus Mr. Denison records: "The Si Baddat and Sikong Dyaks had been at war arising out of a Si Baddat going to Sikong and carrying off a man's wife, and on her restitution being demanded it was refused, whereupon Sikong took two heads from Si Baddat who retaliated by taking one from Sikong, but peace had now been patched up between these tribes." (Ch. iii. 32.)

"As the women have so decided a preference for the men whose bravery and deeds of arms are notorious, it readily accounts for the mass of the populace being addicted to war. . . .

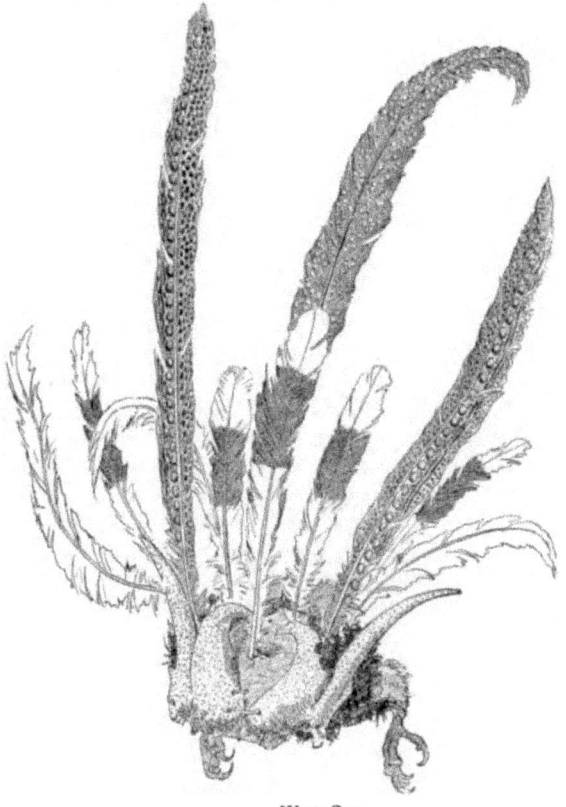

WAR CAP.
Made of split bill of the hornbill bird and of part of its skin, claws and feathers, and with argus pheasant feathers. S.E. Borneo.
(Leiden Mus.)

It may even be doubted whether Europeans might not be found who would take the heads of their dead enemies to gain the smiles and embraces of beauty." (Mundy ii. 3.) As previously mentioned by Mr. Brooke Low, the women urge the men on to war. (See p. 363.)

Very often the cause of war is much the same as amongst ourselves—the mere love of fighting. The following statement by Admiral the Hon. H. Keppel goes far to

WICKERWORK WAR CAP. S.E. Borneo.
(Leiden Mus.)

prove this: "The whole country on either bank of this river is rich and fertile in the extreme. Fields of cotton, sugar-cane, and padi, with cocoa-nut and fruit-trees in variety, grow in the greatest luxuriance. Pigs in hundreds, ducks and poultry without number, proved that these people were robbers from choice, and not from necessity. In every house cotton-looms for making cloth were found. The country at each mile improved in beauty: the scenery was varied by hill and dale; while a succession of open spaces, cleared for cultivation, gave evidence of a dense population well able to enrich themselves by honest industry. Our party were informed that, if they continued to advance for the next four days, they would still find the country continue to improve." [1] (Meander i. 173.)

"A Mahomedan Pakatan named Japer lost two grandchildren, so to ease his sore heart he went on a war expedition and massacred a tribe of harmless Punans." (St. John ii. 62.)

Among the Singé Dyaks: "If one tribe claimed a debt of another, it was always demanded, and the claim discussed. If payment was refused, the claimants departed, telling the others to listen to their birds as they might expect an attack. Even after this, it was often the case that a tribe friendly to each, mediated between them, and endeavoured to make a settlement of their contending claims. If they failed the tribes were then at war. Recently, however, Parimban has attacked without due notice, and often by treachery, and the Sow Dyaks, as well as the Singé, practise the same treachery. The old custom likewise was, that no house should be set on fire, no paddy destroyed, and that a *naked woman* could not be killed, nor a woman with child. These laudable and praiseworthy customs have fallen into disuse, yet they give a pleasing picture of Dyak character, and relieve, by a touch of humanity, the otherwise barbarous nature of their warfare." (Mundy i. 331.)

WAR EXPEDITIONS.

"Sea Dyak warfare is far from despicable, although it is undisciplined, and when the command is assumed by a person of sufficient influence to enforce obedience, the force at his disposal becomes more formidable than it otherwise would be; but this is not so often the case now as it was formerly." (Brooke Low.) Once "upwards of 100 boats, with certainly not fewer than 2,500 men, had been at Saräwak a week, asking permission to go on an expedition." (Keppel i. 216.) Sir Chas. Brooke's force against the Kayans consisted "of about three hundred large boats, averaging over forty men in each; besides a large portion are still behind, and will be coming up for a week or more." (ii. 259.)

"It is customary to announce a coming war expedition for such and such a season at one of the great feasts, when the village is thronged with guests

[1] "The *Orang blonda* (white men)" said Rajah Dinda of Long Wai, "have been killing the Dyaks and Malays on the Tewéh by hundreds,"—referring to the Dutch war in the Doesoen district in 1859-64,—" because they want to take their country and collect more rice and gutta; and why should they object to our killing a few people now and then when our *adat* (custom) requires it? We do not care for the instructions of the white men, and do not see why they should come into our country at all." (Bock, p. 216.)

War Hat.

Made of the fish scales, sewn with finely-split rotan on to a plaited cap. The cap is made of a soft, bast-like material. Diam., 6½in.; depth, 4½in.; weight, 4¼oz.

(Leggatt Coll.)

The double thread (A) as seen on the outside.

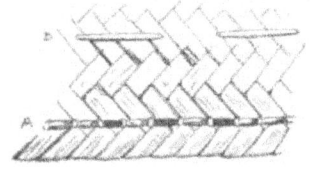

Inside of the War Hat.

Showing (B) how the thread holds the scales, and (A) also how the double thread runs round the edge inside.

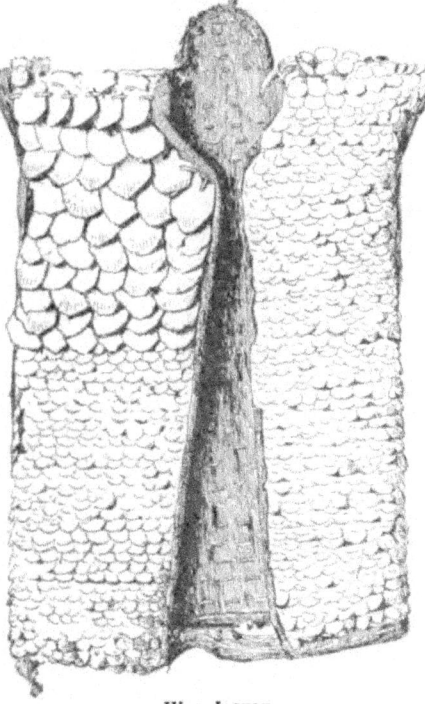

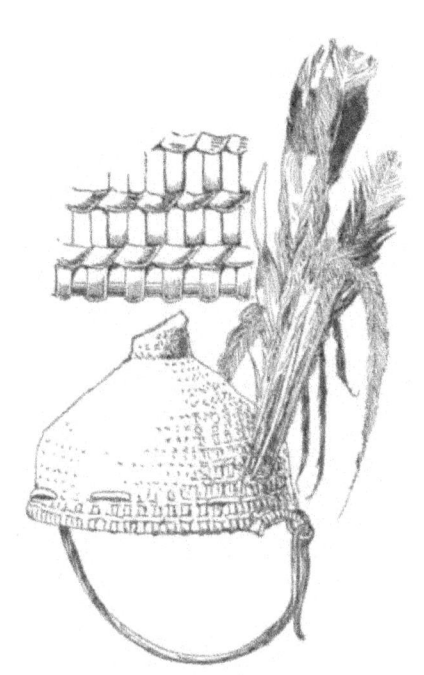

War Jacket.

Made of thick bark furnished with fish scales! The larger scales on the left hand side sewn on with finely-split rotan, the smaller scales with strong thread (fine cord). The whole edged with dark blue cotton as tape. The portion covering the right breast is about 1¼in. broader than that covering the left breast. Dr. A. Günther informs me that the scales are those of a scaroid fish, *Pseudoscarus marine*. Weight, 2lb. 10oz.; length, 25½in.; breadth, 16½in.

(Leggatt Coll.)

In the Brooke Low collection the hat is called *hatupu kaloi* and the coat *baju empuran*.

Dyak War Cap.

Made of coarsely-plaited rotan, lined inside with pandanus leaf; to one side are fastened some hornbill's feathers. Height, 17in. diam., 7½in.

(Brit. Mus.)

from the country far and near, and when there is sure to be an unusual gathering of powerful chiefs. The speaker, who must be a great chief, gives his reason, that his people wish to put off mourning, or that his people have been slain and he must have some revenge, and he ends by inviting all present to accompany him on an incursion upon an ancient enemy. If he be a chief of any real influence he is sure to secure an ample following, in reality more than enough for his purposes, but his ambition expands as his numbers increase and his warpath assumes grander proportions. The women lend their assistance to induce their husbands and lovers to join the warpath. Before this, however, the chief whose mind is set on the business gets together a circle of chiefs and warriors, which before the end of the proceedings resolves itself into a council of war. The expediency of the campaign and the exigencies which demand it are then openly debated, and if the majority or even a strong party are in favour of it, the chief who originally broached the topic, if he feels confident of a following large enough to effect

Lutong KAYAN HAT.
Made of plaited rotan with armadillo scales sewn on. Chin strap made of European two-coloured band.
(Hose Coll.)

Kalupu. DYAK WAR CAP.
Made of a single skin of the porcupine pushed up to a peak in the centre, with fur edging, inside matwork. Weight, 22oz.; diam., 7in.; almost round. Baram River.
(Peek Coll.)

his purpose, announces his intention of becoming a leader and the date of the departure for the enemy's country. All present are invited to accompany him and to bring their friends and relations. The details are then discussed, the amount of *bekals* (baskets) necessary, the route, the character and number of enemy, etc. The period usually selected for any expedition on a large scale is that immediately after the seed planting or after the harvest; the former time is preferred when available as they can spare the time better, and have three months clear before they are required to gather in the harvest. In the latter case they would probably have no farms at all for that year, as they would have no dry weather to dry the clearings, which, therefore, would not burn well.

"As the time draws near for the expedition to start, a spear is sent round the country from village to village with a *tembubu toli*, to signify how many days are to elapse before the commander-in-chief is able to make a start; a place is also mentioned where he will await the force." [His Highness once had some trouble owing to a Malay sending a spear round amongst the Sakarans. (i. 256.)] "The women are everywhere busy preparing

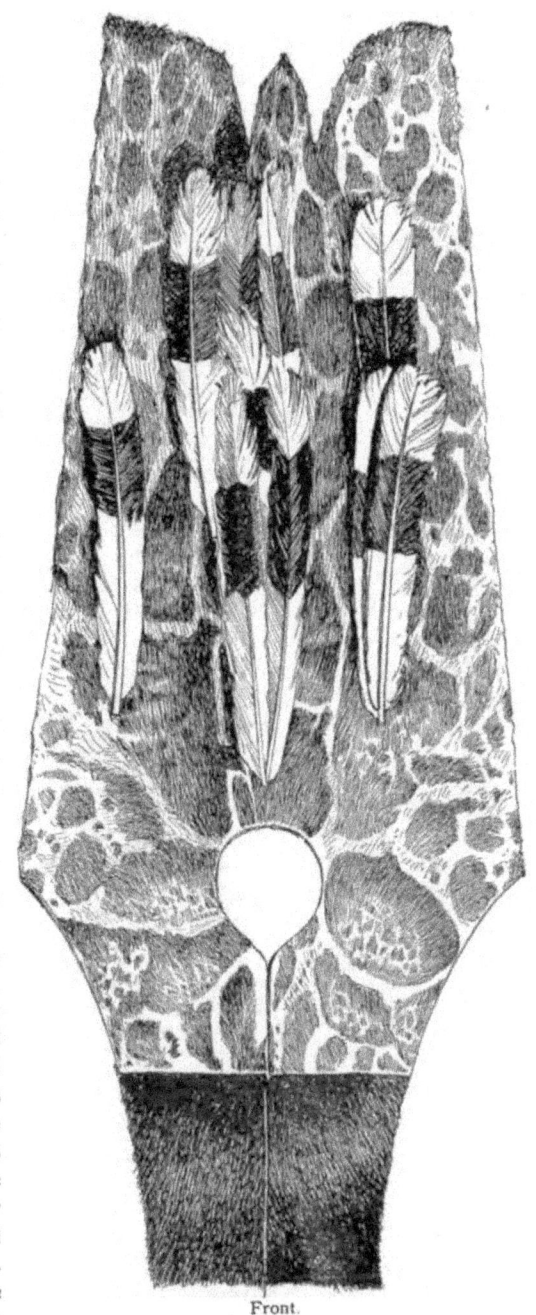

Front.
WAR DRESS
From Sarawak. Skin of the *Riman Dahan* (or tortoise-shell leopard), with an opening for the neck; attached to it are eleven feathers of the hornbill. Length, 47in.
(Brit. Mus.)

the *bekals*, and the produce of the gardens are taken to the nearest market to exchange for tobacco, *chunan*, *gambir*, etc. The men on their part have been busy in getting the war boats ready, launching them into the river, lashing on the planks and fitting them up with palm leaf awnings and bamboo floorings. Those who are able to purchase the material, plane the bottom of their canoes to make them smooth and tar them to preserve them, make figure heads for the bows, and paint the side planks in various patterns. They take nets with them to fish by the way, and dogs to hunt with if the distance is so great that they are likely to run short of food, but their chief support on an expedition of this kind is what they find on the banks and in the forest—especially the wild sago. The men are very busy furbishing up their arms and sharpening their weapons and decorating their helmets and war-jackets." (Brooke Low.)

" As long as the men are away their fires are lighted on the stones or small fireplaces just as if they were at home. The mats are spread and the fires kept up till late in the evening and lighted again before dawn, so that the men may not be cold. The roofing of the house is opened before dawn, so that the men may not lie too long and so fall into the enemies' hands." (Crossland, Gosp. Miss. 1871, p. 166.)

" If one of a war-party slips down and grazes his skin shortly after the setting-out of the expedition, he had better return home at once, or he will be brought back wounded." (Chalmers in Grant's Tour.)

" The chief is always the first to leave the village, and as the first and chief part of the journey is by water, he pulls away in his canoe, and at some convenient distance from the village, he bivouacs for the night to *beburong*— to consult the omen birds. If the omens by birds are favourable, he proceeds to the tryst and there awaits the force as it dribbles in one by one or few by few.[3] When all or most have arrived the flotilla moves on uncontrolled until it reaches the *pengkalan* or landing-place, whence the overland route commences. There is no attempt at order or regulation as long as they are in the water and in their own country, every boat stopping and moving much as it pleases, but all trying, nevertheless, to reach the pengkalan at once. If this is close by there is a dash for it, but if it is several days' journey there is a good deal of loitering by the way to increase their stock of provisions or to

[3] " When the chief of this tribe has decided to go out kidnapping and head-hunting, the people, women as well as men, are called together to confess. Should it appear that some youthful members have infringed the recognized laws of the tribe as regards marriage, or that the sanctity of the marriage vow has been violated, certain penalties are inflicted on the offending parties, such as a fine of a fowl or a pig; and when the offence is purged, and the moral character of the tribe is, according to their opinion, re-established, a ' prophet ' is sent out with twenty or thirty penitents, to observe omens either in the air or in the woods. These penitents are youths who appear at birth to have had certain marks, signs of misfortune, on them, and who, in order to get the marks to disappear and to prevent the evil which their presence forebodes, must atone, or go through penitential performances, such as depriving themselves during a certain portion of their lives of salt or fish, or of every kind of clothing. This party of omen observers proceed a day's march into the depth of the forest, and regular communication is maintained between them and the rest of the village, so that they can be informed of anything that happens while they are away from home. Should any one die in the tribe they must return to the village, taking up their dwelling in a shed specially built for them. As soon as the funeral is over they resume their journey, not returning until they have satisfied themselves that the omens are favourable for the expedition about to be despatched." (Bock, p. 218.)

Back.

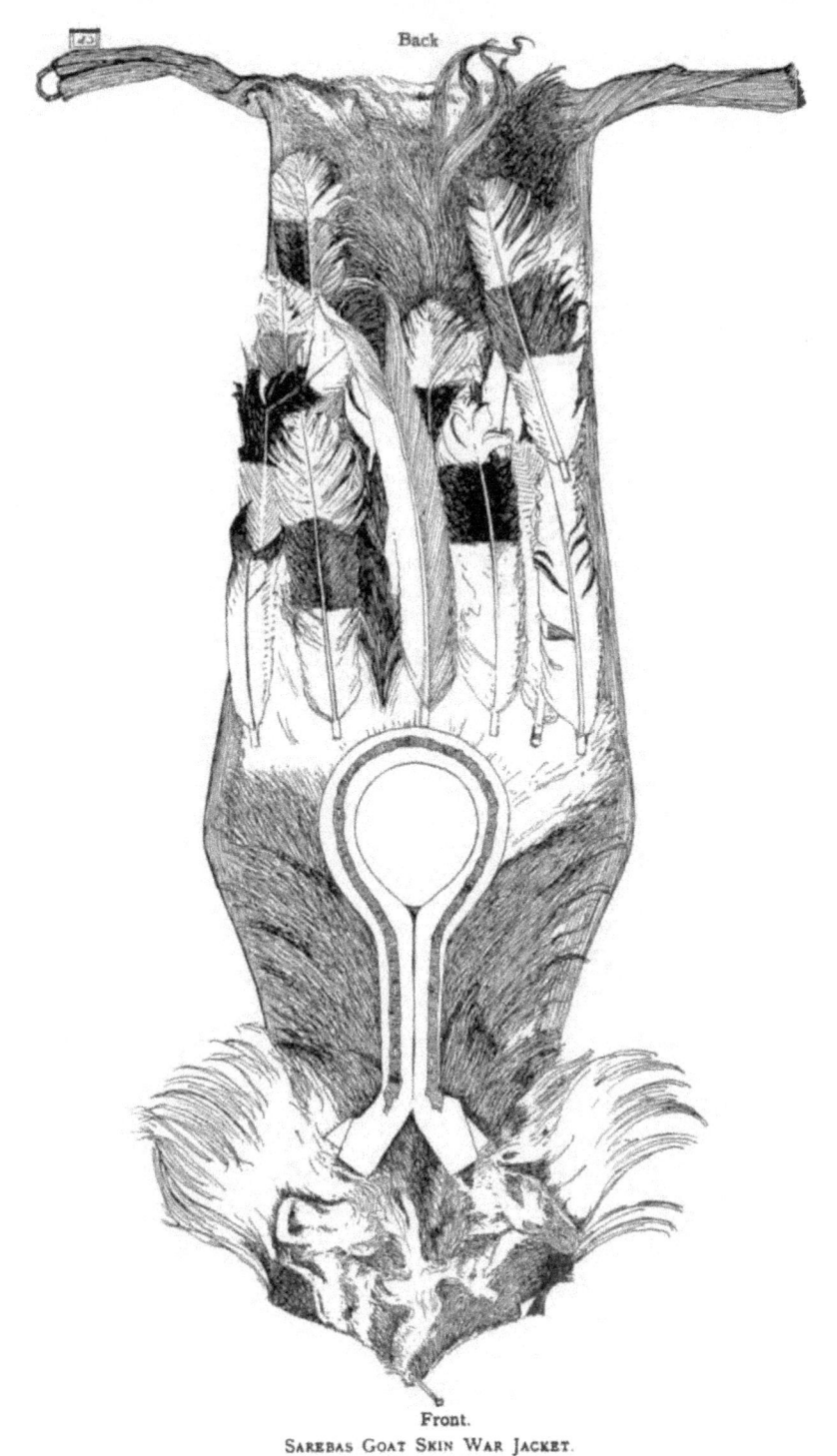

Front.
SAREBAS GOAT SKIN WAR JACKET.
Edged with red calico and yellow woollen cloth. Length, opened up as shown, 3ft. 3in.; width, 13in.
(Edinbro' Mus.)

equip themselves more fully with *kejangs* (deer), poles, *tukahs* (pegs), etc., and cords for hauling rapids." (Brooke Low.)

"The Dyaks are never in a hurry in setting off. They cook and feed at leisure, and commence walking about half-past seven, and the morning meal keeps them going until late in the afternoon; they certainly get over more ground by following this plan." (Brooke ii. 178.) Occasionally, however, the delay is so great that the force becomes useless for the purpose for which it was called together. Such a case happened on the Batang Lupar. (S.G., No. 161, p. 5.) This is quite in accordance with the natives' inability to appreciate the value of time. When on the Limbang Sir Sp. St. John notes (ii. 26) "that they start with, perhaps, two days' provisions, and trust to hunting for food. If they find a spot where game is plentiful, they stay there till it is exhausted; if the jungle produce no sport, they live on the cabbages taken from the palms, on the edible fern, on snakes, or anything, in fact, that they can find. If they come across bees' nests, they stop to secure the wax and honey. Time is of no value to them, as they generally start after the harvest, and many parties are said to have taken six months."

"The chief brings his musical instruments with him and plays on his gongs and *lawahs* as he sweeps along. The line of advance is most irregular, the canoes not moving up in a line but with wide gaps, some outstripping each other, others lagging behind to cook and angle, others deterred by bad omens and adverse dreams, obliged to halt for the day, others to dry their things capsized in the rapids, etc.

"It is a grand sight to see these canoes, filled with dusky warriors, whose naked arms and bodies are just visible beneath the awning, pulling away with a uniform and vigorous stroke, each arm with its white shell bracelet, and the chief standing up in the stern steering the rudder with hand and foot. The canoes hold each from twenty to seventy men.

"Arrived at the landing-place, a camp is formed, but the huts are not arranged in any military fashion, but line the banks of the river. The *langkan*, or hut is built sometimes to accommodate a whole boat's crew; the warriors lie side by side, their spears are stuck in front, and their shields and swords in their hands, so that they can spring to their feet, arms in their hands, in the twinkling of an eye. The roof slants upwards from the ground and forms an angle with it. It is thatched with leaves and branches; the flooring is of the same material with a layer of bamboo or sticks. A fire is lit hard by to keep off the mosquitoes and sandflies, who are often troublesome. These huts are meant to last a single night, or several, according to the care with which they have been built; but stronger huts are reared when a stay is expected to exceed a few days." (Brooke Low.) "The floors are always raised above the ground to preserve the inmates from the attacks of leeches which abound among the dead leaves." (Low, p. 245.) "Kayans, when they make their camp, strew dead leaves outside the fence so that no one, not even a dog, can approach without being heard. Punans make their camp in a circle, each hut facing a different direction, so as to prevent a surprise." (Brooke Low.) These precautions are, however, not always efficient. "Some of the enemy had quietly walked through the camp at night; their tracks were seen in the morning—probably some

SPEAR.

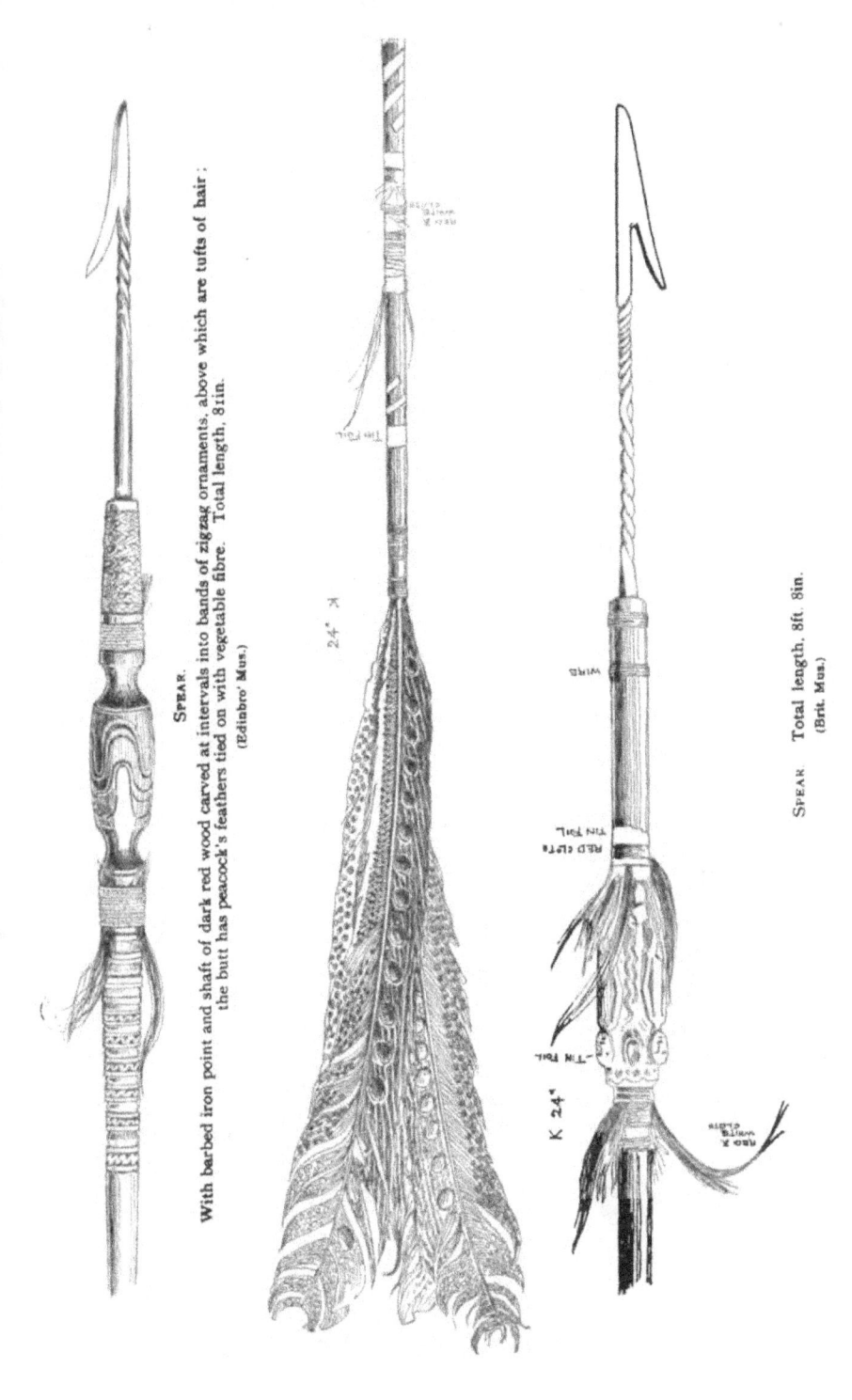

With barbed iron point and shaft of dark red wood carved at intervals into bands of zigzag ornaments, above which are tufts of hair; the butt has peacock's feathers tied on with vegetable fibre. Total length, 8 in.
(Edinbro' Mus.)

SPEAR. Total length, 8ft. 8in.
(Brit. Mus.)

venturous spirit who wished to ascertain how strong our force really was." And on another occasion, on the same expedition : "One of the enemy took a dexterous aim with a barbed spear as an old Dyak was warming himself before a fire in camp, sitting with his hands crossed to shade his face from the flames.

SPEAR.
(Leiden Mus.)

The spear pinned both his hands together in this position, and fortunately so, for it kept the weapon from his chest and saved his life. The spear-head was cut off before it was extricated." At the camp "a halt is made of several days' duration, to explore the neighbourhood, and to permit stragglers to come up. The canoes are hauled up and concealed in the forest, and the track examined." (Brooke i. 310.) "The boats, if any, are rendered safe from any sudden night surprises; each party watch abreast their own boat." (*ibid* i. 294.)

SPEAR (? FISH SPEAR).
(Leiden Mus.)

Section.

Lower Pattern. Upper Pattern.
UNDUP SPEAR HANDLE.
½ real size.
(Crossland Coll.)

GOURD.
Trained into shape by binding it with a cloth while young. Used as a powder flask. James Motley.
(Kew Mus.)

"A war-council is held, and the route marked, and the situation of the enemy discussed, and on a given day the march commences, each one shouldering his pack and stepping out in Indian file—the guides ahead, and closely followed by a few of the hardiest, boldest, and most experienced men at their heels. This line of march reaches many a mile if the war party be a numerous one. The pace is rapid so long as they are in neutral territory, but slackens as soon as they reach the borders of the enemy's country. The leaders then proceed more warily as the enemy, if forewarned of their approach, are pretty sure to be posted in ambush by the way." (Brooke Low.)

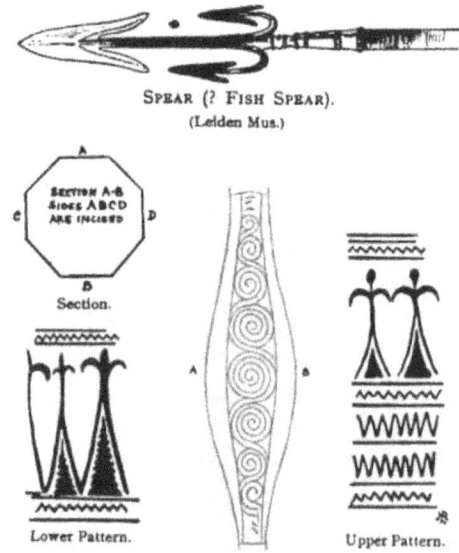

"It is really curious to witness their movements, when the order is given to go out to skirmish,—one by one, with a quick pace, yet steady and silent tread, they glide into the bushes or long grass, gain the narrow paths, and gradually disappear in the thickest jungle." (Mundy i. 262.)

"Sometimes a war-party would decoy a party of traders, and murder them for the sake of their heads; while a trading party, if opportunity offered, never failed to act in a similar manner." (Horsburgh, p. 14.) "At night they would drift down on a log, and cut the rattan cable of trading prahus, while others of their party would keep watch on the bank, knowing well where the stream would take the boat ashore; and when aground they kill the men and plunder the goods." (St. John.)

"When a tribe is on a warlike excursion, it often happens that their track (or 'trail') is crossed by another tribe. Those who strike the trail guard it at some convenient spot, apprehending the party to be enemies; they plant *ranjows* in the path, and wait till the returning party are involved amongst them to make an attack. If enemies, and they succeed, all is well; but if friends, though no attack be made, it is a serious offence, and mostly gives occasion to war, if not paid for." (Keppel i. 302.)

WAR ALARMS.

The alarm caused by the rumour of an enemy is well described by the Rev. Mr. Crossland : " During the last few days we have been living a rather exciting life. Four men went up the country to take bees' nests. Two of the four went up at night and began to take the nests, when their attention was drawn to a series of fires on a mountain not far off, perhaps two miles ; at once they concluded that there was an enemy, and came down the tree, and set off home, leaving the greater part of their things in a hut. They never said a word to any of the people living near, but came straight home and reported there was an enemy. I happened to go to the house and heard the news, which for the moment alarmed me; I could not help thinking of our people who were up there, and of their defenceless wives and children. I said I could scarcely believe it, and they had better all keep quiet. If there really was an enemy we should hear the tom-tom from the up country. Next morning a lot of the other men, with the four, went off to spy out the enemy ; but before they got to the river-side they saw a cobra ; this was a sign that they should not be eager to find the enemy, so they returned home. About an hour after there was a screeching and squalling cry of enemy. Men were rushing off from the house away from us, with spears, shields, swords, etc., to seek the enemy. The women began to beat the tom-tom ; I stopped them, told them that my ears had been open all day, and I had heard no tom-tom, and until I did they must keep quiet. Not long after, up came some of the neighbouring tribe of Sakarran, inquiring after the enemy. The men who had first rushed off came back from a neighbouring house, saying there was no tom-tom sounding. Next day men kept on going up in search of the enemy ; I always said, ' Go if you like,' when they asked. Yesterday a man came saying the tribe were gathering at a house up country to resist the enemy, and so this morning they all went off, save one head-man, who laughed and said, ' If there was an enemy, our people would have come home at once, and since they have not come I don't intend to tire myself for nothing ; ' so off he went to his farm with his wife and daughters. Before long a man came to tell me of a dream he had had. He thought he found a basket with a durian fruit in it. 'Oh,' said I, 'then you expect to get the head of an enemy if the dream is true.' 'I shall,' said he, 'what was your dream, Tuan?'" (Miss. Life, 1867, p. 70.)

DEFENCES.

When describing the houses we referred to the palisading: "The fortifications of the Land Dyak villages consist principally of a strong palisading of bamboo stakes, or sometimes of hard wood, which are strengthened and fastened together by split bamboos being woven amongst the perpendicular posts, the ends of which, sharpened to points, project outwards in all directions, presenting an impassable barrier of spikes, like chevaux-de-frise, to the invader. This *pagar* or fence, is about six feet high, and surrounds all the village, in accessible positions: two gates are made in it, over each of which the worked spikes are carried, and when the entrance is shut, it presents an uniform appearance with the remainder of the fence." (Low, p. 285.) "Once Lang Endang, with his Sakarang and Balau party, returned without success: they found the enemy had collected in force with a strong *pagar* (fence) around them on the top of a steep mountain called Katimong, situated between Kanowit and Katibas." (S.G., No. 21.) "The waterside, the landing-places, and the approaches to the village, are all spiked, and also the foot of the ladder, and they dig pit-falls in the pathway. Their valuables they conceal in the adjoining forest, or in the vicinity of their farms. The moment the enemy appears the sound of the *tawah* begs to announce their condition to their neighbours, and to summon them to their assistance. If they are heard help is sure to arrive *instanter*. If they feel confident of their ability to repel the enemy, they keep their women at home; but if there is any doubt about the matter, they conceal them with their treasures on the hills and flee into the forest to rejoin them at a rendezvous when resistance becomes hopeless." (Brooke Low.)

On one of his great expeditions Sir Charles Brooke writes: "Although the enemy ran off in haste, they had time to hide many things, but our Dyaks allowed no leaf to pass unturned; at a place where I had been sitting and bathing for hours to-day along with hundreds of Malays I was surprised to

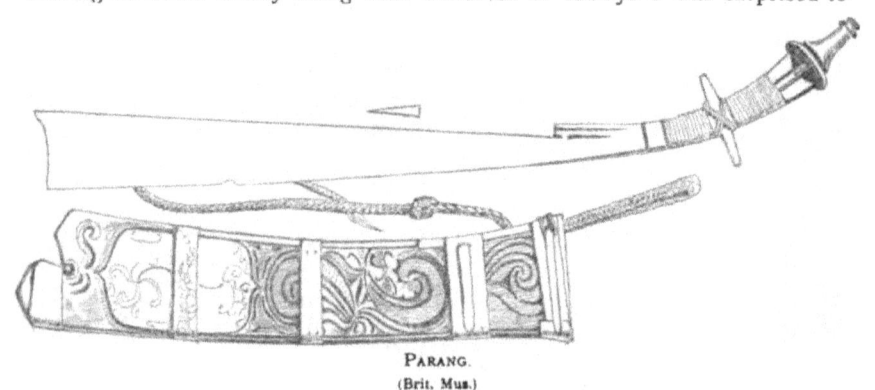

PARANG.
(Brit. Mus.)

LANUN SWORD.

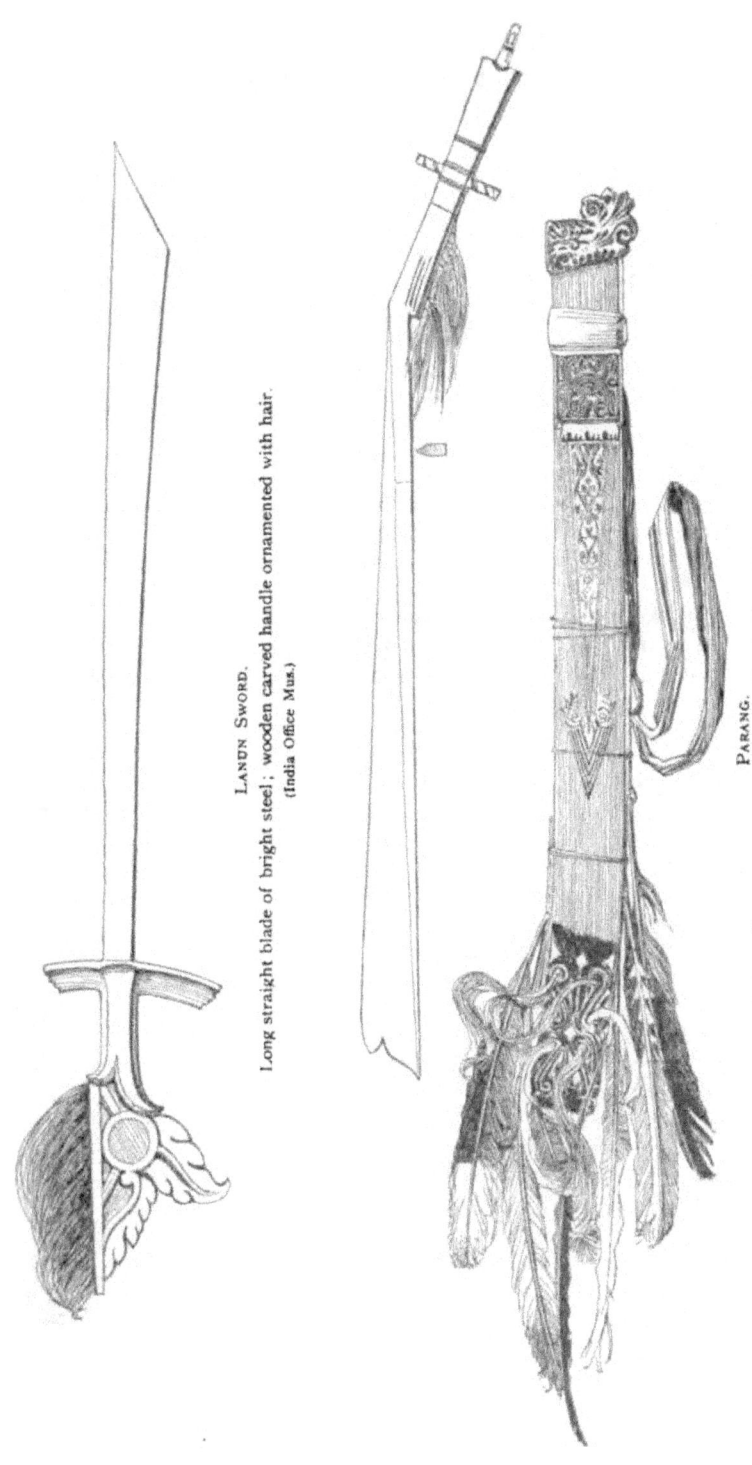

Long straight blade of bright steel; wooden carved handle ornamented with hair.
(India Office Mus.)

PARANG.

Made entirely of steel; flat handle, with cross-guard covered with tinfoil and brass; sheath of red wood, carved. Length of blade, 2ft. 4½in.; length of sheath, 2ft. 8½in. ? Kapuas River.
(Brit. Mus.)

see towards evening a few Dyaks come to take their last duck before retiring after their day's work; when lo! and behold, they traced a small line to a twig, and brought up a large brass gun. Such is their quickness of vision; only Dyaks can kill Dyaks." (i. 188.) Later on he says: "When clearing places for our night abode many found some property concealed among long grass and under trees." (*ibid;* 301.) "If the attacked party are in no hurry they fire the village before they leave it; if on the other hand they wish to gain time, and to divert the pursuit, they leave it for the enemy to plunder and burn." (Brooke Low.) Many burnt houses are met with on the expeditions—generally the burning has taken place when defence has been given up." (Brooke i. 299.)

"The Brāng people placed great reliance in the difficulty of approach up their steep hill; the men quietly sat and 'ate their rice,' and the women went to the top of the peak above the village and openly defied the invading force. They turned their backs to the invaders, and screamed yells of defiance." (Grant, p. 25.) "On one occasion the Balleh Dyaks ascended the river Mujong, into an almost inaccessible part, and made a stockade on the top of a steep hill defended by precipitous rocks over the path of ascent." (S.G., No. 148, p. 8.)

"On the Baram when attack is expected the house is fortified by a sort of chevaux de frise placed round it, and though this is limp, the ends of the bamboo being pointed and very sharp make it a very difficult obstacle to break through."[*] (Hose, J.A.I. xxiii. 162.)

AMBUSHES.

"A favourite stratagem of defence is to entice the leading boats of the enemy into an ambush on shore. As everybody in the attacking party is anxious to be foremost in the race for heads, there are sure to be one or two boats so far in advance of the rest as to make it worth the defenders' while to put them to their mettle. Some convenient spot is selected and a strong defending party placed in ambush among the trees. One or two men are thrown out to stroll upon the shingly bed to lure the enemy to their destruction. The moment they are caught sight of, the boats give chase, and as the warriors leap ashore, the men in ambush spring from their covert to their feet and hurl stones to shatter the shields, and engage with spears and swords in a short but desperate conflict. As the main body is seen winding up the river, whooping and yelling, and crashing up in clouds of spray and with a rush of waters, they plunge into the thicket with the heads they have obtained, and are far away before the enemy have recovered from their discomfiture, and are prepared to follow." (Brooke Low.)

This sort of thing happened more than once during Sir Charles Brooke's Expeditions. (i. 38.)

"Another stratagem is one of ambush without luring. When the head of the column is close upon them (the ambush), they discharge their muskets [*sic*], leap from their ambuscade, and engage in a hand to hand combat.

---

[*] According to Mr. Hupé they erect palisades 500 ft. long, 100 broad, and use up 5,000 tree trunks sunk into the earth some feet deep. (p. 314.)

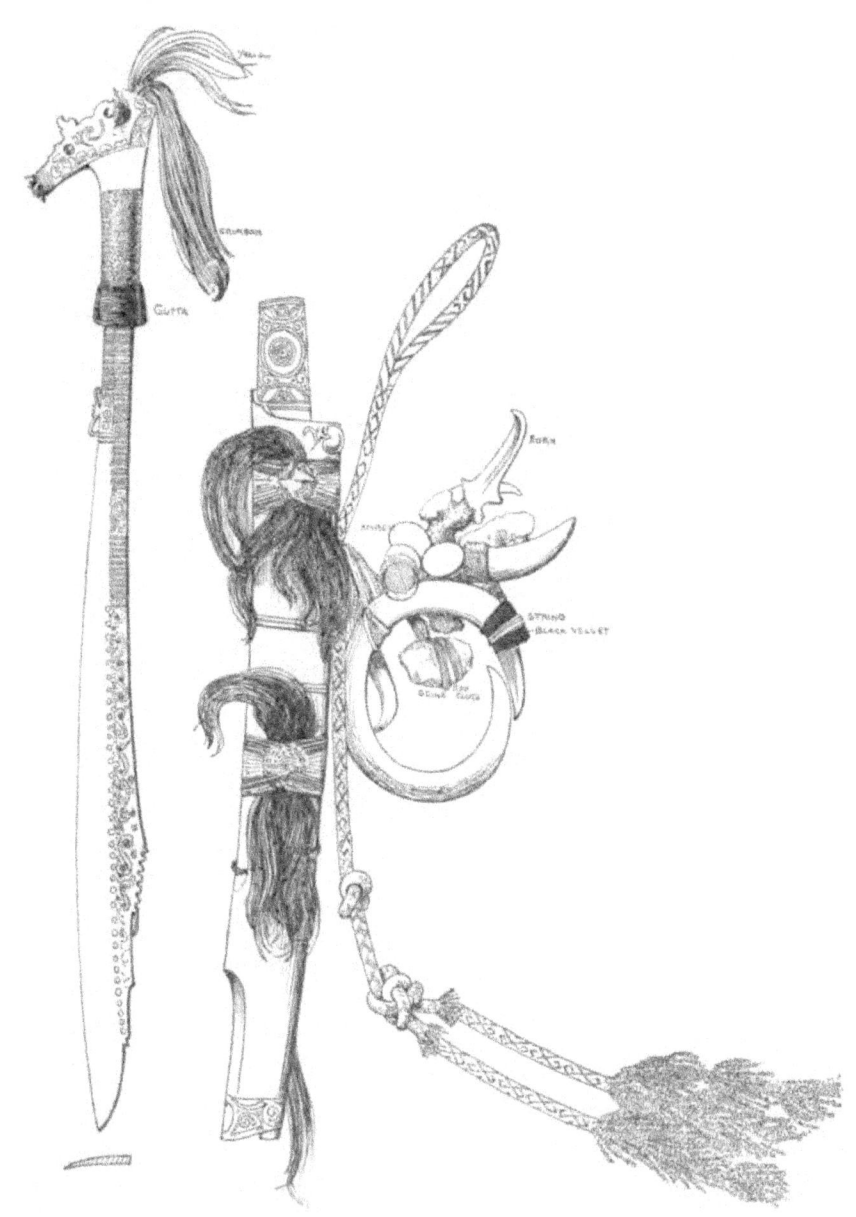

KENNIAH PARANG ILANG.

The sword is made of stream ore found by the Kenniahs in the Baram head-waters. The charms are of specific value: one looks like portion of a mason wasp's nest, another is a piece of stone. The usual dirk attached to the sheaths of these swords is thrust in a piece of attached bark, covered with yellow and black beadwork. The dirk [not shown] itself is ornamented on one side of the blade, into which little brass discs have been melted: the haft looks like English cherry-tree wood, and at the end is beautifully carved like some of the dish ends shown on p. 383. Baram River.

(Hose Coll.)

The Dyaks always waylay on the right-hand side of the line of march, as that side of the body is unprotected by the shield, which is carried in the left hand. A short, but desperate fight ensues, a few heads are taken, and the defenders scamper off with their dead and wounded before the main body can come up. The invaders pause a while until reinforced, and then pursue, but the enemy have taken advantage of this delay to plant *tukaks* in the path and *ranjaus* in the water-way. Some are sure to get spiked, and another delay ensues. The ambuscade is by that time beyond pursuit. If the defenders are plucky, they form several ambuscades, and so impede the progress of the *bala* (war-party).

"When acting on the defensive, if it is intended to entrap the invaders by water, it is customary for the entire force to divide into two equal portions, and to be hid in two branches of the main stream, sufficient distance apart, and when the enemy are in between, to dash out simultaneously and take them in front and rear. If the invading force is too numerous to try this, it is customary to lure the leading boats by a decoy boat into a position where by reason of the rapidity of the current and obstacles in the river they can be taken at a disadvantage, and to scamper off with a few heads after a desperate and hurried fight before the main body comes up.

"It is a defensive measure to blockade the passage up the river with huge trunks of trees felled right across, which form a temporary barrier to quick progress; stakes and *tukaks* are placed in all suitable places, and in the shallow beds to impale the feet, as the men have to tumble out of the canoe to haul it over the rapids, &c." (Brooke Low.)

While the Meanders boats were punishing some pirates "A few select ruffians of this fleet lingered behind, after the main body had quitted the river, having dressed themselves in the spoils of their victims, and put on the broad-brimmed hat used by the labourers on the farms. Thus disguised, these miscreants stealthily dropped down the river in the small canoes which they found on the banks; and, imitating the Sadong dialect, they called to the women to come out of their hiding-places, saying that they had come to convey them to a place of safety. In many instances the stratagem was but too successful; and the helpless women, rushing down with their infants in their arms, became the prey of these wolves in sheep's clothing." (Keppel Meander i. 144.)

The *ranjaus* above referred to are practically calthrops and are also by the way used in times of peace. Thus Mr. Grant relates: "At one part of the road our guides stopped to draw a lot of *ranjows*, or sharp-pointed bamboos, out of the ground. Some man had left his farm-house, and protected it from thieves by sticking these *ranjows* for some distance around it." (pp. 22, 80.) Sir Chas. Brooke's party once had unpleasant experiences with these articles. The country was "thickly spiked by some Dyak enemy many years ago. These were not yet rotten, and the grass had grown sufficiently to make them very blind. The leading Dyaks took a start to pull them up, as only those can who are in the habit of resorting to such schemes of warfare. They are mostly of bamboo, about six inches long, and sharpened to a point, and, as a band is retiring from an enemy's country, these are stuck in their wake to

Ambushes.

prevent any others from pursuing; they are very simple but dangerous obstacles to those who have bare feet." (ii. 188.) "Occasionally the *ranjaus* are poisoned." (Crossland.)

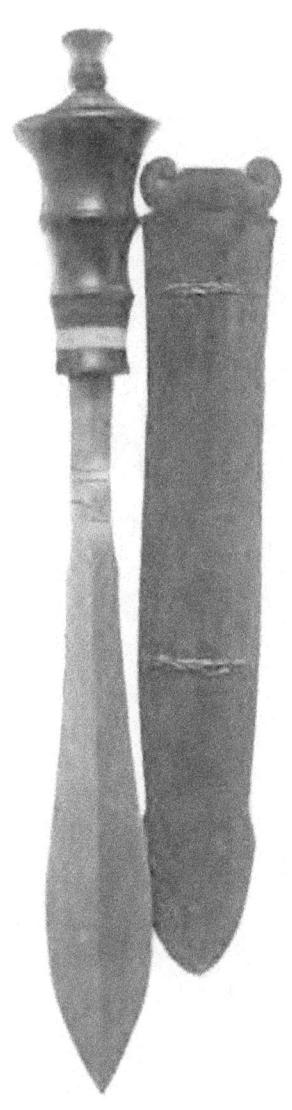

Dopong DAGGER.
Used at funeral feast, *Tiwah*.
S.E. Borneo.
(Leiden Mus.)

DAGGER.
Said to come from S.E. Borneo.
(Leiden Mus.)

SWORD-SHEATH BELT
KNOT (?)
(Brooke Low Coll.)

"With lelahs or brass guns, muskets, spears, &c., they will keep their strongholds, while parties will go sneaking about the jungle in search of stray enemies: and when they have successfully resisted an attack, and see the enemy retreating, they will harass his rear, securing as many heads as possible to take home as trophies." (Grant, p. 92.)

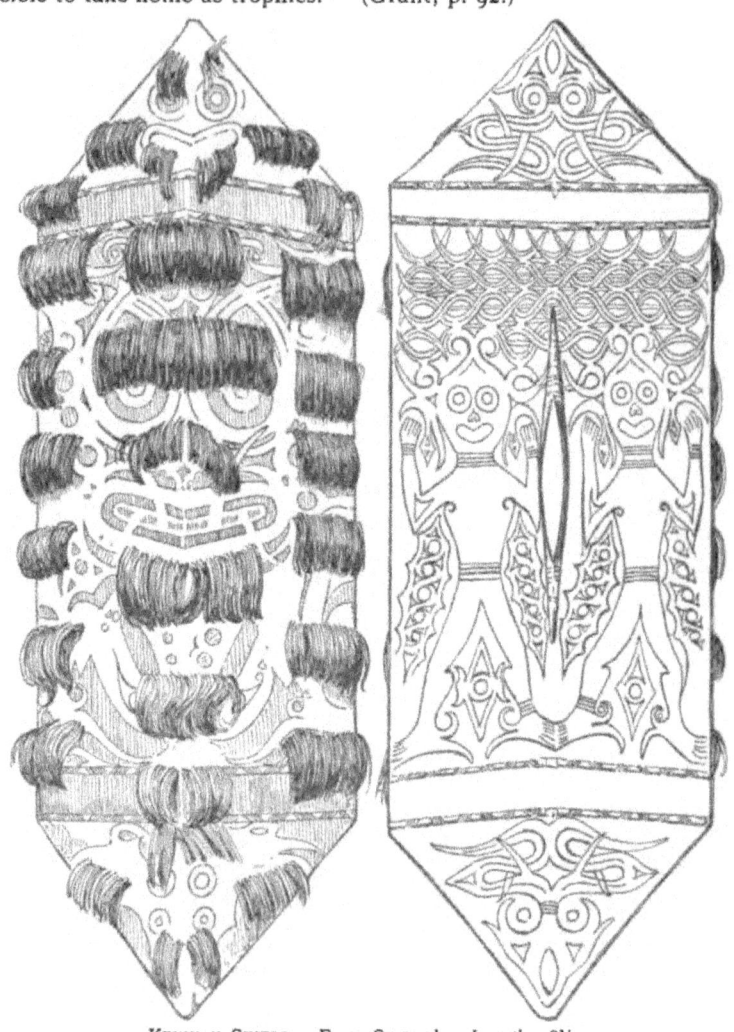

KENNIAH SHIELD. From Sarawak. Length, 48¼in.
(Edinbro' Mus.)

SURPRISES.

On one occasion the Sauhs had driven off the Sarebas and Sakarans, their hereditary enemies, and were in grand spirits at this their victory—a victory never before achieved against these foes. "But their joy was short-lived;

Surprises. 117

they had reckoned too much on their security, and forgot the bitterness created in the hearts of their foes by their repulse and loss. It was not many months afterwards, on a fine sunny day, when most of them were busily engaged at their farms, that, with the suddenness of a flash of lightning, and

Front.   KAYAN SHIELD.   Back.
From Sarawak. On the front, along the median ridge, there is a rib of iron twisted at both ends. Decorated with human hair. Length, 49½in.
(Edinbro' Mus.)

without any warning, the Sauhs found themselves surrounded by their lately discomfited enemies. And that day the Sauhs were no longer victors, but vanquished; between 300 and 400 dead bodies lay strewed on or around the farms. Besides the heads, the enemy carried off as captives 100 women and children." (Grant, p. 92.)

"As Dyak warfare consists of surprises, they do not attack a village, or a cluster of villages, if their approach has been discovered and the population is on the defensive, but they content themselves with cutting off stragglers, and lie in ambush at the waterside for people going to bathe or to examine their fish-traps, and in the forest for individuals out hunting or produce collecting." (Brooke Low.) Mr. Horsburgh says: "If a small war-party of six or seven men embarked in a fast boat, they would conceal it in the umbrageous creeks near an enemy's house, and then prowling about in the jungle, would pounce upon any unfortunate who might stray near them. Sometimes they would even get into the wells of their enemies, and, covering their heads with a few leaves, sit for hours in the water waiting for a victim. Then when any woman or girl came to draw water, they would rush out upon her, cut her down, take her head, and flee into the jungle with it before any alarm could be given." (p. 13.) "It was much in this way that the Dusuns drove out the Lanuns who had settled north of the Tampassuk. No people in Borneo could cope with the Lanuns in battle; so the Ida'an kept hovering around the Lanun villages to cut off stragglers. At last, no one could leave the houses even to fetch fire-wood, unless accompanied by a strong armed party." (St. John i. 239.) "When old Japer was about to attack the Punans, he stripped off his clothes one night, and crawled up to the house. To find his way back he had let out some string as he went on." (*ibid*, ii. 62.) "But if their approach be unknown, they so manage as to reach the settlement before daybreak; generally they draw a cordon round it at midnight, and tighten the circle before day-break. If the ladders are down they rush up to the house and take it by storm; if they are drawn up they hurl lighted javelins into the thatch and fire it."[5] (Brooke Low.)

"The mode of attack adopted by the Kanōwits shows the system of warfare of these barbarians. The first house attacked was of the largest size, built on piles. A body of four hundred men approached—no arms were used, not a spear was thrown, or an arrow shot; but the Dyaks, covered with their shields, crouching along the ground, slowly marched under the house, and commenced cutting and burning the posts. The defenders, about fifty in number, with their wives and children, cast down between the crevices of the bamboo floor every implement they could collect, together with boiling water, but in vain. Their fate slowly but surely approached. The fire and the steel did their work. The besiegers retreated. The house fell with a dreadful crash, and ten men were killed, and fifteen women and children were captured, the remnant escaping into the jungle." (Mundy ii. 69.) Later on Sir Jas. Brooke

[5] "Upon their arrival near a village, if the party be small, they take up their position in the bushes close to some pathway, and attack a passer-by unawares. If the party be large, they are bolder in their operations, and an attempt will perhaps be made to surprise the whole village. For this purpose they will remain concealed in the jungle, on the banks of the river, during the day, and at night will surround the village so completely as to prevent the escape of the intended victims; and an hour or two before daybreak, when the inhabitants are supposed to sleep their soundest, the attack will be commenced by setting fire to the houses, and their victims are destroyed as they endeavour to escape." (Earl, p. 268.)

Surprises. 119

records a very similar case : " The invading force of tattooed warriors was, however, too numerous to be long withstood, and the piles being eventually either hacked to pieces or burnt down, the lofty buildings fell with a crash to the ground, when, with the exception of a few able-bodied men, who may have

KENNIAH SHIELD.
(Edinbro' Mus.)

escaped to the jungle, the whole tribe was made captive and carried away in triumph to Kanōwit. The young and lovely of the women were, of course, the greatest prizes." (*ibid* ii. 124.) So Sir Sp. St. John relates of the cutting off of the Orang Kaya Kiei, with his family, in a farmhouse at the foot of the Ladan range, by Kayans : " The Kayans set fire to the rice stalks under the house, and as the family rushed out they were killed ; a few, who either saw the fall of their companions, or were bewildered by the smoke, stayed in the house and were burnt to death : ten women and children lost their lives." (ii. 31.) Bishop McDougall is reported to have said that chillies are burnt under the houses on account of the suffocating smoke they make. (Mrs. McDougall, p. 84.) Is it, however, an ascertained fact that chillies when burnt are more offensive than wood smoke ?

During the punitive attack on the tribes who murdered Messrs. Fox and Steele, "the Dyaks advanced madly until they were close, and some underneath the house, tumbling over obstacles, dashing right and left, in search of some place where they might ascend. The enemy were blowing poisonous arrows at them. Our Dyaks commenced clambering up the posts, carrying their arms and spears ; and after one had got a footing, peeping through the crevice, or removing some fragments occasioned by the shot of yesterday, there would be a momentary skirmish, and down they would all go to the ground again. A short time after, this scene was repeated, and then one had entered. In about five minutes out he came, and down they all jumped to the ground, evidently having encountered the enemy inside. One foolish and daring fellow had climbed to the top of the roof : of course he was killed. One lot entered, and had a fight, sword to sword, with the enemy, in which two of our party were killed. And then a man brought a burning brand, and set the ends of the building on fire, which immediately after was blazing furiously. Now came the horrors of war indeed. Some were burnt, some killed, some taken prisoners, and some few escaped. So ended that fortification. Its roof fell with a crash, leaving only its smoking embers to tell where it had stood. Our Dyaks were mad with excitement, flying about with heads ; many with fearful wounds, some even mortal. One lad came rushing and yelling past the stockade, with a head in one hand, and holding one side of his own face on with the other. He had had it cut clean open, and laid bare to the cheek-bone, yet he was insensible to pain for the time ; but before five minutes elapsed he reeled and fell exhausted. We then doctored him the best way we could, by tying his cheek on as firmly as possible, in the hope that it would unite and heal. This it eventually did, leaving a fearful disfigurement." (Brooke i. 353.)

A favourite method is to attack as the Batang Lupar Dyaks did, "a house of Bugau Dyaks under Dutch jurisdiction ; the attack was made while the men were absent at their farms. Thirty women and children were killed and taken captive." (Brooke i. 118.) " This sort of surprise is generally made about the time of sowing, weeding, and cutting the rice-crops." (Keppel i. 301.)

A correspondent of the S.G. (No. 104) reports that "a party of Poi Dyaks called at the house of a Kayan chief named Uniat, by whom they were fed and kindly treated. In return for this kindness the wretches attacked a party of 17 women and children, ' Anak biak,' Uniat who were living by themselves in a farm. They killed 14 of these unfortunates, amongst them being the two children of their late entertainers."

Sir Sp. St. John gives quite a list of treacherous attacks made in different parts of the country. Amongst others (i. 42) that " before the

Kanowit was well guarded, a Sakarang chief with fifty war boats arrived at a village of Pakatan Dayaks, his allies; he took the men as his guides to attack some Punans, who, however, escaped; mortified at this result he killed the guides, and on his return carried off all the women and children as captives." There is also the record of the treacherous way in which the Kayans possessed themselves of a Murut village in the Blait country. Some captured Muruts were sent as deserters into the village and at the end of six months they let the Kayans in at night. Their heads were also taken by the Kayans. (*ibid.*)

HOMERIC COMBATS.

" The great object in their combats is to obtain as many of the heads of the party opposed as possible; and if they succeed in their surprise of the town or village, the heads of the women and children are equally carried off as trophies. But there is great difficulty in obtaining a head, for the moment that a man falls every effort is made by his own party to carry off the body, and prevent the enemy from obtaining such a trophy. If the attacking party are completely victorious, they finish their work of destruction by setting fire to all the houses, and cutting down all the cocoa-nut trees; after which they return home in triumph with their spoil." (Marryat, p. 18.)

This is confirmed by Mr. Brooke Low: " In fighting, the warriors cluster round their chiefs and are indifferent to the fate of the others so long as the chiefs escape with life and limb. Similarly relatives cluster together, preferring to entrust their lives to the tender mercies of one another, rather than to a stranger; a relative would bestride his fallen kinsman and protect his body from mutilation, when a stranger might decline the combat and leave him to his fate. They carry away the dead and wounded when possible; the former they bury, but, if hurried, often so imperfectly that the enemy scent them out, dig them up and carry away the heads. When unable to carry away the dead, they have sometimes severed the head from the trunk and carried it away with them to bury in the forest, rather than let the treasure fall into the hands of the enemy."

During a skirmish on the Sarebas river, "Janting, with a son-in-law on each hand, advanced, followed by his people, and opposed the party with drawn swords; one of his sons cut down his man, decapitated him, and Janting himself had come in contact with another, when his other son-in-law fell with two spear wounds, and would have lost his head, if his father had not most opportunely dealt a terrific blow at his adversary, and then stood guard over his wounded relation, while the enemy had time to make off, fighting indiscriminately with our people." (Brooke i. 275.)

Admiral Keppel gives a graphic account of such hand to hand encounters: " Three brothers were advancing through the jungle in the usual single file, the second leading, when a tiger-like spring from the bush was made on poor Bunsie, and he was cut down. His slayer was the redoubtable Dyak chief, Lingire himself, near to whose residence the flotilla were advancing. A fierce and desperate struggle ensued between the youngest, Tujong, and a Malay, named Abong Apong; he was son-in-law to the Laksimana of Paku, the chief who led the late recent severe foray at Sadong. Each combatant was armed with shield and sword: but assistance coming to his enemy, Tujong received the fatal blow; before, however, the fallen man could be decapitated, a musket-shot fired by Tujong's party passed through the shield, and entered the body

KAYAN SHIELD. From Koti River. Length, 55¼in.
(Edinbro' Mus.)

of the man who had come to Abong Apong's assistance, making him likewise bite the dust. Kalong, the eldest of the three, who was in rear of his brothers, saw the danger just in time to fall back, and bring up the assistance which saved his youngest brother's head, but not his life. Kalong had also had his share of fighting. On the night of the late action, the moon was

DYAK SHIELD. Length, 33in.
(Edinbro' Mus.)

shining brightly, and he had chased one of the Serebas bangkongs aground. A young pirate chief jumped out, and invited any one of his pursuers to single combat. The challenge was immediately accepted by Kalong: wading on shore, he was soon engaged in mortal strife with his enemy, whom he shortly slew. The younger brother, Tujong, was to be seen standing in the water, ready to take up the combat, should Kalong have been worsted."[6] (Meander i. 166.)

EXCITEMENT OF WARFARE.

During the Kujulan expedition, "when one party thought they had met the enemy, the other part of the force was perfectly mad, throwing off their covering, arranging their arms, and making the most fearful noise." (Brooke i. 173.) During the great Kayan expedition the same intrepid commander writes: "We were now close on the rear of the leaders, who were legion, and their din and murmuring were audible for many miles, like an immense swarm of bees." (*ibid* i. 293.)

On another expedition: "There was a motley group of some hundreds of Dyaks congregated on all sides of my abode, dressed in war costume, and vociferating at the top of their voices, declaring that they would rest with their forefathers, or die, rather than not have the blood of the enemy. Their spitting and spluttering of vengeance was astonishing." (*ibid* i. 351.)

But the Dyaks do not always agree on these expeditions, and are apt to fall out over the booty. Sir. Chas. Brooke writes: "On reaching our force I found our Dyaks were fighting among themselves, and disputing over the head of an enemy. They were making a fearful commotion, the boats drifting across each other, and men standing with drawn swords in their hands. I saw there was little time to lose, so rushed down the mud bank to the dingy, and shoved into the midst of this promiscuous mêlée. Janting was the leader, vociferating in true Dyak fashion with the utmost exasperation. His temper was hot enough to drive him to commit any mischief when once aroused. I closed with his boat, placed my hand on his shoulder, spoke a few quiet words, asking him not to cast disgrace on the whole of the force by fighting with his own friends. He at once silently slunk inside his boat, the sounds died away, and peace was restored; but such rows are exceedingly dangerous and unpleasant. No Malay attempted to interfere, and it was only by knowing the man that I was able to succeed without resorting to severity, when one drop of blood might have led I don't know where." (i. 277.)

They do not appear to mutilate their enemies on the warpath, but Admiral Keppel says he "saw one body, afterwards, without its head, in which each

[6] When the chiefs engage hand to hand, they, after the spirit of chivalry, throw these (shields) away; after skirmishing with the sumpit they usually come to close quarters; what the chiefs principally aim at is a surprise, but the adverse party knowing his enemy is in the field, always provides against this, and as one side is as cunning as the other, they usually in the end come to open blows; their personal combats are dreadful; they have no idea of fear, and fight until they are cut to pieces; indeed their astonishing strength, agility and peculiar method of taking care of themselves, are such that I am firmly of opinion a good European swordsman would stand little chance with them, man to man, as, except at their arms, he could not get a cut at them. The temper of the steel with which they make their mandows is such that a powerful man is not required to cut through a musket barrel at a single blow. The Diaks, in fighting, always strike and seldom thrust; indeed their *mandow* is not calculated for it, but the small sword would be useless against them as it would not penetrate the thick skin in front, over which, about the navel, they attach a very large shell. (Dalton, p. 50.)

passing Dyak had thought proper to stick a spear, so that it had all the appearance of a huge porcupine." (ii. 65.)

"The ancient custom was, that anything by the roadside is anybody's when on an expedition, and this is generally adhered to." (Brooke i. 241.)

Original Dread of Firearms.

Originally all the natives had a great dread of fire-arms. Writing of the Sarebus tribes, Sir James Brooke remarks: "They are by no means so warlike

SHIELD. From Sarawak. Length, 45½in.
(Edinbro' Mus.)

as the others, and from their great dread of fire-arms, may be kept in subjection by a comparatively small body of Malays. The sound of musketry or cannon was enough to put the whole body to flight; and when they did run, fully the half disappeared, returning to their own homes." (Mundy i. 236.)

"If the Dyaks, in a fortified village such as that above described, are enabled to resist their invaders for one or two days, they generally escape, but should these be assisted by fire-arms, they have little chance, as they are so terrified at the report of them, that they generally desert their houses, and seek protection in the depths of the forests and the caves of the mountains." (Low, p. 285.)

KAYAN SHIELD. From Rejang River.
(Dublin Mus.)

"Pañgeran Mumein justly observed, that as long as the Kayans were unacquainted with the use of fire-arms, it was easy to defend the country; but that now the Bornean traders were supplying them with brass swivels and double-barrel guns, he thought that the ruin of Brunei was at hand. But the fact is, that though the Kayans are now less frightened at the noise of heavy guns and muskets than they were, they seldom employ them in their expeditions in the jungle, as they cannot keep them in working order." (St. John i. 87.) The Lanuns "are very fond of boasting of their courage, and say, if the Europeans would but meet them sword in hand, they would fight them man to man."[7] (*ibid* i. 240.)

[7] "The Dyaks entertain the greatest dread of fire-arms, believing that there is no limit to their range, and that an object which can be perceived, however distant, may be struck by a musket ball." (Earl, p. 269) "They no sooner hear the report of a gun than they run deep into the jungle; if they are in boats they leap into the water, and, after gaining the shore, never stop until they are out of hearing of the report. The most sensible of the Diaks have a superstitious idea of fire-arms; each man, on hearing the report, fancies the ball is making directly towards himself; he therefore runs, never thinking himself safe as long as he hears the explosion of gunpowder; thus, a man hearing the report of a swivel five miles off, will still continue at full speed, with the same trepidation as at first. They have not the least conception of the range of gun-barrels. I have been frequently out with Selgie and other chiefs, shooting monkeys, birds, &c., and offended them in refusing to fire at large birds, at the distance of a mile or more; they invariably put such refusal down to ill-nature on my part. Again, firing at an object, they cannot credit it is missed, although they see the bird fly away, but consider that the shot is yet pursuing and it must fall at last." (Dalton, p. 50.)

MR. DALTON'S NOTES ON WAR.

"The ravages of these people are dreadful; in August, 1828, Selgie returned to *Marpow* from an excursion; his party had been three months absent, during which time, besides detached huts, he had destroyed seventeen campongs, with the whole of the men and old women; the young women and children were brought prisoners. The former amounted to 113, and the latter about 200. He had with him forty war-boats, or large canoes, none less in length than 95 feet. . . . The perseverance of the Diaks during an expedition is wonderful; they generally get information of distant campongs from the women taken prisoners (no man ever escapes to tell the tale), who soon become attached to the conquerors. In proceeding towards a distant campong, the canoes are never seen on the river during the day-time; they invariably commence their journey about half-an-hour after dark, when they pull rapidly and silently up the river close to the bank. One boat keeps immediately behind another, and the handles of the paddles are covered with the soft bark of a tree, so that no noise whatever is made. (In Selgie's last expedition, he was forty-one days before a campong was surprised, although several canoes were cut off in the river owing to the superior swiftness of Selgie's boats.) After paddling all night without intermission, about half-an-hour before day-light, they pull the boats up upon the banks, amongst the jungle and thick trees, so that from the river it is impossible to see them, or discover the least track of their route. Here they sleep, and feed upon monkeys, snakes, or any other animals they can reach with their sumpits; wild hogs are their favourite food, and they are in abundance ;—if these fail them, the young sprouts of certain trees and wild fruit will answer the purpose; nothing comes amiss to the stomach of a Diak. Should the Rajah want flesh, and it cannot be procured with the sumpit, one of the followers is killed, which not only provides them with a good meal, but a head to boot. Whilst part of the people are employed in hunting and cooking, others ascend the highest trees to examine the country, and observe if a campong or hut be near, which they discover by the smoke. Should it be a solitary hut, they surround it, and take care no one escapes; but should it be a considerable campong, they go much more warily to work. When the boats have arrived within about a mile of a campong, they prepare themselves; about one-third of the party are sent forward, who penetrate the thickest part of the jungle, arriving at night near the houses; these are surrounded, men are placed in every foot-path leading from them, for the purpose of intercepting all who may attempt to escape into the woods. In the meantime, the remainder of the party in their boats, arrive about an hour before day-light, in perfect silence, within a few hundred yards of the campong, when most of the warriors put on their fighting dress, and creep slowly forwards, leaving a few men in each boat, likewise about a dozen with the women who remain in the jungle. About twenty minutes before day-break, they commence operations by throwing upon the attaps of the huts lighted fire-balls, made of the dry bark of trees and damar, which immediately involves the whole in flames. The war-cry is then raised, and the work of murder commences; the male inhabitants are speared, or more commonly cut down with the mandow, as they descend the ladders of their dwellings in attempting to escape the flames, which Selgie remarked to me, give just sufficient light to distinguish a man from a woman. The women and children endeavouring to gain the jungle by the well-known paths, find them already occupied by an enemy, from whom there is no escaping ; they, of course, surrender themselves, and are collected together, with the assistance of day-light, which they manage so as to be certain of at this moment. When the signal is first given (always by the Rajah), the people in the boats pull rapidly ; some are placed up the river above the campong, some below it, and the remainder abreast of the huts, so that should any of the unfortunate beings gain their sampans, they are certainly cut off in the water. Their principal object is to prevent a single person escaping to give intelligence to other campongs, and to arrange the time so that the day shall dawn about ten or fifteen minutes after the slaughter begins, which enables them to take their stations, and fire the houses in the midst of darkness, and afterwards affords sufficient light to secure their prey. On moonlight nights they keep concealed in the jungle, only acting in the dark. Heavy rains just previous to the attack are not considered favourable, as the attaps will not burn readily, but a smart shower at the moment is always wished for, the noise preventing their operations being heard, besides they imagine people sleep soundest about an hour before day-light, particularly if it rains. After the women and children are collected, the old women are killed, and the heads of the men cut off ; the brains are taken out, and held over a fire, for the purpose of smoking and preserving them. The women and children are only secondary considerations ; the heads are what they want, and there is no suffering a Diak will not cheerfully endure to be recompensed by a single one. From the last excursion Selgie's people brought with them 700 heads —of which 250 fell to the share of himself and sons. The women and children all belonged to him in the first instance. . . . I have been present when Selgie has taken two campongs ; the inhabitants were surprised and the fighting consequently all on one side, but in a few instances resistance was offered. I did not observe them attempt to parry the blows with their weapon, these were either taken on the shield or contrived to meet the bamboo cap : as the men of the campong had no time given them to cover themselves, they were easily cut down ; the noise is terrific during the massacre (for it can be called nothing else), and joined in by all the Rajah's women who accompany him in his excursions. An old Diak loves to dwell upon his success on these hunting excursions, and the terror of the women and children when taken affords a fruitful theme of amusement at all their meetings." (pp. 48-51.)

WEAPONS.

GENERAL WAR COSTUME.

" The general Sea Dyak war costume consists of a basket work hat, called a *katapu*, and a skin-jacket, called a *gagong* ; in lieu of the latter the *klambi taiah*, a quilted jacket, is used. These form but poor defensive armour for the body ; reliance is placed upon the shield." (Brooke Low.)

" The costume of a Kayan warrior consists of a round cap (*lavong*), covered with hair of various colours, and two huge eyes to represent a face, with long tail-feathers of the hornbill stuck into the top ; a war jacket (*simong*) made of a goat skin, with a butterfly worked in beads between the shoulders, and a large thick shell (*blasung*) on the breast, and the whole of the back covered with hornbills' feathers. Underneath this a quilted jacket is often worn as a protection against poisoned arrows, and a small mat about 18 inches long and a foot wide, hangs behind, and is used for sitting on when in the jungle. He carries a spear (*bakin*) in his right hand, and a shield (*kalavit*) in his left, while his long sword (*parang ilang*) in its sheath, is fastened round his waist on his left side, if he is a right-handed man. He carries his rice and other small requirements in a description of basket (*sarut*), provided with two straps, on his back. Only chiefs, or those who are known as the *bangsa rajah*, are allowed to wear the feathers of the helmeted hornbill, which is called by them *tebououl*, but they are not so particular about the feathers of the rhinoceros hornbill which are black and white, though a youth of no importance would not be allowed to wear even these. If a man has taken the head of an enemy, he is made much of by the women, and, if unmarried, mothers and fathers are anxious to secure him for a son-in-law." (Hose, J.A.I. xxiii. 168.)

Dyak Shield.
(Oxford Mus.)

Dyak Shield.
(Oxford Mus.)

"The Muruts were furnished with war jackets and helmets. The former were well padded, and thickly covered over with cowrie shells; the latter was of the same material, with flaps hanging, so as to protect the wearer's neck from poisoned arrows." (St. John i. 90.)

"The *katapu*, or helmet, in general use, is a round skull cap of wickerwork, with a rush lining and occasionally a skin covering, surmounted by either a metal plate or two of fanciful pattern or the scaly armour of the *tenggolieng*. The crown is decorated with the plumage of birds, and the sides with tufts of human hair. The rim is bordered with scarlet flannel, and embroidered with nassur shells. The Kyans and Kiñahs wear on their head-pieces the tail plumes of the helmeted hornbill—each plume signifying a dead enemy." (Brooke Low.) See pp. 99 *et seq*.

Klawang, SHIELD.
S.E. Borneo.
(Leiden Mus.)

KENNIAH SHIELD.
54in. long.
(Hose Coll.)

"The *gagong*, or Sea Dyak war-jacket, is a skin with a hole and slit in the neck of it to admit of the insertion of the warrior's head, the animal's face falling on his stomach, and its back hanging over his shoulders and reaching below the waist. This dress is by no means universal among the Dyaks, as suitable skins are not so easy to obtain. Goat skins are preferred by them to any other, being long haired at the shoulder, and black is preferred to white; bear skins and panther skins are also in use but more sparingly. The animal's face is usually covered with a metal plate, or a mother-of-pearl shell, to protect the pit of the stomach, and the back is decorated with bunches of hornbill feathers. The gagong is worn more for its warlike appearance than for any real protection it affords the wearer. It may possibly divert a wooden javelin, but it is no defence against the thrust of a spear. The Kiñahs wear the mandibles of the *Bucerotidae* (hornbills) in pairs on the breast of their war-jackets of skin, to record the number of persons they have killed with their own hands—one pair for each person killed. See pp. 103-105.

The *klambi taiah* is the *baju tilam* of the Malays, and is a padded or quilted cotton jacket, for the most part sleeveless and collarless. The striped variety is the one most in request. It is thick enough to be able to protect the body from the blow of a wooden javelin, but it is useless against a spear." (Brooke Low.)

SMALL SHIELD.

One end narrower than the other. Handle at back, cut out of the solid pale-coloured wood. Angular front carved with a cross, which with the ends and border is painted dark crimson and coated with tinfoil. The interspaces are painted yellow; they are coloured with indigo and dark crimson and also partially coated with tinfoil. Length, 23in.; width, 8½in.

(Brit. Mus.)

"They have no covering or protection for their thighs or legs, but leave them as on ordinary occasions." (Low, p. 180.) "The Borneans, in fighting, wear a quilted jacket or spencer, which reaches over the hips, and from its size has a most unservicelike appearance; the bare legs and arms sticking out from under this puffed-out coat, like the sticks which support the garments of a scarecrow." (Keppel i. 155.)

SPEARS.

"Among the Land tribes, particularly those of Sadong, each family generally possesses a spear, the haft of which is made of balean wood, and towards the brass plate, which binds the blade into the handle, are carved

BORNEO WOOD SHIELD.
Painted red and decorated with an incised foliated design ; edged with cane. Length, 21in.
(Edinbro' Mus.)

rude representations of the human figure in high relief. These stand with their backs to each other, and are from three to five in number : like those on the war-boats of the Sea Dyaks, these figures generally represent indecent attitudes. Their spears are also ornamented with sheets of tin foil, with which the haft of the weapon is covered, and also with the feathers of the argus pheasant and the rhinoceros hornbill, which latter are usually stuck on three little prongs, into which the handle has been cut for that purpose." (Low, p. 313.) See pp. 107, 108.

"The Sea Dyak *slighi* is a wooden lance, the point of which is hardened in the fire. It is used as a missile and is hurled at the enemy. It is usually of ironwood (*bilian*), but the palmwood javelin, especially *imbery*, is also used. They are showered upon the enemy at the commencement of an engagement before the parties are close enough to use the spear, which never, or rarely, leaves the hand.

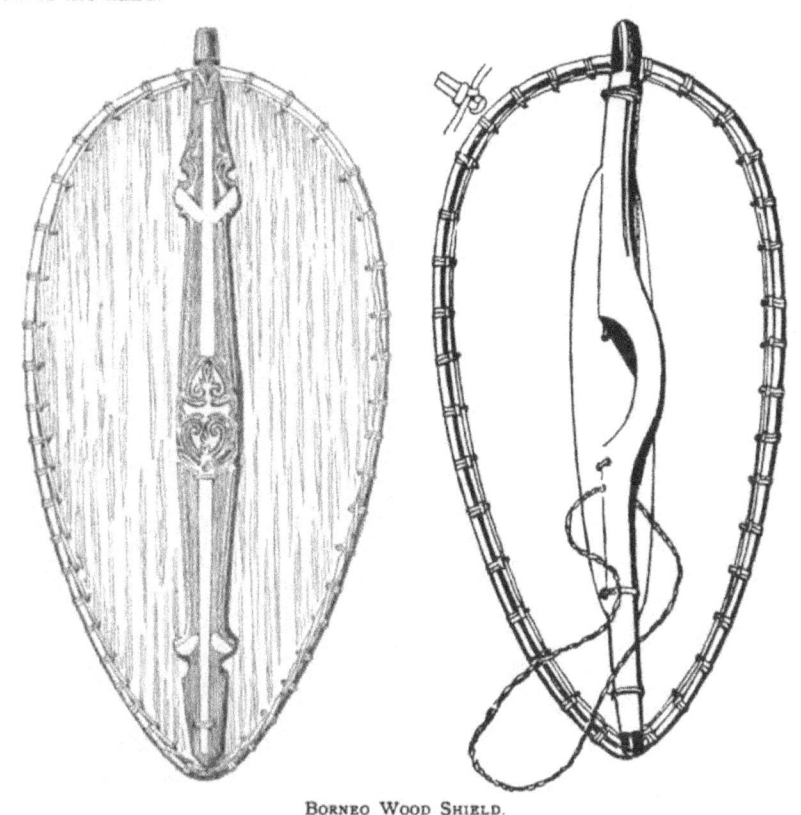

BORNEO WOOD SHIELD.
A band of red wood down the middle with engraved ornament, and overlaid with lead-foil.
Length, 32½ in.
(Brit. Mus.)

"The Sea Dyak *sangkoh* is a long wooden shaft with a steel spear head. The shaft is usually of ironwood, with a spud of bone at its butt end. If it has no spud it is pointed so that it can be stuck into the ground. It is always held towards the point, rather than by the centre, and over the right shoulder, the butt end up in the air, and the point towards the ground. The blade is of steel, and is 12 inches in length, and broad towards the point; the tang is not inserted in a slit in the wood, but is bound on to the stern with cane or brass wire, and is very firm. The spear is used at close quarters to thrust with, and is held in the right hand—the shield occupying the left.

The shaft is occasionally carved, but more often plain. I have one in my collection with six or seven brass rings, indicating the number of warpaths made by its owner." (Brooke Low.)

Swords.

"The swords of the Hill tribes differ from those of the Sea Dyaks in having no wooden handle; this part of the weapon being of iron, and a mere continuation of the blade. The handle of this weapon and its sheath are

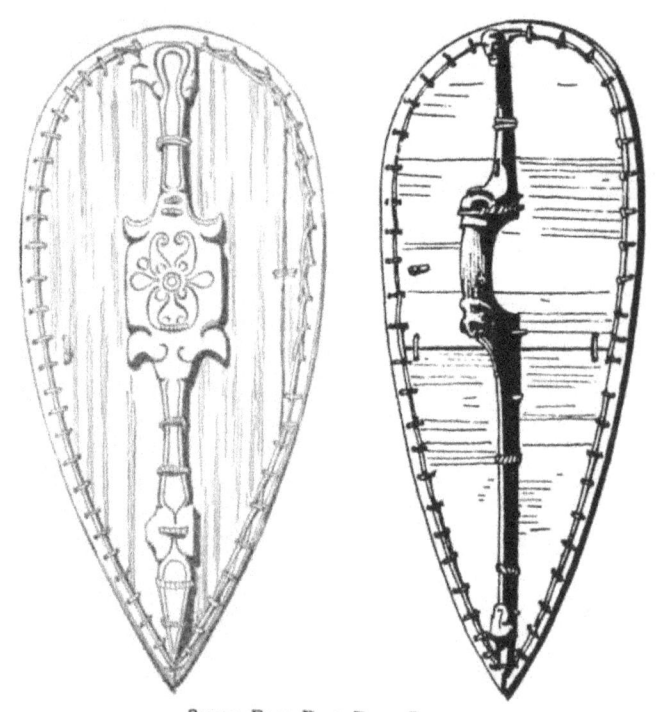

SMALL FLAT BAST DYAK SHIELD.
Painted dark-red and blacked; with cane rim. Wooden handle at back, and carved slip of wood along the middle of the front.
Length, 23in.; width, 9½in.
(Brit. Mus.)

ornamented with hair, instead of with the feathers of the argus pheasant. But this is put on sparingly, and in small tufts only at the extremities. The sheath is always stained red, and very rarely carved, and if such decoration be attempted, it amounts to nothing better than mere scratching."[*] (Low, p. 313.) See pp. i. 399; ii. 110, 111, 113.

[*] "The sheath is carried by a belt made of very finely plaited rattan; the buckle or fastening consists of a loop at one end of the belt, through which is passed a piece of shell, or the upper mandible of the hornbill, or, as I saw among the Tring Dyaks, the kneecap of a human being fastened at the other end of the belt." (Bock, p. 193.)

"The *dukn*, or *parang pedang*, is the scimitar so much worn by the Malays, and differs only from it in being thicker and heavier. It is formed after the pattern of a German cavalry sabre, and has a cross-handle of brass. The blade is two-edged at the point, so that it can be used for thrusting as well as cutting. The sheath is of some light wood, and is stained crimson with dragon's blood. The Undups and Balaus in particular have their sheaths covered with silver work, and the hilt with silver. The hollow of the hilt is decorated with human hair, and the edge of the sheath is adorned with a row of the wing feathers of the hornbill. The Malays wear the sword with the edge upwards but the Dyaks wear it with the edge outwards.

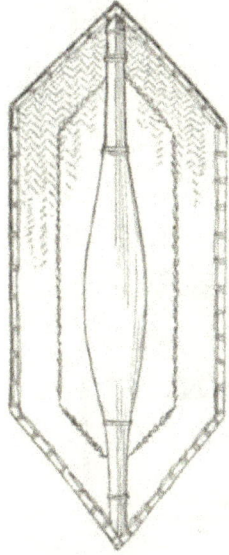

Trabai Temiang.
DYAK BAMBU SHIELD.
(Brooke Low Coll.)

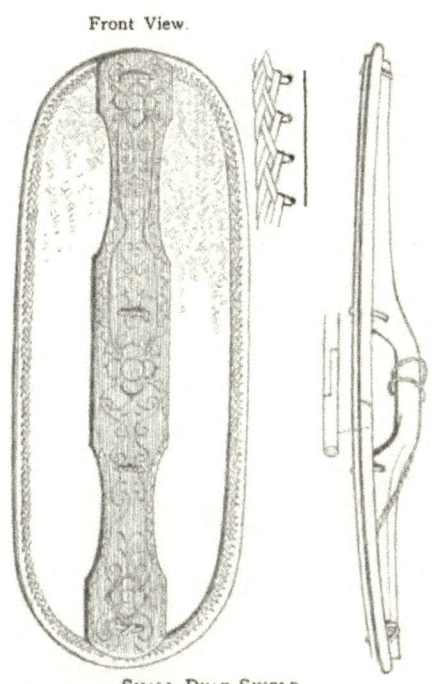

Front View.

SMALL DYAK SHIELD.
Made of cane; the front covered with plaited buff-coloured reed, rimmed with rotan and with a carved slip of dark crimson-painted wood along the middle. The handle, which is the full length of the shield, is fastened through on to the slip of wood in front. Length, 20in.; width, 7in
(Brit. Mus.)

"The *parang ñabur* seems to be the only really genuine Sea Dyak weapon. The *parang pedang* they have copied from the Malays, and the *parang ilang* is altogether a Kayan weapon, and beyond their powers of imitation. The *ñabur* in ordinary use is a short curved sword with a bone handle. This style of sword is broadest at its point of curvature. It does not curve like a scimitar from the hilt, but is straight for some distance, and takes a sudden curve towards the end, and when the sword is long, as is one in my collection, it becomes top heavy and requires both hands to wield it effectually.

"The *parang ilang* is the Kayan *malab* (*mandau* elsewhere), and is preferred to any other side arm by Malays as well as Dyaks. It is the ambition of every Dyak lad to be presented with one of these." (Brooke Low.)

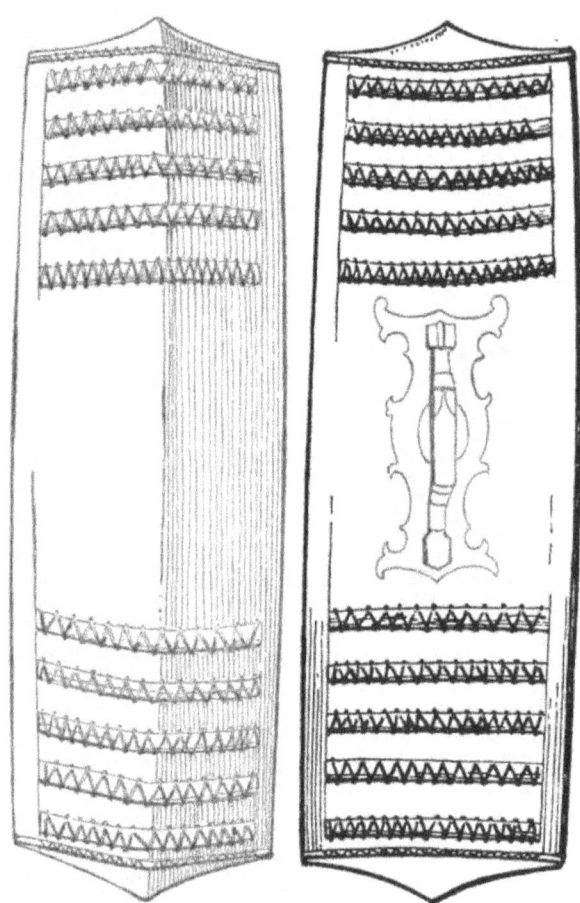

Utap. SEA DYAK SHIELD.
Painted red, ornamented (? strengthened) with strips of cane.
Length, 44½in.
(Edinbro' Mus.)

"The *isau* of the Balaus is a pretty weapon, and *I am told* that at one time custom required that it should be manufactured only from odd scraps of steel and iron collected at odd times, which were first twisted together, then welded, and afterwards beaten into shape. The handle, of hard wood or of horn, was strengthened and decorated with a number of rings, which were demanded from the inhabitants of the long village house, each family contributing at least one of either brass or silver. The smith is also said to have asked no payment for making an *isau*." (F. W. Leggatt.)

"The Uma Bawangs are famous for their *parangs*, which they make out of their own iron ore." (Brooke Low.)

Speaking of the Land Dyak tribe, Si Panjangs, Mr. Denison remarks (ch. v. p. 57): "They left Sarawak owing to the oppression of the Malays, who were jealous of their skill as workers of iron (to this day the Si Panjangs maintain their ancient fame and their swords are much sought after throughout the district), and finally drove them out of the country."

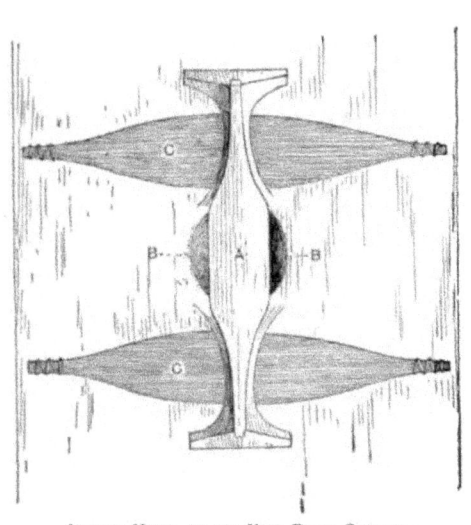

INSIDE VIEW OF AN *Utap* DYAK SHIELD.
A, handle, being of one piece with the shield; B B, concavity to admit of fingers under the handle; C C, two strips of flat dark wood let in through slits under the handle and fastened with rotan at ends. The shield is in other respects similar to that figured on p. 136. It is 46in. long and 17in. wide. In the same collection is a Kenniah shield, taken at the attack on Long Si Balu in 1887; it is split and the split sewn up by means of thin strips of rotan and strengthened by a piece of square iron wire running along the median ridge, hooked in top and bottom, similarly to that of the shield illustrated on p. 117.
(Hose Coll.)

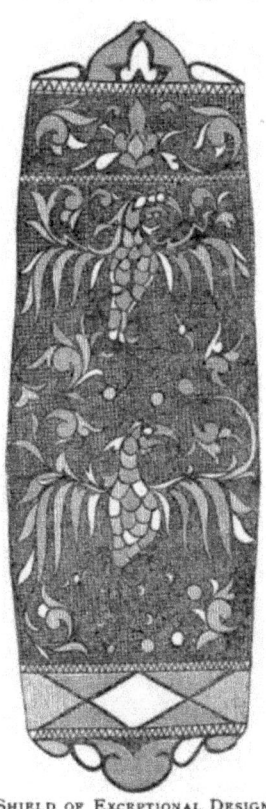

SHIELD OF EXCEPTIONAL DESIGN.
From Koti River, Dutch Borneo.
(After Prof. Hain. p. 83. Amsterdam Mus.)

"The Kayans make the curious complex manufacture of short swords (*parang ilang*) possessing concave and convex blades, which are capable, by this means, of penetrating either wood or flesh to a surprising extent; but much practice is required to use them properly, as a mistake in the angle of cutting, would bring the weapon round and often wound the holder." (Brooke i. 50.) "It is made either right-handed or left-handed." (St. John i. 121.) "Some of the divisions of the Kayans manufacture their own iron, as well as short swords, which fetch as much as £10, if of superior workmanship." (*ibid* ii. 301.)

"The Kayans are very good blacksmiths, possessing forges and anvils, and in former days they smelted their own iron; their workmanship is neat and serviceable, and the engraving with which they adorn their weapons, &c., is finished and artistic." (Hose, J.A.I. xxiii. 162.)

SHIELDS.

"In action, the left hand of the Sea Dyak supports a large wooden shield, which covers the greater part of his body. It is made of the light wood of the plye or jelutong, about three feet long and twenty inches broad, convex towards the centre, and of the same breadth throughout, but cut off angularly from each side at the ends, so that its greatest length is the middle." (Low, p. 212.)

"The *trabai klit klau*, or shield, is with its handle hollowed out of a single block of wood. Its form is oblong and convex, with a ridge along its centre. It is held in the left hand well advanced before the body, and is not meant to receive the spear point, but to divert the spear by a twist of the hand. It is often coloured with red ochre, or painted some elaborate design or fantastic pattern. It is large enough for its purpose, but it is small compared with the shields manufactured by the Sibus and others. There are also seen in use among

SHIELD.
From Batang Lupar. The ends furnished with strips of rotan. Height, 56in.; width, 17in.
(Leggatt Coll.)

them wicker-work shields of plaited bamboo, corresponding to the wooden ones in length and size." (Brooke Low.)

According to Bishop McDougall, "the shields of the Sea Dyaks were of two kinds: one, long in form, called *Utap*; another, round, called *Pricei*. The way they used the first kind of shield was this: they tried to catch the point of the sword upon it; if this succeeded, it would stick in and be held gripped by the wood, and before the antagonist could get it out, the other fellow would have sliced his head off." (T.E.S. ii. 32.)

BOWS AND ARROWS.

Mr. Skertchly has remarked that it is strange for the natives to have no bows and arrows although they have what may be called a bow trap. Mr. Crossland tells me the Undup children played with bows and arrows but that the grown-up men had none. No writers appear to mention bows and arrows excepting Mr. Earl (p. 265), whose words when speaking of the sumpitan are, " Some of the tribes possess bows and arrows." There is an old attendant at the State Ethnographical Museum at Leiden who was once a soldier high up on the Banjer river and he is very positive that the natives shot at him and his comrades with bows and arrows. He was. cross-questioned in my presence by Dr. Serrurrier, but persisted in his statement. Dr. L. Lewin in the introduction to his paper on Borneo arrow poisons (Virchow's Archiv. für. Path.-Anat., 1894, p. 317) says "it would appear that formerly bow arrows were also used in the island." I wrote to Dr. Lewin asking his authority for the statement, but I am still without reply, and on Mr. J. D. E. Schmeltz similarly writing him, the answer was the papers had been put away and Dr. Lewin could not remember his authority. Under the circumstances his statement must be accepted with caution, and the whole question as to whether some of the natives do really make use of this weapon requires further investigation.

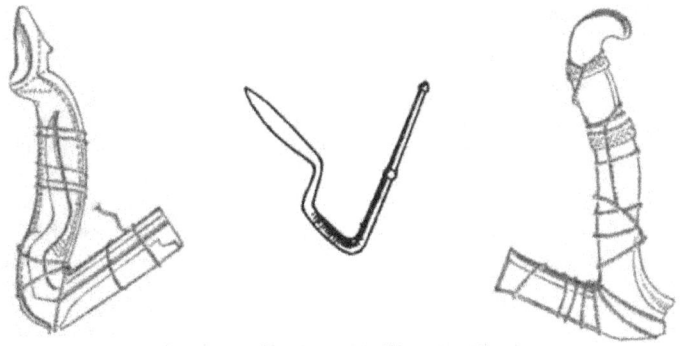

SPURS AND SHEATHS FOR FIGHTING COCKS.
(Brooke Low Coll.)

CHAPTER XXI.
HEAD-HUNTING.

THE PASSION FOR HEADS: An old custom—Recent increase—Malay evil influence—Memorial of triumph—Pleasing to the gods—Scalps *versus* heads—Desire for heavenly slaves—Heads for burial feasts—To mollify the dead spirit—Pride—Heads from corpses—Attempts to outwit the Government—Preventing raids—A head "a blessing"—Enumeration of heads—Children's admiration. DECAPITATION AND PRESERVATION: Manner of decapitation—Various methods of preserving—Ornamentation—Origin of ornamented skulls—Meyer's remarks—Placement—Other bones—Brutal sport. HEAD HOUSES: General description—Comfort of—Varieties of. STRANGE COLLECTIONS. PROPERTY IN HEADS: Division of heads—Chief's rights and obligations—Halves—Dividing block. COWARDLY PROCEEDINGS: Women and children equally bagged—Cunning—Man pushed into river—Attacks on sleepers—Treacherous murders—A sweetheart's head—A relative murdered—Some fishers' fate—The "finest way possible"—Model of child's head—The fate of slaves. WOMEN'S INFLUENCE: Legendary origin—No head no marriage—Various facts confirming women's influence—Pounding a head—Prisoners plead women's wants—Allies killed—A sole survivor—A lover's trouble. RECEPTION OF HEADS: Received by women—Singe head feast—Balau head boat return and reception—*Penyala* poles—Lundu feast—Sea Dyak feast—Bantings' feast—Land Dyak feast—Curious Murut feast. MENGAP, THE SONG OF THE SEA DYAK HEAD FEAST, by the Ven. Archdeacon Perham.

"THE practice of head-hunting has no doubt obtained among the Dayaks from the earliest times, and when carried on by the interior tribes very few lives were lost; but it much retarded the progress of the country, as it rendered life and property insecure. The Sakarang and Seribas, within the memory of living men, were a quiet, inoffensive people, paying taxes to their Malay chiefs, and suffering much from their oppressive practices,—even their children being seized and sold into slavery. When the Malay communities quarrelled they summoned their Dayak followers around them, and led them on expeditions against each other. This accustomed the aborigines to the sea; and being found hard-working and willing men, the Malays and Lanun pirates took them out in their marauding expeditions, dividing the plunder—the heads of the killed for the Dayaks, the goods and captives for themselves. Gradually they began to feel their own strength and superiority of numbers. In their later expeditions the Malays have followed rather than led. The longing these Dayaks have acquired for head-hunting is surprising. They say, 'The white men read books, we hunt for heads instead.'" (St. John.)

Sir Hugh Low writes to a like effect: "The passion for head-hunting, which now characterizes these people, was not formerly so deeply rooted in their characters as it is at present, and many of the inhabitants of Sarawak have assured me that they well recollect the tribes first visiting the sea with that ostensible and avowed object. In a limited extent the custom is probably as ancient as their existence as a nation; but though other tribes appear to be equally addicted to the practice, there can be little doubt that it is a corruption of its first institution [as a memorial of triumph, *ibid*, p. 165], unless, as Forrest says [p. 368] of the Ida'an of the north of Borneo, they consider human sacrifice the most pleasing to the divinity, and lose no opportunity of presenting it ; but having conversed with the Dyaks frequently respecting this practice, they gave no such reason for it, and merely accounted for it, in their usual method, by saying, that it was the *adat ninik*, or custom of their ancestors." (Low, p. 188.)

" The headmen of the village of Serin told me, *though I know not what truth to attach to their statement*, that when the Land Dyaks first settled in Sarawak territory from Sikong, there were no Sea Dyaks in their proximity, and head-hunting was unknown. It was not until after they had settled some time in various parts of the country, that the Sibuyau Sea Dyaks, in attacking them, taught them the custom of head-taking, which they have never followed so persistently, or with so much ardour, as the Sea Dyaks, for the simple reason that it was not their original custom." (Denison, ch. vii., p. 78.)

" The Serambo Dyaks say, when they first came from Sikong, they only took the hair (the scalp I suppose), but a Peninjauh woman, one Si Tuga, told them it was no use taking hair only, the country was put to shame by this half measure ; why not take the whole head of their enemies ?" (Denison, ch. ii. 14.) " These Dyaks say they will not take a head from a corpse. On this account they obtained few heads during the Chinese insurrection. They tell a story of Tabiah Dyaks, during the insurrection, killing and taking the head of a Chinese whose companions came up afterwards and hurriedly buried the body. Some Sakarran (Sea) Dyaks, who were following the Chinese, perceiving the newly-made grave, opened it in hopes of getting the head, and were disappointed for their trouble." (*ibid*.)

" The Uru Ais believe that the persons whose heads they take will become their slaves in the next world." (Brooke Low.) Bishop Chambers speaking to the Banting Dyaks of Heaven in accordance with Christian ideas was once interrupted by one of them to tell him of "their belief, that the persons whose heads had been taken in this world would in the next become the servants of the warriors who had taken them." (Miss. Field, 1868, p. 222.) The Ida'an also believe " That all whom they kill in this world shall attend them as slaves after death. . . . From the same principle they will purchase a slave, guilty of any capital crime, at five-fold his value, that they may be his executioners."[1] (Dalrymple, p. 42.) See *infra*, p. 163.

---

[1] " That portion of their creed which obtains the greatest influence over their mode of life, arises from a supposition which they entertain that the owner of every human head which they can procure will serve them in the next world. The system of human sacrifice is, upon this account, carried to so great an extent that it totally surpasses that which is practised by the Battas of Sumatra, or, I believe, by any people yet known. A man cannot marry until he has procured a human head, and he who is in possession of several may be distinguished by his proud and lofty bearing ; for the greater number of heads which a man has obtained, the greater will be his rank in the next world ; and this opinion naturally induces his associates to consider him entitled to superior consideration upon earth. A man of consequence cannot be inhumed until a human head has been procured by his friends ; and at the conclusion of peace between two tribes, the chief of each presents a prisoner to the other to be sacrifice t on the spot. . . . The chiefs sometimes make excursions of considerable duration for the sole purpose of acquiring heads, in order that they may be assured of having a numerous body of attendants in the next world." (Earl, p. 266.)

Sir Hugh Low (p. 335) has mentioned that "among the Kayans before a person can be buried a head must be obtained."[1] "I once met the Orang Kaya Pamancha of Seribas, the most influential chief in the country. He was dressed in nothing but a dirty rag round his loins, and thus he intended to remain until the mourning for his wife ceased by securing a head. Until this happens they cannot marry again, or appease the spirit of the departed, which continues to haunt the house and make its presence known by certain ghostly rappings. They endeavour to mollify its anger by the nearest relative throwing a packet of rice to it under the house every day, until the spirit is laid to rest by their being able to celebrate a head feast : then the Dayaks forget their dead, and the ghosts of the dead forget them." (St. John i. 71.) The Pakatan Japer, who had 35 people murdered to ease his heart when he lost two grandchildren, "denied that head-hunting is a religious ceremony among them; it is merely to show their bravery and manliness, that it may be said so and so has obtained heads ; when they quarrel it is a constant phrase, 'How many heads did your father or grandfather get ?' If less than his own number, 'Well, then, you have no occasion to be proud !' That the possession of heads gives them great consideration as warriors and men of wealth ; the skulls being prized as the most valuable of goods."[2] (*ibid*, ii. 27.)

The desire for the possession of heads is well exemplified by the persistence with which the Dyaks still try to get permission to go head hunting. Mr. Denison was once present at a meeting of which he thus writes: " It seems that a Sea Dyak's relative had died, and, therefore, they wanted a head. Some one had told them that a head belonging to one of the Lanun pirates killed off Bintulu was available there, and they wanted permission from the Resident to go and find it. R——— talked them over, and sent them all home again. Had he granted the permission they asked, the whole story might have been a myth, and instead of proceeding to Bintulu to look for an old smoke-dried skull, they might very quietly have picked up a fresh head without the owner's knowledge or consent—a little game these people are fond of playing among themselves." (Jour. Straits Asiatic Soc., No. 10, p. 181.)

Sir Charles Brooke also tells us : " Our Dyaks were eternally requesting to be allowed to go for heads, and their urgent entreaties often bore resemblance to children crying after sugar-plums. . . . Often parties of four or five would get away to the countries of Bugau and Kantu, in the vicinity of the Kapuas river, whose inhabitants are not so warlike as the Sakarang and Sarebas Dyaks. As soon as ever one of these parties started, or even listened

---

[1] Mr. Dalton says the same of the Koti Kayans. (p. 9.)

[2] "Nothing can be done without them [heads]. All kinds of sickness, particularly the small-pox, are supposed to be under the influence of an evil spirit which nothing can so well propitiate as a head. A Diak who has taken many heads, may be immediately known from others who have not been so fortunate : he comes into the presence of the Rajah and takes his station without hesitation, whilst an inferior person is glad to creep into any corner to escape notice." (Dalton, p. 49.) "Whenever a man has distinguished himself in securing heads he is entitled to decorate the upper part of his ears with a pair of canine teeth of the Borneo leopard." (Bock, p. 187.)

to birds of omen preparatory to moving, a party was immediately dispatched by Government to endeavour to cut them off, and to fine them heavily on their return, or, in the event of their bringing heads, to demand the delivering up of them, and the payment of a fine into the bargain. This was the steady and unflinching work of years, but before many months were over my stock of heads became numerous, and the fines considerable. Some refused to pay, or follow the directions of the Government; these were declared enemies, and had their houses burnt down forthwith, and the people who followed me to do the work, would be Dyaks of some other branch tribe in the same river." (i. 142-3.)

Feasts in general are "to make their rice grow well, to cause the forest to abound with wild animals, to enable their dogs and snares to be successful in securing game, to have the streams swarm with fish, to give health and activity to the people themselves, and to ensure fertility to their women. All these blessings, the possessing and feasting of a fresh head are supposed to be the most efficient means of securing. The very ground itself is believed to be benefited and rendered fertile, more fertile even than when the water in which fragments of gold. presented by the Rajah, have been washed has been sprinkled over it; this latter charm, especially when mixed with the water which has been poured over the sacred stones, being, next to the possession of a newly acquired head, the greatest and the most powerful which the wisdom of the 'men of old time' has devised for the benefit of their descendants." (St. John i. 194.)

If further evidence were wanting as to the hold which head-hunting maintains over the people the large numbers of heads preserved by them will give it. The number is still large in spite of the numerous conflagrations, whether the result of accident or an act of war. From Mr. Denison's Journal of his tour I have compiled the following figures : p. 15—95 and 41 heads; p. 19—129, 27, 9, 25, 14, 12 and 16 heads; p. 24—9 heads; p. 27—2 skulls; p. 28—6 heads; p. 33—5 heads; p. 39—12 skulls; p. 46—20 skulls; p. 54—none, but some diamonds highly valued because they had been exchanged for some skulls and their fixings; p. 61—30 skulls; p. 62—9 skulls; p. 70—14 skulls; p. 72—16 and 15 skulls; p. 73—13 skulls; p. 76—none, but a fine peal of gongs instead; p. 78—50 skulls; p. 84—41 skulls; making a total of 610 heads met with on his journey. After such a list it sounds strange to read Sir Hugh Low's remark : " But on account of the bloodless nature of their wars the heads are seldom numerous and frequently would not equal in number the heads in the possession of a single family of the Sea Dyaks." (p. 282.)

From other sources I have compiled the following list :

20	Heads	Hornaday, p. 356	Sadong.
21	,,	St. John, p. 157	Peninjau.
30	,,	De Windt, p. 72	
30	,,	Sir J. Brooke, Keppel i. 55	Sibuyaus.
32	,,	St. John; 157	Bombok.
33	,,	St. John; 157	Sirambau.
36	,,	Pfeiffer, p. 76	

36 Heads		{Witti Diary, 24 Nov. {Hatton Diary, 11 April	Danao Dusuns.
42	,,	Hornaday, p. 485	Peninjau.
50	,,	Mundy ii. 222	Mambakut Kiver.
about 50	,,	Burbidge, p. 287	Dusun village.
over 50	,,	Whitehead, p. 70	
85	,,	Crossland Miss. Life, 1874, p. 94	Katibas; obtained on a single expedition.
numberless	,,	Mundy ii. 218	Kimanis R.
baskets full of (in several houses)	,,	Burbidge, p. 64	Muruts near the Lawas R.
hundreds of	,,	Sir J. Brooke, Keppel ii. 34	Singeh.
several great baskets full of	,,	Wallace i. 84	Menyille.
piled up in pyramids to the roofs	,,	Marryat, p. 81	Lundu R.
500	,,	Earl, p. 319	Near Bruni, "on the authority of an American gentleman."
1000	,,	Hornaday, p. 450	Sentah, said to be mentioned by Sir J. Brooke in "Mundy's Narrative."

A correspondent of the Sarawak Gazette (Nos. 103-104), writing from Pulau Majang, on the Dutch border coast, after describing a feast given in his honour, continues: "I have often, after looking at these grim spectres, [the smoked head] tried to discover in the faces of the little children around, some sign of disgust or disapproval of these horrid spectacles everlastingly facing them, as they play up and down the common flooring in every Dyak house, in front of the apartments of the married men. But no; there was no sign of anything, but that of perfect satisfaction. Whenever I asked if the sight of them was not sad, the answer I received invariably was ' No!' On the contrary, they would be glad to see more of these spectres hanging up above their own heads. There can be no doubt, the being allowed to retain skulls, no matter of what age, is, in itself, a source of great evil. The young savage does not consider himself entitled to the admiration of his brother savages until he has added his own contribution to the gory pile."

Mr. J. B. Cruikshank told Mr. Grant a funny story about the redemption of a head. "A Mahomedan named Seriff Amit was killed by a chief of the Sibuyow Dyaks, who took his head. Some years afterwards Amit's relations came to redeem the head; they offered for it two sacred jars of the value of $70, but the Dyaks denied all knowledge of it. The Malays, however, persisted that it was there—so the Dyaks said, ' If you do not believe us, search the house.' This, however, was not necessary, for the Seriff, being a supposed descendant of the Prophet, would decidedly object to leave his head in an unbeliever's house. Immediately on the Dyaks denying that they had the head, that article fell down from the roof of the house—where it had been concealed—and landed at the feet of the assembled relations. It was then taken away, and buried at Pulo Burong; the jars were left with the Dyaks and Seriff Amit has been a Kramat (or saint) ever since—happy man!"

(p. 93.) Once Sir James Brooke " recaptured some heads from the mountain of Singé and offered them to the relatives of the original owners. They declined, however, taking them, alleging as a reason that it would revive the sorrows of their relations. It was sufficient, they said, that they had been brought from the mountain, and that I might dispose of them." (Mundy i. 330.)

As we have incidentally seen, the Dyaks are fond of referring to the original owners of the heads, as they hang in their houses: " While in the circular building, a young chief (Meta) seemed to take great pride in answering our interrogatories respecting different skulls which we took down from their hooks: two belonged to chiefs of a tribe who had made a desperate defence; and judging from the incisions on the heads, each of which must have been mortal, it must have been a desperate affair." (Keppel ii. 37.)

Similarly, Mr. Burbidge says of the Dusuns: "The individuality of the skulls seemed well-known to one old man, who pointed out several to me as having once rested on the shoulders of some of the Chinese settlers. . . . Others were pointed out as the heads of their old foes the Lanun, whom the Dusun people detest, saying that they formerly came up to the hills with the ostensible purpose of trading, but adding, that they really wanted to steal their children as slaves." (p. 287.)

METHODS OF DECAPITATION AND PRESERVATION.

"The way of cutting off the head varies with the different tribes. They do not always cut it off the same way. The Dyaks and Bakatans have each a different way, and by the manner of it it is known whether it is a *pumjong iban* or a *pumjong Bakatan*. The Sea Dyaks sever the head at the neck, and so preserve both jaws." (Brooke Low.) Sir Sp. St. John writes me saying he thinks the head is merely chopped off in the quickest manner possible.

Mr. Hornaday describes some heads among the Hill Dyaks which had "been very carelessly taken. . . . They had been split open or slashed across with parangs; and from some large pieces had been hacked out. One I noticed had a deep slash diagonally across the bridge of the nose." (p. 485.) Madame Pfeiffer says: "They cut off the head so close to the trunk,[4] that one must conclude it is done by an extremely practised hand" (p. 89). She continues: "Among the men who surrounded me were many who carried at the side the little basket destined to receive a stolen head. It was very neatly plaited, ornamented with shells, and hung about with human hair. Only such Dyaks who have obtained a head are allowed to wear the latter decoration." (p. 107.)

The Sea Dyaks " scoop out the brains through the nostrils, and hang the head up to dry in the smoke of a wood fire—the fire, in all probability, at which they are cooking their victuals. Sometimes they tear off a bit of the cheek skin and eat it as a charm to make them fearless. They cut off the hair to ornament their sword-hilts and sheaths, &c. If the jaws drop they fasten them up, and if the teeth fall out, or if they extract them, they fill up

---

[4] On the Koti river, according to Mr. Bock (p. 199), the native "finds it more convenient to decapitate his victim below the occiput, leaving the lower jaw attached to the body."

the cavity with imitation ones of wood. They put studs in the eye sockets, but do not carve the skull, as do the Kayans. They generally plug the nostrils with wooden stoppers. The tongue is cut out." (Brooke Low.) Mr. Horsburgh says (p. 28): "The eyes are punctured with a parang, so as to allow the fluid

DYAK MODE OF DRYING HEADS.
(By Mr. B. U. Vigors, *Illus. Lond. News*, 10 Nov. 1849)

contents to escape." The brains are, however, not always extracted through the nostrils. "The operation of extracting the brains from the lower part of the skull, with a bit of bamboo shaped like a spoon, preparatory to preserving, is not a pleasing one." (Keppel ii. 65.) Both Sir Hugh Low (p. 214) and Madame Pfeiffer (p. 89) say the brains are extracted by the occiputal hole.

Mr. Hornaday mentions a fire " burning on a bed of earth, and above it hung a bundle of about twenty human heads, or rather skulls, for not a vestige of flesh remained on any of them. Each skull was bound round securely with rattan, evidently to keep the lower jaw in place. All were black and grimy with smoke and soot, and those at the bottom of the bundle, nearest the fire, were quite charred." (p. 357.) Regarding this drying and smoking the same traveller elsewhere (p. 485) refers to a collection of forty-two heads, which " was in very good condition, the specimens being moderately clean and not at all smoked." Mr. D. U. Vigors describes some heads "undergoing the operation ; and within two feet of it the Dyaks were coolly cooking some wild boar chops for their dinner, and inhaling the mingled perfume of baked human and hog's flesh." (Illus. Lond. News, Nov. 10, 1849, p. 31.) " This head cooking was the most disgusting part of the whole affair." (Helms, p. 189.)

" The heads of the enemies of the Hill Dyaks are not preserved with the flesh and hair adhering to them, as are those of the Sakarran Dyaks; the skull only is retained, the lower jaw being taken away, and a piece of wood substituted for it. These ghastly objects are hung up in the Pangah, which Admiral Keppel facetiously calls the 'skullery,' and are often painted with lines of white or red all over them; they are occasionally blackened with antimony, and have cowrie shells placed in the apertures of the eyes, with the flat or white side outwards, which in some measure resembles the closed eye, the little furrows appearing like eye lashes." (Low, p. 303.) After the Chinese insurrection Mrs. McDougall describes : " Two Chinese heads, laid side by side on a flat basket, with a mixture of all the various eatables before them. They had been smoked, the eyes taken out, and the nostrils filled out with bits of cork. Each head was tied in a fine rattan basket." (Gosp. Miss, 1857, p. 117.) Mr. Whitehead found among the Muruts that " many of the heads were ornamented with a boar's tusk, which was stuck in the nose, the curve pointing upwards." (p. 71.)

Regarding the carving, or rather the incising of patterns on the skull, above mentioned by Mr. Brooke Low as being a custom of the Kayans, Mr. C. W. Pleyte Wzn (Amsterdam Mus.) informs me that the painted and engraved skulls come from the Olo Ngadju, in the south-east of Borneo. Thus Mr. Doty (p. 300) writing from those parts says: " Human heads are suspended over us as we write. As usual they are ornamented with various figures, carved in the bone with a knife, and also ornamented with bunches of rattan." The accompanying illustrations give an excellent idea as to the nature of these ornamentations, and, while on the subject, I cannot omit to reproduce to Dr. A. B. Meyer's very pertinent remarks as to the origin of some of these skulls.

" We have still to discover the exact origin in Borneo of these ornamental skulls. The Dresden Museum possesses four, of which two are painted and covered with lead or tin and come from the west (Wassink's Coll., 1854, Nos. 828, 829), and two engraved ones from the north-west (Kessel's Coll., Nos. 1356 and 1357). I formerly (Mith. Zool. Mus., 1878, iii. 337) described these two as coming from the interior of Borneo, which, however, does not agree with the information given in Kessel's catalogue, which at the time I had not by me. By engraved I do not mean superficial incisions which may follow the outlines of the painted ornaments, but I mean patterns deeply carved in the bone. In the above-named catalogue it says: '*Kapala Gatong*, skulls which are hung up in the houses for ever as trophies; they are mostly ornamented and overlaid with lead. The grass [wanting] fastened to the sides is called *daun gernang*; with regard to its signification I only know that

LEFT MOIETY OF CRANIUM OF NATIVE BATTA.
East coast of Borneo. Orbits filled with gum, in which are stuck a large cowrie in the centre with small ones radiating round it.
(Van Kessel Coll., No. 740, in Mus. Roy. College of Surgeons, London).

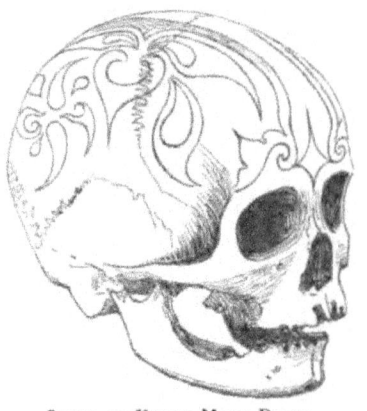

SKULL OF YOUNG MALE BATTA.
From E. coast of Borneo.
(No. 739, Van Kessel Coll., Mus. Roy. College of Surgeons, London).

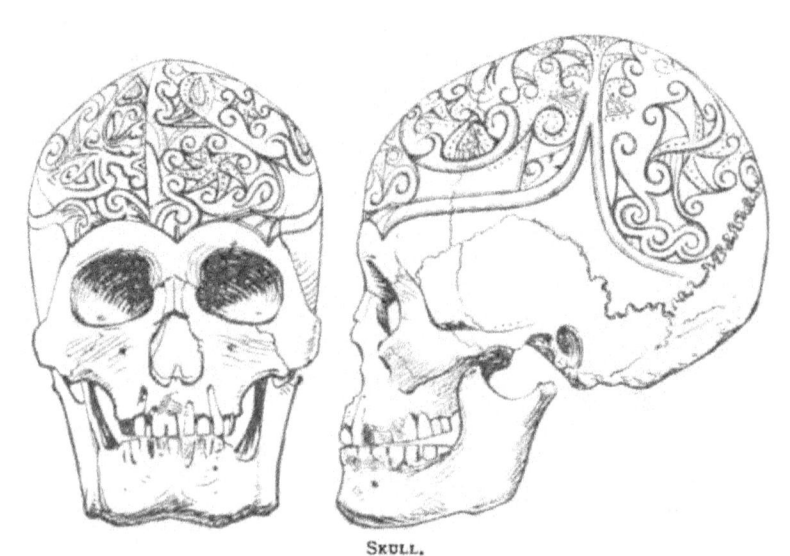

SKULL.
From east coast of Borneo. Roughly incised; wooden blackened teeth.
(No 736, Van Kessel Coll. in Mus. Roy. College of Surgeons).

Head-Hunting. 149

at funerals these leaves are planted on the grave and hence probably the adorning of the skulls. Kessel also mentions (Z. Allg. Erd., Berlin, N.F., 1857, iii. 393) that the branch *Daun Germis* or *Daun Kapak* is planted on the grave. Filet (Plantk. woordenb., 1888) does not mention these names. Bleeker (Afmetingen van Schedels Nat. T. N. Ind., 1851, ii. 513), refers to a bundle of long grass hanging on the cheek bones. I perceive from a photograph sent me by Dr. Stolpe that a skull in the Copenhagen Ethnographical Museum, overlaid with lead, has such leaves on the right cheek bone. Kessel in his catalogue says in general of the Dyaks of the north-west of Borneo 'they alone ornament their weapons and skulls with lead and tin, which ornamentation is not found amongst other tribes.' As, however, just the two skulls, Nos. 828 and 829 (and the third one about to be mentioned from thence), are only engraved and not overlaid, they must either not have come from the north-west or engraving is also customary there. I think the former more

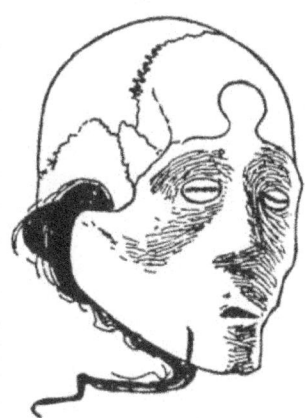

CRANIUM OF FEMALE DYAK.
Lower jaw of wood tied on with rotan, the hair is caught up under and inside the jaw and held there by finely-plaited cord of human hair. Face covered with tinfoil.
(No. 738, Van Kessel Coll., Mus. Roy. College of Surgeons, London).

A VERY CURIOUSLY PREPARED SKULL.
The lower jaw is stained inside a deep red with gum dragon, and is fastened on with pieces of rotan. Pieces of soft wood have been put into the places of the missing teeth (which are *all* absent), into the nostrils, and in the position of the ears ; other inequalities are filled up with a reddish brown resin ; the entire skull has then been covered with tinfoil, two cowry shells represent the eyes, the eye-brows and a small tuft of beard are made of stiff black hair, on the vertex and sides of the calvarium there is an ornamental, regular, and symmetrical device cut through the tinfoil and coloured red. A string passing through a hole in the sagittal suture for suspension in the head-house. District of Sango, Sambas Kapoeas.
(No. 970, Mus. Roy. College of Surgeons, London).

likely as I have reason for mis-doubting Kessel's statement as to their origin. In the Paris Museum in des Murs Coll. (Quatrefages & Hamy, Crania Ethn. 1882, 451, note 7, and Montano, Cranes Boughis et Dayaks, 1878, 59) there is half a skull engraved and coloured red-brown to which apparently the other half in the Dresden Museum from Kessel belonged (according to Kessel's catalogue from north-west Borneo). The latter was consequently sent to Paris in the year 1880; it was then found out that the two halves did not fit, perhaps the other half of the earlier Dresden piece is the same as No. 740 of the Roy. Coll. of Surgeons in London (Flower, Cat. 1879, 124), which was likewise collected by Kessel. I do not know whether Kessel is right when he says that if two Dyaks together obtain one head they cut it in two so that each may preserve one half.[6] The references in the literature of the subject, in so far as I have been able to ascertain, give no certain indication as to the locality whence these ornamented skulls originate. Swaving (Nat. T. N. Ind. 1861, xxiii. 256; and 1862, xxiv. 176, 178, 181), describes four overlaid or painted skulls from West Borneo, but none engraved and none ornamented from anywhere else; Flower (Cat. Coll. Surg. 1879, 123-125) describes seven ornamented skulls from Borneo, including the above-mentioned half: four engraved ones from the N.E., E. and S.E. Borneo, one from E. Borneo engraved and at the same time overlaid with tin, one similar one, locality not certain, and one overlaid, locality uncertain, all from the Kessel collection. If the correctness of the localities given by Kessel are accepted, they certainly seem to me doubtful (it is already suspicious that we have specimens from every important place in the east), it would mean that engraving and tin overlaying occur together, therefore perhaps they are not to be separated geographically

ORNAMENTED SKULL WITH MENDED JAW.
(Brit. Mus.)

INCISED PATTERN ON CRANIUM OF MALE DYAK
This cranium is likewise ornamented with tinfoil and has cowries for eyes; the face is similar to No. 738.
(No. 734. Mus. of Roy. College of Surgeons, London).

[6] Kessel is quite correct regarding such division of the trophy. See p. 158.

and that solely engraved skulls only come from east Borneo, while the two Dresdener skulls of Kessel come from the north-west. I certainly do not know whether that which Flower calls carved corresponds to the deep chiselings of the Dresdener skulls. Accordingly no conclusion can be drawn as to the approximate origin of the ornamented Dyak skulls described by Quatre-

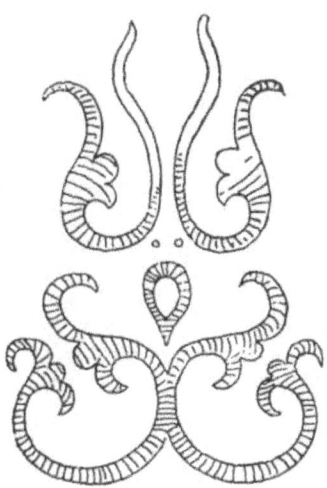

FRONTAL BONE ORNAMENTATION.

With tinfoil across the supraciliary region and above this with symmetrical carving, which extends along both parietals; the two holes for suspension are on the upper part of the frontal bone. The face and lower parts have been stained with gum dragon.

(No. 982, Mus. Roy. College of Surgeons, London).

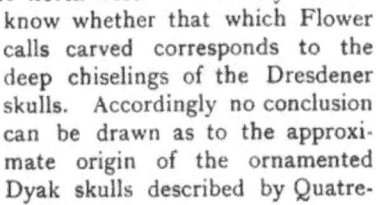

CRANIUM OF MALE DYAK.

From S.E. coast of Borneo. Incised and covered with tinfoil. The false teeth are all of wood.

(No. 735, Van Kessel Coll., Mus Roy. College of Surgeons, London).

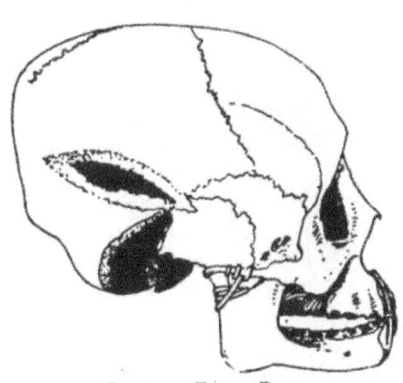

SKULL OF BUGAU DYAK.
W. Borneo.

(From a drawing by Mr. C. M. Pleyte, Curator, Amsterdam Ethnograph. Mus.

INCISED PATTERN ON CRANIUM.
From S.E. Borneo.

(No. 741, Van Kessel Coll., Mus. Roy. College of Surgeons, London).

fages and Hamy as Negritoe skulls from the heart of Borneo. Others who describe Borneo skulls generally omit to mention the origin; so for example, Barnard Davis (Thes. Cran. 1867, fig. 291) describes three engraved skulls, Nos. 1307, 1308, 1411, and one engraved and overlaid (No. 1406, fig. 83) all without mentioning origin and he only mentions the origin of one (fig. 284) overlaid and engraved from Sambas Kapuas, that is west Borneo; Dusseau (Musée Vrolik, 1865, 113) describes two overlaid with tin without stating origin; then Stolpe describes one (Expos. Ethn. Stockholm, 1881, pl. 68) engraved and painted without mentioning origin. Besides the one ornamented with leaves already mentioned as being in the Copenhagen Museum there is one engraved and painted red. In the *Catalogen der Anthropologischen Sammlungen Deutschlands* there is mention of only a very few ornamented Borneo skulls: Gottingen (1874, 50) has one overlaid, origin not mentioned, and Leipzig (1886, 139) has one engraved and one overlaid, origins not indicated. In *Ausland* (1867, p. 305 fig. 1) Lungershausen illustrates an engraved skull from Sambas on the west coast. Perhaps by means of other accounts such as I have not at hand and by means of the style of ornamentation it may be possible to localize the origin, for it would be contradicting the experience of Ethnography were the same sort of decoration to be

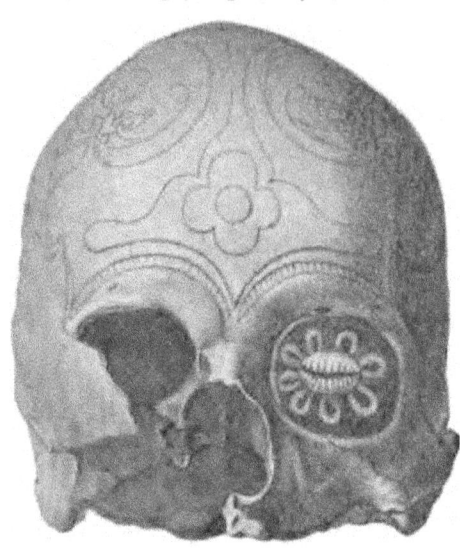

DYAK SKULL IN STOCKHOLM MUSEUM.
Front view.
(From "Crania Ethnica.")

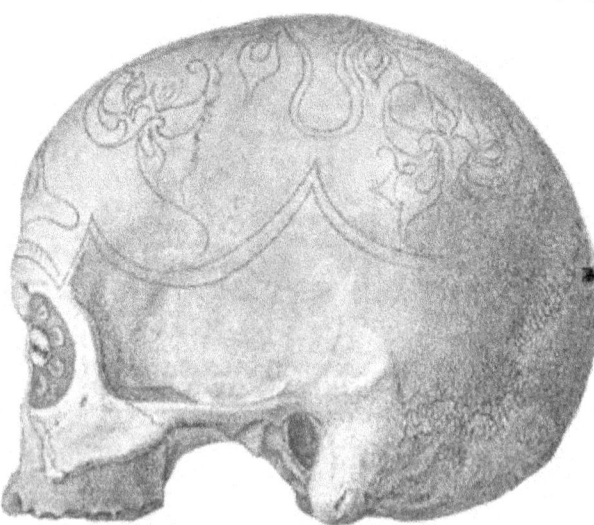

DYAK SKULL IN STOCKHOLM MUSEUM.
Side view.
(From "Crania Ethnica.")

Head-Hunting. 153

found in fashion over the whole of Borneo. We should have to distinguish between engraved skulls, overlaid skulls, and skulls engraved and overlaid as well, and each of these three classes would be combined or not with painting." (The Negritos, Dresden fol., 1893, p. 72.)

"Occasionally the heads are hung up in a net" (Mundy ii. 115); and Madame Pfeiffer describes the skulls as "hung up like a garland."[6] (p. 76.) Mr. Hornaday speaks of heads hung in a semi-circle round the room. (p. 485). Mr. Pryer says the same on the west coast. (J.A.I. xvi. 233.) Lieut. Marryat thus describes (p. 13) the heads hung up in a Land Dyak *pangga* or head-house: "The beams were lined with human heads, all hanging by a small line passed through the top of the skull. They were painted in the most fantastic and hideous manner; pieces of wood, painted to imitate the eyes, were inserted

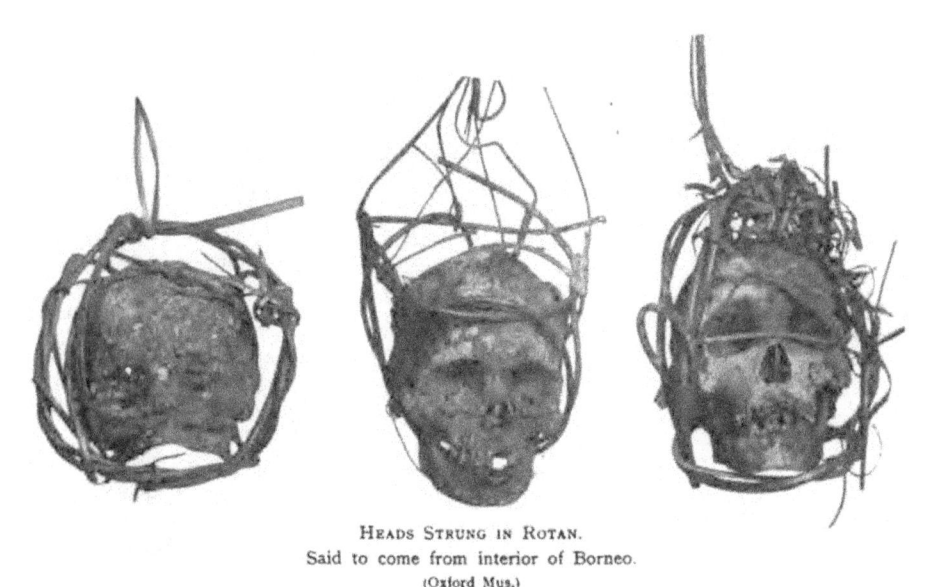

HEADS STRUNG IN ROTAN.
Said to come from interior of Borneo.
(Oxford Mus.)

into the sockets, and added not a little to their ghastly grinning appearance." The wind rocked them about, and "what with their continual motion, their nodding their chins when they hit each other, and their grinning teeth, they really appeared to be endowed with new life, and were a very merry set of fellows."

The same author, in describing a Lundu head dance, says: "The heads were encased in a wide network of rattan, and were ornamented with beads. Their stench was intolerable, although, as we discovered upon after examination, when they were suspended against the wall, they had been partially

---

[6] The heads obtained on these occasions are dried and brought home by the captors, and are then stuck up in the most conspicuous places about their houses, the teeth being sometimes extracted and worn round the head and neck, in lieu of beads." (Earl, p. 268.) "On the Koti river the dried skulls are said to be wrapped in banana leaves." (Bock, pp. 84, 199.)

baked and were quite black. The teeth and hair were quite perfect, the features somewhat shrunk, and they were altogether very fair specimens of pickled heads." (p. 85.) Sir Jas. Brooke (Mundy ii. 115) likewise refers to the use of the net by the Sibuyaus. Admiral Keppel (Meander i. 172) speaking of their condition among the Sakarrans says: " In every house evidence was found of their fondness for human heads; they met our senses in every stage of what was considered preservation,—from the old and dried-up, and therefore less offensive, to the fresh-baked, and therefore very unpleasant specimen."

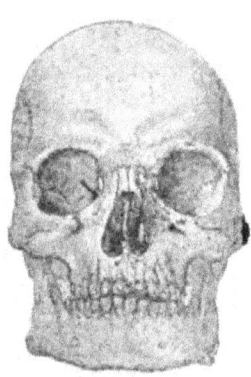

Sir James Brooke also refers to "the *numberless human skulls*, pendant from every apartment, and suspended from the ceiling in regular festoons, with the thigh and arm bones occupying the intervening spaces." (Mundy ii. 219.) Later on he refers to the packages of human bones found with the heads. (ii. 222.)

SKULL OF A BANDJERMASSING MAN.
(No. 279, Barnard Davis Coll., Roy. College of Surgeons, London.)

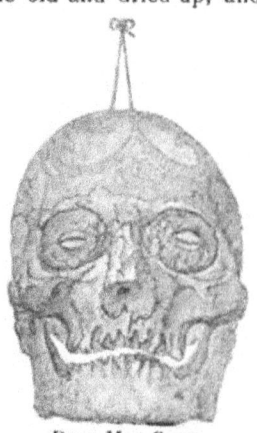

DYAK MAN SKULL.
(No. 1406, Barnard Davis Coll., Roy. College of Surgeons, London).

Muruts "also cut off the first joint of the limbs, which they bring back with the head; these, he said, they amused themselves with by throwing at their women on such occasions. I should quite imagine Murut brutality equal to even this." (Whitehead, p. 72.) At Pangeran Sarfudin's, among the Dusuns, under Bruni rule, Mr. Witti saw "a human hand and forearm nailed up on a door-post." (26 May, Diary.)

Among the Sea Dyaks the heads "are preserved with the greatest care, and baskets full of them may be seen at any house in the villages of the sea-tribes, and the family is of distinction according to the number of these disgusting and barbarous trophies in its possession; they are handed down from father to son as the most valuable property, and an accident which destroys them is considered the most lamentable calamity. An old and grey-headed chief was regretting to me one day the loss he had sustained, in the destruction by fire, of the heads collected by his ancestors." (Low, p. 214.)

LAND DYAK PRESERVED SKULL.
(After Mr. Marryat).

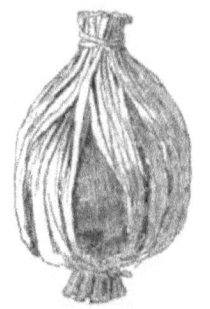

DRIED HEAD TIED UP IN LEAVES.
S.E. Borneo.
(Leiden Mus.)

At Unbuckun, a Dusun village, Mr. Von Donop was shown the there " usual custom of displaying wisps of straw on the house tops, each of which

DYAK SKULLS.

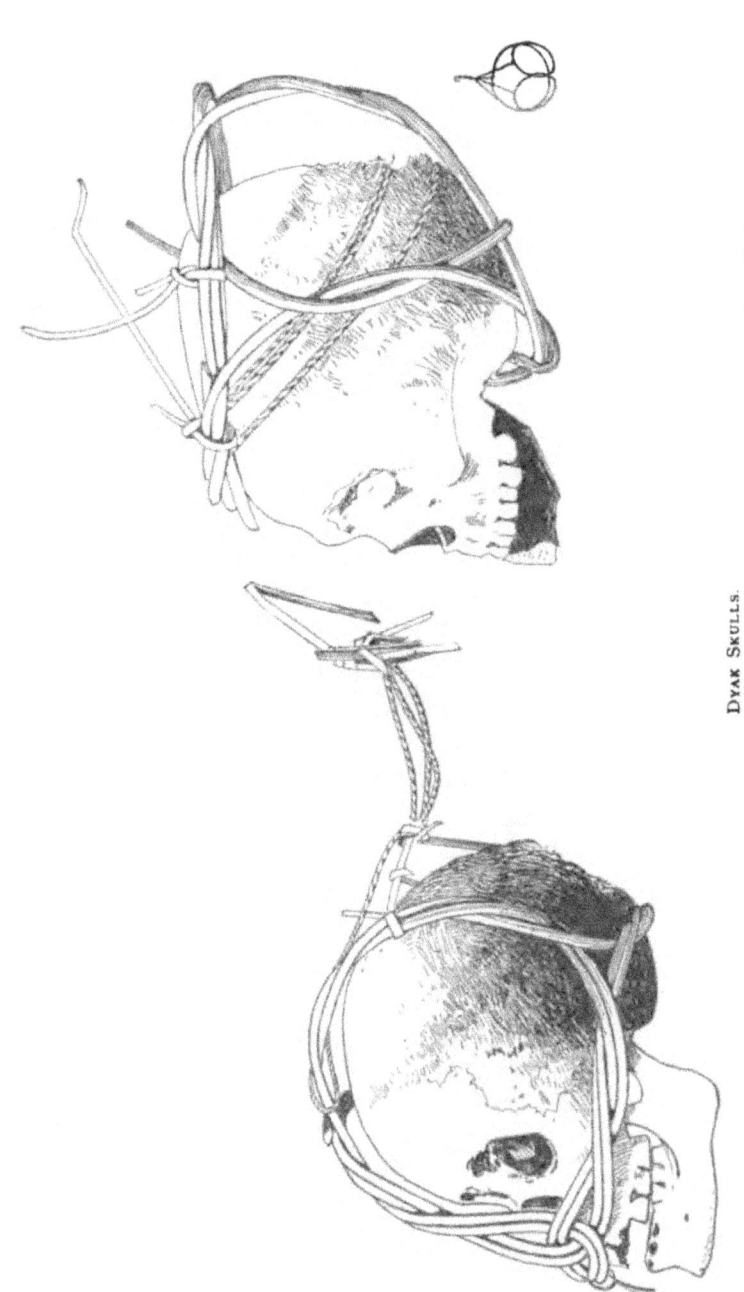

Smoked quite black: portion of the skin and the hair remain on the scalp: no decorations of any kind.
(Mus. Roy. College of Surgeons, London).

denotes a head; but on entering the house they were not to be seen."[7] (Diary, 27 May.)

HEAD HOUSES.

While, as seen above, the Sea Dyaks, Kayans, and others ornament their dwellings with the captured heads, the Land Dyaks have houses specially built for their reception, and these houses form the bachelor's quarters. " In the villages of all the tribes of Land Dyaks are found one, and sometimes more houses of an octagonal form, with their roofs ending in a point at the top. They always stand apart from the others; and instead of having a door at the side, these, which are never built with verandahs, are entered by a trap door at the bottom, in the flooring. These houses vary in size, according to the wants of the hamlet by which they are built; but are generally much larger than ordinary domiciles. The term by which they are distinguished is *Pangah Ramin*, being the Dyak word for an ordinary house. The Pangah is built by the united efforts of the boys and unmarried men of the tribe, who, after having attained the age of puberty, are obliged to leave the houses of the village; and do not generally frequent them after they have attained the age of eight or nine years. A large fire-place of similar construction to those of the ordinary residences, is placed in the centre of this hall, and around its sides are platforms similar to those used by the women in the other dwellings of the village." (Low, p. 280.) Sir Sp. St. John (i. 130), however, says: "They are circular in form, with a sharp conical roof. The windows are, in fact, a large portion of the roof, being raised up, like the lid of a desk, during fine weather, and supported by props; but when rain or night comes on, they are removed, and the whole appearance is snug in the extreme, particularly when a bright fire is lit in the centre, and throws a fitful glow on all the surrounding objects. Around the room are rough divans, on which the men usually sit or sleep."

SERAMBO HEAD HOUSE.
(After Capt. Sir E. Belcher, p. 26).

[7] " Nearly every village has its special symbol, in recognition of the distinction which its inhabitants have gained in successful head-hunting, consisting, generally, of a large wooden post placed in a conspicuous position in front of the village, ornamented with some local device or crest. At Long Wai this crest is merely a ball, with a spike on the top. At Dassa and Langla, it was a monstrous head ; at Long Puti, a figure representing a crowned Rajah in a very inelegant attitude." (Bock, p. 220.)

Mr. Collingwood's description is very much like the last one. (p. 237.)
The comfort offered by the head house is attested by Mr. Wallace, who describes it as "a circular building attached to most Dyak villages, and serving as a lodging for strangers, the place for trade, the sleeping-room of the unmarried youths, and general council chamber. It is elevated on lofty posts, has a large fire-place in the middle, and windows in the roof all round, and forms a very pleasant and comfortable abode." (i. 103.) Mr. Denison makes frequent references to these head houses, and mentions variations in their size, build, cleanliness, and comfort. "At Grogo the head house was clean but surrounded by filth and refuse. (ch. iii., p. 24.) Among the Aups it was insecure, he dared not enter it. (ch. iii., p. 33.) At Tringas it was small and dirty; it was not round but irregular, but it had the fire-place in the centre. (ch. iv., p. 39.) At Si Badat the two head houses are constructed with higher roofs, not round, but irregular in shape, small and dirty. (ch. v., p. 46.) At Sigu it was remarkably lofty and steep; it was new, clean, and comfortable. (ch. vii., p. 73.) At Jinan it was in "good order, square in shape (the first of the kind I had yet met with), constructed of planking, with split bamboo floor and a narrow verandah on two sides." (ch. viii., p. 83.) At Lanchang there "are four head houses; some of these panggas are circular in shape not large, but, with a *very* high steep pitched roof, the upper portion of which is perpendicular and made of attaps, and the lower part of planking. The head house, however, in which I stayed was large square and parallelogram shaped, and perhaps twelve feet from the ground with a low pitched roof. The walls were constructed of planking, and instead of the roof being made to be raised as is the case with the Land Dyak house in general, narrow doors were introduced at irregular distances. There were six of these besides the entrance door, and they opened on a small narrow verandah of split bamboo (*lantis*) two feet broad which ran round the whole building. The floor was made of lantis, there was as usual a cooking place in the centre of the room and a few raised sleeping places." (ch. viii., p. 83.) "The head house [at Mungo Babi] which I occupied was clean, and differently constructed from that of Lanchang, being circular in shape, with the perpendicular straight pitched roof, and windows as usual of attaps which could be raised or lowered at pleasure." (ch. viii., p. 84.) The Dusuns would appear to have head houses, for Mr. Burbidge speaks of a "little flat topped hut which served as a head house." (p. 287.)

PANGAH, OR LAND DYAK HEAD HOUSE.
(After Sir Hugh Low. p. 281.)

Some of the Dusuns do not preserve the heads of their enemies. (De Crespigny, Proc. R. Geogr. S. ii. 348.) The Bakatans and Ukits[a] do not value heads (Brooke i. 74), but will take them out of revenge. (St. John ii. 66.)

STRANGE COLLECTIONS.

In connection with this mania for human head collecting, these people also occasionally add that of an animal to their store. Mr. Hornaday found the skull of a young orang utan amongst the human heads. (p. 485.) Sir Sp. St. John mentions, amongst a batch of heads, "the skull of a bear killed during a head-hunting expedition." (i. 157.) Mr. Witti, in the Langsat country, remarks: "Curious that in sifting the human heads I came on the skull of a sun-bear (*ursus malayanus*)" (Diary, 26 May); and at Tambunan, "In most villages the skulls of monkies are preserved; in others, those of deer or pigs; in many, only the lower jaws of deer, the carapaces of land tortoises, the bladders of goats, and the drum-sticks of fowls." (Diary, 29 Nov.) Mr. Whitehead enumerates the skulls of monkeys, deer, pigs, rats, &c., &c. (p. 109.) In 1869, Mr. A. Hart Everett, at a Singgè village says: "I lit upon a veritable tiger's skull, preserved in one of the head-houses (*panggah*). It was kept with other skulls of the tree-tiger, bear, muntjac deer, &c., in certain very ancient sacred dishes, placed among the beams of the roof, and just over the fire-place. It was so browned and discoloured by soot and dirt, and the Dyaks were so averse to my touching it, that I was unable to decide whether it was a fossil or a recent skull." They said it came in a dream to them, and had no recollection of its first arrival. "The dish on which it lay was of a boat-like form, and was of camphor-wood, and quite rotten. On a second visit I made an attempt to purchase it, but the people were so horrified at the idea of its removal, that I reluctantly desisted. The chief of the village declared that, in consequence of my having moved the skull on my last visit, the Dyaks had been afflicted by heavy rains, which had damaged their farms; that once, when a Dyak accidentally broke a piece of the bone, he had been at once struck dead with lightning; that its removal would bring about the death of all the Singghi Dyaks, and so forth. Afterwards the Rajah of Sarawak kindly endeavoured to persuade the Dyaks to part with it to him; but they begged that he would demand anything rather than this skull, and he therefore did not push the request."[b] (Jour. Straits Asiatic Soc., No. 5, p. 159.)

PROPERTY IN HEADS.

Property in the heads seems to vary in different tribes. "When two or more tribes of Land Dyaks combine to attack another tribe, and one head only is obtained, it is divided, so that each may have a part; in honour of this moiety, all the same ceremonies are observed, as if they had a whole head."

---

[a] The Bukkits do not go head-hunting. (Bock, p. 244.)

[b] "Among the heads is a small bowl, carefully tied up with cord. On enquiring its use and meaning we were told that it is a challenge from a rival Dyak Kampong of the Mempawa region. This seems to be an emblem chosen by common consent, as a warning for any village receiving it, to look out for their heads." (Doty, p. 300.)

(Low, p. 304.) Speaking of the Sea Dyaks the same authority says: "These trophies are not, as amongst the land-tribes, the general property of the village, but the personal property of the individuals who capture them, though the honour of the tribe is augmented by their being in the village." (p. 214.) On the other hand, however, Mr. Brooke Low, discussing these people, says: "The head does not, in an expedition, belong to the person who takes it. It belongs to the chief, and if there are several it is distributed among the leading chiefs. If only one head is obtained, and there are many claimants to the honour of *salai*-ing it, it is broken into pieces, and a fragment given to each; but this is not popular with the Dyaks, and it is more usual for the most powerful chief to keep it. But the chief who salais a head undertakes a great responsibility, as he by that act aspires to be a war chief, and must lead the people on the warpath. They look up to him, &c. They do not mind his keeping the head as long as he gives them an opportunity of cutting off others. When brought home the head is hung up in the verandah of the house outside the chief's apartments, along with the smoke-blackened cluster of heads depending from the sloping roof and overhanging the fireplace."

Admiral Keppel, describing a collection of skulls, continues: "Among other trophies was half-a-head, the skull separated from across between the eyes, in the same manner that you would divide that of hare or a rabbit to get at the brain—this was their division of the head of an old woman, which was taken when another (a friendly) tribe was present, who likewise claimed their half. I afterwards saw these tribes share a head." (ii. 37.)

Among the Dusuns Mr. Witti was shown a sort of natural clearing in the jungle, where "there is a stone block [10] on which the division of skulls is made. These Dyaks are said never to go beyond quartering a head, smaller shares being made up in kind. On that block could be seen stains of blood. Near by is a rude scaffold which serves to exhibit the trophies. But the queerest feature of that spot was a young sugar plant, sprinkled with blood, and carefully fenced in,—why not a forget-me-not?" (Diary, 26 March.)

Cowardly Procedures.

"Among the Dusun the men that took heads generally had a tattoo mark for each one on the arm, and were looked upon as very brave, though, as a rule, the heads were obtained in the most cowardly way possible, a woman's or child's being just as good as a man's."[11] (Pryer, J.A.I. xvi. 233.) "The maxim of these ruffians [Kayans] is, that out of their own country all are fair game. 'Were we to meet our father, we would slay him.' The head of a child or of a woman is as highly prized as that of a man; so, as easier prey, the cowards seek them by lying in ambush near the plantations." (St. John ii. 66.) The Mount Dulit Dusuns told Mr. Witti (Diary, 16 Mar.) that they had no skulls in their houses or elsewhere, but they say the Limberan

---

[10] Mr. Hupé (p. 720) mentions a stone used for preparing the skull, and refers the reader to his report for details, but I have not succeeded in tracing them.

[11] "The possession of a human head cannot be considered as a proof of the bravery of the owner for it is not necessary that he should have killed the victim with his own hand, his friends being permitted to assist him or even to perform the act themselves." (Earl, p. 267.)

people, a day's journey off, "collect the crania of their enemies. That is to say, whatsoever cranium they can get hold of somehow, providing it was procured by violent death. Thus, such a skull might be stolen and yet genuine." In trying to make a settlement between Jeludin and the Peluans (see *supra.*, vol. i. p. 98) Mr. Witti found that the latter would not count as against themselves heads obtained on head hunting excursions, but only those of people who had been making peaceful visits, &c. In fact "the sporting head hunter bags what he can get, his declared friends alone excepted." (Diary, 25 Mar.)

The cowardly method in which heads were taken is illustrated by many an anecdote. Admiral Keppel, when a Dyak was naming the individuals to whom the heads originally belonged, says, "the skulls, the account of which our informant appeared to dwell on with the greatest delight, were those which were taken while the owners were asleep—cunning with them being the perfection of warfare." (ii. 37.)

"Here are a couple of extracts from Mr. Hatton's Diary: "Only seven days ago a head was taken at a tree bridge over a torrent. A Dampas man was walking over a felled tree (which in this country always constitutes a bridge), when four Sogolitan men set on him, pushed him down the steep bank and jumping down after him took his hand and head and made away. I saw the victim's head and his hand in a house not far from the scene of the murder. (18 March.) . . . A great many people have left owing to a fright of the Muruts, who made a raid here about seven months ago. The people from Lebu came down on Danao at night and firing a volley from their sumpitans into the sleeping house, they rushed in, took seven heads from one house and three from another, one a woman's. During the fight one of the Lebu men fell, and his head still new, hangs in the Danao house. The method of attack of these Muruts and indeed of all the tribes, is cowardly in the extreme. It ought to be called *head stealing* not *head hunting*. They wait in the bush watching the house all day, and about 3 o'clock in the morning, when every one is asleep, they enter the house, take as many heads as possible and decamp at full speed." (11 April.)

The following treacherous head murder [12] is related by Sir Chas. Brooke: "A party of five Malays, three men and two women, left Sakarang to go to Saribus for the purpose of meeting some of their relations. Thus they met a boat's crew of Dyaks while in Saribus, and spoke together, saying they were traders, and they were also seeking for fish. When the Malays were leaving Saribus to return, the Dyak boat followed in their wake, entered this river together, and on the following day proceeded to carry out their sly and murderous design. In the morning they offered their swords for sale, and sold or exchanged one, permitting the Malays to make an exceedingly

[12] " A year after my arrival on the coast, the entire population of Slaku, a town situated a few miles distant from the mouth of the Sambas river, was cut off during a night attack by a powerful tribe of wild Dyaks from the north-west coast ; and although the town, which was occupied chiefly by Chinese, contained large quantities of rich merchandize, they were contented with the iron and trifles, with which, together with the heads of their victims, they departed unmolested to their homes." (Earl, p. 269.)

profitable bargain; they then proposed fishing with a hand net on the mud bank, and persuaded a Malay named Limin (who was well known and considered a brave man) to separate from the others, to cast the net; this was done for some time, and they were successful in bagging fish, and were going further and further from the boats. At length the net fouled on a stump at the bottom, and one of the Dyaks immediately off sword and dived down, as poor Limin thought, to clear it, but instead of doing so the wily rascal twisted it firmly round and round, came up to take breath, and then again dived, and again twisted it in divers ways round the stumps; he then rose, and said he could not clear it, but asked Limin to try. Limin unsuspectingly took off his sword, dived, and on approaching the surface breathless, the two Dyaks struck and decapitated him without a sound. They then took his head and returned to their boat. A third [sic] Malay was persuaded to administer some cure to a Dyak's foot, which was bleeding slightly; while the Malay was leaning over and looking to the wound, one of them chopped off his head from behind. After this the women were decapitated. They lost one head, which tumbled into the water, but the other four, with all the property belonging to the Malay party were taken and carried away to Sadok." (ii. 124.)

A still more dastardly head murder is mentioned by Sir James Brooke (Mundy ii. 66): A young Sitakow Dyak went up country with a Chinese trader and on his way up made the acquaintance of a young woman of the Saribas (Dutch) country. He kept company with her and on his return he again visited her. Then he slew her and ran off with the head. "Had he been on a war path and taken the head of an enemy, though that enemy were a woman, he, as a Dyak according to the Dyak code of morality, incurred no guilt; but on the contrary, if he tempted and deceived this woman and treacherously murdered her even as a Dyak, he would be considered guilty amongst Dyaks."

"An atrocious case happened many years ago up the Batang Lupar, where a young man started on an expedition by himself to seek for a head from a neighbouring tribe. In a few days he came back with the desired prize. His relatives questioned him how it was he had been away so few days, as they had never been able to do the same journey in double the time. He replied gravely that the spirits of the woods had assisted him. About a month afterwards a headless trunk was discovered near one of their farms, and on inquiry being made, it was found to be the body of an old woman of their own tribe, not very distantly related to the young fellow himself. He was only fined by the chief of the tribe, and the head taken from him and buried." (St. John, i. 69.)

The cool matter-of-fact way in which those who have taken heads behave is quite extraordinary. They cannot possibly have any idea as to the wrong they are doing. At Bintulu, writes His Highness: "A fine young Kayan chief sat near me, an independent-looking fellow, and head of a long house many miles further inland. One of the inhabitants lodged a complaint against this young fellow for having killed two of his people about a year ago, and asked me whether he might demand a fine of the tribe. I gave him permission to do so, according to the custom which had been in vogue previous to the country coming into our possession. On inquiring of the young chief if such had really taken place, he said, 'Oh yes; my brother killed them and took their heads while they were fishing a little way below our house." He evidently looked on it as a natural consequence, because their heads were required for a Kayan holiday, as wild deer's flesh might be required to satisfy hunger. There was no use in lecturing or reasoning, and I was not in a position to command, so the matter was permitted to rest." (ii. 223.)

"In 1857, when all the Europeans were making their escape from the Chinese, who attacked and occupied Sarawak, the bishop collected the women and children and non-combatants, and embarked them on board a native craft to sail away to another river where there was a mission-station. It was a dreadful night, and all the poor creatures were huddled together below vainly endeavouring to keep themselves dry, as the deck, being native fashion, was made only of matting and laths, and leaked throughout. The closeness and steam below, during the night, were most trying; but there was besides a horrid stench, which the bishop's wife and others said they could not possibly endure any longer; so as soon as ever the vessel was brought to in smooth water, a search was made; and a Chinaman's head was found beneath the place where Mrs. McDougall and her children were sitting: it was in a Dyak basket or Tambuk, and it plainly belonged to a young Dyak who was on board the boat. On being questioned about it, he proudly said it was his, and that he procured it in the '*finest way possible*.' He was prowling about the fort at Sarawak, which the Chinese had taken and occupied, and while they were in it and had myself in their hands there, he went into one of the rooms, lately occupied by the English commander of the fort, and saw a Chinese admiring his own face in a broken looking-glass hanging on the wall. The man did not see him; but his bare neck and stooping head were in so tempting a posture for decapitation, that the Dyak could not resist the temptation, he whipped out his sword, smote off the head at one blow, popped the coveted trophy into his basket, and walked away through the Chinese outside, while the headless trunk of their comrade was yet quivering on the floor of the inner room." (Bishop McDougall, T.E.S., ii. 30.)

Mr. Witti mentions two heads being taken from children. (Diary, 24 Nov.) The Sibuyaus showed Sir Jas. Brooke several heads, but they said they only took heads of women when enemies. (Keppel i. 86.) Mr. Whitehead relates that he once saw "a small wooden model, resembling somewhat the shape of a man, which I at first took to be a Murut household idol; but when I enquired of our host what this peculiar model really was, they answered that it was the model of a child which they had killed on one of their expeditions, but, as the skull would not keep, they carved out this as memento of their bravery." (p. 70.) Elsewhere (p. 76) he again refers to dummy wooden skulls among these people.[13]

[13] "It is said that some of the tribes consider the heads of women and children to be more valuable than those of the men, but this is merely hearsay; and though perhaps, on some occasions,

"During the famine in Sooloo, in 1879, a great many slaves and captives were taken over to Booloongan and there sold, and in most cases the purchasers cut off their heads for that reason. The number of slaves and kidnapped people so taken over was estimated at 4,000." (Pryer, J.A.I. xvi. 233.) Mr. Hatton speaks of a captive at Sinorant being killed for the sake of his head. "The unfortunate was a slave of Datu Serikaya, of Tandu Batu, in the Labuk. This man was sold to Degadong, the Dusun chief, of Tanaorunn, for gutta, paddy, and a gong. Degadong, getting tired of his slave, sold him to some travelling men of Sinorant, who took him home to their village and made him work in the fields. He tried to escape, and so the savages took his head; and his skull, still white, hangs in the house, on a line with those which were taken ten years ago." (Diary, 11 April.)

"A hundred years ago, it was reported that the Ida'an were in the habit of purchasing Christian slaves of the pirates, in order to put them to death for the sake of their heads. If it were ever true, I believe it is not so now, as we never noticed dried skulls in any of their houses, except at Tamparuli; and if they had been given to any such practice, the Bajus, who never missed an opportunity to malign them, would have mentioned the subject to us." (St. John i. 345.) Mr. Burbidge was once told "that a party had been out head-hunting for a fortnight, but had failed to pounce upon any Murut of another tribe; so to end the suspense they had seized one of their own slaves, who had in some way offended them, and had made a scapegoat of him." (p. 65.)

WOMEN'S INFLUENCE.

From all accounts there can be little doubt that one of the chief incentives to getting heads is the desire to please the women. It may not always have been so and there may be and probably is the natural bloodthirstiness of the animal in man to account for a great deal of the head taking. Mrs. McDougall relates an old Sakaran legend which says that the daughter of their great ancestor "who resides in heaven, near the Evening Star, refused to marry until her betrothed brought her a present worth her acceptance. The man went into the jungle and killed a deer, which he presented to her; but the fair lady turned away in disdain. He went again, and returned with a *mias*, the great monkey [sic] who haunts the forest; but this present was not more to her taste. Then, in a fit of despair, the lover went abroad, and killed the first man that he met, and throwing his victim's head at the maiden's feet, he exclaimed at the cruelty she had made him guilty of; but, to his surprise, she smiled, and said, that now he had discovered the only gift worthy of herself." (p. 64.) As is the nature of legends this one is of course only an after-explanation. Sir James Brooke writes of the Sintah's collection of heads: "The heads were clearly stated to be the heads of enemies: they would take no others. If a white man,

the helpless portion of the community may be accidently made victims, I am convinced that the practice is not general, the women and children being more frequently retained as slaves." (Earl, p. 268.) Noticing some men guarding women in the fields, Mr. Doty (p. 289) remarks: "This brought to our minds the remarks of some writer, that the Dyaks are very careful to defend their females, hence in their system of head-taking, the heads of females are more highly valued than those of the men, inasmuch as it requires more artifice and bravery to obtain them."

Chinaman, or Malay were to come into their country, they would not kill him for his head, but if they quarrelled and fought, and he was killed, they would then secure the prize for the ladies! They would rather not kill a stranger Dyak who came as a friend amongst them. It was *absolutely necessary* to be the possessor of *one* head previous to marriage. If a man wanted to get married and could not procure an enemy's head, he accompanied a party of perhaps fifty or one hundred men a long way into the interior, and then attacked anybody for the sake of the head. The chief, Cimboug, was particularly examined on this point, and insisted it was only on such an occasion they made these excursions, and then always a long way from home!"

Sir Jas. Brooke was told by the Sibuyaus (Keppel i. 55) "that it is indispensably necessary a young man should procure a skull before he gets married. On my urging them that the custom would be more honoured in the breach than in the observance, they replied, that it was established from time immemorial, and could not be dispensed with. Subsequently, however, Sejugah allowed that heads were very difficult to obtain now, and a young man might sometimes get married by giving presents to his lady-love's parents. At all times they denied warmly ever obtaining any heads but those of their enemies; adding, they were bad people, and deserved to die." After the burning out of the robbers of the Mambakut River, Capt. Mundy writes (ii. 222): "No aristocratic youth dare venture to pay his addresses to a Dyak demoiselle, unless he throws at the blushing maiden's feet a net full of skulls! In some districts it is customary for the young lady to desire her lover to cut a thick bamboo from the neighbouring jungle, and when in possession of this instrument, she carefully arranges the *cadeau d'amour* on the floor, and by repeated blows beats the heads into fragments, which, when thus pounded, are scraped up and cast into the river, at the same time she throws herself into the arms of the enraptured youth, and so commences the honeymoon. The usual practice, however, is to guard the skulls, pickling them with care, as from the extreme heat of the climate, constant attention is required to preserve them. This account was given by a native to Mr. Brooke and Captain Maitland."

Among the Dusuns the possession of a head appears to be a certain method of ingratiating oneself with the fair sex." (Pryer, J.A.I. xvi. 233.) According to Mr. Everett's reports (S.G., No. 78) when two Dyaks were tried for the murder of a Chinaman and a Dyak both of the prisoners pleaded guilty and threw themselves entirely on the mercy of the court, the only defence they had to make, being that they were incited by the women to obtain heads. A correspondent of the same paper (S.G., No. 104) writes: "At this moment there are two Dyaks in the Kuching gaol, who acknowledge that they took the heads of two innocent Chinese with no other object in view when doing so than to secure the pseudo affections of women, who refused to marry them, until they had thus proved themselves to be men."

The influence of the women is alleged in the following case. A young chief "longing to see the world took with him thirteen young men; he travelled on till he reached a Kayan tribe with whom his people were friends, and stayed with them for a few months. One day their hosts started on a head-hunting expedition, and invited seven of their guests to accompany them: the latter never returned, having all been killed by the Kayans themselves. Why or wherefore it is impossible to tell, but it is supposed that having failed in their head-hunt, and being ashamed to return to their women [14] without these trophies, they had fallen upon their guests." (St. John i. 42.) It must not be supposed that head hunters are always successful. A Kayan, one of a party of several hundred, returned half starved and reported he was the only survivor. (*ibid*, i. 118.)

"One young fellow of about eighteen years old had been brought over from Saribus Fort in chains. He was now in irons here. His account was as follows, and it portrays the matrimonial preliminaries required by Dyak ladies:—His name was Achang, he said; he had been living on Sadok since his house was burnt down on the lower ground. Many had then retired there, and were living in the midst of considerable drawbacks and difficulties, as water was scarce, and all the necessaries for household purposes were far away on the lower ground. Then he had been of late enamoured of a damsel younger than himself, and had been refused, in consequence of his never having proved himself a warrior in cooking a head. She said, 'Why don't you go to the Saribus Fort, and there take the head of Bakir (the Dyak chief), or even that of the Tuan Hassan (Mr. Watson), and then I will deign to think of you and your desires with some degree of interest.' The young man after this rebuke agreed, with another lad of his own age and inexperience, to set off for the purpose required, and after the preparatory proceeding of dreams, birds, missing their road, and many other hindrances, he reached the vicinity of the fort, and very sensibly arranged with his companion that it would be desirable to find shelter in a Chinaman's house, under the plea of wishing to purchase some of his goods. They were kindly received, and ate their meal in peace with the Chinaman, and retired in the evening, with the intention of taking the Chinaman's head, instead of the Tuan Hassan's or Bakir's, as the first, if well cooked, would pass off for anybody else's. At midnight they agreed to strike the blow,—the time came, and the inhabitants were aroused by the piteous howls of the owner of the house. People rushed to the place, which was only twenty yards from the fort, and before five minutes were over, fifty people were on the spot, finding the poor Chinaman with his face gashed all down one side. The young fellow's companion had done this. Achang himself was still fast asleep, in total ignorance of what had taken place. He was now aroused, pulled neck and crop into the fort, and placed in chains. They wished to cut him down then and there, which he really deserved, but

---

[14] Mr. Earl refers on two occasions (pp. 266 and 267) to the necessity of obtaining a head to grace marriage. "The more heads a man has cut off, the more he is respected, and a young man cannot marry until he can produce heads procured by himself; nor can the corpse of a person of rank be inhumed until a fresh head be acquired by the nearest kin. Should he be of high rank, great rejoicings take place on his return from a successful expedition; the heads, which probably still bleed, are seized by the women, who rush into the water, dip the heads and anoint themselves with the ensanguined water which drops from the skulls. A man of *great consideration* may have fifty or sixty skulls suspended in his premises. It has been known that two years have expired before a young man could be married, or in other words, before he could procure a skull." (Dalton, p. 9.)

it was the wiser plan to send him to Sakarang the next morning. He was brought over the twelve miles of road with a long chain attached to his waist, as if he had been a wild animal, and hungry Dyaks were following around, wishing to bribe his keepers, and holding a kind of auction within the unfortunate lover's hearing for his head. The companion, on hearing the Chinaman bluster so loudly, decamped, and although immediately pursued, could not be found. Poor Achang was left in irons for over a month, and then released. He afterwards became very useful in gardening and other occupations, and was a general favourite. A more innocent youth could scarcely be seen anywhere. He had slept so soundly in consequence of a partial deafness. The march over to Sakarang the day after the event brought grey hairs on his head, although he was not yet nineteen years of age."[15] (Brooke ii. 93.)

[15] "No Diak can marry the daughter of a warrior unless he has previously taken a head or two. Neither will one of the great chiefs allow a marriage with one of inferior celebrity. On a proposition being made to wed, it is referred to the Rajah, who calls before him the lover and the father of the girl; the former is asked what number of heads he has taken, the same question is put to the father; if the old man can produce ten heads the young one must have five, as according to Selgie's reasoning, by the time the lover is of the age of the girl's father, he will, in all probability, be likewise in possession of ten. Should the young man not have so many, he must get them before he presumes to take another step in the affair. He then musters a few friends, takes a swift-boat and leaves that part of the country, and will not return until the number is complete (they are often absent three months). To return unsuccessful would expose him to ridicule ever after. Women's heads will not answer the purpose; they, however, generally bring back with them a few young women and some children, as an acceptable present to the Rajah, and to attend the wife. They wend their way to some unprotected campong, taking advantage of the absence of the young men, and kill the old ones, or some poor straggling fishermen; it makes no difference whose heads they may be, so they do not belong to the Rajah's friendly campongs. Having procured the desired number, they paddle quickly back and send immediate intelligence to the intended bride, who puts on all her ornaments and with her father and friends advance to meet the heads; these are in the first instance always placed on a spot about halfway between the dwelling-places of the two partners, and near the Rajah's house. On the approach of the young lady, the lover meets her with a head in each hand, holding them by the hair; these she takes from him and he gets the others if there are sufficient, if not, they have one each. . . . . . They then dance round each other with most extravagant gestures, amidst the applause of the Rajah and his people. After this ceremony, the Rajah or some warrior of his family, must examine the heads to see that they are fresh; for this purpose they are not allowed to be smoked or the brains taken out, which destroys the smell, but must bring them in a green state in full proof that old heads have not been borrowed for the occasion. (I have frequently seen heads which have been cut off a week or more, the smell of which to me was intolerable, but to them nowise offensive.) The family honour of the bride's father being now satisfied, he asks the Rajah's consent, which is always given (the young women and children taken during the expedition are at this interview presented). A feast is now prepared, at which the young couple eat together, this being concluded, what clothes either of them may have on are taken off, and sitting on the ground, naked, the old women throw over them handsfuls of paddy, repeating a kind of prayer that the young couple may prove as fruitful as that grain. At night, the bride attends her husband to his dwelling. . . The warrior can take away any inferior man's wife at pleasure, and is thanked for so doing. A chief who has twenty heads in his possession, will do the same with another who may have only ten, and upwards to the Rajah's family, who can take any woman at pleasure. The more heads a man has the braver he is considered, and as the children belong to the husband, he is happy in his future prospects. On the contrary, a man of inferior note to think of the wife of a superior is entirely out of the question, perhaps such a circumstance never occurred." (ibid, 52-54.)

"It is generally supposed that head-hunting had its origin in the fact that no man could court a girl without presenting her with a human head as a token of his valour; but this idea is contradicted by every Dyak worthy of confidence, whom I consulted on the matter. From the greater mass of the information we gathered on this question, it would seem that this horrible custom is another of

Reception of Heads.

"The heads are taken, but after being used at the feast are not valued. Some of the divisions on the coast, after obtaining the head of an enemy, exhibit it in a public place, where the women, dressed in their best clothes, repeat incantations, and walk past in procession; each one taps the head with a piece of wood. After this ceremony it is thrown away." (Brooke i. 74.) "Although the Millanows do not preserve the heads of their enemies, a young warrior will occasionally bear home such a trophy with the same sort of pleasure with which a young fox-hunter takes home his first brush. On this occasion, a juvenile aspirant to love and glory, who had accompanied the expedition and wished to display a prize he had won, was met on landing by the women, who had already spied the relic from their elevated platform on the bank. They descended to meet it with a stick in each hand, and began to play on the unfortunate head, as if it had been a tomtom. After this performance, each in turn rushed into the river, as if to cleanse herself from the pollution. Although these gentle creatures did not strike with any violence, it was as much as the young hero could do to prevent his trophy from being pommelled into a jelly." (Keppel Meander i. 171.)

Exceptionally curious treatment of heads is mentioned by Madame Pfeiffer: "As they handled the heads they spat in their faces, and the boys banged them and spat on the ground. On this occasion, the otherwise quiet and peaceful faces of the Dyaks, became strongly expressive of savageness." (p. 89.)[16] As a comment on this Mr. Crossland tells me he has seen women, when a head was brought in, kiss it, bite it, and put food in its mouth.

the fruits of the religious superstition which has given birth to so many other monstrosities of the kind. Thus, for example, when a Dyak takes a head he is only fulfilling a vow he made under some difficult or important circumstance; and consequently the unhappy victim, unexpectedly attacked in a forest, or during an excursion, or while at work in the fields, and falling under the blows of a fanatical assassin, is offered by him to the manes of some recently deceased parent, or to the spirit of the superstition to which he attributes the re-establishment of his health, or the success of an enterprise, or of a long journey. What does it matter to the murderer that he attains his end by an act of bravery and an open attack, or by treachery and foul play? Equally what does it matter to him that the being he sacrifices is a young man or an old man, a middle-aged woman or a young girl, or even an infant. He has promised his divinities one or more heads, he owes them these, and without any remorse he brings them in triumph to his village. . . . The head is placed on a mat in the middle of the habitation, and the *bilians*, as well as the majority of the men who are present at the ceremony, dance around it with diabolical contortions. The conqueror receives exaggerated praises on the valour he has displayed, which do not fail to excite to the highest degree the jealousy of others, and decides them only too easily to merit as soon as possible, by similar means, similar flattering distinctions." (S. Müller ii. 364, 365, 366.)

[16] "It really appears the Dayak character is made up of extremes. As we see them at their homes, they are mild, gentle, and given to hospitality, but when they exchange their domestic habits for those of the warrior, their greatest delight seems to be to revel in human blood, and their greatest honor to ornament their dwellings with human heads, which are the trophies of their inhuman barbarity. Shocking as it may appear they carry about with them tokens of the number of persons they have killed. This they effect by inserting locks of human hair corresponding to the number of persons decapitated, in the sheath of their war knife, which is always attached to their persons, when from home. We fell in with a man this evening just returned from his labor, with a basket in which he had carried out the necessaries for the day, and to which was fastened a lock of human hair. The lock was ten inches or a foot long. He informed us that it was a token of his having cut off a head during the past year." (Doty, p. 288-9.)

On Singe mountain, writes Sir Jas. Brooke, we found "five heads carefully watched, about half a mile from the town, in consequence of the non-arrival of some of the war-party. They had erected a temporary shed close to the place where these miserable remnants of noisome mortality were deposited; and they were guarded by about thirty young men in their finest dresses, composed principally of scarlet jackets ornamented with shells, turbans of the native bark-cloth dyed bright yellow, and spread on the head, and decked with an occasional feather, flower, or twig of leaves. Nothing can exceed their partiality for these trophies; and in retiring from the 'war-path,' the man who has been so fortunate as to obtain a head hangs it about his neck, and instantly commences his return to his tribe. If he sleep on the way, the precious burden, though decaying and offensive, is not loosened, but rests on his lap, whilst his head (and nose!) reclines on his knees. The retreat is always silently made until close to home, when they set up a wild yell, which announces their victory and the possession of its proofs. It must, therefore, be considered, that these bloody trophies are the evidences of victory—the banner of the European, the flesh-pot of the Turk, the scalp of the North American Indian—and that they are torn from enemies, for taking heads is the effect and not the cause of war." (Keppel i. 300.) "On the following morning the heads were brought up to the village, attended by a number of young men all dressed in their best, and were carried to Parembam's house amid the beating of gongs and the firing of one or two guns. They were then disposed of in a conspicuous place in the public hall at Parembam. The music sounded and the men danced the greater part of the day; and towards evening carried them away in procession through all the campongs, except three or four just about me. The women, in these processions, crowd round the heads as they proceed from house to house, and put sirih and betel-nut in the mouths of the ghastly dead, and welcome them! After this they are carried back in the same triumph, deposited in an airy place, and left to dry. During this process, for seven, eight, or ten days they are watched by the boys of the age of six to ten years; and during this time they never stir from the public hall—they are not permitted to put their foot out of it whilst engaged in this sacred trust. Thus are the youths initiated. For a long time after the heads are hung up, the men nightly meet and beat their gongs, and chant addresses to them, which were rendered thus to me: 'Your head is in our dwelling, but your spirit wanders to your own country; your head and your spirit are now ours; persuade, therefore, your countrymen to be slain by us.' 'Speak to the spirits of your tribe: let them wander in the fields, that when we come again to their country, we may get more heads, and that we may bring the heads of your brethren, and hang them by your head,' &c. The tone of this chant is loud and monotonous, and I am not able to say how long it is sung; but certainly for a month after the arrival of the heads, as one party here had had a head for that time, and were still exhorting it." (ibid i. 303.)

"If the boat in which the fortunate captor sails is one of a large fleet, no demonstrations of success are made, lest the head should excite the cupidity of some chief; but if she has gone out alone, or accompanied only by a few others, she is decorated with the young leaves of the nipa palm. These leaves, when unopened, are of a pale straw colour, and, when cut, their leaflets are separated and tied in bunches on numerous poles, which are stuck up all over the boat. At a little distance, they present the appearance of gigantic heads of corn projecting above the awning of the boat, and amongst them numerous gay-coloured flags and streamers wave in the breeze. Thus adorned, the boat returns in triumph; and the yells of her crew, and the beating of their gongs, inform each friendly house they pass of the successful result of their foray. The din is redoubled as they approach their own house. The shouts are taken up and repeated on shore. The excitement spreads; the shrill yells of the women mingle with the hoarser cries of the men, the gongs in the house respond to those in the boat, and all hurry to the wharf to greet the victors. . . . It has been said by former writers that it is stuck upon a pole, and its mouth filled with choice morsels of food, but I never saw this done, nor did any Dyak whom I have questioned know anything of such a custom. As to the opinion that they endeavour to propitiate the souls of the slain, and get them to persuade their relatives to be killed also, or that the courage of the slain is transferred to the slayer—I am inclined to think that these are ideas devised by the Malays, for the satisfaction of inquiring whites, who, as they would not be satisfied till they had reasons for everything they saw, got them specially invented for their own use.[17] The grand event of the day, however, is the erection of lofty poles each surmounted by a wooden figure of the *burong Penyala*, which is placed there 'to peck at their foes.' (See *supra* i. 255.) The figures are made some time previous to the festival, and a day or two before it are carried about to the different houses in the vicinity, accompanied by gongs and flags, to levy contributions for the benefit of the feast. The poles on which they are to be elevated are young trees, some of them about forty-five inches in circumference at the lower end, and eighty feet in length; posts so long and so heavy, that it may well be matter of surprise how men, unaided by ropes and pulleys, could erect them. The method employed, however, is both simple and effective; the posts are carried up, and laid on the platform of the house, and two frameworks, about twenty feet high, and thirty feet long, are erected parallel to, and within a yard of each other, on the ground at the end of the platform. These are constructed some days previously, and are so placed that the lower end of the post, when launched off the platform, may pass between them. When it is intended to erect the post, the burong Penyala, together with a proper amount of flags and streamers, is fixed on its upper end; and it is then pushed along the platform till its lower end, projecting beyond it, and passing between the frameworks, is overbalanced by its own weight, and falls to the ground. The post then lies at an angle of about twenty degrees to the horizon, one end resting on the ground, while its middle is supported by the platform. One of the Dyaks below then advances with a fowl in one hand, and a drawn parang in the other; and placing the neck of the bird upon the end of the post, chops its head off, and smears the

---

[17] As we shall see, however, there is ample evidence that the heads are propitiated—different tribes having different customs; the Rev. Mr. Horsburgh only knew the Balau Dyaks.

base of the post with its blood. After this sacrificial ceremony, the signal for raising it is given. The Dyaks swarm upon the two frameworks before mentioned, and putting their shoulders under the post, while its lower end is kept fixed upon the ground, they mount up by degrees to the top of the framework, and thus gradually elevate it. The beak of the Penyala is then pointed in the direction of the foe whom they wish it to peck at; and the mast-like pole, securely lashed to the two frameworks, stands at once a trophy of victory and a symbol of defiance. Eight or ten such posts are erected, a fowl being sacrificed on each; and about half-way up the largest, which is erected first, a basket of fruit, cakes, and siri is suspended, as an offering to the spirits. Meanwhile, those who remain in the house still continue the feast, and those who have been engaged in erecting the posts return to it as soon as their labour is finished. The festivities are prolonged far on into the night, and they are resumed and continued, though with abated vigour, during the two following days." (Horsburgh, pp. 28-33.)

The Lundu called the head feast *Maugut*. "In one house there was a grand *fête*, in which the women danced with the men. . . . There were four men, two of them bearing human skulls, and two the fresh heads of pigs; the women bore wax-lights, or yellow rice on brass dishes. They danced in line, moving backwards and forwards, and carrying the heads and dishes in both hands; the graceful part was the manner in which they half-turned the body to the right and left, looking over their shoulders and holding the heads in the opposite direction, as if they were in momentary expectation of someone coming up behind to snatch the nasty relic from them. At times the women knelt down in a group, with the men leaning over them." (Keppel ii. 35, and Mundy i. 345.)

A somewhat different account is given by Sir Hugh Low: "The feast held on the reception of a head is a disgusting ceremony to a European, though the Dyaks view it only with sentiments of satisfaction and delight. The fleet, returning from a successful cruise, on approaching the village, announce to its inhabitants their fortunes by a horrid yell, which is soon imitated and prolonged by the men, women, and children, who have stayed at home. The head is brought on shore with much ceremony, wrapped up in the curiously folded and plaited leaves of the nipah palm, and frequently emitting the disgusting odour peculiar to decaying mortality; this, the Dyaks have frequently told me, is particularly grateful to their senses, and surpasses the odorous durian, their favourite fruit. On shore and in the village, the head, for months after its arrival, is treated with the greatest consideration, and all the names and terms of endearment of which their language is capable are abundantly lavished on it: the most dainty morsels, culled from their abundant though inelegant repast, are thrust into its mouth, and it is instructed to hate its former friends, and that, having been now adopted into the tribe of its captors, its spirit must be always with them: sirih leaves and betel-nut are given to it, and finally a cigar is frequently placed between its ghastly and pallid lips. None of this disgusting mockery is performed with the intention of ridicule, but all to propitiate the spirit by kindness, and to procure its good wishes for the tribe, of whom it is now

WAR DANCE OF THE LUNDU DYAKS.
(From the plate in Admiral the Hon. Sir H. Keppel's "Voyage of the Dido.")

supposed to have become a member. . . . . During the drinking the dancing generally commences; this is performed with the recently-acquired heads suspended from the persons of the actors, who move up and down the verandah with a slow step, and corresponding movements of their outstretched arms, uttering occasionally a yell, which rises fierce and shrill above the discordant noises of the gongs, chanangs, and tortewaks, to which the dances move. Another amusement at these festivals is carried on by two persons standing or walking with a theatrical air and peculiar step, and with canes in their hands, reciting to each other in a rude extempore verse, the heroic deeds of their fathers and their ancestors, to which, if they live under a Malayan government, and the prince has any share in their affections, they add his memorable achievements and exploits. I heard them once, in this interesting manner, recount the whole of the events of the Seniawan war, the arrival of Mr. Brooke, &c." (Low, pp. 206-208.)

An account of a Banting Dyak Head Reception is given by Mrs. Chambers: "Janting, the chief man of the house, and six others united to give the feast to the heads of their enemies obtained in the late insurrection. Some days before the men of the house were busy seeking for poles of sufficient length, called *tras*, to be raised as trophies. The second morning of the feast, when found, they were placed on the *tango* or uncovered verandah. . . . On the tango opposite each door of the donors of the feast, a pig was laid bound to the lanta; the old manang marked each with yellow, and then he and some old woman stepped backwards and forwards over the pig, the first seven times, the second six, and so on; piggy was then fed with cakes and rice, which he greedily devoured, all-unconscious that his life was to be sacrificed the next morning at the elevation of the tras; a procession was then formed, headed by the Orang Kaya, each man first dipped his feet in water, then took a sword in his right hand, a bunch of leaves in his left, and walked up and down the tango, giving the pigs a kick every time they passed; one or two indulged in a Dyak yell, and hit them rather hard, which the pigs resented by struggling and grunting very energetically. A long procession of women, each carrying a small basin of rice, which she scattered to the right and left as she passed, headed by the old manang and a drummer, walked three times up and down the house. We received our share of rice. One of the women who came to see me a few days after, said she was so 'shy,' she did not look about, and did not know we were there. The next morning the tras were raised, and the pigs killed, which was notified by the firing of a gun. The women who do not belong to the house go home before sunset, but the men remain, and generally drink arrack till their senses are quite gone. . . . For weeks after, the women went from house to house in procession, carrying a head with them, singing or rather chanting in a loud monotonous tone, and demanding a plate at the door of every house they visited." (Gosp. Miss., 1858, pp. 65-73.)

Sir Sp. St. John says of the Land Dyak head feast: " The head feast is the great day of the young bachelors. The head-house and village are decorated with green boughs, and the heads to be feasted are brought out from their very airy position, being hung from one of the beams. . . . An offering of food is made to the heads, and their spirits, being thus appeased, cease to entertain malice against, or to seek to inflict injury upon, those who have got possession of the skull which formerly adorned the now forsaken body. A curious custom prevails among the young men at this feast. They cut a cocoa-nut shell into the form of a cup, and adorn it with red and black dye. Into one side of it they fasten a rudely carved likeness of a bird's head, and into the other the representation of its tail. The cup is filled with arrack, and the possessor performs a short wild dance with it in his hands, and then with a yell leaps before some chosen companion, and presents it to him to drink. Thus the 'loving cup' is passed around among them, and it need not be said that the result is in many cases partial, though seldom excessive, intoxication." (i. 186.)

"The most important of all Murut ceremonies is the feasting of a new head, this takes place at the first new moon after the head has been obtained and the preparations cause considerable excitement in the house; everything else is left to take care of itself; the farm is neglected and nothing is done except to prepare for the feast. The first thing is to erect three poles placed in a triangle some twenty feet apart varying from thirty to fifty feet in height, bamboos are tied to the tops of these poles and droop down some ten or twelve feet; these are decorated with tassels made of some grass or rush but resemble fine shavings, being curled; at the end of one of the bamboos is a dried gourd with a red flag tied above it, the gourd representing the head. Bunches of tassels are hung all along the eaves of the house and all the old skulls are brought out and one put over each door; this has a most gruesome appearance. In the centre of the triangle formed by the three poles a mound of earth is raised and fashioned in the form of an alligator, the dimensions of which are about six feet in width in the middle, and from thirty to forty feet long, some three feet deep. On the day when the feast takes place all the inmates of the house and the guests, of whom there are not a few, they having been called from every place far and near, walk round and round the poles in two processions, the men headed by the hero of the day in one, the women headed by his wife if he has one in another; whilst walking round they shout—the women and men alternately 'Ko Kuay,' 'Ho Ta,' varying the note occasionally and the women come in at intervals with other words. During this performance there are intervals for refreshments when they all go into the house and gorge themselves with pork, buffalo, etc., copiously washed down by arrack; in the afternoon the processions cease and the time is devoted to drinking bowl after bowl of arrack so that by evening there is not a man, woman, or child that is sober. (I may as well state here that I have seen children of four years old drinking raw gin.) The women when not occupied in drinking dance up and down the house stamping on the floor to the time of 'Ho Ta Ho Ta' shouted in quick succession; this combined with perhaps over two hundred people all shouting, yelling and talking, the firing of guns, and the squealing of pigs being sacrificed for the collation, produces a din more easily imagined than described. The guests leaving the party in the evening, or rather such as are at all capable of doing so, is perhaps the only amusing incident, as many tumble into their boats or out of them into the mud, make off with some one else's boat and career wildly about the river singing snatches of Murut songs, or 'Ko Kuay,' and finally in many cases landing somewhere, fall into the scrub, and pass the night there. Sometimes instead of an alligator between the poles a huge snake is made in concentric circles with the head in wood in the centre raised about four feet above the body; the head is ornamented in colors." (O. F. Ricketts, S.G., No. 348, p. 18.)

MENGAP, THE SONG OF THE SEA DYAK HEAD FEAST.[18]
By the Venerable Archdeacon J. Perham.

The principal ceremonial feasts of Sea Dyaks are connected with three subjects: farming, head-taking, and the dead; and are called by them respectively, Gawè Batu or Gawè Benih, Gawè Pala or Burong, and Gawè Antu; the Stone or Seed feast, the Head or Bird feast, and the Spirit feast. The first mentioned are two distinct feasts, and not two names of one; but both refer to the farm. It is with the Gawè Pala or Burong that this paper is concerned.

When a house has obtained a human head, a grand feast must be made sooner or later to celebrate the acquisition; and this is by no means a mere matter of eating and drinking, although there is an excess of the latter, but is a matter of much ceremony, of offerings and of song. The song which is then recited is well-known to differ considerably in form from the ordinary language, and the European who may be able to understand and to speak colloquial Dyak may yet find the "Mengap" (as it is called in Saribus dialect) mostly unintelligible. But I believe the difference is only that between a poetical and prose language. Certain requirements of alliteration and of rhythm and rhyme have to be fulfilled, which, together with native metaphor and most excessive verbosity, are quite sufficient to mystify an uninstructed hearer. Another reason for the difference lies in the fact that the language of the Mengap remains stationary, whilst the ordinary spoken language is continually changing and developing new forms. But the object of this paper is not to discourse about Dyak poetical language, I only attempt to give a sketch of the Mengap of the Head-feast, so that the reader may have some idea of the meaning of what has perhaps sounded to some a mere senseless rigmarole.

In Dyak life the sense of the invisible is constantly present and active. Spirits and goblins are to them as real as themselves. And this is specially true of these ceremonial feasts. In the feasts for the dead the spirits of Hades are invoked; in those connected with farming Pulang Gana, who is supposed to reside somewhere under the ground, is called upon; and in the Head-feast it is Singalang Burong who is invoked to be present. He may be described as the Mars of Sea Dyak mythology, and is put far away above the skies. But the invocation is not made by the human performer in the manner of a prayer direct to this great being; it takes the form of a story, setting forth how the mythical hero, Kling or Klieng, made a Head-feast and fetched Singalang

[18] Jour. Straits Asiat. Soc., No. 2, 1878.

Burong to it. This Kling, about whom there are many fables, is a spirit, and is supposed to live somewhere or other not far from mankind, and to be able to confer benefits upon them. The Dyak performer or performers then, as they walk up and down the long verandah of the house singing the Mengap, in reality describe Kling's Gawè Pala, and how Singalang Burong, was invited and came. In thought the Dyaks identify themselves with Kling, and the resultant signification is that the recitation of this story is an invocation to Singalang Burong, who is supposed to come not to Kling's house only, but to the actual Dyak house where the feast is celebrated ; and he is received by a particular ceremony, and is offered food or sacrifice.

The performer begins by describing how the people in Kling's house contemplate the heavens in their various characters :—

"They see to the end of heaven like a well-joined box."

"They see the speckled evening clouds like a menaga jar in fulness of beauty."

"They see the sun already descending to the twinkling expanse of ocean."

They see "the threatening clouds like an expanse of black cloth ; " "the brightly shining moon;" "the stars and milky way;" and then the house with its inmates, the "crowned young men;" and "hiding women" in high glee, and grave old men sitting on the verandah—all preparing for high festival. The women are described decorating the house with native cloths; one is compared to a dove, another to an argus pheasant, another to a minah bird—all laughing with pleasure. All the ancient Dyak chiefs and Malay chiefs are called upon in the song to attend, and even the spirits in Hades; and last of all Singalang Burong. To him henceforward the song is almost entirely confined.

We must suppose the scene to be laid in Kling's house. Kumang, Kling's wife, the ideal of Dyak feminine beauty, comes out of the room and sits down on the verandah beside her husband, and complains that the festival preparations make slow progress. She declares she has no comfort either in standing, sitting, or lying down on account of this slackness; and by way of rousing her spouse to activity, says the festival preparations had better be put a stop to altogether. But Kling will never have it said that he began but could not finish.

Indah keba aku nunggu,
Nda kala aku pulai lebu,
Makau benong tajau bujang.

Indah keba aku ngaiyau,
Nda kala aku pulai sabau,
Makau slabit ladong penyariang.

Indah keba aku meti,
Nda kala aku nda mai,
Bulih kalimpai babi blang.

Indah keba aku manjok,
Nda kala aku pulai luchok,
Bulih sa-langgai ruai lalang.

Kitè bisi tegar nda besampiar untak tulang,
Kitè bisi laju ari peluru leka bangkong,
Kitè bisi lasit ari sumpit betibong punggang,
Sampurè nya kitè asoh betuboh ngambi ngabang.

"When I have gone to fine people,
"Never did I return empty handed
"Bringing jars with me.

"When I have gone on the war-path
"Never did I return unsuccessful
"Bringing a basketful of heads.

"When I have gone to lay pig-traps,
"Never did I return without
"Obtaining a boar's tusk.

"When I have set bird snares,
"Never did I return unfruitful,
"Getting an argus pheasant.

"We have a strong one, the marrow of whose bones never wastes.
"We have one swifter than a bullet of molten lead.
"We have one more piercing than the sumpitan with ringed endings.
"Sampurè we will order to gather companions and fetch the guests to the feast."

So Sampurè is ordered to fetch Singalang Burong who lives on the top of a hill called "Sandong Tenyalang." But Sampurè begs to be excused on account of illness; upon which *Kasulai* (the moth) and *Laiang* (the swallow) offer themselves for the work, with much boasting of their activity and swiftness. With one bound they can clear the space between the earth and the "clouds crossing the skies." So they speed on their way. Midway to the skies they come to the house of "Ini Manang," (Grandmother Doctor) who asks the meaning of their hurried arrival covered with dirt and perspiration. "Who is sick of the fever? Who is at the point of death? I have no time to go down to doctor them."

Agi lelak aku uchu
Baru pulai ari tuchong langgong Sanyandang
Di-injau Umang
Betebang batang pisang raia.

"I am still weary, O grandchild,
"Am just come back from plain-topped Sanyandang;
"Having been borrowed by Umang
"To cut down the grand plantain tree."[19]

They answer that they are not come to ask her to exercise her medical skill, but simply to inquire how far it is to the country of Salulut Antu Ributt (the spirit of the winds). Ini Manang, joking, gives them this mystifying direction. "If you start early in the dark morning you will be a night on the way. If you start this evening you will get there at once." Whether this

---

[19] This refers to a particular performance of the Dyak Manangs, i e. Medicine men [J.P.]

reply helped them or not they get to their destination at last; and the Wind Spirit accosts them.

>   Nama siduai agi bepetang, agi malam?
>   Bangat bepagi belam-lam?
>   Dini bala bisi ngunja menoa?
>   Dini antu ti begugu nda jena baka?
>   " Why come you while it is still dark, still night?
>   " So very early in the dawn of morning?
>   " Where is there a hostile army invading the country?
>   " Where are there thundering spirits in countless numbers?"

They assure her they bring no evil tidings; and they tell her they have been sent to fetch Singalang Burong, and desire her assistance in the matter. Here I may give a specimen of the verbosity of these recitations. Kasulai and Laiang wish to borrow Antu Ribut to,

>   Nyingkau Lang Tabunau
>   Ka Turau baroh remang.
>   Nempalong Singalong Burong
>   Di tuchong Sandong Tenyalang.
>   Nyeru aki Menaul Jugu
>   Ka munggu Nempurong Balang
>   Nanya ka Aki Lang Rimba
>   Ka Lembaba langit Lemengang,
>   Mesan ka aki Lang Buban
>   Di dan Kara Kijang.

>   " Reach up to Lang Tabunau
>   " At Turau below the clouds.
>   " Strike out to Singalang Burong.
>   " On the top of Sandong Tenyalang,
>   " Call to grandfather Menaul Jugu
>   " On Nempurong Balang hill.
>   " Ask for grandfather Lang Rimba
>   " At Lembaba in the mysterious heavens.
>   " Send for grandfather Lang Buban
>   " On the branch of the Kara Lijang."

These five beings described as living at five different places all refer to Singalang Burong, who is thus called by many names in order to magnify his greatness, to lengthen the story and fill up time. This is a general feature of all " Mengap." But to go on with the story: Kasulai and Laiang desire Antu Ribut to take the message on because they would not be able to get through " pintu langit " (the door of heaven), whereas she, being wind, would have no difficulty. She could get through the smallest of cracks. At first she objects on the plea of being busy. " She is busy blowing through the steep valleys cut out like boats, blowing the leaves and scattering the dust." However at length they prevail upon her, they return and she goes forward: but first she goes up a high tree where she changes her form, drops her personality as a spirit, and becomes natural wind. Upon this everywhere throughout the jungle there arises the sound of mighty rushing wind "like the thunder of a moon-mad waterfall." Everywhere is the sound of driving wind and of falling leaves. She blows in all quarters.

Muput ka langit ngilah bulan
Muput ka ili ngilah Santan.
Muput ka dalam ai ngilah karangan,
Muput ka tanah ngilah sabaian,
Muput ka langit ntilang remang,
Nyelipak remang rarat,
Baka singkap krang kapaiyang,
Nyelepak pintu remang burak,
Baka pantak peti bejuang,
Menselit pintu langit,
Baka tambit peti tetukang.
Nelian lobang ujan
Teman gren laja pematang.
Mampul lobang guntor
Ti mupur inggar betinggang.
Nyelapat lobang kilat
Jampat nyelambai petang.

The above describes how Antu Ribut blew everywhere,

" She blows to heavenwards beyond the moon.
" She blows to seaward beyond the Cocoanut isle.
" She blows in the waters beyond the pebbly bottom.
" She blows to earthward beyond Hades.
" She blows to the skies below the clouds.
" She creeps between the drifting clouds,
" Which are like pieces of sliced kapaiyang.[20]
" She pushes through the door of the white flocked clouds,
" Marked as with nails of a cross-beamed box.
" She edges her passage through the door of heaven,
" Closed up like a box with opening cover.
" She slips through the rain holes,
" No bigger than the size of a sumpitan arrow.
" She enters the openings of the thunders,
" With roarings loud rushing one upon another.
" She shoots through the way of the lightning
" Which swiftly darts at night."

And moreover she blows upon all the fruit trees in succession making them bear unwonted fruit. And so with sounds of thunder and tempest she speeds on her errand to the farthest heaven.

Now amongst Singalang Burong's slaves is a certain Bujang Pedang (Young Sword) who happens to be clearing and weeding the "*sebang*" bushes as Antu Ribut passes, and he is utterly astounded at the noise. He looks heavenward and earthward and seaward but can see nothing to account for it. On comes the tempest: he is confounded, loses heart and runs away, eaving half his things behind him. He falls against the stumps and the

[20] A kind of fruit. [J.P.]

buttresses of the trees and against the logs in the way, and comes tumbling, trembling, and bruised to the house of his mistress,

> Sudan Berinjan Bungkong
> Dara Tiong Menyelong,

which is the poetical name of Singalang Burong's wife. He falls down exhausted on the verandah and faints away. His mistress laments over her faithful slave; but after a time he revives, and they ask him what frightened him so dreadfully, suggesting it may have been the rush of the flood tide, or the waves of the sea. No, he says, he has fought with enemies at sea, and striven with waves, but never heard anything so awesome before. Singalang Burong himself now appears on the scene, and being at a loss to account for the fright simply calls Bujang Pedang a liar, and a prating coward. Whilst they are engaged in discussion Antu Ribut arrives, and striking violently against the house shakes it to its foundations. Bujang Pedang recognizes the sound and tells them it was that he heard under the "*sebang*" bushes. The trees of the jungle bend to the tempest, cocoanut and sago trees are broken in two, pinang trees fall, and various fruit trees die by the stroke of the wind; but it makes other fruit trees suddenly put forth abundant fruit.

> Muput Antu Ribut unggai badu badu.
> Mangka ka buah unggai leju leju.
> " The Wind Spirit blows and will not cease, cease,
> " Strikes against the fruit trees and will not weary, weary."

Everybody becomes suddenly cold and great consternation prevails. Singalang Burong himself is roused, and demands in loud angry tones who has broken any "*pemali*" (taboo), and so brought a plague of wind and rain upon the country. He declares he will sell them, or fight them, or punish them whoever they may be. He then resorts to certain charms to charm away the evil, such as burning some tuba root and other things. In the meantime Antu Ribut herself goes up to the house, but at the top of the ladder she stops short. She is afraid of Singalang Burong whom she sees in full war-costume, with arms complete and his war-charms tied round his waist; and going down the ladder again she goes round to the back of the house, and slips through the window in the roof into the room where Singalang Burong's wife sits at her weaving. Suddenly all her weaving materials are seen flying in all directions, she herself is frightened and takes refuge behind a post; but when she has recovered her presence of mind and collected her scattered articles, it dawns upon her (how does not appear) that this Wind is a messenger from the lower world, bringing an announcement that "men are killing the white spotted pig." Now she entertains Antu Ribut in the style of a great chief, and calls to her husband; but he heeds not,

> Nda nyaut sa-leka mukut,
> Nda nimbas sa-leka bras.
> " Does not answer a grain of bran,
> " Does not reply a grain of rice,"

(that is to the extent of a grain, &c.) The lady is displeased and declares she would rather be divorced from him than be treated in that way. This brings Singalang Burong into the room which is described as

> Bilik baik baka tasik ledong lelinang.
> "A room rich like the wide expanse of glistening sea."

It appears that Antu Ribut does not speak and tell the purport of her message, for they still have to find it out for themselves, which they do by taking a "*tropoug*,"[21] (telescope) to see what is going on in the lower regions. They see the festival preparations there, the drums and gongs, and thus they understand that they are invited to the feast.

Before Singalang Burong can start he must call from the jungle his sons-in-law, who are the sacred birds which the Dyaks use as omens. These are considered both as spirits and as actual birds, for they speak like men and fly like birds. Here will be observed the reason why the festival is called Gawè Burong (Bird feast). Singalang Burong the war-spirit is also the chief of the omen birds. The hawk with brown body and white head and breast, very common in this country, is supposed to be a kind of outward personification of him, and probably the king of birds in Dyak estimation. The story of the feast centres in him and the inferior birds who all come to it; hence the title Gawè Burong. To call these feathered sons-in-law of Singalang Burong together the big old gong of the ancients is beaten, at the sound of which all the birds immediately repair to the house of their father-in-law, where they are told that Antu Ribut has brought an invitation to a feast in the lower world. So they all get ready and are about to start, when it comes out that Dara Inchin Temaga, one of Singalang Burong's daughters and the wife of the bird Katupong, refuses to go with them. On being questioned why she refuses, she declares that unless she obtains a certain precious ornament she will remain at home. She is afraid that at the feast she will appear less splendidly attired than the ladies Kumang, and Lulong, and Indai Abang.

> Aku unggai alah bandong laban Lulong siduai Kumang.
> Aku unggai alah telah laban Kalinah ti disebut Indai Abang.
> "I wont be beaten compared with Lulong and Kumang.
> "I wont be less spoken of than Kalinah who is called Indai Abang."

This precious ornament is variously described as a "lump of gold," a "lump of silver," and compared in the way of praise to various jungle fruits. A great consultation is held and inquiries made as to where this may be found. The old men are asked and they know not. The King of the Sea gives a like answer, neither do the birds above mentioned know where it is to be obtained. At length the grandfather of the bird Katupong recollects that he has seen it "afar off" in Nising's house. Nising is the grandfather of the Burong Malam[22] (night bird). All the sons-in-law set out at once for Nising's house.

[21] This must be a later addition to the story. [J.P.]

[22] This is not a bird at all, but an insect which is often heard at night, and being used as an omen comes under the designation "Burong," as do also the deer and other creatures besides birds. [J.P.]

Arriving there they approach warily and listen clandestinely to what is going on inside; and they hear Nising's wife trying to sing a child to sleep. She carries it up and down the house, points out the fowls and pigs, &c., yet the child refuses to stop crying much to the mother's anger. "How can I but cry," the child says. "I have had a bad dream, wherein I thought I was bitten by a snake, which struck me in the side, and I was cut through below the heart." "If so," answers the mother, "it signifies your life will not be a long one."

"Soon will your neck be stuck in the mud bank.
"Soon will your head be inclosed in *rotan-sega*.
"Soon will your mouth eat the cotton threads.[23]

"For this shadows forth that you are to be the spouse of Beragai's [24] spear"; and much more in the same strain, but I will return to this again. After hearing this singing they go up into the house and make their request. Nising refuses to give them any of the ornaments, upon which they resort to stratagem. They get him to drink "*tuak*" until he becomes insensible, when they snatch this precious jewel from his turban. Soon after Nising recovers, and finding out what has been done, he blusters and strikes about wishing to kill right and left; but at length they pacify him, telling him the precious ornament is wanted to take to a Gawè in the lower world, upon which he assents to their taking it away, saying that he has many more where that came from. They start off homewards and come to their waiting father-in-law, and deliver the "precious jewel" into the hands of his daughter, Dara Inchin Temaga.

Now this ornament, on account of which so much trouble and delay is undergone, is nothing else than a *human head*, either a mass of putrifying flesh, or a blackened charred skull. The high price and value of this ghastly trophy in Dyak estimation is marked by the many epithets which describe it, the trouble of obtaining it, and the being for whom it was sought, no less a person than the daughter of the great Singalang Burong. It shows how a Dyak woman of quality esteems the possession of it. This is that which shall make Dara Inchin more spendidly attired than her compeers Lulong and Kumang, themselves the ideal of Dyak feminine beauty. And, moreover, the story is a distinct assertion of that which has often been said, viz., that the women are, at the bottom, the prime movers of head-taking in many instances; and how should they not be with the example of this story before them?

The meaning and application of the woman singing a child to sleep in Nising's house is the imprecation of a fearful curse on their enemies. The child which is carried up and down the house is simply metaphorical for a human head, which in the Gawè is carried about the house, and through it the curse of death is invoked upon its surviving associates. In the words I have quoted above their life is prayed to be short, their necks to rot in the mud, their mouths to be triumphed over and mocked, and their heads to be hung up in the conquerors' houses as trophies of victory. And this is but a

---

[23] This refers to cotton which in the feast is tied round the head. [J.P.]
[24] The name of a bird. [J.P.]

very small part of the whole curse. It is this part of the song which is listened to with the greatest keenness and enjoyment, especially by the young who crowd round the performer at this part.

With this "ornament" in possession Singalang Burong and his followers set out for the lower world. On the way they pass through several mythical countries, the names of which are given, and come to "*pintu langit*," of which "Grandmother Doctor" is the guardian, and see no way of getting through, it is so tight and firmly shut. The young men try their strength and the edge of their weapons to force a passage through, but to no purpose. In the midst of the noise the old "grandmother" herself appears, and chides her grandchildren for their unseemly conduct. She then with a turn of a porcupine quill opens the door and they pass through. Downward they go until they come to a certain projecting rock, somewhere in the lower skies, where they rest awhile. Dara Inchin Temaga, in wandering about, sees the human world, the land and sea and the islands; upon which she describes the mouths of the various rivers of Sarawak.

The following may be given as specimens :—

Utè ti ludas ludas,
Nya nonga Tebas;
Ndor kitè rari ka bias,
              glombang nyadi.

Utè ti renjong renjong,
Nya pulau Burong,
Massin di tigong
              kapal api.

Utè ti ganjar ganjar,
Nya nonga Laiar,
Di pandang pijar,
              mati ari mati.

Utè ti linga linga,
Nya nonga Kalaka,
Menoa Malana
              ti maio bini.

Which may be rendered as follows :—

"That which is like a widening expanse
"Is the mouth of Tebas; (Moratebas)
"Whither we run to escape the pattering waves.

"That which is high peaked,
"Is the island of Burong;
"Ever being passed by the fire ships.

"That which glistens white,
"Is the mouth of the Laiar, (Saribus)
"Lit up by the setting sun.

" That which heaves and rolls,
" Is the mouth of Kalaka ;
" The country of Malana with many wives."

Soon after this they come to the path which leads them to the house of Kling. As the whole of the performance is directed to the fetching and coming of Singalang Burong, naturally great effects follow upon his arrival, and such are described. As soon as he enters the house the paddy chests suddenly become filled, and any holes in wall or roof close themselves up, for he brings with him no lack of medicines and charms. His power over the sick and old is miraculous. " Old men having spoken with grandfather Lang become young again :—The dumb begin to stammer out speech. The blind see, the lame walk limpingly. Women with child are delivered of children as big as frogs." At a certain point the performer goes to the doorway of the house, and pretends to receive him with great honour, waving the sacrificial fowl over him. Singalang Burong is said to have the white hair of old age, but the face of a youth.

Now follows the closing scene of the ceremony called " *bedenjang*." The performer goes along the house, beginning with the head man, touches each person in it, and pronounces an invocation upon him. In this he is supposed to personate Singalang Burong and his sons-in-law, who are believed to be the real actors. Singalang Burong himself " *nenjangs* " the headmen, and his sons-in-law, the birds, bless the rest. The touch of the human performer, and the accompanying invocation are thought to effect a communication between these bird spirits from the skies, and each individual being. The great bird-chief and his dependants come from above to give men their charms and their blessings. Upon the men the performer invokes physical strength and bravery in war ; and upon the women, luck with paddy, cleverness in Dyak feminine accomplishments, and beauty in form and complexion.

This ceremony being over, the women go to Singalang Burong (in the house of Kling, according to the Mengap) with "*tuak*" and make him drunk. When in a state of insensibility his turban drops off, and out of it falls the head which was procured as above related. Its appearance creates a great stir in the house, and Lulong and Kumang come out of the room and take it. After leaving charms and medicines behind him, and asking for things in return, Singalang Burong and his company go back to the skies.

At the feast they make certain erections at regular intervals along the verandah of the house, called "*pandong*," on which are hung their war-charms, and swords, and spears, &c. In singing the performer goes round these and along the " *ruai*." The recitation takes a whole night to complete ; it begins about 6 p.m. in the evening, and ends about 9 or 10 a.m. in the morning. The killing of a pig and examining the liver is the last act of the ceremony.

In Balau Dyak the word " Mengap" is equivalent to " Singing" or reciting in any distinctive tone, and is applied to Dyak song or Christian worship: but in Saribus dialect it is applied to certain kinds of ceremonial songs only.

CHAPTER XXII.

THE SUMPITAN AND OTHER POISONS.

THE SUMPITAN. TUBE: Description—Length—Spearhead—Sight—Remarkable straightness—Primitive boring apparatus—Tediousness—Dusun name. DARTS: Variety—Length—Neatness—Barbed with fish bones—Butt of pith—How made to fit—War and sporting arrows—Quivers—How darts are held—Charms—Girdle prong. SHOOTING: Range—Accuracy—Exaggeration. POISON: Bakatan preparation a mixture—Appearance—*Tasam* tree and *akar* creeper—Antimony—*Antiaris toxicaria*—Decaying human flesh—Dalton's account—Hatton's account—*Pali nikus* or Rat's Upas—Punan preparation—S. Müller's account *siren* tree and *ratoes* creeper—Ingredients mixed. EFFECTS: Dalton's account—Earl's opinion—Fatal to small animals—Slow effect on orang utans—Kayan opinion—Weakened by exposure—Mortally poisonous—Small puncture—Somnolent death—Feverishness—Thirty men wounded—Effect on ant eater. DR. LEWIN'S EXPERIMENTS: Mixtures—*Siren* is *Antiaris toxicaria*; *Ipoh* is *Strychnos tiuté*; *Aker tuba* is *Derris elliptica*—Effects—Difficulty in obtaining poison—I.: The pure poison—Chemical Tests—Frog—Pigeon—Rabbit—Strychnine—No Brucin. II.: Description—Rabbits—Frogs—Chemical tests—Antiarin obtained—Frogs—Pigeon—Rabbit—Fishes. III.: Strychnine. IV.: Description—*Antiarin*—Fishes. ANTIDOTES: Earl's opinion—Crawfurd's opinion—Man wounded—Sucking wound—Brandy—Liquid ammonia—*Ingo*—Wounds aggravated. FOOD: Not poisoned. MANUFACTURERS: Punans—Lugats—Pakatans—Other tribes.
OTHER POISONS. A white powder—Mixed with sirih—Arsenic—Belief in poisoning—Poison plants—Kapuas poisoning—Bambu spiculæ—Murut poisonings.

THE SUMPITAN.

TUBES, DARTS, AND QUIVERS.

" THE sumpitan, or blow pipe, is a wooden tube of about eight feet in length and an inch in diameter, through which small poisoned arrows are blown. . . . Sometimes the spear and the sumpitan are combined, a spear head being lashed upon the tube of the sumpitan, thus in some degree affording the advantage of a musket and bayonet." (Horsburgh, p. 38.) On the Mambakut River, "the length of the longest sumpitan I saw was between seven and eight feet, and much resembled the cherry-stick pipes of Turkey." (Mundy ii. 226.) The Adang Muruts have sumpits "as usual of dark hard red wood, and had a spear-head, lashed on very neatly with rattans on one side of the muzzle, and an iron sight on the other." (St. John ii. 89.)

In " Sarawak " (p. 330) Sir Hugh Low was I think the first traveller to call attention to the fact that the little iron hook fastened at the outlet end of the sumpit is a " sight." Mr. C. A. Bampfylde writing to the " Field " newspaper from Fort Kapit on the Rejang, Feb., 1882, says: " Mr. Hugh Low is certainly correct in describing the small iron hook on the end of the sumpitan, or dart tube, as a sight; I have also seen on some 'sumpitans' a white backsight, made of bone for use at night."

"The beauty and straightness of the bore is remarkable." (Mundy ii. 226.) "The boring of a sumpit by a skilful hand is performed in a day. The instrument used is a cold iron rod, one end of which is chisel-pointed and the other round." (Burns, Jour. Ind. Arch. iii. 142.) "The bore of these blow-pipes is as clean and bright as that of a gun-barrel, and is about six feet long, and drilled through a log of hard wood; the log is then pared down and rounded to less than an inch in diameter." (Whitehead, p. 75.) The most complete account of the boring process is that given by Mr. Crocker, who saw it performed by a Bakatan: "A hard piece of wood had been selected the length required and reduced to the size of a man's wrist, this was fastened to a post forming a part of a raised platform to the house. The operator stood underneath and bored upwards with a long piece of round iron the length of the sumpitan and sharpened at one end like a chisel. Two bits of round wood, about 8 inches long, were fastened by rings of rattans to the iron forming a movable handle. The iron was beautifully round and made out of native iron like the Kayan weapons; the rod or chisel in question had been in the tribe as long as any of them could recollect. The traveller is naturally astonished to find the holes of the blow-pipe so straight, when he sees the simple contrivance employed; besides a good eye they must be possessed of more than ordinary perseverance, as the method of boring is tedious to a degree. After the hole is bored a piece of rattan is worked through until the desired smoothness is obtained, when the outside is reduced to the usual size and polished by constant rubbing." (S.G., No. 123, p. 6.)

SUMPITAN.
Pattern inlaid with tinfoil. Length, 80⅜in.; bore, ⅞in.; weight, 29 oz.
(Oxford Mus.)

SUMPITAN.
with concave convex blade bound on to the ejector end by two coils of brass wire. Butt end of the pipe encased in brass and encircled by a series of shallow grooves. Length, 6ft. 4½in; length of blade, inclusive haft, 16¼in.; diam. of bore, ⅜in.; weight, 44 oz.
(Oxford Mus.)

Mr. Witti (Diary, 20 Nov.) says the Dusuns calls the blow-pipe *Sopok* and not Sumpitan, but *Sopok* also means a spear.

"The darts are of various sorts." (Dalton, p. 51.) "The arrow is a small splinter of nibong about as thick as a stocking wire, stuck into a small hemispherical base of very light wood, so as to afford a surface for the breath to act upon. The point is cut sharp." (Horsburgh, p. 38.) Mr. Brooke Low describes the darts as "made of the palm called *apieng*," while Sir Sp. St. John describes those in use by the Adang Muruts as "slips of wood, tipped with spear-shaped heads cut out of bamboo." (ii. 89.)

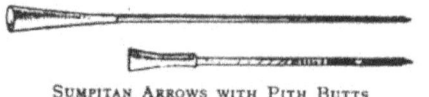

SUMPITAN ARROWS WITH PITH BUTTS.
(Brit. Mus.)

WOODEN BODKIN WITH BRASS PIN.
Used for making the butts, from sago palm midribs, for blowpipe arrows (see text).
Length, 8¼in.
(Edinbro' Mus.)

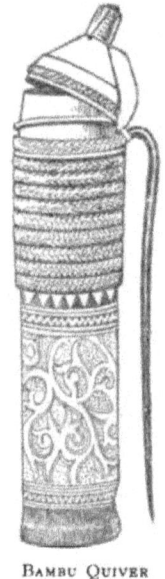

On the Mambakut River the "arrows are nine inches long, of tough wood, not thicker than moderate-sized wire, very neatly made, and generally barbed with sharpened fish bones . . . . and in order to give greater velocity to the arrow, the head of it is made to fit exactly to the size of the tube, and is formed of a sort of pith, or of very soft wood." (Mundy ii. 226.) According to Mr. Whitehead (p. 75) the "darts are made from the stem of a palm-leaf—as hard as the tough nebong fibre—which is cut into slender strips, tapering into a needle-like point and nearly a foot in length. The resistance to the air is obtained by piercing a small piece of dried pith (from a species of mountain sago-palm) on a brass needle, which is fixed in the centre of a small length of rattan, previously pared to fit the barrel; then by paring the pith towards the needle a neat little cone is formed, already pierced exactly in the centre, the base of which, being the same

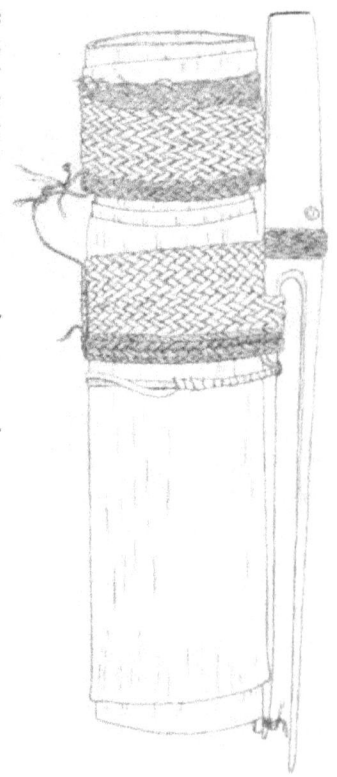

BAMBU QUIVER
(S.E. COAST).
Bands on upper portion are dark brown and yellow rotan. The two ends of the quiver painted dark crimson. The belt hook is of iron.
(Brit. Mus.)

BAMBU QUIVER.
Cover appears to have been inset with gutta at one time. Length, with cover on, 13in.; length, without cover, 10⅞in; weight, complete with 27 darts, 13¾oz.
(Oxford Mus.)

size as the rattan, exactly fits the barrel. In this cone the heavier end of the shaft is fixed. . . . War-arrows differ from sporting arrows by having a loose barbed point attached, either of tin or bamboo; this point is besmeared with poison, and when shot home would remain in the wound with most of the poison."

The arrows are "carried in very neatly carved bamboo cases." (St. John ii. 89.) When the Kyans face an enemy the quiver at the side is open; "and, whether advancing or retreating, they fire the poisoned missiles with great rapidity and precision: some hold four spare arrows between the fingers of the hand which grasps the sumpitan, whilst others take their side-case." (Sir Jas. Brooke; Mundy i. 260.) "The quiver for these arrows is really curious, beautifully made from the large bamboo, and besides, the darts usually contain a variety of amulets or charms, in the shape of pebbles, bones, and odd pieces of wood, with the skins of monkeys." (*ibid*, ii. 227.) Mr. Whitehead also speaks of the "neatly made bamboo case, with a prong at the side for fixing in the chawat, and ornamented with rattan plaits." (p. 76.)

Shooting.

"In advancing, the sumpitan is carried at the mouth and elevated, and they will discharge at least five arrows to one compared with a musket. Beyond a distance of twenty yards they [the Kayans] do not shoot with certainty, from the lightness of the arrow, but I have frequently seen them practise at the above-named range, and they usually struck near the centre of the crown, none of the arrows being more than an inch or two from each other. On a calm day the utmost range may be a hundred yards." (Sir Jas. Brooke, Mundy i. 261.) Capt. Mundy says: "At twenty yards distance, the barb meeting the bare skin, would

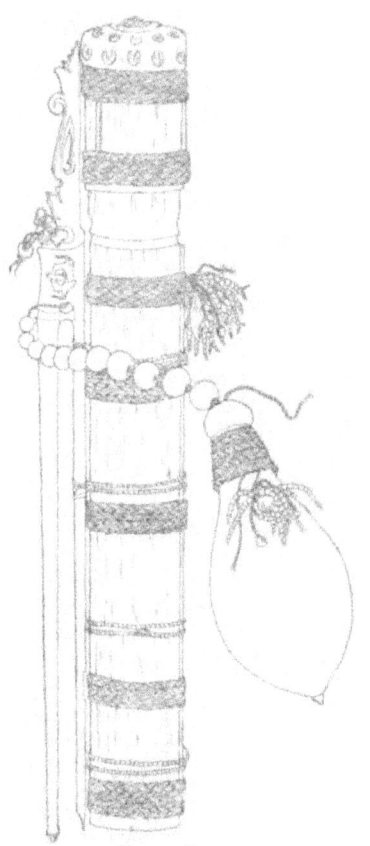

BAMBU QUIVER.

The small tassel at the side is made of strings of variously coloured glass beads, with a canine tooth in the middle. On the same side as this tassel, that is opposite the belt attachment, there is a thin square strip of bambu which is fastened in its place by all the bands of plaited cane passing over it. The bottom of the quiver is formed by the natural joint. The cover is likewise formed by the natural joint; on the top is the flattened spiral of a shell *(conus)* embedded in gutta, surrounded by two inches of small shells *(nassa)*. Three equi-distant thin square strips of bambu are found attached between the two bands of plaited rattan. On the free string from the belt attachment are strung a series of graduated opaque turquoise blue beads, and at the end is a small gourd with a wooden plug. In the midst of the bead tassel on the plug is a small brass hawk bell. Total length, including cover, 15¾in.; length of quiver only, 13in.; weight, including gourd and 24 darts, barely 14 oz.

(Oxford Mus.)

bury half the arrow in the flesh, but would not penetrate cloth at a distance of forty yards; the extreme range may be eighty or ninety yards." (ii. 227.) On the Koti river the Kayans "will strike an object at 40 yards, and will kill a monkey or bird at that distance; when the darts are poisoned, they will throw them 60 yards, as in war, or at some large ferocious animal which they seldom eat." (Dalton, p. 51.) Mr. Horsburgh gives (p. 38) the wounding distance as 30 yards. The Ukits are said to use the tube with deadly aim. (S.G. 169, p. 54.) A correspondent at Saratok (Dutch Borneo), writing to the S.G., No. 95, records good aim at 30 paces with a six feet sumpitan, at a target slightly bigger than a man's head.[1] See also Chapter on Hunting and Fishing; pp. 446, 462.

PACKET CONTAINING SUMPITAN POISON.
½ real size. S.E. Borneo.
(Leiden Mus.)

BAMBU BOX CONTAINING SUMPITAN POISON.
½ real size. S.E. Borneo.
(Leiden Mus.)

MANUFACTURE OF THE POISON.

The Bakatans told Mr. Crocker that they manufactured the poison thus: "They made incisions in the Epo tree (Upas) and the gutta, which exuded, they cooked over a slow fire on a leaf until it assumed the consistency of soft wax; when it was required for use they grated the bark of a tree and mixed with it, when it became a potent and deadly poison. Both of those trees they described as being of large growth." (S.G., No. 123, p. 6.) "The poison looks like a translucent gum, of a rich brown colour; and when dipped into water of a temperature of one hundred and fifty degrees, it began to melt immediately; but on being withdrawn and placed over the flame of a lighted candle, it instantly became hard again. . . . The natives say also, that the juice from one kind of creeper is even more virulent than that of the upas." (St. John ii. 89.) Sir Jas. Brooke also refers to the sap of two sorts of creepers being used to mix with the original poison." (Keppel ii. 146.)

Mr. Brooke Low mentions the juice of the *tasam* tree, which is dried over the fire until it becomes a hard paste, and is then softened with the juice of an *akar*, creeper."

Mr. Crossland informs me he was told

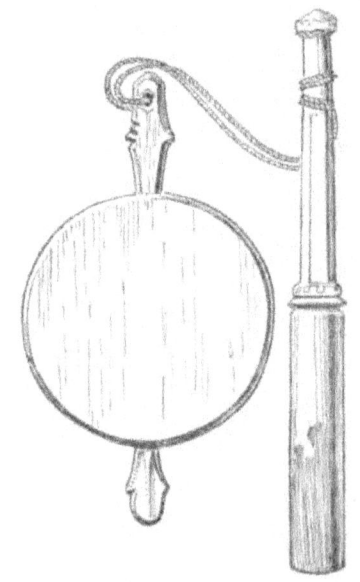

CIRCULAR PLATE of hard brown wood; attached rolling pin of light wood. Said to be used for preparing sumpitan poison. Poonans at Long Wai.
(Brit. Mus.)

---

[1] But "E T.S." writes to the "Field" newspaper (the date of which I have unfortunately mislaid), saying, from his own information he knew Dyaks to blow their arrows to 150 yards to a certainty, and he would not mind betting on their doing 200 yards. This writer makes other statements which may be equally well doubted.

antimony was mixed with the poison by the Undups. Mr. Burbidge writes me (16th Oct., 1894): "I was always told that the arrows for the sumpitan were first steeped in juice of upas (*antiaris toxicaria*), and then, that they were stuck into a portion of a decaying human body, in full sunshine, for a month or more." According to Mr. Dalton, with the Kyans, on the Koti river, "each man carries about with him a small box of lime juice; by dipping the dart into this immediately before they put it into the sumpit, the poison becomes active, in which state they blow it. . . . . And darts used in war are poisoned by dipping them into a liquid taken from a young tree, called by the Diaks *upo*." (p. 51.) Mr. Hatton's account is very curious; on 31 March (Diary) he writes: "To-day some men came in from collecting upas juice. I asked how it was obtained, and they said they make a long bamboo spear, and, tying a rattan to one end, throw it at the soft bark of the upas tree, then pulling it out by means of the rattan, a little of the black juice will have collected in the bamboo, and the experiment is repeated until sufficient is collected." Mr. Witti remarks on a tree which made itself noticeable through the manner in which its bole was scarred. The Dyaks call that tree *Pali Nikus*, or "Rat's Upas," although in individual appearance it has nothing in common with the upas proper. Its sap is said to be just virulent enough to poison rats. The tree is shaggy topped, and has a straight stem, free of branches up to 60 feet. The simple undivided leaf has an obtuse apex and an obvate form. (Diary, 17 March.)

The Punans prepared poison as follows: "They had a bundle of arrows by their side, and as soon as the poisonous matter was hot they took a small quantity and smeared over a wooden plate by means of a wooden instrument resembling a pestle, till the plate was covered with a thick layer. Then taking an arrow they rolled the head across the plate, so that it became coated with the pasty matter. Next they made a spiral incision in the arrow-head and again rolled it over the plate. The arrow was then ready for use." (Bock, p. 73.)

Mr. Bampfylde (as quoted above) says the two juices "are mixed together and placed over a fire until they congeal. Different tribes vary in some of the ingredients but all use the upas juice."[1]

"The Bakatan and Lugat are the chief manufacturers of the sumpitan." (Burns, Jour. Ind. Arch. iii. 142.) The Adang Muruts, although large users, cannot manufacture the "sumpitan themselves, but purchase them from traders, who procure them at Bintulu and Rejang from the wild Punans and Pakatans and are therefore very dear, and highly prized, and no price offered

---

[1] The varieties of the poisons are thus described by the traveller Mr. S. Müller: "The substance of which a coating is put on the point of these little bambu arrows is made of two different poisons, known under the name of *siren* and of *ratoes* or *ipot*. Both are prepared with vegetable matters, although they are furnished by quite different species of trees. The poison is extracted by decoction from the juice of the bark, twigs and leaves of these trees, and after it has been allowed to rest and to ferment properly it is mixed with the juice of other trees and bushes; it is then preserved for use The poison extracted from the *siren* is much more active, violent and dangerous than that furnished by the *ipot*, but it seems its preparation is more difficult than that of the latter. It comes from a lofty tree which might well be the *Pohon oepas* (poison tree) of Java. The *ratoes* or *ipot* on the contrary is a climbing plant which appears to be fairly common in the interior of the country." (ii. 355.)

will induce a man to part with a favourite sumpitan." (St. John ii. 89.) These two last-named people (if they are not identical with the Ukits) seem to have a wide range in Borneo, and hence they must probably be numerous. But as almost every writer mentions the sumpitan, the weapon must have a still wider range than the people who alone are said to produce it, hence we may yet expect to hear that there exist other tribes than these who are also manufacturers.

Effect of the Poison.

It may be that on the Koti river in Mr. Dalton's time an exceptionally virulent form of poison was in use by the Kayans as his report reads very deadly (p. 51): "The effects are almost immediately fatal. I have been in Selgie's boat when a man was struck in the hand; the poison ran so quickly up the arm, that by the time the elbow was green, the wrist was black; the man died in about four minutes; the smell from the hand was very offensive." Mr. Earl writes in a more moderate spirit (p. 265): " The arrows are steeped in the most subtle poison, which destroys birds and smaller animals, when struck with them, almost instantaneously, a slight wound from an arrow on which the poison is strong, being said to occasion inevitable death, even to man. The effects of weapons of this description are always exaggerated by those who use them; the poison, therefore, is not in all probability, so destructive to the human species as it is represented." Most travellers bear out Mr. Earl's general statement. Thus Mr. Horsburgh says "the arrows are dipped again into the poison immediately before using and are used in hunting as well as in war, and kill not only birds and squirrels, but also large animals such as orang-utans. To animals the poison proves fatal, because they cannot pull the arrow out of the wound; but men suffer little inconvenience from it, as their comrades can always extract the missile before the poison has been absorbed by the system. Squirrels and small animals drop a few minutes after they have been struck, but orang-utans frequently clamber about among the trees for a whole day before the poison takes such effect upon them as to bring them down." (p. 58.)

According to Sir Jas. Brooke (Mundy i. 262): " The poison is considered deadly by the Kyans, but the Malays do not agree in this belief. My own impression is, that the consequences resulting from a wound are greatly exaggerated, though if the poison be fresh, death may occasionally ensue; but decidedly, when it has been exposed for any time to the air it loses its virulence." [3]

Sir Chas. Brooke refers to the effects of the poison three times in the course of his expeditions. On the first occasion he writes: " Many men had been struck by sumpitan arrows which were most mortally poisonous." (i. 353.) These were Kanowit arrows. On the following page he continues: " Before one hut there lay a fine strapping fellow, having just breathed his last. I waited to look at the body, as he seemed only to sleep. He had been struck in the chest by an arrow, which left no more mark than the probe of a

---

[3] The first poisons from Malay Peninsula experimented with by Prof. Sydney Ringer, F.R.S. gave negative results. (Kew Bulletin, No. 50, p. 26.)

pin. After receiving the wound, he dosed off to wake no more, and died half-an-hour after he was struck."

Finally, when fighting the Kyans, he writes : "Some had been wounded by poisonous arrows, but the only effect was feverishness." (ii. 297.) But he appears to have given details of the effects of this Kanowit poison to Sir Sp. St. John, who writes as follows: "In 1859, the Kanowit tribe, instigated by Sherif Musahor, murdered two English gentlemen, and then fled into the interior. Mr. Johnson [now Sir Chas. Brooke] who led the attack on them, tells me he lost thirty men by wounds from the poisoned arrows. He found the bodies of Dayaks who had gone out as skirmishers without a mark, beyond the simple puncture where a drop of blood rested on the wound." (i. 45.)

Of the effect of the poison on an animal we have an eye-witness in Mr. Motley, who, having in his possession an ant eater (*manis javanica*), but being without its necessary food, "he determined to destroy it for a specimen, and he accordingly got a native to administer to it one of his little poisoned darts, from the sumpitan or blow-pipe; the dart, which had apparently been dipped in some black juice, entered the skin of the belly about a quarter of an inch, and in a quarter of an hour the creature was dead. It died very quietly, having gradually ceased to move about, and then lay for three or four minutes in a state of torpor; after which, death came on with a very slight tremor, passing of the fœces, and protrusion of the tongue. On dissection, the aorta and the large artery leading to the strong muscular tail were gorged with dark venous blood, as was also the left ventricle; there was no arterial blood to be seen anywhere, and, indeed, very little in any other part of the body, except in the air-cells of the lungs, where a number of vessels were ruptured; all the vessels of the head and brain, in particular, were perfectly empty and collapsed; the diaphragm was most strangely contracted and corrugated." (Motley and Dillwyn, p. 52.)

In the Kew Bulletins, Nos. 50, 58-59, 102-103; Feb., 1891, Oct.-Nov., 1891, and June-July, 1895, there are described the experiments made with poison from the Malay Peninsula, but the following account, which I have translated from the German, I give here, as the experiments were made with poison obtained from Borneo.

THE ARROW-POISONS OF BORNEO.

By Dr. L. Lewin (Pharmacological Private Laboratory, in Berlin.)

Virchow's Archiv., für Pathol. Anat., 1894, pp. 317-325.

According to an eye-witness, the outer bark of the stem is removed, and the rest rasped and pressed, and the juice boiled down in iron saucers to the consistency of an extract. The upper layer of this extract is the more powerful poison, and is kept by the makers for their own use; the lower layer, which is weaker, is sold. Before being covered the arrows are wetted with water in which *akar tuba* has been soaked, and are then dried for half-an-hour in the sun. . . Cuts are made in the siren tree, which then exudes sap, which at first is not poisonous, but which is said to become so when allowed to lie until it has turned black. After being allowed to lie for a few days, it is mixed with the sap of *akar tuba* on a stone or board. It is then mixed with the ash or charcoal of *poetjoe semamboe, kaijes sitik, kaijies tjaboet, moeho, kaijes sikap, rottan boeloe, koelit kapoijan* and *koelit doeko*. Before being used it is said to be mixed again with the juice of *aker tuba*. Different substances are afterwards added to the preparation; thus the sap of *moehon* or *moeho*, a water plant (*Mal. kladi*), is added to the siren sap, or the juice of the gadung (*dioscorea hirsuta*), used in Malacca, also the juice of the tuba root, and also tobacco water, and the mixture is boiled up ("gekocht.")[1]

Ipoh is considered to be a kind of strychnia, probably *Strychnos tieuté*, and *Siren* is considered to be *Antiaris toxicaria*, while *aker tuba*, as I have already stated several times, is *Derris elliptica*.

There is also stated to be a sort of a sub-species of *siren* poison called *Mantalat* poison, probably named after the kampong Mantalat, which is characterized by the addition of the wing covers of *Lytta gigantea*.

In Borneo it is difficult to get fair quantities of the poison Small bambu cylinders, 6 decimetres long by ½ decimetre outside diameter, cost 17 shillings; and much circumspection must be used, as on discovery of a purchase by the natives, the lives of both the purchaser and the salesman are put in danger.[2]

The few experiments made with Borneo arrow poison (most probably siren poison) on animals, resulted in disturbance of the respiration, and final death through heart failure.

I have received fair quantities of arrow poison. . . . .

I. Brought by Mr. Grabowski, originating from south-east Borneo, called *ipoh*, is a brown mass, partly crumbling and partly capable of being cut, mixed with sand. It is soluble in cold water with a yellow colour. The solution had a distinctly alkaline reaction. After acidifying it gave the following reactions: with potassium-ferri-cyanide a slight turbidity, and after a few hours a granular deposit; with phosphotungstic acid a white precipitate; with phosphomolybdic acid and picric acid a yellow precipitate; with platinum chloride it gave a crystalline precipitate, at first yellowish-white but afterwards became a reddish brown; with bi-chloride of mercury a white deposit; and with potassium sulphocyanide at first nothing, then a deposit of small crystalline needles.

The test for strychnine with bi-chromate of potassium and sulphuric acid gave at once the characteristic violet coloration. The experiment on animals had at first led to the supposition that we had here to deal with the presence of strychnine. Frogs, after an injection with a Pravaz syringe, of an aqueous solution of ·002 grammes of poison, showed, after 6-7 minutes, decided tetanus, which was preceded by increased reflex excitability. It became apparent that an extremity (limb), of which the blood supply was cut off, suffered also from convulsions, but that the limb did not do so if its nervous connection with the spinal cord was cut off. *Experiment* No. 5, 12 Dec., 1889. A solution of ·002 grammes of poison, dissolved in water, was injected into a pigeon subcutaneously. Two minutes after there was strong trembling with wing clapping. After three minutes it fell on its back, opened its beak, and a few tetanic convulsions followed. Every muscle trembled at the same time. At the end of five minutes the head was raised a little, then fell back and death supervened. The heart stood absolutely still in systole. *Experiment* No. 6, 12 Dec., 1889. A solution of ·005 grammes of

---

[1] From a communication by Mr. J. D. E. Schmeltz, of Leiden. [Dr. L.]
[2] Mayer. [Dr. L.]

the poison, dissolved in water, was injected under the skin of a rabbit; 4·30 injection; 4·43, sudden trembling of the whole body, in its attempts to get away accompanied by the well-known tetanic scratching of the paws on the table; 4·44, tetanus and the standing up of the animal; 4·45, it fell down, tetanic stretching out, opisthotonus; 4·47, a second attack after a short intermission; 4·48, third tetanic attack, death.

To obtain the active principle the weakly alkaline solution was shaken up with ether. After distilling off the ether light yellow coloured sharp pointed crystalline needles remained, which after several re-crystallisations out of alcohol became colourless. They gave the reaction for strychnine and had the following composition:

    a The elemental analysis ·1749 grammes dried at 100° C. gave ·04832 grammes CO_2 and ·1055 grammes H_2O.

    b ·1454 grammes at 748·5 mm. Bar. and at 20° C. gave 11·1 c. cm. N = 8·59%. N.

Found—	Calculated—
C 75·35%	C 75·45%
H 6·70%	H 6·58%
N 8·59%	N 8·38%

We have therefore to deal with strychnine which is present in the *ipoh* poison. We shall not err if we consider *strychnos tieuté* as the source of this poison, as in spite of many endeavours I did not succeed in discovering even a trace of *brucin* in the poison.

II. Dyak poison (*Siren*) received in 2 samples from the State Museum at Leiden.

The poison consists of thick, hard, dry, easily powdered pieces which form a grey black powder almost completely soluble in water. When hydrochloric acid is added it becomes turbid and the solution after long boiling with this acid shows the presence of a glucoside.

Experiments on animals showed a very decided virulence. With a subcutaneous injection rabbits died in 10-12 minutes with the following symptoms: restlessness, trembling, drooping of the head, then sudden tumbling over, dyspnœa and apnœa. The heart stood absolutely still. The character of a poison belonging to the digitalis group was still better brought out with frogs in which after subcutaneous injection the ventricle stops in systole.

The chemical examination of the poison was as follows: The poison was entirely extracted in a reflux condenser with hot 96% alcohol. On cooling of the alcohol a white mass separated out which after filtering and drying proved to be amorphous and free from ash. The alcohol was almost completely distilled off from the residue and the small quantity remaining driven off in the water bath. During this some more of the originally white but now yellowish mass separated out, besides which a resin-like substance made its appearance in small quantities, fluid [*sic*] yellow and viscous during the steaming off but hard as stone when cold, and lighter than the white mass; this substance dissolved more easily in chloroform and was therefore the more easily separated off. A solution in benzol gave a white precipitate with alcohol.

Of these white masses so obtained I purified the first precipitate several times in hot diluted alcohol. It proved to be free from nitrogen and not a glucoside. The melting point was 57 to 58° C. Dr. " Privatdocent " Bistrzycki was kind enough to analyse the body and to determine its formula : ·1790 grammes substance gave ·5358 grammes C O^2 and ·1988 grammes H^2 O hence :

Found—	Calculated—
C 81·64%	C 81·82%
H 12·34%	H 12·12%

The composition is similar to that which I found in the *antiaris* resin which I obtained from the Batak poison and more similar than the composition which De Vrij and Ludwig obtained from this resin (C 83·9%; H 11·9%).

TRUE UPAS TREE *(Siren)*, *Antiaris Toxicaria* Lesch.
Botanically it belongs to the Artocarpeæ, or bread-fruit order.
(After Rob. Brown : Plantæ Javanicæ Rariores, pl. 13).

I further tried to purify this resin :—1. by washing with boiling water, drying and dissolving in hot alcohol; 2. by treatment with chloroform and petroleum ether.
The elemental analyses of the substances obtained were :

a ·0971 grammes of substance gave ·2886 grammes CO^2 and ·0989 grammes H^{2}O.

b 0·265 grammes of substance gave ·7895 grammes CO^2 and ·2658 grammes H^{2}O.

Therefore :

Found—		Calculated to C^{18}H^{30}O.
I.	II.	
C 81·06	81·22	C 81·22
H 11·34	11·16	H 12·12

According to this the values have turned out somewhat lower, and with regard to the carbon quantities deviate still more from that of the above-mentioned investigators.

So much of this antiaris resin which had no action on animals, and which had not been used up in experiments on animals, was extracted for a long time with hot water in order eventually to obtain antiarin. The solution was dried up, and the deposited crystals purified as much as possible by pressure and recrystallisation out of the alcohol. The body possessed the character of a glucoside. The melting-point was ascertained to be 218-220°C, by Dr. Bistrzycki, who also carried out the elemental analysis. As regards the carbon the figures came out too high for antiarin, while as regards hydrogen they agreed approximately. The formula $C^{14} H^{20} O^5 + 2H^2O$ requires 7·89 % H, while 8·46 % H were found. In spite of the good agreement of melting-points (220·6° and 218° to 220° C), the substance was still contaminated with small quantities of the antiarin resin, rich in carbon, which I was unable to remove even by further washing of the substance. A second elemental analysis gave too high carbon figures.

Nevertheless, we have succeeded in determining the presence of antiarin, in a real Dyak arrow poison — *siren* poison. The experiments on animals also indicated this. In frogs it showed stopping of the ventricle in systole.

Experiment No. 114, 14 May, 1894. A small portion of the *antiarin* obtained was injected subcutaneously into a pigeon. Vomiting followed in eight minutes, and this was repeated more frequently, then followed dyspnœa, short spasms, and death in 11 minutes. The heart stopped beating. *Experiment* No. 115, 15 May, 1894. About ·005 grammes of antiarin was subcutaneously injected into a rabbit, at 11·5 a.m.; at 11·8 the head sank on to the table, at 11·11 clonic spasms, exophthalmos, and death. In order to determine whether any of the active principle of *derris elliptica* was present in the resinous portions, I did not omit to let it act several times on fishes, in the form of emulsion, without, however, witnessing any change in their condition of health.

FLOWERS AND LEAVES OF STRYCHNOS*(Ipoh)*, *Strychnos tieuté*.
Nat. order: Loganaceæ.
[Strychnia and Brucia are poisonous alkaloids affecting the spinal cord, &c.]
(Ex Blume: Rumphiæ, pl. 24).

III. Dyak arrow-poison, from south-east Borneo, from the State Museum, Leiden. (I. Aft. Ser. 901, Nos. 9 and 10.) I may treat the two preparations together, although they were sent to me as *siren* (No. 10) and *ipoh* (No. 9). They both contain the same active principle, namely, *strychnine*. The *Ipoh*, apparently very old, was in a bambu box, as a brown friable mass, while No. 10, the nominal *siren*, was wrapped in a palm leaf.

The preliminary toxicological determination on a frog and rabbit indicated strychnine reaction at once and it was besides easily determined chemically. But the pure preparation of the active principle was a more difficult matter than with the first mentioned preparation from the Berlin Museum.

I poured a little water over the large quantity at my disposal and this weak alkaline mass I shook up with ether. Chloroform proved itself unsuitable as it extracted more coloured constituents. After distilling off the ether the residue contained crystals embedded in a yellow mass which it was difficult to remove. Purification finally resulted only after repeated treatment with diluted 40% alcohol which dissolved the coloured matter but not the strychnine. *Brucin* should have gone over into the alcohol, but I looked for it there in vain.

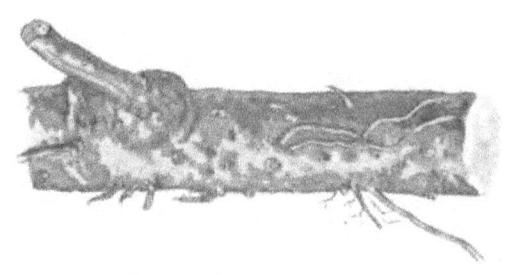

Strychnos tieuté FRUIT.
The poison is in the round thick-edged halfpenny-like seeds *(Nux vomica)* ; the outer covering of the orange-like fruit is eaten with impunity by birds and other animals.
(Ex Blume: Rumphiæ, pl. 24.)

ROOT OF TUBA *(Derris Elliptica)*.
(Ex Blume: Rumphiæ, pl. 24.)
"Porcupines *(Hystrix Crassispinis)*, like the rhinoceros, feed upon the poisonous tuba root, which is almost certain death to any of the other animals in the Bornean jungle."
(Hose, Mammalia, p. 60).

The elemental analysis of the substance claimed to be strychnine was as follows:

    a ·2468 grammes of the substance dried at 100° C. gave ·6788 grammes CO_2 and ·1490 grammes H_2O.

    b ·2357 grammes at 764 mm. Bar. and 19° C. gave 18·1 c. cm. N = 8·87% N.

It was therefore really *strychnine* we had to deal with.

IV. Dusun-Dyak arrow-poison from the State Museum Leiden (iii. Ser. 913, No. 6 and No. 8.)

Both preparations consisted of black pieces, their solutions produced the same symptoms in warm and cold blooded animals, that is the same symptoms as we have already reported as resulting from *antiarin*.

The isolation of the chemical component parts was obtained by the same methods as above described, the antiaris resin was extracted by 96°/₀ alcohol and the *antiarin* by extraction with hot water from the resinous mass. The products obtained agreed in their chemical behaviour with the antiaris resin and *antiarin*. The melting point of the latter is 219° C.

On this opportunity by my several experiments on fishes I endeavoured to ascertain whether *derrid* was present in these poisons, but I only obtained negative results."

THE TUBA PLANT *(Derris Elliptica)*.
A climbing leguminous plant.
(After Nath. Wallish: Plantæ Asiaticæ rariores, pl. 237).

ANTIDOTES.

Although according to Mr. Earl "the Dyaks assert that no antidote is known, yet the preparation of the poison being similar to that practiced by the aboriginal inhabitants of Celebes, for which a remedy has been discovered, the people of Borneo are probably acquainted with it." (p. 265.) When Sir Jas. Brooke asked the Sakarran chief Lingi, whether many of his men were lost from wounds from the Kayan sumpits he was told, "No, we can cure them." "This is one more proof in favour of Mr. Crawfurd's opinion that this poison is not sufficiently virulent to destroy life when the arrow is (as it mostly is) plucked instantly from the wound." (ii. 126.) A servant who was struck by a poison arrow had sulphuric acid and caustic applied and the man recovered, and on another occasion when several men were hit the wounds were sucked by a messmate and no harm resulted. (Mundy ii. 262, 226.) His Highness Sir Chas. Brooke told Sir Spencer St. John that during the Kanowit troubles in 1859, "One man was struck near him; he instantly had the arrow extracted, the wound sucked, a glass of brandy administered, and the patient sent off to the boats about four miles distant. Two companions supported him, and they had strict orders not to allow him to sleep till he reached the landing-place: they made him keep awake, and he recovered." (i. 45.)

Mr. Witti states, but he does not say it is from his own knowledge, at Peluan: "Liquid ammonia, applied externally after free bleeding of the wound and internally at the same time, is a pretty sure antidote. Each of our men carries a vial of that drug tied round his neck. The natives themselves, strange to say, have no such specific, and, consequently, many of them succumb to both dart poison and snake bites. Some Pagalan Dyaks used to cut out the part hit and apply *Ingo*, the Chinese universal medicine. The fatal termination of blowpipe wounds is often aggravated by internal festering through the tips of the arrow breaking off after penetrating into, say, the abdomen. The arrow is purposely formed to facilitate this, and hereabouts does not end in a simple point as with our Dusuns." (Footnote, Diary, 25th March.)

According to Mr. Earl "the Dyaks shew no hesitation in eating animals which have been killed by their arrows, taking the precaution, however, of removing the flesh immediately adjacent to the wounded part. The poison, which is called *ippo* throughout the island, consists of the juice of a tree, and its mode of preparation appears to be perfectly similar to that practiced in Java, and other islands where it is employed." (p. 265.) And Mr. Dalton writes: "I have seen them eat of the flesh notwithstanding it was killed with a poisoned dart; in such cases they boil it before roasting, which they say, extracts the poison." (p. 51.)

OTHER POISONS.

On one occasion, when on the Sekyan river, below Sikong, Mr. Denison with the Dyak tribes was discussing Annum, the chief of the Sikongs and his supposed evil propensities, regarding all of which he expressed his disbelief, and rated them as fabrications. "The Orang Kaya replied that some Landak Dyaks once sold him what they said was poison. It was a powder, white in colour; and he laid it by for nearly a year, not knowing what to do with it. Having a violent quarrel with a Dyak enemy, who had threatened to kill him, he mixed some of the powder in his enemy's chalk, which he used with his siri, 'and do you know, tuan,' said this solemn savage to me, 'he was taken ill, and in four days he was dead.' It is but fair to add that the Orang Kaya at once threw away the poison; it was not Dyak *akat*, he said, to kill an enemy in this manner, besides, having a wife and children, he dreaded keeping it in his possession. This story was told so naturally and coolly, with such a grave and earnest countenance, that I do not hesitate to believe it." (ch. v., p. 48.)

The following is reported by Mr. F. R. O. Maxwell from the Sadong. A Mingrat Dyak, named Suel, poisoned the Pengara of Jenan, and nearly killed some other men. "After the Mingrats had eaten sirih with the Jenans, the Mingrats returned the civility, and gave sirih to the Jenans, with this difference, that, instead of pushing the bag over to the Jenans, as the latter had done to them, Suel made up quids from the bag at his side, and handed it to the Pengara first, and then one to each of the four men, and then immediately got up to go. They left by the opposite entrance to that by which they had arrived—Lanchang road, and no one knows where they went. They had not gone 50 yards when the Pengara, who was still sitting down, fell forward with his arms stretched out and his face on the mat; he then straightened himself up and fell back. He said, 'Suel has killed me, they have given me poison in the sirih,' and then he died. The other men, four in number, were then taken the same way, they fell down one after another and were very ill, and are still very ill. The Pengara turned blue in the body, his nails were yellow, and his eyes red, teeth clenched. The Pengara purged very much but was not sick, the other four men were sick as well (this probably saved them)." (S.G., 1894, p. 103.)

Mr. Crossland informs me he had a case among the Undups where a woman administered arsenic in food to another, having obtained the poison from the Malays. He also states that when his people came back unwell from up country, they invariably believe they have been poisoned by the up country people.

In August, 1874, Mr. Gueritz reported from Simanggang (Batang Lupar) a serious case of poison by which five persons nearly lost their lives. The guilty parties were two women (S.G., No. 85), but he gives no details.

In the S.G., 1894, p. 21, I notice the following in the Batang Lupar notes: "Several specimens of the *Kibang upah*, one of the supposed Bugau poison plants, are now flourishing in the fort garden. They are similar to the *kladi* but with red leaves and stalks. They do not seem to have any known use in this district. Another variety of the *kibang api* is much more red than these. These are, however, probably plants producing poison for the sumpitans."

"I may mention that the crime of poisoning is almost unknown on the north-west coast, but it is very generally believed the people of the interior of the Kapuas, a few days' walk from the Batang Lupar, are much given to the practice. Sherif Sahib, and many others who visited that country, died suddenly, and the Malays assert it was from poison; but of this I have no proof." (St. John i. 30.)

Referring to this statement, Mr. Burbidge remarks (p. 66) : " The nature of the poison used is not exactly known, but it is very generally supposed to be a peculiarly irritating fibre or spiculœ derived from some species of bamboo, the effect of which is to cause a chronic state of sickness and depression, followed by death. Whatever it may be, it is a mechanical rather than a chemical irritant."

Referring to the murder of a headman in 1886 Mr. F. O. Ricketts writes: " Orang Kaya Abai and his followers are what are known as main Muruts. . . . Abai has always been overbearing and defiant and consequently has been at enmity with most of the other inhabitants of the river, he also bears the character of being a poisoner, and it is said that many have met their death at his hand in that manner."

Eight years later the same Resident reports: " There is one tribe of Muruts which originally inhabited a small locality near the source of the Trusan, but few of them left; there are one or two houses in the lower river; these are known as the Main Muruts and bear a bad character, the others being afraid of them; they have the reputation of being adepts in the art of poisoning and one of their ways of administering it is in arrack in the following manner: it is the usual custom in Muruts' houses for the hosts to drink first, this they do, but in handing the arrack to the person they want to poison they slide the thumb into the liquor, the poison being secreted under the thumb nail; how far this is true it is impossible to say—most Muruts are under the impression that it is done. The poison acts slowly, as the victim it is said does not die for some days. Many believe that they can be poisoned at a distance by charms at the hands of this tribe and consequently keep aloof—even those who are on fairly good terms with them avoid having much to do with them. Personal experience has shown that there is something different about these people, who seem reserved and indisposed to become friendly." (S.G., No. 347, p. 214.)

TOOLS USED IN THE PREPARATION OF IPOH POISON IN THE MALAY PENINSULA.

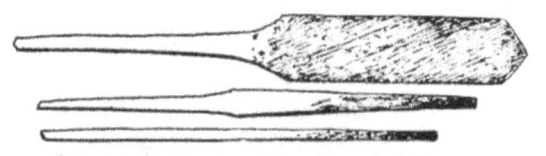

SPATULAS PARTIALLY COVERED WITH *Ipoh* POISON.

The smallest is used to spread the poison on to the arrow tip, and the next size to ladle the sap from the bambu trough and spread it on the largest spatulas. Batang Padang.
(L. Wray, Kew Mus.)

BAMBU FOR COLLECTING *Ipoh* SAP.
The piece of wood is to convey the sap into the bambu.   Batang Padang.
(L. Wray, Kew Mus.)

BAMBU TROUGH
in which the *ipoh* sap is dried by the Sakais.   Batang Padang.
(L. Wray, Kew Mus.)

BAMBU FOR HOLDING *Ipoh Aker* POISON
(Strychnos).
Near S. Maingayi, Batang Padang.
(L. Wray, Kew Mus.)

PROTECTING SHEATH FOR ARROWS.
HOLLOW BAMBU RECEPTACLE FOR POISON.
From Perak.
(Sir H. Low, Kew Mus.)

BAMBU FOR HOLDING *Lampong* POISON
(Strychnos).
Maingayi, Batang Padang.
(L. Wray, Kew Mus.)

CHAPTER XXIII.

PEACE, SLAVES AND CAPTIVES, HUMAN SACRIFICES, CANNIBALISM.

PEACE. Feasting—Symbol of good understanding—Heads, Dr. and Cr.—Peace through a third party—Banting and Sakaran—Peace ceremonies—Fated pigs—A sturdy chief—Meeting of enemies—Slaves sacrificed—Swearing over water—Salt-eating—Fowl-waving—Exchange of knives. BLOOD-BROTHERHOODS: Other brotherhoods.

SLAVES AND CAPTIVES. Slave-debtors—Enemies' children adopted—Sea Dyaks kind masters—Sales of relatives—Ransoms—Gifts of freedom—Kayans brutal masters—Murut slaves—No Dusun slaves. SYSTEM OF INDOOR AND OUTDOOR SLAVES: Origin—Descent—Curious succession—Marriage of slaves—Their work—Slave's property—Inheritance—Freedom—Introducing slaves—Support of slaves—Debts of slaves—Fire makes slaves. SLAVERY IN NORTH BORNEO: Two classes—Marriage—Easy life—No slave gangs—Punishments—Maltreatment—*Brian*—Adoption—Debts—Private work—Infidel slaves—Work for wages degrading.

HUMAN SACRIFICES. Peace-making sacrifices—Malanau sacrifices at house-buildings—Torture—Heart-augury—Kayan house-building victims—Kayan sacrifices for prosperity—Murut women not present—Purchases for sacrifices.

CANNIBALISM. Originally widespread—"To get brave"—Reported Land Dyak cannibals—Circumstantial evidence—A German missionary—The Abbé Langenhoff—Kayans not cannibals—Mr. Bock's statements concerning the Trings—Mr. Bampfylde's rejoinder—Mr. Brooke Low's reply—Malay charge against the Dusun.

PEACE.

AMONG the Land Dyaks: "When peace is made between them, one tribe visits the other, in order to feast together; and on these occasions, whatever the number of visitors may be, they are at liberty to use the fruits of their hosts without hindrance. At their pleasure they strip the cocoanuts off the trees, and devour, and carry away as much as they can, without offence. Of course the hosts in turn become visitors, and pay in the same coin. All the Dyaks are remarkably tenacious of their fruit trees; but on the occasion of the feast, beside taking the fruit, the visitors fell one tree, as a symbol of good understanding: of course it is only once that such liberties are taken or allowed; at other times it would be an affront sufficient to occasion a war." (Sir Jas. Brooke, Mundy i. 210.) This custom existed among the Sadong people, the Engkrohs and Engrats, but Sir Chas. Brooke put a stop to it. (i. 367.)

Among the Sea Dyaks peace is brought about by balancing the head accounts[1] and paying the difference in goods to the other tribe. "In this computation the value of males is estimated at about twenty-five dollars, £5 4s. 2d., and females from fifteen to twenty dollars each; when the

---

[1] See *supra* ii. 98: the Peluan feud.

difference is thus adjusted the two contracting tribes feast and dance together, and are friends until some new occasion of quarrel happens, and disturbs their amity." (Low, p. 213.) "When one party is weaker, or less active, or less warlike than the other, they solicit a peace through some tribe friendly to both, and pay for the lives they have taken: the price is about two gongs, value 33½ reals, for each life: thus peace is concluded. This is the custom with these Dyaks universally; but it is otherwise with the Sarebus and Sakarran. But Sarebus and Sakarran are not fair examples of Dyak life, as they are pirates as well as head-hunters." (Sir Jas. Brooke, Keppel i. 302.)

On the expedition against Pa Dendang in the Sakaran district, "the meeting of the Banting and Sakarang, who had been on terms of deadly feud for generations past, was far from amicable: the former, to whom I was then attached, denying the Sakarangs to have a single virtuous quality. They were cowardly traitors—crafty, false, and never to be trusted. The Bantings drew their boats quietly under the banks of the river, or advanced at a distance, when the Sakarang party were being noticed." (Brooke i. 111.) Sir Charles Brooke's "arrival at Sakarang had the effect of bringing the Lingga and Sakarang Dyaks together; but there was anything but love existing between them, and when apart, they abused each other most spitefully." (*ibid*, i. 137.) In these and many other cases it was the present Rajah's mere presence that kept the peace. One of his many triumphs was the establishment of peace between the Undups (?) and the Kantu Dyaks of the Kapuas river in Dutch Borneo. He says: "An assembly of about three hundred people was present. Sheds had been run up, and people had been waiting on the ground for days. At length, when all were assembled, the spokesman of each division made an oration, and the settlement was finally concluded. The first to draw a sword upon another on any future day, was to pay the established fine of eight jars. This was agreed to by all parties, and then two pigs were killed, the blood sprinkled about, and some was even taken home to touch the house, to wash away any evil tendencies there might be hanging in the atmosphere, and to appease the spirits. After this ceremony, they all mixed in the same circle, and told their different relationships, handed down through many generations, and over a large extent of country, on which were situated their many farming lands and fruit trees, some of them long since abandoned. This is the common practice of Dyaks, and their eyes sparkle with delight on finding a new Scotch cousin, several times removed, although they may have been at feud for years, and only an hour before would have gladly carried each other's head in a bag." (*ibid*, ii. 79.)

The peace made by the late Rajah Muda between the Balaus and Sakarans is described by Sir Spencer St. John: "After orations on both sides, for they all appear to have a natural gift of uttering their sentiments freely without the slightest hesitation, the ceremony of killing a pig for each tribe followed; it is thought more fortunate if the animal be severed in two by one stroke of the parang, half sword, half chopper. Unluckily, the Balau champion struck inartistically, and but reached half through the animal. The Sakarangs carefully selected a parang of approved sharpness, a superior one belonging to Mr. Crookshank, and choosing a Malay skilled in the use of weapons placed the half-grown pig before him. The whole assembly watched him with the greatest interest, and when he not only cut the pig through, but buried the weapon to the hilt in the mud, a slight shout of derision arose among the Sakarangs at the superior prowess of their champion. The Balaus, however, took it in good part and joined in the noise, till about two thousand men were yelling together with all the power of their lungs. The sacred jar, the spear, and flag were now presented to each tribe, and the assembly, no longer divided, mixed freely together." (i. 26.)

Whether Bishop McDougall is referring to this special peace making is not clear, but he says: "One of the fellows at a stroke cut the animal right across, but on one of the parts left a little bit of skin. This, it was disputed, would break the treaty, and the parties would have fought then and there but for the strongest persuasion; which fortunately prevailed." (T.E.S. ii. 30.)

Among Kanowits when peace was made, " a pig was placed between the representatives of two tribes, who, after calling down the vengeance of the spirits on those who broke the treaty, plunged their spears into the animal, and then exchanged weapons. Drawing their krises, they each bit the blade of the other's, and so completed the affair. The sturdy chief of Kajulo declared he considered his word as more binding than any such ceremony." (St. John i. 45.) " It is a very curious custom also, that if two men who have been at deadly feud, meet in a house, they refuse to cast their eyes upon each other till a fowl has been killed and the blood sprinkled over them." (*ibid*, i. 65.) Sir J. Brooke relates at Simpoke "that enemies can neither eat nor drink in company, without desiring a reconciliation." (Keppel i. 309.)

" The following are the customs observed on the conclusion of peace between two hostile tribes. Each provides a slave to be murdered by the other, and the principal person present gives the first wound, which is inflicted on the lower part and in the centre of the breast bone. The other persons of the tribe who may be present immediately follow the example, and fathers encourage their children to mutilate the body with their knives or whatever weapon they can acquire. The slaves sacrificed to peace are not criminals, but generally purchased for this purpose.[1] Besides this, presents are interchanged: these are provisions, gold dust to the value of a few rupees, and Siamese earthen jars, which are highly valued, as the priests use them as oracles, striking them and predicting according to the sound which may be elicited. Peace is generally concluded at the chief village or town of the most powerful tribe. It was thus that a feud which had existed for 5 years between the Sintang and Sakadayo Daya was terminated in 1826, since when they have been on amicable terms." (Dalton, p. 9.)

Something similar used to occur on the Trusan, among the Muruts. " One party claimed a *bangun* of two slaves, one old jar, one kabok, and three tetawaks, to stop a blood feud; and the lives taken were even, and according to Murut custom, the party last killing is required to pay a slave and a gong as a preliminary to making peace. It is usual with Muruts to kill the slave

[1] See *supra* ii. 163 and *infra* ii. 216.

when received as part of a *bangun*. (O. F. Ricketts, S.G., No. 242, p. 46.) The same resident writes later : " Occasionally feuds have been settled between two tribes, the aggressors having made full compensation in payment of jars, brassware, and two slaves ; it was the custom to kill one of these slaves to make up for the relative lost ; on these occasions the same festivities as previously described would take place, as also when reprisals had been made, although no one had been killed, but in the latter case they would be on a much smaller scale, and the clay alligator or snake would be absent ; these are only present when a head has been taken.

" A feud is not actually settled until peace has been made by swearing an oath, which with Muruts is binding. The ceremony is undertaken by the chiefs of the two tribes, and is generally conducted over a stream, there being suspended, above the log they stand on, a bamboo filled with hair charms and tiger-cat's teeth, the latter are set great store by and must be used ; then each chief, as he goes through his oath, holds on to the bamboo. There is, however, one more test, after which the two parties feel themselves perfectly secure against any renewal of hostilities from each other, and that is when they have eaten each other's salt ; it is the place of the aggrieved side to ask the other's first, and this is not done usually until they have shifted their houses three times ; this may mean 4 or 5 years, as they do not move oftener than once a year and sometimes once in two." (S.G. No. 328, p. 18.)

The custom of waving fowls over the heads of guests, as has been referred in the description of the festivals, " is supposed to conduce to good and friendly feeling, and to prevent either party from quarrelling and fighting." (Brooke i. 111.)

At Muka, a feud during which three lives had been lost on both sides, was arranged by a promise to exchange knives. . . . Boling and Tama Nideng [the two principals] put an end to their feud. Boling stroked the breast of each Penan present with a naked parang, repeating some formula in the Penan language ; he then presented Tama Nideng with the sword. The latter then performed the same rite on Boling with a spear, and afterwards presented him with it." (De Crespigny, S.G. No. 188, pp. 42, 44.)

The curious custom of making brothers was first described by Mr. Dalton. " Selgie requested I would make *sobat* with him ; on my gladly consenting, he went in person and stuck a spear into the ground above his father's grave. This being the signal for a general assembly, each of the chiefs sent a person to know the Rajah's pleasure ; it was that every warrior should assemble around the grave by twelve o'clock the next day. Some thousands were present ; a platform of bamboo was raised about twelve feet above the grave, and on this Selgie and I mounted, accompanied by an Agi, his high priest. After some previous ceremony, the Agi produced a small silver cup, which might hold about two wine glasses, and then with a piece of bamboo made very sharp, drew blood from the Rajah's right arm : the blood ran into the cup until it was nearly full ; he then produced another cup, of a similar size, and made an incision in my arm, a little above the elbow, and filled it with blood. The two cups were then held up to the view of the surrounding people, who greeted them with loud cheers.[8] The Agi now presented me with the cup of Selgie's blood, giving him the other one with mine; upon a signal, we drank off the contents amidst the deafening noise of the warriors and others. The Agi then half-filled one of the cups again from Selgie's arm, and with my blood made it a bumper; this was stirred up with a piece of bamboo and given to Selgie, who drank about half; he then presented the cup to me, when I finished it. The noise was tremendous; thus the great Rajah Selgie and I became brothers. After this ceremony I was perfectly safe, and from that moment felt myself so during my stay amongst his people. Drinking the blood, however, made me ill for two days, as I could not throw it off my stomach. The Rajah took his share with great gusto, as this is considered one of the greatest ceremonies, particularly on this occasion, between the great Rajah and the first European who had been seen in his country. Great festivities followed, and abundance of heads were brought in, for nothing can be done without them. Three days and nights all ranks of people danced round these heads, after being, as usual, smoked and the brains taken out, drinking a kind of toddy which soon intoxicates them; they are then taken care of by the women who do not drink, at least, I never observed them." (Dalton, p. 52.)

"The following was observed on my initiation into the brotherhood with Lasa Kulan, the chief of Balaga on the Rajang, and of Tubow on the Bintulu river. Two days previous to that on which the bloody affair came off, the great hall of the chief was garnished with the weapons and gaudy skin war dresses of the men, and dashed with a fair sprinkling of the finery of the women kept more for show than use. On the day appointed, a number of the neighbouring chiefs having arrived, several of them commenced proceedings by haranguing on the greatness and power of their own selves, and of all the wonders they had heard of the white people, and of their satisfaction in being visited by one of them, of whom their fathers had heard so much but had never seen. Next a large pig, provided for the occasion, was killed, the throat cutting part of the business being performed by one of the fair sex, seemingly with great satisfaction to the attendant crowd of men. Next were brought three jars full of arrack of three sorts, severally made from rice, sugar-cane, and the fruit tampui. In pieces of bambu it was dealt out in profusion to all present, the ladies excepted. On the chief taking a bambu filled with arrack, we repaired to the balcony in front of the house, and stood side by side with our faces towards the river. The chief then announced his intention of becoming the friend or brother of a son of the white man; on which one of the attending chiefs gave me a small sharp-pointed piece of bambu, with which I made a slight incision in the right fore-arm of the chief, and the blood drawn was put on a leaf. The chief then, with a similar instrument, drew blood from my left fore-arm, which was put on the same leaf and mingled with the other. The blood was then mixed with tobacco and made up into a large cigar which we puffed alternately until it was finished, when my new friend delivered himself of a long and eloquent speech, invoking their god Tŭnangan,

[3] Two wine glasses full would mean about 8 oz. of blood. In the days of cupping about 10-16 oz. used to be the limit.

the sun, moon, and stars, and rivers, the woods and mountains to witness his sincerity. Three times during this declamation he sprinkled the arrack on the ground towards the river. My speech being delivered, several of the principal chiefs present held forth both long and loud enough. We afterwards returned to the hall, and the cheering beverage went round more merrily than before, calling forth their good nature and social disposition. Although no toasts were given, still each successive bumper was accompanied by a merry and noisy chorus. The feast came afterwards, and the whole affair was wound up by music and dancing which lasted until about midnight." (R. Burns, pp. 146-7. Mr. Hose says of this ceremony, "the smoke is inhaled into the lungs in some cases, to show the sincerity of the bond." (J.A.I., xxiii. 166.)

Sir Chas. Brooke refers to the custom, and adds: ". . . . After this matter is consummated, the stranger is designated 'Nian,' or friend; but it is not desirable to attempt such experiments, as they require a number of presents, and unless one has some ulterior object, it is needless, as no one could ever trust a Kayan's faith or word. They are false in the extreme, neither proving true friends nor steady enemies, and always committing some acts of treachery upon a weaker tribe. Their names have been extolled preposterously." (ii. 224.)

Sir Sp. St. John was made blood brother of Siñgauding, a Kayan chief. The ceremony is called *berbiang*. The ceremony seemed to be similar to that Mr. Burns underwent, but instead of a sharp piece of bambu being used for the blood-letting, there was used "a small piece of wood, shaped like a knife-blade, and slightly piercing the skin, brought blood to the surface." Among the Kiniahs "a pig is brought and placed between the two who are to be joined in brotherhood. A chief offers an invocation to the gods, and marks with a lighted brand the pig's shoulder. The beast is then killed, and after an exchange of jackets, a sword is thrust into the wound, and the two are marked with the blood of the pig. . . . . As the Kayans believed some misfortune would happen to us if I went anywhere but straight on board the ship, or if Siñgauding left his house during the day, I remained quiet, and talked over affairs with the Malays." (i. 107, 110.)

The brotherhoods mentioned by Mr. Frank Hatton are very different, and more like the welcome ceremony described above by Sir Chas. Brooke. "At about 12 o'clock the Dusuns commenced arriving, boat load after boat load, until some hundred men had collected, all armed with spears and swords. The chief now came up, and we at once proceeded with the ceremony. First the chief cut two long sticks, and then sitting down, he had a space of ground cleared before him, and began a discourse. When he came to any special point in his discourse he thrust a stick into the ground and cut it off at a height of half-a-foot from the earth, leaving the piece sticking in.[4] This went on until he had made two little armies of sticks, half-a-foot high, with a stick in the middle of each army much higher than the rest, and representing the two leaders. These two armies were himself and his followers, and myself and my men. Having called in a loud voice to his god, or Kinarringan, to be

[4] See *supra* i. 77, efforts of memory, and i. 356, sticking fowls' tail feathers in the ground.

present, he and I took hold of the head and legs of the fowl, while a third person cut its head off with a knife. We then dropped our respective parts, and the movements of the dying fowl were watched. If it jumps towards the chief his heart is not true, if towards the person to be sworn in his heart is not true; it must, to be satisfactory, go in some other direction. Luckily, in my case, the fowl hopped away into the jungle and died. All my men fired three volleys at the request of the chief, and I gave some little presents all round, and sent the people away pleased and delighted. . . . The Dusun headman, Degadong, was very kind. He presented me with a spear, and I gave him a long knife. This exchange of weapons is customary after the fowl ceremony." (Diary, 27, 28 March.) " To-day I was initiated into the brotherhood of the Bendowen Dusuns. The old men and all the tribe having assembled, the ceremonies began. First the jungle was cleared for about twenty yards, and then a hole dug about a foot deep, in which was placed a large water-jar. In this country these jars are of enormous value: $30, $40, and even $100 worth of gutta being given for a single jar. The bottom of the jar in question was knocked out, so as to render it useless in future. The clay taken out to make the hole was thrown into the jar, and now the old men commenced declaiming, 'Oh, Kinarringan, hear us!'—a loud shout to Kinarringan. The sound echoed away down the valleys, and as it died a stone was placed near the jar. Then, for half-an-hour, the old man declared that by fire (which was represented by a burning stick), by water (which was brought in a bamboo and poured into the jar), and earth, that they would be true to all white men. A sumpitan was then fetched, and an arrow shot into the air to summon Kinarringan. We now placed our four guns, which were all the arms my party of eight mustered, on the mouth of the jar, and each put a hand in and took a little clay out and put it away. Finally several volleys were shot over the place and the ceremony terminated." (Diary, 4th April.) Two days later on he had to submit to a similar ceremony. On the banks of the Lilompatie, " No water-jars were buried, but three stones were placed in a triangular fashion, and two fowls were slaughtered. The spot selected was close to the woodland path; this is an important point. We fired three volleys, and I held the feet of the two fowls, whose bodies were allowed to rot." (Diary, 8th April.)

Mr. Whitehead also mentions the ceremony. "The Melangkaps are anxious to make brothers of our party, and are going to sacrifice a cow to celebrate this occasion. Their object in doing this is to make us, by accepting their gifts of food and returning other like presents, vow always to be friendly with the tribe, and in our absence never to do them any harm. Strange as it may seem, the aborigines of Borneo believe that people have power over each other though separated by many miles." (p. 123.)

"The Ida'an are very strict keepers of their oath, which they take by pronouncing in their language some execrations against perfidy, and then cut a rattan: you do the like in yours; the friendship is then cemented with all the district with whose oranky this oath was exchanged. They then consider you as a brother, and also everybody related to you; if anyone knows of such an engagement, and pretends to be a relation of the person they will take his word for it, and behave to him in the same manner as if they were under an oath to himself." (Dalrymple, p. 43.)

SLAVES AND CAPTIVES.

Among the Land Dyaks "though slavery, in its degrading form of trading in the liberties of our fellow creatures, is not practised by them, the system of slave-debtors is carried on, though to a very small extent. In scarce seasons, poor families are compelled to borrow of the rich, and it sometimes happens, that being unable to repay the debt, they live in the houses of their creditors, and work on their farms. They are just as happy, however, in this state, as if perfectly free, enjoying all the liberty of their masters, who never think of ill-using them." (Low, p. 301.)

" The slaves of the Sea-Dyaks do not in general appear to be hardly treated, as in their wars only such as are young are taken captive; these, after living with their captors for some years, lose the remembrance of their families, or, perhaps, only recollect that they were destroyed, and consequently fall into the customs and practices of the people amongst whom they live, and from whose power they soon lose all hope of deliverance. In many instances children, who have been taken from the Land-Dyaks, become so endeared to their conquerors, that these latter adopt them as their own, and they are then admitted to all the privileges of the free-born of the tribe, and inter-marry with the sons and daughters of the other inhabitants of the village. Instances are not uncommon when children thus treated have forgotten their parents, and expressed, when the opportunity of returning to their tribe has presented itself to them, an unwillingness to avail themselves of it, thus causing to the parents who had so tenderly cherished the remembrance of them, infinite agony; but, when they have once arrived at their native village, and experienced all the kindness of parental affection, these impressions soon wear away, and they are always finally glad that they had been restored. In the villages the slaves are not distinguishable from their masters and mistresses, as they live all together, and fare precisely the same, eating from the same dish, and of the same food." (*ibid*, p. 200.)

Sir Spencer St. John says "though it is contrary to ancient custom for the Sea Dyaks to keep slaves they have the habit of keeping a few slaves, and are generally kind masters; but the system has been a very bad one, as many unfortunate people have become so in consequence of the debts or the crimes of their parents or grand-parents. It is scarcely right to give the name of slaves to these people, as on the payment of the original debt or fine they become free." (i. 72.) Sir Chas. Brooke refers to "the sale of relations and even of children, though not common among some of the less settled Milanau tribes, when pressed for food " (i. 75); much as the Muruts used to do to the nobles of Brunei (St. John ii. 30), but such sales cannot be regarded as customs.

"The Sea Dyak captives are generally ransomed after peace has been concluded between the tribes, and instead of exchanging prisoners according to civilised modes, they exchange captives for jars, each of which is supposed to represent the value of a man's life." (Brooke i. 245.)

" The Sea Dyaks too often spare neither man nor woman nor child, but sometimes, when more humanely inclined, or when the opportunity offers, they carry the women and children away with them into captivity. But it is a remarkable fact that there are so few slaves, or persons of servile descent, among the Dyaks. Other tribes keep their slaves in a condition of perpetual servitude, but the Sea Dyaks allow their friends to ransom them, and if they still remain on their hands they adopt them into the tribe and enfranchise them. The ceremony is usually performed at a great feast, the owner announcing that he has freed so and so and adopted him as a brother, and he is presented by the chief with a spear, with which he is told to slay the man who dares hereafter call him a slave. They are not cruel to their captives, but humane." (Brooke Low.)

A writer on the Kayans in the S.G. (No. 130, p. 28) says: " The difference in appearance between the master and slave is so marked as to be noticeable by the most careless observer. The slave is but little removed from the animal either mentally or physically, while the master is a well-to-do looking warrior who rolls about and looks as if the earth is too small for him."

" The Muruts have slaves and will sell their children to pay their debts. They follow a fixed custom in not selling a slave to another person, unless with the slave's consent. Dusuns will not have slaves, nor will they sell their children, nor will they give up runaway slaves." (Denison Jour. Straits Asiatic Soc., No. 10, p. 185.)

Mr. Brooke Low has summarised the laws or rules relating to the position of the slave on the Rejang river as follows: "*Out*door slaves become so either by descent, by purchase, or by an amelioration of condition from having been *in*door slaves. *In*door slaves become so by purchase or descent. In cases where both parents have been *out*door slaves the *tabusan* (purchase or freedom money) is 40 reals (= \$28·80), or one picul of guns, unless the child is of tender years, when the tabusan is 80 catties (= \$21·60). In cases where one or both parents have been *in*door slaves, but have become *out*door slaves at marriage, the children are *out*door slaves.

" When one parent is an *in*door slave and the other an *out*door slave, the children are divided between the owners of the parents, the first child following the condition of the father, supposing there be more than one child, *e.g.*: the father is *in*door slave of A, and the mother is *out*door slave of B; a child is born and sex being immaterial to the question, it becomes half *in*door slave of A and half *out*door slave of B. The *tabusan* of an indoor slave having been fixed by the practice of the courts at 60 reals (= \$43·20), and that of an *out*door slave by descent at 40 reals, it will be clear that the *tabusan* on account of this first child to A is in this case 30 reals, and to B 20 reals, should the parents decide on purchasing the freedom of their child, subject, however, if very young to reductions as above. But when two children are born, the first becomes *in*door slave of A and the second *out*door slave of B, the *tabusan* to A being 60 reals or 1½ piculs, and that to B 40 reals or 1 picul.

" Where the parent is free on one side, and the other parent either an *in* or *out*door slave, the first child follows the fortunes of the father, the second that of the mother, and so on in succession, and this rule is unalterable. For example, a claim was lately made upon a boy, whose father was an *out*door slave, and whose mother was a free woman. The boy was third of a family of five and both parents were dead. The owner of the late father claimed this the third child, but the friends of the boy said that before the father died he had declared that the second child should be slave, and that the third child should be free, the second child being also dead. The court decided that the father had no right to alter the succession, and decided in favour of the plaintiff.[5] In cases where both parents are originally slaves, and after children are born one parent frees him or herself, the children born after the event follow the above rule.

" In cases where an *in*door slave, man or woman, has become an *out*door one upon marriage, and has sought his or her own living, the children, so far as he or she is concerned, become *out*door slaves, but he or she is still liable to pay his or her full *tabusan* to the master, no reduction being made unless the slave has become aged.

" The owners of *out*door slaves have a right to demand the services of one child to work as *in*door slave until marriage, when he or she quits the master's house and returns to his or her position as an *out*door slave; if a girl the master is on no account to receive *barian* (purchase-money)[6] from the husband, and if a boy the master must provide *barian*, or at least assist in the matter for the reason that the boy has hitherto worked for his master and has had no opportunity of acquiring property for himself. The above rule is seldom enforced by the owners. The owner of an *in*door slave, if the slave be a man, is expected to provide *barian* when the slave marries, and in such a case he becomes co-heir in the slave's property at death: if the slave be a woman, the owner receives the *barian*, and is still co-heir in case of death. In this case the husband generally prefers to pay the *tabusan* and to make his wife free. In no case whatever may an *out*door slave become an *in*door one except in the case of a child for a time as above.

" It having come to the notice of the courts that in certain cases masters exacted as much work from an *out*door slave as from an *in*door slave, and that in other cases *out*door slaves could not be induced to do any work at all, a rule was made by which *out*door slaves became liable to be called twice a year to work for their masters, twelve days on each occasion, failing which they would be subject to a month's hard labour on the roads. No *out*door slave is to be called upon to work out of his river's district.

" The property of slaves is now strictly protected, it having been found that masters sometimes helped themselves as a right to their slaves' property. In a case lately settled at Oya, a widow, *in*door slave of a *pangeran* (high Malay official), possessed three sago plantations, and complained that her master had felled six trees, he having no land of his own. The *pangeran*

---

[5] Among the Punans the law seems a little different, the sex being of consequence; thus there was the case of a freeman who had married an indoor slave and a son and daughter were born. The son is free, following the condition of the father, the daughter is bond, following the condition of the mother. (B.L.)

[6] This is rather the price for the virginity of a bride, and appears to be a Malay custom of late introduction.

pleaded that he only did what was customary; it was held, however, that he was wrong, and he was ordered to pay $9—the value of the trees and the costs of the suit.

"The master of an *in*door slave becomes as above-stated co-heir with the slave's other relations in case of death if he has provided *barian;* if not, his position on this point is as the master of an *out*door slave. The master of an *out*door slave may become co-heir only when the slave has no children. No master can refuse permission to his slave to free him or herself, or his or her children, whether *in*door or *out*door, nor can he refuse permission to a slave to seek a new master, but he can complain to the courts if he has reason to think anyone has endeavoured to entice away his slave, and the person, if found guilty, would be heavily fined.

If a master seduces a slave she at once becomes free. There was a case in court where it was found that a master and his slave girl had lived as husband and wife for many years, and he had had children by her. The man died and his relations brought a case against the woman and her children to exclude them from the succession to the property of the deceased; but judgment was given in favour of the defendants on the ground that, though no marriage ceremony had ever been performed, the man and woman had been recognised by all their relations as husband and wife during the lifetime of deceased.

"The fine for bringing a slave into the country from foreign parts and selling him or her is $100, and the slave is to become free. There was a case where a man brought a family slave into the country, whose *tabusan* was three piculs, and as no permission had been given to the man to bring him here the slave was allowed to seek another master who had to pay one picul only to the previous master. There was another case where a man was allowed to bring a family slave from Brunei, he having first asked permission, and the slave himself having been questioned by me at Brunei as to whether he liked to come here, and permission being obtained at the same time from the authorities at Brunei.

"Where it can be proved that a master has not supported an *in*door slave, nor called upon him or her to work for five years, the slave is entitled to become free. The court would, however, be very careful about giving judgment in the case of *out*door slaves, they being very nearly independent. On one occasion, one family brought a case into court against another and very numerous family, to compel the latter to pay the *tabusan* and become free, as the latter positively would not work when called upon, the defence being that they were already free, having been P. Dipa's slaves, who had been declared free. After a long investigation into their antecedents and genealogy, the case was given against the defendants, it having been found that since P. Dipa had left Maka none of the family had really worked for the plaintiffs, and that one of them had freed himself. An appeal was made to the then resident of the Third Division, but the previous judgment was confirmed, notwithstanding a letter from P. Dipa himself in favour of the defendants.

"When *in*door slaves contract debts, if such debts be trifling, amounting to only a few dollars, the masters are expected to pay; when the debt is considerable, should the master pay it, the amount is added to the *tabusan*, for which the slave is already responsible. Should the master be unable or unwilling to pay, the slave is assigned to work for him until the debt is paid off at the rate of $2·50 a month. Slave debtors are unknown. When a freeman becomes hopelessly in debt, he is either imprisoned or assigned to his creditor to work off the debt as above, the creditor providing food and clothing; or the terms of the assignment may be that he sail in his creditor's *prahu* (boat) during the whole season—$7·00 a voyage being allowed to and from Kuching, or $12·00 a voyage to and from Singapore. During the close season the debtor must work in his creditor's house, and have such reductions made off his debt as may be agreed upon by the court. It has happened in a few cases that a relation has paid a man's debt and the man has been assigned to work for his relation until the debt is cleared off; no monthly diminution being allowed, but even in this case the term slave-debtors has not been used." " Every transfer of slaves must be made before the court." (Brooke Low.)

"In the old days, according to the old Dyak laws, people who were careless enough to set a house on fire rendered themselves liable to become slaves to those who had been burnt out, and this may have gone on for two or three generations, so that the grandchildren were slaves by birth. On one occasion the son of an old woman, whilst smoke-drying some fish, fell asleep through weariness. The fire caught the thatch and spread rapidly through the long Dyak house, melting the people's guns and cracking jars. A neighbour told the woman what had occurred, and she, forgetful of the altered state of things, at once gathered her children and said to them " Death is better than slavery," paddled with them to the Dyak graveyard, where she ate and gave the children to eat *tuba* root, and only one child survived to tell the story." (Crossland.)

This account may be well supplemented by that of Mr. Witti, as published by Mr. Treacher: "The late Mr. Witti, one of the first officers of the Association, at my request, drew up, in 1881, an interesting report on the system of slavery, in force in the Tampassuk district, on the west coast, of which the following is a brief summary. Slaves in this district are divided into two classes—those who are slaves in a strict and rigorous sense, and those whose servitude is of a light description. The latter are known as *anak mas*, and are the children of a slave mother by a free man other than her master. If a female, she is the slave, or *anak mas*, of her mother's master, but cannot be sold by him; if a boy, he is practically free, cannot be sold, and if he does not care to stay with his master, can move about and earn his own living, not sharing his earnings with his master, as is the case in some other districts. In case of actual need, however, his master can call upon him for his services.

"If an *anak mas* girl marries a freeman, she at once becomes a free woman, but a *brihan*, or marriage gift, of from two to two and a half pikuls of brass gun—valued at $20 to $25 a pikul—is payable by the bridegroom to the master.

"If she marry a slave, she remains an *anak mas*, but such cases are very rare, and only take place when the husband is in a condition to pay a suitable *brihan* to the owner.

"If an ordinary slave woman becomes *enceinte* by her owner, she and her offspring are henceforth free, and she may remain as one of her late master's wives. But the jealousy of the inmates of the harem often causes abortion to be procured.

"The slaves, as a rule, have quite an easy time of it, living with and as their masters, sharing the food of the family, and being supplied with tobacco, betel-nut, and other native luxuries. There is no difference between them and free men in the matter of dress, and in the arms which they carry, and the mere fact that they are allowed to wear arms is pretty conclusive evidence of their not being bullied or oppressed.

"They assist in domestic duties and in the operations of harvest and trading and so forth, but there is no such institution as a slave-gang, working under task-masters, a picture which is generally present to the Englishman's mind when he hears of the existence of slavery. The slave-gang was an institution of the white slave-owner. Slave couples, provided they support themselves, are allowed to set up house and cultivate a patch of land.

"For such minor offences as laziness and attempting to escape, the master can punish his slaves with strokes of the rattan, but if an owner receives grave provocation and kills his slave, the matter will probably not be taken notice of by the elders of the village.

"An incorrigible slave is sometimes punished by being sold out of the district.

"If a slave is badly treated and insufficiently provided with food, his offence in endeavouring to escape is generally condoned by public opinion. If a slave is, without sufficient cause, maltreated by a freeman, his master can demand compensation from the aggressor. Slaves of one master can, with their owner's consent, marry, and no *brihan* is demanded, but if they belong to different masters, the woman's master is entitled to a *brihan* of one pikul, equal to $20 or $25. They continue to be the slaves of their respective masters, but are allowed to live together, and in case of a subsequent separation they return to the houses of their masters. Should a freeman, other than her master, wish to marry a slave, he practically buys her from her owner with a *brihan* of $60 or $75.

"Sometimes a favourite slave is raised to a position intermediate between that of an ordinary slave and an *anak mas*, and is regarded as a brother, or sister, father, mother, or child; but if he or she attempt to escape, a reversion to the condition of an ordinary slave is the result. Occasionally slaves are given their freedom in fulfilment of a vow to that effect made by the master in circumstances of extreme danger, experienced in company with the slave.

"A slave once declared free can never be claimed again by his former master.

"Debts contracted by a slave, either in his own name or in that of his master, are not recoverable.

"By their own extra work, after performing their service to their owners, slaves can acquire private property and even themselves purchase and own slaves.

" Infidel slaves, of both sexes, are compulsorily converted to Muhammadanism, and circumcized, and even though they should recover their freedom, they seldom relapse." (Treacher, Jour. Straits Asiatic Society, No. 21, p. 88.)

" Mr. W. B. Pryer, speaking for the East Coast, informed me that there were only a few slaves in the interior, mostly Sulus who had been kidnapped and sold up the rivers. Among the Sulus of the coast, the relation was rather that of follower and lord than of slave and master. When he first settled at Sandakan, he could not get men to work for him for wages, they deemed it *degrading* to do so, but they said they would work for him if he would *buy* them! Sulu, under Spanish influence, and Bulungan, in Dutch Borneo, were the chief slave markets, but the Spanish and Dutch are gradually suppressing this traffic. (*ibid*, p. 90.)

HUMAN SACRIFICES.

We have seen above that human sacrifices used to take place at the burials, peace makings of the different tribes, and that captives and slaves were killed for the sake of their heads. (See i. 157, 163, 204.)

" Human sacrifices were common among the Milanos previous to the cession of the country to Sir James Brooke. At Rejang village, a young virgin was buried alive under the main post of a house." (Denison, Jour. Straits Asiatic Soc., No. 10, p. 182.) They are described as a cruelly disposed people, and are in the habit of putting their enemies to death by horrible and barbarous tortures. (Brooke i. 74.)

Of these people it is more circumstantially " stated that at the erection of the largest house, a deep hole was dug to receive the first post, which was then suspended over it; a slave girl was placed in the excavation, and at a signal the lashings were cut, and the enormous timber descended, crushing the girl to death. It was a sacrifice to the spirits. I once saw a more quiet imitation of the same ceremony. The chief of the Quop Dayaks was about to erect a flag-staff near his house: the excavation was made, and the timber secured, but a chicken only was thrown in and crushed by the descending flag-staff." (St. John i. 35) The same writer says : " Not many years ago, Rentap, the pirate chief, who formerly resided in a stronghold on the summit of the Sadok mountain, took a Sakarang lad prisoner. Although one of his own race, he determined on putting him to death, remarking—' It has been our custom heretofore to examine the heart of a pig, but now we will examine a human one.' The unfortunate boy was dragged about for some time by the hair of his head, and then put to death and his heart examined." (Brooke i. 64.) According to His Highness, the Kayans used to treat their captives very badly. " On one occasion seven captives were tortured by slow degrees to death." (*ibid*, ii. 271.) " On another occasion eleven captives were divided out among Yonghang's followers, and were carried, on their way up the river, into every house, where they were received with delight, and tortured by the women. On arriving at Yonghang's abode, one of them named Boyong was singled out to be a victim in the sacrifice for Yonghang's son, who had lately departed this life. Boyong was to be buried alive under a Salong (a large wooden pillar) early the succeeding morning. Boyong, however, and one of the others, managed to effect their escape that night, ran into the jungle, and found their way, after twenty days' wandering, to the foot of the first rapids. . . . Boyong is now living, and shows the marks about his body where he was tortured by the Kayans. . . . The remaining men were all strangled by the Kayans." (*ibid*, ii. 272.)

"The Kayans strenuously deny the practice [of human sacrifice] at the present day, but it would seem to have been prevalent amongst them formerly, especially on the occasion of the King or principal chief taking possession of a newly-built house, and also on the occasion of his death. They acknowledge that an instance of this most revolting custom took place about two years ago [1847] on the occasion of the chief Batu Dian taking possession of his new house. The victim was a Malay slave girl brought from the coast for the avowed purpose, and sold to the chief by a man who was also a Malay. It is said to be contrary to the Kayan custom to sell or sacrifice one of their own nation. In the case alluded to the unfortunate victim was bled to death, the blood was taken and sprinkled on the pillars and under the house, but the body was thrown into the river." (Burns, Jour. Ind. Arch. iii. 145.)

Sir Chas. Brooke tells us: "It is a Kayan custom, named 'Jahum,' when captives are brought to any enemy's country, that one should suffer death, to bring prosperity and abolish the curse of the enemy in their lands. The deed is generally performed by women, who torture with sticks, &c." (ii. 304.)

"As for the presence of women at religious ceremonies, here at the swinging ceremonies they are always present, and also when feasts are held in honour of the padi spirits. So far as I had power of observing, women do not become spectators of human sacrifices, even though the victim be a woman. The Muruts never sacrifice one of their own people, but either capture an individual of a hostile tribe, or send to a friendly tribe to purchase a slave for the purpose. The Dusuns do not sacrifice human beings, even when they build their houses."[7] (Denison, Jour. Straits Asiatic Soc., No. 10, p. 184.)

Capt. Forrest, however, writing in 1780, says (p. 368): "In this north part of Borneo, is the high mountain of Keeneebaloo, near which, and upon

---

[7] Mr. Hupé writes the following (pp. 330-331 footnote) referring to the still (though secretly) practiced human offerings: "The missionary Huperts writing on 26 October, 1842 (see Barm. Missionsblatt, No. 7, 1848) about this, says: 'A clandestine sort of murder still exists here amongst the Dyaks [*sic*] in the interior, and still many sacrifices are offered to the devil, but secretly, and excepting the Dyaks hardly anyone knows anything about them. They still slaughter the fairly-aged slaves, whom they take into the interior without their knowing what is to come; they dig a deep hole, and place the poor man bound in it, when they chop off his head and hang up the skull in their huts. I have this information from the mouth of two Dyaks, especially from the mouth of a 35 year old Dyak who now works at the mission station here; his name is Andang and he fled to us, with which fact his master must need out of fear be satisfied, for the masters are much afraid especially as regards the Dutch Government when such shameful deeds become known. A widow slaughters one or more slaves in order that her husband should have servants in the spirit world. Only a short time ago a Dyak named Tondau killed twenty such slaves.'" See *supra*, ii. 163 and 204.

the skirts of it, live the people called Oran Idaan or Idahah, and sometimes Maroots. . . . An Idaan or Maroot must, for once at least in his life, have imbrued his hands in a fellow creature's blood; the rich are said to do it often, adorning their houses with sculls and teeth, to show how much they have honoured their author, and laboured to avert his chastisement. Several in low circumstances will club to buy a Bisayan Christian slave, or any one that is to be sold cheap; that all may partake the benefit of the execution."

CANNIBALISM.

As yet no European excepting Mr. Dalton appears to have actually *seen* any traces of cannibalism. Nevertheless there is plenty of circumstantial evidence that the custom must at one time have been fairly wide-spread in Borneo.

Of the Hill Dyaks in general Sir Hugh Low writes (p. 304): "So much have these people been maligned, when called cannibals, that if told such a race of people do exist, they cannot credit it, and do not believe such enormities possible." Mr. Denison states: "Among Dayak and Milano tribes, in many parts of the country, it is the practice still to cut up and consume the raw heart of "a brave," killed in battle, under the idea that the partakers will in time become braver. (Jour. Straits Asiatic Soc., No. 10, p. 182.) Later on he repeats: "I have never met with cannibals in Borneo, although I am sure, from all I have heard, that the practice of eating human beings has not long died out, and I think it very likely it may still exist in obscure and little-known places in the far interior." (*ibid*, p. 185.) In his earlier jottings he states: "I was assured by the Orang Kaya, that when he visited the Meribun and Tincang or Jincang Dyaks, he found them to be cannibals. These Dyaks live on the Batang Munkiyang, near Muntong and Muntu, not far from the head-waters of the Sadong river, near Senankan Kujan. The Sekyam is descended as far as Tanjong Prin, whence you ascend Sungei Meribun, where these monsters are to be met with. When in their village, the Orang Kaya himself saw them eating a body. The custom is to take only the heads of the enemies, but, when an individual of the tribe dies, the body is sold, and even women and children partake of the flesh. The man in question was not old, and his corpse was exchanged for a *tajow*, the Dyaks seeming to relish most the soles of the feet and palms of the hands. These Dyaks who are credited with making and using poisons, treated the Orang Kaya well while he was in their village; they are great cowards, and ten of these Dyaks will run from one of another tribe. The Malay, Abang, confirming this story, said that when he was collecting revenue at Muntang and Muntu, which belong to Sarawak, the party he was with were always on their guard against the Meribun and Tincang Dyaks, and at night erected fences studded with *ranjows*, as a protection against these brutes. Malays and others who frequented these Dyak villages were well received, and their presence was in fact sought after. Draham, my Malay cooly, said he had seen *with his own eyes*, palms of hands and soles of feet over the fire-place, when he was in one of their villages. I have made some enquiries into the truth of the above statement, and I am assured, by the Resident of Sadong, that they are untrue. 'Whatever may have been the propensities of these Dyaks,' says he, 'there is no foundation in the report that they now indulge in this inhuman practice.' Abang Pandak, *pembakal* of the Sultan of Sangouw, told me, when I met him in Sarawak, that the story was a fabrication, but his denial carried no conviction, as it appeared made from motives of contradiction, and in defence of the Raj under which he served; he confessed to having heard the stories, but had never visited the Dyaks in question. I have since learnt from Mr. Crocker, the President of Sarawak, that when he was on a journey from the head-waters of the Sadong, to Silanteh, he put up one night at a Dyak house. Entering into conversation with the inmates, he discovered an old Malau Dyak from the Kapuas district. This man, called Jamon, who had led a roving life, told him that the Mualangs, of Jincang, who inhabit the head-waters of the Kapuas river, in the vicinity of the Sekyam, are or were cannibals. Jamon went on a head hunting expedition against these Jincangs, and killed four of them, losing two of his friends. The Jincangs ate his friends, leaving only their entrails. These Dyaks have not only given up this practice, but are so ashamed of it, that the mere mention of the former custom is a grave offence."[8] (Denison, ch. v., p. 49.)

Mr. Earl was of opinion (p. 270) that there is very little doubt that some of the tribes are cannibals, but the system does not obtain among those in the vicinity of Sambas, although these latter assert that the people immediately beyond them are greatly addicted to it. But he adds that such statements must be accepted with caution.

Writing of the Singhi Dyaks, Sir Henry Keppel informs us: " They seem to have no idea of cannibalism or human sacrifice, nor did they accuse their enemies of these practices." (i. 230.) In his second work, however, he gives the following account received from others by Sir James Brooke, the first Rajah of Sarawak:—

" The following is the testimony of three intelligent Dyaks from the interior, given during several months' residence with us, in the most frank manner to be conceived,—as direct and unimpeachable evidence as I ever heard offered, sometimes when they were altogether, sometimes by individuals apart, in conversation with numerous persons. I examined them myself, and entertain no doubt of the correctness of these statements, as far as their personal knowledge is concerned. The witnesses themselves stated over and

[8] " In the district of Sangau, extending several days in every direction, there are three tribes of Dyaks, numbering 500 *lawangs*, and probably 3,000 souls. Two of these tribes are several days in the interior, on the banks of the Skiam. One of these, the Janakang, is addicted to the horrible practice of cannibalism. Except this, and a single tribe on the eastern coast, we have not heard of any other portion of the people who eat human flesh. That the practice prevails to no inconsiderable extent among this tribe there is no longer in our minds the shadow of a doubt. One man with whom we conversed had seen them making their meal on the human frame. They themselves confess it with boasting, and give as a reason for the horrid custom that it makes them courageous. How could we be brave, said one man, if we had never tasted human flesh. They do not eat indiscriminately all parts of the body, but with a most horrid kind of epicurism, feast with the greatest relish upon the tongue, brain, and muscles of the leg. The men of this tribe file down their front teeth to a point like the teeth of a saw." (Journal of a tour on the Kapuas in 1840.—Jour. Ind. Arch. I New Ser., No. 1, 104.) [Noel Denison.]

over again, with the utmost clearness, how much they *had seen*, and how much heard. There was such perfect good faith and simplicity in their stories as to carry conviction of their truth.

"The three men were named Kusu, Gajah, and Rinong; and stated as follows: "'We are of the tribe of Sibaru; which is likewise the name of a branch of the Kapuas River. The tribe of Sibaru contains 2,000 (or even more) fighting men (tikaman) and is under the government of Pangeran Kuning, who resides at Santang, a Malay town on the Kapuas. We have none of us been up to the interior of the Kapuas, where the Kayans live, but they often come down to Santang where we meet them. The Kayans are quite independent, very numerous and powerful: they are governed by their own Rajahs, whom they call Takuan. Some of these Kayan tribes are cannibals *(makan manusia)*; it is generally reported, and we know it to be true.

"'Pangeran Kuning of Santang was at war a few years ago with Pangeran Mahomed of Suwite (Suwight), a Malay town situated on the Kapuas, between Santang and Salimbow. A large force was collected to attack Suwite. There were Malays (Laut) of Santang and Sakadow, and the Dyaks of Sibaru, Samaruang, Dassar, and of other tribes; and besides all these, was a party of about fifty Kayans. We never heard the particular name of this Kayan tribe, for we did not mix with them, nor did we understand their language. Suwite was not taken, but a few detached houses were captured, and one man of the enemy was killed in the assault.

"'Kusu saw these Kayans run small spits of iron, from eight inches to a foot long, into the fleshy parts of the dead men's legs and arms, from the elbow to the shoulder, and from above the ankle beneath the calf to the knee-joint; and they sliced off the flesh with their swords, and put it into baskets. They carry these spits, as we all saw, in a case under the scabbard of their swords. They prize heads in the same way as the Dyaks. They took all the flesh off the body, leaving only the big bones, and carried it to their boats, and we all saw them broil (panggang) and afterwards eat it. They ate it with great relish, and it smelt, while cooking, like hog's flesh. It was not we alone that saw them eat this, but the whole force (balla) saw it.

"'Men say that many of these interior tribes of Kayans eat human flesh—that of their enemies; most, however, they say, do not, and all of them are represented to be good people and very hospitable; and we never heard that they ate any other than the flesh of their enemies. It made us sick to see them, and we were afraid (takut), horrified.

"'This was not the only time we have seen men eat human flesh. The Dyaks of Jangkang are likewise cannibals. They live somewhere between Sangow and Sadong, on a branch of the Sangow River, called Sakiam. The Jangkangs had been out attacking the Ungkias tribe; and after the excursion they came to our village with several baskets of human flesh, for they had killed two men. They cooked and ate this outside our house, but it had been broiled (panggang) before. I knew it to be human flesh, for I saw one of them turning the hand (with the fingers) of a dead man at the fire; and we saw them eat this hand on the bank of the river, close to our house. We talked to them about it, and they did not make any secret of it.

"'The Jangkang people, according to report, eat Malays or Dyaks, or anyone else they kill in war; and they kill their own sick, if near unto death, and eat them. There was an instance of this at Santang. Whilst a party of this people were staying there, one of them fell out of a mango tree and broke his arm, besides being otherwise much hurt; and his companions cut his throat (sambilih), and ate him up. None of us, however, saw this happen, but we heard it from the Santang people. It is likewise said, but we do not know it for a truth, that, when they give their yearly feast (makantaun), a man will borrow a plump child, for eating, from his neighbour, and repay in kind with a child of his own, when wanted. We do not, however, know personally anything beyond having seen them once eating human flesh; but we have heard these things, and believe them; they are well known.'

"Sheriff Moksain corroborated this latter statement generally, as he declared there was no doubt of the Jangkang tribe being cannibals; but he had never seen them eat human flesh: and Brereton likewise heard of a tribe in the interior of the Sadong being cannibals. There is clue enough, however, to settle the point; and, without being positive in an opinion, I can only say that the evidence I have put down was as straightforward as any I ever heard in my life, and such as I cannot doubt, until it be disproved." (Meander ii. pp. 111-115.)

Referring to the above charge, at the making of which he was present, Sir Spencer St. John remarks: "I do not remember having heard any other persons actually affirm that they had seen the Kayans eat human flesh, till the subject was brought up last year before the present Sultan of Borneo and his court, when Usup, one of the young nobles present, said that in 1855 some Muka men were executed at Bintulu, and that a few of the Kayans, who had assisted in their capture, took portions of the bodies of the criminals, roasted and ate them. This was witnessed by himself and many others who were then present. The Kayans had not, as a body, joined in this disgusting feast; but, perhaps, some of the more ferocious may practise it to strike terror into their enemies." (i. 124.)

In the Basel Evangelisch Missions Magazin for April, 1889, the editor in his review (*Rundschau*) states of the Dyaks, p. 167: "In some districts the skin of the forehead and the heart of the killed are cooked and given to the boys to eat in order to make them plucky and brave." This may be true. But when the same writer makes the following gross misstatement regarding Sir Jas Brooke his sayings must be taken with every reserve: "The romantic story of the white rajah is to put it shortly this: In 1829 he bought a small piece of land on the north-west coast from the Malay rajah and then married the daughter of the neighbouring Sultan of Bruni and received from the latter an important gift of land as dowry." ! ! ! (*ibid*, p. 172.)

The Abbé Langenhoff (as to his credibility, see Bibliography) says: "In 1836 two Americans had undertaken the journey he made, and had been gone two or three weeks when the guide who had accompanied them returned and told the Dutch authorities that they had been killed and eaten by the natives." . . . "These latter," he continues (p. 512), "are cannibals; they eat certain portions of the bodies of their enemies, especially the palm of the hand." Later on (p. 515) he says: "I knew I was risking myself among cannibal peoples." It may be true that the Abbé got amongst cannibals, but he brings forward no evidence whatsoever, and, under the circumstances, his statements cannot be accepted.

Then we have Mr. Dalton's statement about the Kayans: "Many of Selgie's tribe are cannibals; some will not eat human flesh, whilst others refuse to do so except on particular occasions, as a birth, a marriage, or funeral." (p. 49.) He also states that on war expeditions, when food was wanted, a follower was killed and eaten. See *supra*, foot note, i. 127.

Sir Hugh Low, writing in the forties, says of the Kayans: "They are not, as they have been hastily stigmatised, cannibals; nor does any race practicing the horrid custom of feeding on the bodies of their own species, exist on the island." (p. 336.) Of these Kayans Sir Chas. Brooke writes: "This tribe are cowardly, untruthful, and treacherous, and are capable of committing many horrors, but the gravest attached to the Kayans, I feel confident, is without *foundation*, namely, that of *cannibalism*. For, during the expedition of 1863, there was no sign of it, and I had abundant opportunities of making strict enquiries in the very heart of the country. Many reports of this description are spread by the enemies of a people to degrade them in the estimation of Europeans. . . . Such reports are purely fabulous, and I do not believe any tribes are cannibals in this part of Borneo, although stories go far to lead one to a contrary belief. For instance, some Malays told me, only a short while ago, that on an expedition against the Engkayas, who live on a tributary of the Kapuas, and are under the Dutch jurisdiction, they met with pieces of bamboo, which these people had thrown away in alarm; these hollow canes were filled with human flesh, used as provisions. I regret that I am unable, positively, to contradict such statements; but it is my firm conviction cannibalism is not practised on any part of the island of Borneo." (i. pp. 74, 55.)

Captain Mundy, in reply to enquiries made of the Malays, was told that only the Pakatans were suspected of being cannibals. (i. 209.)

Mr. Carl Bock, in Eastern Borneo, "noticed that the other Dyak tribes did not go near the Trings during their stay at Moeara Pahou, not disguising their fear of them, and their disgust at their cannibal practices. . . . Among the visitors was an old priestess, who gave full details concerning the religious beliefs, &c., of the tribe. This information was elicited by the Boegis] kapitan, and interpreted by him to a Malay writer, who took down the statements on the spot. These statements have since been translated for me. . . . This priestess, in the course of conversation, told me—holding out her hand—that the palms were considered the best eating. Then she pointed to the knee, and again to the forehead, using the Malay word *bai*, *bai* (good, good), each time to indicate that the brains, and the flesh on the knees of a human being, are also considered delicacies by the members of her tribe. . . . At that very time, as he [*i.e.*, a cannibal chief] sat conversing with me through my interpreter, and I sketched his portrait, he had fresh upon his head the blood of no less than seventy victims, men, women, and children, whom he and his followers had just slaughtered, and whose hands and brains he had eaten. . . . The Bahou Trings, again, are the only cannibals in Koetei. According to Dr. Hollander's work, 'Land en Volkenkünde,' there is another cannibal tribe in Borneo, the Djangkangs, in Sanggouw, in the Sintang district.

"Other tribes have human sacrifices on the occasion of their Tiwa feast; not from bloodthirstyness, but from the superstition that the sacrificed serve the departed as slaves in their future abode. . . . To the ordinary horrors of head-hunting—the simple murder of their victims for the sake of their heads as trophies, practised by all the Dyaks—the Bahou Tring tribe add the tenfold worse practices of cannibalism and offering of human sacrifices; not only killing their enemies according to the Dyak reading of the maxim, 'Live and let live,'—' Kill or be killed,'—but taking captive those that they do not put to death and eat on the spot, and reserving them for slavery and ultimate death by torture." (Bock, pp. 133, 134, 135, 210, 218.)

It must be remembered that Mr. Bock saw no evidences himself, and also that all that was told to him was translated from the native tongue through a Malay into Dutch; *i.e.*, it came to him quite second hand. It may be true what he was told, but it must not be forgotten savages usually reply according to the way in which they believe their interrogator wishes them to answer. Mr. Bock's statement brought forth the following letters from Mr. C. A. Bampfylde (Kapit Fort, Rejang River, February, 1882) and Mr. Brooke Low (Sarawak, 20th September, 1887):—

"All exaggerations undoubtedly contain portions of the truth, more or less, this particular exaggeration being no exception. Among nearly all head hunters there is a custom, which, loathsome enough in itself, falls far short of cannibalism, as understood by the term; and, moreover, the Tring people do not stand alone in the practice of this custom. After a successful raid, or on any occasion on which a head has been obtained, it is a custom of warriors to take a portion (the minutest will suffice) of the skin or flesh from the head and swallow it, on the supposition that it inspires bravery, and also because it is a traditional *Penalli*; but the women and children do not indulge in the practice. This is the truth and the whole truth concerning cannibalism, as far as this tribe is concerned. C. A. BAMPFYLDE."

"I have just been reading a second time in 'Head-hunters of Borneo,' and in connection with it, Mr. Bampfylde's remarks, together with Bock's rejoinder. I have been asked by the former gentleman to testify to his credibility, and shall therefore feel obliged if you will be good enough to insert these few lines for the information of the public.

"I have been 400 miles up the Rejang River since the publication of the above volume, and though I had not yet read the book, I took it with me and showed the plates to the natives of the interior; so true were they to life that resemblances were found in the portraiture to their own friends, and every detail provoked roars of laughter.

"Mr. Bampfylde has, however, been over six years in Rajah Brooke's service, therefore his testimony, I feel sure, is preferable to that of a mere traveller.

"I fully believe, with Mr. Bampfylde, that the natives were poking fun at Mr. Bock when they declared the Trings to be cannibals. I do not believe them to be such, for if they were I should have heard of their propensity long before Mr. Bock ever set his foot in Borneo, for we have occasional intercourse with some of the tribes of the Upper Mahakan, among whom Mr. Bock should have travelled instead of stopping short at Mount *Pehau*, which can be reached from the sea by steamers, and which feels the influence of the spring tides. Had he accomplished the ascent from this point upwards, he would have endangered his neck, it is true, but he would have travelled over new ground, and added to our knowledge. A few months ago I received a visit from a Long Gelat, named Bau Dias, who lives at the foot of the Mokan ranges, and I put the question relative to the alleged cannibalism of his neighbours, the Trings. He seemed surprised at my asking such a question, and said, 'Of course it is not true, such a practice is unknown to us at Mokan.'

"I do not accuse Mr. Bock of wilfully publishing an untruth, but I fully believe his credulity was practised upon by his companions to discourage in him any desire to penetrate further into the interior.

"I do not think Mr. Bock will require to return any answer to what I have written. I, for my part, do not wish to engage in any controversy, and disclaim any obligation to make further reply. BROOKE LOW."

Mr. Brooke Low elsewhere (see *supra*, p. 145) confirms Mr. Bampfylde's statement, that to make them fearless the conquerors will eat a piece of the flesh of the vanquished. See foot note p. 218.

Mr. De Crespigny was told by the Malays that the Dusuns were cannibals (Zeit. Berl. N.F., p. 330); that traveller makes no further mention of the subject. Mr. Alex. Dalrymple (p. 46) practically says he never heard of cannibalism among the Dusuns.

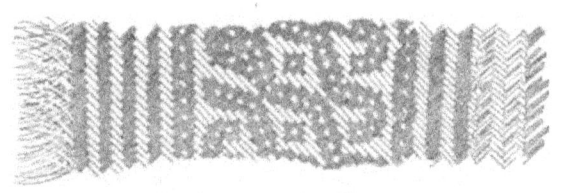

MAT PATTERN. S.E. Borneo.
(Leiden Mus.)

CHAPTER XXIV.

GOVERNMENT, TRADE, MINING, MENSURATION, NATURAL PRODUCTIONS.

GOVERNMENT. GENERAL GOVERNMENT: Grades of chiefs—Their duties—No arbitrary power—Assistance given to chiefs—Power by general consent—Decision in capital crimes—Nature's gentlemen—Independence of people—*Tuahs* hard worked—Good chief means general prosperity—Unpopular chiefs—Prerogatives overworked—Abuse of power—Malay interference—Five chiefs—A goose of a chief—No chief—Election—Village councils—Long discussions—Just administration appreciated—Punishments—Fines—Neighbours must not be molested—Decisions sound and sensible—Fines—Retort in kind—Barbarous punishments. INHERITANCE: Grandchildren—Curious Malanau case. MALAY MISGOVERNMENT. LAW OF DEFIANCE.

TRADE. Primitive ideas—Currencies unknown—Quick in trade—Extension of currency—Trading with Kayans—*Tamels*—Frauds—Kiaus *v.* Bajus—Malay cheats—Wealth—Hidden treasures—Change of fashion.

MINING. IRON: Blacksmith—Sea Dyak forges—Iron ore—Kayan forges and metal. GOLD: From river beds—The Malaus—Natives not gold seekers. DIAMONDS: Method of digging.

MENSURATION TIME: No count—Harvest seasons—Pleiades—Sun-dials—Vague measurement of time—And of length—A pig's measurement—Dusun cloth measurement. COUNTING: Dusun—Fair knowledge of counting. DISTANCES: Curious methods—"So many boilings."

NATURAL PRODUCTIONS. GUTTA—RUBBER—NIPA PALM—ROTAN—BAMBU—DAMMAR-TAPANG TREE—OILS.

GOVERNMENT.

GENERAL GOVERNMENT.

"Each Land Dyak tribe has an *Orang Kaya* (literally, 'rich man'), who is chief; under him is a *Pañgara* (or 'superior'), who wears a white jacket, and a *Pañglima* (or 'military chief'), who wears a red jacket. Every long house has a *Tuah* (or 'elder'), who lives in the centre room, settles squabbles, and does the hospitality." (Grant, p. 5.)

The *Orang Kaya* and *Pengara*, who in external affairs is the mouth of the tribe, "are selected by the suffrages of the *laki bini*, or married men, subject to the approval of the Rajah's Government, one of whose officers publicly invests them, by giving them a jacket and head handkerchief, to be worn on state occasions; moreover each long house in a village is under the charge of a *tuah* or old man, and all the tuahs act as a council to the *Orang Kaya*. The *Orang Kaya* and this council are the magistrates; try and punish offences (chiefly by fines), and settle where the *ladangs* or farms for the year are to be made. It is the *Pengara's* duty to look after offenders and to bring them to justice. As regards its own internal affairs and minor offences, every tribe is perfectly independent of the Rajah's rule." (Chalmers, O. C., p. 1; Miss. Field, 1859, p. 80; Low, p. 187.)

"The Orang Kaya does not appear to possess the slightest arbitrary power; the office is not hereditary, and the person filling it is generally chosen on account of the wisdom and ability he displays in the councils of the tribe, and which appear to fit him for the duties of their representative, in all their relations with their Malayan masters, or with the neighbouring villages. The only real advantage which accrues to the chief of a tribe, besides the standing and consideration his title gives him amongst his people, is the assistance he receives in his agricultural operations, the whole people combining to construct and take care of one large farm yearly for his benefit, the produce of which he receives. But in many tribes, this institution is neglected, and has dwindled into occasional assistance, when the chief chooses to demand it, on the land cultivated by his family." (Low, p. 228.)

"The Government of the Dyaks seems to be administered more by general consent than from any authority lodged in the chief. His power, indeed, is one of persuasion, and depends upon his personal ability, nor can he in any way coerce his people to obedience. Amongst the Hill Dyaks the laws are based on the same principle." (Sir Jas. Brooke i. 211.) "The chief never decides himself in capital crimes, but calls a council of the elders, and consults them as to the judgment or punishment to be inflicted." (Bishop McDougall, T.E.S. ii. 26.) So also among the Kayans, as related by the Rajah, when a chief allowed his people to commit some murders. His words are: "I felt very angry with Balang, who had been so true a friend to us in other ways, and imposed a fine of twelve rusa jars (£120) on him as an example, to prevent such an abominable practice getting foot among Dyak tribes. This was the heaviest fine that could be imposed. He paid it down; and on my meeting him a short time after, he said, '*Tuah*, you know it was not my heart that was in fault; but I could not govern my people, who did this deed when I was away." (ii. 305.) Otherwise the "Kayan and Kenniah chiefs are much looked up to by their followers, and have great power over the people; they are usually very intelligent and well-behaved men, and have the manners of gentlemen rather than of savages."[1] (Hose, J.A.I., xxviii. 171.)

Some of the Dusuns visited by Sir Sp. St. John paid no "tribute, though many chiefs on the coast call them their people; but it is merely nominal, no one daring to oppress them. Each village is a separate government, and almost each house independent. They have no established chiefs, but follow the councils of the old men to whom they are related." (i. 375.)

"This chief of a house *Tuah* is usually much harder worked than his followers, as he has his judicial and political duties to attend, over and above

---

[1] "The Rajah of the country of Waagoo has seventy chiefs under him, all of whom are likewise called Rajahs. Sedgen has fifty, whilst Selgie has more than one hundred and forty. The latter chief is by far the most powerful in this part of Borneo; he possesses an immense extent of country, over which he exercises the most despotic control. Selgie calculates the people under his sway at 150,000; they are under strict command, and divided into three classes, one of which does nothing but fabricate arms, such as *mandows*, spears, shields, *sumpits*, and darts: another attends to the culture of paddy, making war-dresses, and articles of ornament for the women; the third is composed of the finest men, selected for war; these are marked in a particular manner, and have great privileges over all other." (Dalton, p. 48.)

the ordinary daily labour, in which he rarely has slaves to relieve him of his manual work, as among the Kayans." (Brooke Low.)

"The Serebas and Sakarrans, whose large houses or villages are often placed widely apart, follow different customs. With them, the head of a house is in himself a sort of *Orang Kaya*, who, adopting the name of his eldest child, assumes the prefix of *Apai* (Father)—thus, *Apai* Bakar, the Father of Bakar." (Grant, p. 5.) "Upon the conduct of this chief depends the number of families a house contains. If he be brave and upright in his dealings, numbers will settle under him; if otherwise, he will quickly lose his friends, who will migrate to other houses, and he will sink to the level of an ordinary man." (Gosp. Miss., 1860, p. 37.)

And unpopular chiefs are to be met with. "The ground of complaint appeared to emanate from the Orang Kaya, who loudly stated, evidently meant to reach my ear, that his tribe paid him little or none of the respect and deference due him as chief of the tribe, and that the ringleader was the Pengara. In collecting the birds' nests, for instance, the first gathering went to the people, the second to the Government, 200 nests of which were his perquisite, of these he had as yet only received 100 nests. The Dyaks also, according to custom, were bound to work five days for him in the year on his farm; this they refused to do, and led on by the Pengara they disobeyed his orders, and cared little for him or his authority. The Pengara, in an excited but sarcastic tone of voice replied, that Murung knew how to manage his people if he liked, but that instead of looking after his tribe he preferred running about the country, and when the Dyaks wished to work for him he grew angry and abused them, saying he could carry on his own farm without their help." (Denison, ch. iv. p. 37.)

As mentioned above the Land Dyak tribes "assist the Orang Kaya in making his farms; in fact, it is one of the most lucrative of his perquisites. Mita of Sirambau had pushed his prerogative too far, and had forced his people to make him three farms, and from this and many other reasons, he had ruined his popularity." (St. John i. 157.)

If, however, the chiefs generally are unable to abuse their power and position, as Sir Jas. Brooke found, there must be exceptions to the rule. "I have noticed that Bindarri Sumpsu is the hereditary lord of Sabuyow, all of whose relations share in his privileges. This claim to authority over the tribe arose from the payment of some debts by the Bindarri's ancestors, long beyond the memory of the present generation, being since a broken tribe, part only are at Lundu, the rest dispersed in different places at Sadong. The Lundu people have always resisted any undue exactions or claims; but those at Sadong, less strong, have been subjected to them. These claims have gradually risen in proportion to the distance of time, the weakness of the Dyaks, and the increased want of principle in the chiefs. At first the Dyaks paid a small stated sum as an acknowledgment of vassalage; by degrees, this became an arbitrary and unlimited taxation, and now, to consummate the iniquity, the entire tribes are *pronounced slaves, and liable to be disposed of*. This fate has attended them in many instances, upwards of thirty having already been sold by the rapacious relations of Bindarri. Not so the Orang

Kaya Tumangong, who has maintained his liberty, and openly asserts it, with great vehemence declaring that whoever wishes to make his tribe at Lundu slaves, must first fight with them." (Mundy i. 301.)

Where the Malay influence is strong they have not in their election of chief always been able to hold their own, thus: " A few years ago an *Orang Kaya* and a *Pañgāra* were installed by the Rajah, and soon afterwards a Malay, who was sent to collect the revenue, had, after the custom of his predecessors, appointed a second *Orang Kaya* and a second *Pañgāra* at (he said) their own request. In addition to these, there was an old *Orang Kaya*, and as these five chiefs did not act together, it was a case of 'too many cooks,' and there were complaints of too many *Becharas*, and much lack of unity." (Grant, pp. 61, 62.)

The same administrator on another occasion speaking of a village chief says : " I was at a loss to understand why the people had chosen such a goose of a fellow for their chief. He had not a word to say for himself, wore the most common of *chawats*, or waist-cloths, and a turban of bark, and he looked so much more up to the art of hewing timber than of holding sway over his fellow-men, that I began to question the policy of appointing him ; but beyond his being the son-in-law of the old man, and 'very clever in holding his tongue,' no reason was assigned, so we installed him." (*ibid*, p. 54.) Mr. Denison once finding himself in a village which had no head says: " The men seem wanting in energy, and the sooner an Orang Kaya is appointed the better." (Ch. vii. p. 77.)

In the chapter on Character the difficulties Mr. Grant had to contend with in getting a chief elected were set forth, but perhaps Mr. Chalmers' account will be also found interesting : " Before investing, however, on one occasion Mr. Grant tried to see if the person elected was universally acceptable, by calling on all present, who were content, to hold up their right hand. This was a step too far in advance, and failed utterly to our great amusement, and that of the Dyaks also. A verbal assent was then demanded, and given by a thundering burst of ' Suka.' The new officer then had his ' robes of office ' given him and he was exhorted to govern justly." (O.P., p. vi.)

" All Hill Dyak affairs connected with the prosperity or welfare of the village, are discussed by a council of the men of the tribe, which is always held in the *pangah*, and at which every male of the hamlet may be present, though seldom any but the opinions of the old men are advanced—the younger people paying great respect to the advice of the elders at this council. If the chief be a man of known and reputed ability, his opinion—which is generally given in a long and forcible oration while the speaker is seated, and without much gesticulation, excepting the waving of the head—is of very great weight, and his arguments most frequently convince the assembly, unless some other opinion be advanced and supported with equal ability, when the approvers of each, in succession, address the members of this little parliament—a fair and impartial hearing being given to all—though the discussions are often protracted till near morning from the preceding dusk, when one party either yields its opinion to the other, or the minority is compelled to give way—these assemblies are never riotous, but always conducted in a quiet, grave, and business-like manner." (Low, p. 289.)

Another account is given by Mr. Chalmers of these people: "I was much amused at a *Bechaer*, or council, this morning in noticing the same different kinds of character among the Dyaks as among their more civilised brethren. At the *Bechaer* all was done in due order, one man speaking after another, and each allowed to have his say uninterrupted. There was the *Pengara* speaking with all the gravity of age and office; another old graybeard [sic] illustrating and enforcing his arguments with pieces of pinang placed on the floor, each signifying some person discussed of; one man loud and opinionative, evidently a Dyak Radical; another grave and earnest; and the Orang Kaya dignified and thoughtful, only putting in a word here and there, but that weighty and conclusive. It was truly pleasing to witness their childlike confidence in the government of the Rajah." (Miss. Field, 1859, p. 85.)

"The Sea Dyak administration of law among themselves supplies many admirable precedents. Unfortunately, their ties of relationship and want of substantial principle, are impediments to the carrying out of justice: at the same time, they are peculiarly alive to the advantages of a just administration, which never fails to secure the aid and support of the majority. In the event of one tribe commencing war upon another, by killing without provocation, the aggressor would incur a *hukum mungkal*, or fine of £75, according to custom. In cases of adultery, the husband or wife in fault is liable to be beaten with sticks by the aggrieved parties, on the open ground, as their houses are held sacred. Their system of justice in this case is of a very beneficial character, as the female suffers alike with the male. Petty cases of theft are punished lightly, as well as all other trivial cases, but nobody is allowed to molest his neighbour without incurring a fine. For instance, if a party of people should ever damage the drinking or bathing well of another house, or hack at the sticks on the landing place, they would be mulcted. In quarrels about land, they are supposed only to use sticks, and they fall to in earnest: the most pugnacious keep very barbarous spiked and thorny ones for the express purpose, and many use bark hats and jackets to ward off the blows of these implements. Cases of premeditated murder are very unusual among them, although at one time the attack of one party on another was often attended by death. A few examples of heavy fines, inflicted with a strong hand, have greatly decreased this evil. A chief leading such a party is, in most cases, a man of property, and in the event of one of his followers being killed, he pays a jar worth £9 to the deceased's parents, or nearest relations." (Brooke i. 60.)

"There is no doubt, when uninfluenced by prejudice and relationship, the decisions of natives are very sound and sensible. . . . Nothing artificial or extraneous, in the shape of gilt or tinsel, will help to gain the confidence of the natives. They are too matter of fact, and only admire and respect strength in its entirety." (Rajah Brooke's Hints, pp. 6 and 7.)

"Punishment is usually by fine, imposed by a council of old men. In cases of murder, retort in kind is allowed and justified; but, unlike the law of the Arabs, the retaliation must be confined to the individual murderer. If one man kills another, a brother or friend of the deceased kills him in return, and the business ends; but they can likewise settle the matter by paying a fine, provided both parties give their consent. In all other cases fines prevail; and as far as I have yet heard, no severer punishment is ever inflicted for crime." (Sir Jas. Brooke, Mundy i. 211.)

"Some of their punishments are very barbarous and cruel: I have seen a woman with both her hands half-severed at the wrists, and a man with both his ears cut off." (Marryat, p. 77.)

"The Idahan punish murder, theft, and adultery with death." (Forrest, p. 371.)

INHERITANCE.

Property in land and trees has been described in Ch. xiv., 418 *et seq.*

Among the Sakaran Dyaks the law is as follows: "Property is divided equally between all the children, irrespective of sex, but if these children die before their parents the grandchildren inherit equally with their uncles and aunts; thus a man, A, has four children C, D, E and F, these all have children, but C dies before A, leaving, say, three children, then these three children will inherit equally with D, E and F, so that instead of the property being divided up into 4 equal portions only, it is divided up into six equal portions. Adopted children share equally with the other children." (F. W. Leggatt.)

A very curious case of inheritance is given by Mr. de Crespigny (S.G., No. 42) as customary among the Milanaus: "Balang and Biam lived happily together for many years in a long house, relic of old times, of which they were possessors of half a *sirang*. Before marriage Balang had taken as adopted children two young girls; and, after marriage, Biam had taken as an adopted child one young girl. Balang became thus the pro-father of the last girl, and Biam the pro-mother of the two first; all three having thus equal rights. There were no children born to Balang and Biam, and about 20 days ago Biam died. Nipiak, the sister of Biam, sent to Balang for her share in Biam's estate. Balang did not deny her right, but proposed that the matter should be settled in Court; and the Court decided thus, after carefully taking the opinion of sundry Tuahs who were present, the defendant, Balang, acknowledging that the arrangement was according to *adat* (custom).

"The whole estate, consisting of guns, plantations, share of a house, share of a slave, ornaments, and even cooking utensils, to be sold, and the husband to take his one-half. With regard to the share of deceased, the defendant, her husband, got nothing. Had there been children born to them, two-thirds of Biam's share would have been theirs, and one-third the inheritance of the adopted children had they been foster children (*anak meninsu*); but as they were not, so they were only entitled to a *tanda*, although the Court gave them, in this case, one-ninth each, making one-third to be divided between them, and gave the other two-thirds to Nipiak, the sister of deceased, who would have had no claim at all had there been a child to inherit.

"That which appeared so curious to me, was the fact that the husband was entitled to nothing at all, and only got his half of all the property which belonged in common to him and his wife during the lifetime of the latter. I found upon inquiry that she might have made a will in favour of her husband or others, either in writing or verbally before witnesses, but this not having been done, had there been no relatives at all to claim inheritance of her share of the property, it would have gone to the state, and the husband, even under such circumstances, could claim nothing. The Tuahs say that this has been the custom from time immemorial."

The natives, in spite of their wars and feuds and disputes, governed themselves better than the Malays governed them. In 1850, the nephew of the then Sultan, with his whole party, was killed by some Bisayas when dunning them for an imaginary debt. There was in the time of the Bruni nominal control "a system in this country called *serra*, or *serra dagang*, or forced trade, but it is carried on in the neighbourhood of the capital to an extent unknown elsewhere. Every noble of any influence that thinks proper goes to a tribe with some cloth, and calling the chief, orders him to divide it among his tribe; he then demands as its price from twenty to a hundred times its value. He does not expect to get the whole at once, but it enables him to dun the tribe for years after. Not content with taking their goods for these imaginary debts, they constantly seize their young children and carry them off as slaves. The tribe who killed the Sultan's nephew had actually paid their serra to thirty-three different nobles that year, and had been literally stripped of all their food, before, giving way to passion, they destroyed the whole party above referred to." (St. John ii. 46.)

Mr. Denison relates a very similar story of Malay misgovernment. "Whilst Pangêran Anak Chuchu (whose property the Meri district is) was proceeding from Sarawak to Brunei in his schooner, he met with head-winds, and brought up in the Meri river; and, finding this a good opportunity for replenishing his exchequer, levied a tax of 20 pikuls. The people had to borrow these, and in borrowing had to pay for them 60 pikuls of gutta, or in other words had to pay $2,400 for a forced loan of $1,500. The Pangêran carried away plunder from the unfortunate natives to the extent of $9,000, leaving the population so deeply in debt that it will take them years to recover themselves." (Jour. Straits Asiatic Soc., No. 10, 177.)

Babukid is a Land Dyak mode of defiance, and appears to have been first mentioned by Sir Jas. Brooke. "I find it is appealed to as a final judgment in disputes about property, and usually occurs in families when the right to land and fruit trees comes to be discussed. Each party then sallies forth in search of a *head*; if one only succeed, his claim is acknowledged; if both succeed, the property continues common to both. It is on these occasions that the Dyaks are dangerous, and perhaps an European, whose inheritance depended on the issue, would not be very scrupulous as to the means of success. It must be understood, however, that the individuals do not go alone, but a party accompanies each, or they may send a party without being present. The loss of life is not heavy from this cause, and it is chiefly resorted to by the Singè and the Sows, and is about as rational as our trials by combat." (Mundy i. 331.) It would seem to have more the character of an ordeal. At the village of Lanchang, on the Samaharan river, there were, owing to Malay intrigues, five Orang Kayas, and, in consequence, there was much quarrelling. "One proposed that, to settle the matter, they should sally out into the neighbouring countries, and the first who should bring home a head should be declared victor, and have the case decided in his favour. It was their ancient custom." (St. John i. 223.) Compare *bunkit*, i. 70.

TRADE.

The natives' ideas of trade are primitive. "Two old Dyaks were heard discussing the advantages of sago planting, 'Ah,' said the one Apai, 'but supposing the whole country were planted how cheap sago would be, the sale would hardly repay us for working and filling it.' 'Yes,' replied the other, 'then how cheaply we could live and so we would eat the sago and sell all our rice.'" (S.G., No. 183, p. 109.)

When His Highness presented Sandown, a Sakaran chief, with a rupee the man asked him the use of it and whether it would purchase padi. A very few years later this man was an active trader, and gained considerable riches. . . . But generally speaking "a Dyak has no conception of the use of a circulating medium. He may be seen wandering in the Bazaar with a ball of beeswax in his hand for days together, because he can't find anybody willing to take it for the exact article he requires. This article may be not more than a tenth the value of the beeswax, but he would not sell it for money, and then buy what he wants. From the first, he had the particular article in his mind's eye, and worked for the identical ball of beeswax with which and nothing else to purchase it." (Brooke i. 140, 156.)

Sir Sp. St. John found the Sea Dyaks "exceedingly quick in commercial transactions;[2] and most of them who did not know the value of a piece of money six years ago *circa* 1856 are now active traders." (i. 71.) The Sibuyaus are keener traders than the Land Dyaks (*ibid*, i. 208), and Lieut. Marryat found the Lundu Dyaks always ready for barter. (p. 78.) The proximity to, and the influence exercised by, Brunei where a debased iron medium of exchange was in use (*ibid*, p. 113) would have made it likely that the natives might have known something of a currency, but they do not appear to have understood or appreciated it. The Chinese, too, must have handled *cash*, and the coast nations at least might be supposed to have seen this medium.

"Prior to the cession of the Baram district to Sarawak by the Sultan of Brunei, money was not used, and the trade consisted of merely an exchange of jungle produce for cotton goods, grey shirting, turkey red and yellow cloth. The district has now been under Sarawak rule for ten years, and in consequence of the enormous increase of trade, the current dollars and cents have found their way far into the interior, so that even the Punans know the purchasing power of dollars, and it is common now to see the dollar coin on necklaces worn by children." (Hose, J.A.I. xxiii. 161.)

The method of trading with the Kayans seems to have been peculiar but it must probably be considered Malay rather than native Bornean. It is thus

---

[2] Mr. Earl long since pointed out that freedom of commerce would soon improve the Dyaks for, said he, "they are greatly addicted to commerce, and spare no pains to procure articles of foreign manufacture for which they have acquired a taste." (p. 272.)

spoken of by Sir Jas. Brooke: "A trader from the coast, whether Malay or Dyak, when he ascends the river with his small boats, stops at an assigned place, and sends word of his arrival, with a description of his tribe, object, and cargo, to the chief, who orders a party of his people to bring the goods to the village; and though this may be four or five days' journey in the interior, it is done without the slightest article being pilfered. The merchant entirely loses sight of his wares, which are carried off by the Kyans, and he is himself guided by a body of the superior members of the tribe. On arriving at the village, a house is allotted for his use, his merchandise is placed carefully in the same habitation, every civility is shown him, and he incurs no expense. After a few days' residence, he moves his goods to the mansion of the chief, the tribe assemble, and *all* the packages are opened. Presents are made to the head men, who likewise have the right according to their precedence of choosing what they please to purchase; the price is afterwards fixed, and engagements made for payment in bees' wax, camphor, or birds' nests. The purchasers then scatter themselves in the woods to seek for these articles, and the merchant remains in his house feeding on the fat of the land for a month or six weeks, when, the engagements being fulfilled, he departs a richer man than he came; his acquired property being safely carried to his boats by the same people. If he has a large cargo and proposes going farther into the interior, they carry his goods to the boundary of the next tribe, and he returns at the period agreed upon to receive the price of his commodities." (Mundy i. 263.)

Sir Sp. St. John's account is very similar, but the Kayans " were seldom very welcome guests at a small village, helping themselves freely to everything that took their fancy; but this only occurred, as a Malay shrewdly observed, in places where they were feared."[2] (i. 124.)

"Many Dusuns go three or four times a month to the *tamels*, which are generally held in dried-up river-beds. To the *tamel* they will often make a two days' journey, with a few articles of their own manufacture—such as bamboo baskets and hats, bark ropes, and, where they grow it, tobacco. The women are the beasts of burden and on these occasions the men often get drunk and fight." (Whitehead, p. 107.)

On the other hand the Dusuns complained to Mr. Hatton of the Dampas men very much, saying that they stole their goods and swindled them. "The headman showed me a common pinfire revolver, worth about $5, for which he paid 40 pounds of gutta; also a string of beads, worth about 20 cents, which he had purchased for 8 pounds of gutta. He complained also of the Dampas men's scales and weights, saying that one pikul of gutta in the Labuk country on arriving at Sandakan weighed two pikuls." (Hatton's Diary, 9 Mar.) Mr. Burbidge mentions incidentally (p. 75) that the natives adulterate the gutta. In Sir Sp. St. John's time the Bajus used to visit the Kiaus. The

[1] "It is very important for all travellers to note that the Dyaks as they are at present know nothing as to payment or barter—with regard that is to the common articles of livelihood; that they therefore, unless they do it from the start without asking, cannot be brought to do what is wanted by means of presents and that they on the contrary find it quite right if one allows one's people to take as many fowls and as much fruit as one requires. In the same way they know nothing about theft and do not hesitate to help themselves to the fruits in your garden or to the tobacco in your hand as much as they are immediately in need of. They never take more." (Hupé, p. 722.)

Kiaus bullied the Bajus and now the latter "seldom visit these distant villagers, who are thus compelled to take their own produce to the coast, to be cajoled or plundered in their turn, which is one of the reasons why cloth and iron are so rare among them." (i. 312.)

Although the Sea Dyaks "are said to be more acute than Malays, so that even the Chinese find they cannot cheat them after the first year. . . . the Malays sometimes make good bargains with them by using soft and flattering language, but the Dayaks often repent of being so wheedled and will claim justice before the courts." (*ibid*, i. 71.)

"The Kayans in the Baram appear, from all I can learn, to be very unsophisticated in matters of trade, and their ignorance and simplicity are taken advantage of by a lot of Malays for their own ends, who cheat and swindle these aborigines to their hearts' content. The Malays, however, all tell the same story, namely, that it is easy to humbug the Kayans, but dangerous to bully them; they barely acknowledge the rule of the Sultan, if they do so at all, which appears very doubtful." (Denison, Jour. Straits Asiatic Soc., No. 10, p. 178.)

"The Sarawak Malay can as a rule get on very fairly well with the Land Dyaks, better, perhaps, than he can with Sea Dyaks up coast; he can *pèjal*, that is he can force his wares upon those who really have no real use for them or who are not particularly in want of the goods hawked by the Malay pedlar, and whilst the Dyak is turning over his mind as to whether he will purchase or not, the seller sits patiently by smoking and singing the praises of his wares; a Land Dyak usually takes a considerable time in forming his mind in making a purchase, but time is of no particular object to either party, and the bargain completed, and the pedlar having obtained the customary cent. per cent., he packs up his baggage and departs to the next house or village as the case may be. But the present Malay system of trading with the Land Dyaks is rotten to the core. Dyak bintings or villages are perpetually being visited, and the commonest articles of trade thrust upon the Dyaks at exhorbitant rates, which they could purchase ever so much cheaper at any of the numerous Chinese shops scattered throughout the river, and which are easily accessible in a day's journey even from the remotest Dyak habitation; such commodities as waist-cloths (*chawats*) and petticoats (*jamos*), trimmed with a little common Turkey red cloth, are sold previous to the rice harvest, to be repaid in paddy at many times their respective values, nor does it end here, the purchaser being expected to deliver his payment to the house of the Malay merchant, entailing, perhaps, a long journey on foot, or miles of boat travelling; and again, he is expected to fully provide for those traders stopping in his house such necessaries as rice, firewood, provisions, and the like, which he does without the slightest grumbling." (S.G., 1894, p. 98.)

"Wealth is not so much the accumulation of cash, as the possession of gongs, brass guns, and jars; and if a chief is deprived of his wealth, he is also deprived of his power, and the people losing faith in him look out for another who owns 'thousands.'" (Grant, p. 24.) So Mr. Chalmers states: "The wealth of a family is generally estimated by the number of gongs, jars, cups, pigs, fowls, and fruit-trees it possesses." (O.P., p. 1.) The Sennah tribe were considered well off, possessing plenty of *tawaks-tawaks*, *chanangs*, jars, etc., and boasting a splendid peal of gongs."[4] (Denison, ch. vi., p. 65.) The Bukars wealth is shown by the great amount of silver coins and ornaments they possess, "sheaths of swords and parangs being covered with this metal, while silver coins were worn round the edge of the petticoat, and mixed with *sabits* of the same metal round the waists and loins of the women." (Denison, ch. viii., p. 84.)

"The returns for their rice and gutta, the Sozongan Dusuns hoard up in the darkest recesses of the bush, consisting of brass in every conceivable shape,—that is the only thing their heart is set on." (Witti, 19 May.)

"Some of the things the natives of Brit. North Borneo buy are most expensive, sixty and seventy dollars is frequently given for a single sarong. Men of industrious habits can easily be overburdened with the quantity of goods they can acquire. Up the Labuk, where large earthenware jars are what the people most covet, I have seen some of the family residences crammed full, top and bottom, and hung up, to the roof with these rather cumbrous evidences of wealth. It may be said, generally, that whatever they want they buy, from a bundle of tobacco to a gold-hilted creese [Malay sword.] Amongst most of the tribes, brassware of various kinds used to be much valued, a great deal on account of the facility with which it could be hidden in the forest, or even in mud at the bottom of rivers." Collecting parties found these hidden articles. (W. B. Pryer, J.A.I. xvi. 235.)

"When Mr. Low was at Kiau in 1851, beads and brass wire were very much sought after. When we came last April, the people cared nothing for beads, and very little for cloth; their hearts were set on brass wire. We, however, distributed a good deal of cloth, at reasonable rates, in exchange for food and services rendered. We now 1858 found that even brass wire, except of a very large size, was despised, and cloth eagerly desired." (i. 320.)

MINING.

IRON.

"Most Land Dyaks understand sufficient blacksmithery to make their own swords and axes—the latter are small, and, by turning them in their handles, can be used as adzes; they cut down the largest trees with these little tools, which shows that they are not bad steel."[5] (Grant, p. 91.)

[4] A row of gongs of various sizes is referred to as a sign of wealth by a correspondent of the S.G. (No 102) at Pulau Majang in Dutch Borneo.

[5] "The iron which is obtained in the interior is said to be valued by many of the wilder Dyaks even more than gold ; indeed the latter is only sought for as a means of procuring foreign articles for which they have acquired a taste. The iron must either be excellent quality, or the Dyaks must have discovered a method of tempering it, which sets at defiance the competition of more civilised nations. I have heard of musket barrels having been cut in two by a single blow of their swords together with other tales illustrative of their wonderful temper ; and from what I have personally witnessed, I am inclined to give perfect credence to them. To test the capabilities of these weapons I cut a twopenny nail in two and although the temper of the one employed was considered as rather inferior, the edge was not in the least turned. (Earl, p. 264.) "Crimata, a town situated to the southerly end of the Island of Borneo, sends to Bantam a great deal of iron." (A Collection of Voyages undertaken by the Dutch East India Company. Translated. London, W. Freeman & Co., 8º 1703, p. 197.)

IRON ORE SMELTING ON THE BARITO.
(After Dr. Schwaner.)

The Sea Dyak "blacksmith, with the exception of the *manang*, or doctor, is the only person in the village whose time is solely occupied by a profession or trade. If the blacksmith of a village be celebrated for the goodness of his work, he is not only employed in the manufacture of the arms and instruments necessary for his tribe, but those made by him sell for higher prices than those of his neighbours, and he is sure of plenty of employment and considerable profit. The smith's shop is always a little apart from the houses of the village, to prevent accidents from the fire; the bellows precisely resemble those of the Malays, the two bamboos, or hollow trees; a stone is generally the anvil, but when a heavy piece of iron can be obtained it is preferred. His instruments are all of his own making, and rude in their construction; the vessel in which the water for cooling his work is held is a block of wood hollowed out." (Low, p. 209.)

A different description of the Sibuyau bellows is given by Sir Jas. Brooke: "The Dyaks, as is well known, are famous for the manufacture of iron. The forge here is of the simplest construction, and formed by two hollow trees, each about seven feet high, placed upright, side by side, in the ground; from the lower extremity of these, two pipes of bamboo are led through a clay-bank three inches thick, into a charcoal fire; a man is perched at the top of the trees, and pumps with two pistons (the suckers of which are made of cocks' feathers), which being raised and depressed alternately, blow a regular stream of air into the fire." (Keppel i. p. 65.)

According to Bishop McDougall: "They construct a blast of bamboos, and by means of a lever work three or four of their cane cylinders at a time; with these they blow on the iron ore, which is broken up into 'nublets,' or small pieces, and put on a hearth until the fire renders it soft, not melted. In the first state the iron has become malleable and capable of being worked into swords." (T.E.S. ii. 29.)

Sir Chas. Brooke is of opinion "that the iron smelted in the interior of Rejang is second to none for making arms." (i. p. 50.)

The richest specimens of iron ore come "from the Upper Rejang. The Kayan tribes inhabiting this district smelt their own iron, using charcoal only, in their own rude furnaces, and the steel they manufacture is preferred to that of European make." (A. Hart Everett, Jour. Straits Asiatic Soc., No. 1, p. 20.)

"Commonly at every Kayan village there is a place for smelting iron, in all the process of which the community mutually partake. Covered by a shed, the rude furnace consists of a circular pit formed in the ground, three feet deep, and about four feet in diameter. Previous to the smelting process the ore is roasted and broken into small pieces. The coals (charcoal) in the furnace being set fire to and well kindled, the prepared ore is then placed on the top with alternate layers of coals. The ventilators used consist of wooden tubes, ten to twelve in number, about six feet long and placed vertically round the furnace. The bore of each is about seven inches in diameter, the pistons to correspond are framed of cloth or soft bark. Attached to the piston rods are others of considerable length, to which weights are made fast and balanced on the cross beams of the shed. By this contrivance the pistons are moved up and down, and a constant blast produced, which is led by clay pipes from the orifice at the bottom of each tube into the furnace. In the smelting operation there is no flux used with the ore, which yields about seventy per cent. of iron. To make iron either hard or soft as may be required, different sorts of wood are made use of." (Burns, Jour. Ind. Arch. iii. 151.) " In a Kiñah village the smithy is in a central situation. The Kiñahs smelt their own ore and manufacture their own iron ware. I watched the operation and procured a few samples of the metal. There is nothing peculiar to describe; there were an anvil, a couple of hammers, and a pair of twyers as usual, a charcoal furnace, a quantity of impure ore, and the usual primitive bellows. These people temper their own ore with a fragment of European ironware, when they can get it." (Brooke Low.)

"As before stated, the Kayans and Kenniahs for years smelted their own iron, and the weapons made of that steel retain their value to the present day. They are great blacksmiths and skilful engravers on metal, some of their work bearing the closest examination. Their forge is an ingenious, if laborious, contrivance, consisting of several large bamboos into each of which a piston worked by hand forces the air; this is conducted by means of other bamboo tubes into one, the end of which forms as it were the mouth of the bellows, and in which a considerably accumulated pressure of air is obtained. The anvil is likewise ingenious, being provided with many points and small holes by means of which the smith is enabled to bend and work his iron." (Hose J.A.I. xxiii. 161.)

Sir Sp. St. John procured a packet of the iron the Kayans use in smelting; "it appeared like a mass of rough, twisted ropes, and is, I think, called meteoric iron-stone. They use, also, two other kinds. . . . Their iron ore appears to be easily melted."[6] (i. 113, 122.)

GOLD.

"In times of drought, styled by the natives *Kamarow*, or *Tempo Segah*, the bed of the upper Sadong is searched and scraped for gold, generally with success; of course the longer the spell of fine weather the better the results. Sadong gold is of splendid quality, and second to none found in Sarawak, excepting, perhaps, that found at Marup, yclept *Mas Skrang*." (S.G., 1894, p. 98.) "Near the very sources of the Kapuas live the Malau Dayaks, who are workers in gold and brass, and it is very singular that members of this tribe can wander safely through the villages of the head-hunting Seribas and Sakarang, and are never molested." (St. John i. 31.)

[6] The material most used is the argillaceous spherosiderite, which, as already mentioned, is often present in the coal-bearing beds. Usually it is taken from the most accessible spots in the river beds. In these places the ore has been more or less subject to a chemical change, *i.e.* the clay-iron-stone is, in part, converted into argillaceous brown iron-ore, and is then rendered more easily workable. (Possewitz, p. 432.)

On the Doesun river Mr. Müller speaks of villages almost exclusively inhabited by iron smiths, such as Troesan, Siekan Laloenianw, Roedjej, Panoeatawan. The reason being that the metal which they work is extracted close by the villages in the very bed of the Doesun when its waters are low, and principally along the right bank of the river near the affluence of the little Soengi Patakej. The metal is found spread in the mud of the river in masses of 5, 10 and even 100 pounds weight and more. (ii. 359.)

"In connection with the consumption of gold in the Brit. North Borneo Territory, it may be remarked that none of the savage tribes of this part of Borneo seem ever to have made use of this metal, notwithstanding their intercourse with Malays, and in a less degree with the Chinese, during at least several centuries past. I have never known an instance of a Sea Dyak or Land Dyak, a Kyan or Bakatan, seeking gold on his own account, and manufacturing it into any description of ornament, however rude." (A. Hart Everett, Jour. Straits Asiatic Soc., No. 1, p. 19.)

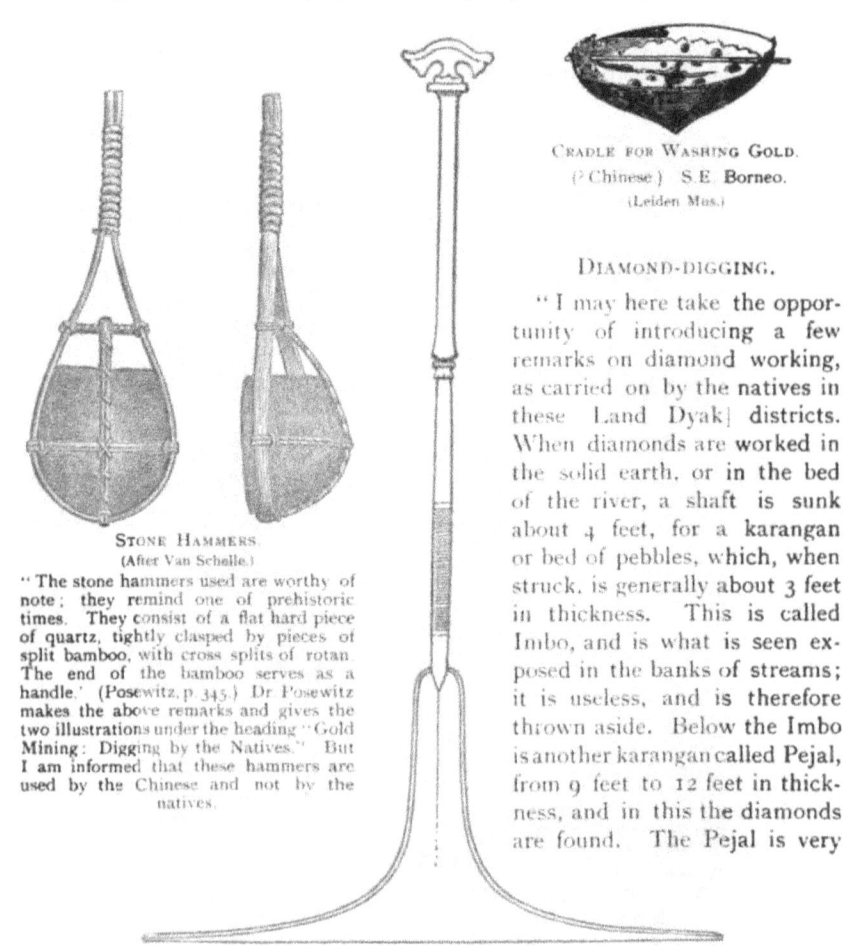

CRADLE FOR WASHING GOLD.
(? Chinese.) S.E. Borneo.
(Leiden Mus.)

STONE HAMMERS.
(After Van Schelle.)
"The stone hammers used are worthy of note; they remind one of prehistoric times. They consist of a flat hard piece of quartz, tightly clasped by pieces of split bamboo, with cross splits of rotan. The end of the bamboo serves as a handle." (Posewitz, p. 345.) Dr. Posewitz makes the above remarks and gives the two illustrations under the heading "Gold Mining: Digging by the Natives." But I am informed that these hammers are used by the Chinese and not by the natives.

DIAMOND-DIGGING.

"I may here take the opportunity of introducing a few remarks on diamond working, as carried on by the natives in these Land Dyak districts. When diamonds are worked in the solid earth, or in the bed of the river, a shaft is sunk about 4 feet, for a karangan or bed of pebbles, which, when struck, is generally about 3 feet in thickness. This is called Imbo, and is what is seen exposed in the banks of streams; it is useless, and is therefore thrown aside. Below the Imbo is another karangan called Pejal, from 9 feet to 12 feet in thickness, and in this the diamonds are found. The Pejal is very

LAND DYAK IMPLEMENT USED IN GOLD WASHING.
Made of heavy brown wood, painted bright red, with yellow edges and lines. Blade thin and flat.
Length, 3ft. 4in.; Width of blade, 2ft. 4½in.
(Brit. Mus.)

hard, being made up of a conglomerate of small pebbles, and is worked with a crowbar, it is carefully placed aside, washed in circular wooden trays, and the diamonds separated from the pebbles. Under the Pejal a stratum of boulders or large stones is met with, to which is given the name of Ampan. With this the shaft is abandoned, as no diamonds are found in or below it, but only mud and sand with perhaps a little gold. The size of the shaft varies according to the number of persons working: one man will sink a shaft one fathom square, while a party of four will not be satisfied under anything less than 4 to 5 fathoms. The shaft is driven down the perpendicular, and should water be met with, the diggers work in the water and drive for the Pejal. One way of working, adopted both in the river and on 'terra firma,' is to sink a shaft till the Pejal is met with, and then drive another at right angles, following the course of the Pejal. This is dug out and brought to the perpendicular shaft, where it is handed up to the surface in baskets."[7] (Denison, ch. vii., p. 71.)

"Diamond digging is not at present carried on in the Sadong river." (S.G., 1894, p. 98.)

MENSURATION.
Time.

"The Land Dyaks generally take no count of days, and months, and years; when they do reckon time at all, they do so by what they call the *Taun Padi*, a period about equal to six of our months." (Chalmers, O. P., p. 7.)

"They make alliances by the rice harvests, and not by years of which they have no knowledge." (Pfeiffer ii. 93.) "Sometimes they explain lapse of time by the height of the sun." (Brooke i. 58.)

As we have seen (i. 401), the Kenniahs judge of the season for planting by a sort of sun dial. "The Kayans, and many other races in Borneo, fix the time of the year for planting paddy, by observing the position of the stars, though it is more usual for Kayans to be guided by the sun. In the case of reckoning by the stars they consider that when the Pleiades appears just above the horizon as daylight breaks (five o'clock) that the right time of the year for sowing has arrived. But paddy may be planted and produce a good crop within three months; the low country people are much later than the hill people, and those who plant swamp paddy even later still. The Kayans measure the shadow of the sun from a horizontal post at twelve o'clock; other shadows cross the large shadow, and the man in charge of this sun-dial has various scales on pieces of wood, but these, and the methods of calculation, together with the sun-dial, which is enclosed by a high fence, are all kept a close secret. But I must admit that they are able to reckon by these measurements how long it is to the time of planting, and I have found that they do not vary much one year from another. I hope some day to have all this explained to me.[8]

[7] Mr. S. Müller states the natives reject platinum as they do not understand how to manipulate it. (ii. 377.)

[8] "The Dyaks reckon their periods of time by the full moon, half-moon, and new moon." (Bock, p. 212.)

"The Dyaks in general appear to know nothing of numbers above ten, and hence they always give us their reckonings in this way, saying, 'one ten,' or 'two, three, four,' or 'many tens,' as the case may be." (Doty, p. 288.)

"A man wishing to describe the time he will be away, says, 'I shall be away so many nights,' not, so many days. If asked what time you will arrive, he will answer, 'when the sun is in *that* position,' pointing to the sky; if wishing to indicate nightfall, he will say, 'when the sun has gone under'; and early dawn, 'when the sun has come up.' A man desirous of describing a fish he has caught, would say it was as big as his forearm, or if larger, as big as the calf of his leg. The graduated scale of measurements they use, are:— the size of the thumb; two fingers; three fingers; four fingers; the wrist; the forearm; the calf of the leg; then the thigh or the head; and lastly, the body.

"As an equivalent for our inches and feet the natives use fingers—one, two, three, four; four fingers constituting the breadth of a hand; their span consists of that between the thumb and first finger, and a long span in some cases between the thumb and second finger, but the latter measurement is not generally allowed, as the following story will show. Once, while seated in a house talking to the chief, I was a witness of a heated dispute which took place between two of his followers anent the sale of a pig. A pig is sold by measurement, the measurement being taken (by means of a string) of the girth of the body just behind the fore-legs; and for every span's-length of string, a dollar has become the fixed price. Now the buyer wanted to use the span of the second finger and thumb; the seller of course objected, as in a large pig the use of the longer span would materially decrease the price. After a heated discussion, both parties appealed to their chief to give a decision. I was anxious to see how the old chief would get out of the difficulty, as it was evident he did not wish to offend either of them, and, on the whole, I think he managed very cleverly.

"Both the disputants sat down in front of him, and explained the point of contention, whereupon he said to the buyer, 'now if you were pointing at a man' (pointing at a man's eyes is a form of insult), 'and were to do it with your second finger' (at the same time pointing with *his* second finger), how foolish it would look, would it not?' The buyer was obliged to admit that it would be so. 'Well, then!' said the chief, 'the first finger is the one to use, and we wont adopt any new fads in this house.' The two men went away, satisfied with the chief's decision, and the pig was sold." (Hose, J.A.I. xxiii., pp. 168-170.)

"The Dusun measuring of cloth is rather an amusing occupation. All cloth is measured by the fathom or *dapah*, which is seldom more than 5 feet 10 inches, often less, being the length that a Dusun can stretch while holding the cloth between the tips of his fingers across his chest. The villagers invariably hunt up their longest *dapah* stretcher, and he measures the first length, which is cut off—all eyes during this operation being bent on the cloth to see that it is just slack and not stretched in the least. After the first length has been cut, it is best to mark an equal measure on the floor and work from that. The head men generally look on while this is being done, to see that there is no cheating by stretching the cloth, and to secure for themselves any lengths that may have an inch or two over." (Whitehead, p. 113.) The Sea Dyaks count with fingers and toes. (Brooke Low.)

The Dusuns have no "idea of time, beyond the return of the seasons, and they know not even their own age." (De Crespigny, Proc. R. Geogr. Soc. ii., 1858, p. 347.)

The Ida'an "are even ignorant of high numbers, and therefore when they go to war, being very numerous, they do not count their numbers by thousands, but by *trees*. They choose a large tree, and each man as he passes gives it a stroke with his weapon, when the tree falls they count one; they who follow pick out another in like manner." (Dalrymple, p. 42.)

This may be hardly true at the present day, as nearly all tribes can count well up into the hundreds. See Append. Vocabs., Chalmers' p. 145, and Swettenham's p. 140. According to the latter vocabulary, the Punans can count up to 100 and more, while the Bakatans (*i.e.*, probably the same people) can only count up to ten. More evidence is wanted. See *supra* Age, i. 60.

DISTANCE.

"One of the most difficult things in this world is to find out from a [Land] Dyak the distance between one place and another. He always answers that question by saying *Takot kabura*, or *Takot kabula*, which means, 'I am afraid of speaking untruly'; and to remedy this evil, they are apt to fall into the very error they would avoid. If the road is far, you will be told it is very far; if short, very short; and so on. Their ways of reckoning, too, are original. You are told you have gone one, or so many divisions, and have so many more to go; or that you will have to eat rice so many times between such and such a place; or that if you leave a place with the sun in that quarter (pointing with the finger), it will be in such a quarter by the time you arrive at the place you are bound for. You are occasionally told you are so many cookings (or boilings) of rice from your destination (a cooking of rice may be reckoned thirty or forty minutes, but the cook will be better able to inform the reader on that point); or if near, that you can hear a gong from it; or if very near that you can hear the cocks crow from it. Then you are either *jau* (far), *ja-u* (very far), or *jau-u-u* (awfully far) from the place. On the present occasion our distance was, *sa bagi sudah, sa bagi balum* (one half completed, one half yet to do); so down the mountain we scrambled, and at the bottom came to another branch of the *Sarāwak* water, called the *Ayer Tebiak*." (Grant, p. 29.)

"As the Dyaks have no notion of dividing time into hours, their methods of reckoning distances are rather original. The most common way is to call a place a day or half a day's journey, or to point to a certain place in the heavens and say they can reach their destination when the sun is there, or to call a village so many boils distant. A boil of rice may be reckoned at half an hour." (Chalmers, Miss. Field, 1859, p. 136.)

Among the Sea Dyaks: "Short distances are described by arriving at such a place before the hair has had time to dry, or by the time for cooking one, two, or three pots of rice, as the distance may happen to be."

NATURAL PRODUCTIONS.

It may not be out of place to give a short account of some of the natural productions, which have been frequently referred to in the preceding chapters.

GUTTA.

The Gutta "is obtained from four or five kinds of large forest trees, belonging to the genus *isonandra*, by felling the trees and girdling or ringing their bark at intervals of every two feet, the milky juice or sap being caught in vessels fashioned of leaves or cocoa-nut shells."[9] (Burbidge, p. 74.)

The process is thus described by Mr. Hornaday: "The native found a gutta tree, about ten inches in diameter, and, after cutting it down, he ringed it neatly all the way along the stem, at intervals of a yard or less. Underneath each ring he put a calabash to catch the milk-white sap which slowly exuded. From this tree and another about the same size, he got about four quarts of sap, which, on being boiled that night for my special benefit, precipitated the gutta at the bottom in a mass like dough. The longer it was boiled the harder the mass became, and at last it was taken out, placed upon a smooth board, kneaded vigorously with the hands, and afterwards trodden with the bare feet of the operator. When it got almost too stiff to work, it was flattened out carefully, then rolled up in a wedge-shaped mass, a hole was punched through the thin end to serve as a handle, and it was declared ready for the trader. I have seen the Dyaks roll up a good-sized wad of pounded bark in the centre of these wedges of crude gutta, in order to get even with the traders who cheat in weight, but I have also seen the sharp trader cut every lump of gutta in two before buying it. If he found bark, you may well believe he did not pay for it at the price of gutta. The crude gutta has a mottled, or marbled, light-brown appearance, is heavy and hard, and smooth on the outside." (p. 433.) "The juice of ficus and one or two species of *artocarpeæ* is not unfrequently used in addition as adulterants. It is generally adulterated with twenty per cent. of scraped bark—indeed, the Chinese traders who purchase the gutta from the collectors, would refuse the pure article in favour of that adulterated with bark, and to which its red colour is mainly due." (Burbidge, p. 74.) "It is most deplorable to see the fallen gutta trees lying about in all directions in the forest. The gutta trees are a long time in attaining to maturity, and are not easy to propagate, except by seeds." (*ibid.*)

In the Linogu valley, on the southern slope of the Derigi, the "people do not know the gutta percha tree, and of indiarubber they know but little, there being no great demand. When rambling in the bush the experienced eyes of my men noticed gutta trees of the best description." (Witti, 29 May.)

---

[9] With two sharp strokes of a *mandau* a deep notch was cut in the bark, from which the juice slowly oozed, forming a milky-looking mucilage, which gradually hardened and became darker in colour as it ran down the tree. The native collectors of gutta-percha make a track through the forest, nicking the trees in two or three places as they go, and collect the hardened sap on their return a few days afterwards. (Bock, p. 152.)

ANIMALS MADE OUT OF RAW GUTTA.
(Hose Coll.)

Pat, KAYAN TOOL FOR GETTING GUTTA.
Baram River.
(Peek Coll.)

ALLIGATOR OF RAW GUTTA.
(Hose Coll.)

CYLINDRICAL BOX OF GUTTA, with ornaments in relief. Kapuas River. Height, 5¼in.
(Brit. Mus.)

GUTTA as brought to market from Balait River. 9in. × 4in. × 2in.
(Hose Coll.)

DYAK CAP. Made of raw gutta.
(Hose Coll.)

PARANG.
Used to ring the bark of gutta-producing trees in PERAK, MALAY PENINSULA.
(Sir H. Low, Kew Mus.)

Rubber.

"The Bornean *gutta soosoo*, or rubber,[10] again, is the mixed sap of three species of *willughbeias*, and here, again, the milk of two or three other plants is added surreptitiously to augment the quantity collected. The three species of climbing plants are known to the natives as *Manoongan, Manoongan putih*, and *Manoongan manga*. Their stems are fifty to one hundred feet in length and rarely more than six inches in diameter. Their fruits are of a delicious flavour, and are highly valued by the natives. Here, again, the stems are cut down to facilitate the collection of the creamy sap, which is afterwards coagulated into rough balls by the addition of nipa salt. The rubber-yielding *willughbeias* are gradually, but none the less surely, being exterminated by the collectors. They grow quickly, and may be easily and rapidly increased by vegetative as well as by seminal modes of propagation." (Burbidge, p. 74.) "The natives use it to cover the sticks with which they beat their gongs and musical instruments." (Low, p. 52.)

The Nipa Palm.

"The nipa (*Nipa fruticans*, see illustration, ii. 4), though in growth amongst the humblest of the palm tribe, in its value to the natives of this island is inferior to few of them. It is found on the margins of the rivers as far as the salt water extends, and large salt marshes at the mouths of rivers are covered with it to the extent of thousands of acres; its chief value is for covering houses, the leaves of which for this purpose are made into *ataps*, and endure for two years. Salt is made in some places from its leaves by burning them, and in others sugar is extracted from syrup supplied by its flower-stem. The fruit, though tasteless, is esteemed by the natives, and is said to make an excellent preserve. Its leaves, on luxuriant plants, are occasionally twenty feet long, all growing from the centre." (Low, p. 43.)

Messrs. Whitehead (p. 32), H. Pryer (*The Field*, 20 Dec., 1884), and Sir Sp. St. John (i. 233) are equally emphatic in its praises, adding that cigars and cigarettes are rolled up in the fine inner leaf.

Rotan.

The rotan canes are the produce of the *Calamus rotang* and various species of the same genus *Calamus*. They are creeping plants, the stems of which are coated with a flinty bark, cylindrical, jointed, very, tough and strong, from ¼ to 1½in. in diameter, and 50 to 100 feet long, they are easily split and are used for the seat of chairs, wicker work, &c. Some varieties of dragon's blood are obtained from the plants of this genus. When used as cordage "the outer and hard parts only are used, the rattans being split and the inner part carefully removed." (Low, p. 43.)

Bambu.

The bambu is the *Bambusa arundinacea*, a kind of reed which grows in clumps, the individual reeds ranging up to 60 feet in height and five inches in diameter. It has a hard siliceous skin, is hard and durable, and is largely used for furniture, water pipes, houses, bridges, &c.

---

[10] It is frequently spoken of as *caoutchouc*, but as caoutchouc is an aboriginal American name for the sap, the name should not be applied to the East Indian product. (H. L. R.)

Dammar.

This is the largely used resin obtained from the *Agathis* (=*Dammara orientalis*.) "The Dyaks mix it with oil for paying the seams of boats." (Low, p. 49.)

The Tapang Tree.

This tree was mentioned when Honey-getting was described, and it should now be added that Mr. W. Botting Hemsley, of Kew, writing to Mr. F. W. Burbidge, of Trinity College Gardens, Dublin, says that from a hint given him by Sir Hugh Low, he finds "the tapang tree is *Koompassia excelsa* Taubert, syn *Abauria excelsa* Beccari."

Oils.

"Mengkabang, or vegetable tallow [*Dipterocarpus*], is procured in the following manner from one of the wild fruits of the jungle:—When the fruit, a species of nut, has been gathered, it is picked, dried, and pounded, and after being thoroughly heated in a shallow cauldron, it is put into a rattan bag and subjected to a powerful pressure. The oil oozes from the bag, and being run into bamboo moulds is there allowed to cool, in which state it becomes hard and yellow, somewhat resembling unpurified bees' wax. It is principally used by the Dyaks and Malays for cooking, being very palatable, but in this country it is employed for the manufacture of patent candles, for which it is superior to palm oil.

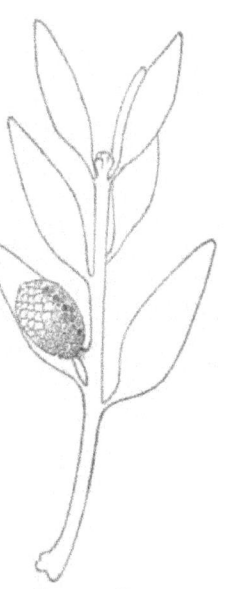

Dammar Fruit.
Agathis (= Dammara orientalis.)
(L. C. Richard's Conifers, t. 19.)

"Katio oil is procured from another wild nut, and is expressed in a somewhat similar manner. It is a beautiful yellow transparent fluid, with a smell very much like bitter almonds, and I have little doubt that it will yet be found a very valuable article of commerce.

"The press employed by the Dyaks in expressing these oils is, like many other of their contrivances, both simple and effective. It consists of two semi-cylindrical logs about 7 feet long, placed in an upright position, their flat surfaces being fitted together and their lower ends securely fastened to each other. On each of their upper ends a stout knob is cut, and a third piece of wood, about two feet long, nine inches wide, and two inches thick, with a hole cut in about a foot long and three inches wide, is put over the knobs so as to clasp them together. Wedges are then inserted between the outside of the knob and the inside of the hole, and these when driven home subject whatever is between the logs to a powerful pressure." (Horsburgh, p. 41.)

Sir Hugh Low mentions several oils used by the natives, one *miniak kapayang* from a tree called *pangium edule*, &c. One wood oil, '*miniak kruing*,' "is extracted from the trees which produce it, by simply cutting a large hole in the tree, into which fire being placed, the oil is attracted. The tree probably belongs to the order Myrtaceæ." (Low, p. 48.)

CHAPTER XXV.

BOATING, SWIMMING, RIDING.

BOATING. BOATS: Plank war boats—Large dimensions—Keel laying ceremony—Method of building—Preservation of planks—Over-landing—Squalls—*Bandongs*—*Kadjangs*—Paddles—Long hours—Speed—Distant voyages. DUG-OUTS: Bintulu *barongs*—Unsinkableness - Surf-running—Fishwives' humour - Muka Regatta—Various descriptions—Method of digging out—The Baram dug-outs—Kanowits—Strength and elasticity. BARK CANOES. POLING: Speed—Expertness—Overcoming rapids—Stirring scenes.
SWIMMING. Mermaids—Good swimmers—Stream crossing—Diving.
RIDING. Bagu buffaloes

BOATS.

"THE Sea Dyak war boats are well constructed and good models, and very fast; some will hold as many as sixty or seventy men, with two months' provisions. The keel is flat, with a curve or sheer of hard wood. A long one does not exceed six fathoms, and upon it they will build a boat of eleven fathoms over all. The extra length of planks which overlap, is brought up with a sheer. They caulk the seams with a bark which is plentiful in the jungle. No other fastenings but rattans are used. They paint their boats red and white,—the former is generally an ochre, but occasionally they use a kind of red seed pounded; the white is simply lime, made from sea shells." (St. John i. 70.) Sir Jas. Brooke states the red paint to be an ochre mixed with oil. (Mundy i. 303.)

Lieut. Marryat describes a fine Lundu war boat "about forty feet long, mounting a gun, and capable of containing forty or fifty men. She was very gaily decorated with paint and feathers. These war prahus have a flat strong roof, from which they fight, although they are wholly exposed to the spears and arrows of the enemy." (p. 83.) He also mentions a Dyak war boat sufficiently capacious to hold from seventy to eighty men. (p. 64.)

KAYAN FIGURE-HEAD FOR WAR CANOE.
An *udoh aso* mythological animal with gibbon in its jaws
(Brooke Low Coll.)

ORNAMENT ON BOW OF ILANUN PIRATE BOAT.
(After Sir Edw. Belcher.)

At Lundu before "the Orang Kaya commenced to build his boat, many plates and dishes were carefully laden with rice and other eatables; sirih and pinang (betel) were also placed so that the spirits could partake of these luxuries and satisfy themselves. Besides this, to the people congregated around the place where the boat was about to be built, arrack was served out, of which they all sipped with the utmost gravity, and the few words that were spoken referred to their enemies, the Sakarangs and Saribus, upon whom their whole attention was evidently concentrated." (Brooke i. 39.)

The Balau war boats are built as follows: "The *lunas*, or keel plank, which is of the entire length of the boat, has two ledges on its inside, each of them about an inch from each margin of the plank. Each of the other planks, which are likewise the entire length of the boat, has an inside ledge on its upper margin, its lower margin being plain, like an ordinary plank. When the Dyaks have made as many planks as are necessary for the boat they intend constructing, they put them together in the following manner:—The lunas, or keel plank, being properly laid down, the first side plank is

DYAK WAR PRAHU ON SKERANG RIVER.
(After F. Marryat).
This boat looks very much like the Ilanun war prahus off Gilolo, figured in Sir E. Belcher's "Voyage of the Samarang."

brought and placed, with its lower or plain edge, upon the ledge of the keel-plank. The ledge of the first side-plank being thus uppermost, it becomes in turn the ledge upon which the lower edge of the second side-plank must rest. The ledges of the keel-plank, and of the first side-plank, are then pierced, and firm rattan lashings passed from the one to the other. The lower edge of the second side-plank is in like manner laid upon the ledge of the first, and these two planks are lashed together in the same way as the first was lashed to the keel. Thus they place the edge of each plank upon the ledge of that immediately below it, lashing them both firmly together; and when they have in this manner put on as many planks as they wish (generally four or five on each side), they caulk the seams, so as to render the boat water-tight. Hence in the construction of their boats they not only employ no nails, treenails, or bolts, but even no timbers—nothing but planks ingeniously lashed together by rattans, and then caulked. It is true that these lashings are not very durable, as the rattans soon get rotten; but this is of little consequence, since, whenever a boat returns from an expedition, the lashings are cut and the planks being separated, are taken up into the house. When she is again wanted the planks are taken down, and the boat reconstructed as before." (Horsburgh, p. 36.)

" As these planks cost the Dyaks—who are unacquainted with the use of the saw or any other instrument for forming them but the 'biliong' or adze of the Malays—no end of time, their preservation is an object of no small importance; two planks only being obtained from a large tree with infinite labour, it being very necessary that the planks of the boat, on account of her construction, should all be of the same length as the *bankong*. These boats, according to their size, carry crews of from thirty to ninety men." (Low, p. 221.)

While Sir Chas. Brooke was once admiring a craft which was exceedingly beautiful an old Dyak said to him, " Tuan, such are our kind of pinnaces; yours are of a different description and better for sea, but ours are regulated for land, and there we beat yours, for we can walk away with ours and build her again in any other direction, in the rivers on the other side of the mountains." (ii. 104.)

" From the nature of these boats, and the slightness of their build, it may easily be imagined that they are not manageable in a sea-way, their length causing them to open at the seams: on such occasions, should they not be near enough to the land to run into smooth water, the crew all jump overboard, and hang by the side of the boat: this I have been assured they have done for many successive hours when the squalls, which are usually short in these tranquil seas, have been prolonged, so as to render it necessary. In this situation they take it by turns for one or two to enter the boat, and cook and eat their rice, until the squall is past." (Low, p. 221.) " They say, when this occurs in places suspected to be frequented by sharks, they each tie a bundle of the tuba plant round their ancles to drive the devouring fish away." (St. John i. 68.)

" The boats used by the Kalaka fishermen are called *bandongs*; they are of crank build and may be classed as skiffs. Their dimensions as a rule are about 30 feet over all, by 3½ feet by 3 feet; they are sharp at the bow and stern, which are both higher than the gunwale of boat amidships. The crew use very large paddles with great strength and skill." (T. S. Chapman, S.G., No. 113.)

Most of the boats are provided with awnings " called Kadjang, which make a roof at once water-proof, very light, easily adjusted, and so flexible that, when desired, each section can be rolled up and stowed away in the bottom of the boat. These kadjangs are made of the long, blade-like leaves of the nipa palm, on the same principle as a tile roof. The leaves are each six or seven feet long by two inches wide. They are sewn together with strips of rattan, each alternate leaf overlapping its neighbour on either side, and so on until a section of roof is formed about six and a half feet square. This section is then made to bend in the middle cross-wise, at a sharp angle, so that it can be folded once and rolled up, or partly opened and made to stand up tent-wise, when it forms the very best kind of roof for such a climate." (Hornaday, p. 354.)

" To propel their boats they employ paddles of about three feet in length —never oars, and seldom sails." (Horsburgh, p. 36.) " The Sakarans ply the paddles with vigour and regularity." (Sir J. Brooke, Mundy i. 235.)

Boats.

"It is no uncommon thing for the Dyaks to pull for eighteen hours, with only short intervals of rest sufficient to boil and cook their rice, and this, from the beautiful regularity of their strokes, and their being long accustomed to the practice, does not appear much to fag them; in smooth water, and, without tides, at their regular stroke, they pull about six miles an hour, but when exerting themselves fully can double that rate of speed." The Dyak bankongs even beat the speed of the Singapore tambangs. "Each tribe of the Dyaks has peculiar strokes in which it delights, so that in the dark a Sarebas or Sakarran boat could tell whether an approaching one was of Lundu, of the Balows, or a Malay. On their cruises the Dyaks, who are not, in their sober moments, friends of boisterous mirth, never make use of the cheering and inspiring songs of the Malayan boatmen: the noise made by each paddle beating time on the gunwale of the boat is to them sufficiently enlivening, and they want no other encouragement to exertion when it is necessary." (Low, p. 221.)

The Ida'an on the Kimanis river build vessels and navigate them to Java. (Dalrymple, p. 50.)[1]

"Until the Sarawak Government curbed their proceedings the Sea Dyaks were known to coast down as far as Pontianak, and occasionally they had been met forty miles out at sea in their rattan-tied boats, some of them seventy feet in length." (St. John i. 68.)

Dug-Outs.

When describing pomfret fishing reference was made to the Bintulu *barongs*. Mr. Crocker thus describes them: "They are particularly adapted for going through the surf which prevails on the N.W. coast in the N.E. monsoon owing to the shallow bars at the mouths of the rivers.

---

[1] It would seem at one time Sumatra was supplied with boats from Borneo. "A world of those Pirogues are made in Bandermassin, a town in the Island of Borneo, where you may buy one laded with bees-wax, rice, dry fish, and other products of the country, at a cheap rate." (A Collection of Voyages undertaken by the Dutch East India Co. Translated. London, Freeman & Co., 1703, 8 p. 202.)

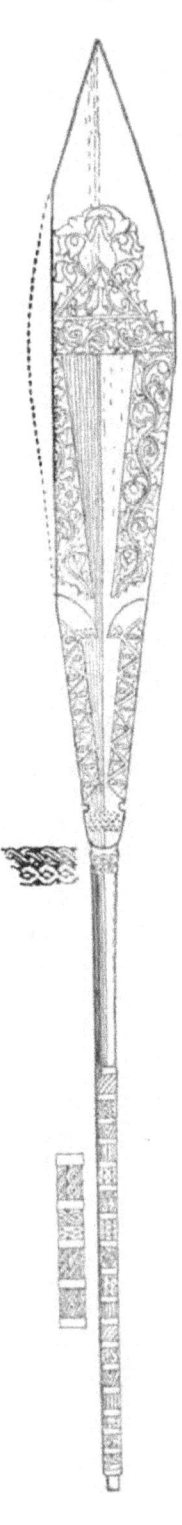

Paddle of Dark Brown Wood. Flat blade ⅜in. thick, with a very slight longitudinal ridge on each side. Round carved handle with smaller square butt, on to which most probably a nut was fixed. The blade has carved borders on the edges of both sides, terminating with triangular capitals. (Brit. Mus.)

They receive the sea broadside on, and the natives manage their craft with such dexterity that, although they often go to sea when a ship's boat could not live five minutes, they never swamp. They are about 40 feet long, the bottom being a simple canoe hollowed out of a tree; planks are raised on each side fastened by wooden pegs: in place of knees they strengthen the boat by several thwarts connecting each plank, a beam runs down the middle of the boat fastened to the thwarts. The ends of the boat are square, fastened by pegs and rotans. They are strong and buoyant and are propelled by short oars fastened on rotan row-locks. The natives use a large sail, and the boats, from being so flat bottomed, sail with great speed before the wind, or when the wind is at all free. The ordinary mode of steering is by two large rudders, one fixed on each side; these however are unshipped when crossing a bar and a long oar substituted." (S.G., No. 122.) Sir Chas. Brooke states these barong look like an oval washing tub only a little longer in dimensions. The Mukah people "have an idea that their boats cannot founder in a high sea unless they go to pieces. They pull short oars with a plunging and splashing stroke, with more jerk than spring, and the tub splashes through the water as dry as a collier, and while coming in through a heavy breaking surf running far over their heads, they watch for the roll, and while in the trough pull with all their might; but when the wave is curling to break, they suddenly slew their crafts broadside on, and so receive it with the exposed side well out of water. Directly it has passed, away they go again as fast as possible, until another roller overtakes them, when they repeat the same manœuvre.[2] It is well known in Mukah, and other places in the

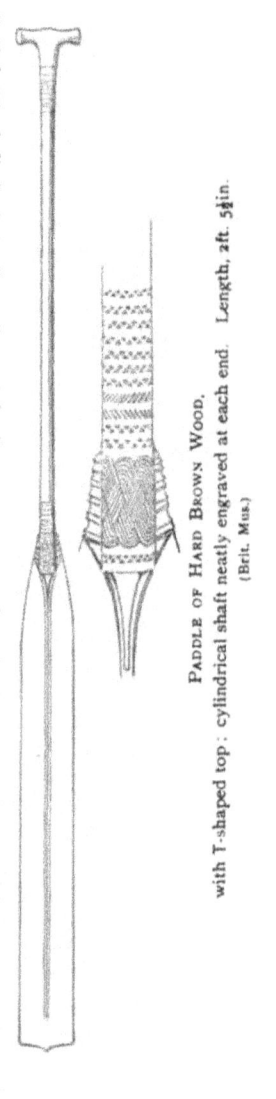

[1] Mr. Hose (J.A.I. xxiii. 158) also describes this surf running.

vicinity, that the wives close their doors and will not receive their husbands unless they procure fish; and this may be an incitement to undergo such

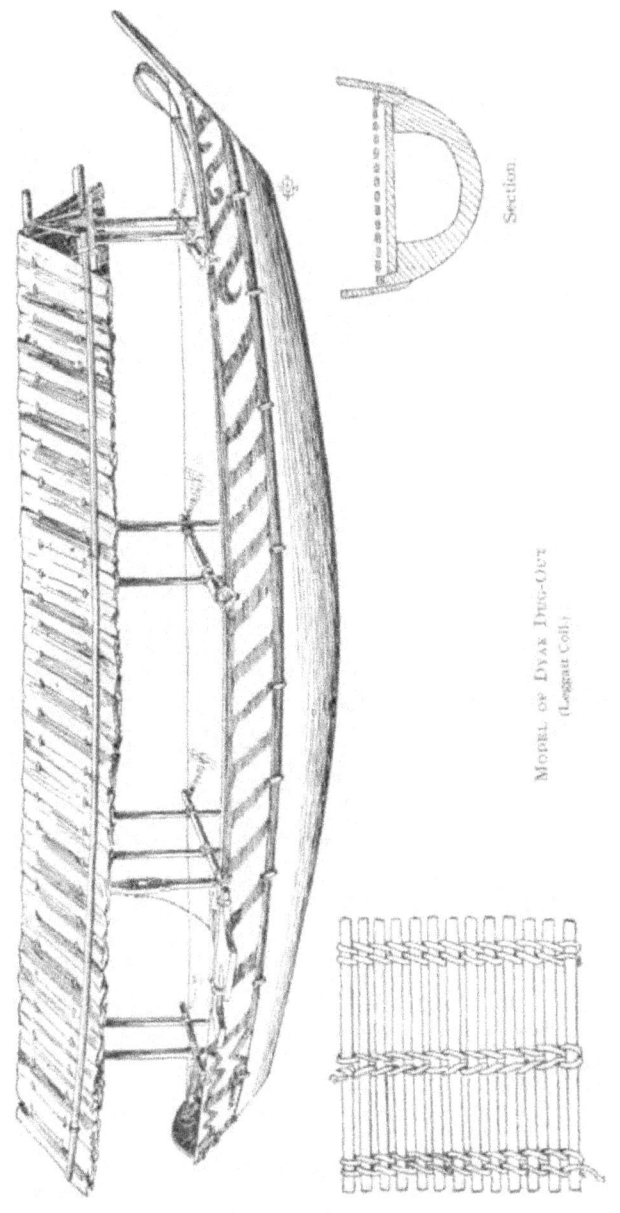

Section.

Model of Dyak Dug-Out
(Leggatt Coll.)

dangers. The women work hard themselves, and make the sagu, which is a remarkably dry condiment without the accompaniment of fish; hence their desire for husbands, plus fish—and the refusal to admit them without that article." (ii. 100.)

The Barong Race, which is the great feature of the Muka Regatta, is undoubtedly a sight to be seen nowhere else. "During the race the crews shriek like fiends, and two men rush up and down the boat with buckets pouring water on the heads of the oarsmen, to prevent their going roaring mad I suppose. This shouting mingled with the creaking and splashing of the oars and the rushing sound of the water thrown up by the great flat bows makes the race very exciting." (Assistant Resident at Muka, S.G., No. 96.)

With regard to the bore on the Sadong (?) river : " Many native canoes went a short way down to meet it, and when its sullen voice was heard they raised loud shouts, and the next instant were whirled along with incredible velocity on the summit of the curling wave." (Sir Jas. Brooke, Mundy i. 214.)

LUNDU WOMEN IN A CANOE.
(After Lieut. F. Marryat).

"The ordinary boats of the Balaus are long, narrow canoes, hollowed out of the trunk of a tree, the sides being raised by planks pinned upon them." (Horsburgh, p. 36.) Sir Jas. Brooke says "their boats are carved about their high sterns, which distinguish them from the plain boats of Sakarran and Sarebas." (Mundy i. 236.) Mr. Crossland mentions a boat eighteen yards long which will easily carry twenty people. "It was cut out of a log, and therefore is all of a piece. As a rule they are not pretty to look at, but are safe boats, and live well in the surf" (Miss. Life, 1870, p. 219.) ; while Mr. Frank Hatton speaks of a Sin Dyak dug-out "of capital workmanship, being carved at the bow." (p. 187.) The Grogo Dyaks are good boat builders ; Mr. Denison mentions one of their boats *jalur* 6½ fathoms long.

"The Sea Dyaks' canoes are hollowed out of a single log by means of fire and the use of the adze. The natives have no measure to ensure accuracy, but are entirely guided by the eye. Generally the canoe shows traces of the fire and water treatment it has received, the inner surface being soft and full of superficial cracks, while the outer surface is hard and close. When the shell has been sufficiently opened out, thwarts are inserted to prevent its shrinking as the wood dries. Planks or gunwales are stitched on to the sides to increase its volume, the seams being caulked with sago stems which are light and porous, and swell when wet and so keep out the water. Each of these side pieces is formed of an entire plank about 12 inches deep and about 1½ inches thick, laced on to the body of the canoe by flaxen cords and united to its opposite plank by the thwarts. The largest canoes have the sides made still higher by means of a narrow plank laced on to the first gunwale, and the seam again caulked. The canoe is alike at both ends, the stem and stern being both pointed, curved, and rising out of the water. There is no keel, and the canoe draws little water. There are no ribs nor is there any figure head." (Brooke Low.)

MODEL OF A *Tukau*. Baram River.
(Hose Coll.)

"On the Baram all the races use boats, excepting those who live far inland and away from the large rivers, as for instance, a few of the Kalabit tribes. The Kayans and Kenniahs use both long and short boats—a long boat, cut out of the trunk of one of the large forest trees (the native name of which is *Aroh*), sometimes measuring thirty-eight yards in length, and seven feet in beam ; a boat of this description will accommodate a hundred men who sit two abreast plying their paddles on either side of the boat simultaneously, and thus propelled it attains a rate of speed enabling it to travel (at a rough calculation) between fifty and sixty miles in a day. The common name given to this boat is *Harok* ; a smaller boat propelled by about twenty paddles is known as a *Temoi*, and they also make use of various little dug-outs of all sizes, for travelling between their houses and rice plantations." (Hose, J.A.I. xxiii. 158.)

On the Kanowit river His Highness describes a boat "sixty-six feet long, shaped like a coffin, and totally devoid of all elegance or beauty. She consisted of a single tree hollowed out, and round at the bottom, but raised a little at her extremities. Many trees split while undergoing the twisting, and the wood requires to be peculiarly tough to stand the hacking in the centre. When the hollowing out is done, a bow and stern-piece are fastened with rattans: they have not a nail in them; two light planks are also tied on to the top, and then they are complete. Some have much speed, and are capable of carrying from forty to seventy men, with a month's provision aboard. They are adapted for passing the rapids and other impediments, but twist and twirl to a great extent in being hauled over difficult places. Although they are buoyant in the falls, they are extremely heavy, and can stand an extraordinary amount of bumping about. The thickness of the wood is not less than three inches in many parts. The crews are able to use a long, sweeping stroke with their paddles, which could not be managed in shorter boats." (ii. 243, 261.)

Bark Canoes.

"To make a bark canoe the native simply goes to the nearest stringy bark tree, chops a circle round it at its base, and another circle 7 or 8 feet from the ground; he then makes a longitudinal cut on each side, and strips off as much bark as is required. The ends are sewn up carefully and daubed up with clay, the sides being kept in position by cross-pieces. The steering is performed with one or two greatly developed fixed paddles." (Brooke Low.)

Poling.

On shallow streams paddles cannot be used, and the Sebongoh Dyaks propel "their boats with long canes of bamboo, which they use more adroitly than any other tribes I have visited; the women are equally expert with the men." (Low, p. 400.)

"Each canoe contained but two Dayaks and one passenger. Our canoes were small, drawing but a few inches of water, and were managed by two Dayaks, one standing at the stem, the other at the stern; with long bamboos in their hands, they impelled us forward at a great pace." (i. 135.)

On the Sekyam river "we were the whole afternoon poling our way down stream, floating over or through the rapids, having repeatedly to stop and re-arrange and bind together our bamboo craft, which was at last so shattered and broken, by contact with stones and boulders, that to this day it is a mystery to me how we managed to cling to it. The skill of these Dyaks which alone saved us from a complete collapse, was beautiful to witness. The strain on the muscles of these poor fellows—as now they poled us over a rapid, now pushed us with their utmost strength from some huge boulder against which the current was forcing us apparently to utter destruction—was great in the extreme. With a turn of the bamboo pole they would send us through a pool of boiling, seething water, past a rock here, over a stone there, and then balancing the long bamboos across their chests, they would pause for an instant as the frail, trembling craft, quivering in every joint, glided swiftly over the rapid into the smooth, fast, flowing stream beyond." (Denison, ch. v., p. 55.)

A lively account of poling under difficulties is given by Mr. Hose: "Giham Tipang, on the Baram, is a particularly dangerous rapid, the passing of which is accomplished at very considerable risk; the volume of water dashing over the rocks, and rising in waves 5 or 6 feet high, makes it appear impossible for a boat to pass. The 'dugout,' however, is tied fore and aft with rattans, and dragged through the middle of the rapids by one half of the men, the others remaining in the boat to work with poles. The noise is deafening, each man shouting at the top of his voice; and after pulling the boat for about an hour, the head of the rapid is reached, and immediately those on the rocks jump into the boat and begin paddling with all their might into some backwater for fear of being carried back over the rapid. For a moment the 'dugout' scarcely moves, but at last their united efforts tell, and the boat begins slowly to make way to the nearest bank. Occasionally the current is too strong for them, and feeling themselves carried back, they jump overboard, holding on to the boat with one hand, while with the other they grasp any rock or bush that they can clutch, thus arresting the boat. One of the party then takes a turn with the rattan around the rock, and so makes it fast until they can start again. Sometimes there is nothing to catch hold of, and then, seeing it hopeless to fight against the stream, everyone turns round in the boat, and seizing their paddles and poles, they allow the vessel to shoot over the fall into the seething waters below. The sensation is undoubtedly singular, but it does not last long. The boat is bumped about in all directions, and carried on at a tremendous rate for a few seconds, the water leaping in on either side and the men *kicking* it out continually with one foot. The moment they are over, the vessel quietly glides round to the nearest backwater, and once more you draw your breath freely. Having thus escaped, they smoke a cigarette before making another attempt to drag up the boat." (Geogr. Jour. i. 196.)

Sir Charles Brooke had frequent experience of poling, and found the small Dyak boats well adapted for this kind of work, "merely consisting of a few thin planks tied into a keel of hard wood. They twist and twirl as they are propelled by long poles, and on meeting any great difficulty the boat's crew jump out and lift them over. . . . Our men worked wonderfully, and some of the attitudes of the crews as they jumped over the rapids were very striking. Every muscle was distended, every pole was planted together to hold the boat still and steady until the time came for another spring, and another five feet were gained." (ii. 172.) Elsewhere he states: "It is a stirring scene to behold this performance, by men who have been all their lives at such work." (*ibid*, i. 240.)

SWIMMING.

Lieut. Marryat describes the swimming of a Lundu girl in the following enthusiastic terms: " She swam like a frog and with her long hair streaming in the water behind her came pretty well up to our ideas of a mermaid." (p. 75.) Mr. Wallace speaks of a Land Dyak girl 10 or 12 years old who swam beautifully. (i. 102.) " The Sea Dyaks seem to acquire naturally the art of swimming, being taken to the river regularly from infancy and dipped and floated on the water." (Leggatt.) " They are fond of the water and both swim and dive well. They swim hand over hand like dogs. They never take a header in diving, but jump into the water upright sinking feet first." (Brooke Low.) The Dumpas men swim like fishes. (Hatton, Diary, 18 Mar.) Sir Sp. St. John saw some young Ida'an cross a stream as if it were no exertion at all; they did it with the surging waters reaching to their armpits and with a half dancing motion. (i. 254.) The Bajus did not attempt to cross a stream in a direct course, but allowed themselves to be carried away a little, and reached the other side about fifty yards farther down. They carried all the luggage over, swimming with one hand and holding the baskets in the air with the other. Two men placed themselves one on either side of us, told us to throw ourselves flat on the water and remain passive; in a few minutes we were comfortably landed on the opposite bank. (*ibid*, i. 257.) Where streams are crossed by walking and not by swimming, " the great difficulty," writes Mr. Burbidge, " is to keep one's legs under one in the strong current, and to facilitate this being done the Dusuns often take up a heavy stone and carry it on one shoulder." (p. 260.)

Of their expertness in diving reference has been made in the chapter devoted to fishing, &c.

RIDING.

" The Baju saddle, made of wood, covered with thin cloth, is very small. Instead of stirrups they have a rope with a loop in the end, into which they insert their big toe, and ride with the soles of their feet turned up behind; and when they set off on a gallop they cling with their toes under the pony's belly. The Baju is essentially a non-walker. He never makes use of his own legs if he can possibly get an animal to carry him. He rides all the horses and the mares, even when the latter have just foaled. Cows are equally in requisition, and it was laughable to observe one of these animals with a couple of lads on her back trotting along the pathways, a calf, not a week old, frisking beside her. The water buffalo, however, appeared to be the favourite, the strong beast constantly carrying double." (St. John i. 234.)

FILE.
Made of fish skin gummed on to wood. S.E. Borneo.
(Leyden Mus.)

CHAPTER XXVI.

MUSIC.

MUSICAL INSTRUMENTS: Jew's Harps—Flutes—Nose flute—*Klurais*—Varieties of—Scale—Violins—Guitars—Banjos—Harps—Drums and gongs—Dulcimers. MUSICAL CHARACTER OF THE PEOPLE. SINGING: Plaintiveness—War songs—Boat songs—Extempore songs.

MUSICAL INSTRUMENTS.

"THE European Jew's harp is a small musical instrument held between the teeth, and having a metal tongue, which, when struck by the finger, produces musical sounds that are modulated by the breath. In the Sea Dyak *rudieng*, the little finger of the left hand stretches the string loop at the left end, and the thumb and first finger hold the metal handle; the cross-piece is held between the thumb and finger, and pulls the concave inside. It is used by a young man to talk to his young girl at night, when they do not wish the mother to overhear their talk—they are able to understand each other in the language of love. The length is $3\frac{2}{3}$ to $4\frac{3}{4}$ inches; the narrow end is $\frac{1}{16}$ to $\frac{1}{4}$ of an inch wide, and the broad end $\frac{3}{8}$ to $\frac{7}{16}$ of an inch wide. It is a perfectly intelligible wind instrument; a metal plate of unequal width, narrowest where it is held in the left hand, and widest where it is held in the right hand. The string is jerked by the tongue, which is likewise metal, vibrates and resounds in the cavity of the mouth. The sounds are modified with the breath. Other tribes in Borneo use a bamboo one; this was no doubt the origin of the Dyak one; the Maloh have taught the Dyaks the use of metal. Bamboo ones are not now in use among them. The case in which it is kept is a bamboo cylinder beautifully carved; the ground is coloured red with dragon's

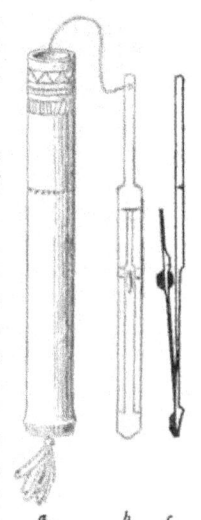

a.   b.   c.

SO-CALLED "JEWS' HARP."

Made of bambu. From Kina Balu. *a*, case, with tassel hanging through a hole in the bottom; by means of the string attached to the tassel the instrument is drawn into the case. *b* and *c*, front and side view.

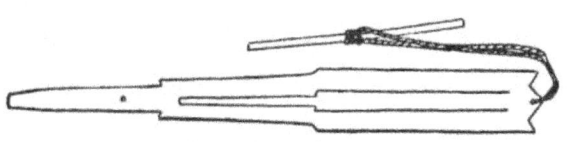

DYAK BRASS JEWS' HARP, *Rodiung*.
(Hose Coll.)

blood; girth about 2¼ inches, fitted with a carved hard-wood stopper. The metal is not flat, but almost imperceptibly concave." (Brooke Low.)

According to Mr. Hornaday (p. 468) the Sibuyau women had a similar "instrument, made of a piece of bamboo like a large organ-reed, the tongue of which was made to vibrate sharply by jerking a string attached to one end. The instrument was held all the while firmly against the teeth and the operator breathed forcibly upon the vibrating tongue of the instrument, thereby producing a few harp-like notes." Mr. Burbidge mentions (p. 178) an "instrument like the Jew's harp made of a single strip of bamboo," and Mr. Whitehead says (p. 108) "a Dusun boy gave him a very cleverly made Jew's harp of bamboo." Mr. Hose tells us the Kayans have the Jew's harp *aping*.

"The *gulieng* is a bamboo pipe, with a plug at the mouth hole, and differs from a whistle in having finger holes, by means of which different tones can be produced. It is blown at the end like a flageolet, and the three finger holes are placed equi-distantly. Four distinct tones are easily obtainable upon it, the lowest when all the finger holes are covered, and the other three by opening the finger holes successively." (Brooke Low.)

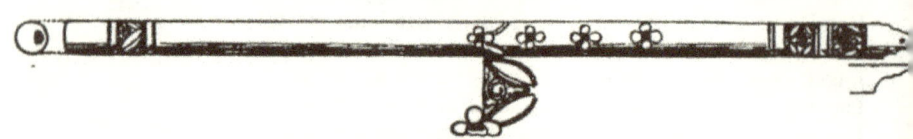

Silingut. KENNIAH NOSE FLUTE. 24½in. long
(Hose Coll.)

"On the Baram," writes Mr. Hose, "we arrived one evening at the house of Aban Lia, and on going inside I found a musician seated in the middle of the verandah surrounded by an audience of about forty persons. The instrument which he was using was a flute (*silingut*) made of bamboo, on which he played not in the usual way with his lips, but through his nose! The notes produced were softer and clearer than the ordinary flute (*ensuling*) which is played with the mouth, and the man was certainly a skilful performer. Finding, however, that much of his wind escaped through the other nostril, he tore out the lining of his pocket and blocked the offending outlet with a small plug of rag. He assured me that his nose, which was undoubtedly a musical one, was slightly out of order, as he had only just recovered from an attack of influenza, but that sometimes he was able to move his audience to tears." (Hose, Geogr. Jour. i. 206.)

Mr. Whitehead tells us: "Much to my surprise, our Murut musician took a small ball of tobacco from his girdle and proceeded to plug up one nostril; in the other he placed the pipe, and continued to play as before. The Murut played really well; perhaps the flat open nostrils of this people are well suited for such a performance." (p. 35.) "Waking during the night, I heard some sounds almost as musical as those produced by a bagpipe; it came from a Murut near at hand, who was perhaps serenading his mistress. I examined the instrument he used, and it was very simple to produce so many notes. Two thin bamboos, about twelve inches long, were fastened very neatly side by side; in one was cut four holes like those in a flute, while the other had a long piece of grass inserted in the lower end. A slight incision was then cut across both towards the upper portion. The performer thrust this instrument rather deep into his mouth and blew, and then, with the aid of tongue, fingers, and moving the grass, produced some very agreeable and wild tunes. I watched him for some time as he sat by the side of a flickering fire, but being tired, it at last lulled me to sleep." (St. John i. 135.)

"The *klurai* is a wind instrument, constructed of a number of tubes, placed in a calabash with a long snout which serves as a mouthpiece, and which are thus sounded together; notes and combinations of notes or harmony can be produced from it. The finger holes are, some of them, placed laterally, others on the upper surface, and others again on the lower surface." (Brooke Low.)

"Modifications of the *cheng*, or calabash pipes, are made both by the Kayans, on the Baram river, and also by the Dusun villagers, near the Kina Balu. There are distinct differences between the instruments as made by each tribe. That from the Baram consists of seven pipes; six arranged in a circle around a long central one, all seven being furnished with a free reed at the base, where they are inserted in a calabash-gourd. Holes are cut in the six outer pipes for fingering; the central pipe is, however, an open or drone-pipe, the tone being intensified

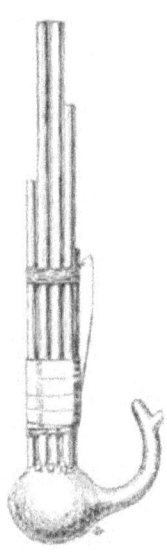

DYAK *Engkruri*, with seven reeds fitted into a gourd by means of gutta. Some of the notes appear to be F A C F—F octave nearly; two holes in one reed note unascertainable; two reeds appear to have no note. Longest reed (one which has no note) to junction with gourd, 31in.; diam. of gourd, 3⅜in.
(Edinboro' Mus)

KAYAN *Keluri*. Four pipes produce the chord of F (F A C F, with upper and lower tonic). A fifth has a faint suspicion of a flattened ninth ᴅ (of course from the lower tonic), while a sixth pipe adds the phuperfect fourth ʙ. It is played by suction and is tuned by shortening the pipes. $FA^DCF\frac{c}{b}$ 36¾in long; weight, 10½oz
Baram River
(Peek Coll.)

by fixing a loose cap of bamboo on the upper end. It is played by blowing air into the neck of the gourd, or by drawing the breath, according to the effects desired. The Dusun pipes are formed of eight pipes, four short and equal in length, and four long and unequal. Reeds are cut at the lower end in all the pipes, but the fingering is performed on the ends of the four equal short pipes, there being no holes cut in the pipes for this purpose, as in the Kayan instrument." (Burbidge, p. 178.)

Mr. Hose mentions (J.A.I. xxiii. 166) a reed organ (*Kuluri*) amongst the Kayans, and Mr. Whitehead (p. 108) a species of pan pipes fixed in a gourd used by the Dusuns, while Mr. Hornaday speaks (p. 468) of the "pleasing clarionet-like notes of the numerous reeds, made like a shepherd's pipe, which the Sibuyow men, women, and children were so fond of playing upon in concert."

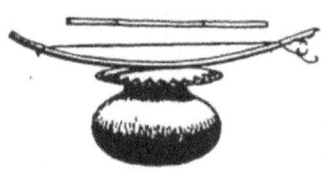

TANJONG *Busoi* AND ARAN.
The wooden disc is placed over a hollow pot. The bow is held across it with its arc resting upon it and the string is struck with a wooden plectrum.
(Brooke Low Coll.)

"The *serunai* is made of a hollow gourd, *selaing*, with a hole, and is one-stringed (*segu* cane), and is played with a bow, the string of which is of the same material. The performer sits on the ground and holds the instrument between his toes, the knees bending outward, and the soles of his feet adjoining. The sound is that of a violin played with a bow, and is mournful, wailing, sobbing, heartrending, dismal and gloomy. The instrument is held slanting, and the sounding cup on the side of the foot, with the stem resting on the left shoulder. The string must be watered with saliva to sound. The stock is 2 feet long, and of hardwood (*bilian*). The cup is 12 inches in cir-

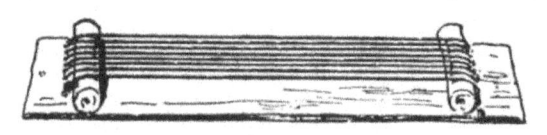

ZITHER.
⅛ nat. size. S.E. Borneo.
(Leiden Mus.)

cumference, and is a gourd shell, called *geno-selaing*, about the size of a teacup, and with a hole at the bottom. The mouth of it is covered up with a circular dish of soft wood, thin and close-fitting, and the seams cemented

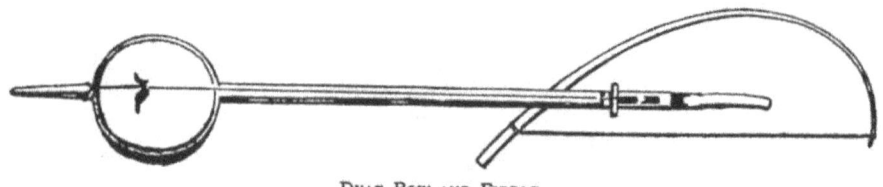

DYAK BOW AND FIDDLE.
(Brooke Low Coll.)

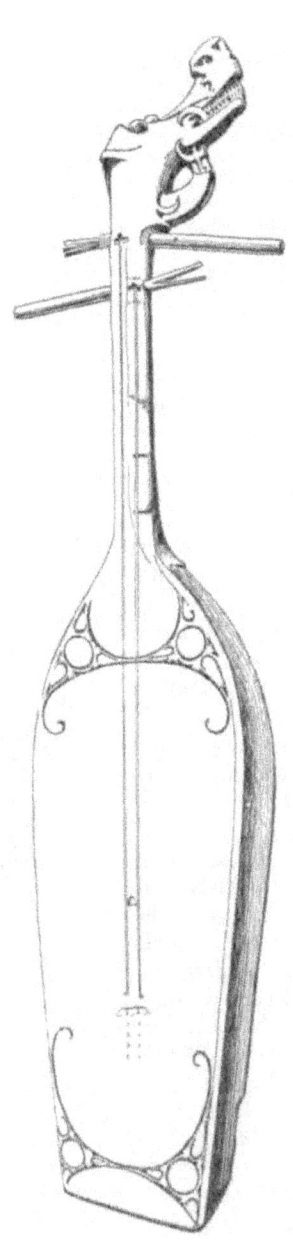

Music.   261

SPECIES OF BANJO WITH TWO RATTAN STRINGS.
Boat-shaped body, open at the back, flat in front with engraved ornament, long neck terminating in a monster's head. Played without a bow. Native name, *impai*. From Long Wai. Length, 3ft. 6½in.
(Brit. Mus.)

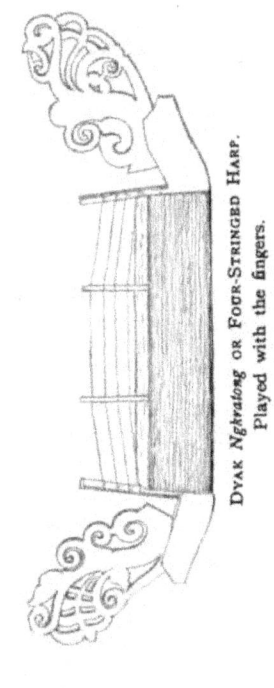

DYAK *Ngkratong* OR FOUR-STRINGED HARP.
Played with the fingers.
(Brooke Low Coll.)

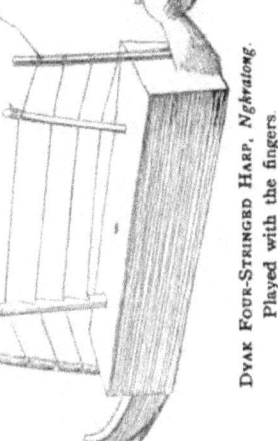

DYAK FOUR-STRINGED HARP, *Ngkratong*.
Played with the fingers.
(Brooke Low Coll.)

with *wild* wax. The bow is a bent cane, and the string a split rattan nearly 12 inches long. There is a moveable bridge on the dish for the string to rest upon. Sometimes the bowl is made of cocoanut-shell.

PRIMITIVE VIOLIN.
Two stringed; sounding board of bambu, open underneath. (Probably of Chinese origin). 23½in. long. Baram River.
(Hose Coll.)

" The *blikan* is a rude-stringed instrument resembling a guitar, and was formerly much in use. It was adopted from the Ulus, and is more frequently found among the Sarebas and Kalakan Dyaks than among any others. It is furnished with two strings (rattan) and two keys. The strings are pressed with the tips of the fingers of the left hand to modify the tone—there are no stops—while the nails of the fingers of the right hand brush the strings. The stock is glued into the beak or bill of a bird, the *kiñalong* or *burong bileh*, and the body is coloured red with the colouring matter of a wild-growing, poisonous fungus. It is 3 feet long from end to end. The *blikan* is hollowed out from the upper surface, and is covered with a thin plate of wood. The *safé*, on the other hand, is hollowed out from underneath, and is not closed up.

" The *busoi* is formed of a bow resting on the ground in a hollow vessel of earthenware or metal, and the string is made to vibrate with a plectrum." (Brooke Low.)

Sir Spencer St. John speaks (i. 109) of a Kayan " two-stringed instrument, resembling a rough guitar: the body was shaped like a decked Malay trading prahu, with a small hole an inch in diameter in the centre; the strings were the fine threads of rattan twisted and drawn up tightly by means of tuning-keys; however, the sound produced was not very different from that of a tightly-drawn string."

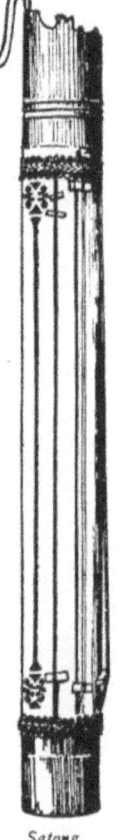

Mr. Hornaday mentions (p. 468) a Sibuyau fiddle " most elaborate and pretentious, the sounds of which were not very pleasing "; Mr. Whitehead a Dusun " extraordinary long guitar with two strings " (p. 108); and Mr. Hose a Kayan sort of banjo (*sapeh*), and a bamboo harp (*paking*). (J.A.I. xxiii. 166.) " The *satong* is a cylindrical bamboo harp, or lyre, played upon with the fingers." (Brooke Low.) It is made of a joint of large yellow bamboo, the nine or ten open strings of which produce notes similar to those of a banjo, when twanged with the fingers." (Burbidge, p. 178.) Previous

Satong.
LONG-KIPUT'S BAMBU HARP.
Length, 31in.
(Hose Coll.)

to this Mr. Burbidge had referred (p. 50) to a Kadyan "native-made violin on a European model, a curious kind of native banjo made of a single joint of a large bamboo, a triangle, or its music rather, being represented by two or three steel hatched heads, which were laid across laths on the floor, and beaten in time with a bit of iron. The music so produced was of a rather melancholy description."

"On arriving at *Kroo*, music from a variety of gongs and drums, beaten in regular time, saluted our ears." (Grant, p. 13.) . . . "The Dyaks possess gongs of all sizes from the deep-sounding *tāwak-tāwak*, which is used for signals in warfare, and can be heard miles off, to the diminutive *channang*. These are sold to them by Malays, who import them from Java. Another musical instrument is likewise imported from that country; it is a box containing a set of six or eight small gongs of different sizes. In beating the gongs and *gundangs*, or tom-toms, a regular time is kept." (*ibid*, p. 5.)

A MALOH (DUTCH TRIBE) *Tengkuang* OR WOODEN DRUM (? GONG) WITH DRUM STICKS.
(Brooke Low Coll.)

"The Malay gong, which the Lundu Dyaks also make use of, is like the Javanese, thick with a broad rim, and very different from the gong of the Chinese. Instead of the clanging noise of the latter, it gives out a muffled sound of a deep tone. The gong and tom-tom are used by the Dyaks and Malays in war, and for signals at night, and the Dyaks procure them from the Malays. I said that the music struck up, for, rude as the instruments were, they modulate the sound, and keep time so admirably, that it was anything but inharmonious." (Marryat, p. 84.)

"The gongs struck up," writes Mr. Chalmers, "not unmusically, but somewhat monotonously. From their mode of striking them, they form no bad imitation of some English country church bells." (Miss. Field, 1859, p. 80.)

DRUM, *Gendang*.
Made of hollowed palm wood, the upper end covered with a piece of monkey skin stretched and lashed on with cane Muruts of Upper Labuk River.
(Edinbro Mus.)

"The Sea Dyak *gendang* is a wooden drum, shaped like an hour glass, one end covered with parchment, which can be tightened or slackened at pleasure, by means of cords; it is not beaten with drumsticks, but is struck with the fingers. . . . The Sea Dyak *krumong* is made of narrow slabs of wood or stone, which upon percussion with a wooden hammer produce a series of tones similar to those obtained on an harmonicon." (Brooke Low.)

"The Kyans also have gongs (*tetawak*) and drums (*gendang*)." (Hose, J. A. I., xxiii., 166.)

"Wooden drums, formed of hollow tree-trunks, and having goat or deer-skin tightly stretched over the ends, are common, and of various sizes. The old war-drums were made thus; but this instrument is now nearly obsolete, being to a great extent replaced by metal gongs, of native manufacture certainly; but doubtless the idea was copied from the Chinese. Nearly every trading prahu or boat carries one of these gongs; and the Muruts are very fond of such music, and keep up an incessant din on these instruments at their festivals. Sets of eight or ten small such are often fixed in a rattan and bamboo frame, and beaten with two sticks, dulcimer fashion; and I have seen similar contrivances formed of iron bars; and even strips of dry hard bamboo wood in the Sulu isles, the scale in this case being similar to our own. It is very uncommon to hear performers playing in concert, unless in the case of gong-beating; indeed, music is at a low ebb throughout the island." (Burbidge, p. 179.)

"As we approach the coast the Dusuns become a tribe musical in brass; the instruments being supplied from Brunei, by way of Patatan. At Mukab the bell-metal pans are going all day long. People further inland have bamboo instruments instead." (Witti, Diary, 25 Mar.) "Among the Dusuns gongs and tomtoms of course take part in all festivities." (Whitehead, p. 108.)

"As night came on the Dusuns struck up a strange kind of music on metal tambourines. A mysterious rhythm and tune was apparent in it, and when I asked if this was *main-main* (*i.e.*, larking), they said no, but that a man was sick, and they must play all night to keep away evil spirits." (Hatton, p. 163.)

THE MUSICAL CHARACTER OF THE PEOPLE.

Mr. Hornaday says (p. 468): "The only amusements I saw among the Sibuyaus were of a musical character. The people of Gumbong's village, with whom I lived at the head of the Sibuyau, were decidedly musical, and scarcely an evening passed without a performance of some kind."

Sir Chas. Brooke writes of the Kayans (ii. 301.): "There is no doubt they possess a much more correct idea of music than any other natives I have met, and the small guitar they play and dance to is monotonous, but possesses harmony, and is fingered and played correctly on two or three strings."

Mr. Hose considers that the Kayans are "a very musical race." (J.A.I., xxiii. 166.)

Mr. Whitehead (p. 109), after enumerating the Dusun instruments, adds: "The performance on all these instruments is, however, feeble."

SINGING.

"When the Hill Dyaks sing, which they rarely do, it is in a low and plaintive voice; but as I did not sufficiently understand the Dyak language, I could never learn anything respecting the composition of their songs. I never heard them but at night, when most of the inhabitants of the village were asleep. They do not practise vocal music at any of their festivals." (Low, p. 312.)

When Mr. Grant left Kroo he wrote (p. 13): "We departed amidst the sound of gongs and the music of the old ladies, who were sitting in a circle singing a most melancholy chant in four notes. I do not suppose, however, they meant it to be melancholy, but it certainly was, and reminded me of the wail of dying people. All these old women were *Borich* or female doctors."

Later on he says, also of the Land Dyaks (p. 84): "Their song is peculiar; often have I heard, as I sat by my window at night, the wild and mournful strain of the Dyak as he paddled past in his canoe."

The mournful character of the song is the same amongst the Sea Dyaks: "The *pelandai* is the recitative in which the natives pour forth their feelings, their sorrows and disappointments, their desires and ambitions. It is full of feeling, and the voice is modulated to express all its shades. The utterance is slow at first, but is rapid towards the end. There is repetition in redundancy of expression and reiteration. The voice is often tremulous with passion, like the wail of a broken heart—a mournful cadence like the dirge of the dead." (Brooke Low.)

Speaking of the musical instruments, Mr. Burbidge remarks: "The pentatonic scale is employed, and the music is monotonous and plaintive in its character. This is especially true of the women's songs, which are mostly of a dirge-like kind. I remember a Kadyan girl who used to sing sometimes during my first visit to the Lawas, and the effect at night more especially was extremely weird and melancholy. She had a rich mellow voice, rising and falling in minor cadences, and dying away sweetly tremulous as a silver bell." (p. 177.)

The inland Dusuns have "pretty songs of their own. The latter are specially taking when given by young girls. They also sing in chorus, when the melodies almost bear the character of hymns." (Witti's Diary, Nov. 25.)

"Very different are the Sea Dyak war songs. The bard leading the song, chants in a low monotonous solo, his voice rising and falling as he chants of love or war, and is accompanied by the whoops and yells (fierce, exultant, presumptuous, and cheering) of his companions, and by the clashing of shields and nodding of plumes as the warriors, in their excitement, don their feathers and seize their arms, singing of the deeds of heroes of the olden days and lovely women whose charms gave rise to deadly strife and bloody feuds. These songs have the same effect on the natives of Borneo that the war drum and trumpet-blast have on the soldiers of Europe. The tones of the minstrel are clear, and bold, and tremulous, and culminating at times in a prolonged chorus which the others take up with something like a prolonged yell." (Brooke Low.)

On the Sarawak river, Mr. Collingwood writes: "The boatmen, as usual, enlivened the way with their songs, some of which were wild and musical. They all joined in the chorus; and one of them, of which they appeared particularly fond, had a refrain which ran as follows, the *staccatos* being strokes of the oar:—

Keeping time with their paddles, the song was cheerful and inspiriting, and seemed to help them along." (Collingwood, p. 233.)

Mr. Grant preferred his boatmen to sing, for it made them pull better; when thus singing they will go on with rhymes, generally nonsensical ones, for an hour at a time." (p. 84.)

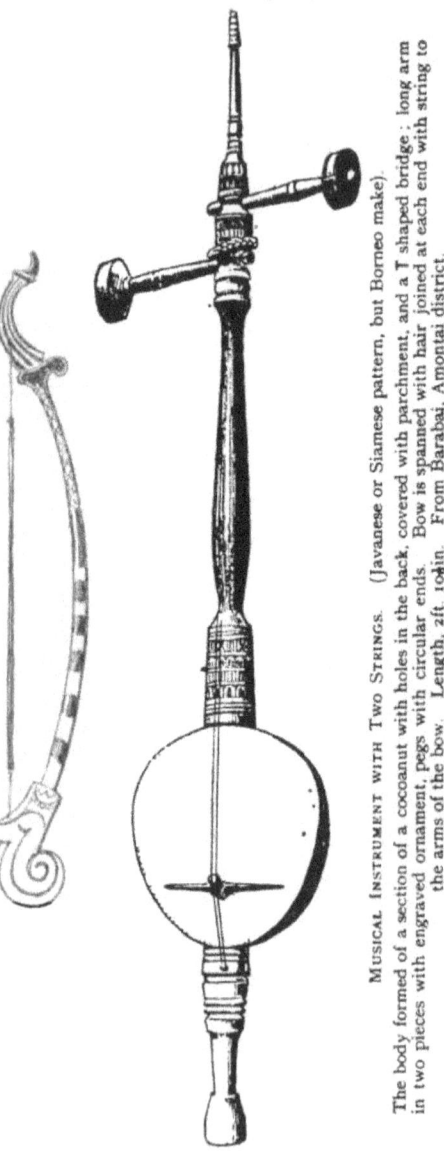

I think it is of the Muruts that Mr. Burbidge says: "The songs of the boatman, on the other hand, are often pleasing and melodious. A good many of their songs are Mahomedan prayers, or chants; but occasionally the theme is on secular, and often very amusing subjects. It is common for one man to strike up a song, improvising his subject as he sings, and then all the crew laughingly join in the chorus. They keep time to the music in paddling; and I always encouraged my boatmen to sing, as it relieves the monotony of the bump, bump of the paddles against the side of the vessel, which becomes very tedious after the first hour or two." (p. 180.)

When peace was made between Sir Jas. Brooke and Tamawan, the Kayan chief, there was a "very excited chorus" as Sir Sp. St. John drank to the friendship of the two nations. "When this was finished, Tamawan jumped up, and while standing burst out into an extempore song, in which Sir James Brooke and myself, and last, not least, the wonderful steamer, were mentioned with warm eulogies, and every now and then the whole assembly joined in the chorus with great delight."

MUSICAL INSTRUMENT WITH TWO STRINGS. (Javanese or Siamese pattern, but Borneo make). The body formed of a section of a cocoanut with holes in the back, covered with parchment, and a T shaped bridge; long arm in two pieces with engraved ornament, pegs with circular ends. Bow is spanned with hair joined at each end with string to the arms of the bow. Length, 2ft. 10in. From Barabai, Amontai district. (Bock Coll., Brit. Mus.)

CHAPTER XXVII.
LANGUAGE, NAMES, COLOURS.

LANGUAGE. LAND DYAK: Affinities with other natives' language—Prefixes—Examples of Sentah—The *Puas* or Lament—Malay stock. SEA DYAK: The letter *h*—Vowel endings—Phonetic spelling—Malay words—Dialectical differences—Malay and Hindu influences—Changes, how brought about. KAYAN. MILANAU. DUSUN: Peculiarities—Different from Lanun and Baju.
NAMES AND TITLES. Land Dyak names—Change of names—Adoption of children's names—Prefixes—Change due to fear of illness—Totem (?) names—High-sounding titles—Ejaculations—Names of places.
COLOURS. Good colour sense—Poor nomenclature—Not colour blind—Table of colour names.

LANGUAGE.
LAND DYAK.

THE following account of the language of the Land Dyaks by the Rev. W. Chalmers is taken from that scarce little volume of the late Mr. C. T. C. Grant: "Each tribe has its peculiarities of words, idiom, and pronunciation, but still the dialect of all the tribes of the two branches of the Sarāwak river is substantially the same, and the dialect of several of the Sambas tribes, as well as that of the Land Dyaks of the river Sadong, are closely allied to it. Indeed, I think it can hardly be doubted, that the dialects of all the Dyak tribes throughout Borneo are varieties of one primitive language: their grammatical construction is formed on one model; and though some of them have far greater flexibility, and are more highly developed than others (as, for example, that of the Olo Ngadjo or Dyaks of Southern Borneo),[1] yet in all the dialects with which I have met—some fourteen or fifteen—there is, in many instances, a *radical* connection which is plainly traceable.

"In common with all its kindred of the Malayan family of languages, Sarāwak-Dyak is rich in derivative words, which are formed by adding certain prefixes to the primitive words, each of which prefixes have a peculiar value and signification.

"Thus—*Pi, Peng,* &c., denote the agent or instrument: as *Kadong,* to lie; *Pengadong,* a liar; *Pang,* to speak; *Punganang,* a word; *usach,* betwixt; *Pengŭsach,* a mediator.

"*Bi, Ber,* &c., denote the quality of possession, and verbs intransitive: as *uri,* medicine; *beruri,* one having medicine—a doctor; *ŭmbai,* a betrothed; *biumbai,* to be betrothed.

---

[1] With regard to New Testament in this language Mr. Chalmers writes: "It seems to me to have no connection with that of the Land Dyaks, but I do trace a connection with that of the Sea Dyaks." (Occas. Papers, p. 9) Is Mr. Chalmers referring to Mr. Hardeland's version? See also *supra.* i. 7, Mr. F. R. O. Maxwell's remark on the Land Dyak language.

"*Ng, m, me,* &c., denote a verb transitive: as *puās*, a lamentation; *muās,* to lament; *ūsach,* an intervening space; *ngūsach,* to come between; *aiyag,* a sieve; *ngaiyag,* to sift.

"*Te, Ti,* denote the perfect passive participle of verbs, and verbal adjectives: as *tekūnūd,* astonished; *tekukah,* wide open, &c.

"*K* and *P* are causative prefixes: as *pijōg,* to make, to stand up; *kudip,* to keep alive, from *udip,* to live; *pibuh,* to drive away, from *buh,* to run away.

"*Re* and *Rūng* are frequently placed before the names of insects, vermin, &c.: as *reggu, retamuch,* worms; *repipan,* a centipede; *rungupod,* white ants, &c. *Si* is also often prefixed to names of persons, places, and things, and to adverbs, adjectives, and present participles. In Sarāwak-Dyak there are no affixes, and the use of the prefixes is also somewhat uncertain; moreover, in number and variety of application, they can bear no comparison with those employed in several other Bornean dialects with which I have met.

"Now for a few examples of the language as spoken in the tribe of Sentah—the people with whom I am best acquainted:—

So kih kāam? Where do you come from?
Moran menūg so Kuching. I have just come from Kuching.
Ogika agach inū? *Meling.* Is there any news? No.
Kowūk-ka? *Bayuch.* Are you tired? Not yet.
An nok jah butan? Will you drink some cocoa-nut water?
Dūch sa. Never mind.
Dūm juan-kih ka umūch-ngan? How much further is it to your farms?
Dūch joh dingè. Not much further.
Kamakih? Where are you going?
Odih ka darūm torun. I am going to the jungle.

"The following is part of the *Puās,* or Lament, made by the female relatives of a deceased person—first in the house, and afterwards on the road to the grave.

"'Kun mūch tinggē-mūch tūgan oku, kun mūch tinggē boba pūnganang di oku; meting yun ku nyadu, yun ku dāan boba pūnganang daya sekambuch sepagih. Asi-asi kiech, prigiag priasi sekambuch sepagih. Yun-ma tinggē; burōm oku nang metak miūn, metak meraman so ogi märi! Awang ku bisa nūpa, bisa nai! Burōm ku an bisa pijōg, boda oku mun, boda oku būsan ūmah-ūmah-i! Mun būtang, mun būngang. Awang ku an pijōg, awang ku an kakat, &c.'

"'Thou hast left me! thou hast forsaken me! thou hast ceased to speak to me! henceforth I can speak to you, I can talk to you no more. We are desolate, we are forsaken, henceforth and for ever. Thy place is deserted. O that I could say, that thou wert gone to stay awhile at the farm! for then thou wouldst return again. Would I could fashion you; would I could create you anew! O that I could make you stand up, that I could give you back your old appearance, your old likeness! Thou art like a fallen tree-trunk, like a log. Would I could make you stand up, that I could make you arise once more!'

"The vocabularies printed in the Appendix will, as Mr. Chalmers observes, show that there is a great affinity betwixt the Dayaks of Sarawak, Sadong, and some Sambas tribes. This connection is not so visible in the dialects of others, as, for instance, the Silakau tribe, who formerly lived on a stream of the same name between the Sambas and Pontianak. In the dialects of the Sea Dayaks, there are perhaps a few words radically the same as their correspondents in Land Dayaks, but only a few which are not derived in common from Malay. In the dialect of the Dayaks of Banjermasin, I have also noticed words the same in form and meaning, but they are not very frequent." (St. John i. 194.)

"The Sennah dialect of the Dyak language is the softest I have heard, and yet there is more of the guttural in it than in the dialect of the other Sarawak tribes. The Land Dyaks of Sarawak turn *l* into *r*; for instance, *Bula* (a lie), of the Malays, they pronounce *Bura*. The Sibuyows (Sea-board Dyaks) turn *r* into *h* guttural; for instance, *Besar* (large), they pronounce *Bessah*; *Orang* (man) becomes *Ohang*." (Grant, pp. 24, 29.)

SEA-DYAK LANGUAGE.

The Ven. Archdeacon Perham, than whom there is no better authority, tells us: "In English we do not pronounce a final *h* when preceded by a vowel. The Hebrew names of the Old Testament ending in *ah*, as in Isaiah, Jeremiah, &c., are pronounced as though they ended in *a*; and so indifferent are we about the *h* that the word Halleluiah is as often spelt without as with an *h*. These cases although they are words simply transferred into English from another language show the tone of our pronunciation. We have hardly any of our own that end in the same way; but sirrah and hurrah are sounded as sirra and hurra. It may possibly arise from this that when we come to write new languages we may be apt to think that the addition or omission of a final *h* is a matter of no importance; but in Sea-Dyak at least this is a great mistake, as will be seen I believe by examples to be quoted. When a new language has to be reduced to writing the only plan to adopt is to write it phonetically; and no preconceived notions borrowed from other languages ought to interfere with the simple representation of the sound as far as our letters will do it. The questions with any particular word should simply be, How do the natives pronounce it? and so our system of orthography and grammar would be built upon the facts of the language.

"Now I believe the Sea Dyaks have no initial aspirate, but as if to compensate themselves for this they have a final one; they have words ending in *ah, ih, oh* or *uh*; and it is necessary to write and to pronounce this final *h* in order to distinguish such words as have it from others spelt exactly the same with that exception but widely different in meaning. This will appear by examples. *Muda* means young, but *mudah* easy: *Nyala* is to fish with a cast-net, but *nyalah* to accuse of wrong: *dara* means an unmarried female, but *darah* blood: *nampi* is to sift rice, but *nampih* to draw near to: *nyepu* to blow an instrument or the fire, &c., but *nyepuh* to dip a thing into water; *bau* is the shoulder, but *bauh* means long; so *au* yes, but *auh* the sound of rushing wind or wave. Many other instances might be cited, but these are enough to show the final *h* has a real function to perform, and ought not to be a silent letter.

"I do not know whether a sentimental objection is not sometimes felt against this final *h* sound as being harsh and uncouth; but surely such an idea if ever entertained is altogether out of place. Once begin to alter the language to suit our ideas of refinement and we lose the only principle we have to write by; and we moreover incur the charge of ignorance whenever an intelligent native who is able to read sees our writing of his language. But in truth this sound, if not pronounced in an exaggerated way (and the natives do not), is not a particularly rough sound, and not so uncouth as our final *th* or *sh*.

"But further, in words ending with vowels there is a difference in the pronunciation of the final vowel which cannot be referred simply to a transposition of the accent. These final vowels have two sounds which I can only call a long and a short vowel sound, so that words spelt with exactly the same letters are only distinguished by the quantity given to the final vowel. Thus *nganti* means to exchange, but *nganti* to wait for; *peti* a box, but *peti* a pig-trap; *malu* to be ashamed, but *malu* to strike; *agu* a privy, but *agu* foolish; *tebu* sugar-cane, but *tebu* a kind of wart or corn on the feet; *mangka* is a man's name, but *mangka* to knock against. The difference between these vowel sounds is not much; but slight as it is the natives detect its non-observance in a moment. Before I was aware of it I remember arguing against a Dyak that the word for box and pig-trap was exactly the same in sound, thus tacitly making the foolish assumption that I knew his language better than he knew it himself; but I am now convinced that the rule holds good, at least with the vowels *a*, *i* and *u*; and when it is observed what an amount of meaning hangs upon the right pronunciation the necessity of being acquainted with it will be felt. Some years ago I asked an intelligent native to write down a list of Dyak words. From reading Mission books he had been accustomed to the use of the short mark; and without any suggestion from me he put the mark over every vowel that required the shortened sound.

"This short quick final vowel sound has sometimes been mistaken for a *k* sound, and notably in the word Dyak itself. They do not call themselves Orang Dyak, but Orang Dyă, or more properly perhaps Daia. So also tamă to enter, and belaiă to quarrel. Sometimes it has been represented by *h*, but it is not the sound of that consonant, which moreover is wanted to do its own work. That it is not the sound either of *h* or of *k* will I think appear by the following instances:—

"*Mata* the eye; *mata* unripe, undressed; *matah* to break in two; *matak* to pull. *Gaga* means joyful; *gaga* make; *gagah* great muscular strength. *Isa* is a man's name; *isa* means let be; *Isah* a woman's name. *Niti* is to skin; *niti* to walk over a bridge; *nitih* to follow; *nitik* to drop as water. *Ngali* means to dig up; *ngali* to lie down or rather to lay ourself down; *ngalih* to turn round or over.

"It is true we make ourselves understood by Dyaks without this attention to *h* and to long sounding vowels and short sounding vowels, for the context will generally show what we mean, and they will know how to reply to our inaccurate Dyak just as we could easily talk to a Frenchman although he spoke rather bad English ; but the question is not what will 'do' for the work of conversation, but what are the correct rules of the Dyak language.

"From what has been said it will be seen that by no system of spelling whatever can the language be written phonetically with absolute accuracy without the use of some indicating marks. In writing or translating books perhaps such phonographical exactness as the difference between a and $\bar{a}$ is not necessary, especially if designed for the use of natives themselves, for they naturally pronounce their own language correctly ; but in Dictionaries the right pronunciation might be marked." (S.G. No. 136, p. 79).

"The language of the Sea Dyaks, though altogether different in such parts as having not been adopted from the Malay, is merely a less refined dialect of the language spoken over all Polynesia, and its connexion with that of the other wild tribes, particularly those of Sumatra, is easily to be traced. It is not nearly so melodious in sound, or so copious in its extent, as the Malay, though the Dyaks do not scruple to extend it by adding foreign words whenever they find it necessary, so that a great portion of the words of their vocabulary are from the Malay ; the intercourse, which has been generally friendly, between the two nations has also encouraged this adoption of foreign terms." (Low, p. 173.) As Sir Chas. Brooke says: "Their language bears a strong resemblance to the Malayan tongue, and I have frequently found words from Marsden's Dictionary used in familiar conversation among themselves, and yet unknown to the Malays on the coast." (i. 50.) See *supra* i. 10, Mr. Maxwell's remark.

"I need only observe, concerning the Sea Dyak language, that the Sibuyaus, the Balaus, the Undups, the Batang Lupars, the Sakarangs, Seribas, and those inhabitants of the Rejang living on the Kanowit and Katibas branches, all speak the same language, with no greater modifications than exist between the English spoken in London and Somersetshire. They are, in fact, but divisions of the same tribe ; and the differences that are gradually growing up between them principally arise from those who frequent the towns and engage in trade, using much Malay in their conversations, and allowing their own words to fall into disuse. The agricultural inhabitants of the farther interior are much more slowly influenced." (St. John i. 78.)

In some correspondence I have had with Prof. A. H. Keane it would appear that the Sea Dyak language as we know it is practically a Malay dialect and that if any real Bornean element exist it will be far in the interior. "I fear," he writes, "at present (and probably for centuries back) Malay dominates exclusively around the whole sea board, as indeed might be expected from the results of the contact of the true Malays with *uncivilised* peoples in other parts of Western Malaysia. The language has developed somewhat independently, but still in constant contact with traders, raiders, rovers, &c., of standard Malay speech during the course of over 1000 years, that is, ever since the true Malays of Menangkabau (Sumatra) began to swarm over the Archipelago." Prof. Keane also notices words showing early Hindu influence.

Regarding the origin of changes in words, &c., it will be noticed under the chapter devoted to Manangs that these sorcerers use a special jargon. Bishop McDougall remarks: " A circumstance which came to my notice, when visiting a tribe in the interior, may account for the way in which dialects alter among people in such a state. I was sitting with the Chief and Tuahs, who were conversing with me in Malay and talking with each other in their own dialect, when some strange Dyaks came in. Our friends addressed the strangers in Malay, and spoke to each other in something I could not understand. Upon questioning them about it afterwards, they said they spoke in their war language, as they did not trust these strange Dyaks, and did not wish them to understand what they said. It seemed to me that they used a kind of slang or patter they had invented, calling things by wrong names; and it is possible that, in a long-continued state of warfare with a succession of surrounding tribes, these war-tongues may have become their every-day language, and have quite changed their original dialects. They had many words in use for which we had no equivalents; for example, for 'to-morrow,' 'the day after,' and so on, they had special words for each, of a sequence of ' ten ' or ' fourteen days.' In the same way they had words for ' rice,' according as it was cooked in one way or another." (T.E.S. ii. p. 26.)

KAYAN.

" Like all other aboriginal tribes of Borneo the Kayans have no alphabet, mode of writing or knowledge of letters, nor do they practice any systematical method of representing their ideas by figures. With the exception of local differences, all the divisions of the tribe speak the same language, so as to be intelligible to each other throughout their wide range on the island. The Kayan language is copious, pleasantly soft and comparatively easily acquired." (R. Burns, Logan's Jour. Ind. Arch.) " Their language differs entirely from that of the Sea Dyaks or Land Dyaks." (F. R. O. Maxwell, *supra* i. 18.)

MILANAU.

" They seem to have a common language, which is, however, much diversified in different rivers, causing the dialect of one place to be difficult to be understood by a man coming from a more distant one." (De Crespigny, Jour. Anth. Inst. v. 34.)

" When residing on the north-west coast amongst the Milanows I made a vocabulary of some fourteen different tribes, and although in many instances before they came under the influence of a settled government, the people of one river could not converse with those of another, yet the similarity of language is so great that it proves unmistakably that all these tribes are branches of one great family ; and yet their manners and customs are in some instances so different that one is almost led to doubt whether this inference is a correct one." (Crocker, Jour. Anth. Inst. xv. 425.)

DUSUN.

" They have no written language. . . . The language of the Dusuns sounds at first, from the frequency of words having the accent on the last syllable, and not as usual in Malay on the penultimate, unpleasant from its roughness, but after a little while it is not unmusical to the ear. Some words are identical with the Sulu, many with the Malay, and others very similiar to the latter. The prefix *meng* is common in their verbs, even when the words are different from Malay. I did not remark any affix such as are frequent in the latter language." (De Crespigny, Proc. R. Geogr. Soc. ii., 1858, 347, 349.)

In the Sonzogon country " Dusuns have the peculiarity of pronouncing *yo ya* as *zo za*." (Witti, 19 May.)

"The Lanun and Baju are entirely different from the language of the Ida'an [Dusun]. I have made several vocabularies and many inquiries. At Kiau, we collected above 400 words; at Blimbing on the Limbang, 300; and whilst in Maludu Bay, seven years ago, I likewise made a short vocabulary. These three agree so far that I may say that the Ida'an and Bisaya have two out of three words in common; and on further inquiry, I think that the remaining one-third will gradually dwindle away, as at present many of the words in my Bisaya vocabulary are Malay, for which they have their native word. The result of my inquiries is that all the Ida'an speak the same language with slight local differences. We found all the tribes on the Tampasuk and Tawaran spoke fluently to each other, and one of our interpreters, who had never before visited these countries, but had been accustomed to the aborigines to the south, conversed freely with them. . . . I was certain of a great affinity between the languages, as men from one tribe could freely converse with those of the other, though their dwellings were a hundred and fifty miles apart; but on comparing the written vocabularies, I found a surprising difference. Just before I left Borneo, I spoke to a Bisaya on the subject: he said, ' Repeat me a few words of the Ida'an that are different.' I did so. He answered, ' I understand those words, but we don't often use them,' and he instantly gave their meaning in Malay, to show that he did understand them.

" In making vocabularies at Kiau we found the villagers very careless of their pronunciation; for instance, the word ' heavy ' was at different times written down, *magat, bagat, wagat*, and *ogat;* for ' rice,' *wagas* and *ogas;* for ' to bathe,' *padshu, padsiu*, and *madsiu*, and indifferently pronounced in these various ways by the same people." (St. John i. 383, 194, 321.)

PERSONAL NAMES.

Mr. Chalmers gives a list of names of Land Dyaks as follows:—

Names of Men—
Se Deraman.
Se Kadiŭng.
Se Ganggak.
Se Kushaû.
Nyäet.
Se Ngaiyo.

Of Women—
Se Kŭdi.
Se Risi.
Se Monog.
Sipúach.
Se Karŭm.
Sisub.

And then he continues: " These are what are called ' body names.' When Dyaks grow up into lads and lasses they generally take another name to which the word *Ma* (contracted from *Sama*—Father) or *Nŭ* (contracted from

Sindū—Mother) is prefixed; and when they attain to middle age, this name is frequently put aside for another, to which the word *Bai* (contracted from *Babai*—Grandfather) or *Mūk* (contracted from *Somūk*—Grandmother) is prefixed; thus, the chief man of this village (Kuap), when a boy, rejoiced in the body-name of *Se Mara*; when he became a young man he became *Ma-Kari* (the father of *Kari*), and now he is called *Bai-Kinyum* (the grandfather of *Kinyum*). Among a people who have no surnames, and among whom age is the great title to honour and respect, this custom would seem natural enough, did they get the names of *Ma* or *Nū*, *Bai* or *Mūk* from their own children and grandchildren respectively, as do the Malays, with whom, *e.g.*, the name *Pa Ismail* means that the man who bears it has a son of the name of Ismail. [It may be observed of this custom, that, should the eldest child be dead, or lost, having become a slave to the enemies of the tribe, the parent is called after the next surviving one, or the next in seniority which remains with him. Thus Pa Jaguen was called Pa Belal until his daughter Jaguen was restored to him from Sakarran slavery. (Low, p. 197.)] Dyak impatience for names of honour, however, is too great to be regulated by the ordinary course of nature; little boys and girls are dignified by the coveted titles of *Ma* and *Nū*, and the way they manage to bestow and receive them is this: the children of the elder brothers and sisters of a family are entitled to take the names—with *Ma* or *Nū* prefixed—of the children of their parents' younger brothers and sisters; *e.g.*, suppose the case of two brothers, the elder named *Tingut*, and the younger *Sugu*. *Tingut* marries, and has a son named *Si Rida*; *Sugu* also marries, and has a son, whom he calls *Narik*; upon this *Si Rida* loses his body-name and becomes *Ma-Narik*, the father of *Narik*, although he is really his cousin, and he himself still quite a child. In case a person has no uncles or aunts (younger than his own parents) from whose children he may become a *Ma*, then he has to wait till he has a child of his own, and from its name he gains at length the long-desired distinction.

"*Bai* and *Mūk* (Grandfather of, and Grandmother of) are titles adopted, either when the persons who assume them have a grandchild of their own, or when their elder or younger brothers or sisters are beforehand with them in this respect, and have a *spare* grandchild whose name they may make their own with these honourable epithets prefixed. Thus, in the case supposed above, *Sugu* might become *Bai*, from one of *Tingut's* grand-children, or *Tingut Bai* from one of *Sugu's*. Among the Land Dyaks, relationships are counted up to exceedingly remote degrees, and the words *kaka* (elder brother or sister), *sudē* (younger brother, &c.), and *palunggar* (cousin), are commonly so used as to mean any relatives, from a brother or sister who has sprung from common parents, down to cousins in the third and fourth degree."

On the Barum River: "When a child is born, the father and mother sink their own identity, and adopt the name of their offspring. Supposing a man named *Jau* becomes the parent of a son to whom he gives the name of *Lahing*, the former would no longer be called *Jau*, but *Taman Lahing*, father of *Lahing*. If his child were to die, he would be called *Ozong Lahing*, or *Ozong Jau*; if his wife dies, he adds the prefix *Aban* (widower) to his name; if a brother or sister, *Boi*, and is called *Boi Lahing*. Should he attain the position of being a grandfather, he becomes *Laki*, adding thereto the name of his grandchild, so if the latter is given the name of *Ngipa*, the grandfather is no longer called *Taman Lahing*, or by any other name but *Laki Ngipa*. A widow is called *Ballo*." (Hose, J.A.I. xxiii. 170.)

"Among the Kayans *Kum* and *Yong* are mere prefixes; the former is attached to the name of the father, after the death of any of the younger children, and the latter, *Yong*, when the eldest dies." (Brooke ii. 298.)

"When Land Dyak children are young, should they be liable to frequent attacks of sickness, it is not an uncommon thing for their parents to change their names even two and three times in the course of as many years. The reason for so doing is, that all sickness being supposed to be caused by mischievous *Hantu* or spirits, by this means they are put off the scent, and their intended victim escapes their hands; for when they come to look for him, they hear his old name uttered no more, and so (very rashly) come to the conclusion that he no longer exists!" (Chalmers in Grant.) The fear of spirits which makes them change their names may have something to do with the Bantings' great dislike to tell their own names; if you ask a girl her name she refers you to her companion for it." (Mrs. Chambers, Gosp. Miss., 1858, p. 70.)

"The principal cause of the change of name in grown-up persons among the Kanowits is the objection people have to uttering the name of a dead person. Thus Adun's name used to be Saog until a person of that name died, when his friends changed his name, fearing that he might die too and also because it was unlucky to retain such a name. But the relatives of the dead man would also insist on such a change, as they would not like to be reminded every day of the dear departed by hearing his name daily uttered." (Brooke Low.) "Names of slaves are changed when they are given their freedom." (St. John i. 73.)

"Many of the Baram River tribes adopt the names of animals and common objects such as—*Lang*, a hawk; *Bangau*, a stork; *Apoi*, fire, and so on. Amongst the Kalabits, a chief who wishes to impress people with his greatness often adds the word *langit*, the heavens, to his other names. This implies that he is a very important personage, literally, that the heavens belong to him." (Hose, J.A.I. xxiii. 170.)

His Highness speaks of a Dyak whose "right name was *Egu*, but he had been dubbed *Jowing*, which is the name of the poison barb of the Sumpit arrow." (i. 205.) "One Balau chief was grandly designated *tukong langit*, which, interpreted, means 'the walking-stick of the sky.'" (Sir Jas. Brooke, Mundy i. 237.)

With regard to these sounding titles a correspondent of the S.G. (1894, p. 21) writing from the Batang Lupar of the death of the chief Basek, says: "Old *Tungkujuh Darah* ('the torrent of blood,' as his title may be translated) has joined his many comrades in the Halls of Valhalla. In spite of his high-sounding title, or *nom de guerre*, poor old *Tungkujuh* was a quietly disposed old fellow, at least, within the last thirty years or so, and never gave any trouble to the Government. He is credited with having earned his name in the wild days long ago, when *Rabong* attacked Banting Hill, then the dwelling place or rather refuge of many Malays and Dyak families, and in those stirring times when forays and expeditions used frequently to be made into the Undup, Bugau, and other countries by the adventurous young bloods of the Skarang and Saribas tribes. The chief warriors who joined in these gentle pastimes, now so happily entirely abolished through His Highness' efforts, have nearly all passed away, and old *Tungkujuh* is among the last of them. It is somewhat interesting to inquire into the origin of old titles. The Malay expression to confer such a title is *galar*, and the Dyak, *ensumbar*. These words both mean the same, viz : to ennoble. The Dyak word *julok* is apparently the substantive, signifying, a title, a nickname. It is stated that the custom of *ensumbar* is a Dyak one, and that the Malays adopted it, in some cases, when joining in the forays made upon neighbouring districts. It is pretty clear that those Dyak tribes who held to the custom of *ensumbar*-ing their bravest or most conspicuous men were the Skarangs and Saribas, though other tribes copied them to some small extent. The following names and titles, with attempted translations, have assisted me in coming to the above-mentioned conclusion :—

SKARANG DYAKS.

Name.	Title.	Translation.
Basek,	Tungkujuh Darah,	The torrent of blood.
Kedu,	Langendang,	The soaring eagle.
A. Salleh,	Tedong,	The cobra.
Dandi,	Gasing gila,	The revolving wheel.
A. Jilom,	Buluh balang,	The bamboo (called *gadeng*).
Jelani,	Bulan,	The moon (is in vain).
Bantar,	Mali lebu,	The socialist (lit : the taboo).
——	Langtabang,	The white hawk.

LEMANAK DYAKS.

Ngelai,	Kendawang,	The snake Kendawang.
Lintong,	Moa hari,	The clouds (lit : the face of day).

SARIBAS DYAKS.

P. Renkai,	Bedilang besi,	The iron poker.
Bakir,	Bujang brani,	The brave bachelor.
Malina,	Panggau,	Lucky.
Unggang,	Kumpang pali,	The iron-like wood (of that name).
Cheloh,	Tarang,	A shining light (lit : a lamp).
Linggir,	Mali Lebu,	The socialist.

BALLOW DYAKS.

Anggi,	Jeritan,	The jester.

"Very probably the custom of ennobling the brave men is in use in the Rejang, and it would be somewhat interesting to inquire whether this custom is also in use amongst the Kayan, Murut and other tribes in Sarawak territory."

"Epithets of surprise are often *Apai Indai*, or *Aki Indai*, ' Father and mother,' or ' Oh, mother ! ' This expression seems very universal, for even Europeans appeal to their grandmothers in cases of distress or perplexity."

(Brooke i. 62.) The expression may, however, have something to do with their belief in Grandmother Manang; see *supra* i. 324.

On the Limbang river we are told the people "know the different villages by the names of the chief men, rather than by rivers or hills." (St. John ii. 120.) On the Latong river, however, we are told: "It is extraordinary how every stream and creek of the most minute proportions has come by a name; for I have never yet seen one that the Dyaks do not call by some name or other." (Brooke ii. 184.) Birds are named according to a fancied interpretation of their notes (see *supra* i. 445).

SENSE OF COLOUR.

While the natives, judging from the colour patterns of their cloths and from the colouring of their implements, seem to have a very good colour sense, on the other hand they do not seem to have a good colour nomenclature, as the table on next page will show. In this table I have arranged all the colour names I have been able to find; the abbreviations for the names of my authorities are Ch. = Chalmers; St. J. = St. John; B. L. = Brooke Low; Cr. = Crossland; Br. = Brereton (in St. John's vols.); De C. = De Crespigny; Bu. = Burns; C. = Cowie; K. = Sir Jas. Brooke (in Keppel). The natives seem to have distinct names for black and white; for blue and green the names seem interchangeable—Sentahs, Sea Dyaks, Muruts; but according to Sir Jas. Brooke, Keppel App. ii. 21, the Sau man who gave the information when asked what green was would not or could not give a term but black. When asked the colour of a green leaf he said *singote*, but we are not told whether the leaf was light or dark green, and the word *singote* may therefore have been used as Mr. Crossland tells me the Undups call dark blue *etam*, *i.e.* black, a word which is probably used the same as the Malays often use it, as for example, *bisu itam* = dark blue. Mr. Brooke Low says sky blue is *ñemit*, but this sounds very much like the *nymit* = yellow of Mr. Burns, so that either a sunset blue, if one may say so, must be meant or there is an error in transcription. For red and yellow the names seem to have more decided distinction than for blue and green, still there is interchangeability, thus the Kanowits say *sak mehe* for red and *mehi sak* for yellow; the Muruts say *malia masia*, and *sia* for red and *masilo* for yellow. What is curious in the naming of these two colours is that while the Sentahs call yellow *sia*, the Muruts call red *sia*; the Sentahs call red *bire* (= *mirah* of the Malays) and the Muruts call yellow *birar*. The Sakarans call dark red or brown *mansau tuai* where *tuai* = old, which is the Malay method; *mansau* also means ripe. The Malau for red = *dadara* and is said to be derived from *dara* = blood (K). Gray amongst the Sentahs (Ch.) = *apok* (= *kelabu* of the Malay) but there is a special word for gray hair, viz. *berubuk* (= *uban* of the Malay) while the name for hair is *rambut* (*ubok*, Malay). As shown above the Saus mix black and green and the Bakatan would seem to mix green = *ujang arang* with red *arang-arang* (*ujang* = deer). The fact that some of the natives distinguish gray, and that as far as we know, with the Bakatan exception, they do not mix up red and green, would indicate that they are not colour blind.

TABLE.

Name.	Black.	White.	Blue.	Green.	Red.	Yellow.
Malay	itam	putih	bira	ijau; gadong (Brunei)	mirah	kuning
Sentah	singut, Ch.; singo, K.	budah, Ch., K.	barum, Ch.	barum, Ch., K.	biré, Ch., K.	sia, Ch., K.
Sau	singote, K.	mopu, K.		singote, K.	bile, K.	
Sadong	bihis, St. J.	buda, St. J.			unchalak, St. J.	
Lara	sungut, St. J.	ranaga, St. J.			teransak, St. J.	
Sibuyau	chilum, K.	putah, K.		gadong, K.	mangsow, K.	kunong, K.
Sea Dyak	etam, chelum, Cr., K.; chilum, Br.; chelum, St. J.	burak, Cr., Br., K.; putih, St. J.	udau, Cr.; biru, Br.	udau, Cr.; ijo, Br.	mansau, Cr.; mansoh, Br.; mirah, St. J.; mangsaw, K.	kunieng, Cr.; kuning, Br.; kunong, K.
Kanowit		putih, B. L.			sak, mehe, B. L.	mehi, sak, B. L.
Matu		pute, B. L.	gadong, B. L.	gadong, B. L.	sak, B. L.	kunin, B. L.
Bintulu		mapu, B. L.	biru, B. L.	gadong, B. L.	mila, B. L.	kunieng, B. L.
Malau	an tarum, Br.; lanarum, K.	uteh uteh, Br., K.	biru, Br.		didarah, Br.; dadara, K.	tantu muun, Br.
Malanau	bilam, St. J., De C.; bilum, K.	putih, St. J., K.	biru, St. J.; biruk, De C.	gadong, St. J.; ijau, De C.	sak, sak, St. J.; sak, De C.	kunyit, St. J.; kuning, De C.
Kayans	pitam, Bu., St. J.	putih, Bu., B. L.; borah, St. J.	biru, B. L.; using, St. J.	gadong, B. L., St. J.	bla, Bu., bela, B. L.; belah, St. J.	nymit, Bu.; kunieng, B. L.; jemit, St. J.
Bissaya	maitam, De C.; hitom, St. J.	purak, St. J.	matamo, De C.	matamo, De C.	maragang, De C.; ragang, St. J.	masilo, De C.; silau, St. J.
Muruts	maitam, bata, De C.; mitam, St. J.	buda, St. J.	matumo, De C.	matamu, matamau, De C.	matia, masia, De C.; sia, St. J.	masilo, De C.; berar, St. J.
Dusun	itom, De C.; eitom, St. J.	purak, St. J.		batamau, De C.	malagang, De C.; ragang, St. J.	kuning, De C.; silau
Pakatan	horommorom, St. J.	buak, St. J.		ujang arang, St. J.	arang arang, St. J.	
Lanun	mahitam, St. J.	maputih, St. J.			marega, St. J.	binaning, St. J.
Sulu	itam, itum, C.		bilu, C.	gadong, C.	pulah, lag, C.	

CHAPTER XXVIII.

ARCHÆOLOGY, JARS, ALLEGED NATIVE WRITING, NEGRITOES.

ARCHÆOLOGY. Remnants of Hindu worship—Tradition of Hindus—Hindu articles—Figure on sandstone rock—Chinese articles—Mount Sobis' caves—Mr. A. Hart Everett's cave explorations —Negative results—Stone implements.
JARS. Three varieties of—Values—Descriptions—A proof of riches—Sacred jars—Fortune-bringers —Invoking a blessing—A prophetic jar—Chinese imitations.
ALLEGED NATIVE WRITING. Sign manual—Prof. De la Couperie's statements—Alleged writing on a jar—Dr. Rost's and Dr. Meyer's replies—Other inscriptions—Knotted cords— Indicators—Tatuing records—No native writing—Dr. H. Kern's note.
NEGRITOES. In surrounding countries— Dr. Meyer's conclusions—Travellers reviewed— Quatrefages and Hamy criticised — Mr. Earl's evidence — Dalton's statement — Captive Andamanese—Mr. Man's notes—Quatrefages' and Hamy's negrito skull—Origin doubtful— Statements not proofs—Borneo recent geologically—Existence not proved.

ARCHÆOLOGY.

ON the Samarahan River Sir Sp. St. John found "a stone which proved to be the representation of the female principle so common to Hindu temples : its necessary companion was not to be found." (i. 227.) On the Sarawak river there was at one time the remnant of a Hindu stone bull ; some Malays and Dyaks tried to remove it but a thunderstom frightening them made them think its spirit was vexed so they left it in the mud. Sir Jas. Brooke only received the natives' permission to remove it by promising to have it sheltered, which he appears to have done near his bungalow. (*ibid*, i. 228.) It seems to have been charred and cracked when the Chinese burnt down the Rajah's house (Grant, p. 66); the trough with it, mentioned by Mr. Grant, would appear to be the stone above referred to by Sir Sp. St. John. Since the latter traveller wrote, other remains, " far distant, have been brought to light, with some of the gold ornaments seven feet under ground, as well as many articles of crockery and other utensils. These articles being found much further in the interior, gives the subject additional interest."[1] (Brooke i. 48.) With regard to such Hindu relics His Highness remarks : " Even the Sarawak Malays of the present generation can recollect the time when it was usually said in conversation, in reference to distant bygone dates, ' In the days of the Hindoos,' which expression has become extinct, as the

---

[1] "In the parts of the country I am acquainted with, I have not heard of the existence of any antiquities, unless the big guna, a stone of man's length (most likely an aerolith), called Le Kuyan, which is kept in a house at Seun, be considered as such." (Houghton, M.A.S. iii. 199.)

Mahomedans of late years have been in the habit of going hadji to Mecca, and are now able to use the dates of the Hegira."[1] (*ibid*, p. 47.)

" At the mouth of the Sarawak river many articles of gold and pottery of unmistakable Hindu workmanship have continually been found." (J.A.I. xv. 425.)

The accompanying illustration is that of a "figure on sandstone rock a little under life size. It is situated at the foot of the mountain of Santubong near a little stream. It was discovered by a Malay fisherman in clearing a spot of ground for his garden." (Her Highness The Ranee.)

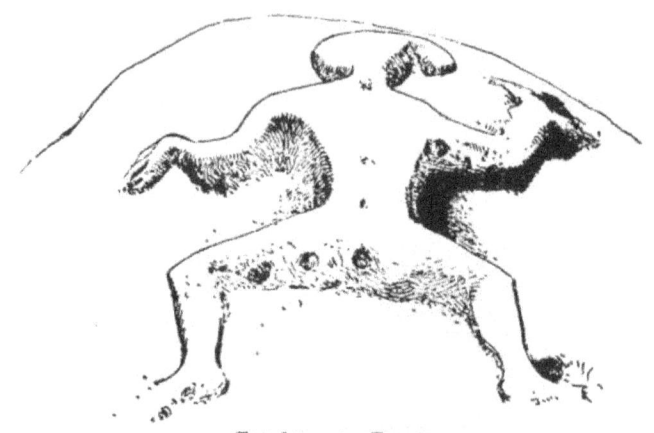

THE LIFE-SIZE FIGURE
found near Santubong Mountain in 1886. "The rock is sandstone, said to be about ten feet high. Remnants of pottery, bits of gold ornaments, and Chinese coins have been found near the rock. The soil round about is rather swampy."
(From a photograph lent by Her Highness The Ranee.)

"Often would the pick or spade, used for the purposes of mineral exploration, reveal thick layers of pottery and china of antique, apparently Chinese, make. On one occasion we found a number of square paving tiles some four inches thick, beautifully made of pebbles, concrete, quartz, &c.: they had been polished, were clearly very old and made by people of a higher civilisation." (Helms, p. 153.)

A visitor to Mount Sobis caves was informed by the natives that old jars were to be found there, but he had no time to examine the place. (S.G., No. 68.) Two of these caves on the Niah river and twelve others on the Upper Sarawak River were explored by Mr. A. Hart Everett: "During my first exploration I discovered embedded at the bottom of a bed of river gravel

---

[1] "Brazen images, ruins of temples, and other relics of Hindu worship are to be seen in the inland districts near Banjar Massin on the south coast, which may be accounted for by the fact that a colony was established at this place from Java during the period in which Hinduism prevailed in the latter island." (Earl, p. 274.) Mr. Bock was shown a small bronze Hindu idol. (p. 119.)

The Stone Implement discovered by Mr. A. Hart Everett "imbedded at the bottom of a bed of river gravel exposed in a section on the left bank of the Siniawan River."
(Oxford Mus.)

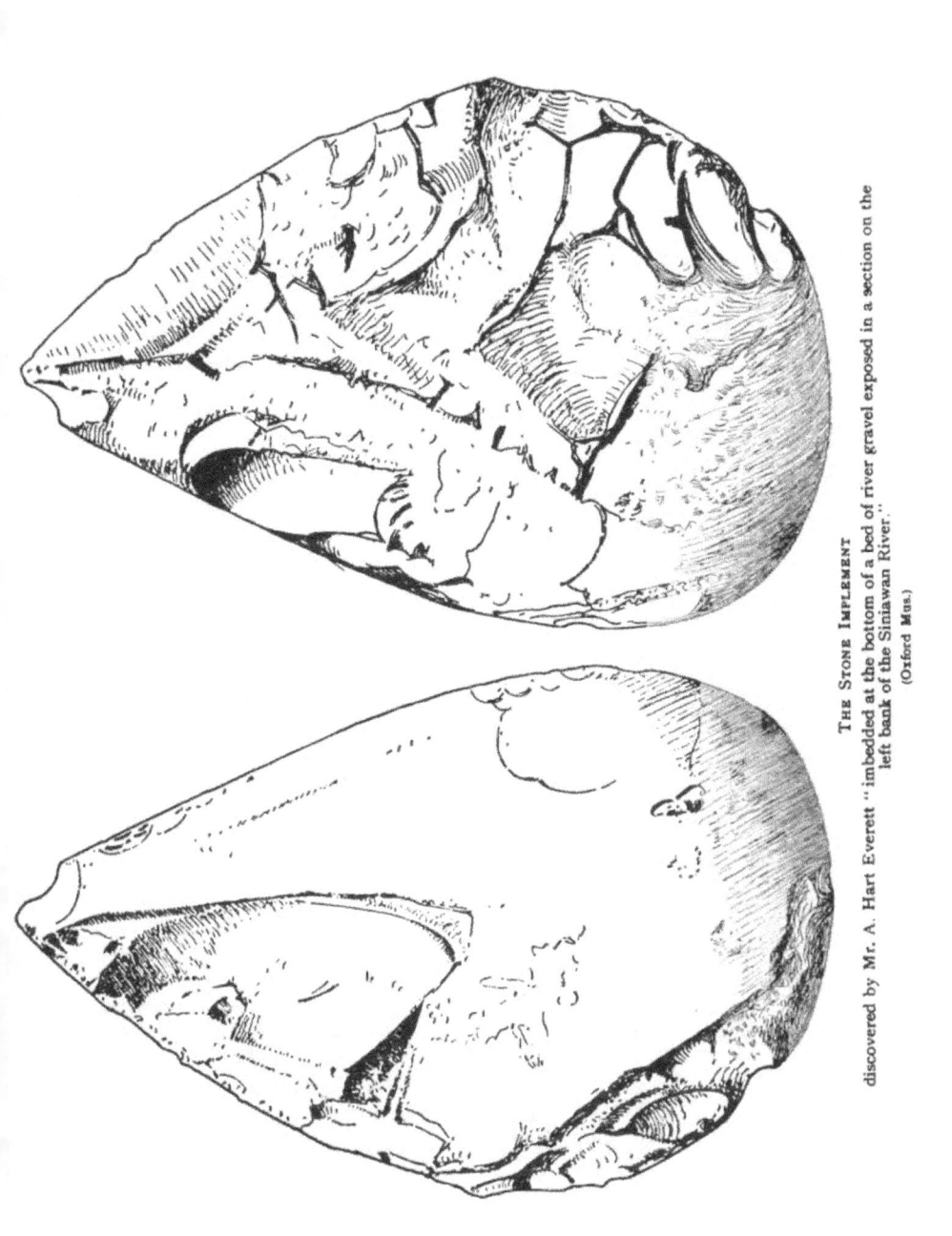

exposed in a section on the left bank of the Siniawan river, a single stone celt. It was forwarded to the late Sir C. Lyell with a note of the circumstances of its occurrence, and was pronounced by him to be of Neolithic type. It is the only existing evidence, to my knowledge, of the use of stone by man for the manufacture of industrial implements yet discovered in Borneo. At present iron seems to be universally employed even by the rudest tribes. In cave No. xiii. a single fragment of stone apparently bearing marks of human workmanship, pieces of burnt bone, fresh-water shells (*Naritina* and *Potamides*) also bearing the marks of fire, the tooth of a tiger cat, with a hole bored through the base, a rude bone head, and a few clean chips of quartz. No stone implements properly so called were observed, though carefully looked for. . . . The quality of the pottery shows that this people had attained a fair degree of civilization. The presence of the marine shells seems to imply that the sea coast was within easy reach of the vicinity of the Jambusan Hill. The remains generally, although of slight interest except to the local archæologist, belong to a ruder stage of art " than articles in the other caves. Mr. A. Hart Everett's concluding remarks are : " The traces of man in the remainder of the eleven caves above referred to consist of human bones, associated, in some instances, with works of art. These remains occur always either just within or but a few yards removed from the entrances of the caves. The caves in which they lie commonly open on the faces of steep mural precipices. That at Ahup, where the largest accumulation exists, is at an elevation of not less than 100 feet above the valley. The bones have belonged to individuals of various ages, they are mostly fragmentary, and they lie scattered on the surface, or but lightly imbedded in the earth without reference to their proper anatomical relations. Their condition will be better judged from the sample sent than from any description that I could give. Occasionally fragments occur bearing the marks of fire. The works of art associated with them include broken jars, cups, cooking pots, and other utensils of earthenware. The pottery is of excellent make, and often glazed and painted. Besides the pottery, beads and armlets of a very hard dark-blue glass, pieces of iron, manufactured gold, and fragments of charcoal have been met with. Similar beads are in the possession of the Land Dyaks at this day, but they can give no account of their origin.

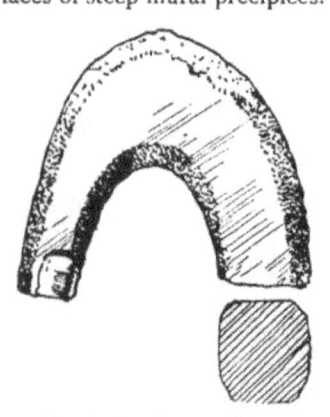

NATURALLY CURVED STONE
ARTIFICIALLY RUBBED FLAT.
Found by Mr. A. Hart Everett in cave.
(Brit. Mus)

BEAD
Found by Mr. A. Hart Everett in cave.
(Brit. Mus.)

" No tradition is extant among the natives with regard to these relics. No tribes in Borneo make habitual use of caves either as domiciles, or as places of sepulture, or for any other purpose. The character of the earthenware, however, and the use of iron and gold point to a very modern date indeed for the people who left these signs of their presence and hence the subject, though curious to a local geologist, does not call for any detailed

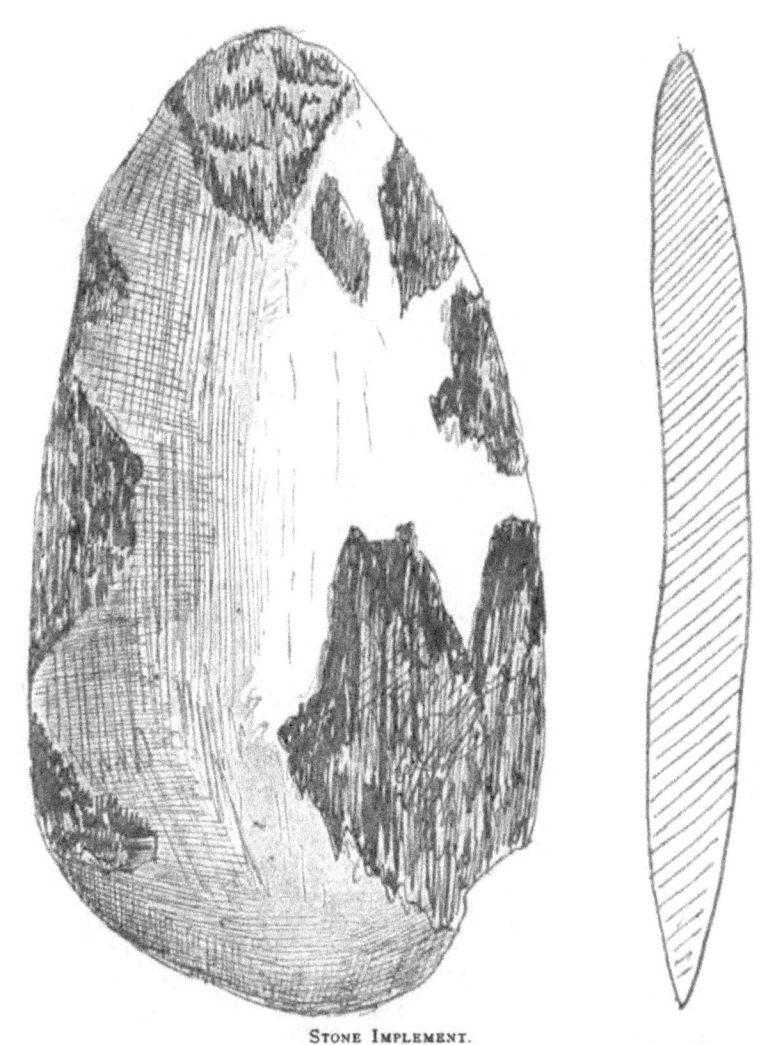

STONE IMPLEMENT.
Said by a London dealer to have come from Borneo, but of very doubtful origin.
(Drawn by Dr. W. C. Pleyte Wzn, Ethnograph. Mus., Amsterdam).

remarks here. It is very possible that the remains date no farther back than the Hindu-Javanese occupation of Borneo, when this part of the island with Pontianak and Banjar were tributary to Majapahit, or they may be of Chinese origin—in either case quite recent."

"The general result of the exploration may be summed up as follows:—The existence of ossiferous caves in Borneo has been proved, and at the same time the existence of man in the island with the Fauna, whose remains are entombed in these caves. But, both from the recent nature of this fauna, and from the fact that the race of men whose remains are associated with it had already reached an advanced stage of civilization, the discovery has in no way aided the solution of those problems for the unravelling of which it was originally promoted. No light has been thrown on the origin of the human race—the history of the development of the fauna characterising the Indo-Malayan sub-region has not been advanced—nor virtually, has any evidence been obtained towards showing what races of men inhabited Borneo previously to the immigration of the various tribes of Malayan stock which now people the Island." (Proc. Roy. Soc., No. 203, 1880, pp. 6, 7.)

JARS.

Of the Sea Dyak jars Sir Spencer St. John says: "There are many kinds of sacred jars. The best known are the Gusi, the Rusa, and the Naga, all most probably of Chinese origin. The Gusi, the most valuable of the three, is of a green colour, about eighteen inches high, and is, from its medicinal properties, exceedingly sought after. One fetched at Tawaran the price of £400 to be paid in produce; the vendor has for the last ten years been receiving the price, which according to his own account, has not yet been paid, though probably he has received fifty per cent. over the amount agreed on from his ignorant customer. They are most numerous in the south of Borneo. The Naga is a jar two feet in height, and ornamented with Chinese figures of dragons; they are not worth above seven or eight pounds. While the Rusa is covered with what the native artist considers a representation of some kind of deer; it is worth from fifteen to sixteen pounds." (i. 27-28.) Of the Land Dyak jars Mr. Grant (p. 94) says similarly: "These jars of supposed antiquity vary in value according to the marks or designs on them—the *Rusa* (deer) is sometimes worth $35, the *Naga* (dragon) $70, the *Ningkah* $150, and the *Gusi* still more."

"Ten jars and *tempayans* of various kinds were brought into the Batang Lupar via Lubok Antu during March, 1894. Amongst these were two *Gusi* jars for which it was stated the owners had paid $500 and $800 respectively. The owner of the latter asked $1200 for it here." (D. J. S. Bailey, S.G., 1894, p. 72.)

"Every Dyak tribe possesses some jars (*tajows*), according to their riches and importance. They are large brown-coloured jars, with handles at the sides, and sometimes figures of dragons on them. No one would suppose, from their appearance, that they were worth more than the common earthen water-pots we use in our bath-houses, but to the Dyaks they have the value of remote antiquity. They say their ancestors bequeathed them to them as the property of the tribe, therefore they never part with them, except by exchange for similar ones, as tokens of amity with other tribes." (Mrs. McDougall, p. 141.)

Sir James Brooke thus describes one of these jars: "Some Dyaks, lately from the interior, have brought one of the celebrated jars; I do not buy it, since it is far too dear as a mere curiosity. It stands three feet high, and is narrow both at the top and bottom, with small rings round the mouth, for the purpose of suspension. The colour is light brown, traced faintly with dragons, and its chief merit and proof of antiquity is the perfect smoothness of the bottom. The ware itself appears coarse and glazed, and those in which the dragon are in alto relievo are valued at a hundred reals. They are not held sacred by the Dyaks as objects of worship, or as venerable relics, though none can be manufactured at the present time; but are collected as a proof of riches, in the same way that the paintings of old masters are in Europe." (Mundy i. 254.)[3]

Another jar is thus described by Sir Chas. Brooke: "One very valuable jar, named *Gusi*, was brought, a common-looking article, small, and one that would certainly have been trampled on by strangers, but it is supposed to possess mysterious qualities—one of them being, that if anything be placed in it over night, the quantity will increase before morning; even water will be found several inches deeper. It is wrapped in cloth, and treated with every mark of respect. People crawl in its presence, and touch and kiss it with the greatest care. They tell me this one is worth £150, and valued most about Brunei and to the northward. Our Sea Dyaks do not hold them as valuable property." (ii. 282.) Nevertheless, some hold them very valuable, for His Highness on one occasion took from the Saribus some jars as hostages for their good conduct during his absence in England. On restoring them he writes: "The Saribus chiefs were inwardly grateful, and blessed every Antu (spirit) under the sun, moon, and stars, for their good fortune in again receiving these jars, each of which they value as much as a child." (*ibid*, ii. 309.)

The Rev. W. Crossland witnessed the following ceremony with a jar: "Two days ago I went to the Undup Dyak house opposite, and found a few old men gathered round a new jar which one of them had just bought. A chicken was caught, and one old man took hold of it, and waved it over the mouth and body of the jar to invoke a blessing. 'This is to make the jar lucky, make it increase with other jars from Europe and China.' This was the invocation. The chicken's throat was then cut, and some of the blood smeared on the jar, and a feather plucked and stuck into one of the handles.

---

[3] A traveller writing from Pulau Majang (Dutch Borneo) writes: I took a stroll through the village, which consists of perhaps forty or fifty houses. Inside of the principal house was a room ten feet square filled with jars, great big fellows standing nearly three feet in height. They represented a portion of the riches of different Dyak chiefs from whom they had been confiscated.

In the event of a house taking fire or the sudden arrival of an enemy, the jars have to be hurried out and buried, which entails both loss of time and risk of life

The appearance of these jars vary but slightly : some are ornamented with a dragon or other reptile in *alto relievo*, others have a small raised figure on either side of the opening. They are usually of a dirty brown colour, and their value in Dyak estimation is simply preposterous. This will be best explained by stating that the "pate" exacted both by the Sarawak and Dutch Governments for a head taken, may be one or more jars. Officials in Borneo talk of heads as in Europe we speak of "lives," and as a punishment for taking one head or more, demand so many jars, in place of so much money. (S.G., No. 102.)

I believe that the Dyaks never acquire any possession without a sacrifice being offered, and though a small fowl may not seem much to give in the eyes of Europeans, to Dyaks it is a great gift." (Gosp. Miss., 1871, p. 165.)

"The old Datu of Tamparuli is the proud possessor of a famed sacred jar. It was a Gusi, and was originally given by a Malau chief in the interior of the Kapuas to a Pakatan Dayak, converted, however, to Islam, and named Japar. He sold it to a Bornean trader for nearly two tons of brass guns, or £230, who brought it to the Tawaran to resell it, nominally for £400, really for nearly £700. No money passes on these occasions, it is all reckoned in brass guns or goods, and the old Datu was paying for his in rice. He possesses another jar, however, to which he attaches an almost fabulous value; it is about two feet in height, and is of a dark olive green. He fills both the jars with water, and adds flowers and herbs to retail to all the surrounding people who may be suffering from any illness. Perhaps, however, the most remarkable jar in Borneo is the one possessed by the present Sultan of Brunei, as it not only has all the valuable properties of the other sacred vases, but speaks. As the Sultan told this with a grave face and evident belief in the truth of what he was relating, we listened to the story with great interest. He said, the night before his first wife died, it moaned sorrowfully, and on every occasion of impending misfortune it utters the same melancholy sounds. I have sufficient faith in his word to endeavour to seek an explanation of this (if true) remarkable phenomenon, and perhaps it may arise from the wind blowing over its mouth, which may be of some peculiar shape, and cause sounds like those of an Æolian harp. I should have asked to see it, had it not been always kept in the women's apartments. As a rule, it is covered over with gold-embroidered brocade, and seldom exposed, except when about to be consulted. This may account for its only producing sounds at certain times. I have heard that in former days the Muruts and Bisayas used to come with presents to the Sultan, and obtain in return a little water from this sacred jar, with which to besprinkle their fields to ensure good crops. In looking over Carletti's *Voyage*, I find he mentions taking some sacred jars from the Philippine Islands to Japan,[4] which were so prized there that the

[4] Mr. Earl gives a curious account of the origin of these jars: "The relics of an ancient people are also to be met with in the inland parts of the west coast, and although the information I was enabled to collect concerning them was extremely vague I came to the conclusion that they were a race distinct from the Hindus of near Banjar Massin. These relics consist merely of tumuli, in which are sometimes found small earthen jars, and being supposed by the Dyaks to be connected in some manner with the ashes of their forefathers, are in all probability graves. The jars are very scarce, and are so highly valued by their possessors on account of their supposed oracular powers, that the offer of a sum equal to five hundred pounds sterling has been refused for one of them. The jars are consulted by their owners before they undertake any expedition, and they believe it will be prosperous or the contrary according to the sound produced, probably by water being poured into it. I much regretted being unable to inspect one of these vessels, as their materials and manufacture might possibly throw some light upon the relation which the natives of Borneo bear to some other parts of India." (Earl, pp. 274-5.)

"The principal luxury of the Dyaks consists in the possession of a sort of large earthenware jar which they assert to have come from the Kingdom of Modjopahit, in the island of Java, but which seemed to me of Chinese manufacture. What confirms me in my opinion is the resemblance I have found between certain figures of dragons with long tails with which these jars are ornamented and the very similar figures as regards form and attitude which are seen on ancient

punishment of death was denounced against them if they were sold to any one but the Government. Some, he says, were valued as high as £30,000. The Sultan of Brunei was asked if he would take £2,000 for his; he answered he did not think any offer in the world would tempt him to part with it." (*ibid* i. 300.)

It is very curious that nearly every one who has something to say about these old jars states that the Chinese have tried to imitate them and to palm them off as new to the Dyaks, who, however, are not to be deceived. No special reference is made to any particular tribe or occasion. Dr. Schwaner appears to have been the first to make the statement.

For illustrations of Jars see *supra* i. 68 and 427.

ALLEGED NATIVE WRITING IN BORNEO.

In the Sarawak Gazette, 1894, p. 169, it is reported: "A rather extraordinary incident happened in this [the Limbang] river with an Orang Kaya, Jahun, who lives some way up river. When asked to pay his yearly tax, he sent a message to the Resident with his *tanda tangan* or signature—which was made by putting his hand in ink and then making its impression on a white sheet of paper—this was then sent with a message that he would willingly come to the fort if he was brought as a prisoner by a policeman, that he would willingly pay the yearly sum, if he was threatened with imprisonment; this, he said, would then show he was forced to pay and would prevent bad odour with the Brunei government." Jahun may of course be a Malay, or he may have learnt the method of signing his name from a Malay. Such signing cannot possibly be a native or Dyak method, for the whole circumstance points to introduced materials.

But in his "Beginnings of Writing" the late Prof. de la Couperie would make us believe that the Dyaks did once understand the art of writing. He states (p. 27): "Among the several writings which were used in Borneo two have left interesting relics and survivals. The Dayaks[s] engrave as ornaments some signs which they obviously understand no more. Some bamboo objects exhibited at the India Museum, London, bear these marks. They are coins of Cochinchina. However this may be, these jars appear very ancient and no doubt they are not manufactured at the present day, without which no doubt on account of their high price the Chinese would not fail to speculate in them. Among the Dyaks these jars are bequeathed from father to son like sacred jewels. The high value they place on these objects gives the jars great importance, and even if they are cracked in various parts and that some portion is wanting, or having been broken and are only held together by rotan bands, their price is none the less considerable. The Dyaks distinguish several varieties of jars which have their proper names, and of which the principal are: 1 —The *Balanga*, a male jar, value from 1,000 to 5,000 florins and over, according to its beauty and its dimensions. A *balanga* which I measured was 70 c.m. high, 48 c.m. in diameter in the middle, and had an orifice of 24 c.m. diameter. On the shoulders were, one on each side, two serpent-shaped dragons with three paws bent under them. 2.—The *Hattot-Halimau*, also a male jar, according to the Dyaks worth 500 to 2,000 florins. The two serpents with dragon heads drawn round the jar had four feet 3.—The *Pasiran-tiaen*, or female jar, and which is only valued at 100 to 300 florins. As for this class of jar, it has much the same dimensions as the two above mentioned; but as handles it has four geckoes, each with four paws. (S. Müller ii 361.)

[s] The name Dyak is here used in its generally but incorrectly accepted application to all natives of Borneo more or less wild.

apparently the survival of an alphabetical writing anciently known there and afterwards forgotten. We find a similar writing on an earthenware vase from the same island belonging to the Ethnographical Museum of Dresden.[6] This vase, as far as I can remember from a sketch communicated to me by Mr. A. W. Franks [Sir Wollaston Franks], is ornamented with two figures of the Chinese dragon, but not Chinese make. Dr. Kern has published some inscriptions found at Koutei in the same island, which are written in the character of Eastern India, the Vengi Chalukya in Kalinga, the same that was carried to Cambodia, to Western Java and elsewhere. . . ."[7] Further on Prof. de la Couperie continues (p. 131): "On a former writing of Borneo,[8] the Chinese records of 977 A.D. give the following information. It is about a letter written by the native King, Hiangta of Puni (Western coast of Borneo), to the Chinese ruler. The letter was enclosed in different small bags, which were sealed, and it was not written on Chinese paper, but on what looked like very thin bark of a tree; it was glossy, slightly green, several feet long and somewhat broader than one inch, and rolled up so tightly that it could be taken within the hand. The characters in which it was written were small and had to be read horizontally."[9]

Fig. 1.

In an appreciative review of the Professor's book in the Athenæum (No. 3518, March 30, 1895) it is said the author shows that the history of writing " is by no means one of progress only, from no writing to pictures, from pictures to phonetics, but that he has discovered not a few instances of graphic systems impeded or decayed, where adverse conditions, such as want of intelligence or want of use, caused the higher thing to degenerate—the honest attempt to write decaying into pictures or charms, and showing in one more department of the world's history a case of failure in the struggle for life. His examples from the Aïnos, Lolos, and Dyaks seem certain enough ; his argument that Chinese writing is another example is not so convincing. . . ."

The reviewer's conclusion about the Dyaks (so called) is true enough when the late Professor's statements only are taken into consideration, but unfortunately the facts on which the Professor's statements are based are not

---

[6] I was acquainted with this inscription through a facsimile sent to my learned friends Col. H. Yule and Dr. R. Rost by Dr. A. B. Meyer, Keeper of the Museum. This writing is not without some apparent connection with one of the writings of Sumatra. . . . [D.L.C.]

[7] Over de opschriften uit Koetei in verband met de geschiedenis van het schrift in den Indischen Archipel. 8vo. Amsterdam, 1882, p. 18.—Also K. F. Holle, Tabel van Oud- en Nieuw-Indische Alphabetten. Bijdrage tot de palaeographie van Nederlandsch Indië (800, Batavia 1882). No 80-1 [D.L.C.]

[8] The vase and its inscription mentioned above is published in the splendid work of Dr. A. B. Meyer, Alterthümer aus dem ostindischen Archipel (Leipzig, 1884, fol), p. 7 and pl. XI. fig. 4. [D.L.C.]

[9] W. P. Groeneveldt, Notes on the Malay Archipelago and Malacca, compiled from Chinese Sources, p. 109. [D.L.C.]

forthcoming. Nor does the Professor show any direct connection at all, between the people who are stated to have made use of the writing in past times and the present generation with their bambu marks, so that there is no evidence of any degeneration. An examination of the illustrations of the three writings as given below will at once convince every student that they are all by different peoples who have passed away and who have left us no proof that the present peoples now living in their respective districts are their blood descendants.

I sent Mr. Charles Prætorius (who has illustrated the greater portion of this work) to the India Office Museum, London, in order to copy the inscriptions on the bambu objects—but these objects could not be found. So I wrote to the late Dr. Rost, formerly of the India Office, whose name is mentioned by the late Professor, sending him a copy of the " Beginnings of Writings," and this is his reply, dated 26th Aug., 1895 :

" It is just possible that Sir Henry Yule, with whom I was up to the time of his death in continuous literary intercourse, showed me the facsimile in question and even that we exchanged opinions about it. But I have no recollection whatever of the circumstances and am very sorry that my name should have been quoted by the Professor, who, I fear, was but too prone to draw inferences from facts not sufficiently established."

I then addressed myself to Dr. A. B. Meyer, regarding the vase,[10] who answers under dates 29th Aug. and 6th Sept., 1895, thus: " I may have sent a facsimile to Col. Yule but I do not remember it and I cannot find an answer from him." Dr. Meyer also informs me that the inscription, if such it be, is on the bottom of the vase (see Fig. 1) and that the vase is decidedly of Chinese make. He writes that " it may represent remnants of a Dayak-writing, as we know that in Pigafetta's time the Sultan of Bruni had 10 writers, who wrote on thin bark of trees,"[11] but the learned Doctor carefully adds in his letter " this is only a supposition."

Whatever writers the Sultan may have had, it does not follow that they were Dyaks or other natives (other than Malays or Chinese), any more than because the Emperor of China received the above mentioned letter from Puni, that that letter was written by Dyaks. As the letter was translatable, it was probably written in Chinese.

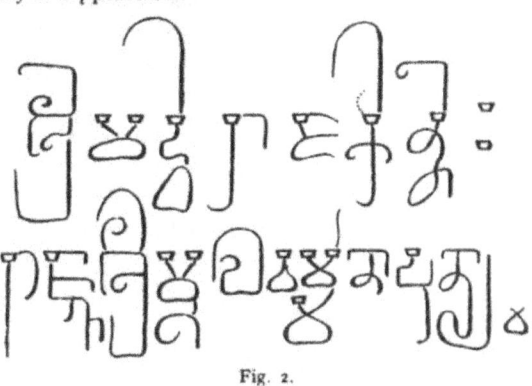

Fig. 2.

[10] The footnote No. 1 on p. 28 of Beginnings of Writings is misplaced and should be placed after the word Dresden, as it refers not to the bambus, but to the vase.

[11] " He has ten scribes, who write down his affairs on thin bark of trees and are called *cherita-tulis*." (p. 114.) Pigafetta, The First Voyage round the World, by Magellan. Hakluyt Soc. vol. lii., London, 1874.

In the Museum at Leiden there are a few good examples of designs, from the so-called Dyaklands in South Eastern Borneo, but there is no correspondence between these and the writings discovered at Koutie (Fig. 2) and decyphered by that eminent orientalist Dr. Kern, nor with the marks on the Chinese jar, nor with the writing (?) on the dagger from South Eastern Borneo of which I submit a facsimile (Fig. 3).[14]

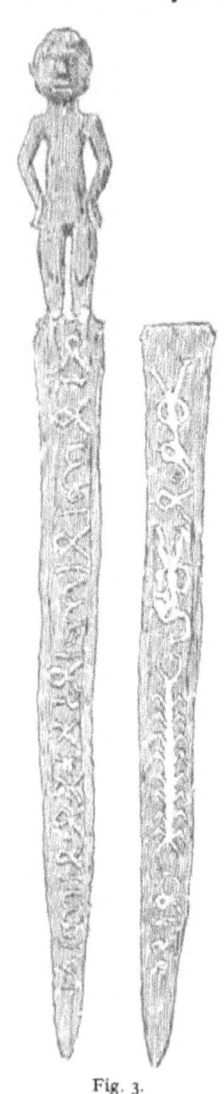

If, however, we speak of writing in its broad anthropological sense of a general means of ocular communication of thought, we shall find the natives have some such methods. Mr. F. R. O. Maxwell, late chief Resident of the Raja of Sarawak, writes me: "Dyak and Kayan chiefs, when sending for their followers, use a spear, and should it be for a war expedition, a piece of red cloth is attached. I know of no nearer approach to writing. They mark days by knots in a piece of cord or rattan. Thus in sending to people to come in a certain number of days, say 30, they will send a piece of cord with 30 knots in it and the recipient cuts off one each day, and when the last knot is gone, he has to present himself. I have used this plan often and it is the only way I could keep Dyaks punctual." In Mr. Brooke Low's notes I find he mentions: "The natives have a kind of symbolic mode of communication by *temuku tali*, a knotted string."

In his Limbang Journal Sir Spencer St. John relates that at the mouth of the Salindong his party came upon a Kayan resting-place where he found marks, which proved that one party had returned. "In the hut was picked up a woman's jacket, with a small net, left behind in the hurry of departure, so it is probable they captured her while fishing on the banks of some rivulet. Though certain they had obtained captives, opinions were divided on the subject of heads. I could find no traces, and old Japer agreed with me that it was uncertain; but it would only be accidentally that we could have discovered indications. They have left a mark, however, to show their countrymen that they had been up the Salindong: it was a long pole, ornamented with three tufts pointing up that stream. The three tufts were supposed by many to show that they had obtained three heads or captives; it might mean either. There were evidently two parties out." (ii. 68.)

Fig. 3.

---

[14] [With respect to the handle and its form this dagger is especially different from the well known ancient Javanese daggers, being made with the handle all in one piece of iron. The ornamentation of one side is partly the same as that on another dagger blade from Bandjermassin, also in the Museum at Leiden. J. D. E. Schmeltz.]

Unless the curious unexplained signs, which Mr. Hose once found put up after a murder had taken place, are also a method of communication by signs, Sir Spencer's record is the only one I have come across. Mr. Hose was returning from the head waters of the Tinjar river; he writes: "On my way down I stopped at Long Tisam at which place the Chinaman, named See Jee, was murdered last month, and I find that posts have been erected with wood shaving, *daun isang*, and seven wooden heads have been placed on the top of the poles. The appearance of which poles being quite new, I enquired of the Malays when they were put up, and find it was about the time of the murder. I therefore stopped at Long Merong and told Taman Liri, the *Penghulu*, to call Aban Avit and find out for what purpose these poles were put up. I now think that there is little doubt that Aban Avit had a hand in the murder." (Sarawak Gazette, 1894, p. 60.) Later on he writes: "Taman Liri, the Barawan *Penghulu*, will not give an opinion as regards Aban Avit being implicated in the murder of the Chinaman See Jee. But Taman Bulan, the Kenniak *Penghulu*, says that if Aban Avit put up posts with heads hanging to them, directly after the murder was committed, he does not think that this was done on account of harvest festivities. But that, if it is Aban Avit's custom at the end of the harvest to use heads and *daun isang* in that way, he will of course have done so in years gone by. Taman Liri, the head of all the Barawans, did not put up anything of this kind after the harvest and Aban Avit, though head of a house, is one of Taman Liri's followers." (*ibid*, p. 74.) We know, of course, that occasionally among the Muruts wooden heads are used to represent the real head trophy (see *supra* ii. 162), but in the above exhibition there must have been some unusual meaning, some special communications to be made to the passer-by.

In some cases tatu-marks appear to be used as a means of communicating a fact. Mr. Burns says that among the Kayans tatuing is distinctive of rank (Jour. Ind. Arch. iii., 145). Mr. Hose tells us the different races are characterised by different designs (Jour. Anthr. Inst. xxiii. 166). Lieut. De Crespigny informs us that among the Dusuns only those who have killed a foe tatu themselves (Proc. Roy. Geogr. Soc. ii. 348). Mr. Witti confirms this (Diary, 19th Nov.). At Tamalan this method, from representing bravery had come to represent cruel murders, for those who had sacrificed slaves tatued themselves. (*ibid*, 30th May.) Mr. Hatton states that Muruts, who had been on bold or risky expeditions, used to tatu and he mentions a case where a Murut, having run away from the enemy, was tatued on his back. (Hatton's Diary, 6th April.) So that we may justly conclude that tatuing among the natives of Borneo is one method of writing.

Mr. Earl writes: "I could not discover any written character among the Dyaks of Western Borneo, but it is said that those of the southern parts near to Banjar Massin possess one." (p. 277).

It may yet be shown that the natives of Borneo have some simple method of communicating their thoughts to one another, something similar to that of the Battas or to such as is referred to by the late Prof. de la Couperie, or it may still be shown that they use as ornament degenerated letters, but so far the proofs are wanting. Perhaps these few remarks may lead those, who are in daily communication with the natives, to make enquiries, the results of which would be looked forward to with interest.

Fig. 4.
THE WRITING ON THE BOTTOM OF THE CHINESE JAR,
Referred to by Prof. de la Couperie. (See *supra*, Chap. XXVIII.)

The above remarks on writing appeared in the Internationales Archiv. für Ethnographie, xi. 57, when Dr. H. Kern, of Leiden, kindly added the following note:—

" There can be no doubt that writing in former times was known to the inhabitants of some parts of Borneo, but it is equally true, as it has been remarked by Mr. Ling Roth, that there is no proof of any connection between those people who made use of writing and the present Dayak tribes. The Sanscrit inscriptions of Kutei are of Hindu origin, of course, and not produced by Dayaks. The inscription on the bottom of the vase published by Dr. A. B. Meyer has quite recently been treated of anew in the splendid publication, " Die Mangainenschrift von Mindoro, herausgegeben von A. B. Meyer und A. Schadenberg, special bearbeitet von W. Foy " (Fig. 4). The result is that the characters belong to one of the Philippine alphabets, the Mangain writing of Mindoro.

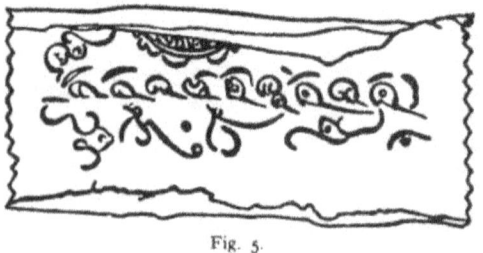

Fig. 5.

"The characters on the dagger (Fig. 3) are decidedly letters of Indian origin, and, if read from left to right, look like $\underset{ma}{\underline{\ }}$ | *maya* | *ma* | *ya* | *ma* | *ma* | *mama* | *ma* | *ya* | *ma* | . No meaning, unless a cabbalistic one, can be attached to this repetition of two letters.

"Another specimen of writing, a facsimile of which is here published for the first time (see Fig. 5), is found near Sanggau on a slab near the river side. The characters shew a debased type of Indian writing. I am sorry to say that my endeavours to unriddle the contents have been fruitless. The first word of the second line may represent *prabhuh*, a well-known Sanscrit word, but it is only with diffidence that I propose this reading. Whether the framers of the inscription were ancestors of the present Dayaks at Sanggau, is a question which cannot be settled before one will have found out the language of the monument." (H. Kern, 16 Febr, 1896.)

NEGRITOES IN BORNEO.

The question, "Are there any Negritoes in Borneo?" is one of great interest, and has been as yet by no means solved.

The interest in the question lies in the fact that while in the surrounding countries the existence of Negritoes has been more or less proved, no European has yet met with a Negrito in Borneo. There are plenty of Negritoes in the Philippine Islands (A. B. Meyer, "Die Philippinen," II, Negritos; Dresden; fol., 1893). Mr. Alex. Dalrymple says there are none in Palawan, Mr. A. Hart Everett also says he could hear nothing of any Negritoes in that part of Palawan visited by him. They exist in the Malay Peninsula. In Sumatra the Kubus had been considered to have at some remote period intermingled with the Negritoes, while their osteology leans decidedly to the Malays. (Dr. Garson, J. A. I., xiv. 132). In Java and Madura I cannot find that Negritoes are proved to have existed, although the Kalangs are said to be like them. In Sumbawa there is a race of people of whom almost nothing is known. (F. H. H. Guillemard, "Australasia, ii. 1894, p. 358), but it is not stated they might be Negritoes. "It is highly probable that a low and primitive race[13] did once inhabit Celebes, but if so, it has, so far as we know, completely disappeared." (*ibid*, p. 288.)

It was for this reason—namely, widespread surrounding negritic population—that, when at the meeting of the British Association at Oxford in 1894, I pointed out we must suspend our judgment as to the existence of Negritoes in Borneo, I was told probabilities were against me, as Borneo was in the midst of a negritic area. Since then, I find that Dr. A. B. Meyer[14] had come to the same conclusion as I did, arguing from a somewhat different standpoint to that which I took up. He has gone so thoroughly into the matter, that I translate his statement.

"Although for a long time past all authors were of the opinion that the reports of the existence of Negritoes in Borneo were not to be trusted, their

---

[13] Not necessarily negritic—nor is this inferred by Dr. Guillemard.
[14] A. B. Meyer, "Die Philippinem," ii., Negritoes. Dresden fol., 1893, pp. 71-2.

existence has lately been repeatedly asserted. Pickering ('U.S. Explor. Exp.,' 1848, ix. 174) notices especially their absence, and Waitz—Gerland ('Anthr.,' 1865, v. 47) express themselves as follows: 'Older reports have mentioned Papuans which were said to have been found in the interior of Borneo, but W. Earl[15] remarks very correctly ('East Seas,' 1836, 256) that no traveller has himself seen them, Kessel[16] also only heard Malay traders speak of them ('Z. f. a. Erdk. N.F.' iii. 379), and Marsden ('Misc.' 37) only mentions that a small Borneo chief spoke of woolly-haired Tammans in the interior; on the other hand, Schwaner ('Borneo,' 1853, i. 64) assures us particularly that with the exception of the Papuans[17] introduced into the north-east of the country, there are no others. Later on Earl ('Races Ind. Arch.,' 1853, 146) found the existence of Papuans in the interior of Borneo somewhat more probable but still without sufficient foundation in fact. Earl's account in question is held to be credible by others, but it is practically a matter of individual opinion whether one believes it or not. It mentions that a ship's captain stranded in 1844 on the north coast of Borneo, at the Berau or Kuran rivers, once met, fifty miles inland, at the foot of Mount Tabur, 17 curly headed small men ornamented with cicatrices, or at least so the man himself told him (Earl), and his evidence must be considered satisfactory. Everything else which Earl brings forward is calculated to weaken rather than to strengthen the case. The district in question has certainly not often been travelled over, but now that north Borneo has been traversed several times, and even Mount Kinibalu has been several times ascended, and no traces of Negritoes[18] have anywhere been found, one must very strongly doubt the credibility of the statement of a ship's captain. Junghuhn ('Battaländer,' 1847, i. 220, note) considers it unimaginable that anyone could have overlooked such a specialised race with woolly hair and black skin in Borneo. Everett, who possesses a profound knowledge of north-west Borneo, leaves the reader in the dark as to whether he believes the statement of the captain or not, nevertheless he seems to be more on the side of the doubters. ("Nature," 1880, xxi. 588.) Giglioli ("Viaggio Magenta," 1875, 253) believes the statement, and adds: "Beccari found no trace of Negritoes in Borneo, 'cioe vide indegeni coi capelli crespi.'" Unfortunately Giglioli

[15] Earl only says that no Dyak whom he met had seen them, notwithstanding that the natives assert their existence; but as they also assert the existence of tailed people, they must not be believed.—A. B. M.

[16] Kessel says that in the interior, "namely, in the north-east," they cultivate the soil. This statement is perfectly incredible.—A. B. M.

[17] These are Papuans from New Guinea, whom the Sulus have brought home as slaves from their widespread piratical expeditions, or whom they have purchased elsewhere, as, for instance, in the Moluccas. Schwaner says, "the few Papuans which were met in the north-east of Borneo come from the fatherland of the Papuans, and have been carried off by the Sulu pirates." He adds also, "that the local traditions there speak against the existence of Negritoes."—A. B. M.

[18] See for example Whitehead ("Expl. Kina Balu," 1893); compare Latham ("Essays," 1860,) 192). Treacher ("J. Str. Br. R. As. Soc.," 1890, No. 1, p. 101), says, "There are no Negritoes in Borneo." Hose ("Journ. Anthrop. Inst.," 1893, xxiii., p. 156) considers the Punans, "the nomadic tribes found at the head waters of all the big rivers in central Borneo," as the real aborigines. (p. 157): " I have no doubt in my mind that this wandering race of people are the aboriginals of the country." The Punans are real Malays.—A. B. M.

says nothing more, and in the year 1876 when he published his "Studi sulla razza negrita" ("Arch., p. Antr.," vi. 315), he said nothing new on the above remark of Beccari; it is therefore only a matter of casual observation upon which no value can be placed. I think this all the more, because when Zannetti ("Arch. p. Antr.," 1872, ii. 159), discussing a Dyak skull of Beccari's collection, speaks against the existence of Negritoes in Borneo, he makes no mention of any contrary opinion of Beccari's. Finally, Hamy ("Bull. Soc. d'Anthr.," 1876, 116) refers to the above mentioned captain's statement, and describes a skull which Jourdan had received at the Lyons Museum as a Negrito skull from Borneo; he says (p. 118) that this skull fully proves the existence of Negritoes in the heart of Borneo. In 1882 Quatrefages and Hamy ("Cr. Ethn.," 195, figs. 212, 213) published an illustration of this skull as such; it is ornamented with incised lines such as we know the trophy skulls collected by the Dyaks of Borneo possess. I do not consider that in this case the conclusion drawn from certain anatomical characters on the race are justified. When, moreover, the Bishop of Labuan[19] informs us ("Tr. Ethn. Soc." N.S., 1863, ii. 25) that the traditions of the Dyaks of north-west Borneo indicate that a black race had preceded them, one must not jump to the conclusion that they refer to Negritoes; besides, according to Waitz—Gerland ("Anthr.," 1865, v., i. 47), the traditions read quite otherwise. On what Flower quite recently supports his short statement ("J.A.I.," 1889, xviii. 82), that Negritoes exist in the interior of Borneo I do not know for certain, but I presume it is on the map in Quatrefages' "Hist. Gen. des Races Hum." (1889, to p. 343), or to the latter's references in "Les Pygmées" (1887, 42), but which, as we saw above, do not stand investigation. How carelessly Quatrefages went about this question I may show by a single example. He says (l.c., p. 76), "A Bornéo, les Dayaks chassent au Négrito comme à la bête fauve," and refers to Earl ("Papuans," 1853, 147); but Earl only reproduces an account of Dalton's on certain tribes of North Borneo, of whom Earl says that they may perhaps be related to the above named more than questionable Negritoes of the ship's captain, in spite of the fact that Dalton himself calls them wild Dyaks. As Dalton lived eleven months on the Koti river, no one has the right to re-christen his Dyaks Negritoes. That which Earl adds to Dalton's account makes it appear as quite settled that these people possibly could have been Negritoes. Compare also Meinicke's excellent remarks on the absence of Negritoes in Borneo. ("Beitr. Eth. As.," 1837, p. 8.) After all this I conclude that there is no proof yet of the existence of Negritoes in Borneo; all the same, we can only then judge with the fullest confidence when the whole interior shall have been fully explored."

So far Dr. Meyer. I give Mr. Earl's statement in full:—

"The interior of this large island is occupied by tribes of the brown race, whose warlike habits, and skill in the use of missiles, will account for the

---

[19] The Bishop's (Dr. McDougall's) words are: "With respect to the races of people, the present occupants were, he thought, the remains of a second wave of immigration. The black race or Papuas, he thought, came in first, and a second wave of Malay or Dyak race followed; the traditions of the country refer to such an event, and people speak of a black race having been there before them. The present race were probably from India." (Trans. Ethno. Soc. ii., 1863, p. 26.)—H.L.R.

disappearance of a less civilised race from the southern and western parts of the island. In the year 1834, when on a visit to the western coast of the island, I was informed by some of the more intelligent among the natives that a wild, woolly-haired people existed in the interior; but the information was mixed up with so many incredible details respecting their habits, that I was led to consider the whole as fabulous; and the subject is treated in this light in the narrative of my voyages, which was published soon after my return to England in the following year.[20]

"During a second visit to the Archipelago, my attention was chiefly directed to the more eastern islands, where the field was comparatively new, and I had no opportunity of obtaining farther information respecting the interior of Borneo until when again on my return to England in 1845. One of my fellow passengers on that occasion was Captain Brownrigg, whose ship, the 'Premier,' of Belfast, had been wrecked on the east coast of Borneo during the previous year, when the European portion of the crew found refuge with the Rajah Mudah of Gunung Thabor, a place about 50 miles up the Buru or Kuran River, whence they were removed after a residence of several months by a Dutch vessel of war, which had been sent from Macassar for the purpose. Captain Brownrigg was so kind as to entertain me frequently with accounts of the people among whom he had been thrown, and who had not previously been visited by Europeans. They appear to me to differ in no essential particular from the other coast tribes of Borneo, except in being rather more advanced, as was evident, indeed, from the hospitable reception he met among them; but my attention having been aroused by a repeated mention of 'darkies' as forming part of the population, I was induced to make some inquiries, when I found that he alluded to an inland tribe that only occasionally visited Gunung Thabor, and who were a short, but stoutly built, people, perfectly black, and with hair so short and curly that the head appeared to be covered with little knobs. This perfectly agrees with the general appearance of the hair of the Papuans, who keep the head shorn; and I have not the slightest doubt that they were unmixed Papuans. He also described the skins of the breast and shoulders as displaying many raised scarifications, apparently similar to those of some New Guinea tribes, but which do not appear to be common among the mountain Papuans. On one occasion, a party of seventeen men, chiefly young and middle aged, visited the settlement for the express purpose of seeing the Europeans. They appeared to live on very friendly terms with the people of Gunung Thabor, from whom they obtained supplies of axes and chopping knives, giving the produce of the forests in exchange.

[20] "The various tribes are said to differ considerably from each other, an assertion I do not pretend to dispute, although my own experience would go to prove the contrary, since I saw individuals belonging to several distinct tribes, who, with the exception of a difference of dialect, might be recognised as the same people, those who lived entirely on the water being much darker than the rest. It is said by the Dyaks themselves, that some parts of the interior are inhabited by a woolly-haired people; but as they also assert that men with tails like monkeys, and living in trees, are also discoverable, the accuracy of their accounts may be doubted. I met with no Dyak who had seen either, but as a woolly-haired people is to be found scattered over the interior of the Malay Peninsula, their existence in Borneo seems by no means improbable."—" The Eastern Seas," p. 225. H L R.

"It should be mentioned that this was Captain Brownrigg's first visit to the Archipelago, and he could scarcely have been aware that any peculiar interest was connected with this information, so that his evidence must be considered satisfactory. I have since searched the published accounts of visitors to the east coast of Borneo, but the only allusion I can find to a people who may be allied to the same race, is contained in the papers of Mr. Dalton, who resided for eleven months on the Coti River, to the south of the Buru, during the years 1827-28. Mr. Dalton's papers were originally published in the 'Singapore Chronicle' of 1831 : and the following extract is from Mr. Moor's 'Notices of the Indian Archipelago,' in which they are reprinted :—

"'Farther towards the north of Borneo are to be found men living absolutely in a state of nature, who neither cultivate the ground nor live in huts ; who neither eat rice nor salt, and who do not associate with each other, but rove about some woods like wild beasts. The sexes meet in the jungle, or the man carries away a woman from some kampong. When the children are old enough to shift for themselves they usually separate, neither one afterwards thinking of the other; at night they sleep under some large tree, the branches of which hang low. On these they fasten the children in a kind of swing; around the tree they make a fire to keep off the wild beasts and snakes; they cover themselves with a piece of bark, and in this also they wrap their children; it is soft and warm, but will not keep out the rain. These poor creatures are looked on and treated by the Dyaks as wild beasts ; hunting parties of twenty-five and thirty go out and amuse themselves with shooting at the children in the trees with sumpits, the same as monkeys, from which they are not easily distinguished. The men taken in these excursions are invariably killed, the women commonly spared if young. It is somewhat remarkable that the children of these wild Dyaks cannot be sufficiently tamed to be entrusted with their liberty. Selgie (the Dyak chief of Coti) told me he never recollected an instance when they did not escape to the jungle the very first opportunity, notwithstanding many of them had been kindly treated for years.'[21]

"It must be remembered that this account, as well as the extract from Valentyn respecting the wild tribes of Ceram, is derived from the information of natives, who avowedly made parties for the express purpose of hunting them, and who are therefore in making them appear as much as possible in the light of wild beasts. Neither of these accounts alludes to the wild tribes as being woolly-headed, but this is a point on which no native is likely to give information, unless the question is expressly put to them. When on the coast of Borneo in 1843, we had a Papuan sailor on board the vessel, who formed one of my boat's crew, and the peculiarity of his appearance was almost invariably a topic of conversation wherever we went, and if any of the natives we came in contact with had ever seen or heard of a people possessing similar peculiarities, the circumstance was nearly certain to be noticed.

"It is probable that information connected with the existence of this race in Borneo, which is of considerable ethnographical interest, may be

[21] Dalton's "Notices," p. 49, G.W.E. The term "Dyaks" should probably read "Kayans."—H.L.R.

found in Holland, among the documents containing the reports of government officers who have been despatched from time to time to make researches on the east coast of the island, as Dr. Roorda Van Eysinga, Professor of Oriental Languages and Geography to the Royal Military Academy of Holland, states in his 'Geography of Netherlands' India,' that 'In the inaccessible parts of the island' (Borneo) 'Papuans yet reside in a savage state, bordering upon that of wild beasts.'[22] No authorities are quoted in the work, but as it is used as a class-book throughout the Netherlands, it cannot be supposed that the statement has been loosely made." (Earl's "Papuans," pp. 144-149.)

The reference by MM. Quatrefages and Hamy ("Crania Ethnica," pp. 194-196) to a comparison between the Negrito skull and that of the Andamans, induced me to turn to Mr. E. H. Man's work "On the Aboriginal Inhabitants of the Andaman Islands" (Lond., 1884), where on p. 119 there is a footnote reference to the kidnapping of the Andamanese by Malays, &c. It runs as follows :—

"Captain J. H. Miller, in a communication to the 'Nautical Magazine,' 1842, says: 'The islands in the west side of the Andamans are frequented during the fine season, from December to April, by a mixed and mongrel race of Malays, Chinese, and Burmese fishermen for *bêche de mer* and edible birds' nests, who are of very doubtful honesty, and it is necessary to take a few muskets and cutlasses just to show them that you are prepared for mischief in case of need. These fellows are also 'fishers of men,' and to their evil deeds much of the hostility of the islanders may be attributed; they carry off children, for whom they find a ready market as slaves in the neighbouring countries. I have been told that formerly they were friendly, and assisted these fishermen, until a large party was invited on board a junk or prow (the Chinese got the blame of it), and after being intoxicated, were carried off and sold at Acheen, and the practice is still carried on by these fellows, who land and carry them off whenever they can catch them. The Andamanians have retaliated fearfully whenever any foreigner has fallen into their power, and who can blame them.'" ("Sailing Directions for the Principal Ports in the Bay of Bengal," by W. H. Rosser and J. F. Imray.) On asking Mr. Man for further information, he kindly sent me the following extract :—" Extract from an article entitled 'One of the earliest accounts of two captive Andamanese,' edited from a paper by the late John Anderson, Esq., Secretary to Government Penang Civil Service, by his son, Capt. T. C. Anderson, B.S. Corps, and published in a magazine called 'Indian Society,' May, 1867 : 'A Chinese junk, manned partly by Chinese and partly by Burmans, proceeded to the Andaman Islands to collect *bêche de mer*, sea slugs (a great treat in China), and somewhat resembling a black snail, which the Chinese dry and eat, as well as edible birds' nests, which abound there. The crew of the junk, which was lying about two miles from the shore, observed eight or ten of the

---

[22] "Ten zuiden van het koningrijk Borneo wonen de wilden volksstammen, Doesoems, K-a-jans, Maroets, en genaamd. In het outoegankelijk gedeelte van het eiland wonen nog Papoeaas in eenen staat van wildheid, welke aan dien der wilde dieren grenst." "Aardrijkbeschrijving van Nederlandsch Indie." p. 76.—G.W.E.

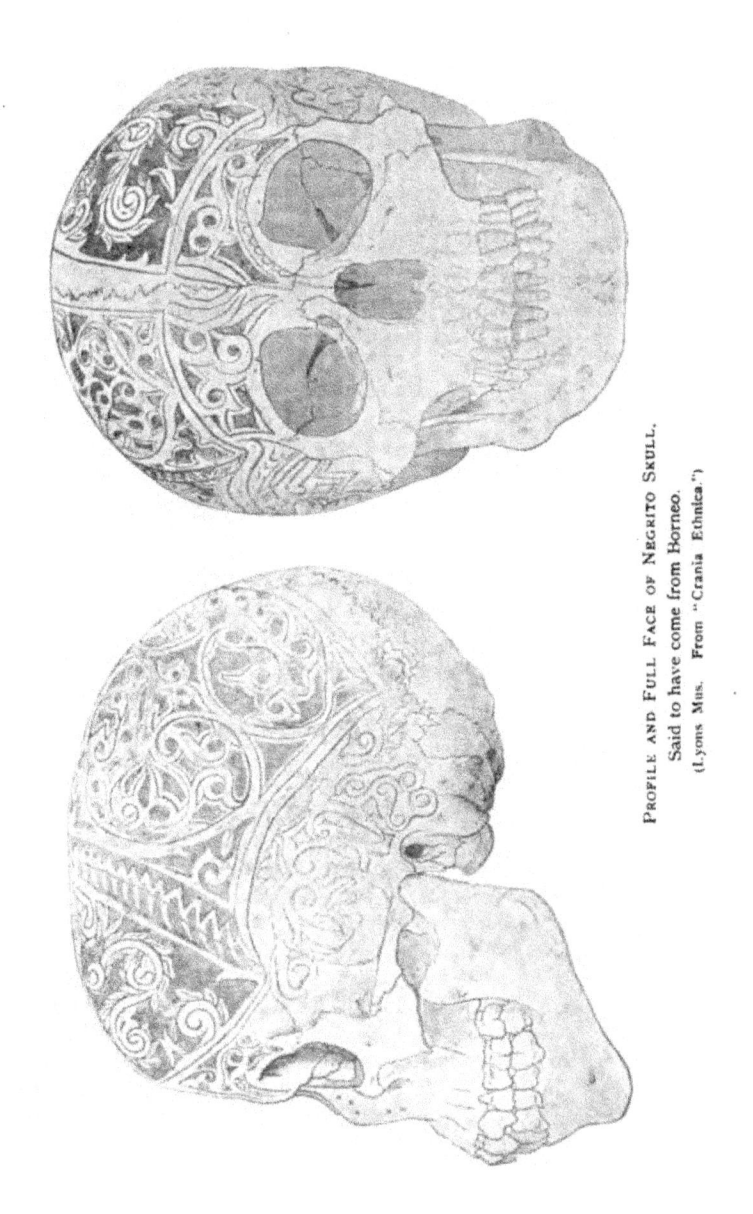

PROFILE AND FULL FACE OF NEGRITO SKULL.
Said to have come from Borneo.
(Lyons Mus. From "Crania Ethnica.")

savages approaching the vessel, and wading through the water. Upon coming within a short distance of the vessel, they discharged several showers of arrows, which severely wounded four of the Chinese. . . . The Burmans gave immediate pursuit in their boat, and after much difficulty captured two of the savages. These were brought to Penang by the Chinese. . . . One of the savages was 4 feet 6 inches, and the other 4 feet 7 inches in height, and each weighed about 76 lbs. They had large paunches, and though they were so small were in good condition. . . .'

"My father, in a work entitled 'Considerations relative to the Malayan Peninsula,' says in a paper on a tribe called 'Semangs,' 'There is little doubt that the degenerate inhabitants of the Andaman Islands in the Bay of Bengal are descended from the same parent stock as the Semangs. . . . Again he says of a Semang whom he saw, 'This man was at the time of his visit to Penang, when I saw him, about 30 years of age, 4 feet 9 inches in height. His hair was woolly and tufted, his colour a glossy jet black, his lips were thick, his nose flat, and belly very protuberant, resembling exactly two natives of the Andaman Islands who were brought to Prince of Wales' Islands (*i.e.*, Penang) in the year 1819.'"

At the same time he wrote to me: "I feel sure, however, that the skulls found in Borneo, which differ so widely from those of Dyaks, can have nothing to do with the Andamanese, none of whom, so far as we know, were ever taken beyond Penang and Perak." But how can we tell to what distance these kidnapped islanders were taken? We have seen Chinese and Burmese pirates visited the Andamans. When the great pirate fleet was destroyed (190 killed or drowned and 31 taken to Sarawak), releasing 390 captives (140 by death only), "among the captives there were people from every part of the Eastern Archipelago, from Borneo, Celebes, Java, the smaller islands, and the Malayan Peninsula." (Helms, p. 212.) The wide range of the pirates, who brought their captives to the Sulu slave mart, is referred to by Dr. Guillemard. (*op. sit.* p. 92.) If Andamanese were carried to the Malay Peninsula, there is every probability of their having been carried further east, and hence possibly to Borneo. On asking M. Ernest Chantre, Director of the Muséum des Sciences Naturelles at Lyons, where the skull is deposited, for further information regarding its origin, he wrote to me under date of 24th January, 1894: "All that I can tell you over and above what is mentioned in the 'Crania Ethnica' is that it was obtained more than thirty years ago, as coming from Borneo, but we do not know under what circumstances it was got. In fact, I do not possess a single document about it. I may, however, add that side by side with this engraved skull we possess another one equally small, not engraved, but blackened by smoke. It was purchased about ten years ago from a natural history merchant of the city of Amsterdam, as coming from Borneo." Further requests for measurements of this second skull failed to elicit any reply. The illustration of this engraved skull shows very characteristic Borneo tracery, and leaving apart the fact that we are not sure from what part of Borneo these engraved skulls are obtained, and also leaving apart the absence of mention by anyone who has seen these engraved skulls hung up by the people who engraved them, we must conclude that this skull must have passed through the hands of Borneo people. But this by no means proves that the skull originally came from Borneo. So much for the artificial evidence. If the skull is so identical with that of Andamanese, as I understand MM. Quatrefages and Hamy appear to think—but which, as seen above, Dr. A. B. Meyer doubts—then it may have been introduced. If, on the other hand, further independent examination should show it to be only generally similar, then it may possibly be indigenous. It may also be accepted as a fact that if the skull can be proved to have been brought from far inland, we shall have good evidence that Negritoes exist or existed in Borneo.

We have seen above how MM. Quatrefages and Hamy have distorted Mr. Dalton's statement, and mis-read that of Bishop McDougall. They further quote M. Domeny de Rienzi and Captain Gabriel Lafond. M. Rienzi writes (Oceanic, p. 258): "As to the Endamens or Aëtas, with woolly hair and sooty colour, hardly any are met with now in Kalemantan,[23] although, originally, they inhabited this island, whence they spread over the rest of Malaysia. The Papuans have overcome them, &c., &c." This is, of course, merely a statement without any proof. Captain Lafond (Bull. Soc. Geogr., 2nd Ser. V. 1836) says (p. 174) that the negro race exists in Borneo, and then adds (on p. 175): "As to Borneo, I did not see any black inhabitants, although I touched its shores twice. But while at Macassar I heard men worthy of credence speak of the existence of blacks in that great island, who lived in the mountains." Previously to this, however (p. 154), he quotes M. Walckenaer (Monde maritime, ch. xv.), who, he says, asserts that "the existence of the maritime negro race in Borneo has been already pointed out." I have not been able to refer to M. Walckenaer's book.

In Professor Sir William Flower's "Catalogue, Royal College of Surgeons" (London, 1879, p. 125), he thus remarks on skull No. 745: "A cranium said to be that of a Dyak. .... It presents more Melanesian than Malay characters, and may be of Papuan origin, as Papuans are often taken to Borneo as slaves." It will be observed, Sir William Flower does not jump to the conclusion that Papuans are indigenous to Borneo.

In this enquiry no reference is made to the presence of the Negrito in prehistoric times. If, as now appears to be generally believed, the negro family, like the rest of mankind, had its origin in the Indo-African continent (Keane's "Ethnology," pp. 229, 242), it may be probable that Negritoes once existed in Borneo. On the other hand, Borneo is comparatively new. It consisted originally of a few islands, which were later on joined together, and ultimately took on a shape very similar to that of Celebes now, the larger portion of the present form of Borneo being recent geologically—tertiary and post-tertiary. (See Posewitz.)[24] As one island it probably did not exist at the time of the disappearance of the Indo-African continent. The only stone implement found so far is the neolithic one found by Mr. A. Hart Everett. (J.A.I. i., P.E.S., p. 39), but others may yet be found. The evidence of a

[23] Old name for Island of Borneo.
[24] "Borneo; its Geology and Mineral Resources." Lond., 1892. pp. 259-260.

pre-historic occupation of the island is still wanting, and with it necessarily any trace of Negrito occupation. The existence of the Negrito in Borneo in the past or in the present has yet to be proved.

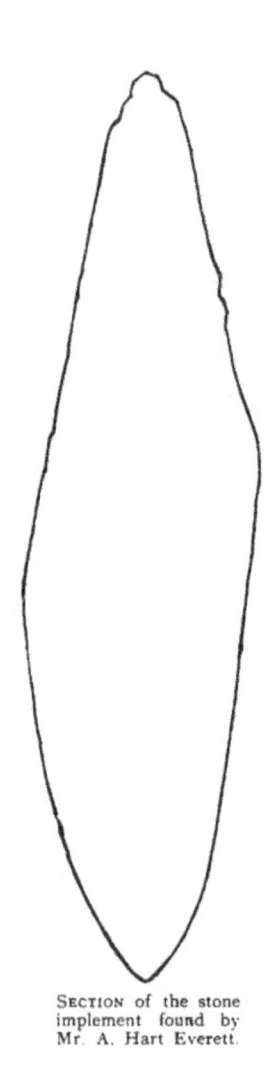

Section of the stone implement found by Mr. A. Hart Everett.

APPENDICES.

I.

SEA DYAK (Rejang and Batang Lupar District), MALAY and ENGLISH VOCABULARY.

With Examples shewing the words in use.

FROM THE NOTES OF MR. H. BROOKE LOW.

SEA DYAK.	MALAY (Colloquial).	ENGLISH. Together with Examples of the use of the word.
abus	abu	ashes.
achok	cuchok	to prick, to thrust at.
ada	ada	to be born; *dini nuan ada*, where were you born?
adap	macham	manner, way how; *nama adap pia*, why is it done so?
adu, ngadu	ator	adjust, arrange; *adu api*, trim the light; *adu tikai*, straighten the mat.
ai	ayer	water; *ai langkang*, low water.
aiam	permainan	a plaything; to play.
aian	tampak	to be visible; to come into sight.
ajat	sumpit	bag made of cane for carrying clothes.
ajih		to enchant, to charm, to work miracles.
akà	dudun	bosom-friend.
akai!	adoh!	oh! alas! *akai indai!* oh dear!
akal	akal	understanding, cunning, deceit.
aki		grandfather.
akiet	lantieng	raft.
aku	sahya	I, me; as a verb to acknowledge, to confess.
alah		overcome; *enda alah*, not to be overcome, i.e. impossible, unable to do; *alah jako*, to be worsted in an argument.
alai	sebab	cause, reason; *iya nadai alai*, there is no reason why? *kati alai*, how can? &c., &c.
alam	dalam	in, within.
alau	buntak besar	locust.
alau!		*alau!* exclamation of surprise.
alit		to close up.
alu		pestle.
ama-ama		*ama dulu, ama dili;* sometimes up river, sometimes down river.
amang		*pia amang*, perhaps so, &c., I wonder, suppose.
amang		to pretend, feign, flourish, brandish; *amang munoh munsoh*, to pretend (go through the actions) to kill an enemy.
amat	benar	true.

SEA DYAK.	MALAY (Colloquial).	ENGLISH. Together with Examples of the use of the word.
ambai	ondé	mistress, love, keep.
ambat, ngambat		to receive, meet, go to meet (one); to await one's arrival; to intercept (hostile sense).
ambi	ambil	to fetch.
ambis, also abis	habis	finished, all gone.
ambu	mengakun	acknowledge, own, claim, adopt.
amboh	nappar	to forge.
ambun	ru	fog, mist; casuarina, only because of the resemblance of the foliage of this tree to a fine veil.
ampa		husk; *ampa padi*, paddy husk.
ampit		to come in for a share.
ampoh	achap	flooded.
amput		to sting; *d'amput*, stung (by bees, wasps, centipedes).
anak	anak	child; *anak laki*, son; *anak indu*, daughter; *anak ambu*, adopted child; *anak menyadi*, brother's child, i.e. nephew or niece; *anak biak*, young children; *anak biak* is "follower" only when contracted *anembiak*.
anang	jangan	don't; *anang begau*, don't bother; *anang guai*, don't hurry, not so fast; *anang pia*, don't do so.
anaraja	neraja	rainbow.
anchau	ampar	to spread (mats); *beranchau*, spread.
andal	arap	to believe, trust, to rejoice.
andau, ngandau		a bridge; to bridge over; *ngandau sungai*, to bridge over a river.
anga		ravenous (the rabid appetite one gets on recovery from fever).
angat	panas	hot, warm; *ai angat*, hot water; *tunggu angat*, a heavy fine; *menoa angat*, infected, plague-stricken country.
anggap		to count up, reckon.
angkabai	sukat	measurement.
angkong	bunut	horse-mango.
anjong	antar	to bring, take, send, convey.
ansah	asah	to sharpen, whet.
ansak, ngansak		to urge.
ansang	miang	the blossom of palms, reeds, &c.
anta		gay, fine, handsome; *anta bendar menyadi dé*, how gay, handsome your brother looks.
anti	nanti	to wait for.
antu	hantu	a spirit; *antu pala*, the smoke-dried head of a person killed in war; *enda betuku antu*, a deceiving spirit; *antu buyu*, *antu grasi*, names of evil spirits; *jai antu*, a demon.
apai	bapa	father; *apai orang*, a father of a family.

Sea Dyak, Malay and English Vocabulary. iii.

SEA DYAK.	MALAY (Colloquial).	ENGLISH, Together with Examples of the use of the word.
apai	bintang	star.
apai-indai	ma bapa	parents.
apin	belum	not yet; even if; *ka apin ĕnggai*, even if I didn't want to.
apit	tapis	to strain, squeeze.
apus	padam	to extinguish; *apus ari*, when the day is extinguished, night; *apus pikul*, the extinction of the measure, full to the brim; *apus ai*, the whole of the river.
aram (contr. am)	marilah	come on, come along.
arang	arang	charcoal.
ari	deri	from.
ari	hari	day, time; *ni ari nemuai, ni ari bumai?* where's the time to visit, where's the time to farm? *mekang ari*, the time is insufficient, &c.; *aku nadai ari*, I've no time, &c.
arok	abu	soot.
asai	rasa	taste, sensation; *kati asai tuboh nuan*, how do you feel?
asi	nasi	boiled rice.
asoh	suroh	to allow, to send, to order.
atas	atas	upon, over, above.
ati	hati	heart, mind, liver; *ati aku tusah*, my mind is troubled; *ati aku enda nyamai*, my mind is ill at ease, uncomfortable; *nyamai ati aku*, my mind is at ease, free from anxiety or worry; *sekut ati*, perplexed; *aku nadai jai ati ĕnggau laut ĕnggau china iang anjong pengeraja kitai*, I have no ill feeling against Malays or Chinese; they bring wealth to us; *gagi ati*, glad, delighted.
au	iya	yes.
auak ka		in order that . . . . let it be that . . . . let be (hence—never mind).
auh		noise, hum, murmur; *auh bala*, hum of the army, *auh ribut*, murmur of the wind.
aya	bapa manakan	uncle.
babas	babas	wood, brush, thicket, new growth, bush; *bulu babas*, leaves.
badas	bagus	fine, handsome, good, nice; *badas rita*, good news.
badi	rughi	to come to grief, go to the wall, suffer loss; *enggai badi ngapa*, I won't suffer loss to no purpose.
badu	berhenti	to stop, end, cease; *badu nuan minta utai*, cease asking for things; *badu enda*, by no means, on no account.

Sea Dyak.	Malay (Colloquial).	English, Together with Examples of the use of the word.
bagas	kuat	always, continually, often; rather zealous to be always doing a thing; *bagas tindok*, constantly sleeping; *dé bagas mabuk, aku jarang*, you are always getting tipsy, I rarely.
bai, mai	bawa	to bring.
baia	buaya	(alligator) crocodile.
baiam		to pet, to play with.
bajai		some winged animal of Dyak mythology.
baka	rupa	like, like to; *baka ka udah*, as formerly.
bakun	dudun	to have a bosom friend.
bala	bala	expeditionary force, a war party; *pengiong bala*, advance guard.
bali	ubah	to change, alter, alter in appearance, color; *bali moa*, to change one's appearance.
baliek, maliek	malik	to look at, look towards.
balu	balu	widowed, widow, widower; *indu balu*, a widow; *laki balu*, a widower.
banchak	tikam	to throw, to thrust.
bandau	biawak	a large lizard.
bangat	brapa	very, exceedingly; *enda bangat mansau*, not particularly ripe; *kati nuan bangat manchal bakatu*, how is it that you are so very mischievous like this? *bangat kalalu*, quite too much.
bangkis	prau papan	a plank boat.
bangkit	banghit	scented flower.
bangkong	prau bertimbo	a boat with a single plank fastened into the dugout at the water line.
bansu	puas, biase	perpetually, accustomed.
bantai	pungga	to expose to view; *bantai utai*, unpack things.
bantun	chabut	to pull out, root out, pull out by the roots, to weed; *bantun bulu mata*, to pull out the eyelashes.
barieng		to roll along.
baroh	rendah	short (stature), low (hills).
baroh	bawa	baroh, low, with prefix *di* (by) below, under; *di barok bukit*, under below the hill, at foot of; *bukit baroh*, low hill.
basieng	tupai pinang	squirrel (smallest kind).
batang	batang	*batang indu*, main stream; in the first sense *batang* means the trunk of a tree, the stem; *batang*, name, own name, proper name, real name, family name, i.e. stem.
batak	tarik	to drag.
batu	batu	stone, rock.
batu		stone.
batu pegai		security, a pledge for something in pawn.

Sea Dyak, Malay and English Vocabulary.

Sea Dyak.	Malay (Colloquial).	English, Together with Examples of the use of the word.
bauh	panjang	tall (vegetation), long (hair); to grow up; *babas kami (nyau) bauh*, our farm land (brush) has grown up; *awak ka buah*, let it grow long.
baum	berpakat	to confer, deliberate, consult, take counsel.
bebakoh	bersahabat	to become friends.
bĕbas	ketas	to pull to pieces, take apart; *bĕbas rumah*, pull to pieces the house.
bedau	masih balum	still, yet, more, not yet.
bedega		bracken.
bedingah		famous, celebrated.
beduan	katcho	to worry, annoy, tease, vex, bother, trouble, persecute; *beduan diri*, worry one's self.
beduru	berbunyi	to roar (a beast of prey), rumble; *prut aku beduru*, my stomach rumbles.
bedus	kambieng	goat.
beg, begau	bego	to set up a hue and cry.
begadai	besik	slowly, cautiously, gently; *bejako begadai*, to speak in a low tone.
begaiang		pierced; *maio-indu tambi di pasar begaiang idong*, many of the Tamil women in the bazaar are pierced through their noses.
begelis		to run a foot-race.
begitang	bergantong	to hang.
beguai	gopo singgaut gampang	to be in a hurry
beguang		used with reference to a married couple; *laki beguang bini*, the husband follows the wife to her people.
bejako	bertutur	to talk, converse with, talk to.
bejalai	berjalan	to walk.
bejali	berpinjam	to lend.
bejamah	bertangkap	to fight, to have a rough tumble.
bekalieng	bersain	to accompany, associate with.
bekalih	pusing	to turn round, from side to side, change one's position, posture.
bekarong	sindir	to be enclosed in a case; *jako bekarong*, disguised speech.
bekau	bekas	a vestige, remains, trail; *bekau kaki*, foot-print.
bekejang	berangkat	to leave (one place for another), to start; *anti tembu nya bekejang*, wait until you have done and we will start.
bekindu	berdiang	to warm one's self in the sun or before a fire.
belaboh	jatoh	to let fall, to drop; *belaboh wong*, to shoot the rapids; *belaboh nugal*, to commence sowing.
belaki	berlaki	to take a husband.
belala	rindu or suka	inclined, pleased; *agi belala bejako enggau dé*, still pleased to converse with you; *agi belala na nuan*, continue to like you.

Sea Dyak.	Malay (Colloquial).	English. Together with Examples of the use of the word.
belaloh		to have over and above.
belama	selalu	always, continually, perpetually.
belawa	berikut	to run, to follow.
belelang	menahun	to sojourn in a strange land, to travel.
beleman	macham-macham	fanciful; *anang beleman*, don't play the fool; *maioh beleman*, very fanciful.
belit, melit	gulong	to coil round, wind round; *melit sirat*, to coil the loin-cloth round.
belut		earth-worm.
benda	tajau or tempian	earthen-ware jar.
bendai	chanang	a shallow gong beaten with wood; *bebendai*, to beat a *bindai*
bendar	benar	indeed, true, very.
benong		while, during, middle-aged; *Benong*, adverb of time or degree, signifies rather a certain point than duration; in the examples given, *iya benong makai*, just when he is very busy eating; *benong berapi*, at the time when we were most engaged in our cooking, &c.; *anang ngawa iya benong makai*, don't bother him in the midst of his meal; *benong berapi, ari ujan*, it began to rain while we were cooking.
bentang	bentang	*bentang tali*, to stretch a rope across a river; *bentang maroh*, a line no one may pass, used when cholera is about.
benyut	gregar	to quiver, rock, shake, quake: *batang benyut*, the log rocks; *tanah benyut*, to quake, of the earth.
bepangkang	seblah	to live next to, to be a next door neighbour to; *aku enggai bepangkang sida nya*, I will not be next neighbour with them.
bepelieng) beselieng)	berblit	to meander, go a roundabout way (of river or road).
beragai	gagah	an omen bird.
berandau	bertutor	to talk, converse, discuss, gossip.
berangkat		to lift, to carry away, to levant, elope with a man's wife.
berap, merap	tangkap	to embrace, catch round, throw one's arms round, lock in embrace.
berapi	masak	to cook.
beratong	beranyut (also Dayak)	to drift with the tide.
beredup		to thump, creak, &c.; the noise of the paddles on the thwarts of a boat when paddling.
berekak	enchekak	to catch by the throat, throttle.
berentak		to ram in, drive in.
berimba		to cut down old jungle, to clear for farming purposes.

Sea Dyak.	Malay (Colloquial.)	English. Together with Examples of the use of the word.
berimbai	bersindi	to lie alongside.
berinsor	surut	to decrease.
berintai	berikut	in sequence, in order, in line.
berumpak	belumba	to run a boat race.
berupai	nampak	visible ; *bangat enda berupai*, hardly visible.
beruran	lapar	starvation, famine, hunger, scarcity.
besagu	tikam k'atas	to raise up, to throw up, toss up; *besagu ringka*, to throw up the football.
besai	besar	large, big, great.
besatup	bertemu, berjumpah	to encounter, meet, clash, come into contact, collision with; *sidaiya mudik kami undur besatup tengah ai*, they were going up river and we were going down river when we collided in mid-stream.
besibil	telessé	to resemble in sound, to rhyme.
besudi		to undergo the hot-water ordeal.
besundang	tuka	to exchange gifts; *besundang ka, munoh ani enggai*, I will exchange gifts (as a token of friendship), but I will not kill a pig (for sacrifice).
betah	lama	of time, long; *aku enda betah nuan*, I cannot be with you long.
betangkai	gumpul	to bunch, to ear (corn); *jako betangkai*, endless talk.
betauing	turut	to accompany, hang on to, follow one about; *kati nuan, lalu betauing iya?* how about you, are you going to follow him about?
betelai	bebisik	to whisper.
betemu		to meet.
beterangau	bertriah	cry out.
betingik	bertingkar	to wrangle.
betis	betis	the calf of the leg.
betu	lukus	scalded, burnt.
betuju (tuju, to point towards)	tentu	unauthenticated; *rita enda betuju*, the relations or narratives do not agree.
betuku	tentu	certain, sure, trustworthy; *enda betuku antu*, a lying spirit.
betunga	berjumpa, bertemu	to turn towards, to meet, have an interview with.
betusi also betusoi	bebisik	to narrate.
bidai	klasa	a rattan and bark mat (large sized).
bidiek		fortunate, successful, lucky.
bilik	bilik	room, apartment.
bisa	bisa	poisonous (sting, bite), potent, telling, effective: *jako aku bisa*, my words are cutting.
bisi	ada	to be, is there? there is, to have.
bla	sama, sama-sama	alike, equally, equal, even; *bla peninggi*, same height.

Sea Dyak.	Malay (Colloquial).	English, Together with Examples of the use of the word.
blah, mlah		to split; *melah pinang*, to split the betel nut, the mode of divination resorted to in the marriage ceremony, to perform the marriage service, to marry (couples).
blaia	berkelai, gadoh	to quarrel; *blaia ênggau pangan diri*, to quarrel with one's own friends.
blanda	(berikut)	to run; *blanda kia, blanda kia*, to run backward and forward; *blanda anchau tikai*, run and spread the mats.
blansai	karong	bag, sack of grass or reeds, ordinarily the gunny bag.
bluit	berlipat	serpentine, sinuous, winding, crooked, round about; *tanjong bluit*, tortuous bend in the river.
bok	rambut	hair of the head only.
bong	bong	war-canoe.
botoh	buto	penis.
brang	brang	upper arm.
brau	bras	rice (uncooked).
brauh	bunyi	a noise; *nama utai nya brauh?* what is that making a noise?
buah	buah	fruit.
buah	sebab	reason, cause, ground; *nama kabuah*, for what reason? why?; *kabuah nya*, for this reason, because of this; *nadai kabuah iya enggai*, there is no possible reason why we should not; *nadai kabuah-buah ngaiau*, no pretext for going on the war-path.
buai, muai	buang	to throw away, fling away, pitch away, toss away; *muai utai ka telok, muai ka lubok*, to throw something into a pond or pit.
budi, mudi	prankap	to entrap, decoy, snare.
buiyah		moth.
buiyan	takut	timid, nervous
bujal		knob or bulb; *bujal tawak*, the knob or bulb in the middle of a gong.
bujang	bujang	bachelor.
bukau	kladi	*kladi*, the cladium.
bulan	bulan	moon, month; *bulan sigi kamari*, last month.
buli		eddy.
bulih	dapat	to get, obtain, procure, catch (fish).
buloh, munti	buloh	bamboo.
bulu	bangsa	1.—hair (body), feather, down; *bulu mata*, eye-lash. 2.—race; *orang nyelai bulu*, men of a different race, kind, tribe, colour.
bumai	buma	to farm.
bungai, bunga	bunga	flower.
bunsu	bungsu	youngest; *anak bunsu*, the youngest of the family.

Sea Dyak, Malay and English Vocabulary.

Sea Dyak.	Malay (Colloquial).	English, Together with Examples of the use of the word.
buntas	beruntas	to disembowel.
buntau, ngantok		drowsy, sleepy, rather the sensation after having lost a night's rest, not the sleepiness which comes in the early part of the night *(ngantok)*.
buntis		*padi buntis*, cleaned paddy.
burai	rambu	tassel (necklace).
burak	putih	white (colour).
burit	burit	bottom, base.
buru	buru	to drive away ; *buru manok*, drive away the fowls.
buruk	burok	rotten; *orang burok*, good for nothing; *buah buruk*, rotten fruit.
but	busok lansang	rotten, putrid ; *bau but*, a rotten smell.
butang		penal, fineable, to render oneself liable to a fine, adultery (*the* fineable offence).
chapak	pinggau	saucer, plate.
chelap	sejok	cold, cool, light (as applied to fines in opposition to *angat*, heavy) ; *tunggu chelap*, a light fine.
chenaga	chuchi	purification ; *chenagu rumah*, house purification.
chiru	jerinih	clear, transparent (water).
chuan	chuntu	a mould, model, pattern.
dagu		chin.
damun	damun	brush (two years' growth).
danau	danau	lake.
dandong	sarong	to wear a *sarong* reaching to the feet, to wear a long skirt.
dara	dara	maid, maiden (a marriageable but unmarried girl).
datai	datang	come.
dedat	pukul	to beat or drum upon.
dejal	sumbat, pakal, libat	to cork, stuff up, stop up (a hole, leak), to caulk.
delapan	delapan	eight.
demam	demam	ague.
deredai, ngeredai		to dry (clothes) in wind.
di	kau	you (singular number).
di		at, by, in.
di ya or di-ia	skarang ini	now (adv.) ; *pukul brapa dia ?* what's the time now? directly; *diya tu*, immediately, at this moment.
dia	sana	there.
diau	diam	to reside, live, keep quiet, stay ; *dini nuan diau*, where do you live ? *diau anang bejako*, be quiet, don't talk.

SEA DYAK.	MALAY (Colloquial).	ENGLISH. Together with Examples of the use of the word.
dilah	lidah	tongue; *dilah tanah*, a tongue of land, promontory.
dingah		hear; fame, distinction, reputation.
dini?	mana?	where?
	begimana?	how?
dini-dini	di mana-mana	wherever, however.
diri		self, oneself.
dudi		after, behind; *dudi ari*, some other time, some other day.
duduk	dudak	to sit, sit down.
dugau		to be idle, have nothing to do, idle about; *puas dugau-dugau*, tired of doing nothing; unemployed, without anything to do, purposeless.
duku	parang tebas	chopping sword.
dulu	dahulu	adverb of place or time, before.
empa		to eat.
empai	belum	not yet.
empalai	kabun	kitchen, garden.
empang	blatt.	
emparu	putus	to adjust, arrange, settle; *emparu laia*, adjust a difference, settle a case.
empasa	ubi bandong	tapioca.
empedu	empeddu	gall-bladder.
empekak		cluck of a hen after laying an egg.
empeleman		mote, an insect which gets into your eyes, also dust getting into the eyes is called *empeleman*.
empran	padang	a plain.
empu, ngempu		to own; owner; *aku empu*, mine.
empurau	semah	a kind of fish.
enchekak nyekak	chepak	to throttle.
enda	tida	not; *enda mé 'tu*, not if I know it; *enda alah*, not able.
endor	tempat	place; *dini endor kita bulih ila?* where are we likely to get some by and bye? *Kati endor iya enda lekat ka ginto?* how did it manage not to stick on the hook? *Utai pandok nadai endor iya enda angat*, things cooked have no place but to be hot.
enggai	tida mau	will not, won't, to be unwilling.
enggau	dengan	connective conjunction, with, and; also as verb, to use, to wear.
enggi	pun	note of possession; *enggi sapa*, whose; *enggi iya*, his; *enggi sapa langkau nyin?* whose is that shed?
enggikami (see enggi)	kita-pun	ours.
engkah	barangkali	perhaps, may be.

Sea Dyak.	Malay (Colloquial).	English, Together with Examples of the use of the word.
engkah	simpan	to put, place, set, deposit.
engkabalu		widowhood; *empai tembu engkabalu*, the period of widowhood is not completed.
engkaiyu	lauk, saior	relish, condiment (vegetable or animal food as an accompaniment to rice).
engkalubang		a pit-fall (hole with calthrops).
engkasak	ngrebat	to writhe, wriggle, struggle with, offer resistance to.
engkelulut		insect, a diminutive fly; *getah engkelulut*, the wax deposited by a fly.
engkila	jaga	to watch, scout, spy; *aku engkila siduai*, I was watching them both.
engklait		wild gambir.
engklaiyu		to fade, to lose colour, tarnish.
engklis	miniak nioh	cocoa-nut oil.
engkraju	tembaga	copper.
engku	aku pun (empu)	mine, contr. from *enggi aku*, see *enggi*.
engkukok		the crowing of a cock.
engkuleh	rimah dahan	tiger-cat.
enjok		to give.
ensana	ari dulu (hari)	day before yesterday.
ensanos	dahulu	
ensapa	siapa pun	whose, contr. from *enggi sapa*.
ensera	cherita	legend, fable, myth, story.
ênsepi or sepi	cheri	to taste, feel, be conscious of, aware of; *ènsepi asi*, taste what it is like; *ènsepi diri parai*, I feel as though I were dead.
b. m. ensiang	luasi	to clear, to prune; *mensiang tapang*, to prune the bee tree; *mensiang jalai*, to clear the road of grass, &c.; *siang*, clear light; *ben-* or *men-siang*, to make clear, to cause to be light.
ensilip	padam	to go out (of life or sun), to fade away.
ensuroh	surok	to crouch; *ensuroh baroh batang*, to creep under the log; *jako ensuroh*, humble, submissive language.
entekai		pumpkin.
entekok	bengok	goître.
entelah		a riddle, conundrum, enigma.
entemu		tumeric.
ênti	jêkalau	if; *ênti benama*, if it should be so.
entighis		source of a river.
entran	batang	shaft; *entran sangkoh*, spear-shaft.
entun, ngentun	tarck, ulur	to pull, haul, launch; *entun prau*, to launch the boat.
gadai	pelehan	*gadai-gadai*, softly, slowly, gently, gradually.
gaga	suka	glad, pleased, delighted; *gaga penapat ati aku*, I am truly delighted.

Sea Dyak.	Malay (Colloquial).	English. Together with Examples of the use of the word.
gagai, ngagai	agar	to pursue, follow after, to arrive at; *nadai utai di gagai*, I am not going after any thing.
gagang	sengkar prau	thwarts (boat).
gaiang	salang	to pierce, make a hole in.
gaiyu	tuah	long-lived; *enda gaiyu nyaua aku*, I am not long-lived.
galau (ngalau)	simpan	reserve, keep by, reserve for another day, save up; *galau nyaka pagila*, keep it for to-morrow.
gama		to touch, feel (pulse, &c.); rather a system of stroking, massage, &c., adopted by medicine men.
gamal	rupa	appearance.
gandong		grip; *gandong prau*, bulwarks.
ganggam	tegoh tegah, telap	sturdy, firm, steady, sure (foot, &c.), secure; *tiang ganggam*, the post is firm; *ganggam moa*, stern, resolute face.
gari	tuka kain	a change of clothes; *nadai mai gari*, didn't bring a change, &c.
gasieng	bergassing	to spin a top.
gaua	gago	busy; *ngaua*, to bother; *anang ngaua udok benong makai*, don't bother the dog while he is feeding.
gauk	rindu	*gauk ka nuan*, fond of you; *gauk nanya rita*, fond of asking for news.
gaum, ngaum	itong	reckon, include, count.
gegusu		curly (hair); *bok gegusu*, frizzled; *rambut bergulong*, curly haired.
gelang	gelang	bracelet.
gelema		furtively; *pindah gelema malam*, in secret, secretly.
gempong	gumpul	to collect into a heap.
gempuru		to collect together.
gemu	gemok	fat, stout.
genap	sabilang, tiap	each, every; *genap taun bulih padi*, every year we get rice.
genggam	genggam	a handful.
genselan		blood offering, propitiatory offering; *genselan padi*, blood offering sprinkled at time of sowing.
gentieng		glen, valley, ravine, gorge, gully.
gentu	pisang kra	wild plantain.
gerar	gelar	to name.
gerigau, nyerigau	gadah	to make a noise; *anang nyerigau*, do not make a noise.
getah	getah	sap, gum; English gutta; *getah tungkun*, i.e. the gutta used for torches; *dammar*.
getil, ngetil	gentu	to pick (flowers), pluck (leaves); to pinch.

Sea Dyak, Malay and English Vocabulary. xiii.

SEA DYAK.	MALAY (Colloquial).	ENGLISH, Together with Examples of the use of the word.
giga, ngiga	anso	to seek, go in quest of, to look for, search after; *ngiga menoa nyamai, menoa grai, menoa chelap, menoa lindap*, to look for a comfortable, healthy, cool and pleasant country.
giliek, ngiliek	gunchang	*ngiliek na pala*, to shake the head in token of dissent.
gilieng	gulong	to roll, roll up.
ginti	kail	fish-hook.
girau		to stir round (coffee).
gitang	guntang	to suspend, hang up.
glumbang	umbak	wave (sea), breaker; *glumbang raia*, enormous rollers.
grah		slack, loose (fit), opposite to tight.
grai	baik	well (health); *menoa grai*, healthy.
grigang, ngrigang	kachoh	to trouble, disturb.
grunjong	anting anting	man's earrings.
guai-guai	singgaut-singgaut	in a hurry (adv.).
gunggo	bayang bayang	shadow.
iban		the laity in contradistinction to *manangs*, medicine men; the Dyaks only in contradistinction to one of another race who may be addressed.
idong	idong	nose.
iga		*iga iya enda nemu!* as if he didn't know.
ikan	ikan	fish.
iku	ikur	tail.
ili	ilis	sea-ward, down stream; (opposite to *ulu*, interior, up stream).
impun, n'gempun	limpan, taroh	to take charge of, care of.
inda (?)		even (?)
indai	ma	mother.
indiek, ngindiek	tinjak	to tread, trample on, step on.
indu	prempuan	female, woman; *orang indu*, a woman, women; *indu utai*, insect; *indu guang*, mistress.
ingat	ingat	to remember.
inggap	inggap	to settle (bees), to perch, alight (birds).
injun, nginjun	gunchang	to shake; *nginjun bilik*, to shake the room.
ingkoh, ningkoh		to cut round, separate from the trunk, detach; *ningkoh bandir tupang*, to cut away the buttress of a bee tree.
insak	ingus	mucus from the throat or nostril.

Sea Dyak.	Malay (Colloquial).	English. Together with Examples of the use of the word.
insit, nginsit	bergerak	move away from, to move, stir; *enda nginsit prahu ari nya*, the boat doesn't move, stir from its place, &c.; *enda nginsit ari rumah diri*, he does not move from his own house.
insor		recede, abate.
intu	ibun	to watch, guard, take care of.
inyak (?)	nyor	cocoa-nut.
ipa, ngipa		to wait for, to meet in the way, to waylay, ambush.
ipak	patul	like, sort, commensurate; *ipak iya, patul dia*, like his sort.
ipar	ipar	brother-in-law or sister-in-law.
ipoh	ipoh	(i.) a species of palm, (ii.) a fermented drink obtained from the palm, (iii.) any strong drink [essence of *tuak*, old *tuak*, strong undiluted *tuak*].
ipoh	upas	poison; *ipoh lajah*, arrow poison.
irau	susah, kachau	distress oneself; *irau ati*, anxious, uncomfortable, anxiety.
iri	tuang	to pour out.
irieng, ngirieng		to guide by the hand, to lead.
irit	tarik	to drag.
irup, ngirup	minum	to drink.
isi		(i.) flesh, (ii.) the body, (iii.) to fill up, i.e. make a solid body of; *isi tunggu*, to pay a fine.
isi	isi	flesh; *pengki isi*, firm flesh as opposed to *lemi isi*, muscular flesh; *badas isi*, fine (good) flesh.
iya	dia	he, she, it, him, her.
jagau		*manok jagau*, fowl marks, i.e. the markings by which game fowl are recognised.
jai	jahat	bad, evil; *jai mati* (emphatic).
jaiau		love-philtre, potion.
jako	chakap	language, speech, talk, saying; *nadai jako, nadai 'ku*, he has nothing to say, never mind.
jala	jala	casting-net.
jalai!	jalan!	go! *jalai dé minta sida sa bilik*, go you and ask that family.
jalai	jeraia	path, a way, custom; *rantau jalai*, on the way.
jalong		bason.
jamah		to pitch into, *jamah asi*, to pitch into the rice.
jamoh		grip, grapple, clasp, handle, tackle.
jampat	pantas	fast, quick.

Sea Dyak, Malay and English Vocabulary.

SEA DYAK.	MALAY (Colloquial).	ENGLISH, Together with Examples of the use of the word.
janggat	kundur	a fruit resembling vegetable marrow.
jani	babi	pig, boar.
jani	babi	pig; *jani menoa*, domesticated pig; *jani kampong*, wild (or jungle) pig.
japai, nyapai	ambil	to pick up (something that has fallen), lay hold of, catch hold of, to reach; *japai roti*, hand me the bread.
jarai, jarang		seldom, rarely (adv.), scarce, uncommon (adj.).
jari	tangan	hand.
jauh	jauh	far, distant, long way.
jaum	potong	to sacrifice, slaughter, immolate (for a superstitious purpose).
jaung	rérang	a species of spiny palm.
jelu jangkiet, nyangkiet	monyet (monkey)	a climbing animal (monkeys, &c.), tree-walking animals.
jemah		ultimately, by and bye, subsequently, some other day, some future occasion.
jeput		as much as can be taken up between the points of fingers and thumb.
jibul		big bottle.
jimbi, nyimbi jimboi, nyimboi	jimor	to dry in sun, put out to dry.
jingkau, nyingkau	ambil	to reach for, fetch, get, pick up (a thing that has dropped), touch.
jingkong		to bend into an arch (as *smambu* for *teladok prau*), to force into a circular shape, bend round, arch.
ju	tulak	to push.
jugau	bodo	senseless, imbecile, ignorant; *kami iban jugau penapat, umpai tulih ka akal*, we are as ignorant as can be, we do not yet understand.
junggur	tanjong	a jutting out, promontory.
jungkang		lofty (prau).
jurieng		pointed; *jurieng mata*, sharp sighted.
ka		to, for, and also to express numerical order, e.g. *sa, dua, tiga*, 1, 2, 3; *ka sa*, 1st; *ka dua*, 2nd; *ka tiga*, 3rd.
ka, deka	mau	to want, wish, desire.
ka-dia	tadi	just now, at present.
kabak	kapala (= head)	skull, cranium.
kaban		company, clan; *samoa kaban kalieng kami*, the whole of our tribe.
kachang	chabi	chili, capsicum, bean.
kadeka	kahandak	wish, desire; *nama kadeka ati nuan?* what is your wish?

Sea Dyak.	Malay (Colloquial).	English, Together with Examples of the use of the word.
kadua-kadua	separu-separu } skeda-skeda }	some others; half-half; *kadua nginti kadua nyumpit*, some are angling, others shooting with the blow pipe; *nginti enda lama bulih ikan mengalan*, we were not long fishing and we caught a *mengalan* fish; *nyumpit enda lama bulih jelu jangkit*, we were not long shooting and we got a *jangkit*; *kadua uda, kadua bedau*, some we have, got, some we have not yet got.
kaiang		undecided; *agi kaiang*, irresolute.
kaiau, ngaiau		to go on the war-path, make war; a war-path, expedition, campaign.
kaioh, ngaioh	berkaiyuk	to paddle.
kaiu	kayu	wood.
kak	gagah	a crow (bird).
kaki	kaki	foot.
kala	kala	ever do, ever have; *kala nuan*, do you ever, have you ever; *enda kala*, never; *enda kala*, never do, never have.
kala		the scorpion.
kalah, ngalah	berbalik (also pusing)	to turn round, turn on one side, change one's position, reverse; *kalah kitu*, turn round this way, to decline, set, go down (sun), to slope, slant; *bekalah*, to change places; *dé na ngalah ka orang*, to want to obtain the superiority over others; to put in the wrong.
kalalu	telaluk	excessive, too far; *bangat kalalu*, quite too much.
kaleman	petang	dark (night); *ari nyau kaleman*, the day has become very dark, i.e. moonless.
kalia	manséa	of old, ancient, former, of yore, once upon time; *adat kalia*, ancient custom; *ari kalia*, from old times.
kalieng	dengan	companion; *samoa kubu kalieng kami*, all our followers and companions.
kaliti	kupak	to peel off (skin).
kamah	kotor	dirty.
kamaia?	bila?	when? *kamaia kabua dia?* how is the fort getting on? *kamaia nuan datai dia?* when did you get there?
kamarau	kamarau	dry weather, drought, spell of hot weather, the dry monsoon.
kamari (ari kamari)	kamarin	yesterday; *limai 'mari*, yesterday evening.
kambut	kandi	satchel.
kamerieng	ngerin	tiger fly.
kami	kita	we; *kami menoa*, we, in contrast to others.
kampong	utan	old jungle, primeval forest (*kyan tuan*, virgin forest).
kanan	kanan	right (distinct from left).

Sea Dyak.	Malay (Colloquial).	English, Together with Examples of the use of the word.
kandong, ngandong	buntien	pregnant (woman, corn, &c.), to get into the family way, to get with child.
kang	kandar	pubes.
kangau, ngangau	tuñggah	to call, shout, call out.
kantok		shoots.
kapa?	apa sebab?	why? what for?
karau	glap	dark, dusty, misty, &c.; *agi karau-karau*, while it is still deep twilight.
kasih	kasih	to have pity on, be kind enough.
kasumbar	kasumbar	soubriquet.
kati	apa	*kati*, what? indeed, affirmative; *kati pemesai rerga*, what is the price?
katong, ngatong	angkat	I lift, remove, carry; *dua ikan, aku katong*, I carry off two fishes; *end' alah katong, tuboh sepuloh*, ten men could not lift it; *katong ka rumah, katong ka ruai*, carry it up to the house, carry it up to the verandah.
kebah-kra	tegal	wherefore? therefore.
kebok	tempayan	a small earthen jar.
kebut	gago	to stir, bother; *anang kebut*, don't bother.
kedil	tebal	dense (population), stout (cloth).
kelaiang, nglaiang	nebrang	to cross over (from one side to another); *tumu aku kelaiang kitu*, I came across quite early.
kelala	kanal	to recognize, to know again.
kelaung, nglaung	larang	to pass over; *aku nggai nglaung jaku tuan*, I will not cross the words of the *tuan*.
kelimat	taroh	to save, keep for by and bye; *kadua kelimat makai*, some of it keep to eat by and bye.
kelui, ngelui	limpas	to pass; *iya udah di kalui kami*, we have passed that; superior to, surpass, past, beyond; *ari chapi nglui, ari rusa ngelui*, pork is superior to beef, &c., to excel, exceed.
kembai	kembang	swollen, to swell.
kembuan	paké, simpan	to keep, treasure; *binda tunggu enda tau di kembuan, kó tuan*, the fine cannot be kept the *tuan* says.
kempang		to feel it in one, feel up to a thing, feel competent to; *kempang nuan munoh orang?* do you think you could kill a man? *Dini aku kempang nanggong umai pangan diri!* how can I take my companion's farm! *enda kempang*, not up to it.
kempat	letas	to cut through; *kempat bok*, to trim the hair; *kempat teladok*, to sever; *kempat tiang*, to cleave a post.
kendua (contr. kami dua)		we two.
kenyalang	kinchallang	rhinoceros horn-bill.
kenyilieng		green beetle *(chrysochroa)*.

b

Sea Dyak.	Malay (Colloquial).	English. Together with Examples of the use of the word.
kepit		to squeeze, jam, squeeze in between.
kerukor	kurungan, sangkar	cage.
kesa	krengga	red ant.
kesai, ngesia	keboh	to splash (of water), brush away, ward off, to shake (mat, blanket).
kesat	sedjok	chilly.
ketas, ngetas	kerat	to sever.
ketau, ngetau	ngatam, beriñah	to reap, gather in the harvest.
ketawa	tertawa	to laugh, laugh at.
ketieng	puki	clitoris.
kia	kasia	thither; *anang kia*, don't go there.
kiba	kiri	left (contrasted with *kanan*, right.)
kibong	klambu	curtain.
kilah, ngilah	blakang, bekas	behind, next to; *kilah kitu*, there and here; *kilah nya*, after that, next to that; *kilah ngetau*, after the harvest; *ngilah bukit*, behind the hill, beyond, &c.; *kilah ensana*, the day before, day before yesterday.
kilat	kilat	lightning.
kikil		wart.
kimbiet, ngimbiet	pelok	to embrace, cuddle.
kini?	kamana?	where to? *kini ka nuan? nok sini kau?* where are you off to? whither away?
kini (amang)	barang kali	perhaps so; *pia kini!* may be.
kitai		we, our, us (inclusive of person addressed).
kitu	ka-situ	hither; *kitu nuan enda lama*, come you here a minute.
klabu		grey.
klai	tanda	token, mark, sign, pattern, mould.
klambi	baju	coat, jacket.
klau	utap	shield.
klingkang		hoop.
koiyu		cheek.
kran	kuat	to be eager; *enti iya bangat kran nan kapala, nadai jaku*, if he is very eager in with-holding the head, never mind.
krawang	alun	passage, channel.
krebak, ngrebak	silak	to part open (curtains), to lift up (petticoat), to open letter (box), to lift open, uncover, lift the cover, remove the lid *(bintang)*.
krembai, ngrembai	ampar	to unfold, spread out (casting net), *krembai ka kajang*, to spread (an awning); *krembai ka surat*, open out the book.
kresa	barang, herta	personal property; *anak kresa utai*, small articles of property.
kresiek	pasir	sand.
kretum	empighit	bug.
krieng, ngrieng	kras	hard, powerful; *ngrieng*, to prepare for; *krieng rekong*, stiff necked.

Sea Dyak, Malay and English Vocabulary.

Sea Dyak.	Malay (Colloquial).	English, Together with Examples of the use of the word.
krimpak	maringka	fragment, piece of brass or earthenware.
kroh	karoh	muddy (water).
krubong		skull.
krukoh	krukoh	scrub (one year's growth; *kyan baié*, first year's growth after harvest).
kuan		wrist; *mesai kuan*, as big as the wrist.
kubal		India-rubber.
kudi, ngudi, jai, rosak	binchi	cursed, to hate, detest; *kudi aku meda*, I hate to see it.
kukok, ngkukok	kokok	a cock's crow, to crow.
kukut	kuku	claws, nails.
kumbai, ngumbai	panggil	to think, fancy, imagine, suppose, to call; *orang ngumbai nuan*, someone is calling you.
kunye	gigit	to chew, bite, swallow, masticate, chaw up (dogs).
kusi, ngusi	kupak	to skin, flay, peel; *menoa nyau kusi*, the country is worn out, worked out.
kusieng	kluang	bat.
kusil, ngusil	getil, ngetil	to pick (flowers or leaves, &c.).
laban	—	owing to; *anti ai langkang nadai jalai merau laban bah*, wait till the water is shallow, there is no road for the boat owing to the freshet.
labang	putch	white; *manok labang*, white fowl; *lang labang*, white kite.
laboh	jatoh	to fall.
labong	dultar	head-covering, cap.
ladong	selabit	a pack-basket.
lagi	ila	by-and-bye, presently.
laia	bichara	quarrel, dispute, case; *laia empa ukué*, a frivolous dispute; *emparu laia*, adjust a dispute.
laja	lajah	a sumpit dart.
laki	laki	husband, man, male.
lali	trima	to receive, accept, harbour.
laloh	lebih	more, over, in excess.
lama	lama	long (time).
lancham, nglancham		to point (a pencil, stake).
landai	rata	inclined only very slightly.
landiek	pannai	clever, ready; *landiek bejaku*, to speak fluently; to be a dab at talking.
lang	menaul	a kite or kestrel.
langgai		the long tail feathers of a bird *(manok, tagai)* as opposed to *pumpun*, the shorter tail feathers of a bird.
langgu		a pendant; *langgu tingga*, ear-pendants.
langkang	kring	shallow, dried up; *ai langkang*, low water.
langkau	dango	hut; *langkau umai*, farm house.

Sea Dyak.	Malay (Colloquial).	English, Together with Examples of the use of the word.
lanji		a basket of a certain size; *sa lanji brau*, a package of rice.
lanjut	lanjar	distended (breasts).
lansiek	trus	clear (sight).
lantang	senang	free from trouble; leisure, convenient, comfortable.
lapang	padang	an opening, open space.
lari	lari	to run away, escape, to take off, away; *lari ka jari dé*, to take your hand away; *lari ka labong*, off with you, &c.
latak	latak	mud, muddy.
lauang, pintu		door.
laun	lambat	long (time), late (opposite to early).
laut	malayu	the sea; the Malay word for sea is *laut*; the Malays came from the sea and were therefore called by the Dayaks *orang laut*.
lebu	nasib jahat	unsuccessful, without success, in vain, to no purpose, fruitless, disappointed.
leboh		point of time, when.
leka, meleka	lepas	to let go, drop hold of.
leka	bighi	*sa leka jako*, a single word, a seed, grain; *sa leka* (one seed); *leka pluru*, a bullet.
lelak	lelah	tired.
lelang	menahun	to sojourn, wander.
lelang		to wander away, stray; *nyangka iya lelang*, it may wander away, to roam.
lemai	lebah-hari	evening.
lemai-mari		yesterday evening.
leman	bangsa	customs, rites, details.
lembaian		wall plate; *lembaian langit*, centre beam; *lembaian rumah*, wall plate of house; *lembaian kajang*, support of *kajang*.
lembau	malas	disinclined, to have no inclination for, indisposed.
lemi	lemɔut	soft, weak, feeble.
lempong	ringan	light (weight).
lempuang	abong-abong	lung.
lengan	lengan	the arm, lower arm, fore-arm; *mesai buah lengan*, as large as the biceps.
lengis		smooth, without irregularities; *parai ambis*, all dead; *parai lengis*, all dead smoothed out.
lengkiang		sword-rack.
lepong		swell.
lesong	lesong	mortar in which rice is pounded.
limpang, nglimpang		to turn aside, wander from the direct path, take a wrong turning; *samoa jako tuan aku nggai nglimpang*, I will not go beyond what the *tuan* says.
lindap	lindang	shady, sheltered; *menoa lindap*, shady district.
lingkau		a species of corn known as "Job's tears."

Sea Dyak, Malay and English Vocabulary. xxi.

SEA DYAK.	MALAY (Colloquial).	ENGLISH, Together with Examples of the use of the word.
lintan		tripe.
lis	halus	fine, thin.
lita	rabi	scar, mark.
lobah	lambat	slow.
lubok	lubok	pool.
lulong, nglulong	kaliling	to surround, encircle; *lulong rumah*, to encircle the house.
lulup		touch-wood.
lumat	alus	fine (minced).
lumiet		*rawai*, women's body ring ornaments.
lumpong	butih	a length, piece, log; *brapa lumpong (kaiu api) bedau*, how many lengths of firewood? *sirat sa lumpong*, not quite the length of a waist cloth; *sago dua lumpong*, two lengths of sago (wood); *lumpong jari*, a hand length; *lumpong kaki*, a foot length.
lunchong	jalor	a small canoe or dug-out.
lungat (?)		slow.
lungau	bodoh	stupid.
lungga	pisau	knife.
lupat	lusa	the third day after to-morrow.
lupong		medicine-case.
lus	lengis	all gone, clean gone, none left; *kati buah, bedau menoa kita?* how about fruit, have you any still up your way? *nadai nyau lus*, no, none, all gone; *parai ambis lus*, all dead, not one left; *lus Batang Merandong ari nanga nyintok ka entighis*, throughout the length of the river *Merandong*, from mouth to source.
má	sikutan	load, burden (carried on the back), verb. to carry on the back.
magang		entirely, all; *kita bedau dia magang?* are you still here all of you? *kajang magang*, all *kajangs*.
maia	uaktu	time; *maia dia*, about this time of day; *kati maia taun kita? benong nugal*, lit. what time is your year, in the middle of planting?
maiau	pusa	cat.
maioh	banyak	many, plenty.
makai	makan	to eat, feed.
mali	pamali	tabu-ed, unlawful (opp. to lawful), prohibited (opp. to permitted), mayn't (opp. to may); *mali bula*, may not lie; *mali rari*, may not run away.
malik	malik	to look *at*, glance *towards*.
manang		a medicine-man.
manchal	gauk	mischievous.

Sea Dyak.	Malay (Colloquial).	English, Together with Examples of the use of the word.
mandieng	tampak	prominent, showy, attractive ; *mandieng jako*, ostentatious talk.
mangah	marah	hot-tempered, quick-tempered, passionate, fierce, vindictive.
manok	aiyam	fowl ; *manok sabong*, game-cock, fighting-cock, champion.
mansang	surong	to go ahead, commence, advance, move forwards ; *ai mansang*, to rise, of water ; *ayer naik*, opposed to *surut*, to fall ; *mansang bumai*, commencement of farming ; *orang* or *anak biak mansang bharu*, the rising generation.
mansau	masak	ripe (fruit, &c.), red (colour).
manyi	lanyi	bee ; *ai manyi*, honey.
mar	mahal (?)	difficult, opposite to *muda* ; expensive.
marik	manit	bead
mata	mata	eye ; *lansiek mata*, clear sight ; *rabun mata*, dim sight ; *tajam mata*, keen sight.
matang		to continue to, persist, keep on ; *iya matang minta*, he keeps on asking.
mata panas	mata hari	sun.
mau	marak	*api nggai mau*, the fire will not burn.
mauieng	benkok	crooked.
mebintang	malintang	cross ways (opposed to *unjor*, length ways).
meda	meliat	to see, perceive, observe.
mekang	alang	insufficient, not worth while ; *mekang ari*, not enough time.
melepu	timbul	to float, buoyant.
mengalan		a kind of fish.
menggi, enggi	akun	to own, to belong to.
mengkang	kekal	lasting, still.
menoa	negri	country, region, district, place, home, abode ; *isi menoa orang menoa*, the people of the country are ; *kami menoa*, we in contrast to others.
mentas		kind.
mentudi	dudi	to be behind, follow behind.
menya, contr. from maya nya	dulu kamari	before (time) ; some time ago.
menyadé, madé	beradik	brother, sister ; *anak menyadé*, nephew or niece.
menyaua		to take breath ; *sakali menyaua*, a single breath.
mepan	pakaian, sinjata, pekakas	costume, equipment, accoutrement ; *nyelai mepan*, a different costume.
merarau		to make a mid-day meal, to dine.
merenieng	ningok	to peep at, peep over, to look at.
merinsah	susah, sakit	suffering, uncomfortable, unpleasant, tiresome.
merong	kawang	to howl (dog).
meruan	kekal	lasting, still.

Sea Dyak, Malay and English Vocabulary. xxiii.

SEA DYAK.	MALAY (Colloquial.)	ENGLISH. Together with Examples of the use of the word.
merunsai	membuka	to unfold, unwrap, take off the wrappers.
merurut		to slip, slide, to come undone (clothes).
mersap	sessat	astray, to wander astray, lose one's way.
mesai, contr. from pemesai	tangah	size.
mimit	sedikit	a little of quantity, slightly (adv.), (adj.), small, little, few ; *mimit 'da*, nearly ; *mimit 'da aku parai*, a very little longer and I shall be dead.
mimpi	mimpi	to dream.
minta	minta	to ask for, and in a religious sense, to pray for ; *minta ari*, to pray for dry weather.
minyarai		a kind of gong.
misah	tuka	to alter.
mit	kechil	small, little in size, young.
moa	muka	face, mouth, front.
mo-ari	pengarak (?)	rain-cloud, lowering clouds, storm-cloud, cloudy sky.
mrau		travel by water (boat), to boat.
mri	kasih	to give.
mubok	buka	to settle ; *mubok menoa*, to open up a country, be the first to colonize it and settle in it.
muda	muda	young, tender.
mudah	mudah	easy.
mudik	mudik	to ascend (river).
munchol	buku	a knob.
munoh	bunoh	to kill.
munsoh	musoh	enemy, foe.
muntang	mintas	to cut across (country); *ari kanan muntang ka jikang*, take a short cut on the right : *muntang tanjong*, cut across the river bend.
munyi	berbunyi	to sound.
murai		(of *paddy*) the stage when the corn begins to form.
nabau		a snake of mythology; *ular sawa tai nabau*, the *sawa* is the excrement of the *nabau;* *sawa* is the python.
naga		dragon.
nakal	tahan	to endure, suffer; *maioh nyamok aku enda nakal enda bikibong*, there are so many mosquitoes I cannot endure being without a curtain.
nama	nama	a name.
nama ?	apa ?	what ?
nampik		*nampik nggau latak*, to splutter with mud, pitch mud at.
nanga	muara	mouth of river.

Sea Dyak.	Malay (Colloquial).	English, Together with Examples of the use of the word.
nanyeng	pingingat	*indu nanyeng*, a kind of wasp.
nekong	keti	to knock, to strike a light, knock at a door.
nempoh		to overwhelm, to attack with overwhelming numbers; *leboh moari nempoh kubu*, when the clouds are overhanging the fort.
nemuai		to visit, pay a visit.
ni, dini?	mana, seni?	where?
nikal	balik	to turn back, double, return to the original point of starting, to fold over.
ninga	dingar	to hear.
ninting	sabilang	each, every; *ninting taun*, each year; *ninting rumah*, every house; *ninting ari*, each day; *ninting tuboh*, every body, person.
ngaba bau		to smell of bad or good (breath); *nyaua dè ngaba bau sema*, your breath smells like a *sema* fish; *bau ngaba*, a strong scent.
ngabang		to go to a feast.
ngadang	jaga	to look out, be on the watch, to expect; *ngadang!* look out (premonitory); *enda ngadang nuan datai*, I did not expect you to come.
ngagai, nggai		to go towards; *bejalai ngagai nuan*, to go off to you.
ngantok		to nod (drowsy).
ngapa		in vain, without result; *iya bejalai ngapa* he went in vain; *kerja ngapa*, useless work.
ngaru	garu	to scratch.
ngau		to say yes, consent, agree.
ngaua (root gaua, to do something).		to hurt, bother, worry, annoy, trouble, ail, to mind, to interfere with; *nama ngaua ka iya*, what ails him? what's the matter with him? *anang takut, nadai orang ka ngaua ka nuan*, don't be afraid, no one will do anything to you.
ngelai, klai		to picture, to mark.
ngeli	gigi	tooth, fang.
ngema		to carry on back.
ngemilut	ngobé	to make faces, make a grimace.
ngenong	changok	to look hard at.
ngentam	tolong	to succour, aid.
ngelalau	ambil madu	to gather honey.
ngelambai		to light up; *baka kilat ngelambai petang*, like lightning lightens up in darkness.
ngelaua	mengagar	to approach.
ngeliat		to stretch oneself (on awakening).
ngeluar		to go beyond, to go outside.
ngentang	kapada, arah	the Latin *apud*, at; *iya diau ngentang kami*, he lives with us; *nanya ngentang iya*, ask him; *utang ngentang aku mudik ngentang nuan*, but ask me to go up and be at your place.

Sea Dyak, Malay and English Vocabulary.

Sea Dyak.	Malay (Colloquial).	English, Together with Examples of the use of the word.
ngeraiap		to crawl (baby) on hands and knees.
ngerantam	garu	to rebuke, reprimand, forbid.
ngerara	melarang	to scratch (with nails, claws).
ngerejang	masok	to penetrate ; *ambi ai nggo ngerejang lubang sumpit*, fetch some water with which to wash through the sumpit.
ngetu	berhenti	to wait, stop.
ngiar	buru	to compel, cause, excite, urge, press, drive, to scatter ; *ngiar ka iya pulai*, urge him to go away.
ngidup	idup	to keep alive, provide for, to nurse (a sick person) ; *ngidup ka nyaua*, to save life.
ngili ai	hilir	to descend a river.
ngimbai		to lie alongside, side by side.
ngimbi	kasih	to give.
nginjun	gregar	to tread heavily, shake with one's stamp ; *nginjun bilik*, to shake the room.
nginsah		to drag (a person by the heels).
nginti	ngail	to angle.
ngipé	lempah	to boil.
ngosong	agar	to arrive at, to visit ; *enggai aku ngosong dé*, I will not visit you.
ngramak	garu	to scratch (nails).
ngranggar (a corruption from Malay)	melanggar	to collide with.
ngrembang		to hold on to grass or trees in descending a hill.
ngrimbas		to graze (of a bullet grazing one's flesh).
ngoyum		to fester.
nguang	presca	to reconnoitre, explore, to pursue.
nguiyo (root kuiyo, the cheeks)		to suck.
ngundan		to follow behind, to be according to ; *ngundan tajau*, to come after a jar.
ngutap	kulit	to bark (a tree).
niang	ramula	late (deceased).
ninyok		to pry, peep through.
nuan	kita, kau	you (singular number).
nubai } nuba }	menuba	to tuba, see *tubai*.
nelap		kind.
nusok		to string ; *nusok marik*, to string beads ; *nusok engkrimok*, to string leaves together, to thread, stitch.
nya	itu	that there ; *bri nya ka aku*, give that to me ; *anang ngaga nya*, don't do that ; *ari nya*, from there.
nyadi	jadi	to create.
nyamai	nyaman	nice, pleasant, agreeable, comfortable.

Sea Dyak.	Malay (Colloquial).	English, Together with Examples of the use of the word.
nyamok	nyamok	mosquito.
nyampau!	kakan!	how!
nyanda		to borrow.
nyandih		to lean upon, lean one's back against.
nyangkar		to cage.
nyau		gone, become; *menoa nyau kusi*, the country is lost.
nyaua	herga, suara	(1) life, voice breath; (2) worth, value; *bidai nyaua*, value of mat; *dinga nyaua aku ngiar China*, hear my voice, drive away the Chinaman.
nyauk		to dip and fill (water gourds).
nyau ka		nearly; *nyau ka lama*, after a while, after some time; *nyau ka datai da*, almost come.
nyelai	lain	different; *orang nyelai bulu*, men of a different race; *nyelai mepan*, different costume.
nyelipak		to creep past.
nyen	nun	yonder.
nyepi	cheri	to feel, to taste.
nyeregu	berdidi	to bristle; *bulu dé nyeregu asai buah nangka*, your hair bristles like jack-fruit.
nyerungkong		to sit with the arms across the knees and the chin resting on them.
nygelancham		to sharpen, point (a stake or post).
nygensong	bersiol	to whistle.
nyidi	ikut	to track.
nyingkar (sinkar—thwarts of a boat)	mebintang	athwart; *batang maioh nyingkar sungai*, a great many trees lie across the river.
nyintok	sampai	until, down to, up to; *nyintok ka dia*, till now; *ari tauas nyintok ka malam*, from daylight till dark.
nyungkup		cf. *sungkup*.
padi	paddi	*paddy* (rice in husk); *padi sumbar*, half ripe *paddy*.
pagi	pagi	morning.
pagila	bésok	to-morrow; *tumu pagila*, early to-morrow morning; *lemai pagila*, to-morrow evening.
paiya	krapa	swamp.
pajoh	antam; kaparat	to slip into; *parai di pajoh lang*, dead from slipping into a chasm.
paku	paku	fern (edible fern).
pala	kapala	head; *antu pala*, head taken in war.
pambar		scattered, dispersed, broken up, separated from.
pambus, mambus	micah	to break (a boil), to burst, to scatter, &c., as *pambar*.

Sea Dyak, Malay and English Vocabulary. xxvii.

SEA DYAK.	MALAY (Colloquial).	ENGLISH, Together with Examples of the use of the word.
pampul, mampul	gengam	to clutch in one's hands; *pampul pala*, to clutch at the head.
panchur		water-fall, a channel, drain.
pandam	bukut	to hit with the fist, beat with the palm of the hand.
panga	simpang	branch (tree, river).
pangan	sahabat	kinsman, clansman, comrade, fellow to a pair.
panggal	bantal	pillow; any horizontal support.
panggau	katil	bedstead.
pangka, manka		to strike severely.
pangkal		scrub, young jungle.
pangkang, mangkang		to live near, in neighbourhood of; *nggai aku mangkang kubu*, I will not live near the fort; *adu ka lembaian kajang barang ka mangkang*, arrange the horizontal side support of the *kajang* whoever is nearest; *enda kala bebuah sakumbang kami bepangkang*, it never fruited as long as we lived there.
pangkong, mankong	tuku, gual	to strike.
panjai	panjang	long.
panjong, manjong	triak	to shout, scream, yell, whoop; a yell, &c.
pansa, mansa	lalu	pass by.
pansap, mansap	sirap	to slice off, scrape off.
pansut, mansut	kaluar	to emerge from, come out of, issue from, exude.
pantang,	lantak	to drive in (nail), to prick, to puncture, sting; *pantang nyamok*, mosquito pricks; *auak iya pantang*, let it bite you.
pantok, mantok	gigit	to dart at, shoot out (snakes), the young shoots of various plants, young leaves not yet opened out.
pantu	rhumbia	wild sago tree.
pantup	kena	to hit, overtake, strike, knock against, come into contact with.
papal, mapal		to clip off, to pare off.
parai	mati	to die, dead; *parai nyaua*, dead of the breath; *parai antu*, dead of the spirit; *parai nyabong*, dead with regard to cock fighting.
pati	simpang	branch (river, tree).
patok	patok	beak (of bird); *patok ketieng*, clitoris.
patong	patong	knee.
paung		a shoot, a cutting for planting; *paung mulong*, sago cutting.
peda, meda	meliat	to see
pedis	sakit	to hurt, sore; *pedis prut*, stomach-ache.

Sea Dyak.	Malay (Colloquial).	English, Together with Examples of the use of the word.
pedil, medil	tahan	to detain; *kapa dé medil ka utai aku?* why do you detain my goods?
pedua	bhagi	to divide.
pejulok		to nick-name.
pekat	pesan	order, command.
pelaba, nglaba	jangka	to guess, surmise, conjecture; *enda aku nemu pelaba*, I cannot venture to make a guess; *aku pelaba ngapa*, a mere guess, surmise; *enti nemu pelaba*, if one might venture to guess.
pelieng, melieng	gulong	to wind round; *melieng ai*, to follow the windings of the river; *aku nggai bepelieng*, I don't want to go a round about way; *umai aku pelieng umai iya*; my farm goes round about his farm.
pelimping	pesaghi	having angles; *pelimping*, four angles = square.
pelulong		to surround, encircle, to beat into a ring (deer, &c.).
pemadu		end, in order of time; *pemadu rumah*, end of houses, last house.
pemai	pesaka	inheritance, heritage, that which one brings.
pemakai	makan	food.
pemanah	elok, chanteh	beauty.
pemandi		bathing-place.
pemangah		asperity, fierceness, ferocity.
pemanggai		a rest, a shelf.
pemanjai	panjong	length.
pemanyak	baniak	quantity, number.
pemarai	kamatian	manner of death or cause of death.
pemedis	ka-sakitan	illness.
pemegai	pegang	a handle, thing to hold by.
pementi		a tabu.
pemerap	pemelok	girth.
pemesa		quantity; *pemesa ai pemesa arak*, how much water, how much arak? *pemesa nuan tungga iya?* how much do you fine him?
pemesai	besar	size (sub.).
pemidick	nasib	fortune, luck.
pemintas	pintas	a short cut, a cut across.
pemrat	kabratan	weight.
pemuput	kipas	a fan.
penabin	demmum	sickness.
penagang		a stopper, preventive; *penagang ari*, something to prevent the rain.
penama	nama	name.
penapat	benar-benar	as well as one is able; *dua ari mudik penapat ingat*, remember with might and main, in two days we go up river.
penatai	asal	origin.
penawan		harpoon, barbed javelin, fish-spear.

Sea Dyak, Malay and English Vocabulary.

SEA DYAK.	MALAY (Colloquial).	ENGLISH, Together with Examples of the use of the word.
pendai	tepian, jilatong	wharf.
pendiau		abode, place of residence.
pendieng	telinga	ear ; *lubang pendieng*, orifice of the ear ; *anang tikup lubang pendieng*, don't close the orifice of the ear ; *tinsa pendieng*, ear-drops.
penebal		thickness.
penedat	blantan	a cudgel, bludgeon, staff, truncheon.
peneka	nafsu	wish, pleasure, desire.
penelap		kindness, good-nature.
penembu	habis	end, finish, conclusion, completion.
penemu	bijak sana	knowledge, understanding.
pengabang		an invited guest at a feast.
pengamat		truth, genuineness.
pengapus		extinction, exhaustion, end, finish ; *pengapus menoa*, throughout the country ; *pengapus ai*, throughout the river ; *pengapus ulu*, throughout the highlands.
pengaroh		a charm.
pengawa	kreja	work, business, occupation.
pengeraja		source of wealth, means of subsistence, means : *aku nadai jai ati enggau laut enggau* China *iya anjong pengeraja kitai*, I have no ill feeling against the Malays and Chinese, they bring us wealth.
pengerang		secondary jungle, which must be cut down with the *biliong* and not the *duku*.
penggau	paké	to wear, use ; *anang di penggau*, don't wear it.
penggi, menggi		to own, possess, to appropriate ; *sapa menggi?* who owns this?
pengiong		vedette, picket ; *pengiong bala*, advance guard, scout ; *prau pengiong*, reconnoitring boat.
pengki		firm, as opposed to *lemi*, soft ; *pengki isi*, firm flesh.
penglantang		leisure, ease, convenience.
pengorang	korang	deficiency.
pengrieng	kuat	strength, hardness.
pengrujak	pengantar	a ramrod.
penguan		succour, reinforcements, pursuit.
penindok	bilik tidor	bed-room, bed-stead.
peninggi		height.
peninjau		vice, prospect.
penti, bepenti		forbidden, proscribed, *tabu-ed, tabu*.
penuai	umor	age, how old?
penudah	dudi	last.
penuduk	krusi	seat, chair.
penyadi		condition ; *kati baka penyadi padi kita taun tu?* what is the condition of your *padi* this year ? *nama penyadi tua?* what is to become of us two?
penyalah	ka salahan	fault, crime, offence, misdemeanour.

Sea Dyak.	Malay (Colloquial).	English. Together with Examples of the use of the word.
penyampau!	kakan!	how! how much? *penyampau badas*, very good; *penyampau ka pinta?* how much do you ask?
penyangkai	pengkalan	landing-place.
penyauh		distance; *penyauh ari nanga?* how far from the mouth of the river?
penyurieng		leader, commander; *penyurieng bala*, leader of a force.
pepat	api-api	fire-fly.
pepat, mepat	chin chang	to chop up, mince, hash, cut into fine pieces.
peraka, meraka		to cross.
perejok, merejok	melompat	to jump, leap, bound, spring (fishes, animals).
perenieng, merenieng	preksa	to look at, examine, inspect.
perok, merok	prah	to squeeze, to strain; *tuak*, spirit.
perong	merong and kawang	a howl (dog); *di dinga perong udok*, as far as the howl of a dog may be heard, a measure of distance.
pesemaia	perjanjian	agreement, compact.
pesok	bubus	to have a hole in.
petunggal	suku pupu	first cousin
pichal, michal	pichit	to squeeze; *pichal tusu indu dara*, squeeze the breasts of girls.
pinchai, minchai	pegang, simpan	to hold, take hold of, to keep.
pindah, mindah	pindah	to remove, to change; *mindah ka penama*, change one's name; *pindah kresa*, to inherit property of a defunct.
pinggai	pirieng	place.
pinjar	suapang	musket.
pipis	nipis	thin.
pisa	bisul	boil.
pisah, misah	ubah	to change (one's name).
pisang	pisang	plantain.
pisang brunai	nanas	pine-apple.
pisau	sumpit	narrow (?)
prai	halus	*tanah prai*, friable mould, loose soil.
pransang, meransang		a stimulant, incentive, to stimulate, urge on, excite; *meransang ukuć, orang,* &c., urge on the dogs, men, &c.
prengka	pekakas	thing, effect, appliances, instruments, tools, toys.
prut	prut	stomach, belly.
pua kumbu	salimut	coverlet, blanket.
puchau, muchau		to mutter, to speak incoherently, to recite an incantation.
puchong		a very small jar, small bottle, phial.
pudut (k'wit)	rambu	a tassel (necklace).
pugar		to scrub, rub; *pugar moa*, clean your face; *pugar pinggai*, clean the plate.

Sea Dyak, Malay and English Vocabulary. xxxi.

Sea Dyak.	Malay (Colloquial).	English, Together with Examples of the use of the word.
pukat, empelawa	sarong, empelawa	cobweb, lit. the spider's nest.
pulai, mulai	balik, pulang	to go home, go back, return, to restore, make restitution.
pulau	pulau	island, jungle which has a clearing round it.
pumpong, mumpong		to cut off, dissever (head from trunk).
pumpun		the short tail feathers of a bird (*manok, tajai, kinyalang*) as opposed to *langgai*, the long ditto.
pun		reason, why; *pun ági aku ka*, all the more reason I should desire it.
punas	punas	sterile, barren (animal or vegetable).
pungkang	korangan	to run short of, be in want of; *kami enda kala pungkang garam*, we are never short of salt.
pungga, mungga		*pungga batang*, to cut a way through.
pupu	bueh	froth, foam; a tax.
pupus	habiskan	to finish.
puput, muput	muput	to fan, breathe upon, blow upon, be blown upon; *aku nyamai, puput ka ribut*, I am comfortable when I am fanned by the wind.
putieng	ujong	end, edge; *putieng rambut, p. biliong, p. rumah*, the point of the beard, the edge of the axe, the end of the house.
rabun	sebun	dim sight, blindness.
raga	pagar	fence.
ragum	janggut	beard; forceps, pincers.
raia		bright, festal, large; *buah raia*, plentiful fruit season; *pasang raia*, king tides; *jalai raia*, well cleared roads, i.e. bright roads.
raja	kaia	rich, well-born, free-born, king royal.
rambai		cock's comb; *minta manok, enti bujang baru tumboh rambai*, ask for a fowl, if it is a young cock, its comb will be just appearing; *anti inda dara, anti laki tumboh rambai*, if it is a young hen, we call *dara*, if a cock the comb appears; also a species of fruit.
rambau	uaktu	what time: *sarambau*, of the same age; *sarambau enggo aku*, my contemporary.
rampas	rampas	to despoil, sack, pillage, loot.
rampu	timun	cucumber.
randau	akar	creeper, parasite.
randau		conversation, talk, conference, discussion, chat; *nadai utai ka randau*, nothing to talk about.

Sea Dyak.	Malay (Colloquial).	English, Together with Examples of the use of the word.
rangai		entreatingly, in a pressing, earnest manner; *rangai-rangai aku ngasoh iya pulai*, very earnestly I asked him to return; *rangai-rangai aku ngasoh iya nganjong pupu*, very pressingly I told him to pay his tax.
rangau		*rangau-rangau*, piteously.
rangkah		lifeless; *parai rangkah*, stiff (of a corpse); *nyau rangkah bangkai*, the corpse has become stiff.
rangkah		greedy.
rangki		*kima* shell.
ranjur	salalu	to pass through; *kati nuan ranjur ka S'wak*, well did you manage to get through to Sarawak.
ransi, ngransi		used up, bare, stript, exhausted; *udah ransi babas*, stripped of bush; to blame, suspect; *takut di ransi iya*, I fear to be blamed by him.
rantau	ranto	a reach on a river; *besabong rantau jalai*, to meet on the way; *kami bepansa rantau ai*, we passed each other on the river.
rarah	gugor	to shed (hair, leaves, blossoms, horns), to drop (ripe fruit).
rau		dead leaves, drift, dead twigs, branches.
raung	katak	frog.
rawan	takut	nervous, apprehensive, timorous, afraid.
redas	kabun	a sugar-cane garden.
regas	sigat	active; *iya regas bendar di tanah*, as active as can be, &c.
remang	awan	light fleecy clouds (not rain clouds, *moari*).
remaung	rimo	tiger.
rembus	trus	through.
rempah	saior	condiments, fruit and vegetables, greens.
rendang-rendang		completely (adv.); *bulih bangau burak rendang-rendang*, we caught a *padi* bird completely white.
renga	ensema	rheum, cold in nose, hay fever, catarrh.
rentap	ruboh	
rentun	chabut	to pluck out, eradicate.
renyuan		honey-comb.
repa	reboh ?	over grown, tangled with grass and weeds.
rerak	pesi	to open, untie (bundle or parcel), to undo.
retak	kachang tandas	a kind of native bean.
ribut	angin	wind, breeze, gale, squall.
rigau		*maioh utai ka rigau di rumah*, many things that noise about the house.
rimba	rimba	a forest-clearing.
rimbai	rakit	alongside; *prau rimbai batang*, the boat is alongside the wharf.
rimbas, ngrimbas		to graze (a bullet the flesh).
rimpak	pitchah	to break into pieces.

Sea Dyak.	Malay (Colloquial.)	English, Together with Examples of the use of the word.
rindang, ngrindang	lékar	detained, to linger, loiter, tarry, dawdle, delay; *rindang duduk enggau orang*, I was detained sitting with the people; *rindang idup menyadi aku sakit*, my sick brother still lingers; *sigi iya ngrindang diri*, he is simply dawdling.
ringat	gusar	angry, vexed, anger : *nama ka ringat nuan?* what are you angry at?
ringin	embrang	otter.
ringka, ringkai		to weave a rattan frame-wo k or basket; *nya japai, mangkok di ringkai*, lay hold of that there, the cup in the rattan-frame; *mati salai, mati ringkai*, die and be smoked, die and be caged (curse).
ringka	raga	a football of cane work.
rintai		to array, set in line, arrange in order.
rintong		a ladle.
rintong	tekoyong	snail.
ripih		*aku ripih sida*, I am for them, I am on the other side, I am retained for the other side, partizan.
rita	cherita	news, information, intelligence.
royak	rosak	torn, undone.
rugin	sulok	a species of plant, the leaves of which are used medicinally.
rujak		to ram down, force down.
rumah	rumah	house.
ruman		the stalk; *ruman padi*, which carries the grain.
rumbang	puang	deserted, empty; *rumbang bilik*, empty room.
rumbau		barren (tree fruit), sterile (soil), unfruitful.
rumpang		to wane (moon); *rumpang ulit*, to go out of mourning, to abolish the *ulit*, the waning moon; *rumah rumpang*, to demolish the house.
rumpong	masak	to come to a head (boil); *nyau rumpong mata*, the boil come to a head; a species of dried prawn.
rungan	beté	*kapai*, as fruit.
runtoh	tumbung	to fall in, tumble in, to give way; *runtoh langit*, the sky falls; *runtoh rumah*, the house is falling.
sa	satu	one (numeral).
sabak, ngabak	nangis	to cry, scream, cry, scream (subst.).
sabau	perchoma	bootless.
sabau	kuah	gravy, juice.

c

SEA DYAK.	MALAY (Colloquial).	ENGLISH. Together with Examples of the use of the word.
sabong, nyabong		to join forces, of cocks to fight; *manok sabong*, a fighting cock; *ai Skerang nyabong Ulu ai Padi*, the source of the Skerang river joins forces with the upper Padi river.
sadau	padong	loft, attic, upper room.
sajalai		the one road, to be the same, to go hand in hand, agree, correspond, coincide, together in company, to keep one company; *jako tua enda sajalai*, our languages are not the same.
sakai		crew, hands; *prau kami nadai sakai*, our boat has no crew.
sakali	sakali	at once.
sakang	tulak, nyilat	to push off, ward off, keep off, repulse, to avert; *aku sakang pia*, I turned off the blow thus; *iya ka merap aku, aku sakang pia*, he wanted to throw his arms round me, but I kept him off thus.
sakumbang		as long as, all the time; *enda kala bebuah sakumbang kami bepangkang*, never fruited so long as we lived near; *sakumpang bulan 'tu*, during this month.
salah, nyalah	salah	to find fault with, to put in the wrong, to make out a case against; adj. wrong.
salai, nyalai	salé	to smoke, dry in the smoke; *salai ikan, salai kain, salai pala*, smoke the fish, dry the clothes (over the fire), smoke a head.
salam, nyalam	bertapok	to conceal.
salapan, samilan	sambilan	nine (numeral).
samegat		soul, spirit.
samembai	klébar	butterfly.
sampal		collectively, all together, all at once.
sampok	ani ani	the white ant.
sampu, nyampu	buka	to open by fire (boat).
samujan	burong maiat	*burong samujan*, a bird.
san	pikul	to carry on shoulder.
sanda nyanda	jamé	to borrow, *nyanda*.
sandiek		to hang round one's shoulder, slung round the shoulder, to carry a child on the hips.
sanentang	sebah	opposite to; *belaboh sanentang rumah*, drop [the anchor] opposite the house.
sanepa		at the same time, simultaneous.
sangka, nyangka	tekan	to imagine, suspect.
sangkai, nyangkai	singga, singgahi	to take passage; *nyangkai manang*, to take *manang* as a passenger.
sapa?	siapa?	who? what?
sarang	sarang	a case; *sarang ipoh*, poison case; *sarang burong*, a bird's nest; *sarang jani*, a pig's stye.

Sea Dyak.	Malay (Colloquial).	English. Together with Examples of the use of the word.
sareba	sama-sama	simultaneously.
sari 'tu	'mi hari	to-day.
sarok, nyarok	menumpang	to take lodging; *nyarok rumah orang*, to put up at somebody's house; *isa aku nyarok orang*, I had better lodge with someone.
sarugan	(duan sulok)	a leaf of a certain plant.
sebrai	sebrang	across, opposite side.
sedi		gambier (wild).
segau		*orang segau-segau*, idle vagabond.
segieng		to foul (of boats); *besigieng enda blaia*, not sailing they fouled.
sekut	sendat, selut, sumpit	narrow, confined (space), cramped up; *sekut dalam*, uneasy (in mind), unhappy; *sekut ati, sekut dalam*, stuffy feeling from cold in head.
selapok	kopiah	cap.
seliah, nyeliah		to run away, move out of the way or aside, clear out, secrete, isolate, separate; *kita ka mimit nyeliah orang lalu undur*, if you will get out of the way a little bit the men can go on; *nyeliah kita*, clear out of this, you; *nyeliah ka napal*, get out of the way of, &c., to clear away (the things after a meal); *badas kayoh mimit ulih seliah kitai*, it is better that we paddle a little and we shall be able to move out of the way; *ninga rita nuan datai iya nyeliah ka tanah*, hearing of your arrival he disappeared; *nyeliah ka pupu*, to move away from the tax; *nyeliah ka pintu*, to push aside the door.
selong		a wire hoop, thence brass wire of a certain stoutness.
semaia	beyanji	to promise.
semerai, nyemerai	ñembrang	to cross over, to swim, to visit.
sempurai		*paddy*, 2 or 3 years old (?).
sengaioh	pengayah	paddle.
sepu	tiup	to blow (out of a blow pipe).
serak		a fold, a layer, an understood period, a generation, time; *serak dudi*, next time, next opportunity; *serak tu*, this time; *rumah 3 serak*, 3 storied house; *klambi dua serak*, two folds of coats, i.e., two coats.
serang, myerang		to attack.
serangkong	tanggong	to take up, to become responsible for.
serara	cherré	to separate, part.
serarai	angus	scorched (by fire), parched.

SEA DYAK.	MALAY (Colloquial).	ENGLISH. Together with Examples of the use of the word.
serta		at same time with, together with ; *sapa serta nuan ?* who, together with you ? *serta-serta*, all together.
serungkai	buka	to open (a bundle), unpack.
seruri, nyeruri	baiki	to mend, repair ; *seruri jala*, mend your net ; *seruri atap*, mend the shingles (roof).
sibali ari	sindiri ari, lain hari	of the one time ; *orang sibali ari*, men of our own time.
sida		them, those, 3rd person, plural, pronoun.
siduai	kita dua	you two, they two, both.
siga		unsafe, dangerous, unsettled, on the alert, vigilant ; *siga* also means wild ; *menoa siga*, wild country, jungle.
sigi	sighir	one seed, or things resembling seeds.
sigi	saja	simply ; *sigi pementi kami ari klia*, simply our *tabu* from times gone by : *sigi iya ngrindang diri*, he is simply dawdling.
siko	sikor, sikor orang	*siko* (*sa*, one ; *iko*, tail) ; of all living creatures, one ; *iya siko sapa penama ?* what is the name of the other one ?
siku	siku	elbow.
silau	silau	bright, dazzle (of sunlight), exceedingly.
silau	jerinih	clear, transparent (water), the grey of the morning or dusk evening ; *silau tauas*, peep of day.
silih	ganti	to exchange.
silok		a fish (*ikan silok*).
silu		home sick ; *dara silu-ilu nubong, ka nyabak*, the girl is very home sick, does nothing but cry.
simbieng		crooked, on one side, aslant.
simbieng	sirong	awry, askew.
sindap	kelawa	bathing.
sinera		a presentiment, harbinger.
singkap		a slice, or sheet, or layer, anything which presents a broad flat surface ; *singkap pinggai*, one plate.
sintak, nyintak	chabut	to draw out : *sintak*, to unsheathe, to catch with a noose.
sirat	chawat	loin cloth.
siti	sabuti	one, of small things.
skali	skali	*sa-kali*, one time : *sa-kali da*, once more ; *skali 'da*, once more, next time, once again ; *skali nyawa*, a single life.
sligi		a wooden javelin.
sua, nyua		to hand, offer, present to.
suah	puas	often.
suba	dulu (time), kamari	the other day, *before* (time), a little while ago.
subang	krabu	ear-ring
subong	kladi	*kladi*, cladium

Sea Dyak.	Malay (Colloquial).	English. Together with Examples of the use of the word.
sukat	ukur	what time; to measure, the measurement, the destined period; *sukat kaki*, one foot long; *sukat iya grai, grai, sukat iya tabin, tabin*, for the destined period of his time he will be well, for the destined period of his illness he will be ill; *sukat angat, angat sukat chelap, chelap penapat angat*, for the proper length of summer it will be hot, for the proper length of winter it will be cold.
sulieng		a flute, a whistle (steamer's), fife.
suman		well after sickness, recovered.
sumbar, nyumbar		to gather the first ears of *padi* just us they begin to turn ripe; *mansang sumbar*, time for gathering first ripe *padi; nyumbar*, to gather the half ripe *paddy; padi sumbar*, first ripe years of *padi*.
sumboh		healed, to heal, heal up; *utai sumboh*, a curable complaint, &c.
sumiet	tighin, loké	stingy.
sumpieng	pasah	peg, screw.
sumpit, nyumpit		a blow-pipe, to shoot with the blow-pipe.
sungai	sungi	river or stream which is a tributary of a main river.
sungkit, ñungkit		to insert, to pierce, prick, hence to vaccinate, occulate.
sungkup, ñungkup		erection over a grave.
sup	benghah	swollen.
suruan, seruan		mediator, interpreter, advocate, go-between.
surut	surut	to fall (opposed to *mansang*, to rise), water; *ai tu sakali mansang, enda surut*, the water is continually rising and does not ebb.
taban	rebut	to seize, carry off, run away.
tabin	sakit	ill, poorly, sick, ailing, feverish, generally fever.
tachu	temparong	cocoanut-shell.
tagang	tahan	to stop, prevent, make to stop (steamer), forbid.
taia	kapas	cotton; *klambi taia*, a padded jacket or coat of quilted cotton.
tajam	tajam	sharp, keen; *tajam mata*, keen sighted.
taju		a sort of jar.
taju	brian (barian)	dower.
takah	antara	between, apart, a division.
takang	tahan	

Sea Dyak.	Malay (Colloquial).	English. Together with Examples of the use of the word.
takar	sampai	a measure, to measure out, until; *takar ambis*, until finished; *takar nyaua parai*, until the hour of death.
takup		fellow to.
tal (Kat.)	tahan	to endure, put up with, bear (pain).
talar		to level, smooth, a row, even line.
talun	papan	plank, board.
tama		to enter.
tamang	poh	name-sake; *tamang aku siko*, a name-sake of mine, or my other name-sake.
tambah	tambah	to add to.
tambai		flag.
tambak		to transplant, a sapling, suckling, shoot, seedlings.
tambit		to close up, to shut, to tie up, to fasten with thongs; *tambit lauang*, shut the door; *tambit moa pisau*, shut up the edge of the knife.
tampal, nampal	tampal	to cover, to patch (a hole in curtains); *tampal mata*, cover the eyes, to bandage.
tampang		a plant; *tampang tebu*, a shoot of sugar cane; *tampang pisang*, banana shoot; vaccine.
tampil, nampil	tampong	to join on, join to; *orang nampil bala*, men just joined on to us (forces).
tampong	sambong	to join on to, to sew on, patch, splice on to; *menyadih tampong pala*, lit. brothers joining heads, i.e. own brothers v. cousins; *tampong orang jako*, add to what he has said.
tampun		to impale, transfix.
tanan	utang	debt.
tancham	salang, tebok	to pierce a hole in.
tanchang, nanchang	ikat	to make fast, fasten, tie.
tanggoi	cherindak	sun hat, umbrella, sun-shade.
tanggong, nanggong	angkat	to lift, raise, to become responsible for.
tangkai	tandan	bunch (fruit); an ear *(paddy)*; *jako betangkai*, collection of opinions.
tangkal, nangkal	tetak, jaku	to notch, make a note of, treaty.
tangkien, nangkien	ikat	to buckle on, gird on.
tangkir, nangkir	grip, timbo	side-plank. to wall in, fence round; *tangkir prau*, put on the side planks of the *prau*; *tangkir umai*, fence in the farm.
tangkong		horn (bird); *tangkong tajai kinalang*, the horn on the beak of the hornbill.
tangkup		*tangkup enggau jalong*, to invert a vessel as a cover.

Sea Dyak.	Malay (Colloquial).	English, Together with Examples of the use of the word.
tanjak, nanjak	pejal	to go against an opposing force, e.g. against wind or tide.
tanjong	tanjong	a point (river, coast), headland, a bend in the river.
tansa		*tansa pendieng*, ear-studs.
tapa	tapak	palm (hand), sole (foot).
tapak	tempat	the whereabouts; *tapak ni rumah nya?* where is that house?
tarang	tarang	brightness, light.
tasau, nasau	tibas	
tasiek	lautan	sea.
tasih	séwar	rent, hire, tax.
tatai	tebieng	precipice.
tatieng		to weigh down, to suspend.
tau		to be able to, know how, may; *enda tau*, mayn't.
tauar, nauar		to beat down in price.
tauas	luas	clear, light; path; (opposed to *repa*).
tauieng, nauieng		to hang on, to tow.
taun	tahun	year; *taun dempa*, last year; *taun padi di sadau*, last year's paddy; *taun ka udah*, last year; *taun kadai, taun padi di tanah*, present year, this year; *taun ka empai*, next year; *taun siti kamari*, last year; *taun siti ka empai*, next year or year after next; *taun dulu kamari*, year before last.
tebah, nebah		to play a wind instrument; *nebah sulieng*, to play the flute, to cause the steamer to whistle; *tebah gendang*, to beat tom-tom; *tebah tauak*, to beat the gong, &c.; *tebah nyaua*, to sing.
tebieng	rinjan	steep.
tebieng	tepi	shore, bank.
tebu	tebu	sugar-cane.
tedai, teda	katiṅggalan	leavings, remains, remainder, residue.
tegalan		the burnt land prepared for seed-planting.
tegar	kuat	strong; *tegar tulang*, strong, powerful; *tegar nyaua*, a loud voice; *tegar blanda* or *blaua*, swift runner.
tegian	hadat (?)	
teguran	bogo	
tekah	tarah	to plane.
tekang		adhesive, clayey, pasty; *tanah prai, enda betekang*, loose soil, not clayey.
tekap		to stutter.
tekat	tegah	to prevent, forbid, stop.
tekenyit	tekejut	sudden, surprised, taken by surprise, astonished, frightened, startled.
tekul	tahan	crowded, confined, prevented by circumstances.

Sea Dyak.	Malay (Colloquial).	English. Together with Examples of the use of the word.
tela, nela	liat	to see, perceive; *tela man!* do you see! *di tela ari nya*, to be seen (visible from thence).
telanjai	tilanjong	naked.
telenga	terbuka	to open, come undone; breach of a rifle, a window, door.
telis	tilis	a cut, wounded, wound.
telok	tilok	a recess, the recess formed in the bend of a river; *telok sungai*, backwater.
telu	telur	egg.
tembrawai	tembang	deserted dwelling, ruins, the site of an old habitation.
tembu	sudah	to finish, be at an end, end, conclude, accomplish, have done; *pechara udah tembu, udah badu*, the case has been concluded, brought to an end; *enti tembu langkau, kadua ñginti kadua nyumpit*, if the shed has been finished some will fish and some will shoot (blow-pipe); *anti tembu makai kejang kitai*, wait till we have done eating and we will start.
tempalong	proam	to fling (ship's lead); *parai di kena tempalong*, it would be death to be hit with the ship's lead.
tempap	tampar	the palm of the hand, to slap; *satempap*, a handbreadth.
tempelak		to confront.
tempias		to beat in (rain), exposed to the storm.
tempong	kampong	cluster (stars), clump (trees), cluster (houses).
tempuan	tempuan	the passage in a Dyak house from end to end, the thoroughfare.
temu, nemu		to know, understand, to discover, find by accident; *nadai temu aku*, I do not know; *enda temu edup*, he does not know how to live.
temuai, nemuai		visitor, to pay a visit.
temuda	temuda	young jungle.
temuku		to knot: *udah temuku ka tali*, he has knotted the string.
tengah, nengah	tengah	to traverse, pass through, go between, follow a beaten path and figuratively to follow a precedent, established custom; *anti ai langkang enda tau tengah merau, jalai orang nengah aku*, wait for the water to ebb, there is no way through for the boat, go along by me.
tenggau	paké	to use, wear; *kati udah enggau dé?* have you done using it? *panjai sirat laka enda alah enggau*, the loincloth is long and so that it cannot be worn.

Sea Dyak, Malay and English Vocabulary. xli.

Sea Dyak.	Malay (Colloquial).	English. Together with Examples of the use of the word.
tenggau	bersuloh, ñuloh	to torch ; *tenggau enggo api*, to light up fire brand.
tengkani	plihara	to feed (animals), rear (fowls, pigs, fish).
tengkebok	lobang	a hole.
tengkira	pakaian	personal effects, effects.
tengkuang		to quiver, vibrate, swing (lamp) ; *batang tengkuang*, the log sways ; *lampu tenkuangkuang*, the lamp keeps swinging about.
tengok	iris	to long, yearn, desire strongly.
tepak	uaktu	*tepak kami pindah tepak iya munoh orang*, at the time that we removed, at that time he killed a man.
tepan, nepan	inggapp, numpan	to settle (bees), to alight, perch (birds) ; *nepan prau orang*, to get into someone's boat.
tepang, nepang		to bewitch, to blight (with the evil eye).
tepanggai		aground, stranded, stuck fast, run aground.
terengkah		fixed, settled.
tiang		pole, post, mast; *tiang kapal*, a ship's mast.
tiap, niap	itong	to count up; *tiap ari*, every day; *tiap orang*, each man.
tibar	kibar	to cast net, to scatter (of seed).
tikai	tikar	mat.
tikal	lipat	to fold.
tikong, nikong	padam	to suppress, smother.
tikup, nikup	tutup	to close, shut ; *anang nikup pintu pendieng*, do not close the doors of your ears.
timbal, nimbal	jawab	to reply, answer, rhyme.
tinchin	chinchin	a ring for the finger.
tindok	tidor	to sleep.
tinggang		to fall upon ; *parai tinggang kayu*, crushed to death by fall of a tree.
tingik	tengkar	wrangle, quarrel.
tingkap	jatoh	to tumble down.
tinja		morsels of food that in eating get into hollow teeth.
tipan	lipat	to fold, fold up; *tipan pua*, fold up the blanket.
tipok	basoh	to lave ; *betipok moa*, to wash one's face.
titi, niti	kupak	to skin, flay, peel bark of a tree.
titih, nitih	ikut	to follow.
tisi	pinggir	brink, edge, frontier, border, fringe, skirt (jungle) ; *tisi menoa*, border frontier ; *tisi langit*, horizon.
tisil	gial	unlucky.
tisil	saiat	*tisil gundai*, to cut off.
trabai	telabang	shield.
trap	trusu	to stumble, trip.
tras	blian	iron-wood.
trebai	trebang	to fly.

Sea Dyak.	Malay (Colloquial).	English. Together with Examples of the use of the word.
trumbu		snag.
tua	kita dua	we two, us two, our two including person addressed; *aram tua bejalai*, come and let us two walk.
tuah		wind-fall, piece of luck, fortunate, God-send.
tuai	tuah	old, a chief, elder.
tuak	arrack	toddy.
tubai (tuba)	tuba	a plant, the juice of which is used to stupify the fish in a river; verb to fish with this juice.
tuboh		body, people, person; *bisi tuboh*, to be enciente.
tubu	rebong	edible shoots of the bamboo.
tuchol, nuchol	tunu	to burn; *nuchol umai*, burn the farm.
tuchong	puchuk	a peak, pinnacle, a shell; *tuchong simpurai*, bracelet shell.
tuchum	siñum	to smile.
tudoh	tiris	to leak, to drop (as water).
tugal		a dibbler used in planting, to dibble.
tujah		to explore, examine; *tujah enggo saugkoh*, to probe (the bottom of river) with spears, feel the bottom; *ambis ulu sungai tujah kami*, we have explored the whole of the head of the waters.
tukang		to open (door, window, or roofing).
tukang		a skilled workman.
tulat	tulat	day after to-morrow.
tulih		to acquire, obtain; *kami iban jagau penapat, umpai tulih ka akal*, we are an ignorant people and have not yet acquired cunning; *jai iban enda tulih ka utai*, a bad people cannot gain anything; *bangat enda tulih ka kresa*, can by no means obtain tools.
tumbit, numbit		to kick with heel.
tumboh	tumboh	to spring out of the ground (as plants), to grow up, to commence, begin; *dini endor tanjong tumboh?* where does the river bend begin? *umpai tumboh matapanas, datai din*, you will get there before sunrise; *ari ni tumboh jako?* how did the argument (words) originate?
tumbok	kali	to bury, to dig up the ground.
tumbong	lubang burit	the anus.
tunda, nunda	turut	to imitate.
tundi		to coax, cajole, to tease, mock.

Sea Dyak.	Malay (Colloquial).	English. Together with Examples of the use of the word.
tunga	tujuh	to turn towards, to aim at, to have an object, reason, cause ; *enti aku salah nadai tunga aku diau di menoa*, if I am in the wrong there is no reason why I should remain in the country ; *kati tunga ?* what is the reason ? *nama tunga baka 'tu ?* what is the meaning of this ?
tunggal		separately, one by one ; *tunggal*, single (adj.) ; *tunggal-tunggal*, singly, one by one (adv.).
tunggu, nunggu	hukum	to accuse, to lay a charge against ; to fine ; a fine ; *tunggu menoa*, a fine for an offence against the people in general ; *tunggu butang*, a fine for an offence against an individual.
tungkah	uaktu	what time ; *tungkah aku mudik kalu*, at such time as I go up river.
tungkal		perfidy.
tungkul	jantong	heart.
tungkun		to light (fire, cigarette), to kindle.
tungkup, nungkup	lunkup	to turn upside down, bottom upwards, to upset.
tunjok		finger, toe ; *tunjok jari*, finger ; *tunjok kaki*, toe.
tunlong		Brookei shell (helix).
tuntong, nuntong		to reach, arrive at.
tupi	ibun	nourish, maintain, keep, support (parents, &c.), of animals to domesticate.
tusok pendieng	krabu	an ear-ring (woman's).
tusu, nusu	insap	the breasts ; to suck, to suckle ; *ai tusu*, milk.
tutok, nutok		to pound, bruise.
tutus		to clip off (prepuce), to lop off (bough), to trim (vine) ; *tutus botoh*, to circumcise.
tuyu	paloi, bodo	silly, idiotic, crazy, half-witted.
uan nguan	ibun	to take care, occupy ; *besai ai skali, kati bisi nguan prau kitai ?* the river (water) is very high (great), have you anyone to look after our boat ? *nguan rumah*, to take care of, be in charge of the house.
ubong	benang	cotton thread.
uchu	chuchu	grand-child.
udah	sudah	it is done, expressed completion of action
udok	asu	dog
udu	kuat, kras, dras, bisa, kinchang	severely hard, strong ; *udu hendar iya bejamah*, he argued very vigorously ; *udu singat nya*, to be severely stung ; *udu ai*, water strong (current) ; *udu ribut*, wind is strong ; *udu jako*, loud talk.

Sea Dyak.	Malay (Colloquial).	English. Together with Examples of the use of the word.
uji	chob	to try, test, prove : *alau uji*, come and try.
ukai	buka	denial, it is *not* ; *ukai benama maioh*, he has not got many names.
ukoi	asu	dog.
ular	ular	snake.
ulieng	kamudi	rudder, helm.
ulih	dapat	to be able to, to get at ; *enda ulih-ulih*, absolutely unable.
ulit, ngulit		mourning, to throw into mourning.
ulu	ulu	interior (opposed to *ili*), up river, up country.
umai	uma	a farm (*paddy*).
umang	miskin	poor.
umbok	ugut, pejal	to urge, press, importune, to force, compel, oblige.
umpan	umpan	bait.
undai	udang sessar	shrimp, prawn.
undur	ilir	to descend (river).
unggoi		spleen.
ungkup	bhagian	share, division, portion, lot.
unjor	bujor	to stretch out (legs, &c.) ; lengthways (opposed to *mebintang*) ; alongside.
unsai	simbur, siram	to splash, splutter, syringe, sprinkle, to water flowers.
unus		bracelets of fine black fibre worn round the calf of the leg or upper arm.
uong	riam	rapid, water fall.
upa	umbut	the cabbage of a palm.
upah	gaji	reward, wages, bribe ; to bribe.
upun		pith of a dart.
utai	barang, ano	a thing, things.
utap		bark canoe.

A VOCABULARY

Collected by the late H. Brooke Low, Esq.

The locality not specified in the MS., but Mr. Hose informs me the Vocabulary is that of a Dialect of a Rejang River Tribe.—*H.L.R.*

English.	Dialect of Rejang River Tribe.	English.	Dialect of Rejang River Tribe.
alive	gosh	fowl	manok
alligator	bahaia	fruit	buah
ant	hieb	go	chib
banana	telui	gold	mas
belly	eg	hair	soöp
bird	chiap	hand	tig (i)
black	lengah	head	chauog
blood	lód	honey	tabal
blowpipe	belau	hot	bud
boat	prahu	husband	tau
body	tù	iron	besi
bone	tulag	jungle	masrok
child	kuad	large	menu
coco nut	ñor	leaf	sêlá
cold	dekad	male	baboeu
come	béï (madoh)	man	sil
day	jungiah	mat	apil
dead	tebus	moon	ghicheh, ghucheh
deer	rusa, penguin	mosquito	sebeg
dog	chuo	mother	oeng
drink	im org	mountain	jelmol
ear	ngentok	mouth	ñaäg
earth	tè	nail (finger-)	charōs
eat	chā	night	laûit
egg	làp	nose	merh
elephant	adon	pig	changgak
eye	mad	rain	ujan
face	kapō (au)	rat	tikus
father	boeu	rhinoceros	agab
feather	sentöl	rice	charoï
female	babō	river	tiu
finger	jarastig	root	tingtek
fire	ōsh		
fish	kañ		
flower	bunga		
foot	jñg		

English.	Dialect of Rejang River Tribe.	English.	Dialect of Rejang River Tribe.
salt	empoig	wife	kedŏl
sea	laut	wind	parug
seed	kebeu	woman	kedol
silver	perak	wood	jihu
skin	gelŏ		
sky	lahu	yesterday	hatab
sleep	selog		
small	mishong		
snake	taju	*Numerals :—*	
spear	bulush		
star	paloy	one	ser — né (nay)
sun	ish	two	dua — năl
		three	tiga (né) — nè *(sharp)* neh
thunder	engku		
tin	timah	four	ampat — ampat
to-day	naté	five	lima — lima
to-morrow	yakal	six	anam — anam
tooth	moin	seven	tujut — tujut
tongue	lantag	eight	lapan — lapan
tree	jihu	nine	sambilan
		ten	sepuloh, né-puloh
waistcloth	wĕb	eleven	né-blas
water	auk (ork)	twelve	năl-blas
wax	keluai	twenty	năl-puloh
white	biorg	one hundred	saratus

A COLLECTION OF VOCABULARIES MADE BY THE LATE H. BROOKE LOW, ESQ.

Where I have been able to do so I have filled in the English equivalents for the Malay by the help of CRAWFURD and others. It will be observed that the Kyan column is almost identical, where the same examples are given, as the Kayan column of ST. JOHN, which speaks well for general accuracy. The Punan and Pakatan columns are also very similar, but not so identical: considering the wandering character of this tribe this is not to be wondered at.—H.L.R.

MALAY (Colloquial).	ENGLISH.	KANOWIT.	KYAN.	BINTULU.	PUNAN.	MATU.
abas	to reconnoitre		kasip	tepán		
abu	ashes		mok	mu-kau		
achap	to overflow	suboh	liñap	adät	ñaän	nuan
ada	to have (possess)	bin	té	taré		
adat	ceremony, custom		bariek	paré, panak		
adih	younger brother		harin, harik, harim	mapun		
adih-kaka	elder brother (?)		peharin	temuok		
aga	to visit	tengoh	pala	ajar		
agas	gnat		hamok	tumbak		
ajar	to correct, teach	nujau	pekalé	akál		
ajok	to poke	tebak	metoh, tenujak			
akal	wisdom					
akan	future		sang	vakah		
akar	root	akai	akah	akau	oak, nuak	akau
aku	I	ako	akui			
akun		akun	ma-apah			
alah	to lose			alah		alah
alang-alang	name of a tall grass		hang-hang	pasu		ririeg
alih	to change	balé	udé	tepá		apan
alu	pestle	tepá	aló	alap; ghi, apan	pen	mun
ambil	to fetch, get, take	apan	ala, api	raput		
ambun	dew, mist		áp	pis		
ampah	to chaff		upeh	lun		ikar
ampar	to spread out	irat	kah			

Malay (Colloquial)	English	Kanowit	Kyan	Bintulu	Punan	Matu
ampas	fling, dash down	per	so	pat		
ampat	four		pat	masi		
ampun	pardon	pejak	asi			
amput			tama			
anak	child		anak	anak		
anak ampang	youth		an-kawá	an-ubo		jimanak
anak-biak	retainer of a chieftain (?)			an-disi		
anak buah	adopted child		pañin	anak paré		
anak ihru	son		an-among	an-iro; an-among		
anak laki	daughter		an-laké	an-manai		
anak perampuan	orphan		ad-doh	an-redo		
anak pernakan	branch of a river		an-nakán	an-menakán		
anak piatu	son-in-law (? step-son)		an-hula	ula		
anak sungai			hangat	ipak sungai		
anak tiri			an-tuack	an-tebas		
anam	six	lungoh	nam	ánam		
añam		lasu	mañam	añam		
anchur	to dissolve	hariu	linoh	ñuño		
angat	hot	tukah	lasu: hanit	pedi	blau	pangai
angin	wind	makat	di	bahué	pawi	
angkat	to stare	pasui	leka			
angkut	to get up, rise, lift up	sidap	biti, tang	ivieng		akat
angus	to carry		masoh	makut		asoi
ani ani	scorched		tutong	megó		sidah
ano	white ant	ngino	tané	anai		
ansoh	in trying to recollect (anso—to seek)		iré			
antah	know, do not		ilo, pebeh	sigau		pinang
antar	to bring	jujoh	jaeh	antad		
antara	between, apart		matar	temelan		
			hang			

antu	spirit	tó	tó	antu	raman
añut	to drift with tide	maman	mañor		wanau
apa	what (inter.)	nau	nun	nu	apoï
api	fire	apui	apui	apui	
arab		arab	kinah		
arang	charcoal		lusang		
ari-ari	groin		retup		aro
arok			angah		
arong	channel			embob	
asah	sharpen	asah		alo	
asal	origin		masa	masá	
asap	smoke	tugun	puhu	asal	
asu	dog	as-o	lisun	sab	as-au
atap	thatch		asó	aso	
atas	above		kapo (leaf);	sapau; sapau	
			kepang (shingle)	kepang	
ati	liver	amo	husun	bau	amau
atur (ator)	to arrange		kenap	kena	ator
au	ho, holloa (?)			ator	
auk	owl		ai		
aus	thirsty (?)		mekong	ok	
awal	early		megang bā		siéng
awan	cloud		iñaup; pesor	awal	awan
ayam			avun	temaai, avus	
ayer	water	siau	hiñap	sezau	anum
		danum	ata (drinking water),	bā	
			telang (juice,		
			gravy); danum	iyo	
			(river water)	danum	
ayer bah	flood	anum subo	danum sohô	ba	
ayer besar			danum aia	ba reni	
ayer kemeh	to make water	anum toōn	telang hugit	meneni	
ayer kring			taga	tombó	
ayer maàni			telang dut	ba temes	ngát

Malay (Colloquial)	English	Kanowit	Kyam	Bintulu	Punan	Matu
ayer madu	clarified honey	lieng, singat, danum	telang hingat	ba juá		
ayer masin	salt water		ata mi	ba pelis		
ayer pasang	flood tide		uap	ba mood		
ayer surut	ebb tide		melah	ba menat		
ayer tawar	fresh water		ata beleh	ba paád		
babal	ignorant					babal
babas	low grassy jungle		talun	mengag		
babi	hog, pig	babui	utieng (*domestic*), bavui (*wild*)	talun bakas	habui	baboi
badak	rhinoceros		temedoh	temedo		
badal	gizzard		belalang			
badan	human body	biah, ñawah	loöng	usa		
bagaimana	how	kemo wa	nuno	lak embah		
bagus	good	jiá	saio	dezá		daáu
bah	flood (?) bedding (?)		sohó	tumbu		beloh; bam
bahu			ligan	karib		
baiar (utang)	pay	sera sakai	jia	barai	jian	baiar
baik	well, good	jiá	bahári	deza		jiá
baja	plough (? steel)		basong			
baju	coat, jacket	bajau	lupak	bajau		bajau
bakat	waves of a rapid		aio	ilai	ikang	
bala	people, war party	lasau (*counting*), balang	balang; iong (*counting*)	tingan (*counting*)		
balang	(? count)					
balas	recompense, revenge	malé	iulé	valo		
balu	widow		bálo			

bañak	many, plenty	buna	mahom, ngahom, kahom	ninâ	kadida (*subs.*), dida (*adj.*)
bandéra	flag		lujok		
bangké	corpse	kabesán	paté	patai	bukang
bango	name of a stork		kuso	papo	
bangun	awake	pegah	maaur	mai	pegah
bahir			lalir	lalid	
bantal	bolster	luan	helan	tegulau	luan
bapa	father	ama	amé, tamé, taman, tamam, tamak	tama	amah
bapa tiri	step-father		taman tuah		
barang	goods, personal property		davan	barang	
barangka li	perhaps	barang tupo			
basah	moist	hasah	apah	vasá	basá
basi	mouldy		basa		
basoh	to wash	musoh	bangé	usé	us-o
batak	haul	uyut	nlaio, maäng	tegang ; nat	
batang ayer	main stream of river		mejiat	tuto tengo	
batok	cough	ngikat	iong	pikad	pikad
batu	rock	bato	nikar	bato	
batu pegang			bató	dudok	
bau	shoulder (?)	bun	sada	vau	
bawa	to bring	ighi	bu	meghi	ighi
bawah	below (subordinate)	iba	gri	lebu	iba
bechara	dispute, case		hida		
bedil	gun		tetangaran	becharà	besarah
begini	how ? how	kidu	benin	bedil	bedil
begintir			nuni	lach iya	batan ieh
begitu	(*bagitu* thus)	kihi	peseliwé		
bego	hue and cry		nutih	lach iré	
bekal	baskets used on war expeditions	pingá	búka		batan idun
			ngoyo	valun	

li.

Kanowit, Kyan, Bintulu, Punan and Matu Vocabularies.

Malay (Colloquial)	English	Kanowit	Kyan	Bintulu	Punan	Matu
bekas	leavings		laān	san		bas
belah	pull in two	pàk	biang, miang	muba	béta	bah
beli		melé	melé	melé		melé
belum	not yet, even if	agat	jian pah	aa gala, malum		nebé angah
benang	cotton thread		talé	benang		
benantu			ivan			
benar	indeed, true	seno	lan	toò		atang
bengal			mádang	midang	buluok	
bengis			mádang			
bengkak	(swollen ?)	matus, matong	betong	vā		
bengkok	crooked	piko	kawi	bingkok		piko
benih	seed (corn)		upan (paddy seed)	upan		
bentuah			ivan	ivan		
benua	country, patria	tang	dalé	paré		betaāi
beradih	(relations ?)		peharin			
berak	to pass excrement	mené, meni	siba			
beranak		menganak	nganak	menganak		
berang	angry (?)		hiño	ranan		
berbantah	wrangle					besingil
berbini	(? berbunyi=jingle)	pesawa	nahawa	pesaba		
berbuni	marry a wife	berserau				
berdagang	to trade		pebelé			
berdaiong		betuna				
berdiri (verb)	to place upright	kedang	nakrieng (stand), biti (stand up)	badazong	nakérieng	tigar
berdiri	upright, perpendicular, to erect a building	redang	tegrang	merié		
berebut	to quarrel	meramah	īilé	pesisi		pedalo
bergagut		pesiin	tiga	pesingin		
bergegar	floored with planks		ngedar			

berguru	play, to chase in play	betujau, siliek	pekisó	prui	betujau
berhenti	to wait, stop	luit	nglarah nungol	pusod	
beribat			paio	pejijan	padang
berikut	to chase	pelirieng	tepurong	pebivo	pamat
berjalan	to walk	melakau	pano	melakau	makau
berkayoh	(paddle)	melá	besé	meda	bepelah
berklahi	(*berklai*=fight with)	pedalo		bedalo	
berkendak	commit adultery	bakut	pékatóyang	bekelo	peramas
herkuap	mouldy		ngavong		
bernang	swim	plangoi	ñatong	pringoi	turun
beroko		peroko		peroko	peroko
beronde	commit adultery	pemakut, pebakeh	pevákeh		bekelo
bertemu	meet	ñakai	pehabong		
beruma	to farm	aioh	ñadui	minjab	
berutang	owe (debt)	gelegoan	ngutang		aiang; ñat
besar	great	tigah; seno	aia; aian (*subs.*sire)	azah, azang	
besi	iron		tité	malat	
betul	just		marong	tigah	tigah
				batin	
betin		alin	dara	meli	
betah	(*kapaias*=fruit)		tudak lulod (*shin*), nurieng (*shin*)	betas, ai	
betis	calf of leg				
bhaghi	share, divide	pido	petular	pinjun	
bhaghian	division	pido	petular	injun	ubas
bharu	new, again	ubah	marieng	vau	
bhasa	language		dahun	kaup	
biak	young	jimanak	ñam	disi	imiet
biasa	accustomed to	pulai, besa, pakijjar	malé	malai	basa
biawak	*iguano*	mujun	parang	kamerad	huong muso
bibir	lips		husung (*upper*), hiveh (*lower*)	bivi	

Malay (Colloquial).	English.	Kanowit.	Kyan.	Bintulu.	Punan.	Matu.
bighi (biji)	kernel, nut, seed	baha mata	uang (*kernel*) uang mata	amad mata		bras
bighi mata	eye-ball			betá		
bikin	make	ñan	ni	tena-au		mena
bila	when	pidan	hiran	mezap		pidan
bilang	to count	iap	mujap	amin		
bilik	room	bilick	amin			lok
binatang	(? beast)		tular	baji		
binchi	hatred	besé	tegal	saba	awan	
bini	wife	sawah	hawak, hawam, hawan			
bintang	star (?)	hetoán	krawieng	bintang		bitang salang
binturun	name of one of the *Mustelidæ*		kitan	betuan		blangah
biras	related by marriage		biang			
biru	blue		biru, ñemit (*sky-blue*)	biru	letuán	biru
bisa	poisoned	mágahán	lait	bisa		
bisak	hole, torn	sirat	birak, mirak	melelak		
bisik	to whisper	singau	pehivok	puñek		
bisok		lau masok	jima	sebab		song naäh
bisu	dumb	ubal	hamang	mubal		
bisul	(*bisól.* boil), to boil		tuku	pesá		
blajar	learn	likut	pekalé	pulong		
blakang	man's back	ták	laong	likod		
bliong	adze or axe	beseloh	asé	hadong		butah
bluku			kelóng, batong			
bochor	to leak		pesit			
bodo	foolish	suo	mengaaúh	mengag		
bottle	bottle		buri klingé			
hoyah	moth		savat			

brahi	brave	moōn	livang	sakat	moōn	jinau
brani	how much	jino	lakin	braé	piro	bras
brapa	husked rice	bahar	kuri (?)	vas	ba	brat
bras	heavy	brat	baba	vat	uo	joh
brat	to give	pubé	bahat	muju	mékan	susi
bri			mai			britah
brisih	news		maāng			turé
brita		dingar	dingah	rengā	mudi	
britan		turé	muré	pulen		
brok	bear	bedok	humang	vadok		bruang
bruang	fruit	makup	buang	bebang	bohuang	bua
buah	calf	buah	bua	ong		
buah betis			hitat			ihat
buang	to throw away	penana	bat, so	sau	tsiu	baiah
buaya	alligator	baia	baia	baza	buai	
bubok	weevil		belabūkan	suvok		
bubu	fish trap		buvo	uvao		
bubus	to have a hole in		habut	metos		
bubut	the crow pheasant			ivo		
bui	froth			stā		
buiya			lurak	sua		
bujang	unmarried		pegé	pussi		
bujok	coax	ngelilo	laké, ñam			bujok
buka	to open	kap	pekalok	ukab	tugong	sukab
bukit	mountain	jugut	tengaáp	meted		gunong
buku	joint		ngalang			
buku ali	ankle	pulieng	bukong	bukieng tumid		
buku tangan	knuckles	buko pang	akieng tudak	bukieng agam		
bula	false	mesebé	bukong ujo	jagoi		
bulan	moon	bulan	pamoh	bulan	bulan	hudé
bulat	convex	gulong	bulan	pelelang		bulan
bulih	to get	mala	buloōng, sinong	kala		
bulih	may, to be able		ala, kelan			
			haman, dang			

Malay (Colloquial)	English	Kanowit	Kyan	Bintulu	Punan	Matu
buloh (bulu)	bamboo	bulo	bulu	vuló		
hulu	hair, down, feather	bulu likau	bulo	vulao		
bulu mansu kemieng	eyebrow		kusap liko	kedidat		
bulu mata	eyelash	bulu mata	kusap mata	vulo mata		bedak
bumi	free-man	pañin	hipui	bumé		
bunga	flower	bedak	pidang	bunga		
buñi	sound		hmoh			beno
bunoh	to kill	kubé	meté	pesu		
buntin	pregnant	betebé	mali	mebé		
buntu	pot-bellied	senubut	aia butit			
buntut (?)	tail, end (?)		avut (*island*)			
burit	human buttocks	kabut	avut	avut		
burok	rotten		maram	burok		manok
burong	bird	manok	manok	manok	jangé	
buru	to drive away, compel	selarau	uga	guga		
busok	putrid, stinking	madim	butong	burok		
buta	blind	mutup	buta	peset	pésuok	
buti	*papaya* (?), *buti*=piece, log (*buto*=penis)		butieng			
butoh		buto	buto utin	vutoh	butu	
chabang	fork	panga	hangat	pipak		jabi
chabi	chilies, capsicum		sebeh	lada		dot
chabut	to draw out, to pull up	abok	nubit, metat	tegang		jaät
chachat	blemish			jarau		
chaching	worm (stomach-)	puba	lak-han			
chakap	talk	jingiloh, kelang	duan	bekaup		
champur	to mix		pehvar	paaur		

chadang	gong (treble tone)			
changkir	cup			piñang
chari	to search	ngino, kino	penganak	
chawan	saucer		ilo; pebeh	
chawat	men's loin cloth	bai	bah	sanang
chayer	liquid (?), *chaya*=bright		lamá lalé	sigau
chekak			mangal	bigo
chémé	one-eyed		sirang	taáp
cherdik	wise, crafty		lalé duan	
cheri	to feel, taste	kuñam	nesak	rurak
cherindok	(Dyak hat ?)	lip	haung	
cherita	history		na long	cherdiek
chermin	*cheremin* = looking glass		klingé	tuñam, ñam
cherré			puli; pelaát	saaung
chichak	house lizard	peká	selawit	
chimburu			ñivohó	cheramin
chinchang	to hack, to cut in pieces	sesap	nesav	pesau
chinchin	finger-ring	krisieng	hisir	tetak
chium	kiss, to smell	panak	parak, arak	ñivaáu
choba	to try, test	ago	sak	susab
chuchi	to cleanse, wash	usok	maio	sisieng
chuchu	grandchild		so	angus
chukup	complete, full, enough	pádá	dang; pudang	tuñam
chukur	to shave	kikih	ñepitieng	musié
chundong	slanting	mila, kat. sudai	ñuhui	azam
chunto				sadang
churi	to steal	tikau	nako	mugo
				beseloi
				teruan
				meñikau
dada	breast	usok	busok	usok
daging	flesh	sin	sin	sé
dahan	branch of tree		daán	anggap
dahi	*dai* forehead	langang	liko	tukok

moñiong

iveg

saong

liko

supi
kuñam
seraaung

seré

titig
isieng
adak

susi
sau
pada

suan
tikau

Malay (Colloquial).	English.	Kanowit.	Kyan.	Bintulu.	Punan.	Matu.
dahun		duun	daun, jela (blade of paddle)	raōn	dauun	
dalam	deep	teban	dalam	dalám		tumal; katumal (depth)
damar	resin	tulé	lutong	tulé		tulé
damun			sapitang			
dango	a house on a farm		lepo	lepau		
dano			bawang	babang		
dapat	get	mala	ala; kelan dang	kala		kenah
dapat	possible / impossible		jian dang lé			
dapat	able / unable	nam letoh	jian lé	kala		keban
dapur	fireplace or cookhouse	daput	avó	á kala		
dara	maid	jimanak mero	doh ñam	paro		
darah	blood	darah	dahá	redoh pusa		dará
darat	dry land, shore	daiah	tana pegieng	ñi		daiah
dasan	a place	sawa	havan	raza		kedau
datang	to come	labé	atang	naá		labé
datu (nini-)	forefathers		huku	iukat	lamok	
dekat	close, near	sega	jélang	tepo	dékin	sega
demam	fever	medam	medam	dani		
dengki=envy				mendam; tenan		
deri	from	keman	man	ñivañu		
destar		bulang	lavong	teri		kuman
dia	he, him, she, her, it		hia		batok	
diam	be quiet	luit	melo	bereman		kedap
diam	dwell		melo	menda		petad
di-atas	upon, above	amau	husun	belebau		
dia orang	they		dahaló			

di-bawah	under, below floor	ibá	hida		butah
di-blakang	behind	likot	baleh		ruang
didalam	within		halam		
di-hulu			hudiek		
diki		tikát	nakar		butah
di-laut			hauh		jawai
diluar	without, outside	awin	awa		
di-muka	in front, before		jinawa		dingah
dinding	wall		lidieng		
dingan	with	sakai	dahin		
dingan kau			dahim		toieng
dingan sahya (*com-pare* kata sahya)			dahiek		demal
dingar	hear	kinam	nerieng	nglengo	badi
dingin	cold	singiam	laram; hngam	belarum; singiam	
dini-hari	daybreak		jelang dŏ		mejad
di-tengah	amidst	dreh	belua		
dras	powerful; rapid		kasi		
dua	two		dua	duo	suné
dualapan	(*delapan*=eight?)		saia		mungo
dudi	behind	mudé	baia	muré	
duduk	to sit down	kedau	meló	murong	siéng
dudun	bosom friend	avop	sevila		
dulu	first, before (place or time)	oné	uná; arieng	sumoi	dua
dukun	doctor		daieng		
duri	thorns	durai, duré	ulang		
durian	durian		dian	rué	
				pakán	
embawa			bé (v.), bé (*load, subs*)	meghi	
enda	(will not?)	belé	jian		

Malay (Colloquial)	English	Kanowit	Kyan	Bintulu	Punam	Matu
endang			petato	kabagag		
empawa			teláwa	ratah		
empran			datah			
entah			jaeh	sedaian		
entilan			lepau	gan		
entran	shaft	gah; lasau	putang			
entuyut			tangghi noyan			
gadieng	ivory		bala	gadong		ayer laut (?)
gadong	green		gadong	velas		rio, sigah
gadoh (gadah)	noise, disturbance		liawan	gagau		
gago	to stir, to bother	serawan	nikiek, nghadvi	tidan		
gaji	(gaja = elephant)	upah	tibah			
gampang	easy (? to be in a hurry)	seripa	kign			
ganti	replace	silih, sang	ngalui	gati		
gantong	hang on peg	tebink	hendang	iak		
garah	loose (not fast)		ngobak	gelua	usien	siah
garam	salt	siah	hnia	tiam		
garu	to scratch	pagaiyut	ngatal	gazau		
gatal	to itch	gatan	katal	mekeli		
gauk	mischievous		bulieng	melaña		
gêbieng			nakaiong			
gegar	to shake (shiver)	gegar	ngedar	gagezap		
geletiek	tickle	pitak	sakirah	mitak		
geli	(gali = dig)			meghien		mikah
gemok	fat, stout			batengan	labu	mesin
genggam	to clutch in one's hands	piong	madong hnggam (open handful)	makop		

gentu	pick (flowers), pluck (leaves)	puté	isé	bakaran	igá
gerak	mad (?)	pegah	goh, megoh	guga	
ghila	chew	bangan	bulieng	pejog	
ghiña	tooth	ñipan	ñepa	ñipan	ñipé
gigi	to bite	gegat	ipa; gaäm (molars)	subot	
gigit	(giling — grind by hand)	matang	maät		
gilieng					
glumbang	quake, quiver	bangat	bangat	lavak	bangat
glumo		pedak	pang, mepang	dudun	goyut
goyang			meghiong	maghilong	
gretak			palang	titai	tengó
gru	neck	laboh	kra	vatok	
guar	stir	balun	ngaäuh	mai	lulun
gugur	to fall down		legrak	belavo	
gulong	to roll up		lemulun	koóng	
gumpul	to assemble, collect		pang, mepang	dudun	
guna	useful	tega	tuman	meted	jato
gunong	hill	gusoh	ngalang	maied	kulong
gusok	(gosok, to rub)	dedohan	muso	tegor	guna
guntur	thunder	midi	blaré	lubi	litoh
guring	lie down	lohoi	miri	mumbang	midi
gusar	angry	lasit	manó	lalad	belag; patang
gusi	the gums		sin ipan		
habis	finished	gelé, geleh	pah	go	majih
halus	fine, thin		lani (smooth)	halus	
hari	time	lau	dó		tamu
hari	day	lau	dó	dau	
hari dahulu	day before yesterday		dó ji atih	dau ji dau	
hari, dini hari	dawn		jelang dó		

Malay (Colloquial)	English	Kanowit	Kyan	Bintulu	Punan	Matu
hari, isok	to-morrow	lau jibrah	dō jima	sebab		
hari kamarin	yesterday		dohálam	sié		
hari, lebah-hari	evening		dō levi	dau ji ah		lau hinan
hari lusa	day after to-morrow	lau jibrah	dō ji	dau mara plaké		
hari satengah naik	about 9 or 10 a.m.		dō ñirang	dau bau		
hari, tengah-hari	(*satengah hari*=noon)		dō negrang			
hari tulat	three days hence		dō ji aia			
hari satengah tur- un	(*turun*=sunset)		dō nihaiah	dau lemengut		
héran	astonished		lipang			
hilir	to descend a river (to recede, abate)	kaba	ñiauh	patong	mio	kaba; tumad kaba
hukun	to punish, fine		tuang		levo	
hulu	interior of country		aur	oŏd		tuā
ibu	aunt	tinak	hiné	kamina		
ibun	take care of, nourish	udong	penga	mipa	urong	udong
idong	nose	mudip	urong	urong	murip	mudip
idup	to live	brah	murip	murip		
ighir			ong, batong (*fruit*), liap (*beads*)	ong		
ijo			gadong	ijau		
ikak		jien	lian	menggah		
ikan	fish	peké	masiek	enjen	baso	ikan
ikat	to fasten, to be together in counting	seloh	katong, natong	mikad		bad
ikur	tail	ikui	loong	apah		
ikur			ikoh; don (*tail-plumes*)	ikoi		
ikut	to follow	tikui	ngovaia, livoh	sun		

ilang	to lose	nihau	padé	tā
inang	nurse (*mamma?*)	tinak	pekurip	piman
ingar	noise	scrawan	ñawan	velas
ingat	to remember	ñidang	livang	suñid	ingat
inggan	as far as		dang	
inggap	to light upon	tegap	nerekap	tegap	ieh
ingus	mucus		irak	redo
ini	this	hi	hané	ia
ipah		nipah	pavang	maáb	lugu
ipar	brother- or sister-in-law		hango	sabai	irib
irit			bé	maieng
isa			ñirut, nisip (*suckle*)	susip (*suck*), suba (*inhale*)
isap	to suck, to smoke	sisip		sé	sin
isi	flesh, meat	sin	sin	jupan	sisi
sisi	fill		pudang	mitam	bilam
itam	black	bilam	pitam	mezap	idun
itong	to count up	iap	mujap	inah	iyo	itong
itu	that (dem. pron.)	ido	ateh		
iya	yes		ai		
jadi	become, accomplished	ñadin		jadé	
jalor	to watch, take care, expect		nesul	alod	
jaga				jaga	
jagong	maize		jilé baha	jagong	
jagu	chin	jaá	jaá	jaá betaáud	jeté
jahat	bad	jiek	jaák	jaás	
jai	cursed	jiek	jaák	jaás	jaáit
jait	sow cloth	milit	jimahot	pejait	ñā
jangan	do not	gap	asam	lu	dong

Malay (Colloquial).	English.	Kanowit.	Kyan.	Bintulu.	Punan.	Matu.
janggut	beard		bulo jaā	janggut		
janji	to promise, bargain, agreement	pejanji	pejanji	jañi		
jarang	scarce	ganang	mijat	jarang		
jari	finger	berangau	ikieng	juju		berangau
jari ibu	thumb	jerangau pau	bateval		kuso tutu	
jari kapur	first finger	jerangau ijo	ujoh		kuso as-a	
jari antu	middle finger	jerangau bebak	ujoh belua		kuso belua	
jari manis	third finger	jerangau durik	ikieng benua		kuso	
jari enchingan	little finger	jerangau ingih	ikieng ok		kuso ikieng	
jari kaki	toe		ikieng tudak			
jarum	needle	toé	lu	jujo ai		
jatoh	fall down	laboh	legak	taju		
jauh	distant	meju	tsu	belavo		jañ
jawab	to reply			jau	mosu	urai
jemur	(*jemu* satisfy)	muré	kledo	suai		aroh
jera				matdau		
jeraia	pathway	sawa	alan	menjaā		
jeramé	an old farm, young jungle		baié	jilu		
				talun		
jerang	(*jering* net, toils)	mida	nā apui	jujag		
jerat	noose		hatoh	maā		
jerneh	clear (water)		tenieng			
jikalo	if		khā			
jilat	lick	ñila	ñila	meñila, sila		
jimat	amulet		jimat			
jinak	tame, quiet (sound sleep?)	lumak, meté	malé	madelun		
jual	sell	jajah	mabat, bat	pebelé		jajah
julieng	cross-eyed		mingit			

Kanowit, Kyan, Bintulu, Punan and Matu Vocabularies.

jumpah	meet				
jungkar	outside platform of house				
e					
juran	fishing-rod	boh	sa	pehabong	
jurieng					
ka	towards		jango	gan silam	ka
ka-hulu				teriset	
kabun	garden	kajo		moöd	kadaiah
kadarat	rich	beram	man, pala	tiná	
kaia		kanaiah	mudiek	raai	
kaiap		kaia	lida tuvu	kaia	
kail	fish hook	piki	bahé		
kain	cloth	tarup	ke uriek	pesé	
kait		sebit		kluma	
kajang	dressed palm for thatch		kawit	kawit	kajang
kak			klubong	klubong	klubong
			kak	kajang	
kaka	elder brother		harin aia	redo (*swivel*),	
kaki	foot	paä	kasa(*instep*),tudak	jula (*gobs*)	betis
			(*leg, foot*)	teká	
kala	scorpion		deripan ketip	ai	
kalaparun	hunger		lian	katib	
ka-laut		kaba	bahauh	melaau	
kali	often, times	ulé	harat	baai	kawir
kaliatan	view	napak	tula	ulieng	kali
kalintit		pejelat	teregak ; ito		
kamah	(? dirty)	mama	masap	ten	
kamana	whither	kahan	hino	jemi	
kamarin	yesterday	loumai	dahálam	tembah	
kamaro	draught		taga	sié	
				peles	lau sabé

Malay (Colloquial)	English	Kanowit	Kyan	Bintulu	Punan	Matu
kamatian	death		paté			
kambing	goat		kadieng	kambieng	kadieng	
kami	we	mé	kami teló	melo	kipat	ulin
kamudi	rudder		muṭę́	ulen	pengulin	suné
kamudian			baja	mendé		
kampong	Malay village	turé	naán uma	kampong		
kanan	right hand		botáau			
kanji	rice water	taau	telang ranan	taáu	tau	aian atang
kapada	at (Latin apud)	tengo	man pala			
kapala	head	ulau	koḥong (rapids), lusong (islands)	ulo	utok	ulau
kapan	shell	keñat	kong kiñat			
kaparat	to slip into	tenam, kabilang	kaparat	apô		kaparat
kapur	lime		apoh	kaám	béño	karam
karam	to sink	káram	kaham	nás		
karangan	writing (?)		naha			
karat	rust		higan			
karoh	muddy, thick		patak	kevo		
karong	bag		karong	uzut		
kasar	rough, coarse		kudal (coarse), kahi (rough) siban	kasar		
kasi	to sneeze	kanai				
kasia	hither	masé	mási	masi		
kasi-han	love, kindness	kahai!	binih!	tiá!		kieh! kidé!
kasitu!	hither			kaup		uba
kata	to speak					
kata dia	he speaks	kuña	kurin-na	kaup no		
kata kau	you speak	kuam	kurim			
kata orang	the people speak	kuña	kurin dahár			
kata sahya	say, think	kuã	kuriek			

katak	frog		bunang uak	atab
katup	shut, close	itom	kap	nô	mau; kaáu
kau	thou	no	im	kazo
kayu	timber	kayo, lasau (country)	kaio	
kawan	companion, follower	sakai	dahin, hatoh	sakai	ko
kebok		selepak	ngawak	kabok
kechil	little, small, young	isit	ok	disi	isut
kejam		ajap	mijap	aram
kekal	lasting, still	agat		kakál
kela	by and bye, just now (future)	naáh	mahaup	nga	nô
kelala		kelala	nerana	kamila
keliling		peklieng	petak aiak	bukalilieng
kembang	swollen, to swell		betong	kambang
kemeh		murók	singit	meneni
kena	hit, mark	buiya	gá ; mega	luká
kenal	acquainted with			suñed
kenang	recollect a person	meñidang	livang	suñed
kendur		deko		pelok
kenieng			liko	kadidat
kentut	(? satiated)		ketut	muput
kepa			laé	vaäng
kepieng			liap	
kepong	to pursue	taban	livoh	matang	sud
kerat	to sever	kirit	munang (cut in two)	mebieng	ták
kerbau			kerbo	kerbau
kerukoh		béé	baié	
keti	to strike a light			mengitiek
ketiak	arm-pit	kelepa	lekarak	pipa
kijang	deer (medium sized)	poi	telaaú (smaller), saho (larger)	pabás	kijang
kikis	scrape		meki	

Malay (Colloquial)	English	Kanowit	Kyan	Bintulu	Punan	Matu
kilan	span		puhak	taäng		
kilat	lightning	sekalit	bekilat	beli		kiñir, kelat
kiñang		beso	besoh	beso		besoh
kinchalang			tingang	berenggang		
kinchang	strong			pejin		
kiri	left hand	bulai	boholé	bulai	bulé	bulai
kirim	to send	prihit	kato, pekato	peghi		
kita	you (singular)		iká	ikau		melau
kita	ye (plural)		keló	nyilo		telau
kita	we		kami telo	melo		buko
kladi	curtain	buko	lué	saä		klamu
klambu	coco-nut	klamu	klambu	klambu		
klapa	(? butterfly)		ñoh	viño		
kléba	bat	sababang	hñap to	kababak		bekuriek
kluang	to go out	semawa	rawat			
kluar	pond	luat	musang	kebai		keban
kolam	able (physically)		bawang	teba		korang
kongang	less, wanting	neto	lé	merigah		
korang	fort (palisades)	korang	korang	korang		tighi
kota	(? dirty)		kerahan			
kotor	ape	royat	masap	jemi		
kra	marsh, swamp		brok	kuzad	mao	saieh
krapa	hard, powerful	moó, kreh	laho	anas		
kras	work, employment	pekrejah	mahieng	tui		
kreja	red ant		ñadui; hadui	kreja		
krengga	sweet potato	kelé	belesó	tubeg		muang
kribang	dry	bahang	uvé	ubé vakah		
kring	eye-lid	kerukup mata	megang	metui		
krubong mata	gravy		blanit mata	kulit mata		
kuah			telang			

kuala	iron pan	léput	lang	menanga		kalé
kuali	always; strong, loud	udau malat	tarieng tité	kabah		mejad
kuat	to pinch	sagam lagah	intan lé	pejin		
kubit		ghitin	ngital	kubit		
kudong	strong (lasting)		putul	pugan		
kukoh	nail, hoof	silo	kaha mahieng	nieraän		silau
kuku	skin, leather (? flesh)	kulit	hulo	silo	ilu	kulit
kulit			laa, blanit (skin), anit (hide)	kulit		
kumbang	mason bee, beetle		abang	kabahang		
kuning	yellow	mehi, sak	kunieng	kunieng		kunin
kuntum		masé				
kupak	to skin, flay, peel	mukiep	méghit	kuka		
kurap	ringworm (? scrofula)		meki	kuás		
kurong	(? cage)		blatong			
kurus	lean, thin	megé	ñiwang	maeg	maii	maäs
kusieng			pedan			
kutu	louse	gutau	kuto	kutao		kutau
labang			keravang	mapu		
labi			teliap	lavai	klavang	
lacho						
laghi	more, besides	agat, balé (again)		malum		udi
laiang	fly	saiap, bekan, adap	tepiii	anodá		silap
lain	distinct	lahau	dap	nielutu	érup	waké
laiyu	faded (dry)	seli	klubé, lumé	menjuok	mesélé	
laju	to move quickly	sawan	nian	vana		
laki	husband		laké akui, hawam, hawa			
laki-laki	male	lai	laké	manai	elé	lai

Malay (Colloquial).	English.	Kanowit.	Kyan.	Bintulu.	Punan.	Matu.
laku	to pass (be current), in request			laku		
lalat	a fly	langau	lango	kezas		katah
lalu	in excess	laloh	lalo	n:eli		danah
lama	long time	alin	darā	mena	mango	katah
lama	old, not new	puin	uná	meli		
lambat	slow, long or late (time)	ilok-alin	dara			
landak	porcupine		ketong	tetong		
lañé	bee		hingat, tañid	mutit		
langit	sky	langit	langit	langit	langit	
lansang	rotten, putrid	madim	butong	burok		
lansat			lasat	benan		
lanté	(? floor, lath)		klasah	letai		
laotieng	raft		akit			
lapar	hungry	jelak	laô	melaäu	palé	
lapis	plait, fold		petebin	telap		
larang	to forbid	ngené		kudá	mepéra	
larong		lungun	lungun	larong		burau
lari	flee, run	burau	lap	buau	buau	
lasak	bald		lasang	blasak		
lautan	high sea	aba	kala, han	raât		
lawan	contrary to	lawán	sakat	melawan		japan abai
lebah-hari	evening	aio	do levi	dau bū		
lébar	broad		berang (*width*)	azang		
lebat	close (thickset)		bava (*rain*), jama (*fruit*)	mekuót		
lebih	more (comparison)	lebih	huin	lebi		lebih
legu	wrist		akieng leku	geluan		

leber	neck	tengó			gelegah
lekas	make haste	seli		jaran	lisoh
lekat			vatok		
lelah	out of breath, fatigued	liso, lelohot	ligah		leté
			pelekát		
lemah	feeble	looī (urat)	vaáng		
lemak	greasy	miñák	velá		tapo
			melema		lemiek
lemas	drown	tuñat			
lembut	soft	lemiek	melu	loma	
lemetak	land		velá		
lengan	forearm		lengán		uká
lenggang	crank (?)	meghila, gilak	beghilong		
lepak	footprint	bah	uvan		saé
lepas	let go	lepuih	ametak		
lesong	mortar for *paddy*		lesong		lemiek
liat	see, perceive	moó	meliat		
liar			makalai		
lichak	muddy ground	lemiek, piek	velá		dudieng
lichin	slippery	jīngelá	jigela	jala	
lidah	tongue	jila	jilá	maré	
lihat	to see	ñinang	pilau		
lilin	beeswax	lilin	lilin		
lima	five		lima		
limpas	to pass by	lilip	jajau		
lindong	to defend, shade		ringáb		
lintah	water leech (?)	matak	kametá (*water*),		
			kamatak (*land lake*) (?)		
lipan	centipede		kipan		
lipat	to fold	lepak	lupak		
loké	stringy		meselam		

out of breath, fatigued — laé; pelaé (*fatigue, subs.*)
drown — lekoh huat
soft — madong (*adj.*), latap (*subs.*)
land — ngené
forearm — lemá
crank (?) — katak
footprint — uso, lavong tedak
let go — tiah
mortar for paddy — ina
see, perceive — tako
 — song
 — hempit
muddy ground — jerá
slippery — lemá
tongue — jilura
to see — jilá
beeswax — hinang
five — laáh
to pass by — lima
to defend, shade — lalo
water leech (?) — hingo
 — hiram

centipede — deripáh
to fold — napal'
stringy — kesap

kra
ipat, tiga

Malay (Colloquial)	English	Kanowit	Kyan	Bintulu	Punan	Matu
lompat	to leap	kajok	hujok	terujok		ñabong
luan	bow (of a boat)	ajak	dulong	ñavong	tukau	
luar	out, without	bawin, awin	awa	laud	awa	
luas	clear; light (? outside, wide)	mesup-giroh		megabah		
lubang	hole, aperture	lubang	luvang	luvang		lubang
lubang idong	nostrils	lubang udong	luvang urong	luvang urong	lirong	
lubok	hole in bed of river	lidong	lirong	levaáu		
ludah	saliva	peluja	lemura	pejula		
luit				alad		alad
luka	wound	tawan	avá	lukú		
lukis	to carve		nalong	temué		
lukus	scald, burn (a person)	lesoh, lekop	ngleso	melasu	ulin	
lumpur	mud		kuvak	emberák		rurab
lunas	to finish			lunas		
lupa	forget	lilo	hado	telilieng		lilo
luput	faint (senseless)	lupat	kava	maát		
luroh		gegah	gak	mereros		
lurus	straight	tigah	tuto	tigah		tigah
lutong			lutong			
ma	mother	ina	hiné, hinan, hinak	tina		tinah
ma tiri	step-mother		hinan tuak	tina tebas		
mabu			ñivo	sak		
mabuk	drunk	mabuk	mavok	mavok	mahan	té
mahal		mahan	mahal	mahal	miap	mahal
mabu		lo	sang (future), mun (like)	ghi; mesat		ba; lo
main		palek	ngeliah			

		Kanowit	Kyan	Bintulu	Punan	Matu
maiang					maiang	
maias	maias				maias	
maiat	to eat		kujuh	pidang	patai	keman
makan	to scold, abuse		kemo	hirang utan	piña	
maki	night		mara	paté	mehani	malam
malam	disinclined		malám	kuman	kelám,	kelalah
malas	evil omen (tabu)		jiekurat ; belé	nuno		
mali, pe:nali	disgrace			malam		
malu	uncle			doya	mali, mengali	
mama	where? what? (inter.)		mia	lali, pelali	meza	tuá
mana	to bathe		han	haih	kamina	gan ; an
mandi	mangosteen		mo	tamé	dembah	temo
manggis	porcelain bowl or cup		kenarah	hino	mendo	
mangkok	sweet		ñalieng	du	kutan	kenarah
manis	bead			kitong	bigo	ñalieng
manit				bengong	tenis	
manok			siau	mi	vaau	siau
manok laki				ino	sezau tra	
manok indu				hiñap	sezau tua	
manok sabong				hiñap aieng	sezau tinjak	
manok utan	raw, unripe		siau tó	hiñap doh		
mantah			tah	hiñap petudak		
				manok data		
				atú ketap (raw rice, underdone)	manta	tá
manusia	mankind		tenawan	klunan	ulun	
marah	angry		lohoi	manó	mumbáng	gusi
marak	to kindle			mengelat	getan	
mari-lah	to come on			teh	tiá	
mas	gold			ma	mas	
masah (maseh)	still (yet)		agat	pegan	kakal	
masak	ripe		sak	sak	mesak	essé	nuan
masak	cook		misam	maro	petaaud	sak
masam	sour		mesam	mesam	mesam	misam
masin	bring		pedi	masin	paád	misam
						pedi

Malay (Colloquial)	English	Kanowit	Kyan	Bintulu	Pukan	Matu
masok		masak	mutang	pasak, temai	mato	masok
mata	eye	mata	matá	mata	matan élo	matah
mata hari	sun	mata-lau	maran-do	matá dau	makovo	matah-lau
mati	to die, dead	kebeh	maté	mesú	maré	matai
meliat	to see, perceive, observe	ñinang	hinang	kaá		dudieng; plingih
melintang	athwart		apat (*athwart*, batang); belaiong (*athwart a boat*)	tepalang		
melompat	to jump, spring	ngkajok, pajuip	ngujok; hujok tukar na	terujok		
memang						
menang			menang	manang		menang
menantu, mentua	(m. & f.)	ibau	ivan	ivan		menatu, mentuah
menaul	kite or kestrel		arum; mangilieng	plakai		memisé
mengail			mesé	meñilám		sorang
mengayuh			ngaio	milai		
mengerti	understand (?)	mengin	jam	merati		
merau	travel by boat	merti	peharok			
mimpi	to dream	nupaé	ñupé	nupai	nupi	nupai
miñak	oil	ñak	ñeñu (*cocoa-oil*), hair-oil); añeh (*oil, grease*)	iñak		
minta	to ask	ñabé	aké	misum	menama	ñabé
mintas	take short cut	kemo, ñirut	pakieng	mutun		
minum	to drink	sak; mehe	dui	sūbá	du	tutang
mirah (? merah)	red		bela	mila		sak
miskin	poor	miskin	jaák	miskin		
modal			davan	modal		
muaari	capital, stock-in-trade		langat			

muara	mouth of river	liput	'lang	menanga	aba
muda	young	jimanak	ñam	pusa	
mudah	easy	keran	melé	mudah	
mudik	to ascend a river	kajo	mudiek, hudiek	mood	muriek silong	mudiek jawai
muka	face	jawai	nang	jabai	
mula mula	at first		hang-hang	jujau song	
mulut	mouth	mujun (lip), bah	bii	bivi	muso	bii
mun			mun		
munggu	hillock		kelaóng	puku		munggo
munsang			munin	munin		
murah	cheap	lumak	melé	murah	lumak	murah
musoh	(? enemy)	belum pupun	aio	ilai		
mutah	to vomit	mutah	muta	puta		
naik	to rise	jaka	moón; tusun	pebá	jaka	kamau
nama	name	ngadan	aran	ngaran	ngaran	ngadan
ñaman	nice, pleasant, comfortable	jia ñam	hlieng	deza ñam		daau ñam
ñamok	mosquito	ñamok	terukok; hrut	agau		
nampak	be visible		tulá	pangah		
nanas	pine-apple		rosan	pisang		
nangis	to weep, scream	nangih	nangi	mengit		menangis
nanti	to wait	naau	kavé, penga	ipa	mengɔ	laú
nasi	boiled rice	nasé	kanan	nekan	kun	nasi
ñawa	breath		hngá	kaán		
nemberang	(? to cross over)	pegetah	lawat	begatas	pata	gutas; kipar
nen	clear		tenjeng	ma		
negri	Dyak village (? country)	tang; atat	dalé	vaié		tad
neraja	rainbow		lingé hatong	tabar		
nerebis			tekrang			
nesal			nginga			

Malay (Colloquial)	English	Kanowit.	Kyan.	Bintulu.	Punan.	Matu.
ngail	to angle		mesé	meñilam		memisé
ngakal			pekalok	mengakal		mengatok
ngantok		turap	ngudo	turap		
nggok			kavok-o			
ngingiet			tilieng			
ngkah		kah	lõ	mela		
ngkuleh		kuli	kuleh	kuli		neka
ngliat		ngetieng	nelier	penat		
ngrais			nghuhok	perabai		
nguap	yawn		muhav			
nini	grandparents	aké	huku (m. or f.)	tepo		ipau
nipis	thin	nipih	ñipi, kawang	melipis		dipis
nitiet	there is not	nabin	jian nun	au kau	gela	
	strike a light		nekiek			
ñor	coco-nut		ñoh	viño		biñoh
numpang	sojourn, go as a passenger		ñangé	menumpang		
ñunpit			ñeput	suput		
nun			anan	iré		
nusu	suck breast	meso	nuso	piti		
orang	human being		daha	ulum; usa, vaié-sira		tenawan
padah, padam	tell	tujau	tira, nira, duan	pesi	péta (? pela)	
	to go out (of life or sun); to suppress; to smother	pajap	maram, param	aram		
padat			ñak			

Kanowit, Kyan, Bintulu, Punan and Matu Vocabularies.

		Kanowit	Kyan	Bintulu	Punan	Matu
padi	rice	padai	paré	herá	pare	padai
padong	loft		parong	tilod		
pagar	fence		kerahan	pagar		
pagi	early in the morning		jibina	bari		
pagi-pagi	early		pesor-pesor			
paha	thigh	paā	hapi	paā		pebá
paia	dangerous, difficult	gurun	peká	anas		
pais			paü utum			
pait	bitter		paii			
pakal	to cork, stuff up		nesang			
paké	use		ñakau, davan			
paké	wear		meté			
paku	nail (iron)		tapak tité			
paku	fern (edible)		pako			
pala lutut	knee		ujong alav	alab		
palit	to scrape (dirt off feet)	bukup	pir, mahit			
paloi	silly	mahau	menggaäung, hav	paloi mengag		lasu : selau
palu	to strike with stick	salimat	ñagá	pedi		
panas	hot (sunshine)	lasu	teli	seludan		
panchur	to gush out		haman	pandai		
pandai	learned	taau	muvui			
panggil	to think, imagine, call		pagar	gatá	avo	lalo
panggo	flying bug (?)		aru	bebat		
panjang	long, not short	lalo	lali tepang	mengalé		
panjang, peman-tang	proverb					
pantas	swift, hastily	seli	ipat; tiga bavah	mesibat		gelegah
pantu		mulong	nangá	eminerak		
panté	mud		tupak			
papan	floor-plank		tasu	ilang		tui, besá
parang	chopping-knife		malat	rasang		
pasak	peg		tapak	riet		
pasir	sand	nai	hait			nai

Malay (Colloquial)	English	Kanowit	Kyan	Bintulu	Punan	Matu
pasong	bind		ngawieng			
patah	to break stick		brong, merong			lepang
patok	to peck	mujun	husong	titok		
paut	pull towards one'self in steering	abat	luvat	avat	avut	abat
pedas	hot to taste		hanit			
peduli		ibo	ikam ñupan	peduli		palah
pegang	take hold of	gam	hivit, sigam	tatag, mán		tegat
pegari			tuiá			
pelahan	gently (not roughly)		pledah			
pelenté		palip, paliek	klañat	perui		
peler	perspiration	betelo	kelöh	kelebang	bekelo	sinak
peloh (? peluh)	to embrace	sinak	mumah	unás		
pelok		sekukut	muko: pekamang nahap ngabádo	mupu		
pelupa	forgetful		akieng			
pematang			takut	peban		
pemintas	short cut	suok	malir			
penakut	ache, stiff, fatigued		bila	mendaáu		dadit
penat		tinam	biek		kivo	
pendam	short	kadit		jibi		
pendé	talisman		pengaroh			
pengaroh	paddle	pela	besé	pedá	bésai	pelah
pengayuh		ipong sagong				
pengerang		klieng (ulau)	livak			
penin (pala)	wasp		belenga			
pehingat	(? landing-place)		sul alan ; latan	panieng		ngelau
penkalan	full		peno	sungun		
penoh						

Kanowit, Kyan, Bintulu, Punan and Matu Vocabularies.

	English					
pépé	flat					
perampuan	female	mero	pedit		redò	merau
perchaya	faith		doh	oro		persaya
pergam	gone, go	taga	kinah			
perghi			pergam			
perna	order, command		te			
pesan			né			uka
pesi	untie	uka	pekato dohò		kas	malam
petang	night-time, dark	dikelam	uvar, muvar		kelam; sedám	
petunggal	first cousin		lidam			
piak	to halve		peharin higat			
			munang			
pichah	loose		lerok		más	
pichit	squeeze, pinch	amé	mesat			
piker	to think		pekenap, pele-			
			mana (*consider*)			
pikul	to carry		ñuûn			pinang
pilih	to select		mili	uai	uai	pindah
pinang	betel-nut		gahat			
pindah			bulak			
pinggan	plate	kenatan	pigan		pinggran	dawak
pinggang	waist, loins	no	kiñong		eng	meñua
pinggir	brink, edge, rim, border		lirin, balan			
pinjam	to borrow, lend	ñua	ujam, mujam		meñubá	
pintu	door	bersukat	betaman	lamé	sekan	
pipi	cheeks	tapa	pinga		pipai	sumiek
pipit	a whistle		pit		kerbás	balak
piring	saucer		pigan			
pisang	banana		puté	blio	balak	
piso	small knife worn at side	balak	ñu		uji radin	
plandok	small deer	planok	bilun		planok	planok
pola		meno, ñen	ná			kenā

Malay (Colloquial)	English	Kanowit	Kyan	Bintulu	Punan	Matu
potong	roof tree		munang			tak
prabong	boat		kulov			
prahu	to examine	saloi	harok	buvong	salui	saloi
preksa	pot	kudan	patnang	jilu		kudan
priok	belly	nieng	tariong			naié
prut	empty, unburthened		butit	menaaung	buré	
puang	often, accustomed to		gohang	tenaé		
puas	pale, faded		ngila			
puchat	origin (?)	poi	ñemit			
puhun	womb	tuké	puūn	tuké	éten	pár
puki	to strike	selimát	tsik	tutau		muli
pukul	to return		nukul	muli	uli	
pulang	wring		uli			
pulas	island	sa	jilivér			
pulo (? pulau)	gum (var. of rice)		busaug	pulau		bé
pulut	to possess	bin	ubak	mukau		
puña	expose to view		hipun			
punggur	second cousin		peloró			
pupu sakali	third cousin		peharin karūñ			jipau janak
pupu dua kali	cat		peharin kateloh			jipau
pusa	navel	pusat	señgo	sieng	ngau	ngau
pusat	to move round		ubut	pusad		
putar	white	puti	peklivak			kelas
putih	dragon-fly		puti	mapu		puté
putin bliong	to break string		kelahaghieng			
putus			butat			
raja	noble (rank)		maran			
rajin	diligent		ñitán	merigah		rajin

rambang	hurl	barang			
rambut	hair (of head)			tujau	
rami	populous			bok	
rampas	to seize		iruok	ramai	rampas
rangka	greedy	melakap		metag (? melāg)	rangka
ranto	(*rante*—river reach)		lulau	tatau	
rapat	close together			rapat	
rasa	to feel, to taste	ñam		ñam	ñam
rasok					
rata	level			ratah	
ratus	hundred			rawan	
rawan	gristle			pibag, bebá	
rebah	fall (as tree)			subu	
rebong	edible shoots of bamboo			susi	
rebut	to seize, run away with, snatch				
rekong	throat			matdo	
rendam				bu	
rendah	low (hills), short (stature)	mediba			
reng	apart			laha	
renggang				kawang	ranggang
rengit				hamok	
riam	a rapid			ghiam	ghiam
riang	crank			ghilieng	beghilong
ribut	squall			bahui	singab
rimba	forest			tuan	
rimbas	adze			palok	
rindu	inclined, desirous of			pejimat	meritu
ringan	light (weight)	pihieng		ñan	meñaai
ringat	itchy	gatan		katal	

(Second section)

nevalang		
bok		
ngeroh		
melieng		
lulo		
mipat, nerekap, hati		
baán		
meté		
datah (*level*), tiah (*even*)		
atu		
kauach		
pevá		
bong		
ñilé		
bengo		
pu, mepu		
liva		

	lo
	liang
	mekiang

Malay (Colloquial)	English	Kanowit	Kyan	Bintulu	Puman	Matu
rosak	torn, undone		lasa, lerok	megegar		
rotan	rattan	uai	ué	bai	ué	
ruboh	destroy, fall into ruin		nasá, tasá	terab		
rué			kué	rebai		
rumah	house	leboh	uma	uma	levo, lavu	lebu
ruman padi	straw	balau	iong paré	gau		balau
rumbia		abau	bato	valau		
rumput	grass		uro	urau		
runga			pugah	ŭgăp		batan
rupa	shape, appearance (? like)	ua	baän, tok	iaŋ		
rusa	name of a deer	paian	paio	pazau	paio	paiau
rusok	(? side)		hŭ	papan		
sabentar	each, every		aki; arieng			
sabilang	side		potang,			
sablah			bahenji, banji-			
			jibang			
sablas	eleven		ji hevin			
sabut	coco-nut husk	tupa	pak.			
sahabat	friend	avop	sevila			
sahaja	simply, purely		tua			
sahinggan			dang			
saiang	pitiful regret	palepá	javá			
saiap	wings		kapit			
saior	fruit, vegetable (or animal food as an accompaniment of rice)		ujo; tangoh			

sakali	once		harat ji, harat dua prah ; medam	j'ulieng perlas	péro
sakit	ill, unconfortable, unpleasant, tiresome (to hurt)	pedih			
sakrat	cut, piece		ji hunang sala	sala	
salah	wrong				salá
salak	to bark		mangang		kukang
salalu	past, beyond	pelarus	petato ; pendo pendo ñihé		
salé	to smoke, to dry in the smoke				
salin	to alter		ngalui tiah ; peji		
sama	alike		tugong	sama	
sama-sama	together	jikahap	pitan		
sambilan	nine		pehembong		jili (?)
sambong	join together		lim	ivos	iri
samua (? samoa)	all		tinan	iré	
sana	there		bakir	inggram	
sangkoh	spear	bakit	dap		
sa orang	alone		balé		gah
saparu	(*saparu saparu* some others, half half)				
sapiak	half		ji unang		
sapu	to stroke		mepá		
sapuloh	ten		pulu		
saputangan			lavong		
sarang	nest	bulang	halah manok	tetep	sarang
sarat	laden	salai	litit		utong
sarong	sheath	tirap	bukar		sarong ; tipak
sarupa	resembling		kluma		aput
satengah	half	tarup	peji		bidak
satu	one		jiunang ji	jiah	samah

Malay (Colloquial)	English	Kanowit	Kyan	Bintulu	Punan	Matu
saut	to reply (?)		ñué			
sebab	because		kenan			
sebrang	across (river)	awin	dipah	ripa	lepa	ipar
sebun			mabat	sabun		
sebut			patap			
sedang	enlighten, fit (?)	padá	dang	sadang		dakut
sedia	ready		au lepak			
sedikit	small, few	sisit, maré	kahang	jimi	sisut	jimiet
sejok	cold	dadam, singiam	laram; hngam			singor; demal
selam ayer	dive (?)	marat	nesar	pesád		
selut	grown up with grass, stuffy, choked		lebak	mesiat		
semengat	spirit, soul		beruá	beruhá		
sempat	leisure, convenient, comfortable	maán	halat			
semut	ant		jelivan, kabirang			
senang			luhé			senang
sendat	narrow, confined	marat	hilat			
senggaut	thwarts	saripa	kiga			
sengkar	lick (?)		gan			
sepan	verandah	sepan	nah			
serambi	with		awa			serami
serang	rinse		ngaio			
serta	hang up to dry		tugong	galau		
sesah	erring, lose way		sup			
sesé			lavé			
sessat		lawang	lingo			
sial	daytime	lau	sekilah		élo	lau
siang	who	hai	malah	sai	é	sai
siapa			hi			

English	Kanowit	Kyan	Bintulu	Punan	Matu
sidar					
siku elbow	sikun	siko	selo		j'apah
sikur what?	jibrah	peteme, namé	geluan, sikau		iná
simpan hold, keep	hiná, kemeh	(keep, pack up)	jiang		
simpang branch (river, tree)		juman	apai		
simpé hoop		hulat	pipak bā		
simpul knot		tebukong			
sindiri self		dap	ita		
singat that which stings		hingat			
singgah to land at		bahé	pukad		betelingi
singit tip, heel		telehieng	telingi		
sini here		tini			
sintak		mejat; jiat			tupat
siñum to smile		pehivok			sepa
sipat measuring-line	sepah	aiap	arih		
sirih pepper leaf		telisé	tia		
sisir comb		kréhini			
situ there		jilut		boön	
skarangini		ávin			
slighi in order that		hikal			
sopaya	tekán	tekan			
sosoh cock's-spur		dahó			
suar					
suara worth, value, voice, life, breath					
sudah past, gone, to complete, finish	mohot	au; lepak	penga	tupu	majieh
sudu		hulok	tidos		
suit		peñapé			
suka happy, contented		ikam			
suloh torch (?)	lo	lutong			lo
sumbat to stop up, cork	siloh	nesang			

Kanowit, Kyan, Bintulu, Punan and Matu Vocabularies.

Malay (Colloquial)	English	Kanowit	Kyan	Bintulu	Punan	Matu
sumbu	wick		subó			
sumpit	narrow (?)		baiong	uzut	upit	sungai meris
sumpitan	blow-tube		humput	sepot	ungé	
sungi	river	seput	hungé	sungai		
sungut	whiskers					
supan	ashamed		haih	meñua		bada
suroh	to order	mia	ñuho	soi		
surong	to shove on					
suruhan	messenger		idé			
surut	water ebb		melah			
susah	trouble, difficult		paiah	pejuran		paiah
susé	history		bara, tingaran	titi		
susu	breasts (woman's)	só	huso			
susur	landslip		teñu			
tadi	just now (past)		dé			
tahi			taé			
tahu	know		jam	taii	jam	taau
tahun	year		duman			
tajam	sharp	mañit	ñáat			
tajar			niar			
tajo	high jar		tajo			
taka	notch	bedot, boót	nakap, namar	mau	boót	medut
takut	afraid		takut			
tali	string, rope	kabang	talé			talé
taman	pole		tekán			
tambah	to add		ñavang			
tampar	slap		nebip			tamah

tampi	winnow					
tampong	cover up a hole					
taña	to enquire	telabau		lemavau		taná
tanah	earth		tap			
tanak	to boil food	penatun	napal, miré	tuvu		patun
tanam	to bury, to plant	kelada	metang			
tanda	token, mark	tangan	tana			
tandan	cluster		maro			
			tuvu, nuvu			
			terana; atap			
			beluhan, tepungun (buah, pinang, (pisang)			
tandok	horn	uan	huang			agam
tangan	hand	pang	kamah		keján	
tangga	ladder		san		agam; gemán	rag
tangkap	to embrace, catch round		halut (capture), hivit (catch hold of)		ligah	
tangkas	quick		ipat		taki	takien
tangkien	gird on (?)		meté			
tangkir			tekulong			
tanjong	point (river), headland	dunguh	tujul, ajui	tuju	tujok	tañong; tughi
tapak	platter	penanga	uit			jalo
tapak	palm, sole of feet		ida kamah; ida kasa			agam
tapeh	yet		taäh			ketip
tapi	to conceal	sihok	barang	meñuok		
tapok	to plane		muhók			
tara	to pull, haul, launch	jat	malok			jiri
tarik (tarek)	to take care of		jiat, mejiat			
taroh	fresh		ló			
tawar	dense (population)	kapan	beleh		makapan	singor
tebal	cut down trees		kapal		tomba	kapal
tebang	cut down jungle		nevang			tubang
tebas	close together		meda; lemiriek			memipig
tebat			nesang			

Malay (Colloquial)	English	Kanowit.	Kyan.	Bintulu.	Punan.	Matu.
tebi	notched	sip oh, taba	pugak : peteh (*chipped of bead*) tekrang			
tebiang	bank of stream, precipice		bahé	laté	buong	mubu
tebing						
tebok	to pierce a hole in		melebu; ngkrivo (*bore*)			
tebu	sugar-cane	tebo	tevó		tavu	tebo
tebus	redeem		nevú			
tegap	firm, fixed		najé			anal
tegar			higan			
telan	to swallow	merenga	ñilú	tumán		looi
telanjang	naked	bajéo	ngaweh	bajau		hetirong
telinchir	slip		telesá	gelar		
telinga	ear	telinga	telinga (*lobe*), apang tiko, tukok	telinga	tunieng	lingah
telok		takar, bukut		teku	téku	rang
telor	egg		teloh		télu	
temado			klého			
tembako		temako	jako		tembako	
tembang	deserted dwelling		lepun (uma) temeneh	lebúan		tembang
tempa						
tempaian			burui			
tempap	slap	kanan	nebap			
tempat	spot	sawa	havan			
temu	find	tupo	pehabong			
temuda	new jungle	damun				
tempurong	coco-nut shell	tabé	ñóh	upong		
tenang			ngelenang, nglulo			
tengah	middle, while, during	buan	belua	kenó	belua	dagan
tenggalong			hunor			

Kanowit, Kyan, Bintulu, Punan and Matu Vocabularies.

tenggilieng					dudieng
tengok					tetu; atang
tentu	east (?)		ham		tigang
tepian			livang		
terajang	startled, alarmed		tenang	pavong	pegelam
terkejut	exceeding, very	tingan	latan		
terlalu	laugh		nekang		
tertawa	chop, cut	melak	tekejat		dié; kewan
tetak	secure, firm		lalo lalé	moŏng	(mast)
tetap	post	nabin	kesieng	gêtop	
tiada			mitang		
tiang			taär	au-kau	nebé
tiba	east (?)	birih	jian loh, jian nun	rié	
tidak	no, not	nam	jihé		
tidak dapat	impossible		mirieng	ăă	tudui
tidak bulih	may not		jian, ăm		
			jian dang	aa kala; aa kebán	
	sleep	melut	jian haman, jian dang		daän
tidor	heel		tudu	megan	
tiga	three		tumir	tumed	
tiga	stringy		teló		
tighin			kesap		
tigoh	to hurl, throw at	moŏ	tagang		
tikam	fine mat	benarang, tin	meso, nevalang	pan	jalé
tikar	mouse (? rat)	jalé	brat		belabau
tikus	mattress	belabau	lavo	tilam	tilam
tilam	to rise		tilam		latog; katong
timbul	rise of moon		nglatieng		
timbul	to strike		musip		
timpa	lame		belepok, beledit		
timpang	cucumber		kepé	mapiek	
timun			tinun		

Malay (Colloquial)	English	Kanowit	Kyan	Bintulu	Punan	Matu
tinggal	to leave, forsake, to remain	leká; luit (*stay*)	melak (*leave, remain*)	melá		tapu
tinggelam	sink (?)		ngené	melu		
tinggi	high	regau	bo	bebat; bau		ñut
tinjak	tread upon		ngaja			
tintieng	ridge		ngluvang ngalang			
tiong (mina)	starling		tiong			
tipu	deceit		pekalok			
tiris	to leak		turu	metos		té
tiup	blow		har, mehar			
tohor	shallow, not deep		ñivo	menat		
tongkat	staff		hengkúr			
trais			nguhok			rarab
trang	light, clear, plain	taé, gagé	midang; pemalah	perabai		
trebang	to fly		madang		nelérang	tilieng
trejun	jump out, down	tahang	nesó			
trekam			ñaám			
triak	to take		neré			
trima			ala			
trusu	to stumble, slip		jatu	pajut		gula
tuah	old; a chief, an elder	laké, ayoh	muku (*agéd*), aia (*old, in comparison*)	azah	tokan	laké
tuak	toddy		burak, pasé, jakan mubang, uak			bang
tuang	to pour out	biah	loóng	usa		bias
tuboh	body	lawa, lasau	loóng	usa		
tuboh	person					
tudong	cover	kap	tabun (*cover*), ban (*lid, cover*), mebán			tabun
tujoh	seven		tusu			

tukar	to change					seloh
tuku	strike top of anything, drive a peg, beat a drum	petoyu nukul				
tukul	hammer					
tulak	to ward off (to push away)	pelebu haro, ñaro				
tulang	bone	urat	tulang			tulang
tulang bangar	collar-bone		tulang bernang			
tulang geram	shoulder-blade	tulang geraăm	*tulang* jaă ligan			
tulat	day after to-morrow		do ji aia			
tuli	deaf		mádang			
tulong			tulong	buluok		tulong
tumbang	to fall as a tree	tugoh	pevá			
tumbok	husked rice		mulo			
tumpah	to upset	kedun	maauh, mubang			
tumpul	blunt		kasal			
tundun	pubes	bekawang	kerap			
tundok	bow (head)		nukam			
tunggah	to call out	tibah	muvui			tugus
tungkun (api)	to light fire	tutok, pangan, nutup	pekatan			
tungkup	boat	belakap				
tunjok	finger		ngaauh ikieng			
tunu	kindle		havat, ñavat, tu-tong, nutong, misak (ikan?)	tutong	tino	
turun	sunset, to descend hill	kiba	ngileh			
turus	stake, post	jerejak	taman			
turut	to accompany, to imitate	duai	han dahin			kiba
tutok	to shut, close	itom	tepá			
tutup			mekap, meban		boai; jaka boai	tutup
			salu			
			ivai			
			tupa	muo		

Malay (Colloquial)	English	Kanowit	Kyan	Bintulu	Punan	Matu
tutur tutur sahya	speech, language	puba	tangaran, dahun dahauk			
ua-ua	what time	klabat	havat	habat		
uaktu	to change		jivang			
ubah	grey-haired		udé			
uban	charm		muban	uban		
ubat	tapioca		ubat	ubat		
ubi kayu	prawn		uvi kele	ubé kelé		udang
udang	again	balé	urang	savak		
udi		avop	ngruar			
udong			sevila			
uga			tungul (stump), asā (snag)	tugru		
ujan	rain		usan	ujan		pog
ujong	end (extremity)	lawé	uyok: uvang	ugau		ujan
ukang			besieng	bakiké	luli	poōn
ulak	backwater	lelang	kluar	ulak		
ular	snake	penganan	ñipa	ñipa		dipah
ulat	worm, maggot		ular; hiat (sago worm)	ulad		
ulih	by		kenan	luka		
ulu	source river		aur	oōd		ajo
ulu	handle		haup (hilt), tapun (handle, paddle)	ulau		
ulun	slave	dipan	dipan	ripan		dipan
ulur	to pull, haul, launch		hor	ulu		iod
uma	arable land, farm		luma	injab		umah
umbang	chips		uvang			pelepak

		Kanowit	Kyan	Bintulu	Punan	Matu
umbut	cabbage of a palm; pith	tajok		huvor	tajok	tajok
umpan	bait			upat	upan	
umur (umor)	age				umur	
undur	to recede, abate	suat		sohor	sot	será
unggun		ungun		humoi	sepok	
unjam	place upright in ground			jak; tapak (tiang?)	dujam	tatap
untong	reward			untong	untong	
upah				tibah	tidan	
upas	poison			tasam	tajam	
upé				upa	ukap	
uras	dust (litter)			leho	ras	
urat	muscle	urat		huat	uat	urat
utak	root			pakat	amut	
utan	brain			utak	utak	
utang	old jungle	ipong		tuan	kiban	tang : guiin
utap	debt			utang	utang	utang
utap	oblong shield			klebit	utap	utap
	bark boat			bohong	boöng	

méo

VOCABULARIES OF NORTH BORNEAN LANGUAGES.

Collected by LIEUT. C. DE CRESPIGNY, R.N. The seven first columns appeared in the Proc. Roy. Geogr. Soc. July, 1872. The last column, referring to the Malanaus appeared in the Jour. of the Anthropological Institute, v. pp. 36-37.

English.	Malay.	Brunei Low Dialect.	Bisaya.	Murut Padass.	Murut Trusan.	Dali Dusum, near Limbang.	Malanau, District of Mukat.
ant	samut	samut	sodom	sodom	liparus	sodom	ngad
ashes	abu	abu	abu	kau	abu		abau
bad	jahat	jahat	jahat	maraht	maraht		jaat
banana	pizang	pizang	pizang	putih	baun	puntih	badak
belly	prut	prut	tinai	tinai	batak	tian	nga-ai
bird	burong	burong	mamanok	lusuit	lusuit	wahu	manuk
black	itam	itam	maitam	maitam	bata	itom	bilam
blood	darah	darah	rah	dadaha	dadaha	lah	dah
blue	bira	biru	matámo	matumo	matumo		biruk
boat	sampan	prau	bidok	badao	alud	padass	saloi
body	badan	tulboh	inam	inan	inan	inan	bia
bone	zulang	tulang	tulang	tulang	tulang		tulang
bow	panah	paneh	panah				panah
box	piti	pati	pati	pati	pati	riti	kaban
butterfly	kupukupu	kulimbambang	kuliambang	kuliambang	kuliambang	kuliambang	balabang
cat	kuching	kuching	kuching	using	using	using	sieng
child	anak	anak	anak	anak	anak	anak biok	anak
chopper	parang	pamarang	ganjow	dasigul	karit	daugal	parang
coconut	kalapa	piasan	piasan	piasan	bua butan	bua butan	beniu
cold	sejok	sagid	sagid	marima	marádam	sagid	singoa
come	mari	mari	mari	dibok	zungi	liti siti	kidigau
day	ari	ari	tungadan	samilan	sang-chow (au)	adan	lau
deer	rusa	payan	tambang	tambang	payo	tambang	payau
dog	aujing	kuyuk	aso	uka	uka	aso	banawang
door	pintu	pintu	panurabun	panurabun	panurabun	paluang	linga
ear	talinga	talinga	talingo	talingo	lalik	talingo	teloh
egg	taber	taber	ampuni	ampuni	taloh	ampuni	mata
eye	mata	mata	muka	muka	muka	mato	jauei
face	muka	muka	ama	ama	ama		tamáa
father	bapa	bapa	bulu	bulu	bulu	bapa	bulau
feather	bulu	bulu	kariam	kalendo	tichu	bulu	tujuk
finger	jari	jari					
fire	api	api	apui	apui	apui	apui	apoi

Vocabularies of North Bornean Languages.

English	1	2	3	4	5	6	7
fish	ikan	lauk	kayanu	pait	lawit	sadar	jikan
flesh	daging	isi	ausi	asi	asi	isi	sei bia
flower	bunga	bunga	usak	usak	usak	usak	bunga
fly	lalat	lalat	laugau	balougad	balougad	lalat	lalangow
to fly	terabang	terabang	tamulud	mausiam	mausiam		tiling
foot	kaki	kaki	gakun	kaleiam	kaleiam	batis	pajag
fowl	ayam	ayam	manuk	manuk	lal	manuk	siau
fruit	bua	bua	bua	bua	bua	bua	bua
go	pergi	pergi	magiduk	magiduk	burra	mogud	tabol
gold	uras	auras	malawan	mulawan	mulawan	amas	mat
good	baik	baik	mubalut	mausui	doh	mausui	diak
hair	rambut	rambut	abuk	abuk	apuk	abuk	bub
hand	tangan	tangan	kariam	kalindo	pichok	tangan	pāa
hard	kras	kras	mukadan	mukataang	mukatang		sahih
head	kapala	kapala	ulu	ulu	ulu	ulu	ulau
honey	ayer madu	ayer madu	roh	dudih	upa		ayer madu
hot	panas	augat	malassa	malassu	malan	malassu	laso
house	rumah	rumah	walai	baloi	rumah	aloi	lebo
iron	besi	basi	basi	basui	basui	besi	besi
island	pulo	pulau	pulau	pulau	pulau	pulau	pulau
knife	pisan	pisan	pisan	pisan	pisan	pisan	uji
large	besar	besar	megayu	kujang	iyo	megayu	mat
leaf	daun	daun	daun	mayu	mayu	daun	dann
little	kachil	damit	kanak	dadanu	dadanu	diok	umit
louse	kutu	kutu	kutu	bobodok	madari	kutu	kutu
man	orang laki	laki laki	mianei	kutu	kutu	mianei	alai
mankind	manusia	jelama	ulun	ngkuyong	ngkuyong	ulun	tenawan
mat	tikar	lampit	lampit	ulun	damulun	ikam	pan
monkey	moniet	ambuk	kara	lampit	lampit	kara	kuyad
moon	bulan	bulan	bulan	jebulau	basuk	bulan	bulan
mosquito	nyamok	rangit	namok	bulan	bulan	kalias	kias
mother	ma	mama	ina	namok	tukong	ina	tina
mouth	mulut	mulut	kabang	bina	tinan	kabang	moba
nail (finger)	kuku	kuku	sandulu	kabang	tahang	salindu	silu
nail (iron)	paku	paku	paku	sandulu	sandulu	paku	paku
night	malam	malam	jutuong	paku	paku	autuong	famai
nose	hidong	hidong	adong	dundum	mora-chapchan	orong	nio
oil	miniak	miniak	uman	adong	isong	uman	babui
pig	babi	bai	baiyo	uman	uman	ramu	di
post	tiang	tiang	tiang	basing	bakar	tiang	
				tiang	tiang		

English	Malay	Brunei Low Dialect	Bisaya	Murut Padass	Murut Trusan	Dali Dusum, near Limbang	Malanau, District of Mukat
prawn	udang	siar	sasangan	sasangan	udang	siar	undang
rain	ujan	ujan	rasam	ruanang	udan	rasam	ujair
rat	tikus	tikus	lano	lano	labo	tikus	labau
red	mirah	mirah	maragang	malia	masia	malagang	sak
rice (in husk)	padi	padi	hilod	bilod	padi	parai	padai
rice (raw)	bras	bras	wagas	bagas	bara	wagas	bras
rice (boiled)	nasi	nasi	nitaid	kalo	noba	nubur	nasi
river	lungei	lungei	barwan	lungei	lungei	barwan	lungei
road	jalanan	jalanan	lalan	dalan	dalun	lalan	jalan
root	akar	akar	wakan	bakag	tiowag		akar
saliva	hudah	ludah	jula				lijang
salt	guram	sirah	usi	usi	tichu		liar
sea	laut	lautan	lisabar	bugus	laud	usun	alud
silver	pirak	pirak	pirak	pirak	pirak	lautan	pirak
skin	kulit	kulit	kongkong	kongkong	tobil	pirak	kulit
smoke	asap	asap	lisun	lisun	lisun	lisun	tugun
snake	ular	ular	nipo	nipo	kukus		dipa
soft	lembeh	lumbut	maluyat	maluyat	maluyat		lamak
sour	masam	asam	ausam	ausam	bualum	unsom	m'sam
spear	lambing	bujak	andewan	bangkow	bangkow	bangkow	besei
star	bintang	bintang	bintang	motitiu	motitiu		bintang
sun	mata hari	mata hari	matuadan	matuadan	matuadan	matuadan	mata lau
sweet	manis	manis	matanus	mamis	mamis	manis	tami
tongue	lidah	lidah	dilah	dilah	dilah	dilah	ji'lah
tooth	gigi	gigi	nipan	nipun	nipun	ipan	ipan
water	ayer	ayu	waig	timug	upa	aig	niam
wax	lilin	lilin	lilin	lilin	lilin	lilin	lilin
white	puti	puti	mapurak	mapurak	buda	purak	apo
wife	bini	bini	sau	andu	andu	anau	saua
wing	sayap	sayak	alad	alad	alad		payang
woman	perampuan	bini bini	aiyunai	daláh	anak adi	kakimu	mahau
wood	kayu	kayu	kayu	kayu	kayu	luton	kayu
yellow	kuning	kuning	masilo	masilo	masilo	kuning	kuning
green	ijan	gadong	matamu	matamau	batamau	biru	ijau
yes	iya	au	aw	iyo	maw	aw	eh
no	tida	dada	kaissa	kalu	naam	unjap	uda

Vocabularies of North Bornean Languages. xcvii.

seek	chari			chari		
find	dapat	unjar		makabanang		piniang
like this	bagini	beluri	chari	koang dagino	gium	k'nah
like that	bagitu	damiani	makuanang	koang dagino		gatanien
formerly	lagi danlu	damiato	manu	dalaid	miano	gatanien
if	kalan	lagi kurato	manu	tanah	miono	tai
to sail	berlayer	amun	dalaid	namkaliku	amun	kalau
to run	berlari	berlarei	tau	lumayag	lumayag	padu
ghost	antu	berlusir	lumayag	kamimbul	samimbul	pabia
corpse	bangkei	antu	menimbul	kalaganang	lamatai	amo
to mix	berchampur	mayat	ragun	bangkei		bakang
naughty	nakal	bergaul	bangkei	nigaul		champur
angry	marah	gauk	nigaul	makagauk	masiau	gauk
tray	dulang	gusa	makagauk	simaugit	talam	m'dalu
winnowing sieve	lusuran	talam	mausiol	talam		dulang
common sieve	ayakan	nira	talam	tapau		niru
to pull an oar	berdayang	ayakan	lilibu	agang	ayagang	ayak
blind	buta mata	berkayu	gagan	maugkabil		pia
to break	pichah	pachah mata	niboasi	mabusa		mapak
to lie	boung	pachah	nabila	napopog	bila	baba
to sleep	tidor	kalaka	umboi	mabanaban	bawa	pamudei
to lie down	baring	tidor	modap	modop	modap	tudui
to get up	berdiri	limpong	lumanag	talobid		p'galang
to awake	bangun	bangun	umberigud	umberigud	tamidong	ban
bottle	botul	bangun	tamidong	tumidong		p'kadang
tin and lead	timah	surai	surai	surai	surai	botul
to meet	jumpa	timah	andurei	samasak	pandurei	timah
headcloth	dastar	bertamu	minta tamu	manamu		tamu
neck	leër	dastar	lugak	ligah	lingal	bulang
different	lain	leber	liau	liog	liog	tengo
here	disini	masing	luei suei	masu suei		wa ino
there	disana	disini	liti	liti		gagito
that	ito	nun	lino	nog-i-nic		gagien
large	besar	ato				ino
small	kechil	bähsa		kachia		
this	ini	damit				
testicles	palir	ani, or ano		balak		
		palir				

VOCABULARIES OF NORTH BORNEAN LANGUAGES—*continued*. ENGLISH AND MALANAU.

English.	Malanau.	English.	Malanau.	English.	Malanau.	English.	Malanau.
there	gagien	sirie	s'pah	to drink	tutang	day before	sili mabei
what	ino	to want	lo	daylight	lau	boundary	niatan
many	ida	a little	sijumi	to cook	misak	news	dangar
when	peia	to make	sibat	to warm at fire	pidau	up river	kamanuju
who	lei	to bring	gé	to eat	kaman	down river	kalud
where	gagahan	to take	gé	perhaps	barangkali	not yet	madanga
to throw away	jiwiek	presently	né	don't	ka'	to lick	sanilak
to walk	makau	not at all	aké	to forget	leitu	across the river	ipa
to die	matai	goods	barang	to remember	singad	to use	baba
to sit	kuduk	arrive at	tapa	to-morrow	suni	village	liko
to stand up	b'kadang	now	ajau itau	day after	sili suni	forest	gun
betel nut	pinang	to carry	s'un	yesterday	mabei		

A COLLECTION OF FORTY-THREE WORDS IN USE IN TWENTY-FOUR DIFFERENT DISTRICTS
Made by the Rev. CHAS. HUPÉ, of the Rheinische Mission.

"Karangan is American Mission at Pontiana; the others I have collected on the West Coast, and others I copied from BROOKE in Sarawak."

English.	Malay.	Buginese.	Banjerese.	Dyak Pulopetak.	D. Karangan.	D. Sinding and Meratei.
one	satu	sedi	asa	idjä	nyeu	ka-ah
two	dua	dua	dua	duä	duweu	duoh
three	tiga	telo	talu	télô	taroh	taruh
four	ampat	ôpa, mpa	ampat	äpat	ampat	apat
five	lima	lima	lima	lima	rima	limot
six	anam	ônong, nam	anam	djehawen	inum	num
seven	tudju	pitu	pitu	udju	idjo	tudju
eight	delapan	harua	walu	hanja	mai	maih
nine	sambilan	hasera	sanga	djulatien	pre	pri-i
ten	sapulu	sepulu	sapulu	sapulu	samung	smui
man (*homo sapiens*)	manusia	(*vergleiche mensch*, mas, ist, *wo es ist unverändert aus dem Malaiischen augenommen*)				
homo persona	orang	tawu	orang	olo	na	nu-uh
man and husband	laki-laki	horo-ani	laki-laki	hatuä		dari
woman and wife	perampuan (*wife*, bini)	makonrai (*wife*, bini)	bini	bawi (*wife*, sawä)		dajung
father	bapa	ambe-ma	bapa	apang	ma	
mother	ma	indo-na	uma	indu	no	
head	kapala	ulu	kapala	takolok		
eye	mata	mata	mǎta	matä		matün
ear	telinga, kupin	dutjuling	telinga	pinding		
nose	hidon	inga	hidong	orong		nukn
tongue	lidah	lila	ilat	djela		djura
tooth	gigi	isi	gigi	kasingä		djapan
hair	rambut	welua	rambut	balau		bôk
hand	tangan	lima	tangan	lengä	ende	tangan
day	hari	so	hari	andau	änó	ndo
night	malam	weni	malam	hamalem		sakalupm
sun (eye of day)	mata hari	mata so	matahari	matanandau		matun anui
moon	bulan	wulan, ulong	bulan	bulan	bulan	bulan
star	bintang	bitoeng	bintang	bintang		taing
fire	api	api	api	apui	api	sepui
water	aier	wai	banju	danum	pitu	pi-in
earth	tanah	tana	tana	petak	tana	tana
good	baik	madatjeng	baik	bahalap	bait	madih
bad	djahat	mejak	djahat	papa	djet	dja-at
dead	mati	mate	mati	matei	kubeus	kabus
big	bĕsăr	maradja	bǎsăr	hai		aijuh
little	ketjil	baitju	kátjil	kurik		si-it
white	putih	mapute	putih	putih		bĕdé
black	itam	malotong	hirang	bebilem		senget
bird	burung	manuk	burung	burung	manok	manuk
fowl	ajam, manok	manuk	ajam	manok	manok	siok
pig	babi	babi	babi	hubui		pangan
fish	ikan	baleh	iwak	lauk		ikei

English.	D. Kajan.	D. Sau.	D. Bulau.	D. Meri.	D. Lundu.	D. Bintulu.
one	dji	indi	siti	si		djia
two	dua	dua	dua	duveh		ba
three	tello	taruh	tigah	tellau		telau
four	ampat	pah	ampat	pat		pat
five	lima	remo	lima	lima		lima
six	anum	anum	anam	nöm		nöm
seven	tudjak	djuh	tudjuh	tudjoh		tudjoh
eight	saija	moi	delapan	madeh		madeh
nine	petan	pri-i	sambilan	supei		supi
ten	pulo	simohong	sapulu	pulo		pluan
man (*homo sapiens*)						
homo persona						
man and husband	daha	dari	laki	lakei (*husband*, ideh)	kneah	manei (*husband*, bubok)
woman and wife	do	indu (*wife*, bini)	dyung	tarei	dyung	reddu
father	tamei	sama	apei	tama		tama
mother	inei	indo	indei	tina		tina
head	kuhong	bak	palla	uho	bak	ulau
eye	mata	button	mata	mata	botön	mata
ear			pendiang	telinga	kedjit	telinga
nose	urong	indong	idong	singota	nong	urong
tongue			dela	djillah	ihra	
tooth	nipun	djepon	gigi	nipön	djapon	nipön
hair	bök	bök	bök	fök	bök	bok
hand	uwau	tangan	langön	tudjoh	tangan	agum
day	dau	ungnu	ari	allau		dau
night	dahalum	narom	mallöm	dillöm		kolöm
sun (eye of day)	mata dau	buttanuh	mata ari	mata döllo	bitarnanu	mata dau
moon	bulan	bulan	bulan	tukka	buran	bulan
star			pandau	fatak		bitang
fire	apui	opui	api	igon	apue	djara
water	danum	pi-in	ai	feh	pe-in	ba
earth	tana	tana	tana	tana	tana	tana
good		pagu	badas	djia		dijar
bad			dji-i			djahas
dead	mati	kobos	mati	matei		misso
big			bisi			adjar
little			mët			disi
white		budah	burak	putei		mapo
black		singut	tjilum	metöm		itam
bird	manok		bjurong	manuk	do-ut	sijau
fowl			manok	ahal	siok	
pig		sijioh	djani	baha	pangan	bakas
fish	masek	ikan	ikan	futah	kaen	djeing

Hupé's Vocabularies.

English.	D. Millanau and Muka.	D. Berang and Sabungo.	D. Bukar.	D. Santan and Gurgo.	D. Sinan.	D. Sumpo.
one	djia	indi	ni	indi	indi	indi
two	dua	duo	dua	dua	dua	dua
three	tellau	taruk	taruk	taruk	taruk	taruk
four	pat	pat	ampat	pat	pat	pat
five	lima	remo	rema	remma	remma	rema
six	nōm	naum	anaum	anung	anung	anum
seven	tudjoh	djoh	djoh	djoh	djoh	djoh
eight	eian	meii	meihi	mii	mi-i	mei-i
nine	ulan	pri-i	pri-i	pri-i	pri-i	pri-i
ten	pluan	somong	simahung	simung	simung	simong
man (*homo sapiens*) homo persona						
man and husband	malei	dari (*husb.*, dyah)	dari (*husb.*, dyah)	dari (*husb.*, dyah)	dyah	dyah
woman and wife	malei	dyong	dyong	dyong	dyong	sawan
father	ama	sama	amang	sama	sama	sama
mother	tina	sindo	anu	sindo	sindo	anu
head	ulau	bāk	bāk	bāk	bāk	bāk
eye	mata	buttoh	buttoh	buttoh	buttoh	buttoh
ear		kadjit	kapin	kedjit	kedjit	kapin
nose	udong	nong	unong	undong	nong	indong
tongue		djeha	djile	irna	irna	djeha
tooth	nipōn	djepo	djepo	djepo	djepo	djepo
hair	buok	bok	burok	ubok	bok	boks
hand	tudjoh	tangan	tangan			
day	lau	gno (s. ungnu)	ungnu	ungnu djava	ungnu	gno
night	mallam	narom	mungaru	ungnu karim	sanarun	narom
sun (eye of day)	mata lau	buttanuh	buttanuh	buttanuh	buttanuh	buttanuh
moon	bulan	buran	buran	buran	buran	buran
star	bitang	bitang	bintu	bintang	bitang	bitang
fire	apui	poi (s. apoi)	apoi	apui	apoi	apui
water	niam	pe-in	umo	aoh	pi-in	pe-in
earth	tana	tana	tana	tana	tana	tana
good	dia	muni (s. mundi)	pagu	kunna	mundi	pagu
bad		ra-as	be-ik	drap	drep	drap
dead	matei	kabos	kabos	kabos	kabos	kabos
big		ba-as	ahi	ba-as	ahi	ahi
little		pi-it	djahek	tju	sjuh	tjuk
white	apo	budak	budak	budah	budah	budah
black	belöm	singut	behis	singut	singut	behis
bird		manuk	manuk	manuk	manuk	manuk
fowl	ahal		siok	siok	siok	siok
pig	babui	i-oh		i-oh	ich	ioh
fish	djikon	kean	ikan	ikian	ikian	ikian

English.	D. Budanok.	D. Stang.	D. Sibugau.	D. Tubbia.	D. Sabutan.	D. Sering. Gugu & Matan.
one	indi	indi	sa	indi	indi	indi
two	dua	duo	dua	duo	duo	duo
three	taruk	taruk	tiga	taruk	taruk	taruk
four	pat	pat	ampat	pat	pat	pat
five	remo	remo	lima	rema	remo	rema
six	anum	naum	anam	anung	naum	anaum
seven	djuh	djuh	tudjuh	djoh	djuh	djoh
eight	mei-	mei-i	delapan	meihi	mei-i	meii
nine	pri-i	pri-i	sambilan	pri-i	pri-i	pri-i
ten	simung	simong	sapulu	simong	simong	simong
man (homo sapiens) homo persona)						
man and husband	dari (husb., dyah)	dyah	laki	dari (husb. dyah)	dyah	dyah
woman and wife	sawan	dyong	indo	dyong	dyung	dyong
father	sama	sama	apei	sama	sama	sama
mother	sindo	sindo	indi	sindo	sindo	sindo
head	bāk	bāk	kapala	bāk	bāk	bāk
eye	buttoh	buttoh	mata	buttoh	buttoh	buttoh
ear	kadjit	kadjit	punding	kadjit	kapin	kadjit
nose	undong	undong	idong	nong	nung	nung
tongue	djeha	djeha	delah	irha	irha	irha
tooth	djepu	djepo	gigi	djepoh	djepoh	djepo
hair	ubok	book	bōk	burok	book	book
hand						
day	ungnu	ungnu	ari	ungnu	ungnu	gnu
night	ungner karim	narom	malam	karom	narom	narom
sun (eye of day)	buttanuh	buttanuh	matiari	buttanuh	buttanuh	buttanuh
moon	buran	buran	buran	buran	buran	buran
star	bitang	bitang		bintu	bitang	bitang
fire	apui	apui	api	apui	apui	apui
water	pi-in	pi-in	ai	pi-in	pi-in	pi-in
earth	tana	tana	tana	tana	tana	tana
good	kanna	kanna	badas	panat	kunna	munni
bad	drap	drap	djai		raap	rāp
dead	kabos	kabos	mati	kabos	kaboi	kabos
big	ba-as	ba-as	besi		ba-as	ba-as
little	sjuh	tji-it			soak	so-oh
white	budah	budah	putih	budah	budah	budah
black	singut	singut	tjilum	singut	bi-i	singut
bird	manuk	manuk	manuk	manuk	manuk	manuk
fowl	siok	siok	siok	siok	siap	siok
pig	pangan	pangan	babi	eioh	da-ung	eioh
fish	ikian	kian	lauk	kian	ikian	ikian

A SHORT COLLECTION

Made by CHAS. HOSE, ESQ., *Resident of the Baram District.*

There are sixteen dialects spoken in the Baram district, the most important being Kayan, Kenniah, Punan, Kalabit, Narom, Sibop, Brunei Malay, and Malay.

I subjoin nine words as an example:—

English	Kayan.	Kenniah.	Punan.	Kalabit.	Narom.	Sibop.	Brunei Malay.	Malay.
wild pig	baboi	bawi	bakas	bakar	san	bakas	bai	babi utan
man	daha	kalunan	ulun	lumulun	ideh	ulun	jilama	manusia
to walk	panoh	massat	malakau	nylan	malahau	malakau	jalan	jalan
a fish	masik	siluang	luang	luang	futar	enjin	lauk	ikan
dog	asau	asu	asoh	uteh	ou	asu	koyuk	anjing
water	atar	sungei	bah	fah	fer	bah	aying	ayer
good	sayoh	layar	dian	dor	jeh	dian	bisai	bagus
no	nusi	naan	bi	naam	naan	abi	nada	tida
a fowl	yap	manok	deek	laal	aal	deek	manok	ayam

(Geographical Journal, March, 1893).

A VOCABULARY OF THE KAYAN LANGUAGE OF THE NORTH-WEST OF BORNEO.

By R. Burns, Esq.

From Logan's "Journal of the Indian Archipelago."

The following is a Vocabulary of the dialect spoken in the district of the rivers Bintulu and Rajang and their branches.

English.	Kayan.	English.	Kayan.	English.	Kayan.
earth	tana lim	shell	seh	sharping stone	batu asa
sky	langit	garden	luvo	chisel	panjok
sea	kala	mountain	knalang	awl	tuel
sun	matin-dow	cave	luvong	spear	bakier
moon	bulan	house	oma	crowbar	kali
star	kraning	room	tilong	hoe	weying
light	mala	door	taman	gold	ma
darkness	lidam	window	batave	iron	titi
lightning	kilat	loft	parong	steel	titi mying
thunder	balari	floor	tasu	magnet	titi lakin
eclipse	sowang	stairs	san	copper	kavat bla
heat	laso	railing	krahan	brass	kavat nymit or knymit
cold	laram	partition	dinding		
cloud	lison	beam	bong	tin	samha
rainbow	langi hatong	boards	liap	medicine	tabar
tide-flow	wap	rafts	kaso	gun	pulet
fire	apui	laths	laha	rozin	lutong
smoke	lison	thatch	apo	camphor	kapon
sparks	wur	nails	tapak	opium	pune
flame	mala	table	talam	trees	pohun
ashes	havo	mat	brat	root	aka
fuel	tyon	mattress	luto	trunk	batang
charcoal	lusong	pillow	hilan	bark	kul
water	atta	curtains	kalabo	branch	dahan
river	hungie	screen	dindingkalabo	leaf	iton
rain	usan	box, trunk	pati	flower, blossom	pidang
current	kasi	basket	alat		
lake	bawang	plate	pigan	fruit	bua
dew	lipot	cup	pigan dui	orange, lime	lavar
fog	ap	knife	knoe	pine apple	orusan
wind	bahoie	handle	houp	mangostin	kitong
storm	ovan	pot	taring	plaintain	púteh
land	tana	jar	goasi	jack [fruit]	badok
country	dali	torch	lutong	mango	sapam
village	dolia	candle	lutong la	durian	dian
town	dali	beeswax	la hingit	beetle-nut	gahat
island	busang	wick	wang	cocoa-nut	knob
cape point	tujol	sieve	ilik	kernel, seed	wang
whirl-pool	ivak	bucket	lima	vegetables	tango
plantation field	} luma	scales, balance	tibang	yams	uvi
		hammer	tukol	sugar-cane	tuvo
plane	tana padit	anvil	taranan	salt	knah
wood jungle	tuan	file	isa	pepper	lia
sand	hyt	gimlet	knivo	ginger	lia tana
rock	batu	hatchet, axe	asey	oil	tilang

Burns' Kayan Vocabulary.

English.	Kayan.	English.	Kayan.	English.	Kayan.
journey provisions	maso	frog	jowi	blood	daha
		toad	bunang	entrails	tanei
sugar	tuvlang	lizard	silowit	lungs	praha
padi	pari	alligator	baya	stomach	batuka
rice	baha	guana	kavok	liver	pley
boiled rice	kanan	tortoise	kalovi	bladder	na
dried rice	kartip	butterfly	langoto	brains	otak
flour	tapa	fly	lango	spirit	brua
fish	masik	mosquito	trokok	mind	kanip
beef	sin	small kind	hamok	love	masi
eggs	tilo	mosquito		anger	mano
boat	haruk	flea	koto naso	joy	barkam
oar	say	bee	hingit	grief	mahal
gun	banin	firefly	ada	hope	lay
ball	panglo	ant	klavirang	dumb	hamang
powder	tabar banin	birds	manok	deaf	madang
wheel	ilier	kite	knahu	blind	pisak
needle	loe	pigeon	poni	cough	nikar
thread	tali	fowls	knap	mad	buling
fish hook	pisey	sparrow	bayong	boil, pimple	tuko
tobacco	jako			smallpox	klapit
cigar	loko	mankind	kolonan	rheumatism	niviksal
surf, wave	bangat	man	laki	scurf	key
throne	tagan	woman	doh	itch	gatan
dress	akave	child	hapang	fever	padam
hat, cap	lavong	body	loang	asthma	ly
coat, jacket	basong	head	kohong	wound	gga
shoes	tadok	hair	bok	sick	prah
cloth	kain	beard	bulo	ague	padam bilong
woollen cloth	sakalat	eye	mata	lunatic	blanin
satin	dasu	face	mang	toothache	prah knipan
		ear	apang	kindred	paharin
tiger	lijow	nose	urong	king	maran
leopard	koli	cheek	pinga	queen	maran doh
bear	buang	tongue	jila	lord	hipoy
dragon	nang	mouth	ba	master, Mr.	hibo
rhinoceros	tandoh	teeth	knipan	nobleman	panyan
deer	payow	neck	kran	slave	dipin
hart	payow wang	chin	jan	husband	laki
roe	payow doh	shoulder	hone	wife	hawa
mouse deer	planok	back	loung	father	amay
goat	kading	heart	kanip	mother	inei
wild hog	bavoi	rib	ha	grandfather	huko
boar	bilangnyan	hand	kama	father-in-law	ivan
sow	miray	right hand	tow	mother-in-law	ivan
pig	uting	left hand	maving	brother	arin
boar	batuan	arm	lipe	brother-in-law	hango
bow	hinan	wrists	uso	sister	arin doh
pole-cat	bukulo	elbow	hiko	sister-in-law	hango doh
dog	aso	finger	ikin	son	anak laki
cat	sing	thumb	taval	daughter	anak doh
squirrel	pinnyamo	nails	hulo	twins	anak apir
rat, mouse	lavo	breasts	usok	orphan	anak ula
monkey	brok	abdomen	butit	uncle	mamo
ape	poinang	knee	aliv	aunt	mamo
mias	orong tuan	leg	itat	nephew	nakan
tail	eko	feet	kasa	niece	nakan
skin	blanit	toes	ikin kasa	bastard	tuyang
snake, serpent	knipa	heel	tumin	friend	savila
boa constrictor	panganan	skin	blanit	enemy	iow
		bone	tulang	God	Tanangan
black snake	jilivan	flesh	sin	Lord	Hipoy
worm	halang	sinew	uat	ghost	knito
centipede	diripan	reins	uat daha	mercy	masi
scorpion	diripan kitip	pulse	uat nitit	time	rua
leech	atak	milk	so	season	doman

English.	Kayan.	English.	Kayan.	English.	Kayan.
beginning	aring	bold	lakin	lost	pabat
end	bya	bright	mala	low	liva
year	doman	broad	brang	mad	buling
month	bulan	cheap	lyang	many	liba
day	dow	clever	haman	meagre	nywang
day-light	dow mala	course	kudal	merciful	limer
mid-day	dow nagrang	cold	laram	middle	tahang
morning	pisol	crooked	kowi	might	likap
night	malam	customary	barik	modest	hy
mid-night	malam kagrang	dark	lidam	more	la'an
		dead	matei	mournful	lumo
to-morrow	jima	deaf	madáng	naked	loang tua
yesterday	dow dahalam	deep	dalam	narrow	jali
last night	malam dahalam	defective	hang hang	near	jilang
		defiled	lumi	neat	diya
to-morrow morning	jima pisol	difficult	baval	new	maring
		dilatory	padara	next	jilang
day after to-morrow	duji	distant	su	nimble	ipat
		drunk	mavok	noble	sayu
		dumb	hamang	noisy	nyom
———		dry	magang	numerous	liba
		easy	malai	old	aya
PRONOUNS.		empty	gohang	open	ovar
		enough	tami	outward	tawa
I	akui	equal	pia	pale	nuwang
thou, you	ika	even	padit	passionate	laso kanip
he, she, it	hia	evil	jak	past	lalu
we	ita	expect	haman	perfect	lim sayu
ye, you	ika	false	kalok	plain	lani
they	da'a	fast	kiga	polite	hy
who	hey	fat	munang	poor	jak
which	nono	feeble	kangan	pretty	diya
what	none	few	ok	proper	marong
my, mine	akui hipon	first	aring	pungent	hanit
they, thine	ika hipon	fit	tinang	putrid	muvok
his, hers, its	hia hipon	foolish	ombak	quick	ipat
ours	ita hipon	free	jitua	rapid	kasi
yours	ika hipon	future	bya	raw	ata
theirs	da'a hipon	glad	ikam	ready	ouna
this	ini	good	saya	red	bla
that	iti	great	aya	rich	kaya
all	lim	guilty	hala	right	marong
every	lim lim	handsome	diya	ripe	sak
either	ini iri	hard	mying	rough	patong
some	bali	heavy	bahat	round	bilong
other	dap	high	bo	rusty	higan
anyone	tilana ji	hollow	goang	same	pia
such as this	nonana	hot	laso	scarlet	bla
such as that	notika	hungry	lou	shallow	nivo
		ignorant	magave	sharp	knat
		improper	diyan tinang	short	bek
———		indigent	jak	sick	prah
ADJECTIVES.		innocent	diyam hala	silent	milo tua
		kind	tigam	sincere	lan
acid	sam	knotty	buki	slack	liko
aged	aya	languid	ly	slanting	alan
alike	pia	large	aya	slow	dara
alive	murip	late	dara	small	ok
bad	jak	lazy	duya	smooth	jilura
bald	lasang	left	maving	soft	lima
bashful	hy	less	korang	sorry	mahal
beautiful	diya	level	padit	spotted	kalong
becoming	marong	light	knyan	straight	tuto
bent	kowi	little	kahang	strong	ley
black	pitam	living	murip	sweet	may
blind	pisak	long	aru	swift	kiga

Burns' Kayan Vocabulary.

English.	Kayan.	English.	Kayan.	English.	Kayan.
tall	bo	catch	sigam	grit	parak
tame	malai	change	patoyu	grind	lani
thick	kapal	chase	livo	grow	tubo
thin	knipi	choose	mileh	halt	milo
thirsty	magang ba	chop	nitak	hang	jat
timid	takot	circumcise	knilo	have	teh
tree	lan	clean	myang	hear	naringa
uncertain	diyan djam	climb	nakar	help	mahap
unequal	diyan pia	collect	mipang	hire	niba
useless	diyan non	come	ating	hope	kina
valiant	lakin	comprehend	djam	inherit	kalui taman
warm	laso	conquer	alla	inquire	mitang
weak	ly	copy	nangrua	invade	nasa
weary	knila	cover	nabon	invite	bara
wet	basa	covet	mipang	itch	key
white	puti	cough	nikar	keep	nymi
wicked	jak	count	mujap	kill	mamatei
wide	brang	crawl	namang	kindle	avat
wise	udi	cut	mitnang	knot	tivukang
wrong	hala	dance	najar	know	haman
yellow	nymit	decay	lala	lade	maso
young	minor	deceive	pakalok	laugh	kasiang
zealous	niga	decide	mitnang	leak	pisit
		delay	padara	lend	mujam
Verbs.		deliver	hom teh	lie	pamo
		descend	nili	live	murip
abide	milo	desire	mon	look	knynang
abuse	avay	destroy	tasa	loose	paday
accept	oukapi	devour	nilo	love	masi
accompany	beh	die	matei	make	kna
advise	lavara	dig	knali	meet	pahabo
answer	tagulang	disguise	nangrua	melt	nilong
arrest	sigam	dive	misar	mend	sayuna
arrive	atang	divide	patular	mix	pahivar
be ashamed	tehy	double	patibin	mount	moan
ask	mitang	drag	jat	murmur	lidah
assist	mahap	dream	nupeh	nail	patapak
awake	mower	dress	nakave	obey	tangaran dyn
bake	noyyo	drink	dui	obtain	ala
bargain	tira	drown	gnini	occupy	tuman
bark	mangang	eat	koman	open	ovar
bathe	doe	ebb	mila	oppose	piti
bawl	nangi lan	end, done	pahna	order	teh aim
be	teh	enlighten	malaka	overcome	alla
bear fruit	tubo	expect	kavi	overturn	takala
beat	nukol	extinguish	param	own	paju
become	murip	fall	lagak	paddle	b.isay
beckon	nyap	famish	palau	pardon	masika
beg	aky	fast	ipat, kiga	part	patular
begin	aring	fear	takot	pay	iay
behold	knynang	fight	panoh	perish	kam
believe	miteh	file	pino	please	ikam
betroth	pahawa	find	ala	point	tujol
bind	katong	finish	pahna	prepare	ouna
bite	mat	fish	misey	promise	kalok
bleed	nisa	follow	livo	pull	jat
blow	mahar	forbid	asam mon	punish	mukum
boil	maro	forget	hado	push	haro
borrow	ujam	forgive	masika	put	dahy
break off	punang	forsake	milo tinan	quench	param
bribe	duoya	founder	kam	rain	usan
bring	gree	fry	naga	reach	utang
brush	mipa	gape	nivanga	receive	oukapi
buy	pavlay	gather	pang	reckon	mujap
call	muvoy	get	ala	rent	nebaka
carry	kna'an	give	my	repair	sayuna
cast account	mujap	go	kaka	reside	milo

English	Kayan	English	Kayan	English	Kayan
return	uli	long since	arupa	one	ji
rise	mower	yesterday	dow dahalam	two	dua
rob	nako	to-morrow	jima	three	tulo
roll	lulon	not yet	diyan pa	four	pat
row	basay	afterwards	bya	five	lima
run	lap	sometimes	halak tesee	six	anam
say	korin	perhaps	mahapa	seven	tusyu
see	knynang	seldom	mijat	eight	saya
sell	bili	when	hiran	nine	pitan
send	kato	much	kahom	ten	pulo
sew	jinhut	little	ok	eleven	pulo ji whin
share	patular	how much	kori liba	twelve	pulo dua whin
shove	haro	how great	kori aya	thirteen	pulo tulo whin
sit	milo	enough	tami	twenty	dua pulo
skin	blanit	abundantly	kahom	twenty-five	dua pulo lima whin
sleep	tudo	wisely	udi		
smell	bun	foolishly	ombak		
smoke	lison	justly	marong		
snatch	nako	quickly	kiga	**KAYAN PROPER NAMES OF MEN.**	
sow	nugal	slowly	dara		
speak	tangaran	badly	jak		
stand	biti	truly	lan lan		
starve	lou	yes	l	Gong	
steal	nako	no, not	diyan	Lerong	
stop	naring	not at all	diyandipa	Madang	Swift
swear	mamyan	how	nonan, kori	Koli	Leopard
sweep	mipa	why	nanonan	Hajang	
take	api	wherefore	non pohun	Sajin	
talk	tangaran	more	laan	Tamalana	
teach	cakali	most	lalu kahom	Samatu	
think	palamana	good	sayu	Knipa	Serpent
throw	bat	better	lalu sayu	Lijow	Tiger
tie	nupot	best	sayu lan	Dian	Durian
trust	kina	worse	lalu jak	Lidam	
turn	kaluvar	worst	jaklan	Parran	
uncover	páovar	again	rua	Lia	
understand	djam			Batu	Rock
use	tuman	**PREPOSITIONS.**		Tuva	Sugar-cane
wait	kavi			Lasa	
walk	pano	from	maniti	Owin	
weep	nangi	at	bara	Akan. This is a prefix applied to the name of anyone who has lost by death one or more of his children, as Akan Lasa, Akan Kinpa. It is more commonly appropriated by the higher than by the lower classes. Laki, the name for man, husband, is also made use of as a prefix to the names of married men to denote that the person to whose name it is prefixed is a father, as Laki Dian, Laki Lidam. Like the former word, it is chiefly applied to the higher order.	
wipe	mipa	by	mutang		
wither	lala	with	dyn		
wonder	dimisi	in	halam		
work	knadoi	into	pahalam		
wound	gga	through	mutang		
wrestle	payo	out	habay		
yawn	nivanga	out of	nymo		
		without	pahabay		
		on, upon	huson		
ADVERBS.		under	hida		
here	hini	between	tahang		
there	hiti	near	jilang		
where	hino	beyond	lawat		
before	ona				
behind	baloung	**CONJUNCTIONS.**		**NAMES OF WOMEN.**	
upward	bahuson				
downward	bahida	and	panga	Tipong	
below	hida	if	jivang	Jilivan	Snake
above	huson	both	koa	Bulan	Moon
whither	hinopa	because	lavin	Pidang	Flower
backward	baloung	wherefore	lavin non	Balalata	
whence	manino	therefore	lavin iti	Sidow	Day
now	mahoup	as	noti	Lavan	
to-day	dowini	though	barangka	Lango	
lately	maringka	yet, also	sica	Puteh	Plantain
just now	mahaupini			Buah	Fruit

St. John's Vocabularies. cix.

DAYAK LANGUAGES.—SAMBAS TO BATANG LUPAR.

For the six sets of Vocabularies which here follow I am indebted to the kindness of Sir SPENCER ST. JOHN, G.C.M.G., who not only gave me permission to re-publish them from his work "In the Forests of the Far East," but also took the trouble to re-peruse and correct them.

In the first set I have here omitted the column of Sarawak words, as the Vocabulary published by the Rev. WM. CHALMERS in 1861 is more complete. This more complete Vocabulary of Mr. CHALMERS I have placed at the end of those published by Sir SPENCER ST. JOHN.—*H.L.R.*

* In forwarding me the four Vocabularies which I now insert, the Rev. WILLIAM CHALMERS mentioned that the Lara people say they came originally from the neighbourhood of Brunei, the capital.

NOTE.—" The Sarawak Land Dyak is in the dialect of the Sentah Tribe. The ü of this tribe is changed into "o" in the other tribes of the River Sarawak. Sentab River is a tributary of the southern branch of the Sarawak.

** The Sadong Dayak is the dialect spoken by the tribes on the River Kadup, a tributary of the Upper Sadong.

*** The Lara is a tribe of Upper Sambas, part of which now resides on the Upper Lundu.

"ë = English a. ü = English u in cub. ei = English ay in lay.
 e = English e in met. au = ow in now. ö = aw in law.
 ü = French u. ai = English i. ch final = German ch."—*St. John II. 383.*

English.	Sadong.	Lara.	Sibuyau.	English.	Sadong.	Lara.	Sibuyau.
able	inshañn	kaán	bulih	before	taiyñ	uru	dulu
across (river)	sisa	pahja	sebrang	behind	{di kiinang {di sundich	buntot	dudi
acquainted with	ümpuon	nümparu	tau	beads	tumbis	turni	marik
afraid	teroun	buut	takut	black	bihis	sungut	chelum
agree	janggi	bepusun	berjanji	bird	manok	manuk	burong
alligator	buoi	buro	gaiyañ	blood	daya	daya	daha
ant	subi	subi	semut	blind	bikap	buta	buta
angry	deroch	baji	bing-at	break (in two)	pütah	patah	patah
arise from sleep	mungkat	kias	dani	breathe	ngashting	misingat	sipuat
ataps, leaf mats	irañ	aro	atap	burn	nyahu	nyahu, ninu	tunoh
above	sombu	samo	atas	bad	biek	jahñ	jai
all	samoa	sfiman-man	samoa	boy	anak künya	kangot	anak biak
ask (beg)	minta	mahi	minta	bachelor	bujang	bujang	bujang
ask (enquire)	pñsik	masikan	tanya	brave	pogan	pagan	brani
bathe	ngumon	mamu	mandi	bridge	linyan	titi	andaü
below	sigan	saroch	dibahóa				

English.	Sadong.	Lara.	Sibuyau.	English.	Sadong.	Lara.	Sibuyau.
BODY (HUMAN)				BODY (HUMAN) *continued* :—			
head	tibo	ungan	tuboh	knee	bak tuod	tukugn	palapatioang
forehead	bak	abak	pala	heel	peniga	tigak	tumit
cheeks	drich	kaning	dai	palm	pipach tiingan	parapa baregn	tapa jahi
eye	piimpi	koko	koyu	lips	bibich	ioshin	mulut
eyebrow	matuch kiin ng	matu	mata	flesh	isi	turang	isi
eyelash	buruch kilat matuch	burun rimin	bulu kaniang	bones	tulang	pusat	tulang
nose	kilat matuch	burun matu	bulu mata	navel	pushid	raka	pusat
nostrils	undung	dudugn	idong	knuckle	bukuck tiingan	parapa kija	buku tunjia
mouth	rubang undung	rubang dudugn	lubang idong	sole	pipach kija	kurit	tapa kaki
teeth	boba	boba	mulut	skin	kulit		kulit
tongue	jipun	japu	pigi	BEASTS :—			
throat	jili	rata	dila	deer (rusa)	paiyu	anyung	rusa
ear	tegunggong	gangogn	batang hukoang	monkey (kra)	kara	kara	kara
chin	kiping	rajak	pundiang	dog	kosho	kashu	asu
hair of head	raang	rang	dagu	cat	sengau	uching	maiau
neck	buruch	abok	buak	pig, domestic	pongan	uwi	babi humah
side	kuko	jangok	hukoang	pig, jungle	laba	lauk	babi kampong
shoulder	tigahang	silet	husua	rat	babu, jupor	tikus	tikus
breast	kowi	kai	bauh	cough (to)	mungkul	mukut	batiak
back	ishuk	sado	dada	come	monig	utung	datei
belly	jaju	rutuk	blakang	cold	bitbi, madud	sangu	chilap
posterior	putong	putugn	pahut	cry out	siak	ngampak	nyawa
loins	pumpi kiinang	rabat	buhiat	cry (weep)	niingis	munse	nyabak
arm—shoulder to elbow	kupong	apagn	punggoang	cook	nimuk	nanuk	nyumai
arm—elbow to wrist	pumpong	barangu	buah langan	companion	dingan	age	pangan
				commit adultery	nyowang	bebaiyu	bambai
elbow	brungo	baregn	langan	covet	kilek	marun	dika
hand	sikuch	siku	siku	cut	kapiig	mimagn	putus
fingers	tiingan	baregn	jahi	come out	luach	mungkas	pansut
nails	buah tiingan	trinyo	tunjia	DRESS :—			
wrist	siruch	siru	kuku	jacket	bojuch	jipo	baju
thumb	iing-giim	ladak	anggam	head-dress	tundo	bung abak	labiang
thigh	indu tiingan	indu baregn	tunjoa indu	petticoat	jomuch	jamu	kaiin
calf	piinch	pa	pa	trowsers	saluar	salauar	tanchuat
foot	bites	batis	betis	"chawat"	tahup	patung	sihat
ancle	kija	kfija	kaki	"tambok"	juach	jua	jua
	tulang kelali	matu dudegn	buku ali				

St. John's Vocabularies.

English				
DRESS—*continued*	tungking	tokeng	tambōak	
"tambok," small, worn on the side				
pinang knife	sinda	sunda	lungga	
sheath of pinang knife	landong	sario	handuang	
parang				
sheath of parang				
day	bukŭ	bai	isau	
dance	sibōng	dohong	tangkin	
deaf	onu	ano	ahi	
destroy	belangi	nari	ngigal	
divide	nyithŭp	man pain	nyieup ai	
doctor, to (bilian)	kaku	awa	bisu	
doctor, a (male)	tebodung	biingal	mandap	
doctor (female)	rusak	rusak	husak	
	bedodŭg	punugn	duman	
			bilian	
			manang	
	dayung pancha, burich	bari		
door	jigan	pintu	pintu	
dead	kibŭŭs	kabis	mati	
diligent	rijung	gŭgah	hajin	
enough	luput	cbukup	umbas	
eat	maăn	uman	makai	
egg	funtulo	tura	telo	
enter	murŭit	maru	masok	
enemy	pŭngaiyu	pengaiyu	munsoh	
fire	opui	api	api	
forbidden (tabooed)	purich	pari	mali	
fish	ikan	ikan	lawak	
fly (a)	tura	nyamuk	lalat	
fly (to)	finchaling, mobur	mibir	terbang	
fat		manu	gumu	
fowl	siŭk, siap	siap	manok	
fall ("jatoh")	rŭbu	mana	labia	
forget	ngkomut	karimut	lupa	
father	ŭmang	sama	apai	
firefly	ŭngkarup	kalamiu	chutlut	

English			
FRUIT:—			
durian	dihtn	dihan	hian
plantain	pisang	barak	pisang
mangustin	gunau	sikuk	langaiin
langsat	iashat	sarikan	langsat
go	oji	anu	jalei
go up	nyumak	maka	niki
go down	muhun	disa	nuhun
girl	anak dayung	angot	anak biak indu
grown up (as brushwood, selut)	jukut	abut	sikut
get	dapud	daput	tŭmu
gape (yawn)	ngkuhab	chabun	nguap
good	paguch	lhmus	badas
God	Tŭmpa	l'enita	Batara
give	jugon	mangkan	bahi
glad	kira, awang	rŭpo	dika-hati
gold	berowan amas	berawan	mas
HOUSE:—			
outside platform	rŭmin	rŭmin	humah
common room	tonyu	buntahan	tanyu
private room	awach	sambi	ruei
garret	rŭmin	ohang	lawang
high	siŭnu	rŭnga	sadau
hill	darŭid	nyŭmu	tinggi
hide	nyukin	munggu	bukit
hungry	seburŭk	nukan	lalei
hear	ngŭping	seburuk	lapah
husband	bonŭch	danga	dingah
hot ("panas")	nyowa, shiru	banun	laki
hot ("angat")	paras	jera	panas
is	aduch	paras	angat
is not	(kadŭ aduch	uni	bisi
	{ inyap raiya		
jump over	melompat	kati	nadai
jump down	timpapu	nyantang	merejōak
jungle	tarun	nyanguŋn	trajun
kneel	unyuch	tarun	kampong
keep ("pliara")	(nagoch	nungkogn	nyerunkoang
	(nyingat	ngingu	ibun

English.	Sadong.	Lara.	Sibuyau.	English.	Sadong.	Lara.	Sibuyau.
know	timpuon	penani	tau, numu	one	indi	usa	sa
kill	kenobus	ngamis	bunoh	once	ni, idah	nisidah	sekali
large	bahas	aihyo	besei	parang, forge a	ngoba	maba	tūmpa
lazy	bojag	tuga	kelalih	posts	oros	nahi	tiang
lean	kurus	kurus	kuhus	poor	babi	papa	seranta
light (in weight)	nyangan	nyaán	lempiang	provisions	bokul	sangu	bekal
little (quantity)	ichiuk	igeat	sikeat	perspiration	udas	adas	peloh
long	ombuch	ūngho	panjei	"pinang" (betel nut)	pinang, bahai	ohe	pinang
"lesong" (a mortar)	lesong	rensungan	lesong	put down	jimpan	nana	ūngkah
"alu" (a pestle)	alu	aru	alu	put by	jimpan	mogan	simpan
laugh	natau	guluk	tawa	paddy	padi	padi	padi
lie down	nguling	guring	gali	pleasant	sidi	ahwan	nyamei
lie (speak falsely)	muding	lachi	bula	quickly	pantas	japat	lekas
many	tibun	kara	banyau	red	tinchalak	teransak	mirah
melt	lilich	luluch	anchuah	return	maring	ure	pulei
merciful	masi	masi	kaseh	remember	tian	ingat	ingat
moon	buran	buran	bulan	road	jitran	pagala	jalei
mother	aiyang, undu	sindo	indei	"rotan"	wi	wi	hutan
morning	pagi	ngakap ano	magi-pagi	remove (pindah)	berpindah	pindah	pindah
mat ("klasa")	krisah	bide	bidei	run away	buhu	boho	iari
mat ("tikar")	umak	bido	kiaia	rotten	modam	modam	buhua
man	nunich, inya	soók	ohang	receive	kira	nyamut	terima
mosquito	prunggang	pintujok	byamuak	rice	bras, boru	nahas	bahas
mud	jijub	lulok	huboah	rice, boiled	sungkoi	nasi	asi
night	ngarūm	ngarum	malam	straight	bujog	tamut	luhus
new	bauch	bahu	bahu	strike (pukul)	nintong	mangkugn	pahu
not	kadti	kati	adai, nda	sick	minam	inam	pedias
not (do)	ba		anang	sleep	kidiik	punok	pandak
now	mate	mati dia	kamaia tu	sun	bius	buus	tindoak
name	gonon	gaān	nama	stars	matūch shiru	matu ano	mat'ari
noon	narang onu	tuno ano	s'tengah ahi	shut (to)	bintang	bintang	bintang
old (man)	nya tuuch	uma	tuei	sandfly	panut, tutu	tutup	tutup
old (thing)	dūmba	tubi	lama	scald	sirap	bihas	singiat
oil	inyo	aiyan	minyak	see	rius	batu	angus
open (to)	tuhas	nukas	silak	sharp	tibūk	meili	peda
other	bukin	lain	lain	shake, to (neuter)	roja	ruja	tajam
outside	luach sopa	sato	di luach		guyut	begote	beguyu

St. John's Vocabularies. cxiii.

speak	besinda	kasena	bejako	wing	arad	sayap
sneeze	bekuch-sh	berusun	berkasi	white	buda	putih
sit down	ngulu	munyung	duduk	well (baik)	paguch	baiak
stand up	mijiŋ	aguŋ	berdiri	walk	jalan	bejalei
spider	tingkuka	tinga	tampa lawa	woman	dayung	indu
steal	ntingku	nangko	chuchi	wife	tishan	bini
sweet	sija	mamis	manis	water	umon	ai
squeeze	michet	nxerachet	pichiat	weary	kunyoch	lelak
satiated	bisó	baso	kenyang	wind (the)	mohu	angin
spacious	nyowa	tawas	tawas	worms (stomach)	tingkiho	belut
sorry	susah-ati	suba-latï	tusah	work (to)	kaminyang	jama
small (size)	ichiñk	inek	mukat, miet	what?	tinich	ai
"sirih"	baid	uit	sirih	whither?	gupich	kini
sky	langit	langit	langit	whence?	sopich	arini
snake	nyipech	nipa	ulah	who?	osi	apa
spit	nguruja	ngeruja	berludah	young	tingid	mudei
spittle	royang	rayang	ai lioch	yesterday	ngtindu	kamahi
stop (to)	ngtindei	madi	bado	year	sowa	taun
still (to be)	mundu	moko	diaü			
take	tumit	tangkap	ambi	Pronouns :—		
touch	tingnich	nyankam	jamah	I	aku	aku
track	indich	tawan, aju	bakaū	thou	omu	köa
to-morrow	pagi	jakap	pagi	he	aiyech	tu
this	siti, siech	dia	tu	we	ami	kami *(exclusive of persons addressed)*
that	saäch	kako, tëan	nyun			kitei *(inclusive)*
throw away	bütan	matan	buei	ye	kita	kita
thirsty	haus	karing ashung	haus	they	aiyech	tu
vegetables	tingkünich	apu	daün kayu			

h

DAYAK LANGUAGES.—Continued.—SPECIMENS OF THE DAYAK LANGUAGE.

"I add now a short Vocabulary, forwarded to me by the Rev. WILLIAM GOMEZ, who has been stationed at Lundu during many years. It involves a little repetition, but is useful to compare with that collected by the Rev. WILLIAM CHALMERS. By Lundu, Mr. GOMEZ refers to the original inhabitants of that river."—*Spencer St. John.*

NAMES OF TEN MEN AND WOMEN IN THE TRIBE.

	Husband.	Wife.		Husband.	Wife.		Husband.	Wife.
1.	Kalong, O. K.	Gunja	3.	Langi	Kinja	6.	Nyinkong	Jeba
2.	Gali	Binda	4.	Itak	Indak	7.	Bulang	Mingga
			5.	Samuling	Kimba	8.	Lunsong	Burong
						9.	Mangga	Sara
						10.	Sageng	Tamo

HEIGHTS.

	Men.					Women.	
OK Istia Rajah	5 ft. 2½ in.	Bulang	5 ft. 3 in.	Lunsong	4 ft. 11 in.	Pungut	5 ft.
Garai	5 ft. 4 in.	Jinal	4 ft. 10½ in.			Ria	4 ft. 10½ in.

English.	Sabuyau.	Lara.	Salakau.	Lundu.	English.	Sabuyau.	Lara.	Salakau.	Lundu.
NUMERALS:—					foot	kaki	kaja	paha	po, on
one	sa	asa	asa	ni	heel	tumbit	tigak	tumit	tiga
two	dua	dua	dua	duo	skin	kulit	kurit	ku, it	kulit
three	tiga	taru	talu	taru	bone	tulang	turakng	tuang	tulang
four	ampat	apat	ampat	pat	flesh	isi	insin	isi	daging
five	lima	rima	lima	rimo	sinew	uhat	uhat	urat	at
six	anam	unum	anam	nom	milk	susu	susu	susu	sisun
seven	tujoh	ijo	tujoh	jo	heart	ati	ate	hati	atin
eight	lapan	mahi	delapan	mahi	spleen	kuha	kura	kura	kura
nine	sambilan	pire	sambilan	pire	brains	umpadu	umpadu	padu	podun
ten	sapuloh	sapuloh	sapuloh	samoong	blood	daha	daya	darah	ouk
waist	punggong	apakng	pinggang	kupong	spittle	di lioh	rayakng	ai uja	daya
navel	pusat	pusat	pusat	pesud	snivel	insak	buduk	edoh	royang dok
knee	pala patong	tukung	tuut	bakorob	tears	ai mata	pain matu	ai mata	eu boton

St. John's Vocabularies.

English								
perspiration	peloh	adas	pau	das	dahi	kaning	kaning	uru
dandriff	daki	dunuk	dati	ing	pisan	kingkek	tangengeng	ponyip
pus	nana	penunu	nana	penona	bulu keneng	bulu rimin	bulu ramang	kening
face	mua	bahas	muha	jawin	mata	matu	mata	botun
dumb	bisu	awa	awa		pendeng	rajak	tere, nyek	kajip
deaf	bengal	bagi	banga	bangam	idong	duduking	idong	noxong
blind	buta	buta	buta	buta	pipi	kuko	koko	panig, ng
dimness	ulon	kabor	kabor	kabor	mulut	baba	mulut	beba
stammer	kat	mah	awah	awah	dila	rata		jera
silly	budon	bagah	bagah	budoh	mulut	bibih	bibir	bibin
mad	gila	gila	gila	mukud	gigi	japu	gigi	jupon
cough	batok	mukut	batok	perkis	hakong	jangok	tegeh	tungoh
boil	bisul	tampusu	bisoan	kirekng	dagu	rikng	jago	rang
sea	laut	laut	laut	mata nanu	blakang	rutuk	ba, ikang	punok
sun	matahari	matoano	mata ari	bulan	kaki	kaja	paha	po, on
moon	bulan	buran	buan	bintang	langan	bareking	angan	tangan
star	bintang	bintang	bintang	tarang	dada	sadoh	dada	sodo
light	trang	tawas	tarang	mapong	tunjok	terinyo	kukot	terinyo
darkness	petang	petakng	petang	putek	kuku	siru	kuku	sirun
heat	panas	jara	darang	modud	prut	putukng	parut	tain
cold	chelap	panut	dingin	gening ayong	api	api	api	apoi
cloud	remang	rahu	niga	kilat	asap	asap	asap	asu
lightning	kilat	kilat	elak	dudu	hujan	hujan	hujan	jan
thunder	guntoh	guntor	guntor	berengan	angin	nyaru	angin	sebak
rainbow	unggoaja	meraje	antu ai	nyaah	bahat	tupan	nyaru	ribut
mankind	manusia		manusia	nyaah dadari	paseh	krasik	krasik	sumat
man	ohang laki	sok	angaki	dayung	batu	batu	batu	batu
woman	ohang indoh	areh	ang bini	genan	bukit	bukit	bukit	doron
body	tuboh	mahu	tuboh	bok	mungu	mungu	muton	motang
hair	bok	unsgan	bu, uk	bak	reboh	muton	ochak	rapak
head	pala	atok	kapala			paya		

English	
forehead	
temples	
eyebrow	
eye	
ear	
nose	
cheek	
mouth	
tongue	
lip	
teeth	
neck	
chin	
back	
feet	
hand	
chest	
finger	
nails	
stomach	
fire	
smoke	
rain	
wind	
storm	
sand	
stone	
mountain	
hill	
mud	

DAYAK LANGUAGES.—*Continued.*

"The following Vocabulary is compiled from materials furnished me by the late Mr. BRERETON. The Sea Dayak language is spoken by the aborigines on the Batang Lupar and all its tributaries, the Seribas, Kalaka, and the streams which flow to the left bank of the Rejang. The Bugaus, who live in the districts bordering the great Kapuas River, speak the same language. There are local variations, but they are of minor importance. The Malau is the language of the aborigines living at the very interior of the Kapuas, and, it is said, not many days walk from the great mountain of Tilong."—*Spencer St. John.*

English	Sea Dayak	Malau	English	Sea Dayak	Malau	English	Sea Dayak	Malau
straight	rurus	mupi	from	arri	aus	white	burak	uteh uteh
crooked	bingkok, simpin	kong kong	all	samoa	byu	red	mansoh	di darah
square	ampat bersgi	kuata	many	meio	tetopit	yellow	kuning	tantu muün
round	bulat sagala	ga gulun	few	mimit	keh kih	blue	biru	biru
long	panjai	ba lankei	small	mit	brah	green	ijo	
broad	besai	broh	large	besai	si bangun	country	benua	
thick	tabal		like	boka	anindehen	earth	benua	
thin	nipauh, mipis	nipis	now	kamiyatu	endisi	stone	batu	
deep	dalam	ba jalam	when	kamiya		gold	mau	mas
high	tinggi	ba lankie	then	pa gila balik		silver	perak	perak
short	pondak		to-morrow	ka mani	mina	iron	besi	besi
without	de ruai		yesterday	tuai	malam	mountain	bukit	bukit
within	dedialam		old	bharu obas	tuah	valley	darong lengkap	lengkap
light (in weight)	lumpong	tanga sauh	new	lobah	baruh	cave	lobang batu	long batu
heavy	brat		slow	jumpat	ba laun	hill	bukit	bukit
above	datas	de asit	rapid	dadat	ba riah	plain	padang	padang
below	de baroh	de yaum	strike	patah kru	malun tongi	island	pulaü	pulau
behind	deblakang		break	telengah	poloh	water	at	danum
before	demua	de roka	open	tutup, tikup	ilakkeinih	sea	tasik	roong jawa
between	antara dua		shut	katon	tulopu	river	suñgei	suñgai
here	kitu, ditu	loku	lift	tampalom	angkat	wind	ribut	ribut
there	kinu duinyin	ke mangeh	throw	basah	keiniko	hurricane	ribat bungat	
far	jauh		wet	rankai		cloud	niga	dom
near	dampi		dry	tawas tumpak	kumbat tor	rainbow	anakraja	
where	nei iya	ampensop	light	petang	manara	rain	uyan	suran
at	de	di selananu	darkness	chilum	raun	lightning	kilat	dolok
to	ka		black		an tarun	thunder	guntur	

St. John's Vocabularies.

English			
day	ari		
night	lamai		
morning	pagi	asoh	
sun	matahari	kau ko	manbin
noon	tingari	mat asoh	dejankat
sky	laigit		
moon	bulan	suan	
star	apei andau	bulan	lasu
hot	api	bintang	
fire	panas	panas	
burn	tunoh	si siak	
smoke	asap	tuton	aloeh
ashes	abus	rimbu	
cocoa-nut	buah miniak-	kutu au	
	unjor		
plaintain	pisang	buah unti	barasam
paddy	padi	asseh	niawar akar
rice	brauh	brauh	mosi berianka
pumpkin	antakai	parangi	
yam	abuk	miah	mamis
seed	banih, igi	tulang ah	
tree	pohn	akak kaya	
root	randah, urat	banarun	
leaf	daun	daunah	
flower	bungai	bukas	
fruit	buah	buirah	
raw	matah	mutoh	
ripe	mansoh	sasak	
deer	rusa	piang	
bear	jugam		meka
cow	chapi, banting		mateh
goat	bedus	kambin	ankan
dog	uduk, ukue	asu	minum
hog	jani	bawi	meta
monkey	kra		
cat	maiau	sih	
mouse	chit		nangis
rat	chit	balau	chisum
squirrel	tupei	but	men janum
bird	burong		la lako
domestic fowl	manok	manok	lingar

duck	itek	riri	
kite	menaul	bau	lambar
sparrow	pipit	dungus	lari
swallow	lelayang		kadin
crow	kak		duduh
cage	krukor	ruar	mumbit
snake	ural	ba ningar	tindoh
frog	rinkak rarigu	lauk	sadin
fish	ikan		
crab	katam		
prawn	undai	undan	
butterfly	maniah		
bee	manyik		
fly	lalat	lalas	
mosquito	niamok		
louse	kutu		
ant	semut	sinsam	
spider	ampelawa		
horn	tandok	tunjan	
tail	iku	inkuah	
feather	bulu		
wings	sayap	sapa	
egg	tuloh	turoh roh	
honey	ai manyik	danum muami	
wax	lilin		
body	tuboh	mantuan	
head	pala	ulu	
hair	bok	rambut	
face	muah	lindoh	
ear	pending	telinga	
eye	mata	mata	
nose	idong	ingar	
cheek	kayuh	tampilik	
mouth	mulut	baba	
lip	bibir	kulit baba	
tooth	gilit n'li	gisi	
tongue	delah	lilah	
hand		tangan	
finger	jari	unjok	
thumb	tunjok indu	unjok tangan	
nail	kukut	kuku	

belly		parut
foot	prut	
bone	kaki	
flesh	isi	
skin	kulit	
fat	gamok	
lean	kurus	
blood	dara	
saliva	ludah	
sweat	peluh	
hard	kriang	
soft	lemeh	
hot	aingat	
cold	chilap	
thirsty	rankei rekon	
hungry	rapah	
sour	masam	
sweet	manis	
bitter	pait	
smell	bau	
fragrant	aingit, nyamei	
stinking	but jaii	
sick	padis, tabin	
dead	parei	
eat	makai, dumpah	
drink	irup	
see	mada	
laugh	tatawa	
weep	niabak	
kiss	sium	
speak	jaku	
be silent	diau	
hear	ningar	
lift	angkat	
walk	jalai	
run	rari belanda	
stand	berdiri	
sit	duduk	
climb	niki	
sleep	tindok	
awake	dani	

English	Sea Dayak	Malau	English	Sea Dayak	Malau	English	Sea Dayak	Malau
recollect	ingat		take	ambi	taioh	salt	garam	kin paroh
know	nemu		bring	bai	iawa	clothes	kain	sauh
forget	na ingat	temu	take away	angkat	tangkong	ear-ring	gronjong, tinga	
ask	tania		kill	bunoh	dunoh	chawat	sirat	
answer	saut	ketu anan	I	aku	tak	house	rumah	pra kayu
understand	nemu udi		mine	akum puh	tak ampunah	wood	kayu	pintu
yes	au, bisi	oh	thou	nuan	ikon	posts	tiang	
no	ingai, nadei	nanok	thine	nuanpuh	ikon ampunah	door	lian	
beautiful	bajik, badas	mam	he, she, it	iya	ninan	ladder	tangku	alik
ugly	nda badas, jaii	[aku	his, etc.	niam puh		bed	penindok	
pleased	gagot hati	sa sau niawa	we (inclusive or absolute)	kita		mat	tikai	
sorry	tusut, tusah hati	sakanutin	our (inclusive or relative)	kitampuh		box	peti	
afraid	takut, rawan		we (exclusive or relative)	kami		road	jalai	relis
shame	malu	bawa	our (exclusive)	kami puh		bridge	jamban	
love	kasih, rindu		you	nuan		spear	sankoh	
hate	na'ndu		your	nuanpuh		sword	pedang	
anger	ringat	nanak meh nia	they	iya		chopping knife	duku	basi
wish	dekah	babu julu	their	iyampah		boat	bangkong	prauh
right	amai	menioh	this	itu		canoe	bidok	bidup
wrong	salah		that	nin, nia		spirit	antu	
good	badas		who	sapa		man	orang laki	ber bakar
bad	jain	mam	what	nama, kati		woman	indu	berbeneh
true	amai, benda	jauh	food	makai, enkaiu		husband	laki	
false	bula	topat	rice, boiled	asi		wife	bini	arineh
wait	netu		sugar	gula		father	apai	amah
come	datai	ako akoh	oil	miniak		mother	indai	indu
go	nurun, pegi	andor	milk	ai tusu		grandfather	aki, nineh	piang
meet	temu		flesh	isi		child	anak	
hide	belalei	sunyan kolu ko	boil	sumei		old	inai, tuai	
search	gigah	men ari	broil	ganggang		young	muda	
find	ulih	kuleh				boy	biak	
give	anjong, unjok	anlat				girl	n'dun	

BALAU NAMES.

Men.		Women.		Men.		Women.
Linggi	Rata	Salam	Nangga	Janting	Musit	Itau	Chula
Jelapiang	Salima	Saripa	Moramat	Anggi	Jisang	Sarika	Rabi

DAYAK LANGUAGES.—Continued.

LANGUAGES OF TRIBES BETWEEN THE REJANG AND BARAM.

English.	Milanau.	Kayan.	Pakatan.	English.	Milanau.	Kayan.	Pakatan.
straight	tigah	tuto		small	gomit, isit	ok	isi
crooked	pikro, pikok	kauwi	mato'	large	ay-ung, ayoh	ayah	uṅgei
square	ampat papak, pak	tepahak	kaliong kaliong	like	sama, pesoh	chepiah	jabalu
round	gulong	biliong	lipat, liṅgit	now	absilu, nahu	krehini	ah
long	lalau	aruh	atup	when	pidang	heran	lipa
broad	aiyoh	berang	ijé	then	suni		para
thick	kapal, kapan	kapan		to-morrow	lesung, laumasuk	jima	lamasok
thin	dipis	ngipi	uṅgei	yesterday	sabi, lau mai	dahalum	alommalom
deep	tumal, tebun	delum	kapan	old	melai, garu-puhun	lumeh	matui
shallow	té		meliring	new	jakin, uba	maharing	uwa
high	regau	bo	melolom	motion	lakau	tepanau	
short	dadit, kadit	biek	mauo	slow	melai, luhuei	tepat.	malia
without	auir, kauir	auwa	ujo	rapid	jiik, seii	nian	maro
within	wang, kadalum	amin	api, lipo	strike	piir	nukal	bek
light (in weight)	paiying	nian	lalum	break	pesa', pelak	brong	mota
			melang	open	kab, ukah	lueh	ukah
heavy	bahat	bahat	mawat	shut	tabin	kap	jinut
above	amau, mamau	usun	mau o	lift	makat	amju	akat
below	ibah	idah	lué	throw	galang, barang	buht	ting
behind	buta, likut	baleh	api lauo	wet	basah	basah	basoh
before	jau-ai	talatan	tobata	dry	miiang, bahung	megaang	adang
between	patas, gahut	hang	gat	sound	seiigau, serau	nau	hau
here	kide, idai	teni	ati	light	tahung	malah dau	alau
there	kidiin, inun	tenan	iri	darkness	padam, kelam	ledam	sigalup
far	mèjù	su	moju	black	bilam	pitam	horommorom
near	segah	jelang	deteri manjo	white	putih	borah	buak
where	gua-an. bahn	santeno	pahen	red	sat, sak	beliah	arang arang
at	gnau		to	yellow	kunyit	jemit	
to	tugün			blue	biru	using	
from	kiman, keman	man	to maia	green	gadong	gadong	ujang arang arang
all	gruh	limlin	hing gaké	country	tád		bila
many	dida, bunah	mahum	uṅgat	earth	tanah	tanah	tanoh
few	jimit, sisit	okedok	mari	stone	sanau, bato	bato	bato

English.	Milanau.	Kayan.	Pakatan.	English.	Milanau.	Kayan.	Pakatan.
gold	mas	mah		seed	bahah	wang	bah
silver	perak	perak		tree	basoh	ketoh	karing
iron	bisi	titau		root	akai	akah	oka
mountain	tugong	ngalang		leaf	duhun	itun	daun
valley	deta, pating	akeng	malat	flower	bedak	idang	buñgo
cave	luboong	lubang bok	tong	fruit	buah	buah	buah
hill	tagah	ngalang ok	gatong	raw	tah	letah	ata
plain	lalang	nha	bobang	ripe	sak	sak	ak
island	sah	busong	tong malui	tiger	koleh	koleh	
water	anim	atah	data	deer	paiau	paiau	
sea	dit, sabung	ngeoh	palui	bear	makop		ujang
river	sungei	ungah	danum	horse	kudah	bruang	makup
wind	paingai, bario	bahoi	kala	buffalo	karbau	kaleo	karbau
hurricane	buingas, bario lagah		bila	cow	sapi marau		
cloud	mabat, duruoh		balu	goat	muh	kadeng	asu
rainbow	iang aiñgan, jajiling	mengah	balu makokop	dog	asau	aso	bauwi
rain	ujan	langat	aun	hog	babui	baboi	kiat
lightning	skilit	lingyating	bukang	monkey	bedok	kuyal	maiau
thunder	litñ, prah	usan	langut	cat	ngau	cheng	chit
day	lau	kilat	bali	mouse	belabau		belauo
night	lemui	barareh	bali	rat	belabau pagong	lavoh	sirik
morning	tumu, masu	dau	alau	squirrel	bap	telih	purit
sun	matalau	malam	malam	bird	manok	manok	siap
noon	kedang lau	niup	alau	domestic fowl	siañ	niap	
sky	lanyit	matadau	matalau	duck	itek		
moon	bulan	dau nagrang	alau marapuru	kite	kiniñ kang		
star	betohun	lungit	lañgit	sparrow	gerit		niau
hot	lesu	bulan	bulan	swallow	kalau pisan, salar	niau	purit
fire	apui	lauing	letuen	crow	kah	tegih	belini
burn	tiñi, sidap	anit dau	melahu	cage	sakar		purit aromarom
smoke	aniis, tugun	apui	apui	snake	dipa, peñganan	bakah	lakit
ashes	abo	tutong	asik	frog	bekñrek, wak	nipa	asei
cocoa-nut	nyoh	lesun	sun	fish	jen	wak	buja
plantain	balak	aroh	au	crab	gatim, tekeh	masih	bajo
paddy	padai	nyoh	tuporu	prawn	padak		nitike
rice	bahar	uteh	jusang	butterfly	belabing, selababang	orang	suat
pumpkin	labo	pareh	pari	bee	añge, señgut	tiñgat	siñgut
yam	obei	baha	benai	fly	lañg au	lañgo	lañgo
		tinun aloh	entakei				
		oveh	ubi				

English					
mosquito	krias	niamok		thirsty	kraṅg	agang
louse	kutañ	kutu	amak	hungry	jilñ	mitil
ant	udap	ula	butoh	sour	masam	masom
spider	bernimong, belakawa		kalirang	sweet	ngialiang	mamis
horn	ohun		kalawa	bitter	byis	mapeit
tail	ikui	uwong	hṅg	smell	bin	bun
feather	bulau	ikui	ekoh	fragrant	jueh bun	boaram (bau-arum)
wings	kalapayang, bebui	bulu	buloh			
egg	teloi	ilap	kapayang	stinking	bun madam	jot bun
honey	jṅrṅ	telur	teloh	sick	baji, madam	maparo
wax	hliṅ	danum siṅgut	telang	dead	kabas, kebeh	makabo
body	apa, biuh	lilin	laha	eat	kaman	kamo
head	ūlaṅ	kuṅga	luhong	drink	tīntang	niup
hair	bok	ulok	kahong	see	niṅdiang, ngiang	mipo
face	nang	belutok	bok	laugh	pagiam	mobong
ear	jauei	ba	nang	weep	naṅgi	
eye	liṅga	bakit	apang	kiss	marak	meṅgaruk
nose	mata	mato	matang	speak	anak, manak	pelabu
cheek	udong	urong	arong	be silent	oba, pubah	koring
mouth	pipei	ba	bah	hear	kadap, sarawan	kariṅgo
lip	bah	bawa		lift	tuyang, ta'ah	akat
tongue	bujul, bujun	liṅgil bawa		walk	makh	makiap
tooth	nyipan	laiṅgoli		run	sibal, lakau	mago
hand	jilah		ipan	stand	buraṅ	manakariṅg
finger	agam, pang	jela	jilah	sit	kadang	muruk
thumb	braṅgau	loigo	usuh	climb	kudu	menikit
nail	braṅgau poh	tuju	ikeng	sleep	tikid, nikad	matarui
belly	silau	inan tuju	ikeng ayah	awake	tedñi, melut	matia
foot	nai, tenaheng	ilu	eloh	recollect	pega, makat	katom
bone	betis, pahuh	puong	butit	know	iṅgat	matiwo
flesh	tulang	bati	udak	forget	tehu	jakunak
skin	sin		tulang	ask	leli	jajam ipo
fat	kulit	oyi	kulit	answer	klabaṅ, nalabau	taiṅgok
lean	maniak, piong			understand	tilang, mulang	
blood	mās megaeh	mapiong	madong	yes	tahau	oso
saliva	darah	me	niyang	no	iyu, niuh	di
sweat	lujah	dah	niyang dah	beautiful	nṅbe, enam	jan
hard	sinak	danum jela	lurah	ugly	dau, juih wah	jut bawa
soft	saiāk	peloi	umah	pleased	batau jahat, jehek wah	luko
hot	dṅmñi, lemeik	makokop	maing	sorry	luh, agen	
cold	lasu	meluko	lemah	afraid	susah	
	siṅgṅr, siṅganiam	lua	lasu		mamo, bout	maut
		maṅgen merarum	ṅgam			

English.	Milanau.	Kayan.	Pakatan.	English.	Milanau.	Kayan.	Pakatan.
shame	miah	tahih	mengala	their	sapat bin	ini	muto
love	tilang	masih	ilo	this	ih	inéh	mona
hate	bĕsi	jan ikum	maparu	that	idun	inoh	hi
anger	müras	busak	lohoi	which	han	inoh ik	hawa
wish	luh	ikum	lu	what	iya saih	inoh	ngoku
right	tiga	marong	mato	who	wanau	kanih	asi
wrong	salah	jan marong	mela	food	kiu	kanan	
good	jiñ	saiyu	jan	rice boiled	naseh		
bad	jehek	jahak	jut	(nasi)			
true	atang, senau	lan	mato	sugar	gula	jatan	nio
false	pemide, selbeh		sakwe	oil	niñh	telang, usun	u
wait	ati, lulau	kavoh	iyo	milk	soh		oi
come	lebih, kahai	nenih	labi	flesh	sin	nahang	faring
go	mule, luwat	kakah	ane	boil	isak, midah		aling
meet	bat pob	sabong	passiba	broil	sirai, bahang	sehe	ijo
hide	plim, sihok	nyok	molim	salt	siah	niah	oingup
search	iniang, nginoh	ilu	ipo	clothes	asak, sungup	davan	subang
find	kena		ala	earring	tading	isan	bai
give	bih	maieh	tuja	house	bai	bah	lau labu
take	alap, apan	apih	apen	wood	lebih	umah	patun
bring	igih	grih	itong	posts	dirih	kayoh	kobuko
take away	igih, agah	grih kap	apen	door	abusukud	jeheh	ojan
kill	benih	itih	kabo	ladder	taga	bataman	lakid maturui
I	ako'	akui	hok	bed	kadau tudñi ideh	sahn	jali
mine	ako bin	akui pun	hok laket	mat	jali	tilong	
thou	kawan, ikah	kalunan	ko	box	kaban	brat	anun
thine	ikah bin	hih pun	ko laket	road	ari, sawah	peteh	ojan
he, she, it.	idun, ngiah	ikah	ero	bridge	jaman	ulan	
his, &c.	ngiah bin	ikah itih pun	ero laket			palang	
we (inclusive or absolute)	telut	itam	ta				
our (inclusive)	telut bin	itam pun	ta laket	arrow	bakit	bakir	bangoing
we (exclusive or relative)	kami	kami	kai	spear	pedang	pedang	butut, garoja
our (exclusive)	kami pat			sword	tui, barogah	malat	
you	ikah	kami pun	kai laket	chopping-knife			
your	ikah bin	ikah		boat	tiinan, saliñi	tamui	alui
they	sepat			canoe	tañ	arok	otu
				spirit		toh	

St. John's Vocabularies.   cxxiii.

English				
man	tulai, tanawan	lakeh		
woman	marau	doh		
husband	lai, sawah	lakeh doh		
wife	marañ	doh dah		
father	ama'	ameh		
mother	ina'	indeh		
grandfather	ipo', akeh	ukuh		
child	ugut	apang		
son	anak lai	anak lakeh		
daughter	ale	anak marau	anak doh	anak oro
brother	oro	janak lai, tatat lai	aren lakeh	naken alé
sister	alé	janak marau, tatat maran	aren doh	naken oro
old	aman	lake'	dah muku	toké
young	inan	jemanak lake	dah niam	iyong
boy	aki	jemanak lai	makeh	iyong isi
girl	anak alé	jemanak linas or marau	nyen doh	iyong oro

cxxiv. H. LING ROTH.—*Natives of Sarawak.*

DAYAK LANGUAGES.—*Continued.*—LANGUAGES OF NORTHERN BORNEO.

English	Ida'an	Bisaya	Adang (Murut)	English	Ida'an	Bisaya	Adang (Murut)
NUMERALS:—				plaintain	punti		
one	iso, san		sabulang	cocoa-nut	piasau		
two	duo		dua	flesh	ansi	ansi	
three	telo		telo	fat	lambon, lunak	lunok	
four	apat		ampat	tobacco	sigup		
five	limo		lima	fish	sada	sada	
six	anam		anam	arrack	i tuak bahar (talak tinamul)		
seven	turo		turo	padi	parei	parei	
eight	walo		walu	milk	gatas		
nine	siam		ewa	oil	umau	umau	
ten	opod		pulo	water	waig	aig	
eleven	opod dam iso		pelud cha	fire	apui	apui	
twenty	duo nopod		pelud dua	smoke	lisun	lisun	
a hundred	atus, san atus			ashes	abun	a'u	
day	adau, tadau	adau	chaw	egg	antalun	lampuni	
night	sedap	mentiong potong	racham	price	arga		
morning	suab nakapia	bukatadau	kamuka	charcoal	tahun		
evening	tawaiig-an			tree	guas, puhn kaya	puhn	
yesterday	kiniab	kiniab	seladi	branch	rahan		
to-morrow	suab	suab	napi	leaf	rahun	daun	
day after to-morrow	suab dina			bark	usak	usak	
light	okalub	miang	machang	root	gamut	amut	
name	naran			gutta	pulut		
use	guno (muni)			fruit	uah	buah	
the same	bagal			seed	linso	umi	
fowl	takanan	akanakan		plants	tanaman		
rice	ogas, wagas	nubur (nasi)		pitcher plants	kaku aiiga		
kaladi	gual			rattan	tuei		
yam	kaso			bambu	ragup		
kribang	wei			"batang" trunk	wabaiigan		
fowl	manok		lahal	moss	raiigilut		
a cock	piak			thorn	rugi		
salt	silan	uson		pinang	lakang		

English	Adang (Murut)
flesh	ba'ong
fat	bēa butan
tobacco	wang
fish	lumo'
padi	lawid
water	pade'
egg	pa
price	apui
charcoal	rapun
leaf	pohun
root	daun
fruit	usak
fruit	war
rattan	buah
bambu	ilong

St. John's Vocabularies.

English					
young pinang	lugus				
country	pagun	pagun			sikan
earth	tanah	tanah			tokong
stone	watu	batu			ritak
river	bawang	bawang	bawang		dra
mountain	bukid	bukid			nga
valley	parong		pa		
cave	luang	luang	turud dita		
plain	kapayan	gana	aroi		
sea	rahat		lobang		
island	pulau	laut	balad		iyor
wind	ibut	pulau	pa nawap		
storm	taig-us	loigos	penulong		
rainbow	meluntong		bario		
rain	rasam	melintong	takang		
lightning	kadumaat	rasam	mudlan		
		kaduma'at, long-ganit	lalam		
thunder	garut	sengkarut, lalam	lugo		
sun	matadau	mata-adau	chaw		duro
sand	oggis				ilad
moon	ulan	bulan	bulan		
stars	rambituan	bintang	gatuan		
road	ralan				
forest	talunan				
lake	ranau				
deer	tambang	tambang	priau		
bear	buhuang				
horse	kuda				
buffalo	karbau				
cow, cattle	sapi				
goat	kambing				
dog	asu	asu	okaw		
hog	bakas	bau-hi	barak		
wild hog		ramo	baka'		
cat	tuig-au	using	kuching		
monkey	kara	kara	koyad		
rat	ikus	tikus			
snake	lanut	lanut			
butterfly	galamambang	kalabang	mampa'		
beetle	anggiloung		beriipang		
domestic bee	kaluhut				

bee	taigtingat		mutit	
mosquito	sisit		kalias	
sandfly				
ant	kilau		kilau	
horn	suñgu			
hair	ulu			
tail	tiku		iku	
feather	alad			
egg	antalu		lampuni	
honey	paha		leng	
wings	tulut		alan	
half	siñggaran			
trade	bilian			
a "dustar"	sigar		alei	
house	lamin, walei			
wood	seduan		rigi	
posts	trigi			
"ataps" (mats)	tahap		kirbon	
door	sesuanan		tukad	
ladder	tukat			
window	tariga-an			
fireplace	dapu-an			
bed (sleeping mat)	tikam modop		lubok	
mat	tikam		ikam	
"priok" pot	kuran			
hut	sulap			
a measure	uñgap			
pillow	roei			
white man	kambura			
man	kadayan		mianei	
people	suang			
a man	kusei, ngulun		mianei	
woman	tandu		kimo	
husband	kusei		ano'	
wife	sawa, sau		sau-o	
father	ama		yama	
mother	ina		indu	
grandfather	adu aki		yaki	
grandmother	adu			
child	anak			
virgin	samandak			

English	Ida'an.	Bisaya.	Adang (Murut).	English	Ida'an.	Bisaya.	Adang (Murut).
kiss	siŋud	narokadong		navel	pusat		
cloth	umut			"kamaluan," m.	tali		
"chawat"	sautut			"kamaluan," f.	tato tata'		
spear	andus	sirot		thigh	paw		
"parang"	daŋol	bangkau		knee	atud		
knife	peis	madi		calf	dakud	atis	
shield	taming			foot	lapak		palad kukud
sword	pedang			bone	tulaong		
a spirit	ragun	lematei		blood	raha	ra	
iron	besi			flesh	ansi	ng giri	wang
brass wire	saring			fat	la'bon	lunok	lumo
"bidang"	ganap			skin	kulit		kul'il
ear-ring	anting anting			saliva	luja	jimpi	aka
needle	dalat			sweat	tumus	umos	pana
jacket	rasuk-garong			elbow	siku		
sheet	ramut			fathom	dapo		
body	inan	inan	burur	string, etc.	toggis		
head	ulu	ulu	ulu	to roll up	lapiau		
hair	tabuk	abuk	bok	cover, lid	sompon		
face	turas	rabas	monong	thief	penakau	munsi	
ear	telinġo	telinġ-o		good	raṅggoi	rat	
eye	mato	mato		bad	arahat	bunoi	
eyebrow	kirei			right	raṅggoi, ingka		
nose	tadong	adong	tang	wrong	sala'		
mouth	kabang	kabang		tall	kawas	auad	rawir
lip	munong			long	naro	riba	benua
tooth	nipun	ipun	lipan	short	sariba	mamis	
tongue	lelah	lelah	lebah	sweet	momis	masom	
cheek	piṅgas	ilan	piṅg-it	sour	onsam		
neck	lio			nice	wasi		
shoulder	liawa			bitter	pait	pait	
armpit	pakilok			sharp	taram		
hand	palad	loṅg-on	tichu, palad	blunt	amo, katagu		
finger	tentuduk	indu loṅgon	buatichu	old (tuah)	lai-ing (lai-aŋ?)	kako	
thumb	malahing	siṅg-ilu	tuju tapo	young	mulok	tari	
nail	sandulu		selon	old (lama)	laid, kilo	laid, matuo	maun
breasts	susu			new	wago	aġo	baro
belly	tenai	tenai	batak	hot	lasu	lasu	

St. John's Vocabularies.

English				
cold	sagid	sagit		
wet	eiapas	masah		
dry	magintu	kala'		
true	ranggoi	bunor		
false	udut	bawa		
ugly	arahat	rat		
pretty	osonang	monsei		
large	gaio, kagaio	gaio		
small	koré	diok		
heavy	magat, bagat wagat, ogat	magat		
light	gan	gan		
all	timong	sangai		
many	gamo, sapo	suang		
few	koré-koré	diok		
different	bagal ("mirad")	sama paras		
like	suei			
slow	boei	boei		
rapid	gompas	deros		
heavy as rain	gompas			
thirsty	tuhan	kalalio		
hungry	losun	mitil		
striking	buntong			
sick	sagid	duol		
dead	matei	matei		
sorry	susah	gagau		
angry	magulau	siau		
straight	tulid	tulid		
crooked	brakilong	belengkok		
square	apat, persagi	ampat pensagi		
round	urud			
broad	kalab	lebah		
thick	kapah	kapah		
thin	mipis	nipis		
shallow				
deep	ralam	lalum		
black	eitom	hitom		
white	purak			
red	ragang	purak ragang		
yellow	silau	chilau		
sore	owal			
raw		tenab	matah'	matah
ripe		bah	mansak	mansak
dirty		takaring	amut	
clean			aro'k	
hard			kadau	kodau
soft			lumi	lembut
enough			ganap	
"korang," wanting			amo, karungut	
pregnant		raya	betian	
slippery		madi	lamau, lamo	
clever		brat	tutun	
quick		rahan	jajarun	
right		abiabi	ganan	
left		mulamula	gibang	
rough		sesut	sanlu	
bold and brave		pahad lea	siau	
I or we		dadan	yeho, yai dugu	jami
you		mauwar	dia	ikan
he or they			idia	iyo
who			sei	iseo
what			nono	a'an
this			iti	tio
that			ina	sulo
here			diti	ditio
there			ilo, dilo	sulu
where			nambo	domboi
far		sun	sadu	sado
near		kelo'	simak, samok	somok
without		lepingpat	saribau	ribau
within		taburor	saralam	selalam
above		raya	kawas	ribau
below		kapal	sariba	sua
behind		nipi	likud	iikud
before		tutun	dibrus	derabas
between			palatan	
to		mitam	ka	
previously		buda	gahulu	
from		sia	masunut	
not yet		berar	eiso po	
yes			aw	awe

tua leia

dini
dinga-a
dapei-a
madi
monáng
lemela
metakap
dungeilun
meilena
katad
lepa monong
rang

English	Ida'an.	Bisaya.	Adang (Murut).	English	Ida'an.	Bisaya.	Adang (Murut).
no	eiso	iñjob	napi	to kill	saṅgat, menian-gat	metai-o	
now	kirakira	kila	idan	to wound	suhat		
when	saṅgira	memburo	muchi	to sow	memambri		
afterwards	turi, tahuri	turi		to plant	meñgasuk		
in this way	inka', pinka'			to fight	meṅgulan, merasang		
in that way	inka-i			to trade	berdagang		
how many	sangkora, gamo			to buy	bili		
presently	ruhei			to sell	taranan		
more	aro			to cheat	menipu		
to eat	mengakan			to steal	menakau, menikus		
to drink	mengiwum			to marry	menasawa		
to see	magintong	lintong		to bear children	berganak		
to laugh	maḡirak	girak		to grow	samuni		
to weep	miad	giad		to shout	meniangkis		
to kiss	maniigud	narokadong		"ada"	warah		
to speak	boras	betuntul		"habis"	awi, ei, nei		
to be silent	mada	gorom		to shade	osorong		
to hear	makinaiigo	koroiṅgo		to swim	samadoi		
to lift	kakatan	teiṅgaiṅgo		to arrive	korokod		
to walk	manau	manau		to wash	miṅg isu		
to run	magidu	midu		to bathe	madsiu, padsiu		
to stand	mindahau	kakat		to want	saga		
to sit	mirikau	koko		don't	ada		
to climb	midakud	nakod		to burn	tutud		
to sleep	modop	modop		"he says"	kadsio		
to awake	tumanag, tuṅgag	tidong		to play	beransei		
to recollect	insam			to tie	kagus		
to know	pandei, mila	pandei		"gurau"	bersibak		
to forget	aliwan	kalamuan		"amput"	berkiu		
to ask for	makiano			to hug	gapus		
to wait	magandad	ninteo		to lay hold of	migit, makahei		
to come	sikei	mikot		to desire	saga'		
to go	maṅgai, paḡidu	midu		to return	saḡulei		
to meet	bertemu			to take a wife	kasawa		
to hide	lisuk	mensusut		to take a husband	memaṅgat		
to search	magi-om	yumo					
to give	noan	menak					
to bring	oito	mito					

St. John's Vocabularies.

English				
high	ulih			kalalio
to strike	pring			mitil
to break	lau			mau
to open				munsei
to shut			sau-at	mutong
to lift			pudo	matei
to throw			petul	sumbarau
to sound			bika	nako
darkness			beno	lemakak
green		basi	tenañg-o	mikum
iron			menokon	ngako
hill		tañgus	katak	baji
hurricane			potong	ngako
west				bunor
east			bukid diok	malak
cloud			ribut	lapo
noon			surapadau	sunsam
sky			matadayau	sinalau
to burn		tudo		subang
to smoke		lisun	tampakadau	langgaio
rice		agas, wagas	adau	pentaran
pumpkin		tawadak	sensuli	padas
yam		kaso	lisun	padasdiok
mouse		ikus	agas	mianei
squirrel				kimo
bird			niamo	sitari
kite			manok	sitari kimo
sparrow			kanio	anak agu
swallow			pirit	
crow			senkalayang	
cage			mangkak	
frog			kuruñgan	
crab			sei	
prawn			kuyu	
fly			tentudik	tutun
spider			pañgat	simara
			senkalang	

English			
wax	dita		
thirsty	mapar	motul	
hungry	ngukab		
smell	nutub		
fragrant	nakang		kiabau
stinking	mapat		buntong
dead	buri		matei
answer	racham		
pleased			
afraid			
shame	belawan		
love	turud, murud		
hate	buri mawar		
wish			
right			
find	laput		
take	topud chaw		
boil			
broil	menunoh		
ear-ring	rapun		
road	brah		
bridge	belabu		
boat	ubi		
canoe	labaw		
son			
daughter	suit		
brother	kanio		
sister	pirit		
girl	kalua		
shallow (as water)	bǝngkak		
tin			wei
sweet potato	sit		gual
kaladi	kra		piak
a cock			makiano
ask for			

DAYAK LANGUAGES.—Continued.

SPENCER ST. JOHN.

English.	Lanun.	English.	Lanun.	English.	Lanun.
straight	matidu	large	mala	sea	kaludan	frog	babak
crooked	becig	like	magisan	wind	tindii	fish	seda
square	becig	now	amei	rainbow	datu bagua	crab	leigan
round	becig	then	mairi	thunder	gintir	bee	tabiian
long	melandu	to-morrow	amag	day	gau-i	tail	ikug
broad	maulad	yesterday	dua gua i den	night	magabi	feather	bumbul
thick	makapal	old	matei den	morning	mapita	egg	urak
thin	manipis	new	bagu	moon	ulan	wax	taru
deep	madalam	slow	maliimbat	star	bituan	body	ginau-a
high	mapuro	rapid	magu-an	hot	mai-au	head	ulu
short	mababa	strike	basal	fire	apūi	hair	bok
without	segamau	break	maupak	burn	pegiau (ángka)	face	biyas
within	sisedalam	lift	sepiat	smoke	bil	nose	ngirong
light (in weight)	demaugat	throw	pelantig	cocoanut	nliig	mouth	ngari
heavy	maugat	wet	moasah	plantain	saging	tooth	ngipan
above	sekapruan	dry	magaligu	paddy	tlau	hand	lima
below	sekababaan	sound	uni	rice	bigas	finger	kamai
behind	selikud	light	maliwaunug	leaf	raun	belly	tian
before	sesunguran	darkness	malibutäng	raw	melau	foot	ay
between	sesunguran	black	mabitam	ripe	mialūtū	bone	tulun
here	sika	white	maputih	deer	selading	flesh	sapu
there	ruka	red	marega	cow	sapi babai	fat	masaibūa
far	muatan	yellow	binaning	dog	asu	lean	megīsā
near	maubé	country	ingud	hog	babūi	blood	rugu
where	autuna	earth	lupa	cat	bedöng	sweet	ating
at	autuna	stone	watu	mouse	ria (maitū)	hard (as a stone)	matagas
to	a	gold	buliiwan	rat (besai)	dumpau	soft	melemak
from	si	iron	putau	bird	papanok	hot	mai atī
all	lahgunyen	mountain	palau	sparrow	papanok	cold	matinggan
many	madakal	cave	pasu	swallow	leliiyang	thirsty	kaur
few	meitu	hill	gunoňg	cage	kurongan	hungry	megitan
small	meitu	water	aig	snake	nipai	fragrant	mapia bau

English		English		English	
stinking	maratai bau	pleased	mesñap	thou	seki
sick	masakit	afraid	kaluk	thine	quomka
dead	matai	shame	kaya	he, she, it	gia
eat	kuman	love	masñat	his, &c.	quon gia
see	ilai	anger	membuñg ut	we (*inclusive or absolute*)	sakûn
weep	semigûd	wish	kiñgan		
speak	taroh	right	metidñ	our (*inclusive*)	quon akûn
be silent	gûmanñg	wrong	masalah	we (*exclusive or relative*)	sakûn
hear	makiañg	good	mapia		
lift	sepuat	bad	marita	our (*exclusive*)	quon akûn
walk	lumalakan	false	biikñg	you	seki
run	melagui	wait	gûmaganñg	they	quon ki
stand	tumatindug	come	makoma	their	gia
sit	muntud	go	sñmong	who	quon gia
climb	pamusug	hide	tapok	what	antiwa
sleep	tûmiriñg	search	pengilei	rice, boiled	antiña
know	katañan	find	makia	oil	bigñs
forget	kalipatan	give	begai	flesh	lanah
answer	sñmbug	take	kia	salt	sapu
understand	matau	bring	sepñat	chawat	timñs
no	da	take away	gñmañ	house	bilad
beautiful	mapia	I	sakûn		wali
ugly	marita	mine	quon sakûn		

English	
bed	tûrñgan
mat	dûmpas
box	kaban
road	malakau
spear	bangkau
chopping-knife	puduk
boat	awang
man	mama
woman	babai
husband	karñma
wife	karñma
father	ama
mother	ina
child	wata
son	wata mama
daughter	wata babai
brother	pegari mama
sister	pegari babai
old	lukus
young	meñguda
boy	wata
girl	raga

VOCABULARY OF ENGLISH AND SARAWAK DAYAKS.

By the Rev. WM. CHALMERS.

[*Originally printed in 1861 at the St. Augustine's College Press, Canterbury, England.*]

THE DAYAK COLUMN is the Dialect spoken by the Sentah Tribe on the SOUTHERN Branch of the River Saráwak. The pronunciation of the other tribes of the same branch of the river varies slightly from that of Sentah, the chief difference, however, is the substitution of the letter "o" for the Sentah "u."

The Dialect of the tribes of the WESTERN Branch of the river is also *substantially* the same as that of those of the Southern Branch, but variations in words as well as in their sound is not unfrequent. Words marked "(W)" belong solely to the Dialect of this branch of the Saráwak River.

Kuap, Saráwak, Borneo,
January, 1861.

W. C.

SYSTEM OF PRONUNCIATION.

ã is pronounced as a in father.	ü is pronounced as the French u.
a somewhat shorter than this.	u „ „ „ oo in too.
ã is pronounced as a in sat.	ũ „ „ „ u in up.
ĕ „ „ „ a in same.	au „ „ „ ow in now.
e „ „ „ e in let,	ai „ „ „ the English i.
ei „ „ „ ay in lay.	ch final „ „ the German ch.
i „ „ „ the English e.	g is always hard, as in goat.
õ „ „ „ aw in law.	
o „ „ „ o in go.	
ŏ „ „ „ o in pot.	

English.	Dayak.	English.	Dayak.
able	shaũn	advance	odi; ponu
able (physically)	shinonu	advance gradually	mupok; mutik (W)
about (future)	an	afflicted; affliction	susah-atin
about (in number)	sekira-kira	afraid	taruh
above	disombu	after that	rasu
abuse (revile)	mangu; ngamun	afterwards	sekambuch sepagi
accept	mit; kambat	again	dingĕ; bauch
accomplished	jadi	ago	much
accompany	dingñn; suah	age	ashung udip
acquainted with	kũnyet	agree	bepaiyu
across (river)	kadipah, porad (W)	agreement	paiyu
across; athwart	ngiparang	agree together	bejerah
accustomed to	kũnyet	air	sobak
accuse	kũdãan	alarm, raise an	ngada
accuse falsely	nũpu; ngitũma	alarmed	{ gugũch-atin
	{ gũgach (*at working*)		{ gupoch-atin
active	· ringgas (*at walking*)	all	perũk
	{ būkĕ (*at carrying*)	all, in; altogether	kaũsh-i; kiang-kiang
adrift	aman	alligator	buai
add	tambah	also	dingĕ; gũch
adjoin	bebãat	alternately	bekirĕãs
adultery, commit	tũngach; bejorah (W)	although	semũki-kach

Chalmers' Vocabulary.

English.	Dayak.	English.	Dayak.
always	seräru; paûch	back, come	pari
always (from beginning)	taûn	back, go	pari
		back, man's	punok
ancestors	somuk-babai	bad	(arap; bûkok
anchor, an	sauh		(penyamun (*rascal*)
anchor, to	berlabuh	bag	putir; rajut
anchorage	labuban	bald	rakas (*in front*); tûnda
anciently	jiman diû; jiman jach	bald, sham	betundō
angel	melaikat	bamboo	buru; buti; taring
anger; angry	tuas; boji	bamboo, split and flattened	tertap
another	bûkûn		
ant	subi	bamboo, young shoots of (used as vegetable)	umugn
ant, white	rûngupod		
anoint	berangir	banish	taran
announce	dāan	bank of stream	pang tûbing
announce (proclaim)		bark of tree	kurit kayuch
any (man)	setûdû-tûdû (*dayah*)	bark, to (as a dog)	nûkang
any (thing)	setûdû-tûdû (*kayuch*)	barb of spear	bûkid
anxious about (one absent)	jâbûng	barren	oboch; manang
		barrel	tong
apart (disjoined)	renggang	basin	makuk
apostle	dah; penyuruch	basket, fishing	sikup; nobang
appearance	(*thing*) mun; (*person*) rah; (*face*) raûn *	basket for carrying	(bakol
			juach; jumōa (W),
			tambōk (*small*) [*l.*]
appeased	munos		(rangi
approach (visit)	tudu	bat, a	kada
arch	burung	bathe	mamuch
arise	burah; mokat	bay	teruk; ungûng
around	mûning; krurung	beard	gagap
arms	bukō burus	beat (strike)	mukōng
arrange	mishûn	beat, with stick	mukōng
arrive	menûg	beat, with fist	mûtûg
artizan	tukang	beat, against a stone	kupok
ascend (a river)	mudëäk	beat out paddy	pûch
ascend (a hill)	māad	beat with open hand	nupāp
as far as	(ngah; nûg (*distance*)	beat, as heart	kamobak; komujût
	(kûd (*height or length*)	beat a drum	māk
ash of wick; ashes	bûtûp; apûk	beads	tumbis; likich (W)
ashamed	mûngûch; dasah	beams of house (cross)	parang
ask (beg)	mitē	beams of house (parallel)	parang
ask from door to door	nyukah		
ask (enquire)	sikyen	beak of bird	tukuk
assemble	nguruk; ngudung; besinun	bear, a	buang
assist	tolong	beans	retak
astonished	tekûnûd; ngōwa (W)	beast	dang
astonished (startled)	gûgûch	beautiful	paguch; romus; sigat
astringent	kûd	because	sebab
at	di	become	jadi
attack, an	serang	become, make to	bodah jadi; bodah
attack, to	nyerang	bee	(bûnyich (*tree*)
ataps (thatch)	ilau		(nyōwan (*house*)
ataps, to make	tō	beetle	beriang; rukuä; berubut
ataps, to make stick (on which the leaves are laid)	räis	before (place, time)	diû; dawû
		beginning (of anything)	tûgûg
atone (by fine)	berutang		
auction	lēlong	beginning, in the	(bungash
avoid (a blow)	saan odûp		(se bungash-bungash
awake	burah	behind	di kûnang; sundich
axe, large	kapak	believe	sabach
axe, small	biliong	belly	täin

* Rev. F. W. Abé's Vocabulary, published by Mr. Noel Denison. See note at end of this Vocabulary.

English.	Dayak.	English.	Dayak.
belch	taūg	BODY, HUMAN - *cont.*	
beloved	nyirŏt	jaw	raang
below	ribŏ ; sogan ; di dau	ear	kojit
bell	loching [(W)	face	jŏwin
bell, hawk	grunung	hair (head)	ubŏk
belt	shishŭt	hair (body)	buruch
bend	nai rikŏg	neck	tungŏ
betel-nut	bai	throat	gang-gŏng
brass stand, on which betel-nut is placed	karas	windpipe	kor
		side	tigang
betray	juah	shoulder	kŏwin
betroth	biŭmbai	breast	sudŏ
betrothed	ŭmbai	belly	tăin
between, interval	băat ; ŭsach	waist ; loins	kupong
between, enter	ngŭsach	navel	poshid ; pisod (W)
bird	manuk	back	punŏk
bite	koŭt	bottom	kŭnang
bite (peck)	ngingŭt	arm (whole)	birĕāng
bite (peck), mark of	berŭn	arm, shoulder to elbow	pupung
bitter	păit		
black	singŭt ; sungot (W)	arm, elbow to wrist	brungŏ
BLACKSMITH :—	pandai	elbow	sukuch
smithy	boran	hand	tangan
smithy, go to	odi ng-ambang	fingers	trinyu
forge iron	moba	nails	siruch ; silun (W)
red-hot iron	masak	thumb	sindu-trinyu
fire-place	dinding	wrist	brungŏ
anvil	dasan	knuckles	buku tangan
hammer	bobah	thigh	pŭŭch
shafts of bellows	tŭba	calf	bitĕs
blow bellows	muput	leg or foot	koja ; pŏon (W
wind box	putan	knee	ubak karub
tubes of wind box	jupen	ancle	buku siŏk
blaze	begirod ; bejireb	sole or palm	pura
bless	ngyen berkat	heel	tiga
blessing	berkat	boil	tanuk ; rŭmu (*water*)
blight (paddy)	bangas	boil rice	tanuk
blind	(kerak komĕăt (*of one eye*)	boil, a	prŭkis
		boiling	didich ; ngigurak
blood	dĕyah	bolt, a ; bolt, to	ŏbut ; ngŏbut
blot out	ngutŏsh	bone	tulang
blow	pŏŏch	book	kitab
blow pipe, see "sumpitan"	jupen	born, be	jadi
		born, first	penuai
blow nose	suan	born, last	sebushu
blue, see "colour"		bore (in river)	benah
blunt	taju	bore, place in which to await the	benahan
blunt (notched)	rŭbang		
blunted (point)	papŭ	bore, to	girik ; tŭbuk
boat	)	borrow	mitĕ minjam
boat, small	) orud	bosom	pukŏ
BODY, HUMAN :—	pŭrŭng ; gŭnan ; tibu	bother (trouble)	owang-owang ; kakŭch
head	ubak	bottle	serăpak ; jabul (W)
forehead	arŭ	bottom (of a thing)	koja ; kŭnang
cheeks	panding ; pŏup	boundary	băat
eye	betŭch	bow (of boat)	ubak
eye-brow	buruch kŭning	bow (head)	mutu
eye-lash	buruch kirat	box	peti
nose	unugn	boy	anak dari ; gishŭ
nostrils	rubang unugn	brain	atŭk
mouth	boba	branch (of tree)	dahan
teeth	jipŭch ; jipon (W)	branch, forked	sokap
tongue	jura	brave	pogan ; berasap ; tŭtŭd (*fearless*)
lips	(bibich ; bibin (W) tukuk (*upper lip*)		
		brass	tambaga
chin	serăka	bread	roti

Chalmers' Vocabulary.

English.	Dayak.	English.	Dayak.
break	popē ; butach	care of, take	kingat
break string	pūtūd	care of children, take	nyudē
break stick	pūtah	carry	bebuat
break off	kadi	carry on shoulder	gūrūng
break law	ngirawan	carry as tambok	kabich
break promise	pūtūd	carry in arms	pukū
breast	sudō	carve, see "engrave"	
breasts, woman's	shishuch	cat	bushing ; ngiau (W)
breath	ashung	catch	nakap
breath, out of	kōwñk ; paiyah ; joro (W)	Catholic Church	Ekklisia Katholika
		cave	tang
breathe	ngashung	ceremony, a	adat
bridge	teboian	certain ; certainly	tūntu
bridge, long, built on posts crossed	besōwūch	centipede	repipan
		chafe against	gingēs
bright } brightness }	bringēäng	chaff	aping ; budang
		chain	pārik
bring	ngah ; toban	chamber	arūn ; romin (W)
bring (convey)	tūd	change	besambi
brittle	rapich	change (alter)	berubah
breadth ; broad	ramba	change (money)	tukar besambi
broken, so as to be useless	bubūch	change (clothes)	kabarui ; nēān
		change (name)	nyirēsh adūn
brother	madich	change (position of body)	terigen
brother, elder	kaka		
brother, younger	sudē	channel	alor ; arong
brethren	sudē-madich	charcoal	ubū
broom	pipis	charm, a	setagan
bruise	kūdas ; butot	chase	bekūduch ; tūdak
buffet	nupap	chasm	rubang
bug	ūkak	cheap	udach
bug, flying	pūngu	cheapen	tawar
bunch	aiyan ; tundun	cheat	mujuk
bundle	mōäs ; bārun	chew	mūpah
		chief of tribe	orang kaya
buoyant	jangan ; tepuang	chief of tribe, second	pengara
burn	mupun ; sigōt ; nyitungan	chief, war	panglima
		chief of a house	tuah
burn (person)	rāus	child	anak
burnt	sauu	chilis	sebarang
burning place for dead	tinūngan	chisel	pūūt
burner of dead	peninu	choke (in eating)	kangūn ; sitūn
burst	rāak	choose	mien
bury	kubur	church	ramin Sambayang ; ramin Allah Taala
busy	duch poiyah		
but	pūk	circumscribed (confined)	kutich
butterfly	berūmbang		
button	kanching ; ōbut	circuit, make a	mūning
buy	mirich	clap	nupap
by	bodah ; dah	clean	bisig
by and bye	tē	cleanse	ngushu ; ngu ; ngutōsh
		clear (water)	kining
cackle (as a hen)	nyitūkāk	clear (affair)	jōwa
cage	kūrungan (large) ; kariru (small)	clever	bijak
		climb	jūkuch
call	bogan (when near)	close (thickset)	pishung ; bringut
call out to	matau (when far)	close (near)	sindūk
call out	nai kiak	close (together)	pūnct
call upon	nishung ; tudu	close (together), place	bedindar
calm	toduch ; saiyah	close (confined)	kūtich ; sekidūn
candle	bian	close to ground	rapat
cane	ui	close up, to	ngobut
cane, a Malacca	semūmu	closed up	papōt
canoe	orud	cloth	benang
care for	paduli	clothes	benang
care, take	ingat ; jaga	clothes, swaddling	putong bodung

English.	Dayak.	English.	Dayak.
cloud	abun	corner	sukuch
cloud, rain	keruman	corpse	tûdang
clump of bambus, a	punan	correct	ngajar
coarse	baga	cotton (thread)	benang
coax	nyibudŏh (*with intent to deceive*)	cough	mokûd; nyingôk itong
cocoa-nut	butan	council, a	
cocoa-nut water	pïin butan; juh butan	counsel together, to take	beritong; minyu
cocoa-nut shell	tapurung; boru (W)	count	niap
cockroach	randing	country	rAich
cold	madud; mobus	course, of	taũn
cold, a	aũn	covenant	paiyu
collapse	kûrûng	covet	lipông
collect	nguruk; besinun	cover, see "cork"	
Colour:—		crab	kiuch
black	singût	craft	akal
blue	barum	crafty	cherdik; bijak
grey	apak	cracked	murăng
green	barûm	crackle	rutop
red	birĕ	crank	ringgang
yellow	sía	crank, to be	muguyung
white	budah; mopuh (W)	crawl	gawang
comb	sinôd	create	bodah jadi
comb, fowl's	terûping	crooked	bedîkok; rikôg; mudug
comfort (console)	nyaduch		
command, to }		cross (river)	mûtash kadipah
command, a }	semainya	cross (hill)	{ môa darûd
commandment }			{ nyirubĕ darûd
commit	nai	cross, a	regang; tebûkang
come	menûg; nũg	crucify	masak ka regang
come along	jameh	crow, to	kukôk
come hither	jah; tep kamati; di kamati	crow, a	kãk
		crowded together, see "in disorder"	
come out through	berambus		
come out of	ruach; rũpus	crumple up	nyiriuk
come to pass	jadi; tũk	crush	rãra
companion	dingãn	cry	sien
company with, in	beaiyo; bepajak	cry out	nai kiak
complete, to }	raput	cucumber	timun
complete }		cunning, see "crafty"	
compass, the	padoman	cup	makuk
compassionate	siũt	curl, see "frizzle"	
complex (not simple)	bisīrat	customs	adat
concave	surŏk; sekibang	curse, a	pangu
conceal	chukãn; miman	cut	kapũg
conceived in womb	bitĕ	cut in two	mûtud
conduit, water	sekibang	cut down trees	tabûng
conduit, mouth of	aiyak	cut down jungle	nauu
conduct, to	tûd	cut (lop off)	nyûbĕ
confused in mind	berishut	cut (split)	mirĕ
conquer	ngarah	cut (chop)	jûpa
conscience	nyãm-atin	cut (in pieces)	nyirib
consult birds of omen	{ ngabah kushah (*day*)	cut (open)	nidi
	{ nyimanuk (*at night*)	cut off the top, as ear from paddy-stalk }	nyangut; mûtûd; ngûtûm
contagion	sawit		
continually	awĕt	cut down paddy }	
contented	munôs	cutting paddy, knife for	kutam
contrary to	ngirawan		
convey	tûd		
converted, be	berubah-atin	dam, a	suang
convex	mudu; mudug	dam (fishing)	jimbai; ranyu
cook, to	tanuk	damp	nyiput; dûpop
cook-house (or fire-place)	apũk	dance	{ berejang { ngigar (W)
cork, to	nyũkub; natũp	dandle	nyandô
cork, a	tutûp	dangerous	mar

Chalmers' Vocabulary.

English.	Dayak.	English.	Dayak.
dare; daring	pogan (*in war*); puus	DISEASE—*continued*:	
dark; darkness	karûm; mopung (W)	enlargement of the spleen	barid
dash down	pān	disjoined	renggang
date-fruit	khrūma	in disorder (crowded close together)	kakok
daughter	anak dayung		
dawn	kök siök; anu jōwah	dissolve	ririch
day, a	anu	distance between places	juan-i
day (opposed to night)	jowah		
daily	ni-anu-anu	distant	jö
dazzled	shiu	disturbed (in mind)	bepūshid
dead	kūbus	disturbance	gutoi
dead body	tūdang	disturbance, make a	nai gutoi; nai dudu
deadened (sound)	puot	ditch	parit
deaf	bungam	dive	ngobu
dear	mar	divide	berutung
debt	hutang	division	utung; kutung
decayed	an nūtash	divorce	ɩ bu; sebarai
deceit	bujuk		ɩ betogan (W)
deceive	mujuk; nyibudoh	do (make)	nai
deceived	budōh	do not	{ dūchnyach; dunyach
deer (large)	paiyu		{ mānyach
deer (medium)	jerak	doctor	dukun
deer (small)	pranuk	doctor (conjurer)	{ barich (*female*)
deep	tūrūp; au-au (*very*)		{ dukun } (*male*)
defend	gerindung		{ dayah beruri }
deficient	korang	doctor, to (by incantation)	barich
deliver	ruach		
demand (a debt)	nunggu	dog	kūshöng
deny	miman	door	tibān
deposit, a	{ pengaroh, (*applied to charmed stones, &c., used by the Dyak "berobat"*)	doting; dotard	babō
		down, let	bisbor; bitun
		drag	tarik; ngajut
		drag on boat	batak
descend (hill)	mun	draw, see "drag"	
descend (river)	ūman	draw out	dimut
deserted	pujam möog	dream	pomūch; p'moch (W)
desire (wish)	handak	DRESS:—	
desire (lust)	lipöng	jacket	jipō
desirous of	gagah	head-dress	{ bung ubōk
deserving of	patut		{ burang (W)
destroy	nūtash; rusak	petticoat	jomūch
destroyed	rusak	trowsers	sinyang
dew	abun	armlets (brass)	{ ruyang } (*women's*)
die	kūbus		{ tanggam }
different	būkūn		{ gerang } (*men's*)
difficult	bisirat (*complex*); mar;		{ serat }
difficulty	paiyah, susah	armlets (shell)	kara
dig	karech	women's leg rings	roti
dip	kujok; kurūm	men's waist-cloth	taup
diligent	būtach; gūgach	basket	juach; jumōa (W)
dirty	kâich; pūder	small basket worn by the side	tambok; pengupa
disabled (for work)	mūtang; būjang		
disappointed (balked)	asa	small knife worn at side	sindah
DISEASE:—	berandam		
boils	prūkich; kibu	sheath of small knife worn at side	randung
dysentery	tūki dēyah		
fever	sungöh	sirih-case	upich
itch	ku	boxes inside tambok	dekan
looseness	merubus; bawosh (W)	ordinary parang, or chopping knife	būkō tūkin
scrofula	bagi		
small-pox	teboro	visiting parang	penat; bai (W)
ulcerated sores	gēdag; būkang	sheath of parang	sibōng; duong (W)
worms	mūnam regyu	waist chains ɩ worn by	ɩ perik
elephantiasis, when the leg is permanently swollen	mutud	waist wire ɩ women	ɩ kawat
		bead necklace	tumbis

English.	Dayak.	English.	Dayak.
DRESS OF THE BARICH		endure; enduring	tāan; kukoh
head-cloth	sepauung; serapai (W)	enemy	pūngānyu; bishirun; penyerang
bead-cap	segubak; sipīa (W)		
bead necklace	setagi; panggīa (W)	engrave	mutik; bitik (W)
bead scarf	semudn; sombon (W)	enough	raput; sedang
drink	nōk; mōk	enlighten	bodah jowah
drunk	mabok	enlarge (widen)	bodah baiyah
drive (nail)	masak	enquire	sikyen
drive (peg)	mabak	entangle	bekarut; jukut
drive away	kushig; pibu	enter	mūrūt
drop, a	ni-titeg	enter to a short dis-	
drop out or off, to	dimbut	tance (as a spear	kudish masuk
drown	rungūd	or splinter into	
drowsy	nunu	the body)	
drum, a	gundang	enter to a consider-	tūrūp masuk
dry	bodūch	able depth	omu masuk
	pishūk (withered)		arūm masuk
dry, to	dōwan (in air)	enter as far as ex-	repuñn masuk
	dān (in house)	tremity	
dry new rice in a pan, to	nyirandang	entwine	bukur
		envy	shinah
duck	itik	equal, see "same"	
dumb	bawa; bakū	erase	ngutōsh
dung	tūki	erring	mānyap
dusk, see "twilight"		espouse, see "betroth"	
dust (ashes)	apñk	ever, for	nūg se tui-tui
dust (litter)	ronash	European, a	Biranda
duty	sedang; patut	everlasting	dūch bisa obo; babū
dwarfish	mukung	every (each)	setiap-tiap
dwell	rūū	every (all)	perūg-perūg; kaūsh-i
dye, a red	semūngū	examine (enquire)	sikyen
dye, a yellow	tūmu	examine (look at)	koduk
		exceeding	raru
ear	kojit	exceedingly	pushē (in size)
ear, in (as corn)	murai		nūkung (in thickness)
ear, full corn in	mūrah	excepting	kiang
ear, an (of paddy)	aiyan; tundun	exchange	besambi
ear-ring	subang (woman's)	exchange labour	ngirich
	ateng (man's)	expand (swell)	būngkak
early	ishan-ishan	expense	balanja
earth, the	ōng	explain	bodah pūan
earth (ground)	tanah	extinguish	pura
earth (dry land)	dēyūch	eye	betūch
ease, at	senang	eye-lid	pūnu betūch
ease oneself	tūki	eye-lash	buruch kirat
easy (to do)	senang; mudah	eye-ball	anak betūch
eat	man		
eat sirih	pah	face	jowin
eaves of house	penogang ilau	fade	rayu; kūrūng
ebb tide	pīin surud	faded (dry)	pishūk
echo	angu	faded (in colour)	bonus; buus
edge (bank)	pang tūbing	faint, to	mujūp
edge of weapon	shiid	fame; famous	beragach
edge, teeth on	shiin	family, having a large	pūpach powun
eddy	ulak	famine	seburūk
effervesce	ngigurak	fall down	robu
egg	turoch	fall out, see "drop out"	
eggs, lay	menuroch	fall (as tree)	rumak
egg-plant	tiung	fall upon	nyatūk; nyondug (W)
elastic	kunyoi	fall in ruins, see "ruin"	
embrace	pukō; dūkūp	fall off (as leaves)	ruruch
	betūpang	false	kādōng
	kūkūn (seat on lap)	fan, a	kipas
empty	ūngan; gagong	fan, to	nyipas
enclose	nyikapung	far	jō
end (extremity)	tubūn	far, how	juan-ki

Chalmers' Vocabulary.

English.	Dayak.	English.	Dayak.
far-sighted (physically)	suki	fish, to, by tubah	nubŭch
farm, a	umŭch	fish, to, by hook	misich
farm, to	berumŭch	first (in order)	sebungash
farm, a house on	bori	first (time or place)	dawŭ ; diṅ
farm, an old	tebai	first-born	penuai
farms, a small collection of	sebubŏ	first-fruits, the	jangut
		first-fruits, gather	nyipāan
farms, large collection of	ratau	first, at	sebungash-bungash-i
		fit	sedang
farm, a, discontinued, after cutting the jungle	bogag	flame	jireb
		flee	bu
		flesh	ishin
		flexible	liat
fast (quick), see "strongly"		float	tepuang
		flock, a (birds, &c.)	kaban
fasten (tie)	mŭŭng ; ngobut (close up) ; bokosh (W)	flood, a	pīin obah ; obah krambu
fasten (nail)	mabak ; masak	flood tide	piin pasang
fasten up by suspending	ngatir	flour	teboduk
		flow out	nyibŭŭk
fat	gŭmu	flower	suat
fat (greasy)	berinyăb		tura (house) [ing
father	sama	fly, a	rŭngŭ (maggot breed-
fathom, a	dŭpŭch		ishĕt (eggs of rŭngŭ)
fatigued	kowŭk ; mara	fly, a dragon	sedanau
fawn (as a dog)	nanyak	fly, a horse, or painted fly	pigŭring ; adŭd (large)
feast	begawai		
female	dayung	fly, to	mukābur ; timirib (W)
feast, funeral	man baiya	flying fox, a	rŭngowat
feast, harvest	man sawa	foggy	kabut
feather	buruch	follow	tundah ; suah ; ngajach ; nudug
feeble	dŭdŭt ; dŭch shinonu		
feel	nyam	follower	dingăn
feel (by touch)	kăp	fold, a	siak
feel one's way	gagap	fold up, to	ngupĕt
feelings	nyam-atin	food	man
feign, to (to give), see under "strike"	piasa ; ngunur	foot	koja
		foot (of hill)	koja ; sigun
fence, a	buang	footprint	inyuk koja
fence, to	bebuang	foolish	bodoh
ferns (used as a vegetable)	pokuch ; baiyam	foolish (mad)	gila
		foolish (doting)	babo
fever	sunghŏ	foolishness	babal-atin
few	nishit ; nishŭ	for (because)	sebab
fickle ; fickleness	bimbang-atin	forbid	nang ; niṅh ; jaman ; jumba ; mapak
fight with	bekai		
fight against	ngirawan	forbidden	parich
fight cocks	besabung	forest	tarun
file, a	kikir	forefathers	somuk-babai
file teeth, to	bertajar ; ngasah	forget	kambut
		forgotten	opung-opung
fierce	rŭkang ; gauk	fork, a	garfu ; garăpu
fill	ngisi	forked	besŭkap
fill rice-pot for cooking	nyukad	formerly	dawŭ ; jiman diṅ
find	dapŭd	formerly (of old)	sarak diṅ
finished	obŏ ; mobŏ ; kubŏ ; mokŏ ; mŭch	fornicate	bejerah ; nainyung
		fortress	kota ; kubu
fine (thin)	ŭnŭk	FOWL :—	siŏk ; siap (Setang)
finger	trinyu	cock	babang
fire	opui	hen	dayung
fire a gun	tinyŭg ; mak	chicken	anak ungŏd
fire at	nimbak	fragment	tŭdŭch
firefly	bŭkarŭp	fragrant	buuch rŭmak
firewood	wang ; shiru (W)	frequently	awĕt
firm ; fixed	bŭkŭt ; tegap	freed	merdika
fish	ikyen	fresh, a, see "flood"	

English	Dayak	English	Dayak
fresh (not salt)	madud	go back from	pari
friend	dingán; dümpu	go down (hill)	mun
frizzle	menikur; budukung	go down (as swelling)	kerŭng
frog	tŭkang; beratak; tegorag; sai	goat	kambing
		God	Allah Taala
from	so	gold	berowan
froth	tegurak	gong (bass)	tertawak
fry	nyirára	gong (medium)	gong
FRUIT:—		gong (treble)	bŭndé
eatable fruits	buah-buah-jijak	good	paguch; kena; sigat; romus
durian	déán		
mangustine	sikuk	goods	buat; perambut
manggo	muporam	good-natured	mŭnich
sibau or rambutan	sibu	government	prentah
small jungle rambutan	pijuan	gradually	mupok; mukun; mutik (W)
jack-fruit	tibudak; nangka	grasshopper	kadich
tampoi	tapui	grain, a (of rice)	ni-sirach
langsat	lishét	grandfather	babai
papaya	payang	grandmother	somuk
plantain	borak	grandchild	sukuch
naw-palm	inyok	grass	(uduch; pai-pasang
nipah-palm	nipah; apong		(pŭdam
fruit (full-grown, but unripe)	tuuch	grate	ungösh
		grate (cocoa-nut)	nukur
fruit, to bring forth	buán	grater	(penukur; kukuran
fuel	wang		(ungösh
fulfil	betŭtŭk	grave, a	kubor
full	pŭnoh; gŭgŭp	grease; greasy	remak; berinyab
fun, make of, or with	berubi; patia (W)	great	bääs
fungus	kulat	greedy	sibut; bedogich; bidi
funnel	churut	green	barum
		grey (hair)	berubuk
gain	ontong	grey (ash coloured), see "colour"	
gambir	gambir		
gap (fissure)	rubang	grieved	susah-atin; ngurid
gape (yawn)	kuab	grin	betŭjit
garden	téyah	grind (by hand)	kisar; giling
gather together	besinŭn; nguruk	groan	nyidéing
gather (pluck)	nyŭked; nupäs; mŭtŭd	grow up	tumbu
		grown up with grass	jukut
gather fuel	nuh wang	growl	ngŭr
gaze upon	tingah	guard	nguan
gaze upwards	ngigurrah	guava	buah jambu
generous	mŭnich; tatich	guess	jangka
gentle	mŭnich	guide, a	malim
gently (not roughly)	nakit	gum	putŭk
gimlet	grodi	gutta percha	nyatoh
ginger	rái	gums	samad jipŭch
gird on	nŭkin	gun (cannon)	(miriam
girl	anak dayung; gishŭ		(léla
give; grant	ngyen; jugan	pop-gun	panah
	(rään-atin	gun-powder	obat bedil
glad; gladness	gaŭn-atin	gush out	menapus; măräsit (liquids)
	(ginaiyŭn (very)		
glisten, see "twinkle"			
glory (renown)	beragach	hades	sabayan
glory (halo)	kŭmakab	hair (head)	ubōk
glory (effulgence)	jowah shiu tingah	hair (body)	buruch
glossy	nyerinyak	half, a	rapŭt
go	odi; di; metak	halve	(nyirapŭt
go (imper.)	shush odi; shush ponu		(miré nyinuŭch
go (visit)	tudu	hammer	bobah
	(mori (from far)	happy	senang
go back (return)	määd (from near)	hand	tangan
	(motash (from near) (W)	hand, right	taŭch

Chalmers' Vocabulary. cxli.

English.	Dayak.	English.	Dayak.
hand, left	bâit	hinder, to, see "forbid"	
handful	ni-agŭm ; ni-akŭp (*both hands together*)	hinderpart	budich
		hire	gagi ; pach (W)
handkerchief, head	(bung ubōk (burang (W)	history	susud (*genealogy*) ; duda ; susĕ ; dundān
handle (sword)	ubak	history, to relate a	nusĕ ; nyiduda
handle (of vessel)	kojit	hit	dog
handrail	ūtag	hit, be	dog jokad
hang	(begatung (beramboi (*by hands*)	hither	kamati ; kamanñ
		hoarse	piau
hang oneself	betukŭ	hold	digŭng
hang up	tŭngid	hold, take, of	digen
hanging down (pensile)	bikidiŭng ; rambĕŭng	hole	rubang
		hole in bed of a river	lubok
hard	riang ; semŭtak	hole, make, in	tŭbŭk ; karech (*in earth*)
hard (hearted)	tŭnyĕāk ; dŭrach		
harlot	perambai	hole, make, through	nubŏt
harvest	ngah ngŭtŭn	holes, in	tubŏt
harvest mid	piaun ngŭtŭn	hollow	perubang ; begagong
	(*1st.* nyipāan (*gather first fruits*)	holy	kudus
		Holy Ghost	Roh Al Kudus
	2nd. nyitŭngid, or man sawa	hook, fish	pisich
harvest feast, keep		hooked on to	begagit
	3rd. nyipidang men-yŭpong, or nyisupen	hope in	harap ; sabach
		honest	tŭnggŭn
		honey	juh bŭnyich
haste, be in	begaut ; gopoh	honeycomb	(penubak bŭnyich (idang bŭnyich
haste, make	likas		
hasten after	bekoduch	hop, to	ngitijong
hasten away	betŭdak	horse	kuda
hastily	likas	horn	tandok
hat, Dayak	serŏung	hot	sekisu gŭnan (*body*)
hate	tuas		paras ; bongo (W) ;
hatred	boji		surah ; petiak (W)
haul up	pāad	hot or heated, as air near hot water	paras begŭngam
have (possess)	ogi ; biŭn		
head, see "body"		hot or heated, as air near large fire	sadak
head-dress, see "handkerchief"		hot to taste	semarach
head house	(pang-ach ; baruk (W) (balŭ (R. Sadong)	HOUSE :—	ramin
		house, small, in jungle	bishŭn
head-hunting, go	ngŭnyu	house, small, on farm	(bori (*on farm*) (purung (*for goods*)
headache	ubak mŭnam		
heal ; healed	buăh	house, small, near village for storing goods	pŭngau
heap	nambun		
hear	(dingah ; keringab (W) (ngojit (W)		
heart (seat of affections)	atin	a Dyak house, containing several doors	bŭtang
heat (sunshine)	surah		
heated, see "hot"		outside platform of a Dyak house	tanyu
heathen	dayah kapir		
heaven	shurga ; rāich shurga	verandah, or common room	awach
heavy	băt		
hell	opui Narāka	private, or family room	arŭn ; romin (W)
heel over	singit		
helm	mudich	fire-place	apŭk
help	turung	wood-place	(paiyuch (poiyŏ shiru (W)
hence	sŏ iti		
henceforth ; hereafter	repas ati	water-place	pawad
here	diti ; digiti ; diginŭ	garret	rŭngah
hiccup	sedu	below floor	ribŏ
hide	chukăn	floor	lantei
high	omu ; segatung	how ?	munki ; semuki
hill	darŭd	how much, or how many ?	kiangki
hill, a low	terunduk ; dug (*long*)		kŭdu kiangki

English.	Dayak.	English.	Dayak.
how large?	mūtiki	jaw	rāang
howl (as dog)	kāong; kieūng	jealous	mishē; monyash (W)
humble	tūkūn temūngūn	Jesus Christ	Isa Almesih
hungry	seburūk; pilai (W)	Jew	orang Jehudi
hunt	ngashu; tūdak	Jew's harp	trāing; setubiūng
hurricane	ribut; sobak-ribut	jingle	jawūn
husband	bonuch	join together	tubu
hymn	pujian	joint	bukuch turang
hypocrisy	bujuk	joists of flooring	geraggar
hypocrite, to act as	mujuk	joke	berubi; patīa (W)
		judge, to	hukum
I	aku	Judgment, Day of	anu kiamat
idol, an (image)	berhala	judgment of God, a	tulah
if	kamui	jump over	melompat; merūkid; menyakir (as frog); metaran
ignorant	babal; bawa		
ill-will	geraka		
impudent	dūch biūn mūngūch	jump down	stabung; nyūngung
in	darum	jump up	menanjong
in jungle	abong tarun	jungle	tarun
incite	ngajak	jungle (old)	tūuch; tuān; tuān randam (trees, large)
incur	dōg		
Indian-rubber	pūtūk Gemuan	jungle (young)	mūrah; tebai
individually	sekūshin-kūshin	jungle (low grassy)	kupai
industrious	gūgach	just (man)	tūnggūn
infant	anak-pira	just (thing)	betul; patut
infect; infectious	sawit	just? is it (or fair?)	pas inap
inflated	meruāp	just come	moran menūg
ingenuity	akal	just now (past)	tējach; jach
inheritance	pusaka	just now (future)	tō
inoculate	sungkit	jut out from	nogang
instead of	ganti; besambi		
interior of a country	sijō	keep (take care of)	ingat; jaga; nguan
interrogative affix	kah	keep alive	kudip
interrupt (talk)	nyirībur	keep (put by)	kingat; shitah
interest (of money)	anak	key	kunchi
interval of rest between the stages of farm-work	penūngūch	kick forwards	ngikak
		kick backwards	nigah
		kill	siū; nyōō (W)
inundation	{pīin ubah {pīin apuch dēyuch	kind; kindness	{tatich; mūnich {masi (merciful)
invest with name or office	bekadūn; bergelar	kindle	tung
		kindled	sūkūt
invite	ngajak	kiss	chium
iron	besi	kite (bird)	bōuch
iron-wood	tāās	Kling, a (native of South India)	tambē
irresolution	bimbang-atin		
is	ogi	knee	ubak karub
is not	meting; doi (W)	kneel	sedikang; bekunyug
island	puloh	knife (large)	bukō [(W)
itchy	ti	knife (small)	sindah
itself, by (not mixed with others)	shidarū	knock at	gutog
		knock off	tampir
INTERJECTIONS:—		know	puan; (redah)
expressing surprise	arūch; adō	know (person)	kūnyet
expressing pain	adi; adoh	know, do not	āntah; dūch puan
		known, make	agach
jack-fruit	{tebudak {nangka	knot, a knot, to	} muku
jacket	jipō; sekindang		
jammed	serupot	ladder (Malay)	tengah ajan
jar (large)	{bonda {ipang	ladder (Dyak)	tungoch
		laden, over- (boat)	sarad
jar (small)	{iron; mando {blanē	laden, over- (person)	gūnggur-gūnggur
		lake	dūnu
jar (high)	tajo; jabir	lame	{nijōug {bojang (limping)
jar (pitcher)	buyong		

Chalmers' Vocabulary. cxliii.

English.	Dayak.	English.	Dayak.
lament over	muäs	lift up in arms	samöt ; taten
lamp	plita ; lampo	light, the	jowah
land	tanah	light (adj.)	jangan
land, a (country)	räich	light, to (fire)	tung
land, dry (not sea)	dëyuch	light upon, to	mäp
land round and between houses and villages	būdag	lightning	kijat
		like as	nimun ; kayä ka
		like to	nimun ; mun
land round a whole village	rimbang	like as if	mīnyam
		lime	binyuch
land near houses, hard and cleared of grass	pūkan	lime, a (fruit)	rimu
		line, a	didi
land at, to	singgah ; ngesah	lining	turap
landing-place	pangkalan	lip	bibich
language	peminyu	litany	litani
large	⎧ bääs ; aiyuch (W)	litter (dust, &c.)	ronash ; sūpok
	⎪ tebonë ; sindu-i (very)	little (bulk)	shiit ; shū ; isō (W)
	⎨ pūndor (in volume)	little (short)	purōk
	⎪ bidor (disproportionately large) ; baër	little (quantity)	nishit ; shiit ; nishū ; arōk (very)
last	būtach ; tāan	live	udip
lasting	tūgoch ; kukoh	lizard, small house	titēk
last night	singomi	load (gun)	⎫
lath	lantei	load (ship)	⎬ ngisi
laugh	tawūch	lock	kunchi
lavish	pruang	lodge	numpang
lazy	sorut	loins	kupong
lead (metal)	timah	long	omu ; rambung (tall)
leaf (tree)	dawun	long time, a	tui
leaf, a (of anything)	ni-kridëan	long time ago, a	mūch tui
leak	⎫ sirēt	long as, as	setūdūn ; tian
leaky	⎭	long for, to (one absent)	jābūng
lean (adj.)	mānyuch ; maiyuch		
lean back or against	menyanich	long for, to (certain kinds of food)	krangas
learn	belajar		
learned	bisa	loose (not tight)	⎧ tūndor
leather	kurit ; ūnyit		⎩ gushōsh (clothes)
leave (forsake)	tinggë ; tūgan	loose (not tense)	kerūng ; miōsh ; renūk
left (remaining)	kidūm	loose (not coherent)	gushōsh ; ragoch
leaven ; leavened	ragi ; beragi	loose (not fast)	tegugë ; kūtok
leech, land	remūtūk	look at	tingah
leech, water	remotah	look upwards	ngigurah
lend	minjam	look in a wrong direction	begayang
lengthen out	kasawich		
lengthways	tūnggūn	looking-glass	cheremin
less	korang	loop, a	sepakūt segarong
let be ; let alone	biar ; isah-i	lose	⎫
let go	ruach	lose way	⎬ mānyap
let go (a string)	pasan	louse	gutich
let down	bishor	louse (of fowls)	kudūb
level	rabak	loud	benah
lick	ngyarēk	loud (voice)	dōr
lid	tutūp ; gudug	love	⎧ riadu ka
lie	kādōng		⎨ atin-awang
liar, a	dayah kādōng	love, to	⎩ rāan ngah
	⎧ guring	love-bird, a	tigēsh
lie down	⎨ sekunyong ⎫ (on	low (in height)	rapat ; purōk
	⎪ sekūdang ⎬ back)	low (voice)	ūnūk ; rūndeng
	⎩ seging (on side)	lucky	budik betuach
lie down (on face)	sepūūb	lull child ⎧ (by dangling)	nyandō
lie on top of	marēt	asleep ⎩ (by singing)	samūn
life		lump together	meruku
life, principle of	ashung	lust	⎫ lipōng
lift up	mokat ; tunduk	lust after, to	⎭
lift up tambok (for proceeding on journey)	beranyuk		
		mad	gila

English	Dayak	English	Dayak
maggot	urud	mispronounced	skioden
maize	jagong	miss (aim)	ashĕt
make	nai	mist	abun
malice	(tuas ; boji	mistake, to	sabuch
	(mūnam atin	mix	begaur
malicious	grobah	mock (tease)	(nūpat
Malay, a	Kirĕăng		(naiya (*by imitating*)
man, a	(dayah ; năan	mock (abuse)	ngamun ; mangu
	(nyăa (W)	modest	mūngūsh ; dasah
man, a (male)	dari	moment, a	ni-kidap ; ni-girū
mankind	manusia	monkey (long-tailed)	oyung
MANNER OF ACTION :		monkey (short-tailed)	kiad
in this manner	kumunū	monkey	(beduch
in that manner	kamuti ; sekūnū		terpiu
mangustine or mango, see "fruit"		monkey (*orang-utan*)	(bojig
			maias
many or much	bogū ; aduch	money	wang
many ? how	kiang ki ; mukudu	monsoon, rainy	jaiyah
many, too	tūkod	monsoon, hot	roga
marbles	guli	month, a	ni-buran
mark, a	tanda	MOON :—	buran
mark (trace)	arok	new	buran băuch
MARRY :—		full	buran turak
betroth	biūmbai	quarters	bulan kudung
marry a wife	sowan	third day after full	buran bubuk
marry a husband	būnan	more (quantity)	dingĕ
marshy ground	(rūboch ; tanah rabak	more (comparison)	robich ; păuch
	(tanah padak	morning	ishan
mat (fine)	ūmŏk	morning, this	ju-i-jach
mat	bumban ; idash	morning, to-morrow	sepagi-ishan-ishan
mat (coarse)	kasa	mortar (for paddy)	lishŏng
matted	bekarut	moss ; mossy	rimut
matter (pus)	penūnah	moth	sebunut
matter (business)	(tūdū kayuch	mother	sindu
	(tūdū pūngănang	mouldy	bekurat
mattress	tilam	mountain	darūd
meaning	ărti	mouse	babu
measure	)	mouth	bobah
measure (length)	} nukud ; nakar	mouth of river	nūngūch
measuring-line	penukud	mouthful, a	ni-sikăum
meddle with	(nambang (*interfere*)	move (shift)	beringar
	(tūma (*touch*)	move (stir)	terigen ; begiring
medicine	uri	move about (neuter)	begugoch
mediator	pengūsạch	much, see "many"	
meet	bedapūd	mud	tawang ; jijub
melon	semangka	mud (on river's banks)	pantei
melt	ririch	muddy (water)	kăruch
mend	nai kena ; nūpung (*anything broken*)	muddy (ground)	(tarĕ ; mamĕăk
			(tawang (*deep*)
mention	nyobut	musquito	prungang
mercy	)	musquito curtains	kelambu
mercy upon, have	} masi	muscle	kuku
merchant	dayah berdagang	must	tūntu
merely	mina ; perchoma	mustard (plant)	sabi
messenger	penyuruch ; dah		
middle ; midst	băat ; rapūt	nail, a	)
middling ; moderately	moa	nail, a wooden, or	} pasak
midwife	penūding	peg	)
milk	juh-shishuch	nail (human)	siruch ; silun (W)
mill, hand	kisaran	naked	(setabet (*woman*)
miscarry (child)	ruus		(setagor (*man*)
mischief ; mischance	genaka ; geraka	name, a	adūn
mischievous	gauk	name, to	bekadūn
miser	bidi ; bedogich	name, have, of	biūn adūn
misfortune, see "mischance"		name, take, of	kambat adūn
		narrow	kupit ; sekīdūn

Chalmers' Vocabulary.

English.	Dayak.	English.	Dayak.
narrow (circumscribed)	kūtich	NUMERALS (cont.):— twenty	dūñch puroh
nation (tribe)	bangsa	one hundred	ni-ratus
naturally	taūn	one thousand	ni-ribu
near	sindūk	ten thousand	ni-laksa
near-sighted	kidu	number, to	niap
neck	(tungñ (in front) (pungō (back of)	O	yah
necklace	(kongkong ; tumbis (seramū (made of teeth)	oath	mangu (asih
necessary	patut	obey	pakai pūngānang
needles	utósh		(pakai prentah
nerve, a	uat	obstinate	madūd
nest (bird's)	sānuk ; sarin	obtain (get), see	
net (fishing)	jala ; pukat	"procure"	
net (a toil)	jering	offer (hold out)	jugan
never	būūn	oil	inyō
never mind	(dūch jerah (dūch isach	old (man) old (thing)	uyambah ; penyibāñs ūmah
new	bāuch	once	ni-sidah
news	agack		ni
nice	sidi		(ni-buah
night	ngarūm		(ni-bidang
night, to-	sekambuch		ni-pūrūng
night, last	singomi	one	· ni-ikor
night, pass the	nyirumun		ni-keping
no	indah ; dūch		ni-kayu
noise, a	gutoi		(ni-lei
noise, make a	(berishut ; nai gutoi (nai dudu	oneself	ni-turap odūp-sādi
noise (sound)	jawūn	oneself, by	sñdi
noise (of animals)	sūk	one's own	odūp-dūpu
noise (of falling water)	gō	onion	bang
noon	! yun anu	only	adū
	(nūnūng repuān	only-begotten	tūmu
noose, a	seringō	open, to	kuka ; mbang (fruit)
noose, to	nyeringō	open (not confined)	baiyah ; tawas (W)
nose	unung	opinion	pikir ; kira
not	(dūch ; mudūch (doch (W) ; di (W)	opportunity or	shuput kūdū
not, there is	meting ; doi (W)	origin	pūun
not, no it is	būkūn	orphan	(patu
not, do	(mānyach ; dūnyach (mba (W)	order, an	(tumang (no father) semainya
not, even	semūki kūn—meting gāch	order, to	(bodah ; dah (semainya
nothing at all	meting mani-mani	order, put in	mishūn
notch (wood), to	nyūbang	order, that, in	parang
notched	rūbang	other	būkūn
now	(tong-i · madin ati ; madin (da adin (W)	ought out outside	patut } disopah
NUMERALS:—		outside, from	sō sopah
one	ni ; ikan (W)	out of, come	ruach
two	dūūch	out through, come	rāpus ; berambus
three	taruch	overflow (land)	apūch dēyuch
four	pat	overflow (vessel)	robich muab ; meliris
five	rimūch	overladen (boat)	sarad
six	num	overladen (man)	(beduru
seven	juh		(gūnggur-gunggur
eight	mai ; mōich (W)	owl	bō
nine	plii	own (possessive)	dūpu
ten	semūng	oyster	sampi
eleven	(semūng-ni (semūng-ni (W)	paddle, a	brosi
twelve	semūng dūūch	paddle, to	kayuh

k

English.	Dayak.	English.	Dayak.
paddy-farm on high dry land	umňch padi	pipe	serubok (bambu) supak (W)
painful	pidě	pin	utŏsh
pale	puchat	pinch, to	kujet
palm (of hand)	purah tangan	pinch, take a	unyut
pan (iron)	kuali	pith	umbud
pan (earthen)	belanga	pitiful	siňt
parallel	tůnggůn	pity upon, have	nyibňra
pardon	ampun ; mňňp	place (put)	nikůn ; nah
parasite (plant)	bůkach	place down	nah
pare off sharp edges of split rotan	pňid	place upright place upright in ground	mejŏg juman
pare off split bamboos	nguus		
part, a	utung-ni	place, a	yůn ; kah
pass (be current)	laku	plain (clear)	jŏwah
pass away	mňnyap	plain, a	tanah rabak
pass over	langkah, kabang	plait (braid)	nyerat
pass beneath	nyerap	plane, a	kůtam
pass on	rasu	plate	jaru ; pinggěn tapak (small)
pass by	nůnan ; rowan		
pass before	budawů	planking	ůdah ; asu (W)
pass through	sŏ	plant, to	perůn
pass, come to (crenire)	tůk ; jadi	plant paddy, make holes in which to	noruk
past	můch mungňm		
past tense, sign of	můch	plantain	borak
passenger, go as a	numpang ; tambang	play (amuse oneself)	mŏňh-mŏňh
passionate (choleric)	boji	play (jest with)	berubi ; patia (W)
pat	nutŏt	pleasant (scent)	růmak
patch	nůpung	pleasant (taste)	sidi
patient	madůd-atin	pleased	rňan
pay	bayer	pledge (promise)	nňňm
peace	damai ; selamat	pluck, to	nyůked
peace, be at	berdamai ; senang	pocket	kůndi ; putir (a bag)
peck, to	nukuk	point towards	tiju
peep at	ngirěng	point out	
pelt	nabur	point, a	tubun
pen	kňlam	pointed	růshing
penitent	sesal	pointed bamboo stuck in the ground as a means of defence	tuka
pepper	lada		
perforated	tubŏt		
perhaps	kůdů—indin ; kůdů	poison	rachun
perish	rusak	poisoned ; poisonous	bisa
perspiration	udňňs	poke	kujok ; ngikir
perspire	mudňňs	pole, when stuck upright in the ground, or	turus
pestle (for pounding paddy)	aruch		
petticoat	jomuch	post, a	tukang
phlegm	ůk	polish	bodah nyirinyňk
pick up	mit ; shun nukuk (as fowls)	pond	důnu
		poor	seburůk ; bůtak ; kůta- charňta ; charňta ; ruga (W) ; papa (W)
pick (gather)	nupňňs ; nyůked		
pickle, to	betůbach ; nůbach		
pickled flesh, fruit, or fish	tubach (fruit) dňňt (fish and flesh)	populous	powůn
		possess (hold)	digung
pickles	bekashům (fruit)	possess (have)	biňn
picture	gambar ; tegundo	possessive case, sign of	důpu
piece, a (part)	ni-pirě		rŏŏs ; tugu (W) pumůůd (short) penakap (long) pumůnůs (of gable)
pierce (stab)	numuk ; tůbůk	posts of a house	
pierce through	ngůtŏ		
pig (domestic)	aiyŏ		
pig (wild)	pongňn	see also "pole"	
pigeon	achang ; merpati	pot	priuk ; ternang
pigeon, wild	punai	pot-bellied	bushung
pile in layers	berapich ; beturap	potatoes, sweet	setira
pilfer	prikěsh	pouch of monkey	kuni
pillow	bantal	poultice	tubi maměňk

Chalmers' Vocabulary. cxlvii.

English.	Dayak.	English.	Dayak.
pound paddy (separate rice from husk)	pûch	provisions for a journey	onyad
pour out	mobâs; rëän	pull	narik; tarik
powder	teboduk	pull down	rubûch; patûb
powder, to	bodah rûnduk	pull up	dimut; ngäjut
powerful	{bûkē} {bogug} (*physically*) {bisa}	pull in two	nyiräak
		pull towards oneself in steering	pawot
praise	puji; parich; sidäru	pumpkin	krûni
pray, to	sambayang	A man is said to be punan, when having rudely refused hospitality of another, some accident befalls him	punun
prayers (divine service)	sambayang		
prawns	udang		
pregnant	bitē		
prepare (arrange)	mishûn	pungent (taste)	semarach
presence of, in	{di jowin} {di serung jowin}	pungent (odour)	pashûk
		punish	nunggu
presence of, enter	ngadap	punishment	hukum, tunggu
presently	tē	pure (clean)	bisig
press down on	digang	pure (clear)	kining
pretend (to do anything)	} nyimauu	pursue	tûdak
		push away	tulak
see "feign"		push on	nganyor
pretty	sigat; romus	push through	tön
prevent	jaman; nang; siût	put	nûngkah
price	harga	put on	nah
price, cost	poko(k)	put down	nikûn; nakit
prick	tûbûk; nyûg	put by or away	nikûn; mishûn
pride	} meruâp; sambuch; asi-asi (W)		
proud (vain)		quarrel	nai gutoi
proud (arrogant)	gruah	quarrel (by words)	bekarit
Priest	Tuan Padri	quarrel (by blows)	bekai
prisoner	dayah takap	quarter part, a	pat pirē
privy, a	bandong	quarter, to	nyikupat
procure (get)	shaûn; dapûd	quick	{likas} {repit (*hurriedly*)} {ka säich} {mû mûch}
prohibit, see "prevent"			
		quickly	
profanity	tapat; patïa (W)		
profit	ontong	quiet	rûrû
promise	bepaiyu; nääm	quiet (tame)	mûnich; rimón
PERSONAL PRONOUNS		quiet, be	rûû
1st—I	aku		
me	oku (W)	race	bangsa
mine	ku	radish	luba(k)
2nd—thou	{küu} {mai (*used to elders*)} {kaam (*and friends*)}	rafters	koshu
		rain	ujen
thee		rainy weather	jaiya
thine	mûu (W); mu	rainbow	ujen bukang
3rd—he	odûp; eiyuch	raise up oneself	mokat
him	i (*affix*); iyoch (W)	raised platform, a	angkat
his	i (*affix*)	ramble about jungle	bedandong
1st—we	kiech	rank (smell)	banguch
us	köich (W)	rap at	gutog
our	ami (*affix*)	rapid	doras
2nd—ye	ûta; ûngan	rapid, a	giam
you	ingan (W)	rare	säät
your	ta (*affix*); ûngan	rattan	ui
3rd—they, them,		raw	mantah
same as "he"		razor	sindah gumbak
theirs,		reach to	nûg; tûngang nûg
same as "his"		ready	sedia
pronunciation (sound)	lagu; ûmpas	ready, make	{mishûn} {besisat (*oneself*)}
prophet	nabi		
prostrate (lie)	mäûb	really	sawû
protect	gerindung; nguan	reap	ngûtûm padi
		rebuke	ngajar

English	Dayak	English	Dayak
receive (into hand)	kambat	reward	upah
receive (accept)	mit	rice (in husk)	padi
recline upon	menyanich	rice (husked)	bras
recollect	(natung	rice (of a sticky kind)	bras pulut
recollect	natich (*a thing left behind*)	rice (boiled)	(tubi (sungkoi (R. Sadong)
recompense	maras	rice (boiled in young bamboos)	pogang
red	birĕ		
redeem	nubŏsh	rice (boiled in the leaves of a herb called "manah")	sukoi ; sungkoi
Redeemer	Penubŏsh		
regret			
regretful of, be	nyibāra	rice, boiled (wrapped in leaves of "manah")	isam
relative (near)	sudara		
relative (distant)	kūda	rich	kaya
RELATIVES :—		ridge of roof	bung bungan
the brothers and sisters of one's father and mother	pimás	right	sawñ ; sedang ; betul
		right to be done	tepakai
		ring (finger)	shishin
one's father and mother's elder brother or sister	sümbah	rings (for arms, &c), see under "dress"	
		riot	gutoi ; dudu
one's father and mother's younger brother or sister	tuah	rise	mäad
		rise up	mokat
		rise up from sleep	burah ; mokat
father-in-law	damúch	rise (the sun)	nushak
mother-in-law		rising ground	terunduk ; dug (*long*)
step-father	sama tiri	river	sungi ; beruach (W)
step-mother	sindu tiri	river, branch	(sūkap sungi (grongan (W)
step-son	anak tiri		
son-in-law	iban	river, main stream of	būtang piin
daughter-in-law		road	āran
nephew ; niece	anak senùkun	road, a bye	sūkap āran
cousin	betunggal	road, make a	nyāran
wife's elder brother or sister	sikĕ	road, repair a	
		road, the trunks of trees laid down to form a	teboian
wife's younger brother or sister	sipar		
adopted child	anak angkat ; anak iru	roast	badang
		rob	nyijārach ; berobut
near relatives	sudĕ-madich	robber	penyamun
relaxed (slack)	tūndur	roe (fish)	turoch ikyen
relish, a (anything eaten with the rice)	kudŏsh	roll up	mārun ; ngārung
		roll about	beraring
reluctantly, or, with difficulty	(bersĕna (bedayah	roll, a	bārun
		roof	tūnyah
remain	(rūñ (*stop*) (kidūm (*be left*)	room, a	arūn
		root	būkach ; uat
remember	ingat ; natūng	root, large, above ground	bandir
remove	beringar		
remnants (leavings)	tūduch	roots of a bamboo-clump left after bamboos have been cut	apung
rent (or "tax")	sashuch		
repent	sesal-atin		
repentance			
reserved (shy)	tūkūn temūngūn	rope	tarich
resin	damar ; upach	rope made from the "gomuti" or "naw" palm	ijok
resist	ngirawan		
rest, see "interval"			
restore (give back)	pari	rotten	modām
	(mori	rough	baga
return	mäad (*from near*)	round	burūng
	(motash (*from near*)	rows, in	bejerri
retribution	maras [(W)	rows, place in	besharad
retribution of God	tulah	rub	gasak ; ngireg
revenge	maras	rubbish, light	sūpok
revolve	(begiring ; bekanding (bepūnding	rude	duch setabi
		rudder	mudich

English.	Dayak.	English.	Dayak.
ruin, fall into	(rubuch ; serukob (patŭb ; bigas	sense	akal
run	bu	senseless (in a faint)	mijŭp
run away	mubu	separate (divide off)	bebāat
run after	tŭdak	separate (part from)	bu
run away, make to	pibu ; kashíg ; kushíg	separately (by itself)	shidarŭ
rust	tegar	servant	bŭtak
rustling-noise, a	garósh	servant (hired)	gagi
		set (sun)	murut sibŏng-i
		settle (a business)	bodah tŭnggŭn
sago		settled	tŭnggŭn
sago-palm	sagu	shade, to	gerindung ; baup
sago, raw	lemanta	shadow	(sengangi
saliva	rujah ; royang (W)		(sebambia (W)
salt	garŭ	shake (be unsteady)	begugoch ; begnynt
salt (briny)	pidĕ	shake (active)	nugoch ; ngunyang
salvation	seramat	shake (shiver)	kamutŭl
salver, brass	talam	shake up	kushok
same	ni-mun	shake out (as clothes)	(ngamui ; ngŭmob
same (in height or length)	berikŭd		(ngŭmbar
		shake off	tŭpich
sand	pasir	shallow	boduch ; dadas ; tubŭs
sand-fly	biis ; korap (W)	shame	mŭngŭch ; dasah
sands	pasir	shame to, give	(ngyen mŭngŭch
sarong, a (Malay cloth)	kain tajong ; sarong		(pemŭngŭch
Satan	Umŏt Shĕtan	sharp	roja
satiated	bisoch	sharpen	ngasah
satiate	bodah puas	shave	begumbak
satisfied, see		shaven (head)	betundŏ
"appeased"		sheath, see	
say	nang ; dāan	"scabbard"	
saying, a	pŭngánang	sheet (of bed)	putong
saying	sŭninang	sheep	biri-biri
scab	tubŭ	shells (land)	(brukong (large)
scabbard	sibŏng ; duong (W)		(brŭkyeng (small)
scald	rāus	shell, cocoa-nut	tapurung ; boru (W)
scales (fish)	sisi(k)	shelf	panggŏ
scales (balance)	kŭti	shepherd	gombala
scar	arit	shield, a	peningin
scissors	gunting	shield, to, see "shade"	
scold	boji	shine	nyirinyak
scorpion	(rekara	shining	bringĕăng
	(liñng otich (W)	ship	kapal
scrape	ngikid ; ngiich	shiver, see "shake"	
scrape (dirt off feet)	ngutŏsh ; ngireg	shoes	sibong koja ; kaus (W)
scrape out leavings	garas	shoot, to	timbak
scratch oneself	gaiyu ; dodash (W)	shoot of plant, young	(shŏk
scratch (score)	garag		(tijuk (of tree)
scratch with nails	geraiat	shop	kadei
scribble	berirŏ	shore up with posts, to	nukang
scum	jurak ; tegurak	shore	dĕyuch
scurf	runŭk	shore, go on	māad dĕyuch
scurvy	bagi	short	(kubŭ ; purok
search	(jiroch ; siroch		(kodŏ (W)
	(karik (W)	short cut, make a	mŭtash
sea	laut	shorten	kosigŭt
secretly	bechukăn	shoulder, see "body"	
secure (firm)	tegap ; tetap		(ngyrais
security for, be	ngarun	shout	ngab (at getting a
see	kirich		(head)
see (behold)	tingah	show	(ngah tingah
seed (corn)	binĕ		(ngyen tingah
seed (of plants)	ruang	show (point out)	tiju
seek, see "search"		shut, to	(ngishugn ; tŭŭp
seize upon	nakap		(ngobut
sell	juah	shut up, be	tŭŭp
send	păit	shut up (enclose)	kurung ; nyikapung

English.	Dayak.	English.	Dayak.
shy, see "ashamed"		slowly	berati; pedanach (W)
shy (reserved), see "reserved"		small (size)	shŭ; isŏ (W)
		small (quantity)	nishŭ
sick	mŭnam	smart (pain)	mojot
sickness	berandam	smell, a	bŭuch
side (of man), see "body"		smell, to	kŭduk
		smell, give forth a	bŭuch
side, a	ni-pirĕ	smear	ngutŏsh
side of, by the	turah	smoke	ashuch
side, inclining to one	singit; kumblăk (W)	smoke tobacco, to	ngudut
sieve	aiyag	smooth (level)	dedap; rabak
sift	ngaiyag	smooth (glossy)	nyirinyak
sigh, see "groan"		snake	jipŭch
sign	tanda	snare	jaring
sign, to	nanda	snare, to	nyaring
silent, be	rŭŭ	snatch	serobut
silk	sutra; dasu	sneeze	pasin
silver	pirak	snore	ngudŏd
sister (elder); sister (younger); see "brother"		snot	budŭk
		suff up	nyiruk
		so	kamuti; sekŭnŭ
site (former) of village or house, or site of former dwelling-place of a tribe	tambawang	so that	parang
		so and so	ŭni
		soak	kurŏm
		sodden	rutus
sin	salah; dosa	soft	dudŭt; gumŏsh
sin, to	nai dosa; nai sarah	soft (flabby)	renuk
sinful	berdosa	soft (flexible)	liat
sing	menyanyi	soft (moist)	tarĕ; tawang
sing songs	buding segumbang	sojourn	numpang
sink	kauum	soldier	(orang soldado
sink, make to	tŭmutŭm; seruman		(orang kubu
sirih (a pepper-leaf eaten with betel-nut)	bŭid	some (a part)	ni-kŭda
		sometimes	ogi anu
sit down	guru	song	pantun
sit (as hen)	ngŭkŭp	son	anak dari
skim off	kadi	soon	likas; tĕ
skin	kurit	soot	ing
skin (rind)	kŭbang	sore	pidĕ; mŭnam
skin, to	ngŭnyit; nyibabak	sort	macham; mun
skinned (abraded)	tebabak	[what sort is it?]	muki mun iti?]
skull	tekurŏk	sorrow	susah-atin
sky	langit	sorry	ngurid; ibuch (W)
slack	} tŭndur	soul	semŭngi; *after death it becomes a* "minŏ"
slacken			
slander, see "blame"		soul (a living), (*i.e.*, a body animated by a soul)	dŭtin
slant	meringgĕ		
slanting	mertang (*as a tree*)		
slave	ulon; bŭtak	sound, see "pronunciation"	
sleep	bŭŭs		
sleepy, be	nunu	sound (noise)	jawŭn
slice, a	{ ni-sirib	sound (of voices)'	sŭk; angu (*distant*)
	{ ni-tŭding (*of flesh*)	sound (of musical instrument)	surā
slice, to	nyirib		
slice flesh, to	nŭding	sound (sleep)	rŭrŭ
slide down	} terusap	sour	mashŭm
slip down		source (of river)	ŭtak pŭn
slip (from its place)	bishor; luchut; rupas	source (origin)	pŭun
slip (down from its place)	beraring	south	selatan
		sow cloth	nyit
slippery	jerŭch	sow paddy (broadcast)	nabur
slope, a	} tanai (*ground*) *see* "*slant*"	sow paddy (by planting it in holes)	minĕ
slope, to			
sloping		space of time, a	sukad
slow	(abŏt; săich	space, intervening	ăsach
	(beridu (W)	sparing of, be	siŭt

Chalmers' Vocabulary. cli.

English.	Dayak.	English.	Dayak.
spark	buah opui; shuat opui	steer	mudich
sparrow	piit	stem, a	tŭngŭn; pŭnamai
speak to or with	beritong; mĭnyu	steps (Dyak ladder)	tŭngoch
spear	jerok; ashul (W) burus	steps (pegs driven into tree for climbing)	tatŭk
spear with one barb	perambut	steps (notches cut in trunk of tree for use in climbing)	subang
spear with two barbs	beraiyang		
spear (sharpened bamboo)	tampun		
		steps, to cut	ngubang
spear (sharpened wood)	serugich	stick, a (walking)	sekud
		stick (to keep open window)	tukang
species	purich		
spell (words)	mengija	stick (on which the leaves are laid in making "atap")	rŭis
spider	tŭkah		
spill	bobŭs		
spirit (soul), see "soul"		stick, to; sticky	rekat
spirit (departed)	minŏ	stiff (inflexible)	boḡŭg kŭkag
spirit, evil	umŏt	st ll, be	rŭŭ
spit	ngirujah	still (yet)	babŭ
spittle, see "saliva"		still water	piin nŭnŭr piin nŭnŭng
spiteful	gauk; genaka		
splendid (in appearance)	sangŭn; gruah	sting, a (that which stings)	butu
splinter, a	ibŭn	sting, to	ningŭt
split in two, to	nyirăak; mirĕ	stinking	rŭshish; modăm rŭngang
split in two	rǎak; tepirĕ		
split open	bubus; jeja	stir (move); stirred, be see "move"	
spoon, wood used as a	sukir		
spoon, a	sunduk	stir about	karu; nguil (W)
spoon, to use a	sŭk	stockings	sibŏng koja
spout (of water)	aiyak	stomach	kuboi
spout of a jar	sishuch	stoop	mutu
spread out	mŭd	stoop down underneath	nyerap
sprinkle	mŭsik; tapich (W)		
spur (of cock)	sikak	stone	batuch
square	pujuruch	stop	rŭŭ; mŭŭ; mokŏ
squat down	sedukung	stop at	nyesah
squeeze	pishŭ	stop (close up)	ngishŭgn
squeeze out	pishŭ (by hand) mŭ	stopping-place by roadside	garang
squint	nyipărang	stopped up (choked up)	papŏt (as a road) puncăt; betăbat badŭg (having no vent)
squirrel	ipas		
squirt forth	mŭrăshit; menapus		
stab	jokad	store-room	sitŭk
stagger	mŭbŭng	storing-place (temporary) for paddy (made of mats), while being dried	gŭdong
stalk (of plant)	tŭgin		
stammer, see "stutter"			
stand up	mujŏg		
stand aside (to let pass)	peraru; seginang		
stand stock still	nyinŭnŭng	storm	sobak-ribut; raban (This is a violent wind and rain sent as a judgment for incest, and requires to be stilled by means of a "berobat")
stand, a brass (used at meals)	par		
stand, a brass (used for Sirih-pinang)	karas		
star	bintang	story (of house)	turap; takach
stare at	tirĕk	story (history)	susĕ
staring (adjective)	bedŭnggor; bederang	story, relate a	dundăn; nyiduda nusĕ
start	gugŭch; gupoch		
startle	bodah gugŭch	straight	tŭnggŭn
startled	gugŭch	straight line, in	
stays (worn by women of W. tribes)	tikach; seladan (W)	strain, to	nyerinir
		strain at	siran
steal	noku	stranger	penŭmi saruch (a new arrival)
steam	ashuch piin		
steel	balan	stray	mănyap
steep	irĕd; ronyug	stretch (be elastic)	kunyoi

English.	Dayak.	English.	Dayak.
strike	} muköng	swallow, a	{ semûngan ; tepírich
strike with stick	}		{ tematok (W)
strike with fist	numuk	swallow, to	turûn
strike with hand	nupap	sway	prentah
strike (thump)	mŭtug	swear	mangu
strike by falling upon	marět ; nyondug (W)	swear at	nyupah
strike top of anything	mabak	sweat	udāās
strike a mark	dŏg ; oboch (W)	sweat, to	mudāās
strike with elbow	nyukuch	sweep	pisěán ; mipis (W)
strike a gong	mäk ; bergong	sweet	{ nibonyich ; senobi
strike against anything by accident	nyandong ; natok		{ sidi
to make feints of		swell	{ kûmbang (as seeds)
striking with sword	ngambar (in fighting)	swift	{ bungkak
see also "feign"	ngawak } (in jest)	swift (water)	laju
and "pretend"	nɡatar }	swim	doras
struck, be	dŏg pukŏng	swing, a (cradle)	bernang ; nanguí (W)
string, a	tarich	swing, to	aiyun
string, to (as beads)	tû	swing, make to	beraiyun
stroke, to	purās	swing by hands	pingěán
strong	{ gûgach		beramboi
	· bûkě (in carrying)	swollen	{ bûngkak ; gůmbul
	{ gogah (W)		· bûbûg
strong (voice)	dŏr	sword	{ bû (as from a blow)
strongly	benah (walk)		pedang
or, with strength	nishin (carry or lift)		
strong (firm)	tetap ; tegoh	tail (of beast)	koi ; ukuon (W)
strong, make	{ bodah tetap	tail (of a bird)	tugang
	{ bodah tegoh	take	mit ; nûmit ; jot
strong (lasting)	tegap ; táan	take (receive)	kambat
stuffed with food	tujuěák ; sindak	take in arms	tunduk
stumble	{ sikak ; sekûkan	take away	mokat
	{ sekakong	take out	dimut
stump	tûûd		{ nyukab (as a lid)
stupid	budoh ; bawā ; bakû	take off (uncover)	{ kadi
stupefied (confused)	berishut atin		{ murai (as wrapping)
stutter	kakû	take hold of	digûng
submit	tundok	take care of	{ ingat ; nguan
succeed (come in place of)	ganti		{ nyudě (of a child)
		talk, to (about business)	beritong
suck	niup		
suck breast	niup shishuch	talk (for amusement)	ngitong
sudden ; suddenly	gugñch	talk with	mínyu
suffer (undergo)	dŏg	tall	omu
suffer (permit)	bodah	tame	{ tatich
sufficient ; sufficiently	sedang		{ rimôn (not wild)
sugar	gula	tangled	bekarut
sugar-cane	tobuch	tap	gutog
suitable	sedang	tapioca-plant	ubi bandong
"sumpitan," or blowpipe for arrows	sipŏt	tares (zizane)	padi babu
		taste	kinyam ; nyam
arrows of sumpitan	raja		{ peti (to Rajah)
quiver for arrows of sumpitan	umbach	tax	- sashuch (hire of things)
sun	betûch-anu	teach	ngajar
support	ngarun	teacher	guru
sure (certain)	tûntu	tear	nyiratak
sure (firm), see "strong"		torn	tubŏt ; jeja ; teratak
surety for (become), see "support"		tears	rendang betûch
		teaze	nûpat
surround	mûning ; krurung	telescope	tropong
suspender, a	katir	tell	dāan ; tanon (W)
sustain, see "support"		tempt (attempt)	choba
swaddling clothes	putong bodung	tempt (try)	kija
		tepid	ngumāt

Chalmers' Vocabulary. cliii.

English.	Dayak.	English.	Dayak.
that	ajech; inŭ; itīa (W); inich (*distant*) (W)		kamuti; sekŭnŭ; sekŭti.—Keiyuch, ŭ-kowang (*used redundantly at the close of a sentence*)
that, in order	parang	thus	
thatch	ilau		
thatch, to	tipan ilau		
thatch, repair	nyurat ramin	thyme, wild	bunga pŭtung
then (at that time)	ngŭnŭ; anu ati	tick (of beasts)	kutid; rekinĕăs (*red*); ligi (*large*)
then (after that)	mokŏ ati		
then, and	rasu	tick (of fowls)	kŭdŭb (*white*); rekinĕăs (*red*)
then (therefore : expletive)	jaŭ; garang		
		tickle	bekitik
thence	sonŭ	tide, flood-	piin pasang
THEOLOGICAL TERMS USED IN BORNEO MISSION :—		tide, ebb	piin surud
		tide, paddle against	bersukul
		tidings	agach
baptize; baptism	baptisa	tie	mŭŭng; ngobut (*close up*); bokosh (W)
charity	masi		
Christian	Kristian	tie two or more things together	begagit
elect, to	mien		
Eucharist	Yukaris	tie limbs	muak
faith	sabach	tight	tarik
grace	kurnla; berkat	tight (dress)	tŭkŭd
hope	harap	timber	kayuch
infidel	dayah kapir	time, times (implying repetition as once, twice, three times)	sidah
Person of Godhead	Zat		
religion	agăma		
repentance	sesal-atin	time (opportunity)	shuput
redeem	nubŏsh	time, the (season)	bang; anu tŏng; kaban
sacrament	sacramen		
sacrifice	sambileh		madin
save	ngyen seramat	time, present	madin ati
Saviour	Penubŏsh		jiman madin
salvation	seramat	time of, at the	jiman; turap; sarak
sanctify	bodah kudus	time, that, at the (when)	kaban; tika
Trinity	Triniti		
there	dinŭ; diginŭ; digijech	time, at that (then)	ngŭnŭ; anu ati
therefore	sebab ati	time, some future	sekambuch tepagi
thick	tebar; tebar nŭkung	a short time ago, *i.e.*,	perajach
thick (close)	pishung	a few days ago	
thief	dayah penoku	a short time ago, *i.e.*,	tĕjach
thin	ridĕ	a few minutes ago	
thing, a	kayuch	a long time ago	sarak diŭ; jiman jach
thing, any	tŭdŭ kayuch	in former times	nun jach
think	kira; pikir; jangka	TIME OF DAY :—	
thirsty	bodŭch ashung	about 7 or 8 a.m.	mun dowan
this	ati; iti; itich (W); ănŭ; inuch (W)	about 9 or 10 a.m.	nyengah
		about 11 a.m.	repuăn
thither	kamănŭ; kamăjech (*distant*)	noon	nŭnŭng repuăn
		about 2 p.m.	kumbĕăng
thorns	roja	about 3 or 4 p.m.	tŭrŭp kumbĕăng
thread	tarich benang	tired	jerah; kowŭk; marah beriruk (*of speaking*)
throat	gunggŏng		
throttle	ngukak; nyiap		ka; di; *as* (dăan di eiyuch, *tell him*)
through	tomus; berambus		
through, pass	sŏ	to	sa; *as* (ngyen sa-i tingah, *let him see it*)
through between two rivers, a passage	trusan		
throw	shing; shĕau	toad	sŏuch
throw out or away	taran; săat	tobacco	bakŏ
throw a spear	jokad	tobacco, Chinese	bakŏ saun
throw up	samŏt	tobacco, Java	bakŏ Jawa; bako dagang
throw down	păăn		
throw about in disorder	mengarĕ	together	sama-samach; bersama; nai powŭn (*in large numbers*)
thumb	sindu tŭngan		
thunder	dudu	to-day	anu ati

English.	Dayak.	English.	Dayak.
to-morrow	tepagi	trouble; troubled	susah
to-morrow, day after	gñnuni	troublesome (a bother)	kakûch
three days hence	guni ajech	trowsers	sinyang
tongue, see "body"		true	sawû; bonah (W)
too (in excess)	binah; pñshē (jipûch	truly	mana (W). (*Used after adjectives in sense of "very."*)
tooth	jipûch bûshē (*front*) jipuch baûm (*back*)	trunk (of tree)	tûngûn (*of living tree*) tunggu (*of dead tree*) bûtang kayuch (*of a felled tree*)
top (summit)	tebung		
top of, on the (upon)	tunduch atuch (*of tree*)		
torch	siruh	trust in or to	harap; sabach
torn, see "tear"		try (attempt)	chuba
touch	tŭmah	try a matter by means of ordeal by two lighted tapers	bepanyut
touch (feel)	kăp		
tough	liat		
towards, see "to"		turn round (body)	kimat
trace, a; track	arŏk; inyuk; diai (W)	turn round (revolve)	bekanding
trade, to	berdagang; berjaja	turn over (leaves of book)	murai
having transgressed bounds of propriety, or, gone beyond proper limits of anything	tepashu	tusk	bubût
		tweezers	anggup
		twilight (morning)	abur dadad
		twilight (evening)	singomi anu
translate	nyirēăs; nyambi		kimirib (*glisten*)
trap, a spring-	pitē	twinkle	kamidil [W] mukidap (*wink*) kidlap [W]
tread upon	digang		
tread out paddy from the ear	ngik gruguch	twist	mûrûs
tree, jungle	tûngûn kayuch		
tree, fruit	tûngûn buah	ugly	arap mun-i dûch romus
tremble	kamutûl		
trial of, make; take on	kija	ulcer, see "diseases"	
tribe	bangsa	unbeliever, see "heathen"	
DAYAK TRIBES ON THE RIVER SARAWAK		unburdened (with nothing to carry)	buruch
On Southern Branch:		unclean	kăich; pŭder
Sempro	Dayah Beparñch Beporoch (W)	uncover	murai
		under, see "below"	
Segu	Bonûk; Bonok (W)	undergrowth (in old jungle)	anak dûdach
Simpok (on River Samarahan)	Sapug	understand	puan
Setang; Sikŏk	Setang; Sikog	understanding, not clear to	bisîrat
Sentah	Sentah; Se Buran Biota (W)	undo; unfasten	kuka
Kuap	Bukuab	undone; unfastened	tebishor
Se Bungo	Dayah Bungñch Bi Bungŏ	unfortunate	genăka
		unite (by adding together)	sinûn
Brang	Brang		
Serin (River Samarahan)	Penyowah	unkind	grobah
		unlearned	dûch bisa
Sennah	Sennah	unless	kiang
Between Southern and Western Branches:		unmarried	bujang
		unripe (fruit)	matah
Tebia(k)	Tebîa(k); Pidîa [W]	unripe (not attained full size)	nyitimun (*used only of the fruit "durian"*)
Sumban	Bimban		
Tringgus	Se ringgus	unskilled, see "unlearned"	
On Western Branch:			
Gumbang	Gumbang	unsteady, see "shake"	
Sauh	Beratak	unsteady in gait	kañg; măbûng
Singgi	Singgai	untie, see "undo"	
Serambo	Se Karuch Brŏich (W)	until; unto	menûg ka
Bombok	Bombok	unwilling, see "do not wish"	
Peninjauh	Peninjauh	unyielding	tûngyĕăk

Chalmers' Vocabulary. clv.

English.	Dayak.	English.	Dayak.
up to (as far as)	kûd		(ngusu ; ngu
upon	(di tunuch ; di atuch	wash	- mambla (W)
	(di sombu		(ngutösh (by rubbing)
upset (spill)	bobās	wash for gold	melenggang
upset boat	kureb	wasp	peningat ; rowûch
urge (incite)	ngajak ; bodah	watch, to	nguan ; jaga ; kingat
urine	kashing	watchman	dayah kingat
use, to	pakai	water	piin
	(guna ; berguna	water, fresh	piin tawar
	"Guna" is also the	water, get	pĕăn
	name of a small house	water, make	kashing
use ; useful	near a Dyak village,		(giam
	in which the magic	waterfall	(piin ûman
	stones, &c., called the		(umak (of sea)
	"pengaroh" are preserved.	wave, a	(băkat (in river)
	(See " deposit "	wave about, to	nyipas ; mosûk
		wax	pûtich
valley	(surok tarun	weak	dûch shinonu
	(surok dau (a gulley)	weak from old age	menyambah
vain, in (in jest or	(ngah tapat	weak (voice)	rûndeng
with profanity)	(ngan patia (W)	wear	pakai
vanish	mānyap	weary, see "tired "	
vapour	abun	web of spider	sebunōt tûkah
vegetables	kudōsh	weeds	uduch
vein	uat	weed, to	nyobu
vengeance on, take	maras	week, a	ni-Minggo
verandah	awach	weep	sīen
verily	sawû	weevil	bubuk
	(rāru, benah, bogū ;	weigh	ngûti
	bonah [W],	weights (for weighing)	tanuch
very	mana (W) (follow	well (adv.)	kena
	adjective)	well (recovered)	asih (after undergoing
victorious	menang ; alah		a doctoring) ; buăh
view, a	tatung ; kirich	well-spoken	mūnich bhasa
view, to	tingah	well-mannered	
village (Malay)	kupoh ; tompok [W]	wet	bisah ; bisah murûng
village (Dayak)	rāich	what ?	(ûni ; mani
violin	sigitot		(osi (person)
virgin	bujang tibûn	what kind ?	muki
visible, be	tatûng ; nanûng		(tûdû-tûdû kayuch
visit, to	tudu		(thing)
visitor	dayah nûmi	whatever	(tûdû-tûdû pĭngā-
	(seruûn ; sûk ; awûn,		nang (word)
voice	(angu (when distant)	when ?	sindē
voluntarily (of own	tûksir	when	komū ; kaban ; tika
accord)		whence ?	sŏ-aki
vomit	(ngutah	where ?	diki ; ki ; dikidoch
		wherever	dûn-dûn kah
wag about	kuting	wherefore ?	uni sebab ; mani
wages	gagi ; pach (W)	wherefore	sebab ati
wages, work for	man gagi	whether (he goes) or	(an (i-di i-di) ûbach
wait	kajûn	not	(keiyuch dûch
wall	sindung	which	adi (seldom used)
walk	ponu ; konu	while (at same time as)	buang
walk fast	bekûduch	whilst	semada
walk to and fro	bejaruch ; bejaja	whirlpool	poshid piin
wanderer	berambē	whiskers	gumis
wanting	korang	whisper, to	begayash ; benănang
war	} nyerang (make an	whistle, to	nyimboch
war, to	attack)	whistle, a (musical	setûboi ; serubai (W)
go out on a war expedition	ngûnyu, ngaiyu (to go out head-hunting in small parties)	instrument) white	budah ; mopuh (W)
		whither ?	kamaki
	(surah ; petlăk (W)	who ?	osi
warm	(paras ; bongō (W)	who (relative). see	
warm oneself at fire	nyinûch	" which "	

clvi. H. LING ROTH.—*Natives of Sarawak.*

English.	Dayak.	English.	Dayak.
whoever	tŭdŭ-tŭdŭ dayah; tŭdŭ kojah dayah	work; work, to	pŭngănai; kaminyang kŭrja
whore, a	perambai	work of a blacksmith, do, see "blacksmith"	
whoredom, commit	nainyung		
why? see "wherefore"		work unceasingly, to	ngaŭn kŭrja
		work at intervals	nyapai
wick, a	sumbu	world, the (this)	dunya
wicked	arap; jäat (W)	world, next	akhirat
wicked (spiteful)	gauk; grobah	world, the (earth)	ŏng
wide (broad)	ramba		retamuch; rotung
wide (spacious)	baiyah; tawas (W)	worms (earth)	regenda (*large*) [(W)
wide apart	săăt		tomuă (W)
widen (make spacious)	bodah baiyah		regyu (*red*)
widow	oban	worms (stomach)	likiyuăch (W)
wife	sowŭn		jakit (*thread*)
will (pleasure)	răan	worn, see "faded" (colour)	
will, to	an; răan (*from* "rŭ" *and* "an" *which both have same meaning*); andak	worn on body, things	penŭkas
willing, be		worship of God	sambayang
wish		worship God, to	
will (verb. auxiliary)	an; shaŭn	worship (do reverence)	sambah; menyămbah
wild (not tame)	siga	wound	towan; kenăman (W)
wind	sobak	wrap	moăs; morut
windpipe	kor	wring out	mŭrŭs
window	komban	write	tulis; nyurat
window stick	tukang	writing, a	surat
window-sill	ubak kaŭs	wrong	sarah
wings	orad; ilad (W)		
wink	mukidap; kidiap (W)	yams	ubich; kuduk
winnow	napan; naju; nyandŏ	yawn	kuŭb
wisdom	akal	year	sawa
wise	cherdik; pandai	yellow, see "colour"	
wish, see "will"		yes	ŭ-kach; ŭ-inŭ
wish, do not	dŭch an; ŭbach; darĕ; dorfa (W)		iyoch (W); anu mijach
		yesterday	sumia (W)
with	ngah; ngan (W)	yesterday, day before	anu perajach; anu diŭ
within	darum; dang (W)	yet	babŭ
without	disopah		
without (deficient)	meting; doi (W)	yet, not	bayŭch; diumboch (W)
wither	rayu		bŏăn (Setang)
withered	pisŭk (*dry*); kurŭng	yield to (submit)	tundok
witness	tŭksi	yield up	ngyen
woman	dayung	yolk of egg	tŭnănang turoch
wood	kayuch	young	mŭrah
wood, fire-	wang; shiru (W)	young (person)	shŭ; onak opod
word, a	pemĭnyu; sŭk	youth, the	anak kŭnya; onak opod
words	pŭngănang; sindah (W)		

THE SENTAH (LAND DYAK) DIALECT.

Mr. NOEL DENISON published a few words of this tribe, which words had been collected by the REV. F. W. ABÉ. With the following three exceptions the Sentah words are identical with those collected by CHALMERS.

a person, naăn; to beat, mukong; leprosy, supach.—H.L.R.

VOCABULARIES

Collected through the efforts of the Hon. F. A. Swettenham, and published in No. 5 of the Journal of Straits Branch Royal Asiatic Society.

* Collected by the Hon. W. H. Treacher, Tampassuk River. "The people style themselves Iranum, not Illanun, and are settlers from the island of Magindano."—W.H.T.
† Collected by the Hon. W. H. Treacher. "The Vocabulary is from Dusuns, on the Tampassuk River, who are in the constant habit of seeing Iranuns, Bajans, and Brunei Malays."—W.H.T. ‡ Collected by the Hon. W. H. Treacher on Sigalitud River, Sandakan. § Collected by Mr. Assoc. Cowie for W. H. T. ‖ Collected by the Rev. J. Holland. ¶ Collected by the Rev. L. Zaender.

English.	Iranun.*	Dusun.†	Bulud Opie.‡	Sulus.§	Kian Dyaks.	Punan Dyaks.	Melano Dyaks	Bukutan Dyaks.	Land Dyaks.¶	Balau Dyaks.‖
man	ton	tulun	ulun	tau	laka	uroh	dale	ele	daya	laki
woman	babei	tandoh	liun	babai	dauh	pawoh	dimrau	oroh	dayang	indu
husband	aki	asouwah	bano	ebana	oang-hawah	eleb	jimanakali	balumko boh	bunuh	laki
wife	karomah	asouwah	mangatak	asawa	oang-punlaka	pawoh	jimanak-mrau	balumko boh	sawun	bini
father	ama	iama	ama	amak	tamak	umak	ama	amai	sama	apai
mother	ina		ina	inak	ini	ini	ina	inai	sindu	indai
child	wata	anak	anak	anak	anak	enak	anak	anak	anak	anak
belly	tian	tian	tarei	tian	butit	buret	neong	bulit	ta-in	prut
blood	rogoh	raha	dah	duruh	dahah	dah	darah	dah	daiya	darah
body	louwos	tinan	bal-uan	badan	loong	umah	biah	likut	tibu	tuboh
bone	tulan	tulong	tulang	bekog	tulang	tulang	tulang	tulang	tuwang	tulang
ear	tulingga	tulinga	tuling-o	tainga	apang	tuning	klingah	tulingoh	kajit	pindiang
eye	mata	mata	mato	mata	nang	mato	mata	mato	butuh	mata
face	bias	muah	angas	baihok	ujoh	chiiong	jawai	ba-ah	jawin	mon
finger	tindoro	tuntoro	tunoro	tudlok	kasah	kusuh	brangan	brangan	trinau	tunjuk
foot	ahi	akad	kasu	siki	bok	biti	pa-ah	pa-ah	kuja	kaki
hair	buoh	buok	buk	buhok		ibok	bok	bok	libok	bok
hand	lima	langan	peh	lima	kamah	tabub-longong	blah		tangan	jari
head	ulu	tulu	ulu	o	ko-ong	utok	pala-ulau	utok	ubak	pala
mouth	ngori	kabang	babpa	sumud	bah	bubah	babah	bawah	baba	niawa
nail	kanuku	kuku	salun	kuku	uloh	ilu	silau	silau	seruh	kukut
nose	nirong	nirong	irong	ilong	urong	urong	udong	urong	undung	hidong
skin	opis	kulit	kulit	pais	blanit	kalatong	kulit	kulit	kurit	kulit
tongue	dila	dila	dila	dilah	jilah	jilah	jilah	lidah	jura	dilah
tooth	nipon	nipon	nipon	ipun	ipah	nyipe	nyipan	nyipin	jipup	ngigi

English.	Iranun.	Dusun.	Balad Opie.	Sulus.	Kian Dyaks.	Punan Dyaks.	Melano Dyaks.	Dukutan Dyaks.	Land Dyaks.	Balau Dyaks.
bird	papanok	manok-manok	karak	manok	manok-madang	jauh-nyilerang	manok-tilip	manok-tiling	manuk	burong
egg	urak	tuntulo	lini	eklug	tuloh-nyiap	telu-yauh	telu-istian	talai-siap	turoh	teleh
feather	bumbul	bubul	bulu	bul-bul	buluh-nyiap	bulap-yauh	balau-siau	bulau	buruh	bulu
fish	sedah	sadah	pait	ista	masik	barauh	jan	bajan	iken	ikan
fowl	manok	manok	manok	manok	nyiap	yauh	siau	siap	sioh	manok
alligator	buaya	buya	buayo	buaya	baiya	buai	baiya	boai	buai	jagu
ant	pila	samut	sitom	sanam	kabirang	ulah	ma-an	samut	subi	semut
deer	saladong	tambang	payow	usa	paioh	paiauh	paiau	kijang	paiyu	rusa
dog	asu	iasu	asu	edok or erok	uko	auh	asau	ahau	kashong	ukwei
elephant	gajah	gajah	liman	gajah						gaja
mosquito	ranggit	takong	namok	hilam	hamok	nyamok	nyamok	nyamok	prunggang	niamok
pig	babui	bakas, boguk	babas, bouhi	baboi	baboe	baboe	baboi	babowi	babu	jani
rat	riah	tikus	sikut	emban-orumban	laboh	blabau	latau	bianwan		chit
rhinoceros	badah	badak	lutah	badak						
snake	nipei	bulanot	ulang	has	nipah	eseh	pungauan	punganin	jipuh	ular
flower	sumping	sumping	pasak	sumping	pidang	barak	budah	barak	bungah	bungah
fruit	ungga	tuah	buah	bungo or bunga-kahoi	buah	buah	buah	buah	buah	buah
leaf	rahun	dahun	daun	dabun	daun	du-um	du-un	daun	dawi	daun
root	wagan	gamut	pasuog-kayu	gamut	pakah	amut	urat	urat	urat	urat
seed	bigi	bigi	lacking	bigi	bunih	upan	patun	bani	ruang	benih
tree	pohun	pohun	batang	kahoi or batang-kahoi	kaioh	kaiu	kaiau	kajau	tungun-kaiyah	kayu
wood	kayu	kayu	daun	kahoi	kaiyu	kayu	kaiyu	kaju	kaiyu	kayu
banana	saging	puntie	puteh	sain	puteh	bliauh	baiak	buah-pisang	barak	pisang
cocoanut	niog	niog	niog	niog	ny-up	ny-up	buah-nyu	buah-nyu	bukan	unjor
rice	bugas	wagas	bughas	brass	bahah	bah	baah	baah	bras	brau
honey	tunub	paha	lawog	tunup	ulang-hingal	wauyi	ling-singat	eti-manyi	ju-banyih	ai-manyi
oil	lana	tumau	lano	lanah	inyeh	lanyi	nyauk	nanyu	ungo	miniak
salt	timus	assin	tacai	assin	nyah	usen	siah	ijuh	garo	garam
wax	taroh	lilin	langut	tagek	lilin	lilin	lilin	lilin	patis	filin
gold	bulowan	amas	mas	balawan	mah	mah	mab		barawan	mas
iron	putau	busi	busi	basi	titeh	milat	luxuan	basi	base	besi
silver	perak	perak	perak	pelak	pirah	piroh	pirak		perak	perak

Swettenham's Vocabularies.

English											
tin	timbarga	saring	mital	tingkah	kupit	kupi	damak	damak	raja	tima
arrow	panah	panah	panah	anak-panah	langah	aui	saloi	aloi	arud	sumpana
boat	awang	alud	alud	dapang	aruk	saltu	jali	jali	ambok	prau
mat	dumpas	ikam	serrah	baloi	brat	uh	mplah	puloh	burari	tikai
paddle	bangkon	gagauh	gu-ud	begsai	buse	busai	tiu	ating	jarok	snayong
spear	sumpit	andus	bujak	bujak	bakir	lapat	niput	upit	sipot	sanko
blow-pipe	bilad	soputan	saput	sumpitan	umput	upit	bai	iveh	ta-up	sumpit
waist-cloth	dalama-kayu	santut	pax	kandit	bah	iveh	ibah	ibah	tarun	sirat
jungle	palau	imbahan	uban	katian	tuan	ipong	ipong	bukit	darud	kampong
mountain	lawas-aig	bukid	bulud	bud	ngalang	tugoong	tugah	bilan	sungi	bukit
river	katudan	bawang	lung	soba	hungai	ungeh	sungai	pasik	bawut	sungei
sea	dunia	laud	pasang	dagat	lang	nunuop	pasi	tanoh	ong	tasik
earth	langgit	pamahgunan	butah	dunia	tanah	tanoh	tanah	langit	rangit	gumi
sky	alungan	langgit	langit	langit	langit	langit	langit	matalau	butuh-anu	langit
sun	ulan	tadan	mat-adan	mata-segah	matando	elo	matalau	bulan	baran	mata-ari
moon	bito-un	tulan	bulan	bulan	bulan	bulan	bulan	butuen	bintang	bulan
star	dalindug	bintang	butun	bitun	butuen	butuen	butuan	dudu	dudu	apai-andar
thunder	kilat	guntur	lugbu	duk-duk	kraning	duduan	duduan	skalit	kijat	guntor
lightning	undu	kilat	barihat	gilat	blarih	sukulit	baru	baru	sa-bak	kilat
wind	uran	anggin	loud	hangin	bukilat	baru	ujan	lujut	ujen	angin
rain	apoi	rasam	uran	ulun	aib	usan	apui	apui	apui	api
fire	aig	tapoi	apoi	kayu	usan	apui	danum	danum	pin	ai
water	daun-dau	waig	sappar	tubig	apui	danum	lau	alau	anu	ari
day		tadau	malowie	hadlan or adlan	atah	elo				
					aoh					
night	magabi	sudop	xappie	dum	malam	malam	malam	malum	ngarum	malam
to-day	imantei	ba-ina	tavano	hadlan-iaun	dohanih	eloini	laui	alaungutu	anu-ati	sa'ari'tu
to-morrow	amug	suwog	mutap	kin-sbum	jimah	elornaubun	lamasoh	alumarok	sa-pagi	pagila
yesterday	kagei-i	kauiab	poxopi-satu	kahapun	da-alam	elomate	lamai	laujong	guriuni	kamari
alive	ouyag ouyag	niau	alun	boheh	murif	murif	dumuaip	murip	udip	idop
dead	matei	matei	matei	matai	mate	mukoboh	kubuh	bukawoh	kabus	mati
cold	matingau	asagit	asalon	hagkut	laram	blarum	dadam	mularum	madud	chelap
hot	mayau	alasu	panas	passo	doh	eloh	lasu	miauoh	paras	panas
large	malah	tugai-uh	axai-o	wakolah	aiah	aioh	aio	ungai	baas	besei
small	ma-itu	akuroh	aitoi	ssivi	hok	ishut	sisit	isi	shu or shut	mit
male	mama	kosei	kosei	eseg					dari	laki
female	babei	tandoh	mangana	omaxak					dayang	indu
black	maitam	aitom	asidom	itam	pitam	murum	bilam	urum	shungut	chelun
white	maputeh	apurak	puteh	puti	putih	baiang	putih	bubuhak	buda	burak
come	mariga	aragang	saro	pakari imper. [?]	tewah	beh	yia	anituloh-lakau	karu-ati	aran

English.	Iranun.	Dusun.	Bulud Opie.	Sulus.	Kian Dyaks.	Punan Dyaks.	Melano Dyaks.	Hukutan Dyaks.	Land Dyaks.	Balou Dyaks.
go	lalakau	mamanau	tunon	matoh or katoh	panoh	bukaiap	lakau	munute	adi	bejalai
eat	kuman	mangakan		kamaim or kaaun	human	kaman	kumaru	kamok	man	makai
drink	minom	minom	munginom	hinom or minom	dui	du	sirut	kamoh-danum	mok or nok	irup
sleep	makaturog	mangudop	turug	matog	tudoh	muturih	mulut	maturoe	bu-us	tindok
one	isa	isa	sa	isa	gth or jih	gth or jih	julrah	jong	ni	satu
two	dua	dua	duo	dua	dua	duo	dua	dugoh	duwuch	dua
three	tulo	tulo	tulo	to	tuloh	tulu	tilan	tauloh	taruh	tiga
four	pat	ampat	pat	opat	pat	pat	pat	apat	pat	ampat
five	lima	lima	limo	lima	lima	limoh	lima	limoh	limuh	lima
six	anom	anam	anom	enam	nam	num	anam	anum	num	anam
seven	pitu	turo	turo	peto	tusu	tusu	tuju	tuju	ju	tujoh
eight	walo	walo	wato	walu	saiah	aian	aian	aian	niai	delapan
nine	siau	siam	siwei	siam	pitan	julan	ulan	ulan	prü	sembilang
ten	sapuloh	opod	puloh	hangpoh	puloh	pulohen	pulohen	pulu	simung	sa'puloh
eleven	sapuloh-wisa	opod isa	puloh-bia-sa	hangpoh-tek-isa	duin	pulohen-jih	pulohen-jubrah		simung-in	sa'blas
twelve	sapuloh-ogo-dua	opod-og-dua	puloh-bia-duo	hangpoh-tek-dua	duain	pulohen-duo	pulohen-dua		simung-duwuch	dua-blas
twenty	duapuloh	duanahopod	duo-puloh	kauhan	dua-puloh	duo-puloh	dua-pulu		duwuch-puruh	dua-puloh
thirty	tulopuloh	tulonahopod	tulo-puloh	katlun	tuloh-puloh	tulu-puloh	tilan-pulu		taruh-puruh	tiga-puloh
one-hundred	magatus	saratus	maratu	angratus	diatu	jiatu	jatus		saratus	sa'ratus

II.
ETHNOGRAPHICAL NOTES BY DR. SCHWANER,
Translated from his work on "Borneo."

I.—THE BARITO RIVER BASIN.

RACE.

THE inhabitants of the Barito River basin all belong to the same race, the Malayo Polynesian. Although they are divided into several tribes bearing different names, there is no reason whatever for considering them as so many different races, neither with regard to their outward appearance and their languages, nor wtih respect to their manners and customs, as was done by Von Kessel, a man who travelled a long time in Borneo.

LANGUAGE.

Their languages generally have one and the same origin, and belong altogether to the Malayo Polynesian family, though somewhat altered in course of time and according to local circumstances.

The different dialects equal in number the tribes of the people, and though to the foreigner they may have the appearance of different languages, are more or less easily spoken and understood by all the natives, the local deviations being soon learned by them. All those dialects are copious in words; the names of each object according to the different circumstances in which it occurs are very numerous, and, as generally spoken, the dialects contain an abundance of vowels, and are melodious. Poetry is only oral (improvisation), or consists of the monotonous recitation of the deeds done by the Sang-Sang (angels) and their circumstances, or in the narration of the ancestral exploits, important historical events, etc. The first mentioned of these arts is principally performed by the Bilians, who recite their extravagant poems with a shrill voice, accompanied by the sounds of the Katampang, a cylindrical drum nearly two feet long and covered with monkey skin, while the gods and heroes are celebrated in songs by old men in an awfully bombastic style; this is done in an old dialect differing from the usual language, called the heavenly or sacred language, or also the Sang-Sang language. Only a few are well versed in it, but the initiated in this science act as priests, and are consulted by the native, when he wishes to communicate his desires to the gods, ask for their assistance, or wishes to have the soul of one of his dead relatives conducted to heaven.

WRITING.

The natives do not possess an alphabet, but they are acquainted with the existence of letters among other nations. According to their traditions, the Creator, having given a language to mankind, had assembled the oldest men of the different nations, in order to communicate the use of letters to them. All of them did receive such writing-signs, but the representatives of Borneo swallowed them, so that they are united with the body and changed into memory. The descendants have therefore their history, their laws, their agreements, etc., printed in their hearts as immutably and surely as other peoples have put them in writing in their books, but at the same time more lively, active, and accessible, for every one is now well acquainted with the history of his tribe, knows the legends of his gods and heroes, their influence on man, their instructions, etc., without the necessity of possessing or studying books, and without fear of forgetting his readings. Indeed, the memory of the natives is admirable, and their traditions bear the aspect of great general agreement.

PHYSICAL AND MORAL CHARACTERS.

In their outward appearance the natives show the greatest resemblance with the peculiarities of the Malay race; nevertheless, the form of the face is often more oblong, the forehead sometimes more flattened, higher and rounder, the teeth are placed perpendicularly, and the eyebrows and beard more developed than with the other peoples belonging to the Malay race. These deviations give a nobler form and a livelier expression to the features. I could often distinguish perfectly regular and beautiful features, by no means inferior to those of the Caucasian race, especially among the men, and their variety is so great that it would be impossible to give an account of the peculiar generally characteristic features of the natives of Borneo; one can only state that more or less all of them show the Malay type. The women's features generally are fuller, have softer outlines, and therefore show more mutual similarity than those of the men. Their expression is, generally speaking, that of pleasing roguishness. Very often the well-opened eyes are found to be of a lighter brown colour than is the case with Malays. The white of them is purer and clearer, which gives them more liveliness and fire, the sensual expression of the Malay eyes being thereby changed into that of a more highly and strongly-developed independence.

The natives are of middle height. Very tall or exceedingly small people are seldom to be met with among them. Their limbs are muscular and well formed, and bear the appearance of strength combined with agility. The women mostly show a more than vigorous development of form; the hips especially are often of a fulness to be envied by many a European beauty. Fat and lame persons are very seldom met with. I only once saw an albino. The hair is of a shiny black, mostly lank, but often also surrounding the head in loose curls. The skin is of a lighter hue than that of the Malays, and very often one may see women of a very light complexion, more resembling the light yellowish complexion of the Chinese than that of the brownish Malays.

Their character is steadier and developed on a nobler base than that of the Malays. They feel deeply, and are persistent in carrying out a once-conceived plan; in love, their enthusiasm often leads to self-sacrifice; in war, they are brave till death; cruel and merciless towards their conquered foes; hard-hearted and incompassionate towards their inferiors, not seldom slaughtering them with solemn ceremonies in order to obtain favours from the gods. I never saw a man shedding tears, and very seldom a woman.

They have great regard for their chiefs and other deserving persons, and are very obedient to them. They never dare object to their orders, and the words of old people are considered as sacred. Towards strangers they are suspicious, but, once gained over, they prove to be well-intentioned, cordial, helpful, and hospitable. In consequence of their distrust they are often fickle in keeping their promises; but that which they have solemnly pledged themselves to, after mature consideration, they stick to with manly loyalty.

Above all, they love the intercourse with the fair sex, and they often allow this passion to lead them into extravagances. They grant great liberties and rights to their wives, who frequently rule with the energy of a man in their houses and among whole tribes, encouraging the men to undertake campaigns, and even commanding the forces in war. In many deliberations the vote of the women is decisive on account of the influence they have acquired over their husbands, although they lack the right of taking part in the deliberations according to the *adat*. For that reason the women are also not very shy, and often more sociable with strangers than the men.

The natives are fond of strong liquor (*tuwak*), and often indulge in drinking to great excess. A sprightliness in conversation at their meetings, an inclination to argue, resulting in long deliberations before forming a resolution, are peculiar characteristics of these tribes.

Being exceedingly superstitious, they are strongly attached to certain formalities, regulating their social condition and their mutual intercourse. Personal insults by words nearly never occur, notwithstanding their frequent drinking-bouts, and never on such occasions, in spite of the contending opinions and the hot disputes, did I see them come to blows. In their mutual intercourse they are modest and ceremonious. At their feasts it is one of the most important occupations of the host to constantly encourage his guests to eat and drink. If not invited, nobody would think of putting in an appearance at a meeting or at a company. In such places where the *adat* still exists in its original purity, the rule is that no judge is wanted where there is no accuser. People at variance with each other choose their own judges, and these pronounce sentence, which is submitted to without protest.

Parents love their children and take care of them, and these in return treat their parents with much regard and filial devotion, nursing them in their old age. They like hunting and fishing, like their ancestors, and nowadays certain tribes still provide themselves with food in this way. All of them have a tendency to trade, and sometimes they are intolerably persistent beggars. In consequence of their inborn curiosity they are fond of travelling, and will journey to distant friendly tribes; but wherever they may be, and in whatever good circumstances and conditions they may live in foreign parts, the love of their native soil always attracts them back to their old home.

The mental abilities of the natives deserve peculiar attention. The experiences made by the missionaries at their schools clearly prove that they are not inferior to Europeans in this respect; in certain arts and handicrafts they have reached a rather high degree of perfection. They are skilful in making *prahus* (boats), in iron smelting, the forging of weapons, the carving of wood and bone; they weave their cloths of homespun and various coloured threads, often adorning them with elegant embroidery. The favourite colours are red and blue. They have their goldsmiths and their coppersmiths; the former make all sorts of native ornaments, the latter forge arm and foot rings, belts, etc., they plait elegant and lasting mats of *rotan* and straw, make ropes, and extract oil and poison out of different plants.

In order to complete this account, illustrating the peculiar conditions of this people, it is necessary to add the observation that in some districts there are public women and worse conduct is not unknown among the men.

Agriculture and cattle rearing are neglected and are confined to the wants of the natives themselves.

Their plays consist in running and leaping races, in wrestling, war-dances and other exercises, developing their bodily strength and giving them the agility and dexterity they want to indulge in in their inclination for warfare. Their dances are mostly performed by the sexes separately, being very singular on account of the slow and ceremonious movements of the performers. They consist in bending the body and raising the arms at the same time, then lowering the arms in the same slow manner as the body is raised. There are besides several plays common to both sexes, but at the bottom of all such entertainments there is wantonness.

Their musical instruments are very simple, especially in the remote interior of the country, where those of the Malays have not yet been adopted. Some differently tuned gongs (a copper disk played on with an iron bar) and a drum consisting of a hollow trunk several feet long and covered at one extremity with skin, are the instruments for noisy music. A flute, a kind of rude two stringed guitar, a harmonica made of a dried cocoanut, to which several long and thin bambu tubes are fastened, like the tubes of our organ, and a mouth-drum, likewise made of bambu, are used by them to beguile their idle evening hours or communicate their feelings to the beloved.

Tatuing may be considered as in general use among all the tribes, though the character and the quantity of figures and lines pricked in the skin are not always the same.

TRIBES.

The natives of the river basin are divided into the following tribes:

1.—*Orang Ngaju*, along the lower *Barito* and the lower and middle course of the *Kapuas*,
2.—*Ot Danom*, along the upper *Kapuas*,
3.—*Orang Dusun*, along the middle course of the *Barito*,
4.—*Orang Menyaän* and *Lawangan*, along the *Karau* and *Patai* rivers,
5.—*Tabayan*, *Anga*, *Nyamet* and *Boroi*, along the *Teweh* river,
6.—*Orang Murung*, and
7.—*Orang Siyang*, in the districts of the same names,
8.—*Olo Ut*, in the northern and eastern interfluvial mountains.

The beauty of their bodily appearance and the adroitness and strength of the natives is the greater the farther they live in the interior. The light complexion and light colour of the eyes also increase in the same proportion.

Of the alleged existence of Papuas living in the interior, with a dark skin and curly hair, as is related, especially by English writers, and considered as the proper aborigines of the island, I never discovered a trace, and I can, according to my personal experience, state with certainty, that their existence is an unfounded tale. The few Papuas, met with in the north-eastern part of the island, are originally New Guinea Papuas, dragged away and brought to Borneo by Sulu pirates. The influence generally exercised by the Sulus in these parts of the island, even in modern times, is sufficiently known.

Whether the present inhabitants of Borneo are the true aborigines of the island, is an undecided question. The existing traditions, however, rather tend to the conclusion that they are not; for according to the tales of the natives their ancestors arrived here in a golden ship and took possession of the islands, whose chief mountain tops were the Buntang, Kaminting, and Raya. Far in the interior of the country one often sees the picture of a ship of a queer form, drawn with charcoal or red paint on the doors of houses, belonging to natives who never in their lives could have seen the sea or even a lake. Whence the ancestors came, which were the characteristics of the population they met on the islands, and whether these islands were inhabited or not at that time, history cannot tell. Anybow, this first colonisation dates from the remote time of the second geological period of the great island; to those times in which the summits of the mountains still rose as separate islands above the sea level, forming an archipelago united in an immense whole by alluvion in the third geological period. The tales of the natives about the former state of their island corroborate this assertion, the exactness of their opinions on this point being moreover confirmed by the geological phenomena.

Let us now pay due attention to the river-basin in general and the manners and usages of its inhabitants.

THE "ADAT." (INHERITED CUSTOM.)

The inhabitants of the river-basin, as mentioned before, all have the same history, the same manners and customs, only a trifle altered by local circumstances, leading also to another manner of life and therefore partially to another way of thinking, and, with respect to social intercourse, leading to different regulations. In all their ideas and institutions, however, there is traceable one common spirit, forming the basis of their social existence.

The contact with foreigners, where occurring most frequently in former times and now, has contributed much to the alteration of ancient usages and to the introduction of new laws. An important influence was exercised in this respect by the Hindus, by the Chinese, and, in modern times, by the Malays.

The Hindus were the first who entered into communication with the wild tribes of Borneo, settled down among them, brought them a certain amount of civilization, regulated their social intercourse, and probably taught them their first religious principles. Many of their actual practices and customs, and some of their ideas on religion and the immortality of the soul after death, bear the undeniable, though not clearly marked, signs of Hindu influence.

On the other hand the Chinese have perhaps a greater influence than the Hindu. As we proceed this opinion will be sufficiently confirmed. Much of their superstitions is but a repetition of Chinese idiosyncrasy, and many branches of their industry point to the fact that they became acquainted with them through the Chinese.

At the same time we may observe every day how their customs are changing under the influence of the Mohammedan Malays, how they are learning new ideas and making progress in culture. Along the banks of the Barito, especially, this influence is very active, and in consequence of this, some rules of the "adat," to which we shall revert later on, have disappeared from these parts.

THE FORMER CONDITION OF THE NATIVES.

The earliest ancestors of the present inhabitants of the river-basin had no peculiar form of government divided into different sections. Being on the lowest degree of civilisation, without laws, unaquainted with agriculture or industry of whatever description, only trying to comply with their scanty natural wants, without fixed dwelling-places, living here and there in miserable sheds, always nomadic, covered with rough clothes made of bark, not knowing any difference of rank or class, they were brought under the sway of the young, rising dynasty of *Banjarmasin*. These princes sent messengers to the remote regions of the interior in order to unite the natives living in small hordes scattered along the banks of the *Barito* into larger groups, and to persuade them to establish common dwelling-places. They were taught the cultivation of rice, the use of salt, and other agreeable necessaries of life.

ON THE SOCIAL SYSTEM AND ITS DIFFERENT CLASSES.

By the appointment of chiefs, by the introduction of fixed dwelling-places, and by the contact of foreign civilisation, there arose a gradual distinction of classes, and the following, now still existing, social degrees, proceeded from it.

1. The earliest *kampong chiefs* with their descendants laid the foundation of the present *nobility*. They gave orders, they gathered the products of the country, carried on trade, and raised the taxes yearly to be paid to the Sultan. They ruled the population by their rank and their superior culture, and availed themselves of it in order to attain their own ends. So the idea of submissiveness was soon awakened and inculcated in the people and the distinction of *masters and slaves*, *Orang Bangsawan* and *Orang Patan* arose from it.

2. The *Orang Patan*, originally the owners and masters of the land, are now *serfs*. They cultivate *ladangs* (fields) belonging to them, gather rotan, dammar, etc., and the profit made out of this is their property. On the other hand, they are obliged to obey the orders of the chief without demur, and to come up as soon as their co-operation is required by him for work affecting the whole kampong or fort or for his own profit. In consequence of this the moral and physical condition of the Orang Patan is absolutely dependent on the chief's will and his benevolence or malevolence; their welfare and their misery is wholly in his hands.

3. The *Orang Mardika* are mostly distant relations of the chiefs; they form the pith of the community, are free from debts; often in the possession of a fortune, and only then obliged to do service when required for an enterprise affecting the welfare of the whole community.

4. *Orang Budak* or insolvent debtors, originating from the Mardika class, are the servants of the chiefs and wealthy Mardikas. The Patans and others too are allowed to keep Budaks, provided that they are able to pay the amount of their

debts. The Budaks have no property whatever, they receive food and clothes from their masters, and may regain their freedom and independence by paying off their debts; after the death of a Budak his unpaid debts however pass to his descendants, these remaining in the same condition as their father until the debts are paid off.

5. The *Orang Abdi* are bought and remain slaves for ever; they are unfortunate people carried away from the coasts of Java, Madura, Bali, Celebes, etc., and imported from Kutai, Tanah Bumbu, etc. The shameful practice of piracy and slave-trade was nearly suppressed after Aji Jawa's death by the energetic measures of the Dutch Government along the eastern coast, and so the importation of Orang Abdi to the interior has ceased; so this class of people has almost entirely vanished since then. The Orang Abdi is a slave deprived of all human rights, and, when not fit for labour, he is slaughtered on solemn occasions.

6. The *Orang Tangkapan* are prisoners of war, mostly women and girls, in all respects on a par with the Orang Abdi.

7. Another division of the inhabitants of a kampong consists of the *Orang Tamoi*, guests or strangers, temporarily staying somewhere, usually for carrying on trade. If the kampong is a *benteng* (fortress), they live for the greater part outside, but they are obliged to obey the orders of the chiefs as long as they are staying there. Strangers often become by marriage permanent members of the kampong community.

The density of the population, forming a community, depends on numerous accidental circumstances. Thus the fertility of the soil, the more or less favorable situation of the kampong itself for trade or defence, the wealth, high descent and mild government of the chiefs all largely contribute to its welfare.

SYSTEM OF GOVERNMENT IN THE KAMPONG COMMUNITIES.

The conditions mentioned below exist in every kampong; for every kampong forms an independent and separate unit. Only in those regions which have been divided by the Dutch Government into defined districts have the kampongs been united into a whole and put under the authority of a district chief. This chief, however, only confers with the kampong chiefs of his district when necessary on account of public works ordered by the Government affecting the whole district. His authority is always very limited and the separate kampong chiefs care little for his regulations and orders.

Every kampong is ruled by a single chief. The community itself, however, is divided into several sub-divisions, the number of which is proportionate to the number of houses, each of these being inhabited by several families.

The oldest person, or another distinguished by ability and goodwill, takes care of the concerns of all the inmates of such a house; only having recourse to the kampong chief when the contending parties do not agree with the decision of this authority. In the latter case the matter is decided by the kampong chief in co-deliberation with a council, composed of the oldest members of the community (*Mandirs*).

ON ALLIANCES AND ON THE RELATIONS BETWEEN THE SEPARATE KAMPONGS.

Alliances of separate kampong-chiefs and communities, in order to attain a common aim, never take place except in case of war. Only when there is a danger threatening several communities do they unite.

A conflict between single kampongs hardly ever occurs. If however it does take place, the friendly chiefs of the neighbouring kampongs join in order to examine the cause of the trouble and deliberate thereon, then the matter gets settled in a friendly way or the party found guilty is condemned to a fine.

LANDED PROPERTY.

Real landed property, protected by right and laws, does not exist; neither the communities nor their members ever possess such a property.

The original conditions of the inhabitants (before the introduction of the first principles of civilisation among them) and their nomadic manner of life, neither ruled by a chief nor by laws, caused the soil to be regarded as public property: an ideal still prevalent now, as may be inferred from the passion for travelling and moving and the removal of entire kampongs, already referred to. A kampong in existence for 10 to 12 years is therefore of rare occurrence. There are various circumstances which cause the removal of a whole community, and its re-settlement in another part of the country. Above all are to be mentioned the attacks of hostile neighbours, as is the case on the *Upper Dusun* and *Murung* by the *Pari* of *Kutai*, or in the north and north-west of *Siang* by the *Ot* and *Ot Danon*; *Kapuas Murung* on the other hand being also attacked by the inhabitants of *Dusun* and *Siang*, etc. Other causes of departure from certain districts are also the frequency of deaths, want of timber, dammar, rotan, etc., sterility of the fields, discontent and quarrels with the neighbouring kampongs, the prospect of greater advantages elsewhere, etc.

It is self-evident that with this inclination to a nomadic life, inherent in the character of the people, the conception of landed property could not arise. The desolate and uncultivated woodlands offer a wide field to meet this inclination, and that without giving offence to another community, for the extent of the soil and the density of the population are not proportionate to one another.

The spot temporarily occupied by a kampong, the space where the native has laid out his fields are the inviolable property of the community or of their individual members so long as it is made use of. As soon as the kampong is left, however, and the fields are no longer cultivated, any other community is allowed to take possession of them; although the first planters of fruit-trees retain the right of returning every year, in order to gather the ripe fruits.

Different from this is the right of property claimed by the communities in certain lagoons and rivers abounding in fish, in sand banks containing gold, etc., which, of course, being taken possession of from the beginning and constituting as a rule the only, but abundant, means of subsistence, are no more abandoned.

The first discoverer of a Tangirang (a tree in which bees have made their nests) has the right to the yearly produce of wax.

Only those people are not liked who, coming from very remote districts, try to settle down anywhere amongst them; such settlement is therefore denied them or at least made difficult for them. The explanation of this, however, is not to be found in the existing ideas about rural property, but in the fear of the inhabitants having their tranquillity and their welfare disturbed by the unknown strangers.

On the Appointment of Chiefs and the Causes of their Election.

In the neighbourhood of the capital the chiefs of the single kampongs or communities are appointed with due regard to the wishes of the population—at least it should be so—by the Dutch resident. In the interior, on the contrary, they are elected by the members of the community themselves out of their number. Cunning, wealth, valour, honesty, knowledge of the ancestral regulations, integrity, and impartiality are qualities by which a man may command claims to the dignity of chieftainship.

On the death of a chief the dignity passes to his first-born son; if, however, this son is not fit for the post by reason of physical or moral defects, then the rank is claimed by some other man eminent for ability and wealth, but in such case it is usually a member of the family of the defunct, whom his fellow-villagers like to see made chief.

No instance has ever been heard of that a chief should be deprived of his dignity by the community, however great his injustices and vexations might have been. It sometimes happens that the people withdraw their confidence and respect on account of injustice and confer them on another more worthy man, from whom they expect the management of their concerns; but this man never undertakes anything without consulting the real chief and asking his advice, if only to keep intact the usual form of government.

Illness and old age are the only circumstances under which a chief may resign his office and confer it on his son in an honourable way; but even then he remains the first man of the community.

ON THE DUTIES AND PREROGATIVES OF THE CHIEF, AND THE DUTIES OF THE INDIVIDUAL TOWARDS THE COMMUNITY.

The duties of a chief consist in taking care of the community's welfare in time of peace and war, arranging its concerns and settling its disputes according to the " adat." It is necessary that he should excel in times of peace by his ability and good deeds, in war-times by his valour, by strategy and self-sacrifice, set a good example to the warriors and take care in general of the honour and reputation of the kampong.

His prerogatives chiefly consist in the power at his disposal to make use of the services of his inferiors, which are profitable to him; as for instance, the laying out of his *ladangs*, the gathering of timber and dammar, the washing of gold, etc. Besides a certain quantity of all fines belongs to him, and he raises a contribution of *padi* (rice), proportionately regulated. At the conquest of a kampong he receives also a part of the spoils even when he has not taken any actual part in the campaign. On the other hand he is bound to give from time to time some little return, consisting, especially after the rice-harvest, of feasts, on which occasions poultry, pigs and sometimes buffaloes are slaughtered, and the *tuwak* (palm wine) has to be poured out in profusion; sometimes he also distributes clothes and weapons.

In *Pulu Petak* all these prerogatives of the chief do not exist, and only at the investigation and settlement of disputes does he claim a part of the costs equal to that of the *Mandirs*.

The members of the community are obliged to put themselves at his disposal when he makes a general convocation; such convocations take place when a war or extensive public works are to be undertaken by their united labours; the absentees are condemned to fines.

Everybody is free to leave a kampong with his family, either to settle down separately somewhere else, or to join another kampong.

THE ADMINISTRATION OF JUSTICE.

Petty differences, as we have already mentioned, are settled by the oldest members of a family, or by the judgment of the chief consulting with some of the *Mandirs*.

More important disputes when all the endeavours of the kampong chiefs or the heads of the families have been unable to decide them, are submitted to arbitrators chosen by the contending parties themselves. It is not obligatory to appoint the kampong chief as a member of this commission. In most cases the chiefs of neighbouring kampongs or other old and honoured men are elected to act as arbitrators. The number of elected *Mandirs* (arbitrators) should be equal on both sides, 3 to 6 according to the importance of the case; so also the number of *Loangs*. The latter join the inquiry and act as intermediaries between the parties and the judges. After the close of the inquiry they get with the Mandirs an equal portion of the costs paid. If the parties don't think themselves capable of explaining and defending their own case, they have recourse to one of those men who are renowned for their ability and sagacity, and who make it their business to defend people; they are called *kamanangan*. Having won their case these kamanangans receive one tenth part of the value or fine in contest, besides the previously stipulated or acquired presents. Every Mandir receives from his elector the *gowat*, a sum of money amounting from 2 to 8 guilders, according to the importance of the case, in addition to his presents consisting of the *lilis*, a *lameang* (agate), worn round the wrist, and of the *tekang hameruan*, a piece of iron of the size of a parang (large native chopping knife). The tekang hameruan is taken between his teeth by the Mandir, who signifies by this act, that the hardness of the iron is emblematic of the iron firmness of the justice, with which he promises to accomplish his task. In order to complete the legally [sic] fixed number of persons, each party has still to designate its *Mandir Jenyanang*, usually chosen from amongst the nearest relations. The Mandir Jenyanangs are present at the deliberation as a kind of mute witnesses, in order to be able to report afterwards whether the sentence given by the Mandirs is just and impartial.

The elections being arranged and the day fixed for the inquiry (*bitjara*) having arrived, the Mandirs assemble in a *Balai* or shed, erected especially for this business in a remote spot in the forest. Anyone not elected to the assembly is not allowed to approach the Balai, even the interested parties, not being authorised to take part in the deliberations, are removed with their kamanangans, in opposite directions, to solitary places on the woody banks of the river.

Affairs of any importance are never treated without eating, drinking, and smoking. The parties have therefore to pay the *Amber Amak*, amounting to 2—10 guilders for each party, and the *saki*, amounting to the same sum, before anything can be done.

The former is to buy tobacco, sirih, gambir, etc., for the members of the assembly, the latter for procuring food for them, consisting of rice, fowls, fish, etc.

After these preparations the members of the assembly give their votes as to whether they agree with the constitution of the assembly, or to lay their objections to any members whom they do not consider fit to take part in the deliberations. Whether the objections are well founded or not, they are decided by a majority of votes, and then another Mandir may have to be elected instead.

The assembly being finally declared in order, each of the contending parties has to deliver up its *gadai*, to be kept provisionally by the assembly. The amount of this is double the value of the matter in dispute. It serves as a pledge of submission to the sentence to be given, and represents the sum to be forfeited by the loser to the winner. Not before then does the enquiry begin The Loangs of both parties are sent, in order to make inquiries as to the plaint and the defence and communicate these to the assembly; this necessitates much going to and fro, and takes up several days before the Mandirs declare that they fully understand the case, and order the parties to be brought before them, one by one, never together, in order to hear the plaint and defence from their own lips, this formality serving at the same time as a test of the truthfulness of the Loangs' reports. As a proof that none of the parties has anything more to declare and intends to stick to his deposition made before the Mandirs, they give the *denda wali* to the assembly, a sum of money varying according to the circumstances from 4 to 10 guilders, to be paid back after the decision, provided that they have really persevered in their assertions; if they have not succeeded and have attempted to deny or to alter their depositions, this sum is forfeited and kept by the Mandirs.

The parties being removed again, the deliberations on the case commence. Then in the first place the Loangs have to give their opinions; afterwards the Mandirs declare theirs. As long as they have not yet made up their minds to a unanimous decision, the discussion continues, and is also often carried on for several days. Finally, all agreeing and having given the verdict, this is communicated by the Loangs to the interested parties, who have to submit to the decision of the Mandirs without protest.

Not unfrequently it occurs in spite of protracted deliberations that the Mandirs cannot agree; this is considered a proof that the real condition of the case cannot be cleared up entirely. Then they are obliged to have recourse to one of the usual ordeals or judgments of the gods.

There is no obligation on the part of the various communities for the mutual extradition of criminals.

RELIGION.*

It is rather difficult to give a well connected and developed account of the religious ideas of the natives. They are very complicated and are made still more intricate by the great number of superstitions. So much, however, is certain, that they believe in a single Supreme Being, who gave the first impulse to the creation of all existing things, and to whose incessant influence the preservation of order in the universe has to be ascribed. They also believe in the soul's existence after death.

Their God, named *Hatalla*,[1] is surrounded by a number of angels, inhabiting with him the highest heaven on the lake *Tasik Tabanteram Bulan Laut Lumbung Matan Andan*.[2]

Next to the first heaven is the second on the lake *Tasik Malambang Bulan Laut Babandan Intan*,[3] inhabited, besides by some demi-gods, by angels of a somewhat inferior class.

Next to it is the third heaven on the *Labeho Rambang Matan Adan Tasik Kalumbang Bulan*.[4] This is likewise inhabited by very powerful angels, of which the most prominent is called *Tempon Tèlon*.[5] Here, too, the souls of the dead have their dwelling place.

The fourth heaven is situated round the lake *Laut Bohawang*.[6] Here lives, among other superior beings, also the *Sangsang*[7] of the *Bilians*.[8]

The fifth heaven is on the lake *Tasik Bulan*,[9] and is inhabited by *Nyaring Dumpang Enyeng*.

Next to this is the earth.

Under the earth is the abode of *Kaloë Taingal Tusseh*,[10] to whose care the plants are entrusted.

All these heavens are inhabited by a great many *Sangsangs* (angels), who partly took part in the creation of the earth, and partly remain in continual contact with man, exercising their influence on his destiny, bringing happiness or misfortune, etc.

The air is filled with innumerable *Hantus*[11] (spirits). Every object has its special Hantu guarding it, and trying to defend it from dangers. These Hantus chiefly confer illness and misfortunes on mankind, and consequently frequent offerings are made to them and to the powerful Sangsangs, the Supreme God, the original source of all good, being neglected.

The Sangsangs are represented as perfectly formed beautiful beings in human shape, brilliantly attired and covered with splendid ornaments; the Hantus are described as gigantic monsters with flaming and sparkling eyes, with long, clawed fingers, and covered with shaggy, black hair, etc.

The ideas of the creation of the earth are not wholly identical in the different parts of the river basin. In those parts where the natives have had more intercourse with Mahommedans, additional Islamitic conceptions are traceable. Farther in the interior, however, there are only two systems of belief.

According to the former of the two systems, the first thing that existed was the water, in which the *Naga Busai*,[12] a monstrous snake, moved about, shining with brilliant colours and adorned with a diamond crown. Its head was as big as the earth, and *Hatalla* having poured out earth on it, the continent rose above the waters as an island, resting on the head of the Naga.

Ranying Atala[13] descended to the young earth and found there seven eggs made of earth, of which he took up two, seeing in one a man and in the other a woman, but both having the appearance of dead human bodies. *Ranying Atala* then went back to the Creator in order to ask him for the breath which was still wanting. In the meantime the Sangsang *Angai*[14] descended to the earth, and breathed the breath

---

* As an explanation of the true or at least very probable meaning of the mythological names which occur here, we have added some notes at the end of this part of the account of Borneo. A full and exact treatment of this exceedingly important subject was at the time impossible, the necessary information for it not being at hand.—*The Editors of Dr. Schwaner's Papers.*

into these human forms, causing them to have life but at the same time depositing in them the germ of death. *Ranying Atala*, who had intended to impart the breath of immortality to man, saw *Angai*'s work on his arrival. Mournfully he returned to heaven, not only taking with him the immortality of man, but also depriving the earth of all other divine gifts destined by him for the human race, such as eternal youth, general and undisturbed happiness, abundance of rejoicing without labour; in a word, the entire bliss of paradise.

The conditions of human society, as they now exist, are regulated by *Angai*. By labour man gains rejoicing, punishment succeeds mischief, grief and illness originate death, war and bloodshed annihilated a part of the human race, etc.

The other eggs contained the germs of all plants and animals.

According to another opinion there were two trees in the realm of the gods, to wit, the *Bungking Sangalang* and the *Limut Garing Tinga*. The former was provided with a globular shoot, called *Bungking*, and on its top the bird *Siñang* moved about, accompanied by the winged angel *Tambarirang*. The boughs stirred by the frolic of its two inhabitants dropped the *Bungking* from the stem, and the shoot fell down into the water of the river *Batang Damon Sangsang* (river of the angels), inhabited by the *Naga Tumbang*. He tried to catch the *Bungking* and devour it, but it fled to the bank and was transformed into the virgin *Budak Bulan Hanjuren Karangan*. She, picking up a leaf of the tree *Kunuk*, changed it into the boat *Lasang Daiü Lunok*, in which she came down the river as far as the lake *Labeho Rampang Mulan Andan Tasik Kalumbang Bulan*. Here floated the trunk called *Gariñ Chenyahunan Laüt*, which, touched by the dashing waves, assumed the form of a man; as such it bears the name of *Garing Banyang Chenyahunan Laüt*. He married the virgin on the rocky island of the divine lake, and the offspring of their union consisted of floods of blood, flowing from time to time and on fit places from the body of the goddess and changing to beings who exercise a great influence on man and his destiny and constituting together the class of the *Hantus*.

So one flood occurs when she is bathing. She gathers the blood on a trunk, drifted ashore on the island *Pulan Tèlopulu*. Here the blood is transformed into the virgin *Putir Rewo Bawin Pulan Tèlopulu*, who, after marrying *Yangong Hadoën Peres*, who is living there, gives birth to all misfortunes and illnesses, bringing unhappiness to man.

From another flood, when she is bathing, the *Indu Reman Lawang* has its origin. This unites with the *Angan Biyai Mamasawang Bungai Peneng Basalo Mamarandang Lagang*, and both become the progenitors of the crocodiles.

A third flood occurs when she is catching fish with a small sieve on the bank of the river. A virgin is born from it, who, marrying *Naga Dambang*, gives birth to six children, all of whom make it their business to cause harm to pregnant women. The latter, therefore, bring their offerings in small casks, hung in the trees on the river-banks.

A fourth flood of blood is poured out on the ground of heaven and develops into the virgin *Kamèlo Lelak Lawang*, who, marrying the *Batu Mambon*, gives birth to seven children, all of them men full of valour and love of war. These are invoked on campaigns, murderous enterprises, etc. They are offered food, spread on a gong. Their assistance is also evoked on the occasion of funeral meals and solemn vows for the success of long journeys.

From a fifth flood the virgin *Indu Melang Sangar* is born, by whom *Tarahem Raja Nandang* begets many children, having the form of eagles, who give their assistance on the occasion of murderous pillaging parties, commercial travelling and illnesses, when honoured by food-offerings and invoked.

To a sixth flood *Kamèls Bumbong Lunok* owes her existence. From her union with *Nyaring Gilahanyi Dumbang Enyen Tingang* many children are born, whose occupation is guarding the deserted houses and the fruit-trees around them; they punish with insanity those who dare desecrate or ruin them.

The seventh pregnancy has a regular course and finishes with the birth of two sons, *Mahadara Sangen and Maharada Singsang*.

Sangen is provided with the germs of all the plants and animals and is sent down to the earth, which is still waste and desolate. Arriving there he finds the miraculous trees, *Limut Garang* and *Limut Gohong*, that unite, and the offspring of this union is an egg, from which rises the lifeless, aerial image of a girl. *Sangen* returns to heaven, in order to fetch from there all the means and powers he requires to complete the formation of the being born from the egg, and impart life to it. In the meantime, *Angai*, a *Bander Atalas*, profits by his absence to accomplish this work with his own powers. He gathers wind for the breath, rain for the blood, *Bading Sangalong* for the bones, and earth for the flesh; unites these elements with the aerial image, and makes an earthly beauty out of them. *Sangen*, coming back from heaven with the *Danom Kaharingan Belom Bohong Banınting Aseng*, in a furious rage at the rash work of *Angai*, breaks to pieces the vessel in which he had brought the water of life, that, spluttering about in all directions, sprinkles the germs of all plants, but, alas, does not reach man. So man, not moistened by the heavenly water, is a victim to death; the plants, even when cut off, continuing living, forming new boughs, and apparently leading an immortal life. The discord of the two gods ends in a struggle resulting in the death of *Angai*. His body is cut to pieces, scattered about, and so changed to snakes, tigers, and all other creatures hostile to man.

Sangen marries the first human being, *Buduk Bulan*, and becomes the progenitor of the human race.

Mahadara Singsang becomes the progenitor of many gods; so *Sangsang Tempon Tèlon*, the mediator between gods and men, is among them. He is invoked in all dangers, in all distresses, and it is he who conducts the souls of the deceased to the abode of bliss.

The natives never make images of the Supreme God, *Atala*, nor of one of the other gods and demi-gods (Sangsangs), although they are generally rather skilful in wood carving. They cannot, therefore, be reproached with being idolatrous.

Many of their Sangsangs may possibly have been historical personages, owing their promotion to the rank of demi-god to their exploits.

Waiving all comparisons and further considerations, I will only observe that the account given above of the natives' opinions on their gods and the creation of the earth affords proofs of a quick, very fertile, and not altogether uncivilised imagination, and shows a considerable resemblance to what is found among other peoples in that respect. Afterwards I shall also have occasion to mention facts, pointing to the existence among them of a fiery and exceedingly sensitive poetry.

The belief in an innumerable crowd of supermundane beings, populating the air, the water, the woods, etc., provided with powers by which they rule all possible actions of mankind, and causing now profit, now loss, exercises a great influence on the mode of life of the natives, hinders them in the development of their intellectual and moral qualities, and prejudices their material welfare. Offerings and prayers to the gods, consulting them on the issue of enterprises, thanksgivings by means of feasts on account of the fulfilment of wishes, etc., occupy a great part of their time, and even during their sleep the influence of superstition still continues, for every dream is considered by them as an omen, causing the performing of certain actions, in order to rejoice in the enjoyment of the good things it foretells, or to avoid the dangers it forebodes. The dreams are also the principal means of communication between the dead and their friends and relations, by which the former may make known their wishes and give them good advice.

When they lay out their fields, gather in the harvest, go out hunting, or take the field for an expedition, when they go out fishing, before and after the contracting of a marriage, before starting on a commercial journey, or any other undertaking of importance, they always consult the gods, offer their sacrifices, and celebrate certain feasts, often losing the best opportunity for the business itself.

A great many talismans, worn on their bodies and weapons, are to protect them against misfortunes and illnesses, give them courage and resolution, or show them the way to welfare and wealth, etc.

The flight of birds, the calls of others, and of some quadrupeds, the crocodile and some snakes are accurately noted in several parts of the river-basin, in order to get at the advice of the gods, and the more important the enterprise is, the more complicated and ceremonious are the formalities observed. So in the case of an intended long journey or a campaign, eight or more months may elapse before the necessary good omens are complete. Not until these preparations are duly finished may one proceed with the execution of a plan; a single bad omen, however, is sufficient to cause an almost accomplished enterprise to be given up or to be stopped entirely. In consequence of such bad omens, *ladangs* nearly ready for cultivation, are abandoned, the merchant, already on the road for several weeks, returns home again, without doing any business, proposed marriages are not contracted, etc.

Without entering into further details, I believe I have already proved by the above-mentioned facts, how deeply the character of the people is imbued with superstition, and how prejudicially it influences all enterprises requiring prompt action.

Still more pernicious to the natives and still more ruinous to their welfare are the feasts they are obliged to celebrate, in consequence of their superstition not unfrequently causing misfortune of their whole family.

The most expensive of these feasts are :—

1. The *Déwa*, or funeral feast,[15] is celebrated on the occasion of the conveyance of the bones of the dead to the sandong, and must not be neglected. It not unfrequently causes an expense of 800—1000 guilders, and lasts seven days and nights.
2. The *Wedding-party* costs some hundreds of guilders.
3. The *Malaho Balai*,[16] a feast of offering to the bad spirits, in order to persuade them not to do harm to pregnant women, costs 30 guilders.
4. The *Nahunan Nakawan*,[17] the birth-feast. It is celebrated seven days after the birth, on which occasion the new-born baby is for the first time brought out of the house. The expenses are trifling.
5. The *Mambandai*,[18] the feast of the first bathing of a child, occasions an expense of 50 guilders.
6. The *Belako Undong*,[19] has as object the imploring of prosperity from the gods, costing 50 guilders.
7. The *Biliankai*,[20] a feast of thanksgivings for the purpose of showing gratitude to the Sangsangs for favours obtained. It sometimes lasts seven days and nights, in some cases even a whole month, and not unfrequently the whole benefit, for the receiving of which it was celebrated, is completely swallowed up by the expenses.
8. The *Harvest-festivity* costs 30—80 guilders.
9. The *Feast* after recovering from a dangerous illness.

The description of all these feasts would take up too much space. I have only enumerated the most important, in order to give an idea of their great number, and of the considerable expense attending them.

Most of these feasts last several days at a stretch, and for the consumption of the large number of guests, buffaloes, pigs and fowls are killed. The *Tuwak* is then poured out liberally, and the Bilians add liveliness and variety to the company. The frequent firing of lilas and rifles announces the beginning of the festivities to the absent inhabitants.

The frequent repetition of such meetings and the extravagance with which their attractions are enjoyed, contribute much to the moral corruption of the natives. There drunkards and libertines receive their education, and idlers and gamesters are made. Business suffers considerably by them, the household concerns are neglected, women and girls are misled into a dissolute life, cause is given for quarrels and law-suits, and the transgression of the laws often originates from them.

The ideas of the natives on the condition of the soul after death are very materialistic. According to their opinion the souls in the other world are in similar circumstances to what they are here, with this restriction only, that they are free from care, that all is found in abundance and perfection, and that every wish or desire is immediately followed by the purest and undisturbed enjoyment. Surrounded by gold and gems they rejoice in heavenly bliss, celebrating continuous revelries. The distinction of classes remains in the life after death. The rich and powerful on this earth remain in that state in the other world ; the slave continues being a slave ; the Budak a Budak, and the poor retain their inferior position ; but all of them partake in their circle of the most plentiful heavenly enjoyments.

They know nothing about being responsible for their deeds to a heavenly justice. Only three sins are acknowledged by which the trespassers are excluded from bliss and banished to the banks of the lake *Tasik Layang Deriaran.* Here the thieves live together, and eternally carry about the stolen goods on their backs, as a penalty for their bad behaviour. The chiefs who were unjust in giving their sentences, live on the shore in the shape of half-deer and half-man. The counsel who, in the course of their investigation, knowingly turn a bad cause into a seemingly good one, so as to give the wrong party a verdict, live, as a penalty, confined in solitary cells.

No crime, however great it may be, is of any consequence to the condition of the soul after death. From this principle those defective ethics result, which are found among all these peoples. After dying the soul is led to heaven by *Tempon Tèlon*, this heaven being situated, according to the opinion of all the tribes, in the river-basin, on the top of the mountain *Lumut*, between the rivers *Teweh* and *Mantalat*. The soul travelling to this place has to endure numerous adventures on its way ; it has to go past burning water-falls, to cross a great many rivers and lakes, go through the abode of the criminals and climb over high bridges, before it reaches the banks of the river *Batang Diawo Bulan Sating Malelak Bulan,*[21] where are seen arising the golden dwellings of their deceased ancestors.

The corpses of men, belonging to the poorer classes, are wrapped up in a mat and buried. Those of richer persons, however, are burnt according to the common custom of the families, the ashes being gathered in pots, which afterwards are put into wooden coffins and placed on high poles. Such coffins containing ashes and bones are called *Sandong dulong.*

In another case the corpses are put into double carefully closed coffins, and after some years conveyed to the *Sandong Naüng,*[22] being larger, though of a similar construction, than the *Sandong Dulong*. Along the river *Teweh* the bones are taken out of the coffin, gathered in pots, and afterwards preserved in mountain caves.

On the occasion of the conveying of the bones to the Sandongs, where they are henceforth to remain, the *Dèwa* or *funeral feast* is celebrated. In certain parts of the river-basin, along the rivers *Kapuas* and *Murung*, Budaks are slaughtered on such an occasion, for services in the other world. In those regions where the influence of the Dutch Government or the missionaries has penetrated, buffaloes are killed instead.

Ambatans,[23] made of wood, having the shapes of human beings, stand on poles around the Sandongs. The placing of these Ambatans is not at all due to idolatrous inclinations, as many consider it to be, but results from the belief that the spiritual image of these wooden figures follows the deceased and serves him.

There are no special priests, nor temples, nor a public service. The persons who commune with the Sangsangs for them are the *Bilians* or the old and experienced members of their tribe.

THE BILIANS.

The *Bilians* are trained for their task from their earliest youth. Free will and inclination are necessary preliminaries to being received into the class of the Bilians. Often the destination of a child to this career is already evident at an early age by certain hysterical fits, during which the patient takes but little food or nothing at all, and sees and tells strange supernatural things.

The Bilians are chosen by certain Sangsangs, desiring to partake of the earthly enjoyments, or wishing in general to be in contact with men for various reasons and to pass into their bodies when occasion offers. When such a spirit has united with a Bilian, she feels endowed with extraordinary powers and with the gift of prophecy; in this condition she cures illnesses, communicates to the gods the wishes of the person celebrating a feast in their honour, and gives the answer of the Sangsangs to the questions put to them. The Bilians can only be dispensed with on a few solemn occasions; for, besides the above mentioned gifts, with which they are endowed, they also know how to agreeably entertain the guests by their rythmically recited songs, celebrating the exploits of the ancestors and still living heroes. On such occasions they often exercise a great influence on the men, either by exciting their imagination or urging them to wars and commercial journeys, which not unfrequently have important consequences. In spite of their sublime vocation as mediatresses between the gods and men, the Bilians also constitute a class of public women, and they know how with peculiar art to attract the attention of the men. Many wealthy natives have lost their possessions by supporting such Bilians. Nevertheless the latter are always in great esteem and favour with the men and women, and the idea of charging them with the licentious life they lead as something bad, never occurs to anyone. They are Budaks to rich people, but they never partake of the field-labour and only a little of the household doings. The profits they bring to their masters result from their being hired as concubines or as singers on the occasion of feasts. The native hiring a Bilian for himself, pays, in addition to a present he has to give to the Bilian herself, 30 cents to her master. For singing the master receives from the giver of a feast 60 cents. There are also Bilians who marry afterwards, and partially continue their business after marriage—*i.e.*, as far as regards the singing and the conjuring of the gods.

THE BAZIRS.

The *Bazirs* are men enjoying the favour of the gods in the same manner as the Bilians. They are dressed like these, and in a way are worse than the Bilians. In spite of their loathsome calling they escape well-merited contempt, and with an impudent face they are seen at festal gatherings, conducting the singing at the head of the Bilians; they are paid better than these, and their number must have been much greater in former years; that of the Bilians was, however, much smaller.

The Bazirs and Bilians are only found with the *Ngajus* of *Pula Patak* and along the middle and lower *Kapuas*. In the regions of the *Barito* river, men only claim the knowledge of the art of curing illnesses by the assistance of the Sangsangs and conveying the wishes of man to the gods. In the regions lying higher up the *Kapuas Murang*, with the *Ot Danom*, these sacred functions are enacted by the wives of the rich.

As the natives ascribe all men's illnesses to the influences of evil spirits, their whole medical art is confined to conciliating these spirits on behalf of the patient, or, when it is supposed that the spirits have entered the body, to driving them out again. Only a few roots and herbs are used as internal and external remedies. By food offerings, the beating of drums and shrill singing, the Bilians summon the *Hantu*, to whom the illness is ascribed, and send their prayers to the superior Sangsangs (as for instance to *Tempon Tèlon*, etc.) to invoke their assistance. The Bilians (in this case sorceresses) then get greatly excited, touch the aching part of the patient's body from time to time with a *Sawang* leaf, and withdraw it with a shrill cry, in order to remove as it were with violence the curse resting on the patient. On similar occasions solemn vows are also made to the gods, to be carried out in case of recovery.

These general remarks on the religious principles and their uses will be sufficient to give an idea of the superstitions, narrow-mindedness of the natives, and the effect this must have on all their actions. At the same time this must be considered as a proof of the truth of my former assertion, to wit, that it is necessary to begin with teaching the natives another religion before it will be possible to get them to strive to attain higher aims and to educate them up to a higher level of civilisation.

On Money and its Equivalents.

In the interior there is no money at all; generally speaking the natives are not acquainted with it, and use the products of their country as a means of exchange.

Along the principal river and at *Pulu Petak* the inhabitants have got acquainted with money and its value by the merchants, and as far as *Siang* the natives know its use. The Dutch guilder is estimated here at 120 *duits*, a division called *uwang tuwa*, in distinction of the *uwang muda*, according to which a guilder is divided into 100 *duits*. On the tributary rivers the idea of money disappears, while in Kapuas Murang, from beyond the Kampong Baru, it is no more accepted, or only in so far as it is fit for making something of, as, for instance, arm-rings, pendants, etc., of the copper, and medallions, etc., of the silver. Money here finds a substitute in gold-dust. We have already mentioned the gold division of weights. This nearly agrees in all parts of the river-basin; only at *Banjermasin* the name *Thail* is in use, and here

One Thail is equal in weight to			2	Piastres Spanish.		
One Guilder	,,	,,	,,	$\frac{1}{6}$	,,	,,
$\frac{1}{2}$,, or *Suku*	,,	,,	,,	$\frac{1}{12}$	,,	,,
$\frac{1}{4}$,, or *Satu*	,,	,,	,,	$\frac{1}{24}$	,,	,,
(*uwang satengah*)						
One *Uwang*	,,	,,	,,	$\frac{1}{72}$	,,	,,
One *Mata burung*	,,	,,	,,	$\frac{1}{144}$	,,	,,

The taxes raised by the Government are paid in the interior by the agency of special messengers, in gold and other products, which, conveyed to Banjermasin, are exchanged for money in order to meet the claims of the Resident. The gathering of the annual taxes affords very considerable profits to the messengers, on account of the low prices at which the products are bought and the high price they are sold at in Banjermassin. These profits are further increased by commercial enterprises undertaken on the occasion of such journeys.

The wealth of the natives consists in the possession of Budaks, clothes, copper, household furniture, gongs, rifles, blunderbusses, *lilas* (small canons), gold-dust, domestic animals (buffaloes and pigs), and other similar articles; chiefly, however, in the possession of certain earthen pots, to which they ascribe peculiar miraculous power, which makes them therefore very expensive. In such pots consists the proper solid wealth of a family.

The Blangas. (Miraculous Jars.)

I will add some further details about these jars, as they act an important part in the households. All the doings and endeavours of the natives are directed towards getting possession of them, often causing long quarrels and extreme enmity.

According to the legend these jars were made at Majapahit in Java, by Ratu Champa, who descended from heaven, of the clay left after the creation of the earth, the moon and the sun, and of which the Supreme Being had formed there seven mountains. Ratu Champa kept his artistically designed jars, besides the other articles produced by his art, gongs, etc., in a cave of a certain mountain and carefully guarded them there. He married *Putir Onak manyang*, daughter of the king of Majapahit, and begot a son, called *Kadèn Tunyong*. Several disagreeable experiences caused Ratu Champa to leave the earth again and return to his native country, heaven. Before carrying out this scheme, however, he informed his son about the caves in the mountain, in which the pots, etc., were stored, and exhorted him to carefully guard them. The careless son, however, neglected the admonition of his father, and in consequence of this those jars, weapons, etc., escaped, and could not possibly be prevented in time. Some of them jumped into the sea and changed to a kind of fish, called *Tampaha*; others escaped to the woods and changed to deers and boars; the weapons became snakes, the gongs tortoises, etc. Nowadays it may happen that a fortunate hunter kills a head of game, sprung from such a vessel, whose shape is re-transformed during the death agony into that of the original jar. It seems beyond any doubt that these jars are of Chinese origin, and were perhaps brought here by the Hindus coming from Majapahit. They are without any particular marks of artistic or elegant make, and are in all respects similar to the modern water-vessels sold under the name of *guchi*. Their exterior glazed surface is adorned with the monstrous images of dragons, with dolphin heads, etc. Besides the earth produced by *Atala*, of which these jars are made, *Ratu Champa* endowed it with some hundreds of talismanic properties, providing the respective possessors with a variety of riches, and also securing to them the possession of distinction, valour, a long life, domestic happiness, etc.

The jars, called by the general name of *Blangas*, are distinguished according to their shape and make, and sold at various prices. The varieties most generally met with are the following:

Blanga lagi	costs fl. 2000
Parampœwan laki	,, ,, 250
Blanga halmauœng	,, ,, 1400
Parampœuan halmauœng	,, ,, 300
Laki Prahan	,, ,, 1600
Parampœwan Prahan	,, ,, 300
Laki Rentian	,, ,, 1400
Parampœwan Rentian	,, ,, 300

Exceedingly beautiful jars of the first variety are sometimes sold for fl. 4000.

On account of their great value the Blangas are carefully kept on specially made shelves in the houses. In the more remote parts of the interior where frequent wars occur between the tribes these jars are buried in the ground or kept in holes, in order to secure them from the greedy hands of the enemies.

To so far back as can be remembered no more *Blangas* have been imported and the art of making them was the secret of *Ratœ Champa* alone. The Chinese have repeatedly tried to imitate them in China and sell them here as the genuine article, but in spite of a striking resemblance the sharp eye of the native soon found out the fraud, and only a few of these so-called false Blangas are in existence.

WAR.

The warriors on going into battle are not commanded by a previously appointed chief. The individual men at first follow their kampong-chief. After the beginning of the battle the man who most distinguishes himself by valour and perseverance is chosen for command, without regard to his social rank. All follow him, attacking the foe in a disorderly manner.

The men called to battle present themselves with their own weapons, and only the absolutely destitute are provided with them at the expense of the chief.

Every kampong-chief brings with him the rice necessary for the support of those under him.

The booty belongs to him who takes it; in most cases however the chief gets the greater and most valuable part as a present.

According to the number of warriors and their object in assembling, two different methods of carrying on the war are known, namely, the *Ngaijau* and *Asan*.

Ngaijau.

A *Ngaijau* expedition only is undertaken by a small number of men, usually not more than 3, 5 or 8. The object is to surprise a few unarmed people, and then to run off into the dense forest with their heads. Solitary *ladang* houses are especially exposed to such attacks. The lives of women and children are not respected on such occasions. The Ngaijau expeditions, in the true meaning of the word, are murderous excursions, on which the spoils are disregarded, while the collecting of heads is the chief aim. Such expeditions are undertaken against tribes living more or less in the interior, often without previous insult; they are also undertaken in regions with whose inhabitants there has been discord and quarrelling for years.

The Ngaijau expeditions are undertaken on the death of a member of the family to whose memory honours are due; they arise also through dreams, vows, ambition, unrestrainable presumption, etc. The wide-spread opinion, that it is obligatory to present a head to one's bride when contracting a marriage, belongs to the realm of fiction.

The Asan Expeditions.

The *Asan* expeditions are of quite a different nature. These require far greater preparations, are undertaken by entire tribes, and are comparable to real campaigns, the largest kampongs being attacked and duly besieged. Very often an Asan expedition is preceded by a declaration of war, by means of which the aim of the enterprise and the day of arrival of the warriors are made known to the hostile tribe.

The motives for such great military expeditions, in which often 800—1000 or more able-bodied men partake, are: frequent Ngaijau attacks, insults given to the tribal chiefs, the death of such a chief, the desire for booty and slaves, the neglect to fulfil promises, etc.

The preparations for an Asan expedition often occupy very much time - months, nay years, being taken up with them. They consist in the making of weapons and praus, the gathering of victuals, and the consulting of the different oracles as to the favourable time for the departure, the result of the enterprise, etc.

The able-bodied men, commanded by the tribal chief, do not leave before all omens are deemed favourable. As soon as the warriors approach the kampong, usually transformed into a *bèntèng* (fortress) by a stockade, the attack on the assembled inhabitants begins. At first they fire muskets and *lilas* singly; the parties having approached so near, that the use of muskets seems unserviceable, they throw themselves upon one another with lances, and the struggle shortly proceeds in so many duels, the respective parties not infrequently exerting themselves so much that they are overwhelmed by fatigue before succeeding in inflicting wounds on one another. The main point of the defence consists in the injury to be done to the enemy at the first attack by the effect of the fire-arms. If the besieged succeed in killing several of the adversaries by some well-directed shots, the latter are overpowered by a sudden terror and a hasty flight is the inevitable result. Consequently the attacking party try to push speedily forward so as to make the use of fire-arms impracticable, and so as to close in with the besieged. If they succeed, the inhabitants of the kampong attacked are obliged to retire within their bèntèng, which then undergoes a regular siege, sometimes lasting for several weeks. Storming is repeatedly tried, and finally when all their endeavours have been frustrated by the bravery of the defending party recourse is had to fire to destroy the kampong. The fate of the conquered is indeed the same, howsoever may be the way of taking the bèntèng by the enemy. The men, the old women and the little children are killed, their heads cut off, and carried away as trophies, the younger women, girls and boys being made slaves, *Orang Tangkapan*. The movables of the inhabitants are collected and the rest left as a prey to the flames. Even the fruit trees standing around the kampong are not spared; these are cut down and burnt, in a word all is destroyed and sacrificed to the fiercest rage.

Such Asan expeditions are often wide spread and entire regions are depopulated by the slaughter of the inhabitants. The upper regions of the Barito river-basin are devastated in the said manner by the Pari of Kutai, while the inhabitants of the tributary rivers have more to suffer from the Dayahs of Passir.

The natives of the middle and lower Barito, as also those of Pulu Pétak, do not now undertake Ngaijau or Asan expeditions, neither have they had to fear any such attacks since 1825. The Siang and Murang people, however, still rather frequently invade the dominion of the Ot Danom, on the Upper Kapuas Murung and on the Malawi; but on the other hand they have to suffer much from these tribes. The inhabitants of the Duson country are attacked from time to time by the Ngajus of the middle Kapuas Murang, and they likewise undertake Ngaijau expeditions to those regions.

The Ngaijau and Asan expeditions, having already brought so much misery on the natives, and having contributed so much to the depopulation of the country, are beginning, however, to become rarer and rarer, and one is quite justified in hoping that they will entirely cease in the course of a few years. The prevention of these infamous practices has been an important part of my business, assisted by a native chief of Pulu Pétak, the Tomonggong of Paliñghan, who accompanied me. I have been fortunate enough to stop many an Asan expedition, to reconcile chiefs who were very angry with one another, and to persuade them to contract alliances of eternal friendship for themselves and their people. The good result of my endeavours in this respect is already evident. Since 1847, the Pari of Kutai have undertaken no further attack on the Barito river-basin; since that time the inhabitants of the tributary rivers live in undisturbed peace, and only the Siang and Murung people, under the supremacy of the intolerant Tomonggong Surapat, are continually at variance with the warlike Ot Danom.

On Marriage.

Marriage is generally here the resultant union of love between two persons of opposite sex.

The marriages vary according to the age at which and the manner in which they are contracted. We shall treat of them in five different divisions.

1. *Marriages of Children.*

Children are often engaged to be married, and are even sometimes married.

This often takes place at the youthful age of three or five years. Frequently the agreement of the two fathers to marry their children is made on the occasion of feasts in a state of drunkenness, and not seldom such agreements are made before the children are born. This custom proceeds from speculative and egotistical, deep-rooted qualities of the native character.

Blood-friendship, wealth, esteem, long descent, etc., together with the parents' fear lest their plans be frustrated afterwards, when the children come to an age of reflection and independence, are also motives for the contraction of marriages at so early an age. After the celebration of the wedding-feasts, these being celebrated in the same way as the marriage of full-grown people, the two children are often, though not always, separated, only to become husband and wife for ever when they have reached the age of puberty. At every opportunity their mutual relation is revealed to them; besides they frequently meet each other, and it is seen with pleasure, when there arises a certain familiarity, not agreeing with our ideas of morality. Having come to a mature age, the young couple look for solitary places, in the *ladangs* and woods, and as soon as this is noticed, the parents no longer hesitate to allow them their own fire-place. Often the young wife is already *enciente* before this measure has been taken.

3. *Marriages of Full-grown People.*

Being beyond the years of infancy, the young people choose their spouses according to their own wishes and feelings; nevertheless they are often guided herein by the wish of their parents. Generally the consent of the parents is required for a lawful marriage. If the parents of one of the parties are content with the match, while those of the other seem to object to it, the consent of the latter may be purchased. If, however, the parents of both parties disapprove of the wishes of their children, these remain unfulfilled.

Before a young man makes known his desire to enter the wedded state, he tries to assure himself of the love of the chosen girl; and not before this assurance has been obtained does he proceed to take the further steps necessary for the accomplishment of his design.

The parents, being content with the choice of their son, or some of the nearest relations taking their place in that case, go to the parents of the girl, to give them notice of the young man's intentions and to ask for their consent. When there are no obstacles in this respect, the assembled members of the family begin to discuss the *belako* or *uwang dichuran*, i.e. the wedding gift to be presented by the son. The amount of this gift is dependent on the class or the wealth, or the beauty or youth of the girl. With distinguished families it usually consists in the presentation of the *Blanga* called *Laki Halmauüng*, about fl. 800 value. With less well-to-do people two *Budahs* are sufficient. Very poor people and *Bedahs* marry without paying any *Belako*. The settlement of the Belako often leads to very long deliberations. The price to be paid by the parents is not to be considered as a debt of the son; the paying of it is a real obligation on the part of the parents towards their sons. When the Belako has been settled, then the *sapot* is agreed on, i.e. the presents the bridegroom has to give to the brothers, sisters and other relations of the bride on the wedding day. The sapot when paid is divided in two portions, one being destined for the brothers and sisters, and the other for the remaining relations of the bride. The amount of the sapot varies, according to the social standing of the parents, from 10—80 guilders. At the same time the *bulan kandang* and *Autup uwang* are discussed. The former is the name of the sum required as a compensation for the expenses of the wedding-party, though this is given in the house of the bride's parents. This amounts to 8 to 20 guilders. The *Autup uwang* is a trifling present in money—from 2 to 4 guilders—to be given by the bridegroom to the grand-parents of the bride if still living. The determination of the sum to be paid by one of the parties for not keeping its word in not carrying out the marriage or in not adhering to the above-mentioned agreements with the other, besides the fixing of the time after which the marriage is to take place, occupies the time of the final deliberations. The said sum usually amounts with rich families to 200 guilders, and with the poor to 60 guilders. Shortly before the time fixed for the marriage, some relations of the bride go to the bridegroom, to receive the *rapen tuwak*. This consists of a gift of 2 to 4 guilders, which is spent in the preparation of the *Tuwak* required for the wedding festivities. As soon as the Tuwak has acquired its proper strength by fermentation, the bridegroom with his relations are sent for, and brought to the house of the bride's parents, with the firing of muskets and the playing of gambalangs, and accompanied by the songs of the Bilians, the bridegroom sitting in a prau beautifully adorned with flags. With various, sometimes ridiculous, ceremonies he enters the house, meeting, besides all the relations and friends of both families, a certain number of kampong-chiefs or other distinguished persons. In the presence of the whole company he pays the previously settled *belako*, *sapot*, *bulan kandang* and *Autup uwang*, and afterwards all indulge in rejoicings for the remaining hours of the day and the whole night; all eating and drinking to excess, and the Bilians performing their dissolute duties. On the next day the betrothed seated on gongs are consecrated to the new state by the oldest member present. To that effect the emblems of prosperity, wealth, fertility, etc., are marked on their breasts, their shoulders, the pits of their stomachs, their knees, etc., with a mixture consisting of eggs, water, earth, rice, blood of a buffalo or a pig, etc., this being done with the reciting of prayers. On this occasion is also fixed the fine to be paid should one of the married couple leave the other in an unlawful manner. This amounts from 100 to 500 guilders. Then the oldest member advances to the centre of the assembly and declares that all the demands of the marriage *adat* have been duly complied with. Everyone present receives some *duits*, to bear well in mind what has taken place and to be able to act as a witness in case of future quarrels. This money is called *timpok tanga*. The house is grandly decorated for the wedding festivities. The room, in which the assembly gathers, is hung with cloth and along the walls are displayed *Blangas* and other objects of great value, partially belonging to the family and partially borrowed from friends. The Bilians sitting on a long bench accompany their songs with the *Katampang*, the men lying at their feet on rotan mats around the jars filled with *Tuwak*. A general inebriety prevails. The young husband usually does not cohabit with his young wife during the first 3 days, but passes his time drinking with the assembled friends, often, however, he is called to the couch of his wife, to eat and chew sirih (betel) with her, to accustom her to his presence and surmount in some way her delicacy of feeling. The wedding-party usually lasts 3 days and 3 nights.

4. *Marriages by Elopement.*

That marriages may be contracted without the consent of the bride's parents, is evident from the fact, that the running away with a beloved girl is not prohibited by the *adat*. Such cases chiefly occur when the young people live in different kampongs. When a young man has got the consent of his parents, but is afraid of rejection by the girl's parents, he runs away with her, brings her to his kampong, and not before then does he open negotiations with her parents about the price he has to pay for her. The girl's parents then repair to the young man's kampong, in order to receive the *Belako*, etc., and to be present at the wedding festivities, which in this case are celebrated in the bridegroom's house.

5. *Marriages by Stratagem.*

The man who has made up his mind to marry a certain girl betakes himself to her house provided with a Blanga, and informs her parents of his immutable intention. Being asked in this way, called *mandai*, for the hand of a daughter, the parents are bound to give their consent, or, if they decline, they must pay the young man an amount equal to the Blanga offered instead of the Belako.

The girls have also the means of securing the men they love. This is called *matep*. In such case the man is inveigled into the girl's house, and as soon as he has entered the door is shut, the walls are hung with cloth of different colours and other ornaments, dinner is served up and he is informed of the girl's wish to marry him. If the man decline, he is obliged to pay the value of the hangings and the ornaments; if he be agreeable, the bride and bridegroom exchange the *Belako*.

The too familiar intercourse of betrothed persons is prohibited under the penalty of a certain fine. Members of the same family are allowed to contract marriage, nay, even the nearest relations, brothers and sisters, parents and children.

After marriage the husband is considered as a member of the wife's family and the wife as a member of the husband's family, both sharing in the occupations of their mutual parents. The husband repairs with the young wife to the house of her parents, henceforth to live there with her. Exceptions to this custom seldom occur. By marrying both are united till death. The husband is bound to provide his wife with food, clothes, and in general to minister to her wants, to protect her from all sorts of dangers, and to treat her with respect and kindness. On the other hand, the wife submits to the will of her husband as a slave, and is bound to do the greater part of the work, the household occupations as well as the field-labour. Only when some work is beyond her strength is she assisted in it by her husband.

Generally speaking, the native is content with having a single wife; only very wealthy men and chiefs have sometimes two or three wives. If a man takes a second wife, he pays to the first the *batu saki*, amounting from 60 to 100 guilders, and, moreover, he gives her presents, consisting in clothes, in order to appease her completely. The second wife kills a buffalo, to make friends with the first, and submits in all respects to her orders, the first wife retaining the management of the household.

The keeping of concubines is not allowed, and is punished if done without the lawful wife's consent. The concubines are usually of low descent, from the Patan or Budak class, and become the possession of a man without any ceremony by his paying off her debts to the former owner. On this occasion the wife receives a present equalling the sum paid for the purchase of the Budak.

The man who commits adultery has to pay the *sapot* over again, and, in addition, a fine of 60, 80, or 140 guilders to his spouse. At the same time he is obliged to slaughter a pig, or sometimes a buffalo, in order to restore domestic peace.*

---

* Though these customs are considered as prescriptions of the tradition (*Adat*), they are hardly ever followed. The *jujur* (marriage-price), etc., described refers exclusively to the Pulu-Petak district. In the Duson district it is different.

DIVORCE.

Divorces seldom occur ; they may take place, however, when by frequent acts of adultery, esteem and love are gone, or when on account of other peculiar causes a mutual aversion has arisen. In this case, those persons who were present at the wedding declare the marriage to be dissolved. The Belako and all the possessions acquired during marriage remain the property of the wife.

Divorce may also take place when a man has several wives who are not able to live in peace with one another. In this case the fine fixed before marriage is not paid. The contrary occurs when a divorce takes place without well founded reasons. If the wife be right she retains the Belako and part of the fortune, the husband being, moreover, bound to pay her the fine fixed for arbitrary divorce. If, however, the wife give cause for complaint, she loses the Belako, and besides her right to a part of the fortune acquired in common, having, moreover, to pay the aforesaid fine to the husband.

If there are children, the party giving cause is considered as dead, and the fortune is disposed of according to the succession-laws. On the other hand, the children are free to choose whether they will stay with the father or with the mother.

Every proposal of divorce has to be brought before a council of Mandirs, who, after having tried in vain with all their might to reconcile the parties, give their decision on the divorce and settle the conditions on which it may come about. Divorce from bed and board is unknown.

When a man remains absent for years without letting his existence or abode be known, or without sending money for the support of his family, a right to divorce is afforded on his return home afterwards ; he is obliged to pay off the debts contracted by his wife during his absence, even if he be compelled to give up his freedom in order to acquire the necessary money. If a wife have committed adultery during the absence of her husband, the latter has the right to claim a sum of 100—200 guilders from her betrayer, and may either keep his wife or get divorced from her ; in the latter case she has to pay back the Belako. In some cases the husband even has the right to kill the betrayer.

If one of the married couple be reduced to the condition of a Budak, neither of them has the right of divorce, but both have to become Budaks with their children.

The running away with a woman is called *manungkon*. In this case the woman remains with the man who eloped with her, but restores the Belako to her former husband, the other being bound to pay her a fine of 100 to 500 guilders. (*Hokkam.*)

If a husband or a wife die the survivor is not allowed to contract a new marriage until the funeral feast has been duly celebrated. The time of mourning lasts until this is held ; during this period the widower is called *boyo* and the widow *balo*.

THE LAWS OF INHERITANCE.

On the death of a wife, her husband remains in the house of his father-in-law until he has celebrated the Dewa-feast. The Belako becomes the property of the deceased's father, who, after paying the expenses for the feast, divides the rest of the acquired fortune with the widower.

The husband dying, the widow retains the Belako and half of the fortune remaining after the Dewa-feast, the other half going to the deceased's father-in-law.

The surviving children receive after their mother's death all that which the father of the deceased woman would have got had they not survived, the widower receiving the legal portion already mentioned. Minors remain with their father ; but those who have already attained their majority are free to choose between their father's house and that of their grandfather by the mother's side.

If the father dies, the whole fortune remains with the mother, in trust for the children.

The children born by a second marriage inherit all the goods acquired during this second marriage, and the mother's Belako besides. The children by the first marriage only get the portion of their share after the decease of one of their parents.

PATERNITY.

Legitimate children are those born from a lawful marriage, and accepted by the father as his.

When a man denies that he is the father of a child, born from his wife, the matter has to be decided by an ordeal, when other proofs are lacking. For this purpose the *Hanyadeng** or *Hasudi* is resorted to. The husband being suspicious as to the paternity of the child, the one suspected has to undergo the trial; if the husband is unable to name the delinquent, the wife has to submit to it. When the accused persons have been cleared of the suspicion resting upon them, the husband is compelled to acknowledge the child as his own, and has moreover to pay his wife a certain fine as compensation for the insult inflicted. This is called *Hokkam*.

A Bilian becoming pregnant informs the Mandirs of the man to whom she ascribes her pregnancy. He, not being able to prove his innocence in a satisfactory way, the *Salam Bichis* is resorted to, and in case this ordeal happen to be unfavourable to the accused, he is obliged to acknowledge the child and attend to his paternal duties towards it. If the man clear himself the child becomes a Budak of the Bilian's owner.

A pregnant Budak must tell her master who is the child's father. The latter, if he do not deny it, must pledge himself to pay the Budak's debts should the Budak die in child-bed, in order to compensate the owner for her loss. He has to pay besides a certain amount to the Budak's master for the time during which the child must be suckled, to make good the loss caused by the pregnancy and confinement of the mother and the first rearing of the child. At the same time he has to pay the *sapot* or money for the dishonour to the Budak's family. If the accused repudiate, then he has to submit to the fire-ordeal, to prove the truth of his words. If he succeeds, then the fatherless child becomes the property of the Budak's master.

The owner is bound to set the Budak at liberty, when he himself is the father; the Budak, however, has to pay a fine to the offended wife, equal to the amount of her debts. If she is not able to do this, the wife has the right to sell the Budak to another master. The husband has to pay besides the sapot to the family of his wife as well as to that of the Budak, and is obliged to acknowledge the child.

A free girl having got with child, is often secretly drowned, in order to prevent the public disgrace. If not, and the designated father also belong to a great family, endeavours are made to bring about a marriage between the guilty couple. In case of denial, the accused has to submit to the fire-ordeal. This resulting in his favour, the child has to be educated by the dishonoured girl's father. Not unfrequently the seducer is killed by the relations of the girl. If the designated father is a Budak, both man and woman lose their lives, or the girl's father takes care of the child's education and the Budak is compelled to pay the double amount of his debt and to leave the house.

Illegitimate children, *Anan Saren*, are hated, and such is the contempt in which they are held that they can hardly marry.

All these severe regulations of the *adat*, however, are unable to check the girls in their dissolute behaviour, the art of overcoming nature being well-known. Generally speaking the morality is not all that can be desired with these tribes.

The father is obliged to educate his children as well as possible, to support them, and to pay the Belako when one of them marries. The education of the children on the other hand is exceedingly simple, consisting only in care for the development of the body. The boys soon join the company of the men and, as far as their strength allows it, try to partake of their occupations and pleasures, the girls managing the household, fetching water, keeping up the fire, etc. In this way the children are already early trained for their future calling.

* To be treated of later on.

To their father they owe respect and obedience, and at the same time they lie under the obligation, especially in the case of the eldest son, to support their parents and entertain them according to their position, when these have grown old and disabled and are past work. The father has the right to pledge his children.

GUARDIANS.

The natural guardian of orphans, *Anak nole*, is the father's or mother's brother. Lacking these another respected person is appointed by the Mandirs. He is entrusted with the care of the parents' estate. The management of the fortune may, however, be left to one of the children, if it have already attained its majority. The property entrusted to the care of a guardian, is delivered to the heirs on attaining their majority in the presence of witnesses.

INHERITANCES.

As we have already seen, the female members of a family also partake of the estate.

The estate left by the parents is equally divided among the children; nevertheless the father is free to confer special privileges on one of them. The division of the estate is done by a Mandir in the presence of witnesses.

The parties concerned are obliged to celebrate the Dewa-feast on behalf of the deceased. The necessary expenses for this are taken out of the inheritance.

INSOLVENT DEBTORS (Temporary Slaves).

Besides the *Abdi* or proper slaves, there is a rather numerous class of natives, deprived of their freedom, called *Budaks*. They may, however, purchase back their liberty. This temporary state of slavery is due to :—1. Descent by a mother who is already a Budak; 2. Debts, which they cannot pay after the lapse of a certain time. Such debts are contracted : *a* by fines ; *b* by unlucky play; *c* by a dissolute life, especially amongst the Bilians; *d* when the interest of a loan is not forthcoming when stipulated ; *e* with the Ngajus also by captivity in war ; for with this tribe the captured booty is divided among all the warriors who take part in the campaign, in proportion to the services rendered by them. Captives of war are taxed, *i.e.* they are compelled to pay a fixed sum to the person to whom they are delivered ; the receiver being on the other hand bound to remit their portions to his fellow-warriors.

The Budak is obliged to accomplish all labours asked of him by his master. If he be negligent or disobedient, his owner is authorised to punish him by blows, or by fines, thus increasing the amount of his debts. The original debt of a Budak may also be increased by laying to his charge the value of the tools broken in his hands. The fines he is condemned to on account of transgressions of the *adat*, are paid by his owner, and are also laid to his charge. Moreover the debt may be increased by the birth of a child. A month after the birth 10 guilders is charged. As soon as the child is full-grown and until fit for labour, the debt is increased by the addition of the estimated amount for the expenses of his education. Then the bodily strength, the personal appearance, ability, etc., are taken into account, and the debt grows in proportion to these qualities of the child ; for the more satisfactory these are the more probable it is that the Budak will be sold for a considerable price. On an average the debt is estimated at 80 guilders. The parents dying the debt passes on to the children. The debt of a Budak is not liable to interest. The owner is entitled to kill his Budaks on the occasion of Dewa-feasts, taking for this purpose those who are of low descent and who cannot boast of free family relatives. The unmarried owner is entitled to an unmarried Budak as his concubine, giving her, however, a small present. The owner is obliged to maintain his Budaks, and gives them for this purpose 80 *gantangs* of rice (*bras*) and 3 *gantangs* of salt a year, altogether amounting in value to fl. 10.70 a head. The furnishing of clothes is left to his generosity.

The means by which a Budak may regain his liberty are the following: 1st. The paying off of his debt by his relations or other persons. 2nd. After the rice harvest the master presents his Budak with a hundredth part of 1000 gantangs, or 1/10 of the produce; it being left to the Budak's own decision whether he will sell the paddy or lend it out on interest. 3rd. Manual labour during the night, as for example the plaiting of mats, the making of *kajangs* (palm-leaves covers), mowing, etc. 4th. At the cutting of rotan the Budak receives a payment of 4 guilders for every 100 *galongs* (bunches). 5th. The rearing and selling of domestic animals.

In this way the possibility is opened to the Budak to gradually lessen the amount of his debt and finally pay it off entirely, provided that he be rather thrifty and the debt be not too great. On the other hand a badly disposed owner has hundreds of ways of wringing the painfully earned possessions of a Budak from his hands and for keeping his debt at the original amount, or even of increasing it, as for instance by fining him for innocent little transgressions, etc.

Every Budak has the right to leave his master, if the latter no longer please him, provided that he looks for another lord, who pays his debt and whose property he becomes thenceforth. A Budak, having escaped on account of bad treatment, the person to whom he has fled is not obliged to deliver him to his former master, but is bound to pay half his debt, without lessening by this the Budak's debt. He thus passes into the service of another master with the full amount of his former debt. A Budak fleeing to his relations, the latter have to pay ⅜ of the debt to his master.

The final paying off of a Budak's debt, when he has succeeded in wiping it off, is accompanied by a great many expenses, to wit: 1st. His debt up to a small residue of 1 or 2 guilders remains unpaid as a proof of his dependence till he has satisfied all the formal exigencies of the *adat*, prescribed for the occasion of emancipation. 2nd. The *Peteng Kayu*. One of the Budak's occupations consists in gathering firewood for the kitchen; as he will no longer do this, he gives his former master a present, usually consisting of cotton to the value of 2 guilders. 3rd. The *Pala Lupat*, i.e. a tax for the declaration of independence, consisting of a sum of 4 guilders. 4th. The *Paki*, i.e. the pig, as an offering to the protecting spirits of the house, in order to persuade these to take care of him and his former master for the future. 5th. A *Tampachat*, i e. a piece of iron, weighing a Parang, serving as an emblem of the durability of happiness. Not until he has attended to these details may he leave the house of his master, and he is then bound by agreement not to enter it again for one or more years; on the other hand he is not allowed to eat or drink anything brought from this house during this period in order to prove his independence by such behaviour. Afterwards he invites his former master, besides many other persons, and celebrates a feast in his own house, at which pigs, hens and Bilians may not be lacking. On this occasion he pays the little residue of his debt, and declares that he has satisfied the conditions of the *adat* and is in the possession of absolute liberty with all the implied rights.

Agreements concerning Debts.

Loans pay 50 per cent. per annum interest. A debtor not being able to pay the interest after a year, the capital remains in his hands on the same conditions as during the previous year, but no compound interest is charged. In modern times, however, the natives of the far interior have begun to imitate the objectionable custom of the Chinese, Banjarese, and Bekompay people, by including the interest in arrears with the capital and asking for compound interest. According to the old custom, fl.100 became fl.150 after a year, fl.200 after two years, etc. Now, however, a sum of fl.100 grows to fl.150 after the first year, to fl.225 after the second, fl.337.50 after the third, and so on.

Butung menteng is the name of the agreement, according to which the debtor is obliged to pay the interest in paddy. The interest for a loan of fl.100 amounts after the first year to 500 gantangs of paddy. The debtor not being able to pay on account of a bad crop, or for other reasons, he has to buy the paddy from the traders; if he cannot do so, he pays the value of 500 gantangs of paddy in ready money; if likewise unable to do this, he may get a year's grace, after which he has to deliver forthwith 1,000 gantangs of paddy.

Loans are contracted in the presence of four to six witnesses.

Different from these are the customs of the paddy loans. With a paddy loan the interest has also to be paid in paddy, and varies proportionately to the higher or lower price of the paddy at the time of the loan. Accordingly the annual interest is put at a higher rate if there be a scarcity of paddy in the region than when the contrary is the case. In prosperous years 100 gantangs are paid off with 200 gantangs after the course of the first year; while in the case of abundance [sic] only 50 gantangs are given. If the debtor be not able to pay at the end of the first year, a new condition is agreed upon, likewise dependent on the temporary price of the paddy. In case of repeated impossibility to pay in paddy or money in several subsequent years, the matter is submitted to the decision of a council of Mandirs, the debtor being condemned to the condition of Budak for so long as he is unable to pay off his debt, which, however, from this moment onward may not be increased by interest. The debts in paddy are commuted on this occasion to debts in money, 100 gantangs of paddy being estimated at fl.20. If the debts be denied, which often takes place when the money has been lent in good faith without the presence of witnesses (*saksi*), an ordeal has to decide the question. This is called *tèser bichis*. The accuser as well as the accused are obliged to deposit at the Mandir's double the amount of the sum in contest. The party found innocent receives, in addition to the sum deposited by him, the whole sum entrusted by the other party. These regulations for the plaintiff are made in order to check unjust demands and frauds.

COMMERCE.

Every free man, being so inclined and possessing the necessary funds, is allowed to carry on trade.

Debts contracted with merchants are paid off by way of instalments, according to agreement between the two parties, the price being also fixed at which the goods have to be accepted in case of the payment not being made in cash.

If he be unable to pay the sum after a time fixed upon, the trader becomes a Budak of the creditor.

ON DEPOSITS.

The person who has accepted money, or goods having been entrusted to his care, is obliged to give them up as soon as required, and is not free from this obligation until he has lost his own belongings, besides the deposit, by fire or theft.

BAIL.

If the debtor be not able to pay, and the price for which he has been condemned to be a Budak is not equal to the debt, the bail is bound to supply the balance.

PENAL LAWS.

In the districts lying within the Government sphere of influence, sentences of death are no longer given by the Mandirs. Only in the far interior does this still occur. Most of the offences, nay, nearly all of them, are punished by fines, payable in money or goods. The prices at which these are accepted are:

A Musket	at fl.20
A Gong, proportionate to its size and weight	,, fl.10-20
A hundred gantangs of paddy	,, fl.6
A big Pig	,, fl.12
A big Goat	,, fl.20
A Buffalo	,, fl.60-80.
A Budak badan orang	,, fl.25
A guchi wangkang (Chinese water vessel)	,, fl.5
Chinese or European plates, dishes, etc. a piece	,, fl.0 30cts.
A "thail" of gold	,, fl.70

Materials for clothes, etc., or ready-made clothes, are estimated.

A murderer who cannot pay the family of the murdered man the stipulated fine, *Balai*, for his offence, forfeits his life. The relatives of the murdered person, however, sometimes undertake a vendetta against the murderer, even if he is able to pay the *Balai*. Not until this is done is the matter brought before the Mandirs, and both parties are then condemned to pay the *Balai* to one another, this being fixed according to the rank and class of the murdered person.

Highway-robbery, or robbery along the river, is called *Menarik*. The deed being done, without any cause being given by the person robbed, the offender has to pay back to him double the amount of the goods stolen, and he is besides obliged to offer him a Budak, a *lilis* (brass gun), and a piece of iron, in order to satisfy him entirely, and to wish him by these presents durable prosperity and a long life.

If, on the occasion of waylaying, wounds be inflicted, the punishment of the robber is increased by an additional fine, according to the greater or lesser severity of the wounds inflicted. If on the contrary the robber be wounded, the attacked party has to pay a fine, which is deducted from the punishment of the former. If the attacked person is killed, the criminal has to pay the *Balai* to the deceased's family, in addition to the punishment for the robbery; the Balai in this case consists of a *blanga* worth fl.1,000. If, on the other hand, the robber is killed, the fine for the robbery has to be paid all the same; the person robbed, however, has to pay to the killed person's family the Balai, the amount of which is dependent on the class to which the person killed belonged.

For a single wounding the *Biat* is paid—a fine fixed according to the depth and danger of the wound and the part of the body injured. This varies from 4 to 100 guilders.

Poisoning and bewitching are punished in the same way as murder.

If a man belonging to a good family sleep with the wife of another of the same class, the offended husband is free to kill him, but has to pay the *Balai* to his family. If he do not take immediate revenge, but submits his case to the council of Mandirs, the adulterer has to pay a fine of 200 to 400 guilders.

A Budak sleeping with the wife of a free man forfeits his life.

A free man committing adultery with the wife of a Budak has to set at liberty the Budak's family or pay their debts.

The entering of another man's house without leave or at an improper time is punished by a fine of 10 to 50 guilders, according to circumstances.

The man who approaches the bathing place of the women during bathing time pays a fine of 50 guilders.

The man who, walking along the river, goes past the bathing place of a girl and steps over her clothes, pays a fine of fl.8.

Indecent words uttered in the presence of girls or women are punished with a fine of fl.10.

A person who offends the moral feeling of a woman by indecency incurs a fine of fl.30.

Children treating their parents badly are bound to give them a Budak or fl.100.

A person purposely setting fire to a house has to pay an indemnity of double the value of the damaged articles. Incendiarism by accident is punished by a fine equivalent to damage done.

Theft in the fields is punished with a fine of 10 to 25 guilders, and the stolen things have to be restored. The same with regard to theft in the house; but in this case the fine is higher.

Common assault without causing bloodshed is punished with a fine of fl.50 when it is committed in a sober state, of fl.8, when in an intoxicated state. If causing bloodshed, the offender has to pay fl.80 if sober, fl.50 if drunk.

Insults by words are punished by fines of 8 to 10 guilders.

The cursing of one's child is expiated by slaughtering a buffalo or a Budak. The child is besmeared with the victim's blood, in order to prevent the evil consequences of the curse.

A person causing damage to the *Batang* in front of a house (*i.e.*, a small raft floating in the river by way of a landing-place), incurs a fine of fl.8. Causing damage to another man's prau is punished by a fine of fl.25.

ORDEALS.

The sentences of the Mandirs being often made dependent on ordeals, as mentioned above, we shall avail ourselves of the opportunity here to give some further details about them.

1st. The *Salam Pinchis* (Malay *bĕlam*, to dive). Two coins, both of the same size and covered with wax, but one of them scoured bright, are put into a vessel filled with water and ashes. Then each party takes one of the pieces out of the vessel and gives it to the Mandirs, who afterwards declare the words of that party to be true who succeeded in taking out the bright coin.

2nd. The *Teser Ulon* (*salam banyoh*). Both parties are plunged into the water by means of a bambu cane put horizontally over their heads. The party emerging the first is considered guilty.

3rd. The *Hagalangang*. Both parties are placed in boxes at a distance of seven fathoms opposite one another, the boxes being made of nibong laths and so high as to reach a man's breast. Then both receive a sharpened bambu of a lance's length to throw at each other at a given signal. The wounded person is supposed to be guilty.

4th. The *Goang Lunyu*. At a distance of two fathoms from one another two parallel roads are made, 70 fathoms long, at the extremity of which, in the middle of the intermediate space, a lance is stuck vertically in the ground. At a given signal both begin to run on the road. The person who first attains the goal, and touches the lance, is considered the innocent party.

5th. The *Salam potong layam*. For this purpose two hens are chosen, of the same strength and colour, and each representing the cause of a party. These are so laid down that the necks are parallel and the head of one touches the shoulder of the other. Then the heads are cut off simultaneously at one blow and the cause of that party, whose hen is dead first, is declared to be lost.

These five ordeals are put into practice at the trial of debt cases, or when Budaks have been stolen, or with disputes about landed property, with quarrels, and with other less important cases.

6th. The *Hanyading*. A certain quantity of *dammar* (resin) is lighted on a board ; as soon as the mass has turned liquid and the flame has expired, the accused person has to stroke the burning hot resin with the forefinger of the right hand. Then the finger is examined, and the accused person, if scorched, is declared to be guilty.

7th. The *Hasudi*. The accused person has to take out with three fingers of the right hand a *Bungkal* (a small gold weight) from boiling water, 1½ inch deep, and is considered guilty when the fingers are injured.

These two ordeals are brought into operation in cases of greater importance, such as for instance in misdeeds concerning women, in accusations of murder, etc.

THE OATH.

The natives, especially the Ngajus, have a certain kind of oath, after the taking of which a case is considered as decided for ever, and the plaintiff is obliged to retract his accusation. It consists in strewing rice by the defendant, and in calling upon the visible universe and the spirits animating it, to witness his innocence, and imploring them to persecute him and his up to the seventh generation with hatred and vengeance, if he may have spoken lies. Then he throws a stone into the water (*halawah batu*) as an emblem of the ruin of his happiness, and cuts asunder a piece of rotan, as an emblem of the annihilation of his welfare, etc., and of the punishment that may fall upon him, if he may have taken a false oath.

TREATIES OF PEACE AND BONDS OF FRIENDSHIP.

The conclusion of treaties of peace and bonds of friendship often takes place with certain ceremonies, when, after the end of a war, or of other quarrels, or of frequent ngaijau expeditions, the vendetta of two tribes has been settled.

After ngaijau expeditions it sometimes happens that the chiefs exchange one or two Budaks as presents, in order to slaughter them as a token of the peace concluded. On the blood of the victims they then wish one another continual peace and immutable welfare; but it is done also in order to reconcile the souls of the men killed, as it is supposed that the souls of the sacrificed Budaks are destined to their service in another life. Sometimes the swearing of friendship and loyalty is also done by the parties holding an axe between them at each end, while a third cuts the helve with a mandau, muttering an imprecatory formula, and imploring ruin upon the head of the party breaking his word, as the axe destroys the tree on whose roots it comes down. In the same manner and under similar circumstances sometimes a rotan is cut off instead of the axe helve.

Another way of contracting friendship is the *Badundi daroh*. Such a friendship cemented with blood is considered sacred and is perhaps the firmest treaty known among the natives and is also seldom broken by them. Agreements of this nature are made chiefly between tribal chiefs and other great personages.

When two persons wish to contract a treaty of eternal friendship for themselves and their relatives, the prescribed ceremonies are directed by a third party, generally some respected man. The latter points out to both parties the gravity and importance of their intention. Then he makes a small cut in their right shoulders and gathers the blood in two small bambu tubes partially filled with water. Holding up such a cup in each hand, he explains the mutual obligations under which both lay themselves and which equal the mutual obligations of brothers. In order to represent still more clearly this relation, he mixes up the contents of the two tubes by pouring them out alternately, while calling down an imprecation on the head of either who breaks this treaty of friendship by thought or deed, foretelling infamous ruin to either with his family who should be guilty of perjury. At the same time, however, he depicts with bright colours the expected happiness if both parties faithfully and sincerely adhere to their treaty. Then he presents each party with one of the bambu tubes, so that they may drink the contents, and after the exchange of gifts, sometimes of great value, a general feast concludes the solemn deed.

With the *Ngajus* the blood is not drunk, but smeared on a sirih-leaf, and so eaten.

Sometimes the marriage of their children is also brought about in token of the eternal and immutable friendship between two fathers.

An old man adopting a younger one as a child, the latter drinks blood from the right shoulder of the former, while blood from the right shoulder of the younger man is drunk by the elder.

THE KAMPONGS AND THEIR DIFFERENT STYLES OF BUILDING.

The native kampongs usually consist of a single house, or of only a few but very large buildings, inhabited by a considerable number of people living together. The custom of living in such a way, close together in a confined space, in which a great many disadvantages as regards personal freedom, ease, cleanliness, morality, etc., must inevitably be inherent, has something unnatural about it, not on a par with the inborn inclination of the natives for liberty and freedom from restraint, and is contradictory to the nomad manner of life of their ancestors. Nevertheless it seems to be a necessary evil. Without doubt this custom owes its origin to the often unexpected attacks of neighbouring warlike tribes; the population is thus compelled to be always ready and to live as closely as possible together, to be thus able to resist the foe with united powers, and not perforce to weaken their resistance by the separate defence of single dwellings.

In the interior the houses are surrounded by palisades and continually kept on a war footing. In the regions situated nearer the sea shore, where for a long time past there have been no hostile attacks to fear, the palisades have disappeared; the ancient custom of living together in large houses has, however, survived.

In the whole district of *Pulu Petak*, the lower *Kapuas* and *Dusun Hilir*, the houses stand on poles three or four feet high, are covered with *kajang* plaiting or mats of thatch, also, often with poor bark like slates, measuring 30 to 40 feet in length, but not very wide. A smooth floor made of laths, covered with mats, but not, as with the other Malays, consisting of several thicknesses laid one above the other, extends throughout the building. In addition to a large apartment, situate in the centre of the house, and serving as a gathering-place for all inhabitants, the dwelling is partitioned into several smaller compartments by means of kajang walls, inhabited by the different families, and opening into the large room by their respective doors. Usually only a single principal entrance leads to the interior of the building, and is reached by a pathway on the riverside, likewise supported on posts, or it consists of a trunk notched across at regular distances like steps.

The compartments for the single families are very small. At the same time they are full of smoke, each of them containing its particular fire-place, and are generally exceedingly untidy. Above the couch of the paterfamilias his valuables are kept, consisting of jars, weapons, and clothes; among the household furniture, lying along the walls on low shelves in the greatest confusion and disorder, some Chinese jars for preserving the precious tuwak are hardly ever lacking. Windows, long and narrow, practically openings made some feet above the ground, through which when sitting on the floor one may look out, are only found in the central room along both sides of the principal entrance.

In front and around the houses are seen the *Ampatons*, dedicated to certain spirits, in order to protect the house from misfortune, illnesses and witchcraft. Often also the *sandongs*, containing the earthly remains of the deceased, are placed in the neighbourhood and surrounded by *Ampatons*.

Along the rivers *Karau* and *Patai* the same style of building prevails more or less. In the districts *Duson Ulu*, *Murung* and *Siang* very great similitude in architecture is found. The houses are all surrounded by high palisades. The buildings enclosed in the *bĕnting* or fence, serve as a common dwelling-place, and consist of two or three large and long houses built on poles 15 and sometimes more feet in height. The front of the house sometimes projects at an obtuse angle, and as the ridge of the roof is considerably longer than the building, the roof itself slopes with acute angles towards the sides of the house, which indeed gives it a strange appearance, for the structure of the roof is just the reverse of what we might observe elsewhere.*

By steps, made of a single long trunk, the common apartment is entered from without, through either a gallery 10—12 feet broad, occupying the whole length of the building, or a roomy, square hall, situated in the centre of the house, to which open out the compartments of the single families. These are also extremely plainly furnished. Along the walls are stuck or hung weapons and clothes, besides a great many charms against evil spirits. Usually a bunch of similar talismans is seen hanging over the principal entrance of the house. In a corner on the floor is the fire-place, consisting of a square receptacle, filled up with earth, while in another corner is seen the sleeping place of the family, usually consisting of several curtains made of coarse stuff sewed together. Along the walls the tuwak vessels are put in a row, and near by hang the drinking horns. Some boxes for keeping clothes in and other things complete the simple furniture.

The exterior walls of the house, as well as the floor and the interior partitions, are usually composed of coarse boards, the roof being covered with *sirap* (small pieces of wood, *i.e.* shingles) or with flattened bambu. For some houses bark is used instead of wood. Between the separate larger buildings or under them, the small rice-stores are erected; they are carefully made closed houses, spacious enough to contain 2 to 6 *koyans*, and supported on poles provided with large wooden discs at the upper end. Within these magazines the rice is kept in cylindrical vessels, or rather in boxes, made of bark. Under the houses also are the rice-mortars which are used day and night, the pig-styes, etc.

The *bĕnting* is composed of a double row of palisades. Many of the poles of which it consists are iron-wood, sometimes 30 feet high, with rough carvings, representing disfigured human faces with long tongues, also monstrous animals,

* This architecture, often met with in the Dutch-Indian Archipelago, to wit, the outward sloping walls, is intended to make defence possible from within with pikes. [EDITORS.]

usually in the form of crocodiles, in order to frighten as it were the attacking foe. So-called *Bandars*, *i.e.* high poles made of several pieces put together, bearing human skulls, stand before or around the principal front of the bênting; they vary in number; beside them are monstrous figures made of wood, and the coffins, surrounded by skulls, in which rest the bones of the ancestors. Within the bênting, where all the living beings are crowded together, there is noise and bustle day and night. Especially must we mention the pounding of rice and the howling of hundreds of dogs, sometimes all yelping together with their shrill penetrating voices.

Along the Tewel and Mantalat rivers the same architecture prevails; but the houses are smaller and the bêntings are in an extremely neglected condition. Here bark is mostly used for closing the houses from without and for partitioning them into different rooms. Bandars are hardly ever seen here, and the coffins are likewise lacking, because in these regions the custom prevails of gathering the bones of the deceased in earthen pots and putting them away in rock caves.*

The houses of the *Ot Danom* lie along the upper *Kapuas Murung*. Their kampongs are very large, usually consisting of three or four very low buildings, whose arrangement does not differ in the least from the houses described above. At several points of the upper side of the palisades are placed small guard-houses, continuously occupied by sentries, to reconnoitre the surroundings of the kampong. At a distance of five feet from the upper inside edge of the bênting there is a circular gallery, on to which open the doors of the family compartments, and from which attacking parties are harassed. In the neighbourhood of the bênting only a few trees are planted, to make an unexpected approach of the enemy impossible. At the same time a great many wooden pegs [calthrops] are stuck into the ground, *i.e.* pointing outward away from the bênting so as to impede a massed advance of the enemy. The bêntings are usually built on the riverside at such places where two river-arms meeting afford an extensive view so that the enemy, which usually approaches in praus, can be readily seen some distance off.

On the other hand all these fortified kampongs, sometimes also called *kotas*, are only safe from the attacks of native enemies; they are not at all capable of offering the least resistance to European means of warfare.

CLOTHES AND WEAPONS.

The clothes and weapons of the inhabitants of this part of Borneo were in former years simpler than nowadays.

The men s clothes consisted of a sort of belt of beaten bark, several yards long, worn round the hips, in order to cover their nakedness in some way. A similar tie was wound round the head to hold up the hair, and a small jacket, open in front, with or without sleeves, covering half the body, likewise of sewed bark or home-woven material, completed the whole outfit.

The women were likewise plainly dressed. Usually they only wore a narrow home-made *sarong*, wound round the hips below the navel and hanging just over the knees, and besides sometimes also a small jacket with or without sleeves, covering the upper part of the body down to the region of the stomach.

Many, nay most of the natives have remained faithful to this ancient custom; others, however, prefer cotton material for their clothes, while some of them have tried to imitate the costume of the Malays.

In Pulu Pétak, where cotton fabrics are to be had at very low prices, the art of weaving has nearly entirely disappeared, the natives preferring to spend their time in more remunerative labour. (Clothes made of bark are very rare here.) The same takes place on the lower Dusun and along the Karau and Patai rivers; nevertheless, the old model has been preserved everywhere. The male inhabitants of these regions cover the loins with belts (*chawat*), usually consisting of a long tie of white or blue cotton; on the head they wear a piece of cloth like the Malays, but more tightly fastened than these have it. The jacket consists mostly of fabrics of a red or other bright colour. To be safe from sunshine and rain they cover the head with

---

* This is done here because this district is situated on the slopes of the *Angé-Angé* mountains.

a coniform hat made of nipa leaves. On the arms they wear rings of copper or polished shells. They also usually tie a string above the calf of the leg, while in the ear-lobes are fastened discs, an inch in diameter, made of wood or horn, and sometimes inlaid with gold spangles. The neck is adorned with chains of long, red polished agates, *laméangs*, consisting of one or more strings and sometimes united with bits of gold-leaf, in the shape of a crescent. These sometimes very costly neck ornaments also cover the upper part of the breast.

One of the chief ornaments is the tatuing of the upper part of the body and the arms and the calves of the legs, which parts are often covered with elegantly and graciously interlacing, symmetrical, black lines and curls.*

The women's dress in Pulu Pétak, Kapuas Murung, and the lower Dusun, consists of the above-mentioned sarong (*saloi*) and the jacket. Both cling tightly to the body and bring their figures into relief. The narrow, short sarong, keeping the thighs close together, only allows them to make short strides, and is the cause of their tripping gait, which is, however, considered very pretty in women. Over the sarong a thin, usually red coloured rotan, called *lintong*, being five or six fathoms long, is loosely tied around the hips, so as to form a kind of cuirass. This lintong is never taken off. The sarong is usually of a dark blue colour and seamed with red cotton. When the women do not wear a jacket, which among the richer classes does not consist of beaten bark but of blue cotton with red borders, then they wrap the upper part of the body, under the arms down to the hips, in a long broad girdle of red cotton, so as to cover the breast.

The whole fore-arm down to the wrist is covered with a great many copper rings, gradually becoming smaller from the elbow to the hand, and fitting close to the arm. The first ring at the wrist and the last at the elbow are made of polished shells. These are called *bĕlusar;* the copper rings, numbering from 20 to 25, being designated by the name of *lasom*. Such arm-rings are already put on to the children of rich people at the age of eight or ten years, and hinder to a not inconsiderable degree the development of the fore-arms; they are only very rarely changed later on, when the girls have attained to a more advanced womanly age, to other, somewhat wider rings. The engendered verdigris injures the skin and causes sores and painful eruption on those parts of the body in continual contact with the rings.

Round the neck the women wear a similar ornament to that of the men, the strings of agates, however, are more in number and more profusely provided with gold-leaves. The ear-discs, too, are like those of the men, but a little larger. The fingers are adorned with a great many copper, iron, silver, and polished shell rings.

The hair is worn separated and combed back sideways, and tied together in a knot with the back hair.

The women protect themselves from sunshine and rain by a round, slightly globular hat, called *tangai*, made of nipa leaves, measuring not seldom two or even three feet in diameter.

The tangai is painted with red figures and lines, and adorned with sea shells sewed on to it.

The teeth of both sexes are sometimes ground down a little when the age of puberty has been attained, and the two incisors are overlaid with bits of silver or copper leaf.

The dress of the inhabitants of *Siang* or *Murung* is generally similar to that of the *Ot Danom* people.

The men, beautifully and robustly built and of a very light brown colour, are naked, except for a whitish or reddish belt made of beaten bark. The long hair is combed backward, and round the head a narrow fillet is wrapped, likewise made of bark, the stiff ends of which stand up in an elegant way on both sides of the temples. The hair is then pulled forward over the back of the fillet and hidden under the upper borders. Some wear the hair in the Pari fashion of Kutai, *i.e.*, cut off for a span at the back of the head, the rest being allowed to grow freely. The longer

* In the south of Borneo this is considered as a sort of costume, usually only worn by those who start on a journey.

hair, thrown back over the fillet, covers the shorter hair at the nape of the neck, protecting this from the penetrating mandau when fighting. Others, especially the wealthy, wear jackets made of home fabrics or of coloured cottons. Even the bark belt is already sometimes substituted by white cotton, and some already wear the Javanese fillet. Jackets of native fabric, usually coloured blue, are also often worn by the men.

The body is extraordinarily richly and beautifully tatued. On the arms single copper rings are often worn, and around the neck the above-mentioned agate necklaces. These, however, are less numerous, nay, usually they consist of single pieces, fastened to a simple string.

The women, who are full and robustly built, and of a still lighter colour than the men, wear, like the Pulu Pétak women, a short and narrow sarong, reaching to the knees and fastened at the hips by folding it and rolling it at the top edge, while it is also kept up by the *lintong*. This whole manner of fastening is, however, very impractical, the sarong only hanging here and there, leaving the buttocks and thighs partially uncovered.

The rotan lintong is sometimes replaced by heavy copper chains, wound several times round the body.

The Ot Danom women have the arms cuirassed with the *lasom* of the *Ngajus*, the Siang women having their arms closely wound with brass wire. The fingers are often provided with a great number of rings made of brass or copper and seashells. The ear-discs are larger than those of the men, sometimes measuring 1½inch in diameter.

Above the calves of the legs is wound a black cord, made of vegetable fibres. The neck is adorned with strings of glass-beads or with agates.

The women are likewise tatued on some parts of the body, as, for instance, on the hands and behind the knees, or along the shin-bone down to the ankles.

When busy outside the house they cover up their bosoms with a linen wrapper of a red colour, or wear a jacket of bark or of blue cotton, with or without sleeves. The sarongs are woven by them out of bambu fibres or grass, and coloured with a blue dye. The hair on the head, often hanging loose, is also sometimes tied up by hair strings.

Men and women are great lovers of smoking, and prefer their cigars rolled in plantain leaves of home grown tobacco to the *sirih*.

The inhabitants of the Dusun as regards dress hold a medium position between those of Siang and those of Pulu Pétak. They are often not tatued at all, and some of them just a little; though they prick certain figures into their skin, attaching a peculiar meaning to them. Thus a figure consisting of two spiral lines interlacing each other and provided with stars at the extremities, pricked on one of the shoulders, means that the man has already cut off heads on various ngaijau expeditions. Two lines meeting each other in an acute angle behind the nails of the fingers, signify a certain dexterity in wood-carving; a star on the temple at the outer corner of the eye is a sign of happiness in love, etc.

The women are not tatued at all, and differ from the tribes already described in their dress, in so far that their short sarongs are not sewn, but are left open at the side, so as to uncover the whole leg at every step.

Along the Teweh the dress custom of the Dusun river people is followed in many respects. Here, too, the men are only tatued a little. On the Upper Teweh, however, the tatuing, especially of the face, becomes more general. I have seen men tatued on the forehead, others on the cheeks, others still on the upper lip. On the other hand they wear a great many arm-rings; the legs are also adorned with copper rings, from the ankles up to the middle of the calves. The ear lobes of the women are more lengthened out than those of the men. At the same time the latter often have a second hole in the upper rim of the ear, in which they wear a tusk of a big species of cat, giving them a very wild appearance. This ornament is especially worn by the so-called Orang Brani (Malay), *i.e.* by very courageous and warlike men. The lintong is not worn by the women of these regions; its place is taken by cords or in some cases by a belt, consisting of a brass chain.

In the uppermost regions of the river basin the women wear head fillets like the men, and their sarong is open at the side. The incisors of the upper jaw are here often covered with bits of copper-plates.

The Orang Boroi men often wear jackets, closely woven out of bambu fibres by their wives. The women also have head fillets and hair cut short, which does not look becoming. The lobes of the ears are exceedingly lengthened out. On the other hand they are decently dressed, with the exception of the left leg, continually uncovered on account of the open sarong. A narrow piece of cotton and a jacket with sleeves chiefly contribute to this decency in dress. The former is adorned with red and blue ribbons sewed on it, is tied round the neck and hangs down over the breast. On arms and legs rings are worn. They like smoking very much and often use rotan tobacco pipes for this purpose.

The weapons of the natives are to be divided into offensive and defensive arms.

To the former belong:

1st. The *Mandau*, a short sword with a rounded off blade, which they know indeed how to handle with tremendous force. I happened to see a Siang man, cutting through the thigh of a captive Melawi man, who was killed with a single blow. On the other hand the mandau is a weapon introduced by the Pari tribe of Kutai into this part of the river-basin only about 50 years ago. Formerly the *parang* was used instead.

2nd. A number of lances, bearing different names according to the different form of the iron points, being either long and narrow, or short and broad, or provided with barbs, etc.

3rd. The blow-pipes, from which poisoned arrows are shot, sometimes provided with lance points.

Defensive arms are:

1st. The shield, *télawang*.

2nd. A waistcoat quilted with kapok (cotton), *baju kapok*, nearly an inch thick, or made of rope.

3rd. The skins of animals, especially of goats and bears, or also of big cats. They protect the breast and the back, are provided with large shells or copper in front, and are called *ayong*.

4th. The covering of the head consists in a semi-globular cap, *tapoh*, of plaited rotan, with an animal skin over it.

No. 1 and 4 are chiefly intended as protection against mandau blows; No. 2 and 3 hinder the penetration of poisoned arrows.

Mandau, shield, lance and blow-pipe essentially belong to the attire of the natives, even in times of peace, and they never leave their houses without them.

A man in full armament, excepting the bare arms and legs, presents but few vulnerable spots to the enemy; he is protected from wounds inflicted by the mandau, and at a great distance even from bullets. But he also knows how to cover the bare parts of the body with great dexterity; for the native fights with the body inclined backward, putting the right or left leg forward, while the weight of the body is resting on the other leg. The shield is put on the ground in front of the advanced foot, and covers the whole inclined body. At intervals only do the fighting men uncover themselves by bold leaps, immediately resuming their stooping positions behind the protecting shields. The battle [*sic.*] having lasted some time in this way and the warriors not having succeeded in inflicting wounds on each other, their rage gets raised to its highest pitch, the shields are thrown away, and a struggle for life ensues, often ending in the death of both combatants.

The warrior wears bark *chawat* round his loins, and is dressed in a thick and solidly wadded waistcoat without sleeves, open in front, kept together by a single button and hanging down to the abdomen. At the neck this waistcoat has a solid collar likewise wadded, covering the back of the head. Above this garment the *sĕnayong* is worn, hanging over back and breast, with the shaggy side turned outward. The front of this is provided with shells or copper plates, either to increase the wild appearance or for the sake of better protection. The hair hangs loosely over back and shoulders and contributes not inconsiderably to safe-guarding these parts. The head is covered with the above mentioned round cap, called *tapoh*; this cap is likewise provided with shells and copper plates in front, and further adorned with bunches of cock feathers, with the quill feathers of the hornbill and with human hair. Sometimes it is shaped like a bear's or tiger's head. On the left hip of the chawat hangs the quiver, filled with poisoned arrows, and the mandau. Then if we put a shield into the left hand of a man so attired and a lance-pointed blow-pipe into his right hand, we get the complete type of a warrior equipped for battle.

We may assume that 25 European soldiers standing behind a palisade parapet, would be able to resist 300 to 400 natives, provided the former kept up a continuous fire. In a hand-to-hand fight, however, I am sure that one native can withstand two or more European soldiers.

ARROW POISONS.

For poisoning arrows the natives make especial use of the juice of two plants, namely, the *ipoh sirèn* or *sadirèn*.

The *ipoh*, also called *ratus*, is gathered from the juice of the *konyong* tree. The konyong has a thin stem and long slender boughs; the leaves have long stalks, are placed in two rows, and are broad and oval; their tops are lengthened out like a thread, and the sappy foliage resembles the leaves of the coffee-tree.

In order to gather the poison, the boughs and the stem are first freed from the exterior thin bark, and the sap-wood scraped off. The latter is thoroughly dried in the sun, and then stewed with water and some dried leaves of the same tree in an iron pan till the liquor grows thick and begins to acquire a brown colour. Then it is filtered through a cloth, to strain off the sap-wood and the leaves, and afterwards it is boiled once more, so that by evaporation it finally acquires a pitchy consistency. The evaporation is completed by continuously shaking the mass in a folded leaf over the fire till it is quite dry. Then the ipoh is further exposed to the influence of the sun for several days, and afterwards may be preserved in dried leaves for months. It is chiefly used for killing small animals.

The *sirèn* or *sadirèn* is gathered from a tree of the same name. It is a lofty tree, the slender, straight-growing stem branching off at a considerable height. The luxuriant foliage is of a dark hue, the shape of the medium sized leaves being a pointed oval. The poisonous juice is drawn by notching the stem, and gathered in bambu cases. As soon as it has acquired a certain consistency by evaporation, it may be used without further preparation.

The *sirèn* is the stronger poison, destroying life with tremendous quickness. It is chiefly used by the natives in war and for killing big animals. A man or an animal shot with an arrow or other weapon poisoned with it dies within a few minutes in fearful convulsions. One of my native travelling companions, wounded by an arrow of the *Punan*[*], died within less than ten minutes in terrible convulsions. The arrow had only superficially wounded him on his right shoulder. The only means by which sometimes the deadly effect may be prevented is the cutting out of the whole wounded part, and the sucking and pressing out of the blood. Once introduced into the blood, both poisons have a quick, nay, an immediate effect; they are less active, however, when taken in food. In this case they cause a slow and gradual decline of the unfortunate victim.

DAILY LIFE.

From what we have mentioned so far, one will be able to derive some notion of the domestic life and the daily occupations of the natives.

[*] This is a tribe living on the Upper Mohakan or Kutai river.

The cultivation of the fields and the domestic occupations are left to the women, the care of the children, the weaving of materials for clothes and the making of them, the plaiting of mats, etc., being also their task. Only at the hardest labour do the men offer their assistance; otherwise they spend their time in idleness or in making and keeping their weapons in repair, mending their house, and watching their families: or they pass their time in gambling, drinking, law-suits, ngaijau or assan expeditions, hunting or fishing, gathering products of the woods, and in trade.

Their daily food is very plain. They eat the produce of hunting and fishing, with rice and other additional meats. Domestic animals are only killed on the occasion of feasts, and only then is the intoxicating *tuwak* drunk. Pastry and cakes are unknown to them and so is opium. They generally like much sirih chewing and tobacco smoking, as with all nations of our globe; their greatest delight, however, is the mutual gossip of both sexes.

The Orang-Ot Tribe.

Before ending this ethnographical part of my account I cannot but add some details about the remarkable *Orang-Ot* tribe and its customs.

This tribe lives on the inaccessible mountains of the eastern and southern watershed. It is spread in the northern Siang, along the sources of the Lahai, Tohop, Marawai, Tahujan and Osoh rivers, and on the opposite side down to their junctions with the Mahakam river, where it touches the Pari tribes, from which it has already copied many habits. The influence from the Barito and Murung side has as yet not had favourable results and has awakened but little confidence; to this we must attribute the great shyness of the *Orang-Ot*, causing them to hide in their dark woods and to shirk all intercourse with strangers. But when compelled to converse with strangers, they turn their backs to them, squatting on the ground, hiding their faces behind their arms on their knees. The alleged reason of this queer habit is that the sight of strangers causes them giddiness, and that their eyes are affected in the same manner as when they look at the sun.

Their build is like that of the already more civilised inhabitants of Siang. They are tall and handsome and of a very light colour.

They are without kampongs and live in the woods and mountains assembled in small families. The sub-divisions of their tribe are called by different names, according to the districts into which they divide their country, and the river-branches along which they live.

Every family has the exclusive right of hunting in the region inhabited by it; poaching often causes bloody wars between them.

The paterfamilias is at the same time family-chief. They take shelter from sunshine and rain in huts made of branches and covered with kajang mats. Like the animals of the woods they lead a nomadic life, only caring for the supply of the necessaries of life. They stay where nature affords them sufficient food for some time, looking afterwards for new means of subsistence for they are not acquainted at all with agriculture of any sort.

Besides sago and wild fruits, they eat all sorts of food, even the most loathsome animals. They do not like salt, supposing that its use causes mortal diseases.

Their whole dress consists of a *chawat* made of bark. The females also do not wear any other clothes than a rotan band round the loins, to which is fastened a strip of bark in front, being a hand-breadth wide, which, pulled between the legs and twisted round the rotan-fillet at the back, is hardly sufficient to cover their nakedness. Neither men nor women are tatued; but both sexes are armed in the same manner. A blow-pipe, provided with an iron or bambu lance point, a quiver with poisoned arrows, a parang, and a shield are their weapons and means of defence. They have a wild, cruel and warlike character. In the dead of night they creep towards their enemies, and, as soon as they have hit them with the poisoned arrows out of their blow-pipes, hastily take to flight. They avoid an open battle. According to what is reported, the Ot-Danom [?] in former years undertook destructive *ngaijau* expeditions under the command of a certain Marong Kain to Siang and Murung, and only retired to the mountains and woods after their commanders had been murdered.

At their marriages the girl's free will acts the chief part. The girl chooses her husband and presents him with a kitchen utensil, with a blow pipe, a shield, and a parang. For the rest the nuptial tie is very loose with them, the sexes satisfying their desires as soon as time and opportunity allow it.

Their dead are buried in an erect position, in the stems of old "iron-wood" trees, the aperture being afterwards so carefully closed up that there is no visible trace left. The tree remains living and the aperture gets overgrown by new bark. A living grave like that is hung with all sorts of talismans, besides the skulls of enemies and the heads of wild boars, deer, monkeys, etc., killed by the deceased during his life. The putting away of the bones into the sandongs, as is the custom with the more civilised tribes, perhaps owes its origin to this custom; the truth of the opinion, that the manner of life of the ancestors of all the natives was originally quite identical with that of the present Orang Ot, is generally confirmed by the similarity of still many other customs, though time and circumstances may have changed them in some way or other.

The *Ot* women have an easy and quick confinement. As soon as the child is born, the mother is placed above a hole, in which are kept burning certain kinds of wood, mixed up with the earth of an ant-hill. The flooding is soon arrested by this treatment, which is repeated several times; on account of the smoke, the humours are dried up, and the mother so soon regains her forces, as to allow her already on the following day to carry about her child wrapped up in bark, and to resume her usual occupations.

When the Ot wish to assemble in greater numbers for some purpose, they strike violently on a hollowed stem. The sound produced is heard very far, and following its direction, the dispersed members of the tribe come up to the meeting-place.

The traders also make use of this expedient to gather their customers, in order to exchange with the Ot wax, ropes, blow-pipes, kajang mats and arrow poison, for utensils, lance-points and parangs.*

---

* The Orang or Olo Ot or Ut carry on the exchange in the well-known manner of *Kubu* or *Lubu* of Sumatra and other similar primitive tribes in Celebes and elsewhere. They never show themselves to Europeans; all that is known about them is on hear-say. The Kutai people relate that their Ot do not contract marriages, have no houses, and are hunted and killed by them like the animals of the wood.

NOTES.

[1] *Hatala*, is neither Indian nor Dyak, but from the Arabic *Allah taâla*. Hardeland has used this name in his Bible version, and it is strange indeed that hitherto no native name for the highest divinity is known.

[2] *Tasik Tabanteran Bulan Lumbong Matan Andan*, i.e. sea moved by the moon and surrounding the sun. We derive *tabanteran* from the Javanese *banter*, and compare this form with the well-known Malay form made with the prefix *tĕr*. *Matan andan* is probably a collateral form of *mata-hara*. In the Malayo-Polynesian languages an inter-changing of *r* with lingual *d* is often met with, and the nasal being put before it is likewise a common occurrence. Only *au* instead of *i* remains unclear. Cf. Balinese *matan-ahi* (sun). See also further on *angai* instead of *angin*.

[3] *Tasik Malambang Bulan Laūt Babandan Intan*, i.e. sea resembling the moon and containing diamonds (or: surrounded by diamonds).

[4] We now arrange the words according to the arrangement in the preceding names: *Tasik Kalumbang Bulan Labĕho Rambang* (on another place *rampang*) *Matan andan*, i.e. the sea surrounded by the moon and more agreeable than the sun. Instead of *Kalumbang* we read *Kalumbung*, as before, in the name of the first-mentioned sea. The words *Labĕho rambang* are unknown, the former is perhaps the equivalent of the Malay *lĕbih*, Jav. *luwih*, i.e. more, the latter a corruption of *ramya* (Old Javanese) i.e. agreeable, Malay *ramai*. The final nasal is also found in the Old Javanese word.

[5] *Tempon Telon*, elsewhere called a *sangsang*, is unknown. According to the details given of this being's functions, one would incline to derive *tempon* from the Jav. *tāmpā* or *tampi*, receive, accept; for *Tempon Telon* receives and conducts the souls like Mercury.

[6] *Laūt Bahawang*. The meaning is not clear. *Bahu* means much in Sanskrit; in Old Balinese also the plural *Bakawah* or, incorrectly, *Bhawah*, is met with.

[7] *Sangsang*, elsewhere called *Singsang*, is undoubtedly the Jav. and Balinese *Sanghyang*, a usual name for the gods, such as *batūrā*, without any distinction of rank, for even the highest deity is called *Sanghyang Tunggal*.

[8] *Bilian*, in Bali *Balian* or *Wawalèn*, see *Atsana Bali* (Tydschrift voor Nederlandsch Indië, 9th year). There are on both isles possessed persons, through whom the deity speaks and cures illnesses.

[9] T.e. the Moon-sea.

[10] *Kalu Tunggal Tusoh*. The first word, *kalu* or *kala*, is probably the God of Death, or of destruction, very naturally having his residence beneath the earth, but at the same time awakening life, in the quality of subterranean fire, and therefore said to keep watch over the plants he produces. *Tunggal* means single, unique; so he is a very great deity. *Tusoh* is perhaps the Malay *tusuh*, prick, stab, a surname given to the god on account of his destructive arms.

[11] *Hantu*, Sanskr., also known in Java; in Bali *Bhuta* is in use, meaning, however, a sort of identical demon.

[12] Compare the *Naga Padoha* of the Bataks in Humboldt's "Kawi Sprache," i. 240. *Naga* means snake; *padoha*, or *paduka*, Sanskr. Malay, prince; the original meaning, however, being *slipper*. It seems not improbable that *busai* is derived from *vasuki* the king of snakes, who acts an eminent part in Indian and Balinese mythology, but who is not said to bear the earth.

[13] Compare *Batada* (Batara) *Yingyang*, the *God Yingyang*, with Humboldt, "Kawis Prache," i. 239.

[14] *Sangsang Angai* is probably *Sanghyang Angin*, the wind-god, also indicated by his functions. In the ending *ai* is to be seen an analogy with *Matan-andan* compared with *Mata-hari*.

[15] *Dewa*, or funeral feast. This may be explained (though *dewa* means god in Sanskr., Balinese, Jav., and Mal.) by the fact that the deceased (the *pitaras*, shadows), are also considered *gods*, and that in Bali up to this present day numerous yearly, nay daily offerings are brought to them. The cremation and the festivity on that occasion, act a greater part in Bali than any other ceremony concerning the mortals.

[16] *Malabo Balai* is possibly to be derived from Old Jav. *labu*, waste, corrupt, and *balé* (as *angai* from *angin*, so *balai* seems to come forth from *balé*) a bedstead, here especially that of a pregnant woman or the nuptial bed. So the words would mean: *corruption of the bed*, and the feast celebrated to prevent this, would bear the name of the feared thing.

[17] *Nahunan Nakawan*. In the second word we think we see the word *anak*, child, perhaps combined with the Old Jav. *wahu*, new, i.e. young. The first word is clearly derived from *tahun*, year, and so the whole signifies the feasts repeated every year, i.e. the feast of birth. [The name should be: *manahunan anak-auau*, the verb, or *tahunan anak auau*, the feast itself, *anak awau* meaning infant. Compare mistake *andan* instead of *andau*.]

[18] *Mambandai*, the bathing feast, to be derived from *mandi*, Mal. (Bathe, Transl.); the ending *ai* is known from other examples; the inter-changing of *m* and *mb* is owing to the organ of speech, and the more natural, because an *m* is preceding, and the connection of *m* with *b* is very frequent in Indian [Malayo-Polynesian] languages.

[19] *Bèlako Undong*. The second word is evidently the Malay *antong*, profit, gain; with the first word we can only compare the Jav. *balākā* or *bēlākā*, sincere. [Should be *balaku ontong*, i.e. the asking for profit or happiness, compare Hardeland's Dict. i. 5.]

[20] *Bilianhai* is undoubtedly a compound of *bilian*, Balinese *balian* or *wawalèn* (see above, note 8). The second word is not clear, perhaps it is only a suffix, corresponding to the Malay suffix *i*, the *h* not being essential. In this case we could trace back the word to *baliani* or *balianin*, i.e. cause to be a *bilian* or possessed person, which agrees with the explanation given by Mr. Schwaner of the Bilians, the gods coming into contact with men by them. [*Hai* is a very common word, meaning *great*, and *balian* means *feast* besides possessed person. So the whole simply signifies "the great feast."]

[21] This name likewise refers to the veneration of the moon, already mentioned repeatedly higher up, which veneration, with that of the sun, seems to form the base of the whole mythology.

[22] The meaning of the words *sandong dulong* is not clear. For *sandong naüng* the latter part seems to agree with the Old Jav. *nung*, i.e. excelling, very well tallying with the description of the matter. [*Naung* should be *raung* = provisional coffin; *sandong raung* means the larger sandong, into which the raüngs are placed; *dulong* is not to be found in Hardeland's Dict.]

[23] *Ambatan* is perhaps to be derived from Jav. *embat*, thinness, slenderness, for they seem to be human images in miniature.

NOTE.—The above Notes are evidently not Dr. Schwaner's.—H. L. R.

II.—THE KAHAIJAN RIVER BASIN.

[*These Notes have been picked out of the text, not having been collected at the end of the volume like those of the Barito Basin.*—H. L. R.]

COURTSHIP AND MARRIAGE.

"Amongst the rich Ot Danums there is sometimes the cruel custom, probably taken from the Chinese, of locking up their young daughters, 8 to 10 years old, for a certain time in a special small apartment of the house and to keep them cut off from all intercourse with other people. The cabin is merely furnished with a small window which only looks out on to a solitary place, so that darkness mostly reigns in the apartment. The captive girl may never and on no account whatever leave the abode. All necessities are carried out in it. Neither father nor mother, nor brother nor sister, are allowed to see her during her term of imprisonment; but only a female slave who is appointed to attend to her has access to her. The poor victim to this custom sits seven years in this way in solitary confinement, occupying herself in making mats and such like handiwork. The development of her limbs, especially the lower limbs, suffer under this want of exercise. After the time of seclusion, which generally finishes when the maid has arrived at a marriageable age, she is freed from her prison and appears bleached lightly yellow as though made out of wax, tottering on small thin feet—which according to the taste of the natives is considered especially beautiful. As though she were new-born, they then shew her the sun, the earth and its productions and the water. A big feast is then held at which a sheep is slaughtered and the maid sprinkled with its blood. This seclusion is called *Bakuwo* and is to endow the daughter with the above-named pretty qualities, to make her name renowned and at the same time through this to attract many rich suitors." (p. 77.)

At Dengan Kami (Melanhoei district) he found morality in an exceptionally low state, almost no marriage ceremonies, and occasionally a man with three wives. There would appear from his report to be something like polyandry without a marriage ceremony, for he mentions a case where several men had to pay a fine each on the birth of a child. (p. 168.)

BURIALS.

"As amongst the Ngajus the coffin with its contents is brought out into open day. Later the bones are cleaned and burned, whereupon the ashes are collected in a jar and placed in the *sandong*. The funeral ceremonies are accompanied by a costly feast at which men, cattle, and pigs are slaughtered and the decapitated heads of the sacrificed offerings hung on the *sandong*. The *tomonggong* Tundan put into the coffin of his deceased wife eight full dresses besides all her ornaments. Immediately she died he killed a *budak*, and over and above that three more when the coffin was brought out of the house. At the cleaning and burning of her bones he had eight *budaks*, sixty pigs, and two bullocks killed." (p. 76.) "Amongst the rich there is a curious custom that the survivor of two spouses must on no pretence whatsoever leave the house for a certain time, which is longer or shorter according to the custom of different families. Often the mourning spouse has to remain from three to seven months sitting idle on a mat." (p. 77.)

On the Katingan River : " In front of the houses stand *ampatans* and *pantars* on the top of which are hornbills carved out of wood. It is strange that most of the pantars do not, as in the more easterly lying districts, consist of high and very straight masts but that tree stems of medium length, crooked, serpent shaped, bent or zig-zag are preferred. This custom coincides more with the idea which one has about a pantar, for the post is looked at in the light of a river (*Batang Damon*) which leads from the earth to the abode of the dead or of the Sangsangs." (p. 121.)

"The corpses are burnt a few days after death and the coffin is placed in the open air and when the flesh has disappeared it is again opened in order to be buried or burnt. Sometimes the corpses are buried and at the end of a year and a day dug up in order to conserve the ashes in sandongs as in the two other cases.

"Mourning ends with the Dewa feast at which offerings are brought to the dead so that they may spread their glory in heaven.

"In the Melanhui district the dead are burnt but children's bodies are buried in living trees. The pantars which they erect at their burial places in front of their houses are only about 15 feet high and ornamented with wooden horns or heart shaped blocks." (Melanhui, p. 195.)

Future Life.

Among the Ot Danum it is believed that the "souls of the dead are led over to their abode in the next world immediately their bodies are put in the coffin, but not as amongst the Ngajus only when the funeral feast takes place. Amid the songs of the *bilian* the soul is led by a Sangsang to the abode of souls over a high bridge which commences at the house of the deceased and whose other end rests on *Kaju Batu Paroh Bulan*." (p. 77.)

"The abode of souls is on the Bukit-Raja, the highest mountain of the district, and on those adjoining it, viz., Kaib, Boran, and Bukit Njait. The Bukit-Raja was very much higher in former times than now, for it reached to the heavens, the seat of the gods and of bad spirits. It served the dangerous spirit, Bojong, as a road to the earth, where he devoured men. But Burong Madeira flew along with his wings and threw him into the depths, whence he rose up as Bukit-Njait, and in doing so gave Bukit-Raja his present shape.

"The souls of the dead are guided by Sangsang Tandeho in a golden boat to Bukit-Rajah with the prayers and supplications of the *bilians*. On their journey to heaven, which rests on the mountain Lumbut, they have, like the souls of the Ngajus, to undergo many difficulties and dangers.

"The natives of the Melanhui district place the abode of the souls of the dead on Mount Balla Kapalla." (p. 195.)

Charms.

A Ngaju, while muttering magic words, "tied to the sash of his *mandau* a piece of wood off one of my drawing pencils, which I had cut into the form of a doll, together with a lot of other charms. As soon as he gets home he will offer a fowl to the spirits who direct the fate of men, in order to bathe in blood this new talisman, which is to provide him with prosperity and riches." (p. 54.)

Omen birds if heard on the right-hand side are bad, if on the left good. (p. 168.)

Medicine Women (Bilians).

"The Ot-Danums have no *bilians* like the *Ngajus*. The business of the bilians is carried on by the wives and daughters of the wealthy, who confine themselves to the cure of the sick by driving out evil spirits, to the guiding of the souls to the abodes of the deceased ancestors, and to the praying of the gods for prosperity and riches (*Belako untang*). The gift enabling them to perform such business is obtained by the *Sangsang* going over into the body of the bilian. While this is in operation, the woman must withdraw herself from all community with her husband." (p. 76.)

"The bilians who know how to commune with the gods in case of sickness and to supplicate evil spirits are women and maids of good family, and always of blameless character."

Basirs (Manang Bali).

The doctor refers to an exceptionally worthy man belonging to this class on the Kaihaijan River. (p. 46.)

Legends.

Dr. Schwaner relates that a certain river is called Gadjah mundor, which means the river bend where the elephant turned round. The legend runs: "Many years ago an elephant came over the seas near the Kahaijan river, and ascended the river up to the above-named place, in order to challenge the animals of the island to combat. With this end in view he let them be informed of his arrival, and gave the herald at the same time one of his tusks so as to give the collected animals an idea of his size and strength, and by this means to strike fear and fright in their breasts in advance. He succeeded in his design so far that fear and desperation filled the assembly, and they were only rescued from their confusion by the cunning of the porcupine, and were thus inspired with fresh courage. It advised them to let the elephant know they were ready to accept his challenge; at the same time they should send the elephant one of his quills so that the elephant might make a comparison between the hair of the porcupine and his own tusks, and then form an idea how great must be the tusks of the animal who owned the hair. The ruse of the little porcupine had the wished-for result, for the elephant, dreading the strife with so powerful an enemy, turned round and went back from whence he came." As there were no wild elephants in that portion of Borneo, and as most of the inhabitants are not acquainted with the existence of this animal, Dr. Schwaner is inclined to think the legend may have some foundation in the mis-carried invasion of the Hindus. (p. 15.)

"In the Labeho Tampang Kahaijan River there is on the left bank a steep rock about which the following story was told me : Many years ago it happened that the inhabitants of the Lepang, a side stream of the Rungan, found many large pieces of the mighty metal while gold digging. Amongst others they found a nugget, which in size and form completely resembled a hart, and with the shape of the animal it combined its shyness and swiftness. Seeing this tremendous treasure the diggers threw themselves greedily upon it, but before they were ready to grasp the animal it got up, reached with nimble legs the grotto of a rock, and vanished quickly into its dark depths out of the sight of its pursuers. At the same time some natives coming down the Kahaijan observed on the heights above Labeho Tampang a golden hart, which, running swiftly, rushed into the foaming whirlpool. According to the opinion of the natives this hart was the king of the gold who was fleeing from the Lepang to the Kahaijan, and by that means had brought over a lot of his riches to the banks of this river." (p. 52.)

"The Ot-danoms call the supreme being Mahadara. He created the earth and all that therein is. In the beginning there was nothing but water, and all endeavours to draw out the dry land remained fruitless, until at last seven Nagas [jars] are taken for a foundation, on to which basis Mahadara threw the earth down out of heaven. As formerly there was nothing but water, now the water and light are suppressed and the universe is overwhelmed with earth. Mahadara stepped down from his seat, and pressed this together into a firm mass, stones, &c.; he formed the mountain ranges and heights, the depths of lakes and seas, the beds of rivers and brooks, so that the water now got its bed in the dry ground. Only after that were men made out of earth, and the rest of creation developed."

"According to the belief of the Ot Danoms there was once a big deluge on the island, on which occasion many inhabitants lost their lives. But the crown of the Bukit Arai at Mendai, which may be a side pocket of the Kapuas Bohang, remained above water, and was the abode of a small number of people who were able to save themselves in praus until the waters, which had covered the land for three months, had abated, and the ground was dry once more."

"The Ot-danoms trace their descent from two different ancestors, who came down from heaven in golden ships, followed by their slaves in wooden and less costly vessels."

AGRICULTURE.

"At times the ears and stalks of the rice are destroyed by insects, at others there are great swarms of rats through which whole *ladangs* (households) are eaten up, or the plants are drowned by the high waters. The results of this are famine and general poverty." (Kahaijan R. p. 21.)

"Here [in Sungei Miri] as well as on the middle and upper Kahaijan the planting of *ujagong*, the most important food of the natives of the Barito and Kapuas Murung in times of rice failure, is completely neglected. In its place we find the

Kumbili Kaju which according to what is said of it must be a healthier and more strengthening root than the *ujagong*. (p. 65.)

On the Kahaijan River he speaks of rice barns "on high poles in the shape of a little house same as with the Ot Danums and Siangers." (p. 24.)

The sacred *Sawang* plant is spoken of at Rasali on the Kahaijan river and on the Katingan river. (pp. 27, 124.)

There is a sacred tree at Tampang, Kahaijan river: "On the top of the Ambon my attention was called to a damar tree, which was held sacred. A large bullet-shaped mass of white damar which had oozed out at the top of the tree may therefore not be taken away, but it serves the traveller as an oracle and is covered with hundreds of darts shot out of the blow pipes. Superstition says that those who miss the damar three times shall become poor and unlucky, while fortune shall favour the lucky shot in the possession of riches which he may carry away." (p. 45.)

GAMES.

Cock fighting and cockpens on the Melahui river are very common and cause great waste of time, &c. (p. 175.)

FOOD.

The salt water rises to the surface and "in order the better to collect it the natives dig a hole in the soil down to the sandstone and place there a cylinder made out of a hollow tree stem. The salt water rises in this pipe and overflowing on to the ground is wasted. Twenty or thirty natives are daily busy preparing the salt by letting the water steam off in iron pans, by which means they obtain about half a gantang of salt per day." They only get salt in this way when the traders omit to bring it to them. (p. 176. Kampong Tumbang Serawai.)

NARCOTICS.

Among the Ot Danums and Ngajus both men and women get thoroughly drunk at their feasts, consequently it sometimes comes to quarrelling. In the evening after a merry feast one occasionally finds a great number of the invited guests in great rage tightly bound on the ground. (p. 77.)

On the Katingan River they smoke home-grown tobacco out of the bambu pipes, and collect carefully the foul juice, out of which they prepare little balls which are fixed on to a thin bambu stick and which from time to time they place between the lips in order to lick them. These tobacco juice balls take the place of cigars amongst them. While engaged or when travelling I did not see them smoke, but I nearly always saw them use these little balls of which almost every Ot Danom carries one stuck behind his ear. (p. 137.)

HUNTING.

"The natives on the Katingan are in the habit of leaving their *kampongs* for long years together and taking their possessions and goods with them to their *ladangs*. Under such forsaken houses where a lot of offal, &c., has been thrown a rich vegetation springs up. Deer, attracted by this at night, are often killed by the lances of the natives who watch for them in the houses." (p. 121.)

DOGS.

At Sakkoi on the Kahaijan R., Dr. Schwaner's little long haired spaniel was taken to be a young steer or a young he-goat and he had much difficulty in convincing them to the contrary. (p. 44.) Among the Ot Danums dogs "have a history and like all animals a soul. It is said they spring from Patti Palankaing, the king of animals. When he was holding an assembly and was about to sit gravely down in the middle, a part of his body which is generally kept covered became visible, and was the cause of a general laugh. Offended at such unmannerly behaviour Patti fell to biting the animals and drove them away in confusion. This action put an end to his dominion; in consequence of an implacable hatred thus taking root in his mind and affecting his issue, it became clever in hunting. The bodies of dogs are wrapped in cloths and covers and buried in the neighbourhood of the houses, rice (*bras*) and salt are given it in the grave and rice strewn over the grave as an offer to the gods to induce them to lead its soul to the heaven of dogs. To its memory a *pantar aso* is erected, on which are hung the jawbones and skulls of the deer and pigs it has killed." (p. 78.)

HABITATIONS.

On the Kahaijan River: "The roofs are covered with *dinger*, a sort of grass, which they say is so lasting that a roof covered with it requires no replacing for 10 to 15 years. The walls are made of tree bark or out of wattlework made of flat pressed bambus. . . . The inside of the houses is very irregularly divided; it is as much as one can do to distinguish a room in the middle on to which a certain number of private family rooms adjoin. The sub-divisions are made by means of bark or bambu wattle, or the walls are made of planks freely ornamented with carving, representing arabesques and foliage. The inside is dirty and black with smoke, which has no other exit than through the door, or here and there through horizontal chinks which act as windows. A quantity of various objects are hung along the walls, as well as all sorts of household utensils, weapons, fishing tackle, clothes, charms, &c. At the same time also gongs in various numbers and sizes according to the wealth of the inhabitants and occasionally on the main post of the building on a very high carriage a leila [brass gun] are fixed. . . . The inside of the house is reached by means of a tree trunk furnished with notches. . . . Along the riverside a few *balai* are erected, the common rendezvous of the inhabitants of the kampong; here also are held the well-attended feasts, while travellers take their night's rest there.

"The size of these buildings is generally out of proportion to that of the dwelling houses which are generally much smaller. Besides they are extremely plain, consisting only of a big, open, long rectangular shed raised on posts about 4 feet high and covered with a very overhanging roof." (p. 20.)

"The landing place is indicated by a small raft, covered with planks, called *batang*, made fast to the bank, which makes intercourse between the river and shore possible. From the batang, by means of a ladder made out of a single beam or out of several small tree stems, one arrives at a small tent house which stands on the bank, and which is furnished with seats right and left; this serves at the same time as a waiting-room for travellers or in general for those who have business on the river. From here there is a plank-way raised about two feet above the ground towards the kampong, where, according to the number of dwellings, it spreads in different directions, so that during rains and floods the inhabitants can get to one another dryshod." (p. 21.)

"The Ot-Danom style of architecture: The houses are long, covered with roofs of trapezoid form, rest on posts, are furnished with but very few small window openings, and closed by means of planks, or bambu wattle, or also with bark.

"The Kampong Tampang is one of the largest, and without doubt the neatest that we have met with in the whole length of the Kahaijan. It consists of a single house 360 feet long, resting on piles 20 feet high, and is surrounded by a palisade of the same height, so that the house towers above it. The floor of the house stretches to the edge of the palisade, and forms a broad gallery round the house which is used for various purposes. The walls are made of planks, while the roof consists of bark. Inside the palisade steps lead to the dwellings of the different families. Underneath are the rice storehouses, the platforms for the rice mortars, &c. In front of the house, on two sides, are spacious yards, which are cleared of grass and kept very neat. There also are two large *balais*, the assembly place of the inhabitants of the Kampongs and for the sojourn of strangers. At each one there is besides a small smithy. The inside of the family dwelling is neatly divided into smaller apartments which serve as bedrooms. One also sees occasionally under the roof small partitions meant for bedsteads. Between the palisades of the benting and the courtyard *ampatons* are set up." (p. 34.)

"The delicately carved ridge-boards of the roofs, projecting much beyond the base of the oblong four-cornered building, gives these houses quite a peculiar appearance. (p. 67.)

DRESS.

On the Katingan River he refers to cases where women have been drowned owing to the heavy copper leg and arm rings which they wear. Ear discs as large as a florin are inlaid with gold plates. (p. 124.)

Higher up the river and in the highlands the natives weave the material for their clothes out of fibre of bambu or of *Daun Lempa*, and also of cotton thread. (pp. 136, 168.)

TATUING.

The Ot Danums' tatuing is more perfect and more intricate than that of the Ngajus, and they cover the whole body except the face. They say that in former times the Ot Danums as well as the Ngajus were but little tatued. The *bilians* have brought the art of tatuing to the present degree of perfection through hearing the description of the pretty tatued bodies of the [mythical] Sangsangs . . . The shinbones of the women are like those of the Siang women tatued to the root of the angle. (p. 79.)

WAR.

"The *benting* [fortress] is built out of ironwood posts 30 feet high, and above it long poles project like masts, on the top of which are placed hornbills with spread wings carved out of wood. These figures sometimes carry a human skull or rest upon one. In front of and inside the benting there are a lot of *ampatans*. The four habitations surrounded by the palisade stand on posts 15 feet high; decayed plank ways, resting on still more rotten supports, lead from one dwelling to the other and throughout the benting. In the middle Kahaijan district the bentings are very scattered, and their number is far exceeded by that of the unpalisaded Kampongs. In case of pressing danger they serve as refuges for the inhabitants of the latter, and they are therefore collectively raised by them, and kept up at communal cost." (p. 26, also p. 54.)

On the Katingan River he refers to a great heap of the skulls of the former inhabitants of the village Jumbang Hangi; there were 160 skulls, and the people had lost their lives through the dispute arising on the elopement of a woman. (p. 152.)

On the same river he found the inhabitants in the greatest dread of the Punans; he adds, "but the murderous destruction carried on by these people along the Rakanur and in other tributaries of the Malahui is truly horrible." (p. 165.)

SLAVES.

"The rich Ot Danums possess a number of slaves. Whenever their number increases too much they are freed of their serfdom; they must thereupon look after their own suppport, and are only bound to serve on special summons. The children of such apparently freed slaves as well as their parents remain subordinate to their original master. (p. 80.)

The "Ot-danoms are partly free and partly slaves. The latter, called *bewar*, are probably of the same class as the present budaks of the inhabitants of the main river whose state I have formerly described, and who have probably descended from former budaks. The bewars are bound to obey and serve their masters as much as these require it. They mostly live in special kampongs, or at least in detached houses. They plant their own rice, and must satisfy their wants out of their own means. They may trade and amass wealth. I know cases in which a bewar was much better off than his master, without, however, altering their mutual relationship. Bewars who have no parents or near relations are employed on domestic work. Sometimes also the full-grown children of living bewars are taken into the house in order to share the work until they get married.

"A free Ot-danom cannot lapse into the state of a bewar.

"The impossibility of paying debts is no reason for falling into slavery. The debt remains in full force, and on the death of the debtor goes over to the children, while they become an object of the *singer*. [See below. Government.]

"There are no real *Budaks*, but those who at the end of three years are unable to pay their debts become slaves, or *samboat*; then they are bound to obey their creditors and to work for them without being allowed their freedom, not even in case they possess the necessary means to satisfy their debt. They remain with their children and grandchildren for ever in a state of subjection.

"On money lent no interest is payable.

"Slaves are sacrificed at the Dewar feasts in the Melanhui district." (p. 195.)

HUMAN SACRIFICES.

On the Kahaijan River "the quantity of skulls one sees placed round about the tombs has been handed down from earlier times or emanates from sacrificed slaves." (p. 22.)

"The Sakkoi of the same river do not lay themselves out to cut off heads and the bad habit of sacrificing slaves does not rule to such a great extent as amongst others of their kinsfolk." (p. 44.)

At Kotta Toembang Menangeh mention is made of a chief having used his sword against defenceless slaves (p. 55), and in the house of the Tomangang Toendan the Doctor refers to 12 skulls of slaughtered slaves. (p. 60.) Every year this man makes human offerings to the spirits of prosperity. (p. 61.) At the head of the river there is "the *balai* for strangers which as everywhere else on the Kahaijan is ornamented with human skulls." (p. 67.) "Among the Ot Danoms, not only at funeral feasts but also on other occasions, as for instance at the conclusion of peace and friendship, men are slaughtered. The Talismans of the house and of a few people are washed in the blood while the concerned parties besmear with it their heads, shoulders, breast, stomach, knees and feet under mutual wishes for prosperity and long life." (p. 77.) The Doctor states that in the Kahaijan River district he induced many chiefs to give up human sacrifices. (p. 55.) In the Melanhui watershed slaves are sacrificed at Dewa feasts. (p. 195.)

GOVERNMENT.

"The chiefs reap certain benefits from those who do not belong to their families, who settle in their districts, or who wish to collect the produce of the country. A right of settlement must be paid for with 100—200 gantangs of rice, besides which the inhabitants of a district are bound to help the chief in any great undertakings. Whoever cuts rotan must pay a bundle of it to the chief; so also with gold washing, every digger has to pay a tax of half-florin to the chief. The chief has also the right to lay a tabu (pamali) on any parts of his district, that is, he may forbid entry and exit for a certain time. This tabu, which may last for several consecutive years, is laid in consequence of the death of some important member of the family. The way in which it is laid—to give it shortly—is as follows: The mouth of the river to be tabued is tied from shore to shore with a rotan rope, on which wooden parangs and short rotan ropes are fastened, while at one spot a little prettily made boat out of bambu is set up, and at one end a small goji, that is a Chinese ewer, is placed. The chief calls the attention of the inhabitants to these preparations to acquaint them with the commencement and duration of the tabu, at the same time informing them that if the tabu be broken a fine will have to be paid of equal value to the ewer above mentioned, and that he who declines to pay the fine shall be forced to do so by means of the weapons whose figures made out of wood are hung upon the rotan rope. I have had ample opportunity of being convinced that the tabu is a very condemnable institution of the adat, as by its means kampongs, whole districts, and important roads are shut off from communication, and that trade and all other business is impeded. It happens not seldom that the tabu entails great loss and important increase of expenses to the merchants. At the mouth of the Senamang I counted no less than six trading vessels which had already been waiting several weeks for the moment when the barrier should be cut through, so to be able to proceed on their journey.*

"From what we have just mentioned it will be seen that in the Katingan districts the dignity of a chief does not depend upon popular election but is hereditary. Should a district fall to a woman on account of the want of male heirs, then the husband of the woman is made chief, an arrangement which shows that no female chieftainship is tolerated." (p. 95.) But Niai Balau, a Kahaijan of great courage and determination, who led her people, mandau in hand, to victory, was a chieftainess. (p. 54.)

"Murder was punished with a fine of 2,000 florins, paid to the family of the murdered man, and a blood feud often supervened." When the matter was ended, slaves were exchanged, and peace made. (Melandui district, p. 168.)

"An important occupation of the free Ot Danums, which occasionally requires the exertion of all their mental powers, is the so-called *singer*. It consists in the renewal of old undetermined law suits, of lapsed debts, unfulfilled obligations, &c., which mostly descend from the time of their ancestors, with the object, but occasionally without well-founded reasons, of robbing others of part or of the whole of their property, and to enrich themselves thereby. The wealth of great grandfathers is thus thrown away among the great grandsons. The *singer* is chiefly a case of memory, and often requires a very thorough knowledge of the genealogical trees of different families and of their circumstances, but also considerable skill in argument. If a defendant does not possess these qualities, or perhaps in not so great a degree as the plaintiff, then he generally loses the case, and must satisfy the demands of his opponent. The custom of the *singer* is for many the source of great wealth, but at the cost of others, who have thereby lost their property and freedom. The collecting of newer debts, of interest in arrears, of fines, &c., can be brought under the *singer* institution." (p. 81.)

"Another very funny custom of the Ot-Danoms is that, during serious conversation, they repeatedly slap the back of their heads with the flat of the hand, in order as it were to knock out the thoughts. This custom is very wide-spread, and appears to be contagious, for several of my comrades shared it." (p. 137.)

Property.

On the Katingan River "The land is divided amongst a few rich and powerful families, and is looked upon by these as hereditary property. The origin of this the people are not able to explain properly; they are satisfied with the saying that their ancestors were already the possessors, as it is, however, demonstrable that various great families at present, who call themselves proprietors of the land, originally did not come from the Katingan watershed, but from another place, more especially from the Upper Kahaijan River, we may not without well-founded reasons consider that their present pretensions have followed upon a provisional usurpation which was supported originally by the riches and the renown of the new comers, and so brought about the present result. These indeed are the only conditions which force the poorer classes of the people with irresistible power into slavish subjection." (p. 147.)

At Tundan, on the Kahaijan River the Doctor speaks of the "*Tomonggong* (chief) possessing 45 costly jars (*blangas*), which may be collectively valued at 15,000 florins, which possession makes him the richest native in the island." (p. 61.)

Trade.

"I may repeat once more that most Ot Danum natives, in spite of their appetite for trade, do not possess the ability for carrying it on with profit; they have not sufficient sense for speculation or calculation, nor method in their affairs, nor quickness in their undertakings. Time is not taken into account in their travels. Only slowly do they learn to set up their wares and to demand the proper price for them. Hence very few return home with any profit to their families, who in the meanwhile

---

* At the new moon, in the Melanhui District, there is one day pamali (tabu), and at the full of the moon there are three days tabu, during which no work must be done, and not even a "singer" undertaken. (p. 168.)

have become impoverished. Many come back laden with debts, and others as poor as when they started. The reason that one sees so many married people along the Kahaijan without children is principally to be found in the licentious life which the traders lead on their year-long travels." (p. 114.)

"Out of superstitious fear the Ot Danums and Ngajus make strangers on their first arrival pay a *balas*, *i.e.*, a sum of money with which, according to the amount, offerings are made, buffaloes and pigs are cooked, and offered to the spirits to reconcile them to the arrival of the strangers, and to induce them not to withdraw their favours from the natives, to bless the rice crop, and to richly fill the *Karangans* with pure gold. Such a balas costs a traveller 40 to 100 florins, according to his means and the length of his journey. (p. 77.)

MINING.

On the Kahaijan River the "whole of the district is covered with gold mines, which consist of square or rectangular, and sometimes also oblong, perpendicular shafts of various depths, according to the depth under the surface at which the gold is found. The shafts are here sunk close to one another, and the gravel is drawn out in an irregular manner, so that in the end the shafts issue into one common opening underground, formed through the taking away of the gold-bearing stratum. None of these shafts are in any way shored up by timber, hence it occasionally happens that they fall in, by which the workers sometimes lose their lives. The sinking of the shafts is the work of the men, while the clearing of the gravel and the washing out of the gold is handed over to the women and girls. The shafts first sink through a 4 to 8 and even 10 foot thick layer of yellowish loam, under which the white *keisand* is found, and which is about $\frac{1}{2}$ to 2 foot thick, and above all things is richest in gold in the lowest part. Under that is found *dorre*, gray solid potter's clay. The gold obtained is washed in the neighbouring river. Of aqueducts the natives have no idea and are therefore only able to extract the gold profitably when it is found near running water. (p. 38.)

At the time of the Doctor's visit "two women were killed through the falling in of a mine and hence the village was made *pamali* to strangers." (p. 39.)

When the gold is in the sand on the bottom of the river bed, in order to get this sand a small raft is made use of which is furnished with an apparatus made out of small tree trunks which has much in common with hinged gridiron. At one end there is a wicker basket (faschine) filled with stones. When the place is reached where gold bearing sand is found the apparatus is sunk with its heaviest end and so serves not only as an anchor but also as a ladder upon which to climb down. With his back leaning against the ladder so as to offer necessary resistance to the current the gold washer steps down, scrapes the sand into flat wooden dishes and then climbs up to wash the gold out of the sand on the raft. He then descends again with the same object. Women also share in this work and it is astonishing how long they are able to stay under water. (p. 74.)

The Serawai river and its tributary the Tjeroendong are noted for the purity of the gold found in their neighbourhood. "The holes which the natives dig are at first not very wide, and only when they are convinced that they have struck the gold bearing sand layer do they enlarge the holes up to 10 to 15 feet square. The depth of the holes varies." The sides of the holes, which do not seem to be much more than 5 (?) feet deep, are supported by timber. "They do not dig up more of the sand than is found at the bottom of the hole, for they do not understand the art of making underground galleries, &c." (p. 178.)

In every Kahaijan village there is generally a small smithy for the repair of weapons and of other iron implements; the kampong dwellers and strangers have the right to make free use of it. (p. 20.)

DAMMAR.

I found children and women busy collecting dammar which they pick up out of the alluvial deposit, standing up to their breasts in water (Kahaijan River). Dammar is never found here in pure sand. (p. 27.)

NOTES EXTRACTED FROM MRS. PRYER'S WORK
(SEE BIBLIOGRAPHY).
Which reached me too late for insertion in the body of the book.

ORDEALS.

Some men were reported to have undergone the hot water ordeal, which is quite a voluntary test. Mr. Pryer examined "the hands that had been in the boiling water; they did not seem any the worse for it. . . . When the man's hand is in the hot water he relieves his feelings by loudly calling on Heaven to help him and bear witness to the truth of his statements." (Kinabatangan R. p. 75.)

NEST HUNTING.

"The candles they made by taking a long piece of thick wick of rolled cloth, and having warmed a lump of beeswax, squeezed it thickly round the wick; ordinary candles do not answer, as they spoil the nests. The pronged forks are made out of thin saplings; they are cut in different lengths, the top end is split into four, and to keep the ends apart little wedges of wood are inserted at the base of the slits and bound into place by rattans, and the beeswax candle is secured just below. . . . One amongst other cave customs was, that if a person below called out 'forfeit,' the collector above had to throw down a nest, so that by these means alone the hangers-on made a good living. . . . The swiftlets which make the nests are of two kinds, the one which makes the black nest having a slightly larger head than the other. I do not know whether this fact is scientifically known." (pp. 56, 66, 67.)

NAMES.

There was a slave woman, rejoicing in the name of Champaka. "*Champaka* is the name of a very sweet-smelling flower. Natives in this part of the world, especially Sooloos, sometimes give their children very odd names. For instance, I have known a man called *Ular* (snake); another, *Ubi* (potato); and another, *Kalug* (worm)." (p. 71.)

HONEY.

On the Kinabatangan R. the wax and honey do not seem to be sought after by the natives. (p. 78.)

FIRE-MAKING.

Fire was obtained by means of bambu, bit of pith and a broken piece of pottery. (Kinabatangan R. p. 81.) The Buludupies' "usual way of producing fire is to take a piece of dry bamboo about ⅛ of an inch thick, scrape it until they have produced a flocky substance, then with a little bit of broken pottery, a piece out of an old plate or tea cup, held between their finger and thumb, they strike it smartly against the edge of the bamboo and a spark is produced which kindles the flock." (p. 98.)

TOBACCO.

The natives do not attempt to ferment it, but simply dry it, cut it up small, and use it in their pipes or rolled into cigarettes, the covers of which are thin young leaves of the nipa palm. (Kinabatangan R. p. 81.)

FOOD.

Snakes, monkeys, rhinoceros and crocodiles are eaten. (Kinabatangan R. pp. 69, 70.)

SICKNESS BOATS.

"We saw a miniature house floating down towards us. It was gaily decorated with flags, and was fitted on to a lanteen or raft. I wished to have it, but the boatmen refused, in their usual courteous Malay fashion, to interfere with it, explaining that someone in a village above must be ill, and that this little house had been launched on the river in the hope that the illness would be floated away in it, and the boatmen were afraid that if they took it, the sickness which they imagined to be on board it, would attack us or some member of our party." (Kinabatangan R. p. 83.)

Trade.

Mr. Pryer attempted at Domingol on the Kinabatangan River to establish a market, but it "went off rather flatly," as being the first, the people did not seem to understand what to do. An old Sulu "woman and her cakes were, in fact, the chief feature of the market." (p. 85.)

Rights in Jungle Produce.

A panglima on the Karamuk River seems to have had rotan cutting rights; both rotan and rights he carefully preserved. (p. 87.)

The Buludupies.

It would seem that we owe it to Mr. Pryer that the Buludupies on the Sigaliud River have not been exterminated. There were only seventeen of them when he came on the scene and they were in despair at the harassing they received on all sides. They are of a mild and gentle disposition and cultivators of the soil. Many of the women are quite fair, almost if not quite as white as Portuguese or Spaniards. (pp. 97, 98.) Mrs. Pryer states: "The character of the face of these people differs in some degree from that of the more typical Mongolian type, their eyes being so round and the bridge of the nose so developed that Dr. Rey, a French scientific man, who visited North Borneo in 1881, was inclined to think they were of semi-Circassian ancestry." (p. 95.)

NOTES FROM PROF. KÜKENTHAL'S WORK.
(SEE BIBLIOGRAPHY.)
Received since going to press.

Agriculture.

The Kalabits irrigate their fields and use the plough. (p. 263.)
The dial post's shadow is measured with the arm. If it reach the biceps it is a good time for augury; if it reach the elbow then is the best time for planting; if it get shorter there is danger from monkeys; if it get to the wrists insects will cause trouble. If the shadow be so small as to reach only between finger and wrist the crop will be good but there will be death in the house, for when there is weeping the hand is used to wipe away the tears, but in the bend of the arm everything can be borne, and hence when the shadow length is equal to it then the best seed time has come. (p. 292.)

Omens.

The white-headed hornbill (*Berenicornis comatus*, Grant,) is mentioned as the most important omen bird. (p. 266.)

Tatuing.

The better class Kayan women are more finely tatued than the lower class women. They are tatued from the hips to the middle of the calves. The tatu instrument has four needles. In the illustration on Plate ix. only two needles are shown. Among the men a finger tatued indicates the owner's presence in a battle, and when the whole of the back of the hand is tatued it means he has taken a head. The rule is not strictly adhered to. (p. 272.)

o

Heads.

A carved piece of wood attached to a decapitated head means that the original owner was a man of importance. (p. 279.) The Kenniahs say that they used formerly only to take the hair [? scalp] of their enemies, but a toad once promised a party of warriors good luck if they would take heads instead. Heads were accordingly taken, and all sorts of wonders followed; hence the custom was started and it remained. (p. 280.)

Sumpit Poison.

It must be renewed every two or three months. (p. 283.) It is said to be very powerful and even to destroy large animals, such as stags, in a few minutes. It is taken internally as a febrifuge. Rhinoceros may eat the leaves with impunity, but if their excrement fall into water the fishes rise stupified. (p. 284.) It would seem from Prof. Leubuscher's experiments that the poison is not that of *Antiaris toxicaria*, but of a probably still unknown poison. Chemical examinations proved that it was certainly not a glucoside and that probably among other and unimportant substances there was an alkaloid mixed with an acid. Physiological experiments showed that the poison acted on the heart exclusively—it did not affect the nerves and muscles. *Antiarin* does affect the nerves and muscles and causes heart stoppage in systole, and it is an alkaloid. Hence the poison brought home by Prof. Kükenthal is not *Antiarin* but probably an alkaloid. It had no effect on fishes, and therefore *derrid* could not have been present. (pp. 284-269.)

Childbirth.

To show that he is expecting offspring the husband ties a vertebra of the plandok round his left ancle, the plandok being sacred here; the vertebra acts like a charm. He is to a certain extent *pamali* as regards his vocation and food; he may not go a hunting for fear the wound he causes may be reproduced on the child and would be a weak spot to it in time of war. Dirt and ape's hair was rubbed on a child's head to insure its not being stolen by apes, and when it had a gumboil an old woman rubbed its mouth with a weed until it became quite raw.

Daily Life.

They have no idea of perspective; in pictures people in the background are thought to be little people.

Burials.

The Professor shows tombs which consist of high posts in a hole at the top of which the dried body is placed.

Coffin Discovered by Mr. C. V. Creagh.
(See opposite page.)

NOTE ON BURIALS.

In a cave on the Kinabatangan River, Mr. C. V. Creagh has recently discovered some "40 bilian (ironwood) coffins, artistically carved with figures of buffaloes, crocodiles, lizards, and snakes, containing skeletons of men, women, and children, and also sumpitans, spears, and articles of Chinese and other pottery, with brass ornaments of native and foreign workmanship. The relics appear to me to be of Javanese origin, but there is no tradition on the river of settlers of this nationality. The carvings and scroll-work on some of the coffins are superior to those now executed by native workmen." . . . The coffins, "ornamented with the protruding heads of buffaloes or cows, contained male skeletons, while figures of snakes, lizards, and crocodiles appeared to be used for the decoration of those of the women and children." The illustration on opposite page of one of the coffins is taken from plate facing page 32 of Vol. xxvi. of the Journal of the Anthropological Institute, by whose permission it is here reproduced.

III.

NOTE ON SKULL MEASUREMENTS.

There are probably not much over 100 Borneo skulls altogether in all the European collections. The measurements prove wide diversity in form; nearly one half of the skulls already measured are dolichocephalic, the other half being about equally divided between the meso- and brachy-cephalic forms. These cranial differences are on a par with the differences in outward physique, customs and language which we meet throughout the length and breadth of the country, proving the mixed origin of the native races both as regards inter-marriage amongst themselves and union with foreigners. The following are the names of some of the chief students who have given attention to the study of Borneo skulls: Prof. Sir Wm. Flower, Jos. Barnard Davis, Professor Virchow, MM. Quatrefages and Hamy, Dr. Mehnert, Dr. Montano, Dr. Swaving, Dr. Dusseau and Dr. Van der Hoeven. For particulars, see Bibliography. The Leiden Collection of skulls does not seem to have been measured, and I have not been able to get any reply to my request for information about it from the Professor in charge. Since Prof. Sir William Flower wrote his catalogue, two specimens have been added to the collection of the Royal College of Surgeons' Museum, and I am indebted to the courtesy of Prof. C. Stewart, F.R.S., for the following measurements of them.

733A. *Skull from North Borneo.*

C 500. L 179. B 125. Bi 698. H 138. Hi 771. BN 104.
Nw 26. Ow 38. Oi 1000. Ca 1380.

743A. *Skull of "Ukiet," Interior of Borneo.*

C 493. L 172. B 135. Bi 785. H 136. Hi 791. BN 100.
BA 89. Ai. 890. Nh 49. Nw 24. Ni 490. Ow 37.
Oh 33. Oi 892. Ca 1375.

Sir Wm. Flower appears to have been the only osteologist who has measured the skeleton of a native of Borneo.

IV.
BIBLIOGRAPHY.

Space prevents me inserting the long list of excellent works relating to the natives of Dutch Borneo. It is therefore with regret I omit the names of a host of such authorities as Horner, Henrici, Grabowsky, Kater, Kühr, Piton, Schadee, Schmeltz, Tromp, Von Gaffron, Von Dewal, and numerous others.

ANON.—Practice of the Native Court at Sibu for Divorce and Matrimonial Causes. 8vo. 9pp. Appendix i., 4 pp. Appendix ii., 1 p. Sarawak: Printed at the Sarawak Gazette Office by D. J. J. Rodriguez.

BASTIAN, A.—Indonesien oder die Inseln des Malayischen Archipel. Part iv. Borneo and Celebes. Berlin. 8vo. 1889. pp. 1-38 deal with Borneo.

BECCARI, O.—" Cenno di un viaggio a Borneo." " Boll. d. Soc. Geogr. Ital." 1868.

BEECKMAN, DANIEL, *Capt.*—A Voyage to and from the Island of Borneo. . . Lond. sm. 8vo. pp. xviii. + 205. 1718.

BELCHER, EDWD., *Sir.*—Narrative of the Voyage of H.M.S. Samarang in surveying the Islands of the Eastern Archipelago. 8vo. 1848. 2 vols.

BETHUNE, C. D., *Capt. R.N.*—Notes on Part of the West Coast of Borneo. Jour. Roy. Geog. Soc. xvi., 1846., p. 294.

BOCK, CARL.—The Head Hunters of Borneo: A Narrative of Travel up the Mahakkam and down the Barito. Royal 8vo. London, 1882. (2nd Ed.) pp. xvi. + 344.

BOYLE, FRED.—Adventures among the Dyaks of Borneo. 8vo. London, 1865. pp. xii. + 324.

BREITENSTEIN, HEINR., *Dr.*—Aus Borneo. Mitth. d. K.K. Geogr. Ges. in Wien. xxviii. 1885. pp. 193 and 242.

BROOKE, CHAS. (*now His Highness Rajah*).—Ten Years in Sarawak. With an Introduction by H. H. The Rajah Sir James Brooke. 2 vols., 8vo. London, 1866.

—— —— Hints to Young Out Station Officers. 7 pp., 8vo. [Sarawak.]

BRITISH NORTH BORNEO HERALD.—Sandaken, 1882 *et seq.*

BURBIDGE, F. W., *F.L.S.*—The Gardens of the Sun; or a naturalist's journal on the mountains and in the forests and the swamps of Borneo and the Sulu Archipelago. London, 1880. 8vo. pp. xx. + 364.

BUSK, GEO., *F.R.S.*—Note on Collection of Bones from Caves in Borneo, referred to in Mr. Everett's Report. Proc. Roy. Soc. No. 203; 1880. pp. 10-12.

CHALMERS, WM., *Rev., of the Sarawak Mission.*—Some Account of the Land Dyaks of Upper Sarawak. Reprinted from the Occasional Papers of St. Augustine's College, Canterbury. Singapore: Printed at the Mission Press. 4to. pp. 12 No date. *See* Grant.

CHAMBERS, WM., *Bishop.*—A Vocabulary of English, Malay, and Sarawak Dyaks. 70 pp., 8vo. Canterbury: Printed at St. Augustine's College Press. 1861.

CLUTTERBUCK, WALTER J.—About Ceylon and Borneo. sm. 8vo.. London, 1891.
COLLINGWOOD, CUTHBERT, M.A., M.B.—Rambles of a Naturalist on the Shores and Waters of the China Seas. Being observations in Natural History during a Voyage to China, Formosa, Borneo, &c., made in Her Majesty's Vessels, 1866-67. London, 1868. 8vo.
CROCKER, WM. M. (*late Chief Resident of Sarawak and late Governor of Brit. N. Borneo*).—Notes on Sarawak and Northern Borneo. Proc. Roy. Geogr. Soc. 1881. p. 193. With Map.
—— —— Exhibition of Ethnological Objects from Borneo. Jour. Anthrop. Inst., 1886, xv., p. 424.
—— —— *See* Von Donop.
DALRYMPLE, ALEX.—A Plan for Extending the Commerce of this Kingdom and of the East India Company. 8vo. pp. iv. + 111. London, 1769. [Advertisement added 1771.]
DALTON, JOHN.—*See* Moore.
DAVIS, JOS. BARNARD, *M.D.*—Thesaurus Craniorum. Catalogue of the Skulls of the Various Races of Man in the Collection of J.B.D. . . . London. Printed for the Subscribers 1867. pp. xviii. + 374.
—— —— Supplement to Thesaurus Craniorum. . . . London. Printed for the Subscribers 1875. pp. x + 90.
DE CRESPIGNY, C. A. C., *Lieut., R.N.*—Proposed Exploration of Borneo. Proc. Roy. Geogr. Soc. Vol. 1. 1857. p. 205.
—— —— Notes on Borneo:—Ascent of the River Limbang; Visit to Maludu Bay. Proc. Roy. Geogr. Soc. Vol. 2. 1858. p. 342.
—— —— Reisen im nördlichen Theile der Insel Borneo (Aug., 1857). Berl. Zeitschr. f. Erdkunde. Neue Folge v. 325.
—— —— On Northern Borneo. Proc. Roy. Geogr. Soc., xvi. 1872. p. 171.
—— —— On the Rivers Mukah and Oyah in Borneo. Proc. Roy. Geogr. Soc., xvii. 1873. p. 133.
—— —— On the Milanows of Borneo. Jour. Anthrop. Inst. 1876. v. p. 34.
DENISON, NOEL (*Assistant Resident, Upper Sarawak*).—Jottings made during a tour amongst the Land Dyaks of Upper Sarawak, Borneo, during the year 1874. Singapore. Printed at the Mission Press. 4to. pp. 52
—— —— Journal from 29 April to 25 May, 1872, when on a trip from Sarawak to Meri on the N.W. Coast of Borneo in the Brunei Territory. Jour. Straits Asiatic Soc., No. 5., pp. 171-188.
DE WINDT, H.—On the Equator. London. pp. viii. + 142, sm. 8vo. [1881.?]
DOTY, E., and POHLMAN, W. J.—Tour in Borneo, from Sambas, through Montrado to Pontianak, and the adjacent settlements of Chinese and Dayaks, during the autumn of 1838. Chinese Repository, viii., p. 283. 1839.
DUNN, E., *Rev.*—The Dyaks of Sarawak. Jour. Manch. Geogr. Soc., iii., 1887. p. 221.
EARL, G. W.—Narrative of a Voyage from Singapore to the West Coast of Borneo, in the Schooner Stamford, in the year 1834, with an account of a journey to Montradok, the capital of a Chinese colony in possession of the principal Gold Mines. Jour. Roy. Asiatic Soc., iii., p. 1.
—— —— The Native Races of the Indian Archipelago—Papuans. pp. xiv. + 239. London, 1853.
EVERETT, A. HART.—Report on the Exploration of the Bornean Caves in 1878-9. Proc. Roy. Soc., No. 203, 1880, pp. 1-12. The two human jaws found are referred to by Prof. Bask in Jour. Anthrop. Inst., I., p. 212, and the stone implement is figured by Col. Lane Fox in Proc. Ethnol. Soc., Nov. 8th, 1870, p. xxxix. Reprinted in Jour. Straits Asiatic Soc., No. 3, 273.

FLOWER, WM. HY., *Sir, F.R.S., K.C.B.*—Catalogue of Specimens illustrating the Osteology and Dentition of Vertebrated Animals. Part I. Man. 8vo. London, 1879.

FORBES, S., *Lieut.*—Five Years in China, 1842-7; with an Account of the Islands Labuan and Borneo. 8vo. 1848.

FORREST, THOS., *Capt.*—A Voyage to New Guinea and the Moluccas, from Balambangan [an island off N. coast of Borneo]. 2nd Ed. London, 1780. 4to. pp. xxiii. + 388. Maps and Plates.

GABELENTZ, H. C. VON DER.—Grammatik der Dajak Sprache. 8vo. Leipzic. pp. 48. 1852.

GRANT, C. T. C.—A Tour amongst the Dyaks of Sarawak, Borneo, in 1858. With additional notes up to 1864. London, 1864. pp. 198. Contains 2 chapters on the Dyak language by W. Chalmers.

GROENVELDT, W. P.—Notes on the Malay Archipelago and Malacca. Compiled from Chinese Sources. Batavia and The Hague, 1876. Large 8vo., pp. 144. (pp. 101-117 deal with Borneo.)

HAMY, E. T. *Prof.*—Les Negritos à Borneo. Bull. d. l. Soc. d'Anthr., 2e Ser., xi. 1876. pp. 113.

HARDELAND, AUG., *D. Th., D. Philog.*—Versuch einer Grammatick der Dajakschen Sprache. 8vo. Amsterdam, 1858. pp. viii. + 374.

—— —— Dajáksch-Deutches Wörterbuch. Imp. 8vo. Amsterdam, 1859. pp. viii. + 638.

HATTON, FRANK, *F.C.S.*—Diary of F. H., Esq., during a Mineral Exploring Journey up the Labuk River and overland to Kudat. [London, 1882.] 4to. pp. 20.

—— —— North Borneo. Explorations and Adventures on the Equator, with biographical sketch and notes by Joseph Hatton, and preface by Sir Walter Medhurst. London, 1885. 8vo. pp. xvi. + 342.

HEIN, A. R., *Prof.*—Die bildenden Künste bei den Dayaks auf Borneo. Vienna, 1890. pp. xiv. + 228. 8vo. (Incorporates his papers "Ornamente der Dajaks" and "Malerei and Technische Künste bei den Dayaks.")

HELMS, LUDVIG WERNER.—Pioneering in the Far East. . . . London. 8vo. 1882. pp. viii. + 408.

HORNADAY, W. T.—Two years in the Jungle. The experiences of a hunter and naturalist in India, Ceylon, the Malay Peninsula and Borneo. 8vo. New York, 1888. pp. xxii. + 512.

HORSBURGH, A. *Rev.*—Sketches in Borneo. Anstruther. Printed by L. Russell. 1858. 8vo.

HOSE, CHAS.—A Descriptive Account of the Mammals of Borneo. London. 8vo. 1893. pp. 78. Illustrated. Map.

—— —— A Journey up the Baram River to Mount Dulit and the Highlands of Borneo. Geogr. Jour. i. 1893. p. 1.

—— —— The Natives of Borneo. Jour. Anthr. Inst. xxiii. 1894. p. 156.

HOUGHTON, EDWARD P., *M.D.*—On the Land Dayas of Upper Sarawak, Sentah, Lihoy, Letung and Quoss. Memoirs of the Anthropological Society, iii. p. 195.

HUPÉ, KARL *Rev.*.—Niemeyers Neuere Geschichte der Evangelischer Missions Anstalten, Halle. 88th to 95th part. Vol. viii. 1842 to 1848.

HUNT, J.—*See* Moore.

KEPPEL, HY. *Hon., Captain, R.N.*—The Expedition to Borneo of H.M.S. Dido for the Suppression of Piracy, with Extracts from the Journal of James Brooke, Esq., of Sarawak, now Agent for the British Government in Borneo. 2 vols., 8vo. London, 1846. (First Edition.)

KEPPEL, HY. *Hon. Capt., R.N.*—A Visit to the Indian Archipelago in H.M.S. Meander, with portions of the private journal of Sir Jas. Brooke, K.C.B. 2 vols., 8vo. London, 1853.
KESSEL, O. VON.—Ueber die Volkstämme Borneo's. Zeitschr. f. Allgem. Erdkunde. New Series iii. 1857.
KÜKENTHAL, W. *Prof.*—Forschungsreise in den Molukken und in Borneo. 4to., pp. xii. + 321. Frankfurt a.M. [Beautifully Illustrated.]
LABUAN, *Bishop of.*—*See* MacDougall.
LANGENHOFF, J. J. *Abbé.*—In the 11th Séance of Congrès International des Orientalistes, 1st Sess. Paris, 1873. I., pp. 502, 505, *et seq.*

[The Author (p. 513) throws doubt on Madame Pfeiffer's travels, but brings no evidence to support his doubt. He says (p. 505) he was the first to get to the centre of the island, ignoring Schwaner, Horner, Henrici, Müller, &c. He says (*ibid*) he left from the Dutch establishment from the east and from the west, but does not say how far he got. His statements must be accepted with caution.]

LEYDEN, *Dr.*—*See* Moore.
LITTLE, R. M.—Report on a Journey from Tuaran to Kiau and ascent of Kinabalu Mountain. Journ. Straits Asiat. Soc., No. 19 (1888), p. 1.
LOBSCHIED, W. *Rev.*—The Religion of the Dayaks. Collected and translated by . . . 8vo. Hongkong, 1866. 3rd ed. pp. 12 + 12.
LOGAN, J. R., *F.R.S.*—The Journal of the Indian Archipelago and Eastern Asia. Singapore. 8vo. 1847-62.
LOW, BROOKE.—Catalogue of the Brooke-Low Collection in Borneo. 13pp. 8vo. Kuching, Sarawak. Printed at the Sarawak Gazette Office by D. J. J. Rodriguez.
LOW, HUGH SIR, *K.C.B.*—Sarawak, its Inhabitants and Productions. 8vo. London, 1848. pp. xxiv. + 416.
MCDOUGALL, F. F., *Bishop of Labuan.*—On the Wild Tribes of the N.W. Coast of Borneo. Trans. Ethnol. Soc. ii., 1863. p. 24.
―― *Mrs.*—Sketches of our Life at Sarawak. 8vo. Lond., 1882.
MARTIN, R. BIDDULPH, *M.A.*—Exhibition of a Fire Syringe from Borneo. Jour. Anthrop. Inst., xx. 1891. p. 331.
MARRYAT, FRANK, *Midshipman H.M.S. Samarang.*—Borneo and the Indian Archipelago. 4to. London, 1848. pp. viii. + 232.
MEYER, A. B.—Uber Künstlich Deformirte Schädel von Borneo und Mindanao. Leipzig and Dresden. 1881. 4to., pp. 36.
―― ―― Uber die Namen Papua, Dajak, and Alfuren. 8vo., p. 18. Wien, 1882.
MEHNERT, ERNST, *M.D.*—Catalog der Anthropologishen Sammlung des Anatomischen Instituts der Universität Strassburg i. E. Brunswick, 1893. 4to. pp. 119.
MIKLUCHO-MACLAY, N. VON.—Uber die Künstliche perforatio penis bei den Dajaks auf Borneo. Perforatio glandis penis bei den Dajaks auf Borneo und analoge Sitten auf Celebes und auf Java. Zeitschr. f. Ethnologie. Berlin, 1876. p. 22.
MOORE, J. H.—Notices of the Indian Archipelago and adjacent countries. 4to. Singapore, 1837, and Appendix, 18... Contains: John Dalton's various papers on Borneo, especially the Essay on the Dyaks of Borneo, pp. 40-54; Dr. Leyden's Sketch of Borneo in Appendix, p. 93; J. Hunt's Sketch of Borneo, or Pulo Kalamanton, communicated in 1812 to Sir T. S. Raffles.
MONTANO, J., *Dr.*—Etude sur les crânes Boughis et Dayaks, du Muséum d'Hist. Nat. Paris. 1878. 8vo. pp. 7'.
MOTLEY, JAMES, and DILLWYN, LEWIS LLEWELYN.—Contributions to the Natural History of Labuan and the Adjacent Coasts of Borneo. 8vo. London, 1854.

MÜLLER, S.—Rapport concernant une partie de la côte méredionale et des districts de l'interieur de Borneo. (Chap. v. of Vol. ii. of Temminck's work).
MUNDY, RODNEY, Capt. R.N.—Narrative of Events in Borneo and Celebes down to the occupation of Labuan. From the Journals of James Brooke, Esq. Together with a Narrative of the operations of H.M.S. Iris. London. 2 vols. 8vo. 1848.
NORTH, MARIANNE.—Recollections of a Happy Life. Edited by Mrs. Symonds. London. 2 vols. 8vo. 1892.
PERHAM, J., Ven. Archdeacon.—The Song of the Dyak Head Feast. Jour. Straits Asiatic Soc., No. 1, p. 123.
—— —— A Sea Dyak Tradition of the Deluge and Consequent Events. ibid, No. 3, p. 289.
—— —— Klieng's War Raid to the Skies; a Dyak Myth. ibid, No. 8, p. 265.
—— —— Sea Dyak Religion. ibid, No. 5, p. 213.
—— —— —— —— ibid, No. 5, p. 287.
—— —— Petara or Sea Dyak Gods. ibid, No. 4, p. 133.
PFEIFFER, IDA.—Meine Zweite Weltreise. 4 pts. small 8vo. Vienna, 1856.
PIGAFETTA.—The First Voyage round the World by Magellan. Hakluyt Society's Publications. Vol. lii. London, 1874.
PRYER, W. B. (*Resident at Sandakan*).—Diary of a Trip up the Kina-Batangan River. [London, 1881.] 4to. pp. 14.
—— —— On the Natives of British North Borneo. Jour. Anthrop. Inst. xvi. 1887. p. 229.
—— ADA (Mrs. W. B.)—A Decade in Borneo. 8vo. London, 1894. pp. iv. + 198.
POSSEWITZ, THEODOR, Dr.—Borneo: Its Geology and Mineral Resources. Translated from the German by Fred. H. Hatch, Ph. D. 8vo. London, 1892. pp. xxxii. + 495.
POHLMAN, W. J.—*See* Doty, E.
RADERMACHER, J. C. M.—Beschrijving van het eiland Borneo. Verhandelingen v.h. Bataviaasch Genoots. d. Kunst on wetens. ii. 1780.
RETZIUS, ANDERS.—Ethnologische Scriften nach dem Tode des Vervassers gesammelt. 4to. Stockholm, 1864. [pp. 143-144 relate to Borneo.]
ST. JOHN, SPENCER, Sir, G.C.M.G. (*H.M. Consul General in the Gt. Island of Borneo*).— Life in the Forests of the Far East. London, 1862. 2 vols. 8vo. (1st Ed.)
—— —— Wild Tribes of the N. W. Coast of Borneo. Trans. Ethnol. Soc. ii. 1863. p. 232.
ST. JOHN, J. G.—Views in Borneo. 4 pts., Roy. 4to. London, 1847.
SARAWAK GAZETTE.—Sarawak, 1870 *et seq.*
SCHWANER, C. A. L. M. Dr.—Borneo. Amsterdam. 2 vols. 8vo. 1853-54.
SKERTCHLY, SYDNEY B. J.—On Fire Making in North Borneo. Jour. Anthrop. Inst. xix. 1890. p. 445.
—— —— On some Borneo Traps. Jour. Anthrop. Inst. xx. 1891. p. 211.
SWAVING, C.—Eerste bijdrage tot de kennis der schedels van volkon in den indischen archipel. Natuurkundig Tijdschr. v. Nederl. Indie. xxxi. 7 serie. Deel i. Aflevering 1-3. Tables viii. and xiv.
SWETTENHAM, F. A.—Comparative Vocabulary of the Dialects of some of the Wild Tribes inhabiting the Malayan Peninsula, Borneo, &c. Jour. Straits Asiatic Soc. No. 3. June, 1880. p. 125.
TAMAT, J.—Vocabulary of English, Malay and Melano. 8vo. Sarawak, 1867.
TEMMINCK, C. J. *Chevalier.*—Coup d'Oeil Général sur les Possessions Neerlandaises dans l'Inde Archipelagique. 3 vols., 8vo. 1842-1849.

TREACHER, W. H., *C.M.G.. M.A. Oxon.*—British Borneo: Sketches of Brunai, Sarawak, Labuan and North Borneo. Journ. of Straits Asiatic Soc. No. 20, 1889, p. 15; No. 21, 1890, p. 19.
UFFORD, IKR. W. QUARLES VAN.—Something about the Land Dyaks of Sarawak. Reprinted from "Tydschrift v.h. Aardrijks. Genootchap." Vol. v. 2 Edit. Trans. from the Dutch by S. Batten. Batavia, 1881. 4to. pp 6.
VAN DER HOEVEN, F.—Catalogus Craniorum divers gentium. Lugduni Bavarum. 1860.
VETH, P. J.—Borneo's Wester-Afdeeling. 2 vols., 8vo. Zaltbommel, 1854-1856.
VIRCHOW, RUD. *Prof.*—Drei Abgeschnittene Schädel von Dayaks. Verhand d. Berl. Gesell. f. Anthrop., &c. June, 1885. p. 270.
—— —— Schädel von Niassern und Dajaken. *ibid*, July, 1892. p. 433.
VON DONOP, L. S.—Diary of travelling through North Borneo or "New Ceylon." The Sabah Government. 4to., pp 12. Ceylon Observer Office, Jan. 3, 1883.
—— —— Official Despatch covering Mr. v. D.'s Report on Silam, dated 13th Feb., 1883. 8vo., pp 4.
—— —— Diary of L. S. von D. during a trip from Papar to Kimanis via Tambounan, Lobo, and Limbawan. London, 1882. 4to., pp. 14.
WALLACE, ALFRED RUSSEL, *F.R.S.*—The Malay Archipelago. Cr. 8vo. London, 1869. 2 vols.
—— —— Notes of a Journey up the Sadong River, in North West Borneo. Proc. Roy. Geogr. Soc., i., 1857, p. 193.
WEBSTER, H. A.—Article, 'Borneo,' in Encyclopædia Britannica. 9th ed. 1876. iv., p. 55.
WHITEHEAD, JOHN.—Exploration of Mount Kina Balu, North Borneo. London, 1893. Fol. xi. + 317.
WITTI, F.—Diary of F. Witti, Esq., during an Excursion in North Borneo, from Marudu Bay to Papar, by the Eastern Slopes of Mount Kina Balu. London, 1880. 4to. pp. 23.
—— —— Diary of F. Witti, Esq., during an Excursion Across North Borneo, from Maruda Bay to Sandakan. London, 1881. 4to. pp. 35. Map.
—— —— British North Borneo. Diary of F. Witti. 4to. pp. 31. Printed at the Singapore and Straits Printing Office (late Mission Press). 1883?
ZANNETTI.—Di un cranio Daiacco. Archiv. per l'Antrop. ii. 1872.

INDEX.

ADAT (see GOVERNMENT).

AGE (see PHYSIQUE).

AGRICULTURE.

Auguries, see Omens
Bambu used as rice stores, 409; private rights in young, 418
Barns, 409, A190, 202, 203
Beburong, 397
Berobat, 403
Bigamy, 401
Biliongs, 399
Birdnesters poor farmers, 422
Children weeding, 405
Chinese influence, 422
Clearing land, 398, 399
Coconuts, 418
Communal property, 419, 420
Dangau, 405
Dibbling, 408
Disputes, fruit trees, 418; land, 420; fighting with sticks, 420
Divination, see Omens
Fallow, 400
Famines, 421; famine foods, A201
Farm houses, 403
Feasts, agricultural, 411; see Harvest
Fences, building, 402; embankments, 421
Floods, 422
Fruit trees, 417; durian, 417; coconuts, 418; abundance, 418; destruction, 418; *Katio* nuts, 418; disputes, 418; private v. communal property, 419, 420
Gardens, 407
Harvest, 76, 82, 408; reaping knife, 408, 409; Land Dyak feasts, 412; Kenniah, 415; Kayan, 415; food wasted at feasts, 421, on the Barito, A173
Hill cultivation, 400
Idols (?) on farm paths, 401
Incest, 401
Inheritance of lands, 419, 420
Insects, 403, A201
Irrigation, 406, A209
Jungle, new *versus* old, 400
Land, tenure, 419; sales, 419; division on death, 419; disputes, 420; communal, 420; rents, 420
Langkau, 403

AGRICULTURE (*continued*).

Mortars, rice, 409, 410, A191
Neglect, A163
Numbar, 406
Oil, 418
Omens, 194, 397; time wasted on, 421, 422
Orang Kaya decides on new grounds, 397
Padi, see Rice
Parangs, 399
Pests, 403, A201
Pleiades, 400
Ploughing, 422, A209
Potatoes treated as marbles, 408
Prayers for heat, 401
Property, in fruit trees, 418; in land, 418
Rats, 403, A201; snaring, 443
Rents, 420
Residence, shifting, 400
Rice, general operation, 402; varieties, 406; doctorings, 411; obtaining soul of, 413; women cleaners, 410
Rights of tenants, 420
Sacred farm flower, 416, ii. 43; plant, A202; tree, A202
Sacrifices, 402; harvest, 412
Sago lands, 91; cultivation and manufacture, 422
Search for new lands, 397
Sowing, 402
Stars, farming regulated by, 307, 400
Storage, 409, A190, 202, 203
Sundial, 400; posts, shadow how measured, A209
Tabu, 401, 402; breaking a, 402; to drive off rats, 403; fruit tree, 419
Tenant rights, 420
Threshing, 409
Tobacco, 408
Weeds, 400; weeding, 405, 418
Winnowing, 409
Women padi cleaners, 410

AMOKING (see CHARACTER).

AMUSEMENTS (see CHILDBIRTH, DAILY LIFE).

ARCHÆOLOGY (see also WRITING and NEGRITOES).
Beads, ii. 282
Bull, native dread of a stone, ii. 279

Index.

ARCHÆOLOGY (*continued*).

Cave, explorations, ii. 280; not used as sepultures, ii. 282; negative results of explorations, ii. 284; artistically carved coffins in, A211
Chinese coins, ii. 280; pottery, ii. 280
Crockery, ii. 279
Everett's explorations, ii. 280
Figure on sandstone rock, ii. 280
Hindu relics, ii. 279, 280 (and note).
Human bones in caves, ii. 282
" In the days of the Hindus," ii. 279
Javanese necklace, 339; era, ii. 283
Ornaments of gold, ii. 279, 280, 282
Paving tiles of concrete, ii. 280
Pottery, ii. 280; Chinese, ii. 280; in caves, ii. 282, A211
Stone celt in river bed, ii. 280, 281, 302; curved stone, ii. 282; celt of doubtful origin, ii. 283
Tumuli containing jars, ii. 286 (note)

BOATING.

Bandongs (Kalaka fish boats), ii. 248
Bark canoes, ii. 254
Barongs (dug outs), 455; ii. 249
Boats, 57, 59, ii. 246; keel laying ceremony, ii. 246; building, 364, ii. 247; skill, A163; builders, 47, 76, ii. 252
Bore (river), ii. 252
Kajangs (awnings), ii. 248
Nails not used, ii. 247, 254
Paddles, ii. 248, 249, 250; paddling, 52, 83, 84
Planks, ii. 247, 250, 253
Poling, ii. 254
Seas, rough, ii. 248; long voyages on, ii. 249
Sickness boats, 283, 284, A208
Soul boats, 144, 145
Speed, ii. 249, 253
Surf running, ii. 250
Taking to pieces, ii. 248
Tuba tied on ankles, ii. 248

BORNEO.

BORNEO, extent of (xv.); note on British settlements (xv.); tribes of, 37

BROOKE.

BROOKE, Sir Charles, work done by (xviii.)
BROOKE, Sir James, high character of (xvi.); reverence for, 65; makes the division of Land and Sea Dyaks, 42

CANNIBALISM.

Birth, to feast at, ii. 221
Body eaten, ii. 217, 219
Brain, ii. 218, 221
Children, ii. 220
Children partake, ii. 217; do not, 222
Cooking, ii. 219
Courage, to obtain, ii. 145, 218, 220, 222

CANNIBALISM (*continued*).

Enemies eaten, ii. 127, 220; to strike terror into, ii. 220
Feasts at, ii. 220
Food wanted for, ii. 127, 221
Forehead, ii. 220, 221
Funeral at, ii. 221
Hand, ii. 219, 221
Heart eaten, ii. 217, 220
Knee, ii. 221
Leg muscles, ii. 218
Marriage, to feast at, ii. 221
Palms of hands, ii. 217, 221
Practise denied, ii. 217, 218, 223
Soles of feet, ii. 217
Statements doubtful, ii. 220, 221
Tongue, ii. 218
Women partake, ii. 217; do not, 222

CHARACTER.

Affection, 75, 86; conjugal, 129
Amiability, 65, 91
Amoking, 95
Amusements, 65, 70, 82, A163; *see* CHILDBIRTH and DAILY LIFE
Apathy, 66, 67, 68
Bajaus, 59
Beggars, 65, 69, 83, A163
Bravery, 92, A162
Brooke, Sir James, reverence for, 65
"Characters," 67, 69, 71, 74, 75, 76, 77, 78, 81, 83, 94, 129
Curiosity, 66, 68, 69, 81
Curious questions, 83
Curious reasoning, 80
Concealment of feelings, 73, A162
Conceit, 71, 91
Conservativeness, 74, 83
Conversion, objection to, 75; difficulties, 75; Mahomedan, 75
Courage, 83
Cruelty, A162
Curses, 86; fine for, A187
Dancing, *see* RELIGION
Decency, sense of, 92
Dirt, 93, 366
Disputes through accident, 78; general, 88; Murut, 94
Election, 72
Energy, 87, 92, 195
Games, *see* Amusements
Generosity, 67
Gratitude, 65, 74, 95
Greediness, 92
Guests must not come to harm, 95
Hair thrown in fire causes sickness, 288
Head-slapping, A206
Help in sickness, 85
Honesty, 65, 66, 67, 68, 69, 73, 81, 82, 92, 93
Hospitality, 65, 67, 72, 73, 86, 87, 91, 92, 94, 95, 117

CHARACTER (*continued*).
Humour, 83
Ignorance, 74
Imitativeness, 80
Indecent language, 86, 92
Indifference to others' suffering, 92, 94
Internal satisfaction, 287, 355 ; communing with dead, A172
Klakar, 77
Lanuns, 59
Laughter, 71, 72, 75, 81, 83, 85, 93
Learning to read and write, 69, 91
Looking-glasses, 71, 91, 93
Lover and the chignon, 84
Lying, 87, 92
Memory, aids to, 77, 356 ; 84
Mental capacity, 65, 68, 69, 133, A163; stationary on arrival at puberty, 83
Miraculous, fondness for the, 85
Modesty, 133
Morals, 66, 68, 76, 94, 117, 131, 132, 133, A162, 163, 173 ; low state of, A199
Murders, 88, 89, 100
Numbers, favourite, 231
Oratory, 71, 78
Pantuns (riddles), 70, 368
Peace, paying for, 70
Politeness, 68, 69, 74, 81, 82, 92
Progress, 65, disappointing, 70 ; capacity for, 73, 80, 82 ; when young, 83 ; Dusuns, 91 ; Muruts, 94
Repartee, 80
Rhyming, 84 ; *see* MUSIC: Singing
School, 82
Shyness, 48, 50, 69, 81
Smallpox, funny scene after, 81
Sociability, 364
Sports and games, 54, 65, 104
Stone-throwing, 72
Suicide, 218
Sympathetic help, in childbirth, 98 ; in war, ii. 104
Tabu, to mention health, 288 ; to praise food, 288
Talkativeness, 52, 65
Temper, 67, 77, 80, 82, 85, 128, 288
Temperateness, 76
Theft, 86, 90, 92, 93
Treachery, Kayans, 87 ; Muruts, 94
Ulit, *see* Tabu
Vaunting or *bunkit*, 70
Vocabulary making, 71, 93
Weeping, unknown, A162 ; at funerals (*see* DISPOSAL OF THE DEAD)
White man, first visit of, 66, 68, 81, 82, 92, 249, ii. 206 ; not wanted, ii. 100
Wit, 83, 86
Women, characteristics of, 85, 92
Women, strange objection between men and, 75, 76, 141

CHILDBIRTH AND CHILDREN.
Abortion, *see* SLAVES
Adoption, 102
Amusements, cat's cradle, 366 ; prisoner's base, 366 ; trial of strength, 367 ; leg swinging, 367 ; natural concert, 367 ; jumping, 367 ; wrestling, 367 ; finger trials, 367 ; spill catching tops, 367 ; whittling, 367 ; football, 367 ; swings, 367 ; greased poles, 368 ; slapping, 368 ; *pantuns*, 70, 368
Barrenness, 102
Blacksmith's child, a, 98
Boys preferred, 10
Cannibalism, ii. 217, 220, 221
Ceremony at first bath, 101
Childbearing age, 104
Chorus, 115, 249
Couvade, 97, 98, A210
Cradle, 99, 100
Death in childbirth, 101
Diet, 97
Difficulty in birth, 98 ; Manang's sympathetic help, 98
Dirt, 366
Dress, 99, 100
Education, 103, A183
Families, size of, 104
Feasts, 102
Girls preferred, 103
Hair thick, 101
Hands, 360
Idiots, 101
Infanticide, 100, 101, 311
Life, 359, 365, 366
Midwife, 97
Miscarriage, 100, 101
Naming, 101
Parental affection, 102, 103, 104, A163
Parturition, 98 ; easy, 99
Pet names, 101
Population, question of, 104-106
Presents, 102
Purification, 102
Sacrifices, 101
School, love for, 82
Shaving, 101
Suckling, 101
Tabu at birth, 97, 98
Twins, 100
Uterogestation, 100
Wallace, A. R., on the population, 105
Weeding farms, 405

COLOUR.
Black used also to designate darkness, ii. **277**
Colour-blindness doubtful, ii. **277**
Confusion of some colours, ii. **277**
Dyeing, ii. 29, 35, 37, 50, 90
Favourite colours, A163

COLOUR (continued).
Good sense of colour, ii. 277
Nomenclature deficient, ii. 277
Pakatans perhaps colour-blind, ii. 277
Table of colour names, ii. 278

CURIOUS MOUNDS.
Added to by every passer by, 357
Added to to prevent sickness, 358
Commemorate a great event, 358
Lie forgotten but heaps still added to, 358
Raised after tabu in consequence of a lie, 357
Raised near scene of murder, 358

DAILY LIFE.
Aqueducts (panchurs), 361; see HABITATIONS
Blacksmith's work, 364
Classes, A165
Cotton weaving, 364
Daily life, 359-371, A195-196
Dancing, 359; see RELIGION
Domestic animals fed, 363
Domestic quarrels, 85; rare, 366
Early rising, 363
Etiquette, 361, A163
Firewood procured by husband, 363
Gossip, A196
Idleness, 364, 366
Mat making, 365
Meal times, 361, 366; preparation, 363
Men's work, 359, 365, A196
Noise in village, 359
Perspective, no notion of, A210
Rice pounding, 82, 359, 362, 364, 366
Sleep interrupted, 360, 361
Social system, A165
Spinning, 364
Vermin, 72, ii. 24
Washing, remarkable, 262, 363
Water carrying, 361, 365; see HABITATIONS
Women's work, 360, A196; see WOMEN

DISPOSAL OF THE DEAD
Affection for the dead, 141, 203
Baiya presents to the dead, 141, 204; jewels, A199
Bones of the dead, 143, 144, 147, 150, A174
Burials, posts used in, A210
Camphor embalming (sic), 149, 150
Cave burial, 149, A211; see ARCHÆOLOGY
Cemeteries, 135 et seq. 204
Coffins, 139, 146, 147-153, 204, A190-191, 199, 211; see Tombs
Cremation, 135, 138, 161, A199
Customs, 135, 136, 137, 138
Dead, communing with, A172
Death, 79
Dividing property with spirits of the dead, 209
Dread of the dead, 209, 211
"Drinking the bambu," 209

DISPOSAL OF THE DEAD (continued).
Feasts, see Gawai
Final dissolution, 218
Food for the dead, 206
Future life, 71, 141; changes in, 217, 218, 219, A174, 200
Gawai Antu Funeral feast, 143, 207, 209, 210
Hades (or Heaven), see Road to; see Sabaian
Heads for funeral feasts, 158, 207
Human sacrifices, 141, 145, 157-159, 190, ii. 204, 216, A199, 205; see HUMAN SACRIFICES
Jars as bone repositories, 150, 151, 152, A174
Kina balu, the Dusun Hades, 220
Legend of Kadawa, the cock fighter, 211
Lying in state, 143, 202
Malays rifling graves, 141, 204
Messages to the dead, 144, 149, 159; pana, 206, 208, 219
Miniature articles at funeral feasts, 258
Mountains inhabited by the souls, 220, A200
Mourning dress, 138; putting off, 209, 258
Mungkul, 133
Naggar's funeral, 142
Names not mentioned, ii. 275
Paluban's funeral, 145; Milanau, 146; Dutch B., 160
Pantars guides to heaven, A199
Puas, or lament, ii. 268
Road to Hades, 140, 143, 151, 202-204; House of Bubut Bird "bridge of fear," "Hill of Fire," 210, 220; difficulties the souls encounter, A200
Sabaian (Heaven), 140, 141, 203, 206, 207, 218, 219, A170; see Future Life and RELIGION
Sermunguþ, 158; see Messages to the Dead
Sextons, 136, 137
Spirit slaves wait upon spirit masters, 141, 158; ii. 141, A189
Soul boats, 144, 145
Souls, seven (simungut), 218
Stone circle, 150
Sumping conveying trophies to the dead, 207
Sungkup, feast of, 130
Tree burial, 149, 152, 205, A200
Tombs, 146, 152, 205; see Coffins
Wailing at death, 136, 138, 142, 146, 153, 154; before death, 202; professional, 203, 206, 207; at feasts, 258
Widows, 130, A182; names, ii. 274

DOMESTIC ANIMALS.
Birds, 426
Bees, 427
Beeswax for candles, 379
Cats, 425
Cattle, 422, 425; neglected, A163
Dogs, 425; eaten, 390; sacrificed, 402, 425; tabued, 425; antus, 426, A191, unknown, A202; legend of origin of, A202; burial of, A202; see HUNTING and LEGENDS

DOMESTIC ANIMALS (continued).
Goats, 425
Pigs, 424
Poultry, 426

DRESS AND FASHIONABLE DEFORMITY.

Armlets, ii. 39, 40, 41, 44, 45, 71-76, A193
Artocarpus cloth, ii. 35, 37
Bambu corsets, ii. 42; fibre dress, A193
Bark or bast cloth, ii. 35, 37, 50, 53
Beads in dress, 140, ii. 39, 40, 41, 44, 45, 46, 53, 65; varieties preferred, ii. 71; necklace, ii. 71, 72; old and valuable, ii. 76, 282
Beards, 63, ii. 81; tale as to Bukar's beards, 3 (note)
Belt of beads, ii. 44, 45 (*see* hip-lace), A194
Blankets, ii. 35, 36
Brass chains, ii. 40, 42, 46, 47
Brass wire, ii 45, 76 (*see* Corsets)
Breast cloth, ii. 44; A193, 194
Bridal dress, 113; drowning through weight, ii. 42, A204
Buttons, substitute for, ii. 32; 42
Caps, *see* Head Dress
Chawats (waist cloths), ii. 35, 37, 39, 41, 44, 54; as a tribal distinction, 55
China armlets, ii. 74
Cicatrices, ii. 80
Circumcision, ii. 80
Colours, ii. 29, 35, 37, 55
Combs, ii. 59, 63; men combing hair, 64
Copper rings, ii. 47, 67; teeth plates, A194
Corsets, ii. 40, 41, 42, 43, 44, 45; weight of, 45; clasps, 46; how removed, 47, A193
Cotton weaving, 364; gin, ii 31
Dandies, 59
Deformation, no, 99; of head, ii. 70
Depilation, ii. 81
Drowning through heavy ornaments, ii. 42, A204
Dyeing, ii. 29, 35, 37, 50
Earrings, ii. 39, 41, 42, 45; manufacture, 65, 71; gold and silver, 69, 70
Ear mutilations, 55, 57, ii. 66, 67, 68, 69, 70, 81; A193, 194
Ear plugs, ii. 44, 66, 68, 70, 71; A193, 204
Embroidery, ii. 50
Eyebrows, shaving, ii. 44, 81
Eyelashes, pulled out, 81, 296
Feathers, ii. 44; in head-dress, 57
Finger rings, ii. 42
Flowers in hair, ii 43, 62
Girdles, *see* Belts, Hip lace
Girl's dress, ii. 42
Gold ear ornaments, ii. 70; armlets, ii. 75; buttons, ii. 42
Hair, cutting, ii 58; length of, ii. 58, 59, 62, 63, 64.

DRESS AND FASHIONABLE DEFORMITY (*continued*).
Hairdressing *see* Head-dress
Hairpins, ii. 44, 58, 59, 65
Hawkbells, ii. 74
Head deformations, ii. 79
Head-dresses, ii. 39, 40, 41, 44, 57, 59, 60, 61, 62, 63, 64, 65; in mourning, 58; A193, 194
Head shaving, ii. 59, 62, 63, 64, 81
Hip lace, ii. 51, 55; *see* Belts
Knife, ii. 39
Jackets, ii. 40, 42, 48; like waistcoats, ii. 49; making, 31, 32, 37
Lamba cloth, ii. 35, 37, 45
Land Dyaks, 49
Lead rings, ii. 45, 69, 70
Leglets, ii. 40, 41, 42, 44, 45, 71-76; A193
Lintong, see Corsets
Looms, ii. 30
Love of finery, ii. 41
Mat seats (tail-flap), 5, ii. 55, 56
Mourning petticoats, ii. 53; head-dress, ii. 58
Moustachios, 59
Necklets, ii. 39, 40, 41, 44, 45, 71, 76
Petticoats, 29, 40, 42, 45; how suspended, ii. 40, 51; in mourning, ii. 53; open at side, A193, 194
Poison-coated trinkets, ii. 71
Polished stones, ii. 51
Rotan corsets, ii. 42
Sacred flower, ii. 43; *see* AGRICULTURE
Saladan, see Corsets
Screws in ear buttons, ii. 69
Sea Dyak, 55
Seams, hems, &c., ii. 38
Sexual mutilations, ii. 80
Shells, ii. 41, 47, 51, 71, 72, 73, 74, 75
Silver coins, ii. 46, 51; teeth plates, A192
Silver, ear ornaments, ii. 70; chains, ii. 71; armlets, ii. 75
Silversmiths, 69
Spinning wheel, ii. 31
Tapang wood armlets, ii. 71
Tail-flaps (mat seat), 5, ii. 55, 56
Teeth, filing, ii. 44, 77, 78, 79; drilling, 77, 78; blackening, 78; plates, 78, 79, A192, 194; ground down, A192
Teeth of animals, ii. 39; as ear ornaments, 67, 68, 69, 73; A193
Thread and fibres, ii. 31, 37
Tin rings, ii. 47
Tribal badges, ii. 32, 33, 34; chawats as, ii. 55
Want of vanity, ii. 93
Weaving, ii. 29, 31, 39
Weight of ornaments, ii. 42, A204

DYAK (THE WORD).

Bampfylde's view, 39
Sir Jas. Brooke on, 39; his division of the people into Land and Sea Dyaks, 42

DYAK (continued).
Everett's view, 40; the word *Iban*, 40
Meyer's remarks, 40
Meaning of the word, probable correct, 42-43
Misuse of the word, 39-43

FEASTS (*see* RELIGION).

FIRE.
Skertchly's exhaustive paper, 371
Fire Syringe 372
　Difficulties with it, 375
　Dyak name and scarcity of, 372
　Kalakas, made by, 372
　Manner of use, 374
　Names and description of parts, 373
　Sakarangs and Sarebus, known by, 373
Fire Drill, 375
　How fire drill not known, the, 377 note
　Description, 375
　Legendary origin of, 301
　Method of operating, 376
　Side groove or notch, the, 375, 376
　Wide distribution, 375
Fire Saw, 377
　Description and method of using, 377
　Flint and tinder struck on bambu, 378
　Forest conflagrations caused by bambu rubbed together in the wind, 378
Bambu and Pottery, 378, A208
　Tinder making, 378
Steel and Flint, 378
Torches, 379
　How light regulated, 379
　Leaf wick, 379
　Made of bambu and dammar, 379
　Strips of resinous wood, 379
Candles, 379; making, A208
Fire not procurable in Hades, 205; fire a "medium," 229; fire appeases hate of birds, 229; messages given to fire, 229; hair burnt in fire causes sickness, 288; "fence of fire," 273; fire kept up during the night, 366; fire place, ii. 1, 3, 10 (and note); firewood, ii. 3; Malay notion of fire, 372; originator of house conflagration condemned to slavery, ii. 213; fines for incendiarism, A187

FISHING
Angling, 460
Barongs (fishing boats), 455
Diving for fish, 456, 462
Drying fish, 455, 456
Floating baits, 461
Hooks, 460
Prawns, 457
Rights, 418, A167
Seines, nets, and scoops, 454-457
Sharks, 455

FISHING (continued).
Spearing, 462
Spins, 461
Sumpitan, 462; *see* SUMPITAN
Tabu, 456
Torchlight, 462
Traps and weirs, 459, 463
Tuba fishing, 458; division of spoil, 459
Weirs, 459, 463

FOOD.
Alligators, 382
Bambu, boiling in, 379; jars, 387
Beans, 407
Beetles, 383
Brine, 385
Buffalo, 383, 385
Cooking: boiling in bambu, 379, 381; in iron pans, 380; roast pigeon, 380; grilled fowl, 380; scalding the feathers, 380; grilling fish, 380; fire place, 380; earthen pots, 381; wild cat, 383; roast rat, 386
Cakes, 385; unknown, A196
Cat, wild, 383
Clay, 385
Cribung, 379
Crocodiles, A208
Cucumber, 379, 383
Curing, 385
Domestic animals seldom eaten, 381, A196
Drinking: arrack, 383; seductive maidens, 391, 392; women not drinkers, 392; drunkards at feasts only, 392; pride in, 392; water, 387, 388; panchurs, 387, ii. 5 (*see* HABITATIONS); bambu jars, 387; at peace-making, 206; fondness for, A163; quarrels while, A163, A202; at marriages, A180; drunkenness incurable; 94
Earth eaten, 385
Famines, 421; foods, A201
Fingers, eating with, 382
Fish, 379, 380, 383, 384
Fowls, 379
Frogs, 382, 383
Fruit, 383
Gourds, 383
Grass, wild, 378
Grubs, 382, 383, 384
High food, 86
Honey, 385
Indian corn, 383, 407
Kaladi, 383, 386
Leaves as plates, 382
Maize, *see* Indian corn
Mice, 383
Monkeys, 380, 382, 383, A208
Mouth washing, 384, 388
Not attacked when eating, 384
Pigeon, 380
Plates, 382

FOOD (continued).
Pork, 379, 385
Pottery, 390
Rats, 383, 385
Rice, 379, 380, 382, 383; mortars, A203
Roots, 386
Salt, 385; manufacture, 386, A202; in food, 385; trade staple, 387; necessity for, 387
Snakes, 382, 383, A208
Spoons, 246
Sugar, 385, 407
Sweet potatoes, 383, 386
Tabued food, vegetables, 388; new rice, 390; goats, 388, 389; ox, buffalo, 388, 389; fowls, butter, 388; fern *paku*, 389; snakes, 389, 390; bears, 389; wild cattle, 389; lizards, 389; tiger cat, 389; fruits, 390; fish with cabbage palm, 390; dogs, 390
Tapioca 383, 421
Toads, 383
Treacle, 385
Vegetables, 379, 380, 381, 407
Vinegar, 385
Waste at feasts, 421
Yams, 379, 383

FOREIGN INFLUENCES.

Alien interference (xix.)
Chinese: Agricultural, 422; cheating, 65, 67; coins, ii. 280; intermarriage, 124; influence, A164; jars, 284, 286; origin of shields (xiii.); pottery, ii. 280
Hindu influence (xiii), A164; "in the days of," ii. 279; relics, ii. 279, 280 (and note)
Indonesian affinities, 63, A209
Javanese era, ii. 283; jars come via Java, ii. 286; Manging's visit to Java, i. 338; musical instrument (xiii); the Siju idol, 340
Malay rifling graves, 141, 204; affinities, 63; affinities in language, ii 273; cheating, 65; derivation of language, ii 269, 271; influences (xiii), A164, oppression (xvi), 67, 70; wheedlings, ii 233
Sulu influence (xiii.)

GOVERNMENT (NATIVE CUSTOM, ADAT).

Adultery, punishment of, ii. 228
Babukid (defiance), ii. 230
Binting Marrow (river *tabu*), A205
Bunkit (vaunting), 70
Capital offences, ii. 225
Chiefs, *see Orang Kaya, Panglima, Pengara, Tuah*
Classes, A165
Councils, ii. 225, 227
Cursing, fines for, A187
Decisions, sensible, ii. 228
Defiance, ii. 230
Destruction of property, ii. 228

GOVERNMENT (continued).
Disputes, about fruit trees, 418; about land, 420, ii. 96; fighting with sticks, 420; settlement of, A166, 168
Evolution, of classes, A166; of property, A166; of heredity, A167
Fines, 89, ii. 228, A186, 187, 206
Guardians, A184
Heads to settle differences, ii. 230
Inheritance, 138, A167; in land, 419, 420, ii. 229; curious case, ii. 229, A182, 184; *see* Property
Malay oppression, ii. 230; intrigues, ii. 231
Murder, ii. 228, 229; curious law, A187, A206
Orations, ii. 227, 228
Orang Kaya, ii. 224; election of, 72, ii. 227; appointment of, A167 office hereditary, A167, 206; women not eligible, A206; power, small, ii. 225; great, ii 225; increased power leads to slavery, ii. 226; farm assistance received, ii. 225, 226; ruined popularity, ii. 226; five chiefs, ii. 227; tabu laying, A205; influence of, A162; duties of, A168; prerogatives of, A168; tax making, A205
Panglima, ii. 224
Pengara, ii. 224
Property, in trees, 66, 418, 453, A167; in land, A166; origin of in land, A206; fishing rights, 418, A167; in game, 453; dividing with spirits of the dead, 209; communal, 419, 420; in bambu, 418; tenants' rights, 420; of slaves, ii. 211, 214; jungle rights, A209; evolution of, A166; *see* Inheritance
Singer, A206
Social system, A165
Theft, punishment for, A187
Tuah, ii. 224; hard worked, ii. 225
Vassalage leads to slavery, ii. 226
Villages separately governed, 225, A165

HABITATIONS.

Altars at, ii. 5
Aqueducts (*panchurs*), 359, 361, 364, 366, ii. 5
Balai, *see* Strangers
Bambu designs, ii. 28
Bark, ii. 18; roofs, A190
Bedsteads, 366, 382, ii. 13, A203
Bridges, ii. 1, 27
Challenge bowl, ii. 158
Communal life bad, ii. 25
Cottages, ii. 23
Decorations, ii. 9, 10, 12, 17, A203; carved ridge boards, A204
Dirt, ii. 4, 10, 17
Divisions, ii. 1, 6, A190
Doors, ii. 1, 3, 9, 10, 17
Fences and stockades, ii. 3, 6, 20, 24, 25, A178, 190
Fire places, 380, ii. 1, 6, 10, 12, 23, 24
Firewood, 363, ii. 20
Flooring, ii. 6, 24, 25
Gomuti palm cordage, ii. 6

HABITATIONS (continued).
Height, ii. 17, 20, 21
Hooks, ii. 16
Household goods, ii. 3; stored in jungle, ii. 6, 10, 16
Human sacrifices at building, ii. 215, 216, see HUMAN SACRIFICES.
Ladders, ii. 1, 5, 6, 9, 16, 26, A190, 203
Land Dyaks, ii. 1; varieties of, ii. 3; Sea Dyaks, ii. 9
Length, ii. 16, 17, 25, A203
Loft, ii. 14, 16
Lower verandah, ii 3
Mats, ii. 10
Mosquitoes, ii. 14; curtains, ii. 35
Nibong palm, ii. 4, 244
Nipa palm, ii. 4, 14, 17, 244
Omens, ii. 14, 16, 20, 24
Punchurs, see Aqueducts
Panggahs (head houses), ii. 5
Partitions, ii. 3, 4, 21, A203
Passages, ii. 3, 9, 22, 23
Paths, ii. 25-27
Picturesque spots, 359
Pillows, 366, 382, ii 6
Planing tool, ii. 24
Planking, ii 4, 18, 20, 23
Plans, ii. 11, 23
Platforms, ii 1, 3, 9, 12, 13, 23
Position and surrounding, ii. 4, 17
Posts, ii. 22; holes, ii. 21
Private apartments, ii 9, 12, 22
Raised seats, ii. 1, 18, 21
Refuse, ii. 4, 10, 17
Removals ii 14, 16
Residence shifting, 400
Roofing, ii. 6, 12, 13, 14, 17, 22, A190
Rotan cordage, ii. 6, 21, 27, 244
Sacrifices, ii. 15, 16, 24
Shelves, ii. 1, 10, 21
Smoke hole, ii. 6, 10, 23, A203
Strangers' place, ii. 1; houses for, A203
Tabu at house building, ii. 6
Vermin, ii. 21, 24
Windows, ii. 1, 3, 9, 12, 22, 27, A190
Women's apartments, ii. 5, 14

HEAD HUNTING.

Accounts, balancing head, ii. 202
Animal heads, ii. 158
Baskets for heads, ii. 145, 147
Bones preserved, i. 258, ii 154
Brain extraction, ii. 146
Brass dishes, ii. 170
Burials, heads wanted for, 158, 207, ii. 142
Captives killed for heads, ii. 163
Care given to a captured head, ii. 168
Carved wood, meaning of, A210
Carving, see Decorated skulls
P

HEAD HUNTING (continued).
Children's admiration of heads, ii. 144; heads, ii. 159-162, A178
Collection of heads, ii. 143; of animals, ii. 158
Corpses' heads, ii. 141
Cowardly procedures, ii. 159
Cunning in taking heads, ii. 160
Decapitation, methods of, ii. 145
Decorated skulls, ii. 145, 146; Meyer's notes on, ii. 147-153
Depopulation due to, A179
Desire for heads deep-rooted, ii. 140, 142
Division of a head, ii. 150, 158, 159
Effect on character, ii. 167
Enemies' heads, ii. 160, 164
Feasts, Head-, 256, ii. 167-174
Festoons of heads, ii. 153
"Finest way possible," ii. 162
Funeral feasts, head for, 158, 207
Gawè Pala or *Burong* (head or bird feast), ii. 174, 256
Houses, Head-, ii. 156, 157
Human sacrifices, ii. 141
Hunting, head, 79, 91, 109
Invoking heads, ii. 168
Klieng at head feasts, ii. 174
Language at feasts, ii. 174
Legend as to origin of head hunting, ii. 163, A210
Lovers' treachery, ii. 161; trouble, ii. 165
Loving cup, ii. 173
Marriage, heads for, ii. 142; heads a necessity for, ii. 163-166, A178; not a necessity, ii. 166 note, A178
Mengap (song of feast), ii. 174
Number of heads collected, ii. 143
Omens, ii. 143
Origin of head hunting, ii. 163, A210
Original owners of heads, references to, ii. 145
Pangahs, ii. 156, 157
Passion comparatively new, ii. 140, 141
Penyala, ii. 169, 170
Perham's Song of Head Feast, ii. 174
Posts, how erected, ii. 169, 173; skulls on, A191
Preservation, methods of, ii. 145-148
Pride in possession of heads, ii. 142
Property in heads, ii. 158
Propitiating heads, ii. 168-172
Prosperity insured by heads, ii. 143
Recaptured heads, ii. 145
Reception of captured heads, ii. 167-174
Redeeming a head, ii. 144
Relative killed for a head, ii. 161
Ruai's chief ornament, ii. 13
Sacrifices of pigs, ii. 172; of slaves, ii. 163
Scalps, ii 141, A210
Schemes for getting heads, ii. 142
Singalong Burong at head feasts, ii 174
Slaves, wanted in heaven, ii. 141, ii. 141; heads of, ii. 163
Smoking heads, ii. 147
Song of Head Feast, ii. 174

HEAD HUNTING (continued).
Spirits at Feast, ii. 174
Spitting on, ii. 167
Stone for head dividing, ii. 159
Straw wisps, ii. 154
Tatu marks, ii. 90, 159
Women, heads of, ii. 159-162, A177, 178; influence of, ii. 163-166, 167, 168
Wooden heads, ii. 162, 291

HOSE.
HOSE, CHAS. List of Borneo tribes, 37

HUMAN SACRIFICES.
Burials, at, 141, 145, 157, 190, ii. 141, 163, 204, 216, A199, 205
Captives and slaves, of, 157, ii. 163, 204, 214, 215, 216, 217, 222, A162, 166, 174, 188, 189, 199, 205
Communal purchases for, ii. 217
Heart examined at, ii. 215
House-building at, ii. 215, 216
Legends relating to, 325.
Peace, at conclusion of, ii. 204, 205, A188, 205
Prosperity, to bring, ii. 216, A205
Spirits, in honour of, ii. 216 (note), A205
Women torturers, ii. 215, 216; not spectators of, ii. 216

HUNTING.
Accidents, 430, 439, 452
Animals, why hunted, 453
Bears, 453
Bees, 451, A208; tapang trees,' 451; ladders, 451; accidents, 452; bears, 453; property in trees, 452
Birds, " calling," 444; birdlime, 445
Cave swift nests, 448; varieties, 448, 450; collecting, 449; value, 450; curious custom, A208
Crocodiles, 446
Deer, 428, 429; snaring, 443; potting, A202
Dogs, 428, 429, 430; *see* DOMESTIC ANIMALS
Frogs, 445
Game rights, 453
Jungle, cry, 430; rights, A209
Pickled food, 430
Pigs, 428, 429; charms, 439
Pitfalls, 444
Property in game, 453; in bee trees, 453; in fruit trees, 66; *see* GOVERNMENT.
Skertchly's description of traps, 430
Sumpitan, 446; *see* SUMPITAN
Tabu, to mention name of animal, 224; against " butter fingers," 430
Tortoises, 445
Traps, 430; Skertchly's description, 430; *Jerat*, 431; *Bubuang*, 433; *Kelung*, 435; *peti*, 437; pig charms, 439; *Peti lanchar*, 440; *Peti* and bow, 441; etymology, 442; rat traps, 443

HUPÉ.
HUPÉ, CARL. Ethnology of Pontianak (xii.)

INTERFERENCE.
Interference of aliens (xix.)
White people not wanted, ii. 100

JARS (*see also* WRITING).
Attempts to deceive Dyaks with, ii. 287
Chinese origin, ii. 284, 286, A177
Exchanges as tokens of friendship, ii. 284
Fines, taken as, per head, ii. 285
Gusi, ii. 284, 285, 286
Heirlooms, ii. 284
Hostages for good conduct, ii. 285
Java, arrival via, ii. 286
Joy at receiving back, ii. 285
Mysterious powers possessed by, ii. 285, 286
Naga, ii. 284
Oracular powers of, ii. 286 (and note).
Price excessive, ii. 284, 285, 286, 287
Room full of jars, ii. 285
Rusa, ii. 284
Sacredness of, ii. 285
Sacrifice to, ii. 285
Sale of by trade goods, ii. 286
Varieties of, ii. 284, 285, 286, A177
Water from sacred, ii. 286

LANGUAGE.
Land Dyak, 7; ii. 267
  Conversion of letter l to r and r to h, 7; ii. 269
  Examples, ii. 268
  Derivatives, richness in, ii. 267
  Malay derivation, ii. 269
  Prefixes, ii. 267
  Puas or lament, ii. 268
  Radical connections with others, ii. 267
  Tribal differences, ii. 267
Sea Dyak, 10; ii. 269
  Archaic Malay words, ii. 271
  Aspirate, importance of, ii. 269
  Final vowel, ii. 270
  Hindu influence, ii. 271
  H versus k, ii. 270
  Malay derivation, ii. 271
  Manang's speech, 269, ii. 174, 272, A161
  Original Borneo element wanting, ii. 271
  Phonetic spelling, ii. 271
  Slang, ii. 271
  Speech at feasts, ii. 174
  Tribal differences disappearing, ii. 271
  War language, ii. 272
Kayan, 18; ii. 272
  Distinct from Land and Sea Dyak, ii. 272
  Local differences
Milanau, 12
  Dialectical differences, ii. 272
  Tribal differences, ii. 272

LANGUAGE (*continued*).
Dusun, ii. 272
    Accent on last syllable, ii. 272
    Affixes not frequent, ii. 273
    Baju quite distinct, ii. 273
    Bisaya likeness, ii. 273
    Conversion of *yo* into *zo*, ii 273
    Lanun quite distinct, ii. 273
    Local differences, ii. 273
    Malay affinities, ii 273
    Sulu affinities ii. 273
    Pronunciation indifferent, ii. 273

LEGENDS (*see also* RELIGION).

Alligators afraid to eat Dyaks, 348; a Dyak meets an alligator, 348, and who marries his daughter, 348; the alligator will not work and so is killed, 349; alligators now dare not for shame look at Dyaks, 349; another version: a Dyak goes under water to cure a sick alligator, 349, and is turned off without his fee, 349

Alligator bird sings to the alligator, 348.

Barich, origin of the.—Sick persons burned to death, 309; a sick woman rescued by Tupa Jing, 310; her veiled return and appearance with doctor's knowledge, 310; another version, 311

Buludupihs, origin of.—During a fire a girl carried off by a spirit; her child the first Buludupih, 304

Buludupih's story of the Kinabatangan cave, 352; a chief sends his son to fight the Sulus, 352; they return successful, 352; are lured into a cave, 352; the cave closes down and only the youngest brother escapes, 352

Cats, men laughing at, turned to rocks, 305

Creation of the world.—Gantallah, the *lumbu*, originates two birds who start creation, 299; dragon, woman and fruit, 300; another account of creation, 300; a third account: world built up on head of Naga the serpent, A170; men born of eggs, A170; Angai gives life with death, A171; fourth account: a woman born from trees after six times bringing forth, A171; produces Sangen, the progenitor of mankind, A172; a fifth account, A201

Deluge.—Trow (Noah), 300; the arc a paddy mortar, 300; after deluge creates women and marries them, 300; the ancestors of the Tringus, 300; men kill a snake and a flood of water issues from his body, 301; the single surviving woman invents fire-drill, 301; birth of Simpang Impang, 301; the adventures of Simpang, 301; matriarchal injunctions, 302; Deluge, A201

Dogs, origin of, A202; men turned to rocks for laughing at 305, 357

Elephant outwitted by a porcupine, A200

LEGENDS (*continued*).
Head-hunting, origin of, ii. 163
Jungle leeches, origin of.—An *Umot* captures a Dyak's wife, 308; her release, and death of the *Umot*, 308; the child a scourge, its cut up body turns into leeches, 309

Kadawa the cockfighter, 211

Kina Balu, Chinese legend of.—Theft of stone from a snake, 304; "celestial" thieves left behind 304; Dusuns' ancestors, 304; lake with imprisoned princess, 305

King of gold mines, A201

Klieng's War Raid to the Skies (by the Ven. Archd. Perham).—Varieties of Dyak legends, 311; Klieng a foundling, 312; his metamorphoses, 312; his wife Kumang (Venus), 312; Klieng appears disguised, 312; proposes to marry Kumang, 313; Tutong's denial, 313; the war path, 314; arrival of the wind, 315; gathering the army, 315; Sampurei's joke, 317; arrival of grandmother Manang, 318; her miracles, 319; counter miracles, 320; approach Tedai's house, 322; the fight with his army, 323; fall of Tedai, 324; Klieng's return, 324; how songs are sung, 324; former human sacrifices, 325.

Klieng, a story of.—Arrival of strangers, 326; the women carried off, 326; the alarm and pursuit, 327; adventures of Bunga Noeing, 327

Klieng, adventures of.—His proposed marriage with Bunga Riman (Kumang), 332; Klieng wanders in the forest, 333; a bird leads him to people fighting, 333; he overcomes them and they give him charms, 333; meets Bunga Riman, 333; a fly helps him, 334; passes the night with Bunga Riman, 334; meets her brother Aji, 334; they fight, Aji's defeat, 334; his prodigies of work, 335; attack the Kayans, 335; the plunder, 335; Klieng's daughter, 336; his return to his people, 336; Klieng's disguise revealed, 337.

Klieng, the tale of old men, 337

Limbang, Ensera, the story of Klieng's youngest brother.—The party goes out hunting, leaving Limbang alone, 328; his strength, 328; a light wanted, 328; he meets Gua the giant, 329; the giant's way of eating, &c., 329; Limbang marries the giant's grand-daughter (Bunsu Mata ari), 330; her jewellery lost, 330; arrival of a Malay suitor, 331; Limbang destroys the war party, 331; meets Klieng, 331; death of Gua, 332; return home of Limbang, 332

Limbang removes Bunsu Mata-ari's house, 337

Manging, the story of.—His arrival in Java, 338; his cleverness and success, 338; the son's search, 339; a bad reception, 339;

LEGENDS (continued).
recognition, 339; Manging's wife, 339; an antique necklace, 339
Mountain spirits, fear of, 356; ghostly buffalo footprint, 356; dragon on Kina Balu, 356; prayer to, 356; Dusun ancestor on, 356; Mount Mentapon angered spirit sends rain, 357; Sadong hill rocks are people turned to stone for laughing at dog, 357. Nini Sit (grandparents Sit) rocks; Lundu famine averting spirits, 354; miraculous night journey, 354; faith is shaken, 355; Temelan rock spirits warn against enemy, 355; spirit communion, 287, 355; no bowing down or worship, 355; pigs turned to stone now sacred, 356
Nating, the adventures of, 338
Orang Outan.—People turn into orang outans, 350; women pregnant by, 350; twins by, 350; orang outans help the Bantings once, 350
Ot Danum's descent, A201
Paddy, origin of.—Se Jura's adventure, 307; maggots, 307; acquires knowledge of farming, 307; farming operations regulated by the stars, 307
Plandok, deer and pig.—Plandok falls in pit, 347; induces a pig and deer to do likewise, he escapes, 347; he gets the deer killed by bees, 347, and the pig by a snake, 348
Plandok and Kikura seeking bamboo shoots, 342; Plandok caught in a snare, and escapes, 343; Kikura caught in a pitfall, 343; induces monkey to change places with him, 344; Kra escapes, 344; the three travel together, 344; Kra deceives and kills a fish, 345; Bruang wants a share and is sent about his business, 345
Plandok, deer, and pig.—Disappearance of their fish, 346; they watch in turn, the giant too much for deer and pig, but Plandok overcomes him, 346
Pulang Gana, see RELIGION
Rats, how came to be eaten, 350; the rats ate up all the rice, therefore it was time to eat the rats, 350
Rocks, men turned into, for laughing at dogs, 305, 357; oath taken by, 353
Sadong chief, ancestor of.—A boy visitor badly treated, 305; he causes them to laugh at a dog, and they are turned to stone, 305; his descendant's dream, 306; discovery of Si Lebor nest caves, 306
Sennahs, origin of, 6 (note)
Sibuyaus, origin of.—*Puttin* not eaten, 303; fish changed to girl, her marriage, child, and her disappearance, 303; other versions ascribe disappearance to ill treatment, 303
Siju idol, history of the.—Its existence denied, 340; Siju dies in Java, and his body carried

LEGENDS (continued).
home, 340; re-appearance as a copper frog, 340; the village guardian spirit, 341; stolen, loses a leg, 341; a miraculous leaf, 341; his recovery, 341; yearly feast in his honour, 341; probably a Hindu idol, 342
Simpang-impang, birth of, 301; mother of Pulang Gana, 177
Singalong Burong and his sons-in-law, Katupong, Beragai, &c., 197, 198, 200
Siu meets a beautiful woman, 198; their son Seragunting, 198; his miracles, 198; get to house of Singalong Burong, 199; more miracles, 199; acknowledged to be grandson of Singalong Burong, 199; return home with knowledge, 200
Snake has a stump tail.—Of a woman's twins, one a snake, 350; the twin brother cuts his tail by mistake, 351
Spooks.—A tree that never sheds its leaves, 351; a sorcerer's home, 351; camphor tree guarded by an ogre, 351; the bones of a dragon, 351; ruins of a gigantic house inhabited by maneating spirits, 351; an invisible tiger, 352
Tails, men with. 351
Toad advises heads to be taken instead of scalps, A210
Turtle, the, with a pearl, 350
Water and rock spirits, 353; warm spring occupied by spirits, 353; a stream infested by antus, 353; cataract's roar caused by antu, 353; the moving stone, 353; the tail end of Bunga Noeing's waistcloth, 353; made known by a dream, 353; an uncanny pond, 353; oaths on rocks, 353; placing a cutlass in a stream, 353
White People, origin of, and survival of books.— An ichthyosic woman's child, the first European, 302; during the Deluge four men escape, fate of the books, Malay bullying, 303

LOW.
Low, H. Brooke, Career of (xi.).

MARRIAGES.
Adultery, 130; punishments for, 130, 131, 133, A181
Ampun, 123
Bergaput, 123
Betrothment, 108, 114, 115, 118
Bigamy, 401
Bilians at, A180
Brian (*berrihan*, *barian*), 115, 124, 125
Caged girls, 121, A199
Ceremony, 109, 110, 114, 115, 202, A180
Chastity, 115, 116, 133
Chiefs' offences, 122
Children, A179
Chinese, intermarriage with, 124

Index.

MARRIAGES (*continued*).
Concubinage, A181
Conjugal affection, 129; fidelity, 115; devotion, 130
Courtship, 108, 109, 110, 118, A179
Cousins considered brothers and sisters, ii. 274
Criminal intercourse, 133
Desertion, 112, 126
Divination, marriage, 202
Divorce, 126, 127, 128, A182; ring, 128
Dreams, 128
Drunkenness at, A180
Early marriages, 45, 46, 115
Elopement, 118, A181
Father-in-law, 125, 302; wife goes to, 348
Feasts, A180
Gifts and Fines, A180
Girls caged, 121, A199
Heads necesssary for, ii. 142, 163-166, A178; not necessary for, ii. 166 note, A178
High class scandal, 115, 116
Incest, 122
Intercourse unrestrained, 116, 117, 132
Intermarriage, 47, 123
Jabu, 116
Jars, 112, 124, 127, 129
Jealousy, 131, 132, 134
Kudi, 116
Love song, 119
Lovers' troubles, 117, 118; lover captured, A181
Male visitors, 109, 110
Matrimonial troubles, 128
Monogamy, 114
Mother-in-law, 112, 126, 302
Ngaiap, 118
Nunghup biu, 118
Omens, 127, 128
Parental devotion, 103
Parents-in-law not to be mentioned, 302; must not walk before them, 302
Perik, 127
Polyandry, 126; a doubtful case, A199
Polygamy, 126, A181
Pride, 118
Prohibited degrees, 122
Relationships, 122; counted to remote degree, ii. 274
Residence, 108, 109, 124, 125, 129, 348, A181
Ring divorce, 128
Sacrifices at, A180
Settlement 112, 124, 126
Suicide, 115, 116, 117, 118
Taju (*tajau*), 124, 127
Wedding dress, 113
Wedlock, a sign of, 114
Widows, 130, A182; widowhood, A182; see DISPOSAL OF THE DEAD
Wife of low rank, 80
Woman's property, A182

MAXWELL.
MAXWELL, F. R. O., tribes of Sarawak, 1-20

MEDICINE MEN (*see* RELIGION).

MENSURATION.
Ages not known, ii. 241
Cloth measurement, ii. 240
Daytime, A153
Distances, ii. 241; measured by hair drying, ii. 241; by boilings, ii. 241
Enumeration, ii. 240
Knotted string, ii. 103, 290
Lineal measurement, ii. 240
Pig measured, ii. 240
Pleiades, 400
Numerals, favourite, 231, ii. 241, A99, 100, 101, 102, 108, 114, 124, 145, 160
Six months' year, ii. 239
Sun-dial, for planting, 400, ii. 239; post, shadow how measured, A209
Time, how referred to, ii. 240, A153
Years not counted, ii. 239

METALLURGY AND MINING.
Blacksmiths, ii. 234; work appreciated, ii. 236; forges, ii. 236, 237; forges common property, A207
Coppersmiths, A163
Diamond digging, ii. 238
Gold in river beds, ii. 237, A207; Malaus the only native workers, ii. 237, A163; rights, A167; methods of mining, A207; river raft, A207
Iron, how obtained, ii. 234, 236, 237; smelting, ii. 137, 235, 236, 237, A163
Platinum, ii. 239
Stone hammers, ii. 238

MUSIC.
Bagpipes (?), ii. 259, A163
Banjoes, ii. 261
Boatmen singing, ii. 265
Character, musical, ii. 264
Chords, ii. 259
Chorus, 115, 249
Drums, ii. 263, A163
Dulcimer, ii. 264
Fiddle, ii. 260, 262
Flutes, ii. 258, A163
Gongs, ii. 263, A163; beaten in unison 263
Guitar, ii. 262, A163
Harps, ii. 260, 261, 262
Jew's harps, ii. 257
Pentatonic scale, ii. 259, 265
Plaintive chorus, 249; music, ii. 265
Reed pipes, ii. 260
Singing, ii. 264; extempore, ii. 266; improvising rhymes, i. 84
Spirits, to keep off, ii. 264
Zither, ii. 260

NAMES.

Additional names, ii. 274
Animals' names adopted, ii. 275, A208
Birds named according to note, ii. 277
Body names, ii. 273
Change in case of sickness, 288, ii. 275; due to dislike of mentioning the dead, ii. 275
Dislike to mention one's own name, ii. 275; or dead persons, ii. 275
Grandfather and grandmother prefixes, curious results of, ii 274
Inversion of Malay nomenclature, ii. 274
High sounding titles, ii. 275
Men, of, ii. 273, A114
Parents adopt children's names, ii. 274; due to impatience of distinctions, ii. 274
Prefixes, ii. 273, 274; for widowers, 274; survivors of brothers and sisters, ii. 274; widows, ii. 275; children, ii. 275
Relatives insist on change of, ii. 275
Slaves, names changed, ii. 275
Streams, all named, ii. 277
Surnames unknown, ii. 274
Surprise expressed by calling upon grandparents, ii. 276
Villages named after chiefs, ii. 277
Widow, ii. 275
Widower, ii. 274
Women of, ii. 273, A114

NARCOTICS.

Arrack, 383, 394
Betel and siri, 51, 86, 100, 111, 114, 131, 137, 143, 202, 260, 272, 359, 394; carved cases, 394; loss of taste due to, 395; ii. 39, A193, 196
Cigars, A208
Coconut wine, 393
Drinking, *see* FOOD
Gomuti palm wine, 393
Oil, an intoxicating, 379
Opium unknown, 395, A196
Palm wine, 393
Quids, A202
Rice beer, 391, 392
Siri, *see* Betel
Spruce beer, 251
Tampoe fruit spirit, 393
Tapioca toddy, 394
Tobacco, 59, 394; cigars, 394; quids, 394; pipes 395; hubble-bubbles, 395; fairly prepared, 395; caladium as substitute, 396; 408, A193, 194, 196, 202

NATIVE CUSTOMS (*see* GOVERNMENT).

NATURAL PRODUCTIONS.

Bambu, ii. 244; rice stores of, 418
Dammar, ii. 245; sacred piece of, A202; collected in river, A207; used for torches, 379; for coffins, 148

NATURAL PRODUCTIONS (*continued*).

Gutta, ii. 242
Nibong palm, ii. 4, 244
Nipa palm, ii. 4, 14, 17, 244
Oils, ii. 245
Rotan, ii. 244
Rubber, ii. 244
Tapang tree, 451, 452, ii. 245

NEGRITOES.

Andamanese carried to Penang, ii. 298
Beccari on, ii. 295
Burmese and Chinese kidnappers of Andamanese, ii. 298
Dalton's "wild Dyaks" *not* Negritoes, ii. 295; his statement, ii. 297
Distribution in surrounding countries, ii. 293
Earl on, ii. 294; woolly haired people, ii. 296
Existence probable but not proved, ii. 301
Flower, no proof given, ii. 295
Gerland on, ii. 294
Giglioli on, ii. 294
Hamy, *see* Quatrefages and H.
Hose on, ii. 294
Junghuhn on, ii. 294
Kessel on, ii. 294
Lafond on, ii. 301
Man, E. H., on, ii. 298
Marsden on, ii. 294
Meinecke on, ii. 295
Meyer's review, ii. 293-295
Negrito skull decorated, ii. 295; origin doubtful, ii. 299
Papuan sailor, ii. 297; inhabitants, 296, 298
Pickering on, ii. 294
Quatrefages and Hamy, Negrito skull in Lyons Mus., ii. 295; careless statements, ii. 295
Rienzi on, ii. 301
Schwaner on, ii. 294
Van Eysinga on, ii. 298
Waitz on, ii. 294
Walckenaer on, ii. 301
Whitehead on, ii. 294
Zanetti on, ii. 295

PATHOLOGY.

Accidents, recovery from, 46
Agues, 289
Albinos, 296, A162
Anthrax, 289
Arrow poison swallowed, 294
Ascites, 289
Bergamah, 83, 245, 251
Bleeding and cupping, 297
Blind people, 131; *see* Opthalmia
Cajput oil, 290
Castor oil, 289
Cauterising, 297
Charms, 291
Cholera, 289, 290; fearful ravages, 290

Index.

PATHOLOGY (*continued*).
Colds, 58
Consumption, 295
Diarrhœa, 289
Dreams, 291
Dysentery, 290
Elephantiasis, 289, 295
Fevers, 53. 289, 294
Goitre, 47, 289, 295
Gonorhœa, 289
Healing wounds, 296
Honey cure, 290
Ichthyosis, 289; *see* Kurap
Inoculation, 292; fear of, 292; efficacy, 292; not submitted to, 293
Insanity, 296; parricide to save from shame of, 296
Kurap (skin disease), 45, 46, 47, 289, 294; native cure, 294; wide spread, 294; due to insanitary conditions, 294
Leeches, 298
Leprosy, 289, 295
Onion cure, 290
Opthalmia, 131, 289, 295; eyelashes extracted, 296; fire smoke, 296
Otitis, 289
Pepper cure, 290
Plantains, 290
Rubbing, 289, 291
Russian influenza, 289, 293
Scab, 289
Scrofula, 289, 295
Setons, 297
Skin disease, *see* Kurap
Snake bites, 298
Small pox, 289; extreme fatality, 290; fear of, 291, 292, 293; inoculation, 291, 292; an evil spirit, 291, 293; spread by pigs, 293
Spices, 290
Spittle, 291, 297, 298
Sprinkling, 289
Syphilis, 289, 295
Tabu, 289
Tetter, 289
Threadworms, 289
Touching cure, 83, 245, 251
Ulcers, 289
Vaccination, *see* Inoculation
Washing, 289
Water from sacred jars, 290

PEACE.
Agreements, ii. 203
Balancing head accounts, ii. 202
Bambu ceremonial knife, ii. 206
Biting opponents' sword blades, ii. 204
Blood brotherhoods, blood-drinking at, ii. 205; blood smoking at, ii. 206, 207, A189
Breast stroking, ii. 205
Brotherhoods, ii. 205-208

PEACE (*continued*).
Cutting a pig in two, ii. 203, 204
Drinking, ii. 206
Eating salt, ii. 205
Exchange of knives, ii. 205
Fines at, 89
Gold dust, ii. 204
Human sacrifices, ii. 204, 205, A188, 189, 205
Jars, ii. 203, 204, 205
Mediation of a third party, ii. 203
Oath keeping, ii. 208, A188
Paying for, 70
Rotan cutting, ii. 208, A189
Sacrifices, ii. 203, 204, 206, 207, 208
Salt eating, ii. 205
Slaves handed over, 94; sacrificed, ii. 204, 205, A188, 205
Sword biting, ii. 204; stroking with, ii. 205
Treachery of Kayans, ii. 207
Trees stripped at peace-making, ii. 202

PERHAM.
PERHAM, The Ven. Archdeacon. Papers on Petara or Sea Dyak Gods, 168; Klieng's War Raid to the Skies, 311; Mengap, the Song of the Sea Dyak Head Feast, ii. 174

PHYSIQUE.
Activity, 52, 54, 55, 57, 58, 59, A162
Age, 60
Ankles, 49; Sea Dyak, 51
Arms, 49
Cheek bones, 45, 48, 49
Chest, 49
Child, ugly, 52
Dusun, 57
Endurance, 53, 56, 77
Eyelid double, 57, 63
Eyes, 46, 47, 48, 49; Sea Dyak, 51, 53, 55; Milanau, 55; Kayan, 56, 57; Ukit, 57; Dusun, 57, 58; Bajau, 59
Face, 47
Family, numerous, 52, 59, 104
Feet, 45
General physique, *see* TRIBES
Hair, 45, 46, 47, 48, 49; Sea Dyak, 50; pride in, 51, 52, 54; Kayan, 56, 87; Dusun, 58; Murut, 59; Bajau, 59, 63, 91, 113; lank and curly, A162
Hands, 45; Sea Dyak, 51
Head, shape, 47
Height, 46, 48, 49; Sea Dyak, 52, 53, 54; Milanau, 55, 56; Kayan, 56, 57; summary, 60, 61; A162
Intermarriage, 47
Jumping, 54
Knees, Land Dyak, 49; Sea Dyak, 51
Legs, Land Dyak, 49; Sea Dyak, 52
Manner easy, 45, 46

PHYSIQUE (continued).

Marriage, early, 45, 46
Milanau, 55
Mouth, Land Dyak, 46, 47, 48, 49; Sea Dyak, 51; Kayan, 56; Dusun, 57
Muscles, Land Dyak, 48; Sea Dyak, 51, 52
Natural grace, Land Dyak, 48; Sea Dyak, 50, 52; Dusun, 58
Noses, Land Dyak, 45, 47, 48, 49; Sea Dyak, 51, 52; Kayan, 56, 57; Dusun, 58, 63; Punans, 18, 19
Odour, 53
Running, 54
Sham fighting, 54
Shin bone protuberance, 57
Skin colour, Land Dyak, 45, 47, 49; Sea Dyak, 50, pride in, 51; fairness in interior, 51, 53, 54; women darker than men, 55, 57; Milanau, 55, 56; Ukit, 57; Dusun, 57, 58; summary, 62, 63; fair in interior, A164
Skull measurements, A240
Teeth, Land Dyak, 46, 48; Sea Dyak, 51; Ukit, 57; Dusun, 57
Tree climbing, 56, 59
Walking, Land Dyak, 45, 49; Sea Dyak, 51; Ukit, 57; Dusun, 92
Weights, carrying, Land Dyak, 45, 46, 47, 48; 52, 57, 58
Wrestling, 54

POISONS.

Bambu spiculæ, ii. 200
Bugau poison plant, ii 199
Fine for poisoning, A187
Powder put in the sirih chalk, ii 199, in arrack ii. 200; arsenic, ii. 199
Thumb-nail, poison under, ii 200

PONTIANAK.

Pontianak, notes on ethnology of (xii.)

RELATIONSHIPS (see MARRIAGE).

RELIGION AND MEDICINE MEN AND FEASTS (see also LEGENDS).

Alla Taala, 168, 182, A170, 197, 200
Alligators, invoking, 187
Ampatons, A174, 190
Angai, the ruler, A170
Angels (Sansangs), A170
Anthropolatry, 189
Antu, 165; *Umots* and *Minos*, 165; called upon in sickness, 179; good and bad, 182; invisible, 182; as monsters, 183; kill people, 183; in dreams, 183; *Girgasi*, 183; tree spirits, 184, 263; magic charms (*ubat*), 185 186; oaths (*sampa*), 184, 240; to *nampok*, 185; cause of sickness, 185; change into animals, 186; Ribai and Ribut (sea and wind spirits), 201, 203; Sikisar's story, 263; leaf, 287; com-

RELIGION, &C. (continued).

muning with, 287; laying a storm antu, 287; antu tree, 286, A170-172
Auguries: pig's heart, 234, 235, 256; pig's entrails, 234; pig's length, 234; pig's liver, 235
Bambu, as ceremonial knife, 254, ii. 206
Bergamah (touching cure), 83. 245, 251
Basir, see Manang bali.
Besant (child invocation), 170
Blessing rice seed, 256
Blood sprinkling, *see* Sacrifices
Borich (*Bilian*), 165, 259, 266, 282; impostors, 259; dress, 259; charms, 260; fighting antus, 260, 263; office and character of, A174; dissolute women, A175; lead the souls to heaven, A200; excellent women, A200; *see also* Manang
Bras Pilut (Rice) 247
Charms, great value of, 238; hailstones, 239; stones, 239; tusk, 240; gourd, 240; seeds, coral, roots, 240; washing water, 240, 241; white cloth, 240; rice, 241; hawk bells, 241, 245, 248, 250, 253, 254; spittle, 241, 251, 260; disagreeable custom, 245; heirlooms, 260; sickness extractors, 260, 261; manangs, 269, 272; marbles, 273, A172, 200; for houses, A190
Cure, no, no blame, 267, 285; *see* sickness and PATHOLOGY.
Creation legends, 299, 300, A170, 171, 201
Dancing, 244; sword and war dances, 244, 249, 250; ridiculous, 244; comical measures, 245, 246, 247; poor performances, 247, 248; " leg" dancing, 249; excitement, 250; unfair dancing, 251; drunkenness at, 252; *main booloogsi*, 252; pole dancing, 252; hard work, 253; gracefulness, 253; conjuring, 253; a divine service, 262; 358, A163
Datu patinggi mata-ari (sun), 200
Dead, communing with, A172
Dewata, *see* Petara
Different people different customs, 263
Divination, 190; of sex previous to birth, 176, 177; *see* Auguries and Omens
Dreams, confidence in, 231, 233; warnings, 231; magic stones presented in, 231; frauds, 231; theory of, 232; lawsuit out of, 132; practical sequence to, 232; deer preserved, 233; concocted, 233; results of bad food attributed to, 233; attention paid to, 233; propitious, 233; A172
Dress at feasts, 242, 248, 251, 252, 254, 257
Drunkenness at feasts, 251, 252
Effigies, cures by, 268
Epidemics due to antus, 186
Feasts, 242; Land Dyak, 412; Kenniah, 415; Kayan, 415; of *sungkup*, 130; nine important ones, A173, 197; *Gawai*, 143, 207, 209, 210; food wasted at, 421
Fire, fence, 273; antidote to bad omens, 229

Index. ccxxxiii.

RELIGION, &c. (*continued*).
Frog reverenced, 177
Future life, *see* DISPOSAL OF THE DEAD
Gawai Antu (spirit feast), 130, 258, ii. 174
Gawai Batu or *Beni* (stone or seed feast), 178, ii. 174
Girgasi, *see* Antu
God, low conception of, 173
Guardian figures, *see Ampatans*
Hands, laying on of, 83, 245, 251
Hantu, see Antu
Idols, 214, 401, A174; no worship, 355
Immorality a cause of plagues, 180; at feasts, A173
Inflicting injury at a distance, ii. 208
Ini Andan, 174
Klieng, *see* LEGENDS
Laying storm antu, 287
Leaf antu, 287
Magic stones, 231, 232, 269; *see also* Charms and Sympathetic help
Main booloogsi, 252
Man turned into a Mias, 286
Manang, 263; importance of, 265; hereditary, 265; blind, 265; mystery of, 266; Dyaks not deceived, 266; regulars and irregulars, 266; male and female, 266, 282; "possessed," 266; payments to, 266, 267; use of European medicines, 266; power of "familiar," 267; no blame if patient dies, 267; blamed, 285; treatment, 267, 268, 273; charms, 269, 272; language, 269, 270; *Manang bali*, 270; dressed as women, 270; gross frauds, 270; a good man, A200; the *bali's* importance, 271; how initiated, 271, 280; mysterious power, 271; fear of cholera and smallpox, 272; *pagarapi*, 273; trance, 267, 274, 285; chant, 274; varieties of cure, 278; three grades of initiation, 280; a doctor not a priest, 282
Medicine man, *see Manang*
Medicine women, *see Borich*
Metempsychosis, 213, 219
Mias (Orang Outan), man turned into, 286; smites with fever, 287
Names changed after sickness, 288, ii. 275
Nampok, 185
Nature worship, 177, 200, 201
Obat, 273
Omens, 165, 191-202, 221-231; birds, 191, 221, 226, A173, 200; legend of birds, 225; complicated system, 191; various animals, insects, &c., 192, 226, 228, A173; rice-farming, 192, A173; cause delays, 192; good and bad, 193; overcoming bad omens, 193, 194; variety of, 193; dead beasts, 194; bees, 194; house building, 194; sickness, 194; killing omen birds, 195, 227; slaves to, 195; bird *cultus*, 196; explanation of, 200; absentees return, 221; foretelling rain, 221;

RELIGION, &c. (*continued*).
disaster to war party, 223; birds are ancestors, 224; the *katubong*, 224; fire an antidote, 229; thorough belief in, 229; curious coincidence, 230; agricultural, 397; agriculture hindered by, 421, 422, A173; war, ii. 98, 104, A178; *bereincornis comatus*, A209
Ordeals, 89, 115, 187; wax tapers, 235; diving, 236, 237, A188; boiling water, 237, 238, A188, A208; salt, 238; land shells, 238; attributed to monkeys, 238; coins in ashes and water, A188; duelling, A188; racing, A188; fowl's death, A188; stroking hot resin, A188
Pelian 263, 273, 278; *see Borich*
Penchallong, Tenyalong, Pennegalon, 255, 256, 258
Perham's Sea Dyak Gods, 168-213
Petara *versus* Allah Taala, 168; as Vishnu, 181; Aratara, 181; names of, 172; the saving power, 179, 180; conception of, 179; not worshipped, 181
Polytheism, 169, 176, 179
Prayer, 200, 215; for sickness, 248, 253, 261; for heat, 401
Pulang Gana, deity of the soil, 176, 181, 200, ii. 15, 174
Rags hung on trees, 358; origin forgotten, 358; compared to passport system, 358
Sacrifices, fowls or pigs, 165, 189, 190, 204, 246, 255, 260, 261, 402, 403, ii. 172, 173; A200, 172
Salampandai, author of mankind, 176, 209
Sampi, invocation for rice crop, 174
Sansangs, A170
Serpent worship, 187-189
Shamanism, 282
Sickness, 179, 185; theory of, 260, 266, 272; *pinyu*, 260; vagrant soul catching, 261, 268; the 'scape' chicken, 261; sesab, 261; food for *antus*, 261, 265; extracting wood, stones, &c., 260, 263, 264, 267; needles, 263; "soul left him," 263; *antus* steal souls, 263; *antus* extracted, 264; *antu* poisoning, 264; invoking *antus* to cause, 264; herbal remedies, 266; pain caused by antus, 267, 272; conversing with *antu*, 267; treatment, 267; curing by effigy, 268; another method, 268; swinging an old woman, 268, 279; begging *antu's* forgiveness, 269; *pansa utei*, 272; securing the soul, 274; various methods of cure, 278; sent adrift in a boat, 283, 284, A208; Milanau cures, 283-286; name changed, 288; *see antus* and *pathology*; touching cure, 83, 245, 251
Simpang Impang (mother of Pulang Gana), 177; birth of, 301
Simungat, 261, 263
Singalong Burong (bird chief), 176, 178, 197, 198, 199, 256; the great teacher, 179; god of war, 179; his sons-in-law, 197, 198, 200; fetched for head feast, 180

RELIGION, &c. (continued).
Soul wandering during sleep, 232
Spirits, see Antus
Strychnos Antu, 286.
Sun, invoked, 200
Swinging, see Sickness
Sympathetic help in childbirth, 98; in war, ii. 204
Tubu, 165, 180; for sickness, 261, 268, 269
Tenyalang, see Penchallong
Theft divined, 79
Trees destroyed, 287
Worship, a magical action, 190

RIDING.
Riding, ii. 256

SARAWAK.
Sarawak, extent (xv.); government (xviii.), (xix.)

SKERTCHLY.
SKERTCHLY, J. B. Description of fire apparatus, 371; description of traps, 430

SLAVES AND CAPTIVES.
Abortion, ii. 214
Adoption into tribe, ii. 210
Adulterers, A182, 187
Bewars v. Budaks, A205
Boys and girls, A178
Brian, ii. 211, 214
Children, forget parents, ii. 209; sold during a famine, ii. 209; captives, ii. 210; not spared in war, ii. 210; Murut, sales of, ii. 210, A183
Conversion, compulsory, ii. 215
Custom on Rejang river, ii. 210
Debtors, ii. 209, 214, A204-205
Enfranchisement, ii. 210, 212, 213, 214, A135, 205
Evolution of slavery (vassalage), ii. 226
Exchanges, ii. 209, A206
Famines, cause of child sales, ii. 209
Fire makes slaves, ii. 213
Humanity to captives, ii. 210
Ill usage unknown, ii. 209, 214
Indoor slaves, ii. 210
Inheritance, ii. 211
Introducing slaves, ii. 212
Kayan slaves badly treated, ii. 210
Land Dyaks, ii. 209
Life of, A204
Markets, slave, ii. 215
Marriage ensures freedom, ii. 213, 214
Sacrificing slaves, 141, 145, 159, ii. 163, 204, 214, 215, 216, 217, 222, A162, 166, 174, 188, 189, 199, 205
Outdoor slaves, ii. 210
Peace-making, handed over at, 94
Property of, ii. 211, 214
Ransoms, ii. 209, 210
Sea Dyaks, ii. 209
Seduction of, ii. 212, 214

SLAVES AND CAPTIVES (continued).
Tabusan, ii. 210
Temporary, A184
Thrashing slaves, ii. 214
Tortures, ii. 215, 222
Transfers, ii 213
Trees of, ii. 212
Tuba eating to prevent slavery, ii. 213
Wage earning degrading, ii. 215
Women captives, ii. 216; not spared in war, 210
Work of, ii. 211, 212, 213, 214

SUMPITAN.
Antiaris toxicaria, ii. 194, A195; taken as food, A195.
Antidotes, ii 198; A195
Brucin, ii. 196
Chemical investigations, ii. 192
Darts, ii. 184; manufacture, ii. 186; loose barbed points, ii. 185, A195
Derris elliptica, ii. 196, 197; tied on to ankles, ii. 248; eaten by porcupines and rhinoceros, ii. 196; eaten to prevent slavery, ii. 213
Eating poisoned animals, ii. 198
Effect on man and animals, ii. 190, A195
Experiments, ii. 190, 191
Febrifuge, a, A210
Glucoside, ii. 195
Ipoh, see Strychnos
Leubuscher, Dr., experiments, A210
Lewin, Dr., experiments with poison, ii. 191
Poison, manufacture, ii. 188; varieties of, ii. 189, A195; a new, A210; see Lewin, Leubuscher
[—— in Malay Peninsula, ii. 190, 191, 200]
Porcupines eat tuba with impunity, ii. 196
Quivers, ii. 184, 186, 187
Rhinoceros eats tuba with impunity, ii. 196, A210; excreta poisonous, A210
Ringer, Prof., experiments, ii. 190
Shooting, ii. 187; range, ii. 187, 188
Sights, ii. 184
Siren, see Antiaris
Strychnos tieuté (ipoh), ii. 195, 196, A195
Swallowing arrow poison, 294
Tuba root, see Derris
Tubes, ii. 184; straightness of bore, ii. 185; manufacture, ii. 185; boring rod, ii. 185, A194, 195, 196
Undetermined poison, A210
Upas, see Antiaris

SWIMMING.
Diving for fish, i. 456, 462
Swimming, 52, 54, 56; ii. 255

TABU.
(mali, pamali, penti.)
Binting marrow, 159, A205
Breaking a, 402
Burials, 137, 154-156

Index.

TABU (*continued*).
Childbirth, 97, 98
Cure by, 289
Dogs to go into upper loft, 425
Farming, 194, 401, 402
Fishing, 456
Food, to praise, 288
Foods, vegetables, 388 ; new rice, 390 ; goats, 388, 389 ; ox, buffalo, 388, 389 ; fowls, 389 ; bears, 389 ; wild cattle, 389 ; lizards, 389 ; tiger cats, 389 ; fruits, 390 ; fish *puttin*, 303 ; fish with cabbage palm, 390 ; dogs, 390
Fruit tree, 419
Health, to mention, 288
House building, at, ii. 61
Hunting, 224, 430
Marriage, 113
Mounds in memory of, 357
Prohibited degrees, 122
Rats, to drive off, 403
Religion, 165, 180
Sibuyau fish *puttin*, 303
Sickness, 261, 268, 269, 289

TATUING.
Clay, pattern marked with, ii. 83
Dammar soot, ii. 83
Distinctive of rank, bravery, head taking, &c., ii. 86, 90, 92, 159, A209
Hammers or mallets, ii. 83, 84
High perfection of the art, A204
Inflammation, rice a preventative to, ii. 84 ; none, ii. 90
Instrument, A209
Gunpowder, ii. 83
Meaning attached to, ii. 86, 90, 92, 159, 291, A193, 209
Needles, ii. 83, 84, 90
Pattern blocks, ii. 84, 85, 86
Tatuing, 55, 57 ; Milanaus not tatued, 56 ; Dusuns, A193 ; Tewehs, A193
Tree dye, ii. 90
Women, A193 ; Kayans, A209

TOTEMS (*see also* FOOD : tabu).
Alligator adjuration, 187
Alligator legend, 348
Animals' names adopted, ii. 275, A208
Birds are ancestors, 197, 229
Rentaps' forefathers once connected with snakes, 390
The orang-outans once helped the Banting people, 350
Totems (probable references to) half-brother to a snake, 350

TRADE.
Bail for debts, A186
Barter, ii. 231
Chinese cheating, 65, 67
Commercial ability, ii. 231 ; inability, A206

TRADE (*continued*).
Debts, A186 ; *see* CAPTIVES AND SLAVES
Decoying traders, ii. 109
Deposits, A186
Dollars, ii. 231
Failure, a, A209
Fashion in trade goods, ii. 234
Goods, ii. 231
Hoards in the bush, ii. 234
Iron a medium of exchange, ii. 231
Kayan system of trading, 87, ii. 232, 233
Licentious life of traders, A207
Loans, A185
Malay cheating, 65 ; trading with Kayans, 87 ; wheedlings, ii. 233
Markets, ii. 232, A209
Money unknown, ii. 231, A176
Primitive ideas, ii. 231
Protection for traders, 89
Swindling, ii. 232, 233
Tabued river a hindrance to trade, 159 (and note), A205
Taxes, on traders, A206 ; spent on propitiatory sacrifices, A207
Useless purchases, ii. 234
Wage earning degrading, ii. 215
Wealth, ii. 233, A176, 203, 206

TRIBES OF SARAWAK AND BRITISH NORTH BORNEO.
Aborigines, 17, ii. 294
Badges tribal, ii. 32, 33, 34 ; chawats as, 55
Bakatans, *see* Punans
Bajaus, 28 ; character, 59 ; physique, 59 ; stature, 61 ; language, ii. 273
Balignini, 35
Bisayans, 20
Borneo tribes, Chas. Hose's list, 37
British North Borneo, peoples of, 20
Buludupis, 22 ; saved by W. B. Pryer, A209 ; Indonesian characters, A209
Chinese elements, 24 ; resemblances, 57, 58, 59
Dalton's " Wild Men," *see* Punans
Dusuns, general characteristics, 22 ; name Ida'an, 22 ; Chinese element, 24 ; Saghais, 26 ; physique, 57 ; stature, 61 ; language, ii. 273
Eraans, 22
Extinct tribes, 105
Hose, Chas., list of tribes in Borneo, 37
Ida'an, *see* Dusun
Ilanun (Iranum), *see* Lanun
Indonesian affinities, 63
Kayans, settlements and list of, 15 ; general characteristics, 17 ; physique, 56 ; colour, 62 ; noses, 63 ; character, 37 ; language, 18, ii. 272
Land Dyaks, 2 ; chief settlements and list of, 3 ; general characteristics, 7 ; physique, 45 ; age, 60 ; stature, 60, A114 ; colour, 62 ; noses, 63 ; hair, 63 ; character, 65 ; language, 7, ii. 267

TRIBES (continued).

Lanuns 26; physique, 59; stature, 61; language, ii. 273
Malay affinities, 61; encroachments, 1
Maxwell, F. R. O., on Sarawak peoples, 1-20
Milanaus, settlements and characteristics, 12; physique, 55; colour, 62; character, 91; language, ii. 272
Muruts, 18; general characteristics, 19; physique, 59; colour, 63; character, 94; Rickett's influence over (xx.)
Orang Ot, see Punans
Pakatans, see Punans
Pryer, W. B., saves the Buludupis, A209
Punans (Bakatans, Pakatans, Skapans, Bukkits, Ukits, Dalton's Wild Men, Schwaner's Orang Ot.) — Aborigines of Borneo, 17, ii. 294; animals, eaten, A196; best-mannered people in Borneo, 16; blind man wishes to see white man, 17; burial in living trees, A197; camphor collected, 16, 16; cannibalism, none, 17; caves, occasionally dwelt in, 16; chase dependent on, 17; cheek bones high, 18; chiefs, A196; children sold for rice, 17; childbirth easy, A197; dangerous enemies, 17, A196, 204; dialects not understood by the different tribes, 17; dress of men and women, A196; Dyaks fear them, 17; dog, large, thought to be a deer, 91; doubtful friends, 17; ear lobes extended, 57; eyes, striking, 57; families, large, seven to ten children, 16; features, good, 17, 18, 57; refined, 19; fish caught, 16; fixed residences, none, 16; forest life, 17; return to, 17; gutta collected, 17; heads not taken, 16, ii. 158; supply Kayans with, 17; of enemies and animals placed on tombs, A197; honest, 16; horse supposed to be a bird, 91; houses, none, 16, 16, 17, 19, A196; on Batang Lupar, 17; hunting rights, A196; huts, temporary, 16; in forest, 17; between buttresses of large trees, 19, A196; imposed about, 17; shamefully treated, 17; driven about, 17; hunted like animals, note A197; jungle fruits, 16, 16; name for everything in, 16; Kayans intercept their trade, 16; supplied with heads, 17; lady in picture asked to come down, 91; language, dialects of, 17; like Tamil, 17; laughter on finding no one behind a mirror, 91; marriage tie loose, A197; nomadic life, 16, 17, A196, nose, aquiline, 18; prominent, 19; nests collected, 16; paddy not planted, 16, 16; begun to plant, 17; left to pigs and deer, 17; poor farming, 17; no agriculture, A196; parang, A196; physique, good, 16, 18, 19, 57, A196; pran fruit collected, 16; property, idea of, learnt from Dyaks, 16; gongs and jars stowed away in, 17; rice food

TRIBES (continued).

taken to, 17, 17; rotans collected, 16; rubber, worked, 16; salt rejected, A196; sago taken to, 17, A196; self defence, fight in, 16; sensible talk, 17; shields, A196; skin, fair, 16, 57 63; diseases none, 16; straightforward talk, 17; sumpitan, very expert with, 16, 16, A196; skilful in manufacture of, 16, ii. 189; boring the tube, ii. 185; making poison, ii. 188, 189; timidity, 16, A196; sounding a tocsin, A197; trees, live in, 16, 17; shelters in buttresses of, 19; tribal divisions, A196; tatued beautifully, 17; head to foot, 17, 57; chin tatued, 18; not tatued, ii. 90, A196; method of tatuing, ii. 90; sounding a tocsin, A197; unselfishness, 16; walkers, good, 57; wax collectors, 16; women fairer than men, 16; carry heavy burdens, 57; word not to be trusted, 17
Ricketts, O. F., influence over Muruts (xx.)
Sabahans, 22
Sarawak peoples, F. R. O. Maxwell on, 1-20
Sea Dyaks, 7; settlements and list of 8; general characteristics, 10; physique, 50; age, 60; stature, 61; colour, 62; noses, 63; hair, 63; character, 73; language, 10, ii. 269
Sulus, 20
Tribes of Borneo, Chas. Hose's list, 37
Ukits, see Punans

WAR.

Alarms, ii. 109
Alliances, A166
Allies' quarrel, ii. 124
Ambushes, ii. 112
Ancient feuds, ii. 97, 98
Bechara, ii. 97
Bows and arrows, ii. 139
Calthrops, ii. 114, A191
Camping arrangements, ii. 106
Cannibalism, ii. 127, 220
Causes of war, ii. 96
Chiefs start first, ii. 104; A177, 178; their musical instruments, 106
Cold-blooded murders, ii. 98
Costume, ii. 128
Councils of war, ii. 102, 108
Cowardice, ii. 97
Debts, a cause of war, ii. 100
Defences, ii. 110; on hills, ii. 112; defensive measures, ii. 114; use of high posts, ii. 20, 118; A178, 204, see HABITATIONS
Defiances, ii. 112
Disputes about land, ii. 96
Enemy enter camp ii. 106; Europeans inferior to natives, A195
Excitement, ii. 124
Expeditions organised, ii. 100; pride in, 53; A178
Feuds, ii. 97
Firearms, dread of, ii. 127
Flotillas, ii. 100; a grand sight, 106

Index.

WAR (*continued*).
Food on expeditions, ii. 104, 105, 127; guard houses, A191
Hand to hand encounters, ii. 121
Harassing retreating enemy, ii. 116
Heads wanted, a cause of war, ii. 96; hunting, 97; smoked and dried, ii. 128
Helens, ii. 99, A204
Helmets, ii. 128, 129
Hiding chattels, ii. 112
Homeric combats, ii. 121, A194
Houses cut down, ii. 20, 118; burning, 120
Iron smelting, ii. 137
Jackets, ii. 128, 129, 130, A194
Knotted string, *tembubu toli*, ii. 103, 290
Leila (brass gun), A203
Murder a cause of war, ii. 96
Mutilations not committed, ii. 124
Not attacked when eating, 384
Omens, ii. 98, 104, A178
Parrying blows, ii. 128, A194
Peluan feuds, ii. 98
Quarrels of allies, ii. 124
Shields, ii. 138; carrying, ii. 114, 128, A194
Skirmishing, ii. 108
Smiths, ii. 136, 137
Spears, ii. 132; sent round, ii. 103, A194
Straggling, ii 104
Sudden attacks, ii. 116
Surprises, ii. 116, 127
Swords not parried ii 128; how used, A194; varieties of, ii. 134-138, A194
Sympathetic practices, ii. 104
Theft, a cause of war, ii. 96
Time of no value, ii. 104
Traders decoyed, ii. 109
Treachery, ii. 100, 121
Tribute, ii. 97
Warpaths crossed, ii. 96, 109
White people not wanted, ii. 100
Women's influence for war, 363; ii. 99; spared, ii. 100; assist expeditions, ii 102, 103; concealed, ii. 110; captured by stratagem, ii. 114; prizes, ii. 119; attacked when men away, ii. 120; captured, ii. 127; terror of, ii. 128

WOMEN (*see also* CHILDBIRTH).
Captives, ii. 210
Care of children, 362, 363
Cotton weaving, 364
Etiquette, 362

WOMEN (*continued*.)
Good paddlers, 83
Hard work a cause of small population, 109
Hard worked, 362
Heads taken, ii. 159-162, A177, 178
Heavy burdens, 360
Importance of, 362
Influence, A162
Influence of on head hunting, ii. 163-165, 167, 168
Names of, ii. 274, A114
Never idle, 364
Not drinkers, 392, ii. 206
Not spared in war, ii. 210
Opinion of a wife's capacities, 365
Politeness, 363
Power, 363
Property, A182
Rice cleaners, 410
Time of rising, 363
Tortures, ii 215, 216
War, influence on, 363, ii. 99; not spared in, ii. 100; assist expeditions, ii. 102, 103; concealed, ii. 110; captured by stratagem, ii. 114; prizes, ii. 119; attacked when men away, ii. 120; captured, ii. 127; terror of, ii. 128
Work, 362, 363, ii. 211, 213, 214
Work on farm, 363, 366

WRITING.
Alleged facts, ii. 287
Communicating thought apart from speaking, ii. 290
De la Couperie's statement, ii. 287
Degenerated letters used as ornament, ii. 287; denial of, ii 291
Examples not forthcoming, ii. 288, 289
Indian inscriptions, ii. 293
Inscription on Chinese jar, ii. 288, 289, 292; on stone, 289, 292; on dagger, 290
Kern, Dr., discoveries of inscriptions, ii. 288, 289, 292; his remarks, ii. 292
Knotted string, ii. 103, 290
Letter to Chinese Emperor, ii. 288, 289
Mangain inscription, ii. 293
Road signs, ii 290, 291
Sanscrit inscription, ii. 292
Sign-manual, ii. 288
Spear symbol, ii. 290
Tatuing a method of writing, ii. 291
Wooden heads, ii. 291
Writing unknown, ii. 291, A161

THE
NATIVES OF SARAWAK AND BRITISH NORTH BORNEO.

LIST OF SUBSCRIBERS.

HER MAJESTY THE QUEEN (for the Royal Library).
HIS GRACE THE DUKE OF ARGYLL, K.G.
RT. HONBLE. LORD AMHERST OF HACKNEY.
SIR HENRY W. ACLAND, Bart., K.C.B., Radcliffe Library, Oxford.
SIR ADAM HAY ANDERSON, F.R.G.S., Chester.
CHARLES ALKEN, Esq., Hilldrop Road, N.
BASIL ANDERTON, Esq., B.A., Public Libraries, Newcastle-on-Tyne.
JAS. ASHTON-GUTHRIE, Esq., M.B., Regent Street, Halifax.
MESSRS. ASHER & Co., London.

H.H. RAJAH BROOKE OF SARAWAK.
H.H. RANNEE BROOKE OF SARAWAK.
RT. HONBLE. LORD BELHAVEN AND STENTON.
VEN. ARCHDEACON BROOKE, The Vicarage, Halifax.
COLONEL BADGLEY, Exmouth.
MRS. BAINES, Elm Royde, Lightcliffe.
HENRY BALFOUR, Esq., M.A., Pitt Rivers Collection, University Museum, Oxford.
JOHN J. BARLOW, Esq., Park Street, Southport.
PHILIP BEARCROFT, Esq., Eggleswick School, Settle.
M. M. MILES BOOTY, Esq., Raymond Buildings, Grays Inn.
JOHN A. BRIGHT, Esq., One Ash, Rochdale.
J. POTTER BRISCOE, Esq., Free Public Library, Nottingham.
D. G. BRUCE-GARDYNE, Esq., Sloane Street, S.W.
MESSRS. JOHN & EDWARD BUMPUS, Ltd., Oxford Street, London.

ADMIRAL COOTE, C.B., College Road, Dulwich.
V. CARY-ELWES, Esq., Manor House, Brigg.
S. J. CHADWICK, Esq., F.S.A., Oxford Road, Dewsbury.
EDWIN CHAPPLE, Esq., Plymouth.
ARTHUR CHICHESTER, Esq., Youlston, Barnstaple.
F. CLAUDET, Esq., F.C.S., Oakhill Park, Hampstead.
JOHN COLES, Esq., F.R.A.S., Altyre Road, Croydon.
MERTON RUSSELL COTES, Esq., J.P., F.R.G.S. (Ex-Mayor), East Cliff Hall, Bournemouth.
WILLIAM M. CROCKER, Esq., Cottenham Lodge, Wimbledon.
JOHN CUTCLIFFE, Esq., F.R.G.S., Heatherside, Bexley.

List of Subscribers.

Sir Alfred Dent, K.C.M.G.
Messrs. Douglas & Foulis, Edinburgh.

J. Edge-Partington, Esq., Westbury Lodge, Eltham.
Andrew Elliot, Esq., Edinburgh.
Thos. England, Esq., Holme Dene, Lightcliffe.
Messrs. Eyre & Spottiswoode, London.

John Ferguson, Esq., St. George's Square, S.W.
Jas. Geo. Fraser, Esq., M.A., Trinity College, Cambridge.
Messrs. Friedländer & Sohn, Berlin.

Matthew H. Gray, Esq., F.R.G.S., Lessness Park, Abbey Wood.
John J. Green, Esq., Prospect House, Halifax.
Messrs. Wm. Georges Sons, Bristol.

Sir Isaac Holden, Bart., Oakworth House, Keighley.
Charles Heape, Esq., Glebe House, Rochdale.
William Highley, Esq., Savile Crescent, Halifax.
Messrs. Hodges, Figgis & Co., Dublin.

Rev. James Jeakes, F.R.G.S., The Rectory, Hornsey.
Henry James, Esq., Holly Bowers, Chislehurst.
Robert Jamie, Esq., Serangoon House, Craiglockhart.

George A. Kennedy, Esq., Seedley Terrace, Pendleton.
Königl. Museum für Völkerkunde, Berlin.

Rt. Hon. Earl of Listowel, K.P.
Sir Hugh Low, G.C.M.G., Kensington.
E. V. Low, Esq., Bush Hill Park, Enfield.
G. G. Lancaster, Esq., The Albany, Piccadilly, W.
Joseph Lowrey, Esq., F.R.G.S., Cornhill, E.C.
Messrs. Sampson Low, Marston & Co., London.

Sir Jas. Maitland, Bart., Stirling, N.B.
R. B. Martin, Esq., M.P., London.
E. H. Man, Esq., F.R.G.S., Palace Road, Surbiton.
Robert M. Mann, Esq., F.R.G.S., Glassford Street, Glasgow.
W. H. Maw, Esq., F.R.G.S., Addison Road, Kensington.
Ludwig Mond, Esq., F.R.S., Avenue Road, Regents Park.
Messrs. Marlborough & Co., London.

Belgrave Ninnis, Esq., F.S.A., Brockenhurst, Streatham.
National Library of Ireland, Dublin.

SIR NORMAN PRINGLE, Bart.
GENERAL PITT RIVERS, Rushmore, Salisbury.
CAPTAIN A. A. CHASE PARR, R.N., Blackheath.
ANDREW PEARS, Esq., F.R.G.S., Isleworth.
PERCIVAL PEARSE, Esq., Warrington.
C. E. PEEK, Esq., F.R.G.S., Belgrave Square, S.W.
R. H. PORTER, Esq., Princes Street, London.

JOHN F. REVILLIOD, Esq., Vaud, Switzerland.
W. A. RICHARDS, Esq., Hillside, Sandbach.
MRS. ROTH, Divonne, France.
BERNARD ROTH, Esq., F.R.C.S., Preston Park, Brighton.

MAJOR-GEN. R. MURDOCK SMITH, Museum of Science and Art, Edinburgh.
JOHN SAMPSON, Esq., York.
DR. A. SCHREIBER, Barmen, Germany.
W. M. SMEETON, Esq., New Road, Halifax.
MRS. LINDSEY ERIC SMITH, Elfinsward, Haywards Heath.
J. A. GERALD STRICKLAND, Esq., F.E.S., Oakleigh, Ascot.
MAXIMILIAN STRONG, Esq., F.R.G.S., Bank of Egypt, Alexandria.
J. H. SWALLOW, Esq., Crow Wood, Sowerby Bridge.
MESSRS. H. SOTHERAN & Co., London.

RT. HON. LORD TREDEGAR.
SIR RICHARD TANGYE, F.R.G.S., Putney.
MAJOR R. C. TEMPLE, Port Blair, Andaman Islands.
REV. EDWARD J. TAYLOR, F.S.A., St. Cuthberts, Durham.
MRS. H. THACKWELL, Rostellan Castle, Co. Cork.
JAMES THIN, Esq., Edinburgh.
EVERARD IM THURN, Esq., F.R.G.S., East India Avenue, E.C.
PROF. E. B. TYLOR, F.R.S., The Museum House, Oxford.
THEOSOPHICAL PUBLISHING SOCIETY, Charing Cross.

GEORGE VACHER, Esq., F.R.G.S., Ewell Road, Surbiton.

HIS GRACE THE DUKE OF WELLINGTON.
HERBERT WARD, Esq., F.R.G.S., Chester Square, S.W.
J. WHITELEY WARD, Esq., South Royde, Halifax.
HENRY S. WELLCOME, Esq., Snow Hill Buildings, E.C.
WALTER M. WILKINSON, Esq., F.S.A., Streatham Lodge, Kingston on Thames.
MESSRS. WILLIAMS & NORGATE, London.